Ic

G000130634

As th planet gleamed in his view that
such a bleak and icy globe could ha the
expe tion had sent in unmanne d: a
native alien life-form, surviving o his
tea re not the first to make contact. Smugglers from his own p had
begun trading with the natives for a new and virulent narcotic – the most
dangerous drug in the universe. Now Sallman would have to find out how he
could survive on a planet so cold that sulphur was solid and water was
liquid – and how to stop the source of the deadly drug!

Cycle of Fire

Stran d on an alien planet, light years from home, wandering from blistering he to searing cold, Nils Kruger was not a happy man. So when he met
anoth being – even though it wasn't human – things seemed to be looking
up. lien might be helpless, or it might be dangerous, but one thing was
for they stood a better chance for survival if they worked together.

Close to Critical

Sh in eternal gloom by its own thick atmosphere, Tenebra was a hostile
a place of crushing gravity, 370-degree temperatures, a constantly
rust and giant drifting raindrops. Uncompromising, yet there was
ligent life – on Tenebra. For more than twenty years, Earth scientists
ed the natives from an orbiting laboratory … and had even found a
in and educate a few of them.

Also by Hal Clement

Hal Clement
SF GATEWAY OMNIBUS

ICEWORLD
CYCLE OF FIRE
CLOSE TO CRITICAL

GOLLANCZ
LONDON

This omnibus copyright © Harry Stubbs 2014
Iceworld copyright © Harry Stubbs 1953
Cycle of Fire copyright © Harry Stubbs 1957
Close to Critical copyright © Harry Stubbs 1964
Introduction copyright © SFE Ltd 2014

First published in Great Britain in 2014 by
Gollancz
An imprint of the Orion Publishing Group
Orion House, 5 Upper St Martin's Lane,
London WC2H 9EA

An Hachette UK Company

A CIP catalogue record for this book is
available from the British Library

ISBN 978 0 575 11015 1

1 3 5 7 9 10 8 6 4 2

Typeset by Jouve (UK), Milton Keynes

Printed and bound by CPI Group (UK) Ltd, Croydon CR0 4YY

The Orion Publishing Group's policy is to use papers
that are natural, renewable and recyclable products and
made from wood grown in sustainable forests. The logging
and manufacturing processes are expected to conform to
the environmental regulations of the country of origin.

orionbooks.co.uk
v.gollancz.co.uk

CONTENTS

ENTER THE SF GATEWAY . . .

Towards the end of 2011, in conjunction with the celebration of fifty years of coherent, continuous science fiction and fantasy publishing, Gollancz launched the SF Gateway.

Over a decade after launching the landmark SF Masterworks series, we realised that the realities of commercial publishing are such that even the Masterworks could only ever scratch the surface of an author's career. Vast troves of classic SF and fantasy were almost certainly destined never again to see print. Until very recently, this meant that anyone interested in reading any of those books would have been confined to scouring second-hand bookshops. The advent of digital publishing changed that paradigm for ever.

Embracing the future even as we honour the past, Gollancz launched the SF Gateway with a view to utilising the technology that now exists to make available, for the first time, the entire backlists of an incredibly wide range of classic and modern SF and fantasy authors. Our plan, at its simplest, was – and still is! – to use this technology to build on the success of the SF and Fantasy Masterworks series and to go even further.

The SF Gateway was designed to be the new home of classic science fiction and fantasy – the most comprehensive electronic library of classic SFF titles ever assembled. The programme has been extremely well received and we've been very happy with the results. So happy, in fact, that we've decided to complete the circle and return a selection of our titles to print, in these omnibus editions.

We hope you enjoy this selection. And we hope that you'll want to explore more of the classic SF and fantasy we have available. These are wonderful books you're holding in your hand, but you'll find much, much more ... through the SF Gateway.

www.sfgateway.com

INTRODUCTION
from The Encyclopedia of Science Fiction

Hal Clement was the working name used for his SF by US author Harry Clement Stubbs (1922–2003); he used his full name for science articles, and painted as George Richard. He held degrees in astronomy, chemistry and education, and was long employed as a high-school science teacher. Clement's first books were very well received; he fell out of favour in his middle years; but his last decades saw him enjoy an Indian summer. He was inducted into the Science Fiction Hall of Fame in 1998, and was given the SFWA Grant Master Award in 2000.

From the beginning of his career, Clement was associated with *Astounding* magazine, where his first story, 'Proof', appeared in June 1942, at the peak of the Golden Age of SF. His work was from the first characterized by the complexity and compelling interest of the scientific (or at any rate scientifically literate) ideas which dominate each story. He was not noted as a stylist, nor was his interest in character depiction very strong. Many of his books – especially the highly abstract later ones – can for pages read like a dramatized exposition of ideas, absorbing though at times disconcerting for the novel reader. This is the case even with his first novel, *Needle* (1950), a rather ponderous Alien-Invasion story with detection elements and a juvenile protagonist in a tale where the invader is a police-parasite chasing another (malign) parasite that has possessed the boy's father; the boy, with the good Alien in tow, helps to drive the bad Alien from his Dad. It is a highly loaded theme, but was published as Children's SF in the Doubleday Young Moderns sequence, and is told without any of the necessary resonance; nor does its sequel, *Through the Eye of a Needle* (1978), written for the evolving Young Adult market, manage to cope any better with the human implications of its material.

Much more famous, and far better, is the work contained in his main series, the loose Mesklin sequence consisting of *Mission of Gravity* (1950), *Close to Critical* (1964) [see below], loosely connected to its predecessor, and *Star Light* (1971), which is a direct sequel to the first, though some of the characters in the second tale appear in the third as well, Elise ('Easy') Rich in *Close to Critical* being the 'Easy' Hoffman of *Star Light*, 25 years older. *Mission of Gravity*, one of the best-loved novels in SF, is set on the intriguingly plausible high-gravity planet of Mesklin, a venue evocative of the Sense of Wonder, and inhabited by Clement's most interesting Aliens. The plot concerns the efforts of the Mesklinite Captain Barlennan and his crew to assist a human team in extracting a vital component from a crashed space probe; the humans cannot perform the feat, because Mesklin's Gravity varies from a mere 3g at the equator to 700g at the poles. Barlennan's arduous trek is inherently fascinating, but perhaps even more engaging is Clement's presentation of the captain as a kind of Competent Man *in extremis*, a born engineer, a lover of knowledge. Though less vividly than in the depiction of Barlennan, these characteristics permeate the texts of everything that Clement wrote, even those stories whose protagonists are no more than pretexts for the unfolding of the genuine text – which is the physical Universe itself.

Clement's most successful novels apply the basic Thought Experiment structure of *Mission of Gravity* to fundamentally similar basic storylines – a character, usually human, must cope with an alien environment, with or without the help of natives, as in *Iceworld* (1953), *Cycle of Fire* (1957) [for both novels see below] and the stories variously assembled in *Natives of Space* (coll 1965) and elsewhere. Clement's only collaboration, 'Planet for Plunder' (1957) with Sam Merwin Jr, demonstrates his fascination with alien environments and viewpoints, as he initially wrote the story entirely from a nonhuman standpoint; Merwin, acting for *Satellite* magazine, where it appeared, wrote an additional 10,000 words from a human standpoint.

In Clement's later novels, particularly *Half Life* (1999), this intense focus on the solving of problems within a strict SF universe becomes even more extreme; *Half Life*, set on another puzzle planet, in this case Titan, confronts various protagonists – none of whom actually meet one another, as they are in mutual quarantine due to the opportunistic plagues which are destroying *Homo sapiens* on Earth – with challenges of a dauntingly impersonal nature; though the creation of disease-resistant strains of life may be the saving outcome. For half a century, Clement almost unfalteringly sought to maintain the relevance and seriousness of Hard SF focused rigorously on the physical sciences. He is a figure of importance to the genre not only for the ingenuity of his applications of science to the universe, but also for the vividness of his imagination, which in his best work overcame any awkwardnesses of narrative technique. What Clement best conveys is something even more important today than in the later years of the last century: a sense that the Universe is wonderful.

The first novel of the three here presented is *Iceworld* (1953), a tale which gives us a traditional Hard SF world, but with a few surprises to keep us guessing. The first surprise comes soon with the realisation that the mild-mannered chemist – who has been asked to visit an unfriendly ice-cold planet in order to track down a deadly drug – and the Iceworld itself are not what we assume them to be. Other surprises follow, all properly prepared for and fine fun, but the heart of the tale is like the heart of any of Clement's best tales: a journey of discovery, a journey whose goal is to unpack a mystery of the universe.

Cycle of Fire (1957), which comes next, plays again with the old SF presumption that humans were more interesting than aliens, and better fitted to rule the galaxy. This time round, a human and an alien are trapped on a planet where conditions are becoming drastically more inimical, and learn that they must cooperate or die. The twist lies in the human's forced reappraisal of not just his own but of *Homo sapiens'* place in the cosmic pecking order. But the friendship survives.

Very loosely connected to *Mission of Gravity* – both novels are set on heavy-gravity worlds – *Close to Critical* (1964) entrancingly explores a planet where gravity is intense, temperatures are oven-hot, and rain is constant: a planet still so unsettled that its crust shifts constantly. Again, humans and aliens cooperate. Again, marvels are in store. Again, solutions are found. The universe is an immense puzzle. How marvellous that Hal Clement made that great puzzle into a playground, and that he invited us to play along with him.

For a more detailed version of the above, see Hal Clement's author entry in *The Encyclopedia of Science Fiction*: http://sf-encyclopedia.com/entry/ clement_hal

Some terms above are capitalised when they would not normally be so rendered; this indicates that the terms represent discrete entries in *The Encyclopedia of Science Fiction*.

ICEWORLD

1

Sallman Ken had never been really sure of the wisdom he had shown in acceding to Rade's request. He was no policeman and knew it. He had no particular liking for physical danger. He had always believed, of course, that he could stand his share of discomfort, but the view he was now getting through the *Karella*'s port was making him doubt even that.

Rade had been fair enough, he had to admit. The narcotics chief had told him, apparently, everything he himself knew; enough so that Ken, had he used his imagination sufficiently, might even have foreseen something like *this*.

'There has never been much of it,' Rade had said. 'We don't even know what the peddlers call it – it's just a "sniff" to them. It's been around for quite a few years now; we got interested when it first appeared, and then took most of our attention from it when it never seemed to amount to much.'

'But what's so dangerous about it, then?' Ken had asked.

'Well, of course any habit-forming drug is dangerous – you could hardly be a teacher of science without knowing that. The special menace of this stuff seems to lie in the fact that it is a gas, and can therefore be administered easily without the victim's consent; and it seems to be so potent that a single dose will insure addiction. You can see what a public danger that could be.' Ken had seen, clearly.

'I should say so. I'm surprised we haven't all been overcome already. A generator in a building's ventilation system – on board a ship – anything like that could make hundreds of customers for whoever has the stuff to sell. Why hasn't it spread?' Rade had smiled for the first time.

'There seems to be two reasons for that, also. There are production difficulties, if the very vague stories we hear have anything in them; and the stuff doesn't keep at normal temperature. It has to be held under extreme refrigeration; when exposed to normal conditions it breaks down in a few seconds. I believe that the active principle is actually one of the breakdown products, but no one had obtained a sample to prove it.'

'But where do I come in? If you don't have any of it I can't analyze it for you. I probably couldn't anyway – I'm a school teacher, not a professional chemist. What else can I do?'

'It's because you're a teacher – a sort of jack-of-all-trades in scientific matters, without being an expert at any of them – that we think you can help us. I mentioned that there seemed to be production troubles with the drug.

'Certainly the producers would like to increase volume. They would like, of course, to get a first-rate production engineer. You know as well as I that they could never do it; no such person could be involved secretly in such a matter. Every competent engineer is well employed since Velio was discovered, and it would be too easy for us to trace one who was approached for such a purpose.

'You, however, are a comparatively inconspicuous person; you are on vacation, and will be for another year; no one will miss you – we expect these people to think. That's why we took such extreme precautions in arranging this interview.'

'But you'll have to publicize me some way, or *they* would never know I existed, either,' Ken pointed out.

'That can be done – in fact, has already started. I trust you'll forgive us for that; but the job is important The whisper has already started in criminal circles that you are the manufacturer of the bomb that wrecked the Storrn plant. We can give you quite a reputation—'

'Which will prevent my ever getting an honest job again.'

'Which will never be heard of by your present employers, or by any respectable person not associated with the police.'

Ken was not yet sure why he had accepted. Maybe the occupation of policeman still carried a little subconscious glamour, though certainly it was now mostly laboratory work. This looked like an exception – or did it? He had as Rade expected been hired by an extremely short-spoken individual, who claimed to represent a trading concern. The understanding had been that his knowledge was to be placed at the disposal of his employers. Perhaps they would simply stick him in a lab with the outline of a production problem, and tell him to solve it. In that case, he would be out of a job very quickly, and if he were lucky might be able to offer his apologies to Rade.

For he certainly had learned nothing so far. Even the narcotics man had admitted that his people knew no one at all certainly connected with the ring, and it was very possible that he might be hired by comparatively respectable people – compared, of course, to drug-runners. For all Ken could tell at the moment, that might have happened. He had been shepherded aboard the *Karella* at the North Island spaceport, and for twenty-two days had seen nothing at all.

He knew, of course, that the drug came from off the planet. Rade had become sufficiently specific to admit that the original rush had been checked by examining incoming refrigeration apparatus. He did not know, however, that it came from outside the Sarrian planetary system. Twenty-two days was a long journey – if it had been made in a straight line.

Certainly the world that hung now beyond the port did not look as though it could produce anything. Only a thin crescent of it was visible, for it lay

4

nearly between the ship and a remarkably feeble sun. The dark remainder of the sphere blotted out the Milky Way in a fashion that showed the planet to be airless. It was mountainous, inhospitable, and cold. Ken knew that last fact because of the appearance of the sun. It was dim enough to view directly without protection to the eyes; to Ken's color sense, reddish in shade and shrunken in aspect. No world this far from such a star could be anything but cold.

Of course, Rade's drug needed low temperature – well, if it were made here, Ken was going to resign, regardless. Merely looking at the planet made him shiver.

He wished someone would tell him what was going on. There was a speaker over the door of his room, but so far the only times it had been used was to tell him that there was food outside his room and the door was unlocked for the moment.

For he had not been allowed to leave his room. That suggested illegal proceedings of some sort: unfortunately it did not limit them to the sort he was seeking. With the trading regulations what they were, a mercantile explorer who found an inhabited system more often than not kept the find strictly for his own exploitation. The precaution of concealing its whereabouts from a new employee was natural.

At a venture, he spoke aloud. After all, the fact that they were hanging so long beside this world must mean something.

'Is this where I'm expected to work? You'll pardon my saying that it looks extremely unpleasant.' A little to his surprise there was an answer, in a voice different from the one that had announced his meals.

'I agree. I have never landed there myself, but it certainly looks bad. As far as we know at present, your job will not require you to visit that world.'

'Just what is my job? Or don't you want to tell me yet?'

'There is no harm in telling you more, anyway, since we have arrived at the proper planetary system.' Ken cast an uneasy eye at the feeble sun as he heard these words, but continued to listen without comment.

'You will find the door unlocked. Turn to your right in the corridor outside, and proceed for about forty yards – as far as you can. That will take you to the control room, where I am. It will be more comfortable to talk face to face.' The speaker's rumble ceased, and Ken did as he was told. The *Karella* seemed to be a fairly common type of interstellar flyer, somewhere between one hundred fifty and two hundred feet in length, and about one third that diameter. It would be shaped like a cylinder with slightly rounded ends. Plenty of bulk – usable for passengers, cargo, or anything else her owner cared.

The control room contained nothing worthy of comment, except its occupants. One of these was obviously the pilot; he was strapped to his rack in front of the main control panel. The other was floating free in the middle of the room, obviously awaiting Ken's arrival since he had both eyes on the door. He spoke at once, in a voice recognizable as the one which had invited the scientist forward.

'I was a little hesitant about letting you see any of us personally before having your final acceptance of our offer; but I don't see that it can do much harm, after all. I scarcely ever visit Sarr nowadays, and the chance of your encountering me if we fail to reach a final agreement is small.'

'Then you are engaged in something illegal?' Ken felt that there could be little harm in mentioning a fact the other's speech had made so obvious. After all, they would not expect him to be stupid.

'Illegal, yes, if the law be interpreted – strictly. I feel, however, and many agree with me, that if someone finds an inhabited planet, investigates it at his own expense, and opens relations with the inhabitants, that he has a moral right to profit from the fact. That, bluntly, is our situation.'

Ken's heart sank. It began to look as though he had stumbled on the very sort of petty violation he had feared, and was not going to be very useful to Rade.

'There is certainly some justice in that viewpoint,' he said cautiously. 'If that is the case, what can I do for you? I'm certainly no linguist, and know next to nothing of economic theory, if you're hitting trading difficulties.'

'We are having difficulties, but not in that way. They stem from the fact that the planet in question is so different from Sarr that personal visits are impossible. We have had the greatest difficulty in establishing contact of a sort with even one group of natives – or perhaps a single individual; we can't tell.'

'Can't tell? Can't you send a torpedo down with television apparatus, at least?'

'You'll see.' The still nameless individual gave a rather unpleasant smile. 'At any rate, we have managed to do a little trading with this native or natives, and found that they have something we can use. We get it, as you can well imagine, in trickles and driblets. Basically, your problem is – how do we get more of it? You can try to figure out some way of landing in person if you like, but I know you're not an engineer. What I thought you could do was get a good enough analysis of the planet's conditions – atmosphere, temperature, light, and so on – so that we could reproduce them in a more convenient location and grow our own product. That way, we wouldn't be forced to pay the price the native asks, too.'

'That sounds simple enough. I notice you don't seem to want me to know what the product is – except that it seems to be of vegetable nature – but that doesn't bother me. I had a friend in the perfume business once, and the way he tried to keep secrets in elementary chemistry was a scandal. I'm certainly willing to try – but I warn you I'm not the Galaxy's best chemist by a long shot, and I've brought no apparatus with me, since I didn't know what you wanted me to do. Have you anything here in the ship?'

'Not in the ship. We discovered this place around twenty years ago, and have built a fairly comfortable base on the innermost planet of this system. It keeps the same hemisphere facing the sun all the time, and we've been able to concentrate enough sunlight in a small valley to make the temperature quite bearable. There's a fairly respectable laboratory and shop there, with a very good mechanic named Feth Allmer; and if you find yourself in need of something we don't have, we can probably afford to get it for you. How does that sound?'

'Very good indeed. I'll take your job, and do what I can.' Ken was a little happier at this point, partly because the job seemed interesting in itself and partly because of some of the other's statements. If this product was a plant, as seemed to be the case, there was at least a slight possibility that he was not on a blind run after all. The matter of the need for refrigeration, of course, had not come up specifically – for all that had been said so far, the planet was as likely to be too hot as too cold for comfort; but what he had seen of this system's sun made that seem doubtful. Then there was the reference to warming the *innermost* planet – no, the place was cold. Definitely. Chances improved again. He switched his attention from these thoughts, as he realized that his employer – if this were really the head of the concern – was speaking again.

'I was sure you would. You can give orders for anything you need, starting now. You may use this ship as you please, subject only to Ordon Lee's veto if he considers the vessel in danger.' The pilot was indicated by the wave of a supple tentacle as the name was pronounced. 'Incidentally, I am Laj Drai. You are working for me, and I am sure we will both be more comfortable if that fact is borne in mind. What do you think should be done first?'

Ken decided to ignore Drai's subtle implication of superiority, and answered the question with another.

'Do you have any samples of the atmosphere or soil of this planet?'

'Of the first, no. We have never been able to keep a sample; probably we did not collect it properly. One cylinder that was collected leaked and burned in our air, for what that may be worth. We do have bits of soil, but they were all exposed to our own air at one time or another, and may have been changed by that. You will have to decide that for yourself. All that I really know is that their atmosphere has a pressure around two thirds of Sarr-normal, and at its base the temperature is low enough to freeze most of the regular gases out of our own air – I believe it would even freeze potassium. Our mechanic claimed that was what happened to one device that failed to work.'

'How about size?'

'Bigger than Sarr – the figures are all at the base on Planet One; it would be easier to look them over there. I don't pretend to remember any of them at all precisely – as a matter of fact, we don't *have* any of them too precisely. You're the scientist, as far as we are concerned; my people are just eyes and tentacles for you.

'We do have remote-controlled torpedoes, as you suggested. It might be well to tell me before you use them; we lost nineteen of the first twenty to reach the planet's surface. We planted a permanent transmitter at the point where the twentieth landed, and we always home down on it now. Just what happened to the others we don't exactly know, though we have a pretty good guess. I'll tell you the whole story at the same time that you look over the other material. Is there anything you'd care to do before we leave the vicinity of the planet and go over to One?'

'Leave the vicinity? I thought you said that world was not the one in question.' Ken waved a tentacle at the cratered crescent.

'That one isn't – that's a satellite of Three, the one we're interested in.'

A chill came back to Ken's skin. The satellite had been frightening; the planet itself could be little if any warmer since it must be about the same distance from the sun. An atmosphere would help a little, of course; but still – cold enough to freeze potassium, and lead, and tin! He had not given real thought to that. His imagination was good – perhaps a little too good; and it began conjuring up out of nothing in particular an image of a world chilled to the core. It was rough, and an icy blizzard played over it, and nothing moved in the dim reddish light – a planet of death.

But that couldn't be right; there were natives. Ken tried to imagine the sort of life that could exist under such hideous conditions, and failed completely. Maybe Laj Drai was wrong about the temperature; after all, he hadn't been *sure*. It was just a mechanic's opinion.

'Let's see this place, since we're so close to it. I might as well learn the worst,' he said at this point in his imagining. Laj Drai gestured to the pilot, and the hull of the *Karella* rotated slowly. The airless satellite slid out of sight, and stars followed it across the field of view. The ship must have spun a full hundred and eighty degrees before Planet Three itself hung in the apparent center of the port. They must be floating directly between planet and satellite, Ken thought. Not wise if the inhabitants had telescopes.

Since the sun was now behind them, the disc of the great world was fully illuminated. Unlike the bare moon, a fuzziness of outline showed that it possessed an extensive atmosphere, though Ken could not imagine what gases might be present. In spite of the definitely reddish sunlight, most of the surface had a decided blue tint. Details were impossible to make out; the atmosphere was extremely hazy. There were definite patches of white, and green, and brown, but there was no way of telling what any of them represented.

8

And yet, foggy as it was, there was something about the sight of the world which caused the shiver to caress the scientist's skin once more. Perhaps it was the things he had been told, and the things he had deduced from the appearance of the sun; perhaps it was nothing objective at all. Whatever it was, the very sight of the world made him shudder, and he turned away abruptly.

'Let's go to One, and look over that data,' he said, striving to control his voice diaphragm. The pilot obeyed without comment.

Earth, really, is not as bad as all that. Some people are even quite fond of it. Ken, of course, was prejudiced, as anyone is likely to be against a world where water is a liquid – when he has grown up breathing gaseous sulfur and, at rare intervals, drinking molten copper chloride.

2

Roger Wing, for example, would probably have been slightly shocked at Ken's attitude. He was strongly in favor of Earth, at least the rather small portion which he knew. He had some justification, for the country around Lake Pend' Oreille is very much worth knowing, particularly in spring and summer. The first glimpse of the lake each June was something to look forward to; all the way up the highway from Hayden Lake the children maintained shrill rivalry over who would be the first to sight the Ear Drop. Even with only four of them this year, the noise was nearly as great as usual; for the absent Donald had never contributed too much to the racket. Roger, left the senior member by his older brother's absence, was determined to make the most of the opportunity; the more so since it was to last only another forty miles or so. Don was expected to fly to Sandpoint with a friend and meet the family there.

It was, all in all, a hilarious group; and the parents in the front seat had only moderate success in maintaining order. However, the northbound highway from Coeur d'Alene is a good one, and the disturbance in the rear was never really dangerous. The principal interruption occurred when the right rear tire of the station wagon went flat near Cocolalla. John Wing was a little slow in stopping the heavily loaded vehicle, and Roger got the first whiff of the sulfurous odor of burning rubber. He was to become much more familiar with sulfur during the course of the summer.

The children were a little quieter after that – the expression on their father's face suggested that his patience might not have much farther to go; but the journey was never really silent. The causeway across the tip of Pend' Oreille was greeted with ringing cheers, which ceased only momentarily while Mr Wing purchased a new tire in Sandpoint. Then they proceeded to the small airport at the edge of the town, and the noise increased again as the youngsters caught sight of their oldest brother standing beside a Cub on the grass parking area.

He was tall, and rather slim, with dark hair and eyes and a narrow face like his father's. Roger, who had grown considerably since the last September, discovered to his chagrin that Donald still overtopped him by half a head; but he did not let the annoyance lessen the exuberance of his greeting. Don shook hands with his father and Roger, kissed his mother and sisters, and swung six-year-old Billy to his shoulder. No, the flight from Missoula had not been eventful. Yes, his final grades had been good, if not outstanding. No, he had no luggage except the little handbag beside him – a Cub has sharp load limitations. They might as well continue their journey, and he could answer questions on the way. He tossed the bag at Roger and moved toward the station wagon, Billy still on his shoulder; and with the crowd settled more or less confortably, they rolled on.

North from Sandpoint; east fork to Kootenai; around the north end of the question-mark-shaped lake to Hope, and on to Clark Fork. There the car was left, in a building that partook of the characteristics of storehouse and garage.

Don and Roger disappeared, and returned with an imposing array of pack and saddle horses. These were accoutered with a speed which suggested the maneuver was not a new one to the family; and the Wings, waving farewell to their acquaintances who had gathered to see them off, headed northward into the woods.

Donald grinned at his father as the town vanished behind them.

'How many campers do you suppose we'll have this year?'

'It's hard to say. Most of the folks who know us have come to mind their own business pretty well, and I didn't notice any strangers in the town; but prospectors seem to turn up when least expected. I don't mind honest prospecting – it lends protective coloration. It's the ones who expect to benefit from our "strike" that bother me. You boys will have to scout as usual – though I may want Don with me this time. If you've really gotten something out of freshman chemistry, Son, you may be able to help solve a problem or two. If he does go with me, Roger, you'll have a bigger responsibility than usual.' The boy nodded, eyes shining.

He had only gradually come to realize the tremendous difference between the way his family and those of his schoolmates spent their summers. At first, the tales of trips to ranches, seashores, and mountains had aroused his envy; then he had begun to boast of his own mountain trips. When he finally realized the atmosphere of secrecy that surrounded certain aspects of those trips, his pride had exceeded his powers of restraint – until he had realized that his schoolmates simply didn't believe that his father had a 'secret mine in the mountains.' Pique had silenced his boasts for a while and by the time he had developed a convincing argument he had realized that silence might be better for all concerned.

That had been the spring when he was ten years old. His father had some-how heard about the whole story, and seemed pleased for some reason; that summer he had extended to Roger the responsibility which Don had been carrying alone, of scouting the territory around their summer home before and during Mr Wing's trips into the mountains. The find, their father had told him, was his own secret; and for reasons he would explain later it must be kept that way.

That summer and the two following he had continued to make his trips alone; now it looked as though there might be a change. Don, Roger knew, had been told a little just before leaving for college the preceding fall; his courses had been partly selected on the basis of that information – chemistry, astronomy and mathematics. The first seemed logical, but Roger failed to see the point of the others. Certainly astronomy seemed of doubtful value in anything connected with mining.

Still, he would find that out in due course; perhaps sooner than Don had, since their father seemed to be letting down the bars. His problem for the moment was to figure out a way by which one boy could keep himself informed about every person who came within a mile of the summer house in any direction – and farther than that in some directions. Roger, of course, knew the topography of the neighborhood quite well; but he began right then planning a series of exploration jaunts to make more certain of some points. He was a young man who took things seriously, if they were presented to him in that light.

Like anyone else of his own age, however, he tended even more strongly to fly off on the interests of the moment; and he was easily aroused from his reverie when Edie caught him in the face with a fir cone slyly tossed over her shoulder. She burst into laughter as he looked around fruitlessly for a means of retaliation – there seemed to be no more cones within reach, and the trail at this point was too narrow for the horses to travel side by side. The pack horse the girl was leading formed, for the time being, an impassable barrier.

'Why don't you wake up and join the party?' Edith finally gurgled out between spasms of laughter. 'You looked as though you'd just remembered leaving your favorite fishpole in Spokane!' Roger assumed a mantle of superiority.

'Of course, you girls have nothing to do between now and September,' he said. 'There's a certain amount of men's work to be done, though, and I was deciding how to go about it.'

'Men's work?' The girl raised her eyebrows in mock surprise. 'I know Dad will be busy, but what's that to you?' She knew perfectly well what Roger's summer duties were, but had reasons of her own for speaking as she did. 'Does it take a man to stroll around the house on sentry-go a couple of times a day?' Roger stiffened.

'It takes more than a girl to do a good job of it,' he retorted. The words were hardly out when he regretted them; but he had no time to think of a way out of the corner into which he had talked himself.

'Evidence!' Edith responded quietly, and Roger mentally kicked himself. She had been playing for just that. Family rules required that any statement made by a member of the family be backed up with evidence if another member required it – a rule the elder Wing had instituted, with considerable foresight. He was seldom caught by it himself, being a thoughtful man by nature.

'You'll have to let me try, now,' Edith remarked, 'and you'll have to give me

a fair amount of teaching. To be really fair, you'll have to let Margie try, too—'
The last was an afterthought, uttered principally for its explosive effect. Roger
almost left his saddle, but before he succeeded in expressing himself a
thought struck him. After all, why couldn't the girls help? He could show
them what he and Don had done in the past, and they might very well have
ideas of their own. Roger's masculine pride did not blind him to the fact that
girls in general, and his sisters in particular, did have brains. Edie and Marge
could both ride, neither was afraid of the woods, and all things considered
would probably make extremely useful assistants. Edith was so near to his
own age that he could not dismiss her as too young for the work, and even
the eight-year-old had at least sense enough to keep quiet when silence was
needed and obey orders when argument would be injudicious.

'All right. You can both try it.' Roger brought his cogitation to an end. 'Dad
won't mind, I guess, and Mother won't care if the work gets done. We'll have
a conference tonight.'

The conversation shifted to other matters, and the caravan wound on up
the river. Two or three hours out of Clark Fork they crossed the stream and
headed eastward toward the Montana border; and there were still several
hours of daylight remaining when they reached the 'summer cottage.'

It was hardly a cottage. Built well up on a steep hillside, though still below
the timber line, it boasted enough rooms to house the Wing family without
any fear whatever of crowding. It possessed a gasoline-powered electric
plant, a more or less limited supply of running water piped from a spring
farther up the hill, and in general bore witness to Mr Wing's luck or skill in
the prospecting which was supposed to be the source of his income.

A short distance downhill from the dwelling was another building which
combined the functions of storehouse and stable. Both structures were solidly built, and had never suffered serious damage from the Northwest
winters. The foundation of the house was part of the bedrock core of the
mountain, and its walls were well insulated. The family could easily have
lived there the year round, and the parents had vague plans of doing so once
the children had all finished school.

The first floor consisted of a big room which did duty as dining room and
parlor, with a kitchen at one end and bedroom at the other. An open stair
well by the kitchen door went down to a basement, containing work benches
cluttered with woodworking and radio paraphernalia as well as the where-
withal for various games. The stair to the second floor was at the other end;
this was divided into six much smaller rooms, one serving as bedroom for
each of the children and the remaining one filled with the various odd articles of furniture and bric-a-brac which are apt to find their way into a spare
room over a period of years.

The Wings dismounted by the porch which ran along the front of the dwelling, and promptly dispersed to their various duties. Mrs Wing and the girls unlocked the front door and disappeared inside. Billy began unscrewing and removing the shutters on the more accessible windows – those along the porch, and the first-floor ones on the uphill side of the dwelling. Mr Wing and Donald began unloading the pack animals, while Roger took the other horses down to the stable, unsaddled, and fed them.

By sunset, the house had assumed an inhabited air. Everyone had eaten, dishes had been washed, Billy and Marjorie were in bed, and the remaining members of the family had settled down for a few minutes of relaxation in the main room. There had been some debate as to whether the fireplace should be used, which had been won by the affirmatives – not so much because of the temperature, though even a June night can be chilly in the Cabinets, but simply because they liked to sit around a fire.

The parents were ensconced in their respective seats on each side of the stone fireplace. Donald, Roger and Edith sprawled on rugs between; Roger had just put forth the suggestion that the girls help in the scouting job. His father thought for a minute or two.

'Do you know your way around well enough, in directions other than toward town?' he finally asked Edith.

'Not as well as the boys, I suppose, but they had to learn sometime or other,' she countered.

'True enough. I wouldn't want you to turn up missing, and your mother can't be expected to do all the housework herself. Well, Roger seems to have let himself in for proving a point, so let's put it this way. It will be a week or ten days before I go out for the first time. In that time the two of you, working together, will turn in a satisfactory map of the territory within three miles of this house, and a patrol schedule that will permit Edie's housework to be done at times satisfactory to your mother. Margie may go with you, but is not to go beyond the half-mile marks alone – the old rules hold for the younger people, still. That is subject to any additions or alterations your mother may see fit to make.' He looked across at his wife, with a half smile on his face. She returned the smile, and nodded.

'That seems all right. Roger has a few duties of his own, I believe; hadn't they better be included in the last item?'

'Fair enough. Does that suit you, Rog? Edie? All right,' as the two nodded, 'time for bed. You seem to have the time for the next few days pretty well filled.' The two youngsters grimaced but obeyed; Don and his parents remained. They talked seriously in low tones far into the night. The four younger children had been asleep for several hours when Donald finally climbed the stairs to his room, but the fact did not lessen his caution. He had no desire to spend the rest of the night ducking Roger's questions about what had gone on downstairs.

In spite of the rather strenuous day just finished, the entire family was up early the next morning. As a 'special favor' to his younger brother, Donald volunteered to take the surplus horses back to town – they kept only a few at the summer house, as fodder was a little difficult to obtain. That left the younger boy free, once the shutters were removed from the upstairs windows, to get out on the mapping job, as far as his own work was concerned. Edith was delayed for a while dusting off china and washing cooking utensils – they had cleaned only enough for a sketchy meal the night before – but Roger conquered any slight distaste he might have had for women's work and helped out. The sun was not yet very high when they emerged onto the porch, consulted briefly, and started uphill around the house.

The boy carried a small Scout compass and a steel tape which had turned up in the basement workshop; his sister had a paper-covered notebook, a school relic still possessed of a few blank pages. Between his father's teaching and a year in a Scout troop, Roger was sure he could produce a readable map of the stipulated area with no further equipment. He had not considered at all carefully the problem of contours.

High as the Wing house was located, there was still a long climb above it; and both youngsters were quite willing to rest by the time they reached the top. They were willing, too, to sit and look at the view around them, though neither was a stranger to it.

The peaks of the Cabinets extended in all directions except the West. The elevation on which they were located was not high enough to permit them to see very far; but bits of Pend' Oreille were visible to the southwest and the easily recognized tip of Snowshoe Peak rose between east and south. Strictly speaking, there was no definite timber line; but most of the peaks managed to thrust bare rock through the soil for at least a few hundred feet. The lower slopes were covered with forest, principally the Douglas fir which is so prevalent in the Pacific Northwest. One or two relatively clear areas, relics of forest fires of the last few years, were visible from the children's point of vantage.

There were a number of points visible within the distance specified by Mr Wing which looked as though they might serve as reference stations, and presently Roger took out the compass and began taking bearings on as many of these as he could. Edith was already making a free-hand sketch map of their surroundings, and the bearings were entered on this. Distances would come later; Roger knew neither his own altitude nor those of the points he was measuring, and could not have used the information had he possessed it. He knew no trigonometry and had no means of measuring angles of depression.

Details began to crowd the rough chart even before they left the hilltop; and presently the two were completely absorbed in their task. Mrs Wing was not particularly surprised when they came in late for dinner.

3

The station on Planet One was a decidedly primitive installation, though a good deal of engineering had obviously been needed to make it habitable at all. It was located in the bottom of a deep valley near the center of the planet's sunward hemisphere, where the temperature was normally around four hundred degrees Centigrade. This would still have been cold enough to liquefy the sulfur which formed the principal constituent of the atmosphere Ken's people needed; but the additional hundred degrees had been obtained by terracing the valley walls, cutting the faces of the terraces to the appropriate slope, and plating them with iron. The dark-colored metal dome of the station was, in effect, at the focus of a gigantic concave mirror; and between the angular size of sun and the actual size of the dome, solar libration never moved the focus to a serious extent.

The interstellar flyer settled onto a smooth sheet of bare rock beside the dome. There were no cradling facilities, and Ken had to don vacuum armor to leave the vessel. Several other space-suited figures gathered in the airlock with him, and he suspected that most if not all of the ship's crew were 'going ashore' at the same time though, of course, they might not be crew; one operator could handle a vessel of the *Karella's* class. He wondered whether or not this was considered safe practice on a foreign planet; but a careful look around as he walked the short distance from ship to dome revealed no defensive armament, and suggested that those manning the station had no anxiety about attack. If, as had been suggested, the post had been here for twenty years, they probably should know.

The interior of the dome was comfortable enough, though Ken's conductor made constant apology for the lack of facilities. They had a meal for which no apology was required, and Ken was shown private quarters at least as good as were provided by the average Sarrian hotel. Laj Drai took him on a brief tour of the station, and made clear the facilities which the scientist could use in his assigned job.

With his 'real' job usually in mind, Ken kept constant watch for any scrap of evidence that might suggest the presence of the narcotic he sought. He was reasonably certain, after the tour, that there was no complex chemical processing plant anywhere around; but if the drug were a natural product, there might not have to be. He could name more than one such substance that was horribly effective in the form in which it was found in nature – a vegetable product some primitive tribes on his own world still used to poison their arrows, for example.

The 'trading' equipment, however, proved more promising, as might have been foreseen by anyone who had considered the planet with which the trading was done. There were many remote-control torpedoes, each divided into two main sections. One of these contained the driving and control machinery and was equipped with temperature control apparatus designed to keep it near normal; the other was mostly storage space and refrigeration machinery. Neither section was particularly well insulated, either from the other or the surrounding medium. Ken examined one of the machines minutely for some time, and then began asking questions.

'I don't see any vision transmitter; how do you see to control the thing on the planet's surface?'

'There is none,' a technician who had been assisting Drai in the exposition replied. 'They all originally had them, of course, but none has survived the trip to Three yet. We took them out, finally – it was too expensive. The optical apparatus has to be exposed to the planet's conditions at least partly, which means we must either run the whole machine at that temperature or have a terrific temperature difference between the optical and electrical elements. We have not been able to devise a system that would stand either situation – something goes completely haywire in the electrical part under those freezing conditions, or else the optical section shatters between the hot and cold sections.'

'But how do you see to control?'

'We don't. There is a reflection altimeter installed, and a homing transmitter that was set up long ago on the planet. We simply send the torpedo down, land it, and let the natives come to it.'

'And you have never brought any physical samples from the surface of the planet?'

'We can't see to pick up anything. The torpedo doesn't stay airtight at that temperature, so we never get a significant amount of the atmosphere back; and nothing seems to stick to the outer hull. Maybe it lands on a solid metal or rock surface – we wouldn't know.'

'Surely you *could* make the thing hold air, even below the freezing point of sulfur?'

'Yes, I guess so. It's never seemed to be worth the trouble. If you want a sample, it would be easier to send a smaller container down, anyway – you can work with it better afterwards.'

A thought suddenly struck Ken.

'How about the stuff you get from the natives? Doesn't that give any clue? Could I work with some of it?' Laj Drai cut in at this point.

'You said you were not a specialist. We have tried to get the stuff analyzed by people who were, without success. After all, if it were possible to synthe-size the material, do you think we'd be going to all this trouble to trade for it? That's why we want you to get the planetary conditions for us – when you've done that, we'll figure out a means of getting seeds from the natives and growing our own.'

'I see,' Ken replied. The statement was certainly reasonable enough, and did not necessarily imply anything about the nature of the material they were discussing.

It did not refute anything, either.

Ken thought that one over for a time, letting his eyes wander over the exposed machinery as he did so. He had a few more questions in mind, but he wanted to dodge anything that might be interpreted as unhealthy curios-ity, if these people actually were drug-runners.

'What do these natives get from you for this product?' he asked finally. 'Is it a manufactured article they can't make, or a substance they don't have? In the latter case, I might be able to draw some conclusions about the planet.' Drai sent a ripple down his tentacles, in a gesture equivalent to a human shrug.

'It's material – heavy metals that don't sulfide easily. We've been giving them platinum-group nuggets most of the time – they're easiest to come by; there's an outcropping of the stuff only a short distance from this station, and it's easy to send a man out to blast off a few pieces. I don't know what they use them for – for all I know they may worship the torpedo, and use the nuggets as priests' insignia. I can't say that I care, as long as they keep filling their end of the bargain.' Ken made the gesture of agreement, and spoke of something which had caught his attention during the last speech.

'What in the Galaxy is a loudspeaker and microphone doing in that thing? Surely they don't work at the temperatures you mentioned – and you can't be speaking to these natives!'

The technician answered the first question.

'It works, all right. It's a crystal outfit without vacuum tubes, and should work in liquid hydrogen.'

Drai supplemented the other answer. 'We don't exactly talk to them, but they can apparently hear and produce sounds more or less similar to those of our speech.'

'But how could you ever have worked out a common language, or even a code, without visual contact? Maybe, unless you think it's none of my busi-ness and will not be any help in what is, you'd better give me the whole story from the beginning.'

'Maybe I had,' Laj Drai said slowly, draping his pliant form over a convenient rack. 'I have already mentioned that contact was made some twenty years ago – our years, that is; it would be nearer thirty for the natives of Planet Three.

'The *Karella* was simply cruising, without any particular object in view, when her previous owner happened to notice the rather peculiar color of Planet Three. You must have remarked that bluish tint yourself. He put the ship into an orbit at a safe distance beyond the atmosphere, and began sending down torpedoes. He knew better than to go down himself – there was never any doubt about the ghastly temperature conditions of the place.

'Well, he lost five projectiles in a row. Every one lost its vision connection in the upper atmosphere, since no one had bothered to think of the effect of the temperature on hot glass. Being a stubborn character, he sent them on down on long-wave instruments, and every one went out sooner or later; he was never sure even whether they had reached the surface. He had some fair engineers and plenty of torpedoes, though, and kept making changes and sending the results down. It finally became evident that most of them were reaching the surface – and going out of action the instant they did so. Something was either smashing them mechanically or playing the deuce with their electrical components.

'Up to then, the attempts had all been to make the landings on one of the relatively smooth, bluish areas; they seemed the least complicated. However, someone got the idea that this steady loss of machines could not be due to chance; somewhere there was intelligent intervention. To test the idea, a torpedo was sent down with every sort of detecting and protecting device that could be stuffed aboard – including a silver mesh over the entire surface, connected to the generators and capable of blocking any outside frequency which might be employed to interfere with control. A constantly changing control frequency was used from our end. It had automatic heat control – I tell you, it had *everything*. Nothing natural and darned little that was artificial should have been able to interfere with that machine; but it went out like the others, just as the reflection altimeter reported it as almost touching the surface.

'That was enough for the boss. He accepted as a working theory the idea that a race lived on the flatter parts of the planet; a race that did not want visitors. The next torpedo was sent to one of the darker, rougher areas that could be seen from space, the idea being that these beings might avoid such areas. He seems to have been right, for this time the landing was successful. At any rate, the instruments said the machine was down, it proved impossible to drive it lower, and it stayed put with power off.

'That was encouraging, but then no one could think of what to do. We still couldn't see, and were not certain for some time whether or not the microphone was working. It was decided not to use the loudspeaker for a while. There was a faint humming sound being picked up whose intensity varied without apparent system, which we finally decided might be wind rather than electrical trouble, and once or twice some brief, harsh, quite indescribable noises which have not yet been identified; the best guess is that they may have been the voices of living creatures.

'We kept listening for a full rotation of the planet – nearly two of our days – and heard nothing else except a very faint buzzing, equally faint scratching sounds, and an irregular tapping that might or might not have been the footsteps of a hoofed creature on a hard surface. You may listen to the records we made, if you like, but you better have company around when you do. There's something weird and unnerving about those noises out of nothing.

'I forgot to mention that the cargo port of the torpedo had been opened on landing, and microphones and weight detectors set to tell us if anything went in. Nothing did, however – a little surprising if there were small forms of wild life; the opening would have made a natural-looking shelter for them.

'Nothing even remotely suggestive of intelligence was heard during that rotation; and it was finally decided to use the loudspeaker. Someone worked out a schedule – starting at minimum power, repeating a tape for one rotation of the planet, then repeating with doubled output and so on until we reached the maximum which could be attained with that equipment. The program was followed, except that the boss was getting impatient and arranged to make the step-up each quarter rotation instead of the suggested time. Some humorist recorded a poem on the tape, and we started broadcasting.

'The first result was a complete cessation of the sounds we had tentatively associated with life forms. Presumably they *were* small animals, and were scared away by the noise. The wind, if that's what it was, continued as expected. The first time we increased the noise, after a quarter rotation of the planet, we began to get a faint echo. That suggested that the sound was at least not being muffled very close to the speaker, and if any intelligent beings came within a considerable radius they would hear it.

'To make a long story short, we got a response after the fourth increase of power. We thought it was a distorted echo at first, but it got louder while our power remained constant, and finally we could tell that the sounds were different. They formed a tremendously complex noise pattern, and every one of us who heard them was sure from the beginning that they represented intelligent speech.

'Eventually we began to hear more footstep-sounds between the bursts of alien language, and we cut off our own broadcast. It became evident that the creature was close enough to detect the torpedo by other means than hearing, for the footsteps continued to approach. At first they were interrupted every few seconds by a loud call; but presently the thing must have actually reached the machine, for the sounds suggested that it was walking around at a nearly constant distance, and the calls were replaced by much less powerful but longer and more complex speech-noises. Probably the creatures can see much as we do, though the light is so much weaker on that planet.

'Presently the photocell inside the cargo compartment indicated that something had cut off much of the light. One of the operators moved to close the door, and the boss knocked him clean out of the control room. He took the torpedo controls himself, and began attempting to imitate the voice sounds of the creature we couldn't see. That produced results, all right! If noise means anything, the native got wildly excited for a minute or two; then he buckled down to producing apparently as wide a variety of sounds as his vocal apparatus would permit. Certainly we couldn't imitate them all.

'That lasted for some time, with nobody making any real progress. Nobody had any way of telling what any of the other fellow's noises meant, of course. It began to look as though we'd gone as far as we could, in learning about the planet, and that the knowledge was not going to do anyone any good.

'Then someone remembered the old swap-boxes. I don't know whether you've heard of them; they were used, I guess, before our race ever left the home planet, when people who didn't speak each other's language wanted to trade. They are simply two trays, hinged together, each divided into a number of small compartments. One side is empty, while the compartments of the other are filled with various articles that are for sale. A glass lid covers each of the full compartments, and cannot be removed until something has been placed in the corresponding compartment of the other tray. It takes a pretty stupid savage not to get the idea in fairly short order.

'We didn't have any such gadget, of course, but it was not difficult to rig one up. The trouble was that we could not tell what had been put in the empty tray until the box came back to us. Since we were more interested in talking than trading, that didn't matter too much at the time. We sent the box down in another torpedo, homing it on the location signal of the first and hoping the flatland people wouldn't detect it, opened the thing up, and waited.

'The native promptly investigated; he was apparently intelligent enough to put curiosity ahead of fear, even though he must have seen the second torpedo in flight. He behaved exactly as expected with the box, though of course we couldn't watch him – he put something in every compartment of the empty section, and presumably cleaned out the other; but he put most of the stuff back. One of the things he gave us proved useful – the stuff we still trade for – so we sent the box back with only the compartment corresponding to the one he had put that stuff in full. He got the idea, and we've been on fine terms ever since.'

'But about the language?'

'Well, we know his words for "yes" and "no," his names for a few metals, and his name for the stuff he sells us. I can give you either a tape of his pronunciation or a written record, if you want to talk to him.'

'Thanks a lot. That makes the whole situation a good deal clearer. I take it you have had no more trouble from these flatlanders?'

'None. We have carefully avoided contacting any other part of the planet. As I said, our interests are now commercial rather than scientific. Still, if you want to send down machines on your own, I suppose we shouldn't interfere with you. Please be careful, though; we'd hate to have contact cut off before we were in a position to do our own producing.'

Ken gave the equivalent of a grin. 'I notice you are still carefully refraining from telling me what the stuff is. Well, I won't butt in. That's none of my business, and I don't see how knowing it could help me out. Right now, I guess, it would be best for you to give me all the physical data you have on the planet. Then I can make a guess at its atmosphere, and send a torpedo down with equipment to confirm or deny the guess. That will be easier than trying to bring back samples for analysis, I imagine.' Drai pulled himself together from the rack on which he was sprawled, and gave the equivalent of an affirmative nod. 'I'm not saying you shouldn't know what we get from the planet,' he said. 'But I shall most certainly make a hammock from the skin of the first member of this organization who lets you find out!' The technician, who had been listening in the background, turned back to the mechanism of another torpedo, and spoke for the first time without looking up.

'That won't be difficult; there's little to tell. The planet is about three-tenths larger than ours in diameter, making its volume rather over twice as great as that of Sarr. Its mass is also over twice ours, though its average density is a shade less. Surface gravity is one and a quarter Sarr normal. Mean temperature is a little below the freezing point of potassium. Atmospheric pressure uncertain, composition unknown. Period of rotation, one point eight four Sarr days.'

'I see. You could duplicate temperature readily enough on this planet, by choosing a point far enough around toward the dark side; and if necessary, there wouldn't be too much trouble in reproducing the periodicity of night and day. Your problem is atmosphere. I'll spend some time thinking out ways and means of getting that, then.' Sallman Ken moved slowly away in the direction of his assigned quarters. His thoughts were not exclusively occupied with the problem of atmosphere analysis; he was thinking more of a mysterious race inhabiting the flat, bleak plains of Planet Three and the possibility of cutting off trade with the planet – always, of course, assuming that its mysterious product was what he feared.

He was also wondering if he had overdone his disclaimer of interest in the planet's chief export.

4

A circle of three-mile radius has an area of slightly over twenty-eight square miles, or roughly eighteen thousand acres. It follows that the map prepared by Roger and Edith Wing was not as detailed as it might have been. On the other hand, as their father was forced to admit, a tree-covered mountainside does not offer too many details to put on a map; and the effort the children turned in did show every creek and trail of which Mr Wing had knowledge. Still more to the point, it showed clearly that they had actually travelled over the area in question. This was the defect in the girl's experience which he had wanted corrected before she was released from the 'stick-to-the-trail' rule.

He looked up presently from the tattered notebook. The family was gathered around the fireplace again, and the two cartographers were ensconced on either arm of his chair. Don was on the floor between the seats with Billy draped across his neck; Marjorie was in her mother's lap. All were listening for the verdict.

'You seem to have done a pretty good job here,' Mr Wing said at last. 'Certainly anyone could find his way around the area with the aid of this map. Edie, how do you think you could do *without* it?'

'All right, Dad, I'm sure,' the girl replied in a slightly surprised tone. 'Do I have to?' Her father shrugged.

'You know best whether you want to carry this with you all the time. No, you don't have to, as far as I'm concerned. How have the two of you made out on the patrol schedule?' Roger took over the conversation, curling a little closer to his father's shoulder and using the map to illustrate his points.

'There are eight trails leading into the three-mile circle at different points. Don and I used to go around the circle each day, going along each one far enough to be sure no one had been using it. There are spots on each which it's practically impossible to go through without leaving some sort of trail. Going from one trail to another we'd try to cut across places of the same sort – where we could tell if people had been through.

'This time we're working it a little differently. I'm still checking the ends of those trails, but we've been listing places from which people could watch anyone bound away from here – there aren't nearly so many of those. Edie can cover nearly all of them in two hour-and-a-half walks morning and afternoon – we've tried it; and I can do the rest when I take the outer trails. That's a lot like the way you've always worked it when you were going out, anyway; you took a zigzag path, and had us checking for watchers, so that one of us could cut across and warn you if we saw anyone – we never have, that I can remember, but I don't suppose that proves anything.' Mr Wing smiled briefly.

'I may be stretching the precautions a little too far,' he said. 'Still I have certain reasons for not wanting the place I get the metal to become known. Half a dozen of the reasons are in this room with me. Besides, I think you get fun out of it, and I know it keeps you outdoors where you ought to be this time of year. If two or three more of you grow up to be scientists, we may be able to do some work together that will let us forget about secrecy.'

The younger girl, who had been displaying increasing signs of indignation during her brother's talk, cut in the instant she thought her father had finished.

'Daddy, I thought I was supposed to be helping with this. I heard Roger say so yesterday, and you said it the first night.'

'Oh? And how did you hear what I said that night? As I recall, the matter was not discussed until after you were in bed. What I said then goes – you can go with either Roger or Edie on their walks, but you still observe the limits when you're by yourself. Billy, you too! There'll be plenty of long trips for all of you, without your having to go off on your own, and there's always been plenty to keep you occupied around here. I've been promising for five or six years to get a load of cement up here if you folks would get enough loose rock together to make a dam out here – I'd like a swimming pool myself. Don doesn't think we need cement for it, but that's something he'll have to prove. I'll be glad if he can do without it, of course.' He leaned back and stretched his legs. Billy promptly transferred his perch from Don's shoulders to his father's shins, and put his own oar into the conversation. He wanted one of the trips before his father went prospecting, and expressed himself at considerable length on the subject. Mr Wing remained noncommittal until the striking of the clock brought relief. He pulled in his legs abruptly, depositing the youngster on the floor.

'Small fry to bed!' he pronounced solemnly.

'Story!' yelled Margie. 'You haven't read since we got here!' Her father pursed his lips.

'How long do you suppose it would take them to be ready for bed?' he asked, as though to himself. There was a flurry of departing legs. Mr Wing turned to the bookcase beside the fireplace, and encountered the grinning face of his second son. 'All right, young man, we need some fun – but some of us need discipline, too. Suppose you and Edie save time by popping upstairs and imitating the excellent example of your juniors!' Still chuckling, the two did so.

For some reason, the story lasted until quite late. The beginning was vastly exciting, but the pace calmed down later, and Billy and Margie were both carried up to bed at the end – though they refused to believe the fact in the morning.

Roger tried at breakfast to make the small boy tell the end of the story and was surprised when Billy refused to accept his inability to do so as evidence that he had been asleep. The older boy gave up at last and went to saddle the horses; he was constitutionally unfitted to hold his own in an argument where the opponent's only words were 'I was not either!'

It was shopping day, and Roger's turn to go down to Clark Fork with his mother to obtain the necessities for the next week. They left as soon after breakfast as the animals could be readied. Edie and the younger children went off on their own; as soon as everyone was away from the house Mr Wing and Don dressed themselves in hiking clothes and headed east. Roger would have given much to see them go.

The trails were good, and for a couple of hours the two made very satisfactory progress. For the most part they followed the creeks, but once or twice the older man led the way over open spurs of rock which involved considerable climbing.

'This is about the quickest way to the transmitter, Don,' he said at one point. 'It's a lot closer to the house than even your mother realizes – though goodness knows I wouldn't hide it from her if she cared to come on one of these hikes. On the regular trips, I follow a very roundabout path I worked out years ago when I was really afraid of being followed. That was just after the first World War, long before I'd even met your mother. There were a number of people around this part of the country then who would cheerfully have tossed me off a hilltop for a fraction of the value I brought back from the first trip. I tell you, I did some pretty serious thinking on the way in from that trip. You'll see why very shortly.'

Don made no immediate answer to this. His attention seemed to be fully taken up with negotiating the slope of loose rock they were traversing at the moment. It was a section practically impossible to cross without leaving prominent traces, and he had been a little puzzled at his father's going this way until he realized that the idea was probably to permit a check on any trailers as they returned. Once across the treacherous stuff and angling back down the slope, he finally spoke.

'You said a while back, Dad, that we were the reasons you didn't make public this source of metal. It seems to me that even that shouldn't have carried weight while the war was on – it might have been better to let the government develop the find and use it. I don't mean that I don't appreciate getting a college education, but – well—' he paused a little uncomfortably.

'You have a point, son, and that was another matter for thought when the war started, with you in high school and Billy just learning to walk. I think I might have done as you suggest, except for the fact that the most probable result of publicity would be to remove the source of metal. Just be patient a little longer – we'll be there in a few minutes, and you will see for yourself.'

Donald nodded acceptance of this, and they proceeded in silence for a short time. The course Mr Wing was following had led them into a narrow gully after crossing the scree; now he turned up this, making his way easily along the bank of the tiny brook which flowed down its center. After some ten minutes' climb the trees began to thin out, and a few more rods found them on practically bare rock. This extended for some distance above them, but the older man seemed to have no desire to get to the top of the hill.

Instead, he turned again, moving quickly across the bare rock as though a path were plainly marked before him; and in a few steps reached the edge of a shallow declivity which appeared to have acted as a catch basin for rocks which had rolled from farther up the hill. Winding his way among these, with Donald close at his heels, he finally stopped and moved to one side, permitting his son to see what lay before them.

It was an almost featureless structure of metal, roughly cubical in shape and a little less than a yard on each edge. There was a small opening on one side, containing a single projection which had the appearance of a toggle switch. Several bolt heads of quite conventional appearance were also visible on different parts of the surface.

After allowing his son to look the object over for a few moments, Mr Wing took a small screwdriver from his pocket and set to work on the bolts, which seemed very loose. Don, lacking tools, tried a few of the projecting heads with his fingers and had little difficulty with them; in two or three minutes, the older man was able to remove several metal plates and expose the interior of the block to view. Don looked, and whistled.

'What is it, Dad? Not an ordinary radio, certainly!'

'No. It seems to be a radio of some sort, however. I don't know what sort of wave it uses, or its range, or its power source – though I have some ideas about the last two. There's nothing to using it; I imagine the makers wanted that to be easy, and there is only the single control switch. I'm not so sure that the interior was meant to be so accessible.'

'But where did it come from? Who made it? How did you get hold of it?'

'That's a rather long story, and happened, as I said, before you were born.

'I was just out of college, and had gotten interested in this part of the country; so I decided to see some of it first hand, and eventually found myself here in the hills. I started at Helena, and went on foot up to Flathead, through Glacier Park, west along the border to the Kootenai, and back along the river past Bonner's Ferry into the Cabinets. It wasn't a very exciting jaunt, but I saw a lot and had a pretty good time.

'I was crossing the brook we just followed up here, just after I had gotten under way one morning, when I heard the weirdest racket from up the hill. I really didn't know too much about the neighborhood, and was a bit on the uneasy side; but I had a rifle, and managed to convince myself that I was out to satisfy my curiosity, so I headed up toward the noise.

'When I got out from among the trees, the noise began to sound more and more like spoken language; so I yelled a few words myself, though I couldn't understand a word of it. There was no answer at first – just this tremendous, roaring voice blatting out the strangely regular sounds. Finally, a little way up the hill from here, on a rather open spot, I saw the source; and at almost the same instant the noise stopped.

'Lying out in the open, where it could be seen from any direction, was a thing that looked like a perfectly good submarine torpedo – everyone was familiar with those at the time, as they played a very prominent part in the first World War. Science-fiction had not come into style then, and Heaven knows I wasn't much of a physical scientist, but even so I found it hard to believe that the thing had been carried there. I examined it as thoroughly as I could, and found a few discrepancies in the torpedo theory.

'In the first place, it had neither propellers nor any type of steering fin. It was about twenty feet long and three in diameter, which was reasonable for a torpedo as far as I knew, but the only break in the surface was a section of the side, near what I supposed to be the front, which was open rather like a bomb bay. I looked in, though I didn't take a chance on sticking an arm or my head inside, and saw a chamber that occupied most of the interior of the nose section. It was empty, except for a noticeable smell of burning sulfur.

'I nearly had a heart attack when the thing began talking again, this time in a much lower tone – at any rate I jumped two feet. Then I cussed it out in every language I knew for startling me so. It took me a minute or two to get command of myself, and then I realized that the sounds it was making were rather clumsy imitations of my own words. To make sure, I tried some others, one word at a time; and most of them were repeated with fair accuracy. Whoever was speaking couldn't pronounce "P" or "B," but got on fairly well with the rest.

'Obviously there was either someone trapped in the rear of the torpedo, or it contained a radio and someone was calling from a distance. I doubted the first, because of the tremendous volume behind the original sounds; and presently there was further evidence.

'I had determined to set up camp right there, early as it was. I was going about the business, saying an occasional word to the torpedo and being boomed at in return, when another of the things appeared overhead. It spoke, rather softly, when it was still some distance up – apparently the controllers didn't want to scare me away! It settled beside the first, trailing a thin cloud of blue smoke which I thought at first must have to do with driving rockets. However, it proved to be leaking around the edges of a door similar to that in the first torpedo, and then a big cloud of it puffed out as the door opened. That made me a little cautious, which was just as well – the metal turned out to be hot enough to feel the radiation five feet away. How much hotter it had been before I can't guess. The sulfur smell was strong for a while after the second torpedo landed, but gradually faded out again.

'I had to wait a while before the thing was cool enough to approach with comfort. When I did, I found that the nose compartment this time was not empty. There was an affair rather like a fishing-box inside, with the compartments of one side full of junk and those on the other empty. I finally took a chance on reaching in for it, once it was cool enough to touch.

'When I got it out in the sunlight, I found that the full compartments were covered with little glassy lids, which were latched shut; and there was a tricky connection between the two sides which made it necessary to put something in an empty compartment and close its lid before you could open the corresponding one on the other side. There were only half a dozen spaces, so I fished out some junk of my own – a wad of paper from my notebook, a chunk of granite, a cigarette, some lichen from the rocks around, and so on – and cleaned out the full compartments. One of the things was a lump of platinum and related metals that must have weighed two pounds.

'Right then I settled down to some serious thinking. In the first place, the torpedo came from off this planet. The only space ship I'd ever heard of was the projectile in Jules Verne's story, but people of this planet don't send flying torpedoes with no visible means of propulsion carrying nuggets of what I knew even then was a valuable metal; and if they do, they don't call attention to the practice by broadcasting weird languages loudly enough to be heard a mile away.

'Granting that the torpedo came from outer space, its behavior seemed to indicate only one thing – its senders wanted to trade. At any rate, that was the theory I decided to act on. I put all the junk except the platinum nugget back where it came from, and put the box back in the nose of the torpedo. I don't yet know if they could see me or not – I rather doubt it, for a number of reasons – but the door closed almost at once and the thing took off – straight up, out of sight. I was sorry I hadn't had much of value to stuff in my side of the box. I had thought of sending them a rifle cartridge to indicate we had a mechanical industry, but remembered the temperature at which the thing had arrived and decided against it.

'It took two or three hours for the torpedo to make its round trip. I had set up my tent and rounded up some firewood and water by the time it came back, and I found out my guess was right. This time they had put another platinum nugget in one compartment, leaving the others empty; and I was able to remember what I had put in the corresponding space on the previous visit.

'That about tells the story.' Mr Wing grinned at his son. 'I've been swapping cigarettes for platinum and iridium nuggets for about thirty years now – and you can see why I wanted you to study some astronomy!' Don whistled gently.

'I guess I do, at that. But you haven't explained this,' he indicated the metal cube on which his father was sitting.

'That came down a little later, grappled to a torpedo, and the original one took off immediately afterwards. I have always supposed they use it to find this spot again. We've sort of fallen into a schedule over the years. I'm never here in the winter any more, and they seem to realize that; but from two to three days after I snap this switch off and on a few times, like this,' he demonstrated, 'the exchequer gets a shot in the arm.'

Don frowned thoughtfully, and was silent for a time.

'I still don't see why you keep it a secret,' he said at last. 'If the affair is really interplanetary, it's tremendously important.'

'That's true, of course. However, if these people wanted contact with mankind in general, they could certainly establish it without any difficulty. It has always seemed to me that their maintaining contact in this fashion was evidence that they did not want their presence generally known; so that if experts began taking their transmitter apart, for example, or sending literature and machinery out to them in an effort to show our state of civilization, they would simply leave.'

'That seems a little far-fetched.'

'Perhaps; but can you offer a better suggestion why they don't land one of these things in a city? They're paying tremendous prices for darned small quantities of tobacco – and a corner drug store could stock them for years at their rate of consumption.

'Don't get me wrong, son; I certainly appreciate the importance of all this, and want very much to find out all I can about these things and their machines; but I want the investigating done by people whom I can trust to be careful not to upset the apple cart. I wish the whole family were seven or eight years older; we'd have a good research team right here. For the moment, though, you and I – principally you – are going to have to do the investigating, while Rog and Edie do the scouting. I expect they'll sneak over to watch us, of course; Roger's curiosity is starting to keep him awake nights, and he has the makings of a man of action. I'm wondering whether we don't find his tracks or Edie's on the way back – he might have persuaded her to go to town for him. There's nothing more to be done here, unless you want to look this communicator over more closely; we might as well head back, and find out how enterprising the younger generation is.'

'There's no hurry, Dad. I'd like to look this thing over for a while. It has some of the earmarks of a short wave transmitter, but there are a lot of things I'd like to get straight.'

'Me, too. I've learned a good deal about radios in the last twenty years, but it's a bit beyond me. Of course, I've never dared take off more than the outer casing; there are parts too deeply stowed to be visible, which might be highly informative if we could see them.'

'Exactly what I was thinking. There should be some way to look into it – we ought to dig up one of those dentist's mirrors.'

'You don't catch me sticking anything made of metal into a gadget that almost certainly uses astronomical voltages.'

'Well – I suppose not. We could turn it off first, if we were sure which position of that switch were off. We don't really know whether you're calling them with a short transmission when you move it, or whether you're breaking a continuous one. If they use it for homing, it would be the latter; but we can't be sure.'

'Even if we were, turning it off wouldn't be enough. Condensers can hold a nasty bite for a long time.'

Don admitted the justice of this point, and spent only a few minutes peering through the openings left by the removal of the plates.

'Most of the inside seems to be blocks of bakelite anyway,' he said at last. 'I suppose they have everything sealed in for permanence. I wonder how they expect to service it? I guess you're right – we may as well go home until the torpedo comes.' He slung the pack that had contained their lunch – or rather, the sandwiches they had eaten en route – over his shoulder, and straightened up. His father nodded in agreement, and they began to retrace their steps down the hillside.

Don was wrapped in thought, and his father forbore to interrupt. He knew how he had reacted to the events he had just described, when he had been very little older than his son was now; also, he had a high opinion of his children's intelligence, and believed firmly in letting them solve problems for themselves as much as was safe. He reflected somewhat ruefully that nothing he could say would be too much help, in any case.

There was no trace of anyone's having followed them at any point on the trail home, though they split up to take opposite sides of the scree they had deliberately crossed on the way out. Neither found this very surprising, for it turned out that Edith had made her scheduled patrols and spent the rest of the day with the younger children, while Roger had gone to town as expected. If he had thought of finding a substitute and following his father, nothing had come of it. Mr Wing was not sure whether he ought to be pleased or disappointed.

5

Laj Drai found his hired schoolteacher beside one of the torpedoes, checking off its contents with loops of one tentacle. The mechanic was listening as he named off the items.

'Magnesium cell; titanium cell; sodium – oh, hello, Drai. Anything going on?'

'Hard to say. You are setting up a research project, I take it?'

'Just checking some hypotheses. I've listed all the elements that would be gaseous under the conditions of Planet Three, and as many compounds as I could find in the Tables. Some are a little doubtful, since I have no pressure data; they might be liquid. Still, if they are there in any quantity, their vapors should be present.

'Then I eliminated as many as possible on theoretical grounds, since I can't test for everything at once.'

'Theoretical grounds?'

'Yes. For example, while fluorine is still gaseous under those conditions, it's much too active to be expected in the free state. The same is true of chlorine – which may be liquid – and oxygen. On the other hand, hydrogen seems very likely, along with hydrogen sulfide and other volatile compounds of both those elements. Nitrogen should be present, and the inert gases – though I don't know how I can test for those.

'I've built little cells containing various materials, along with built-in heaters; and I'm going to warm them up one at a time after landing this torpedo and opening it to the atmosphere. Then I'll bring it back and see what the air did to my samples. I have magnesium and titanium, which should detect the nitrogen, and sodium, and a couple of sulfides which should be reduced if there's much hydrogen, and so on. The report may not be complete, but we should learn something.'

'So I should say, from what little I know about it. Were you planning to send the torpedo out right away?'

'Yes; everything seems to be ready, unless there are complications from your department.'

'Nothing much. We were just going to send one out ourselves; our native signalled a short time ago.'

'Can you control two torpedoes at once?'

'Yes, easily. It occurs to me, however, that it might be best for you to keep a mile or two away from our homing station, and make your descent when that part of the planet is in darkness. The natives are diurnal, we are sure; and it would be a pity to scare them off if any of your chemical reactions are bright or noisy or smelly.'

'Or affect some sense we don't know about. All right, you have a good point. Do you want me to wait until you have finished your trading, or go ahead of you if the chance occurs?'

'I don't see that it matters much. I don't remember whether it will be night or day there when the torpedoes arrive overhead; there's a table for figuring it up in the office, and we'll check before arrival time. I'd say if it was day, we'd go right down while you waited, and if it's night you get first shot.'

'All right with me.'

'You'll have to control from down here – there's only one unit up in the observatory. It won't matter, since you'll be working blind anyway. I'll go up and tell them that you're operating too – we have a relay unit with detection apparatus circling the planet now, and there's no point in having the observers think the flat-landers are out in space.'

'Have you been getting activity from them?'

'Not much. Within the last three or four years we have picked up some radiation suspiciously like radar, but it's all been constant frequency so far. We put quarter-wave coatings of plastic with a half-reflecting film of metal on all the torpedoes, and we haven't had any trouble. They only use a dozen different frequencies, and we're set up for all of them – when they change, we simply use another drone. I suppose they'll start using two or more wave lengths in one area or maybe frequency modulation eventually, and we'll have to get a non-reflective coating. That would be simpler anyway – only it's more expensive. I learned that when I had the *Karella* coated. I wonder how we'll get around it if they learn to pick up infra-red? The torps are enough hotter than the planet to show up like novae, when we happen to start them from the ship just outside the atmosphere.'

'Let 'em hang in space until they cool off,' Ken and the mechanic replied in chorus. 'Or send them all from here, as we've been doing,' added the latter. Laj Drai left without further remark.

'That fellow needs a whole scientific college,' the mechanic remarked as the door closed. 'He's so darned suspicious he'll hire only one man at a time, and usually fires them before long.'

'Then I'm not the first?'

'You're the first to get this far. There were a couple of others, and he got the idea they were poking into his business, so I never even found out what ideas they had. I'm no scientist, but I'm curious – let's get this iron cigar into space before he changes his mind about letting it go.'

Ken gestured agreement, but hung back as the mechanic cut the test controller into the main outside beam circuit – two multiphase signals could be handled as easily as one on the beam, and both torpedoes would be close enough together so that one beam would suffice. The mechanic's information was interesting; it had never occurred to him that others might have preceded him on this job. In a way, that was good – the others had presumably not been narcotics agents, or Rade would have told him. Therefore he had better protective coloration than he had supposed. Drai might even be getting used to having outsiders connected with his project.

But just what did this mechanic know? After all, he had apparently been around for some time, and Drai was certainly not afraid to talk in his presence. Perhaps he might be worked up into a really effective source of information; on the other hand, it might be dangerous to try – quite conceivably one of his minor duties was keeping a watchful eye on Sallman Ken's behavior. He was a rather taciturn individual and Ken had not given him much attention so far.

At the moment he was all technician. He was draped over the rack in front of the control board, his tentacles resting on the various toggles and verniers, and a rising hum indicated that the tubes were warming. After a moment, he twisted a vernier knob slightly, and the torpedo on which Ken had been working lifted gently from the cradle. He spoke without turning his eyes backward:

'If you'll go to the far end of the room, I'll run it down there and we can test the microphone and speaker. I know you don't plan to use them, but we might as well have them serviceable.'

Ken followed the suggestion, testing first the sound apparatus and then the various recorders and other instruments in the cargo chamber which were intended to tell whether or not any violent chemical reactions took place – photocells and pyrometers, and gas pumps connected to sample flasks and precipitators. Everything appeared in working order and was firmly clamped in place.

Assured of this, the operator guided the little vessel to a tunnel-like air lock in one wall of the room, maneuvered it in, pumped back the air, and drove the torpedo out into the vacuum of Mercury's surface. Without further ado he sent it hurtling away from the planet, its control keyed in with a master achronic beam running from the station to the relay unit near Earth. No further attention would be needed until it approached the planet.

The mechanic rose from in front of the panel, and turned to Ken.

'I'm going to sleep for a while,' he said. 'I'll be back before arrival time. In case you care, you'll be making the first landing. It takes one and a half revolutions of Planet Three, more or less, to get the torpedo there when the planets are in their present relative positions – we can't use overdrive on the drones – and the signal must have come during the local daytime. I'll see you. Have me paged if you want me for anything.'

Ken gave the equivalent of an affirmative nod.

'All right – and thanks. Your name is Allmer, isn't it?'

'Right – Feth Allmer.' Without further speech the mechanic disappeared through the door, moving with the fluid ease of a person well accustomed to Mercury's feeble gravity, and leaving Sallman Ken in a very thoughtful mood behind him.

Almost unconsciously the investigator settled onto the rack deserted by Allmer, and stared blankly at the indicators in front of him. One of his troubles, he reflected ruefully, was his tendency to get interested in two problems at once. In one way, that might be good, of course; the genuine absorption in the problem of Planet Three was the best possible guard against suspicion of his other job; but it didn't help him to concentrate on that other. For hours now he had thought of practically nothing but his test project, until Allmer's parting remarks had jarred him back to duty.

He had assumed Allmer was a competent technician, but somehow he had not expected the acuity the elderly fellow had just displayed. Ken himself had missed the implication of Drai's statement concerning the habits of the natives of the third planet; apparently Drai had not even thought of doing his own reasoning.

But could he be that stupid? He, unlike Ken, knew the distances involved in a flight to that world, and the speed of the torpedoes; he had, on his own word, been trading here for years. What purpose could he have in trying to appear more stupid than he really was?

One possibility certainly existed. Ken might already be under suspicion, and facing a conspiracy to make him betray himself by overconfidence. Still, why in that case had the mechanic betrayed his own intelligence? Perhaps he was building himself up as a possible confidant, in case Ken were to grow communicative. If that were so, Feth was his greatest danger, since he was most in Ken's company and in best position to serve as a spy. On the other hand, the fellow might be completely innocent even if the group as a whole were engaged in smuggling, and his recent words might have been motivated by a sincere desire to be helpful. There seemed no way of telling at the moment which of these possibilities was the more likely; Ken gave the problem up for the moment as insoluble with the data on hand.

The other problem was demanding his attention, anyway. Some of the indicators on the board in front of him were fluctuating. He had learned the panel fairly well in the last day or two, and was able to interpret the readings himself. It seemed, he noted, that pressure and temperature were both going down in the cargo chamber of the projectile. Well, that was reasonable. There were no heaters working, and the pressure would naturally drop as the gas cooled. Then it occurred to him that the temperature of Planet Three was low

34

enough to freeze sulfur, and his test units would be covered with a crust of the stuff. Something should be done about that.

As a matter of fact, most of the pressure drop was due to leakage; the cargo door had cooled and contracted sufficiently to let air escape slowly around its edges. Ken, however, did not think of that; he found the appropriate switch and tripped it, watching the pressure drop instantly to zero as the door opened. The temperature was almost unaffected – if anything, it dropped more slowly, for the recording pyrometers were now insulated by a vacuum and the expansion of the gaseous sulfur into empty space had had no cooling effect to speak of. A touch on some of the switches which were designed to heat the test substances showed that the little furnaces were still in working order, and after a moment's thought Ken allowed the magnesium and titanium specimens to come up to melting temperature. Then, sure that they were as free of contaminating gases as could be managed, he watched the recorders as the samples cooled again. Through all this, the torpedo hurtled on, unaffected by the extra drain on its power.

For some minutes Ken continued to wait, one eye roving over the dials and the other glancing casually about the great room; but finally he decided that Allmer had picked a good time to go off duty. He did not feel tired himself, but gradually he became convinced that there must be something a little more constructive to do. He suspected that, even if there were to be any drugs around the station, they would not have arrived yet, so there was no use making a search for them; but preparations might be made to see just what came back in the other torpedo.

As a first step, it might be well to go up to the observatory to find out just who was guiding that missile. If it were Drai himself, it would be a point in favor of Rade; if not, it would be another person from whom information might be obtained. There seemed little doubt that no one would be allowed to run the trading torpedo who did not know, exactly what was being obtained on the third planet – the Planet of Ice, as Ken was coming to think of it (not that he thought of ice as a substance; he had never seen the material and would have thought of it as hydrogen oxide in any case. Planet of Solid Sulfur comes closer to the way he would have expressed the thought).

Ken was basing his supposition on his memory of how Drai had refrained from naming the substance obtained from the planet; and, determined to find at least one small brick of data to add to his edifice of information, the investigator headed up the spiral ramp toward the observatory at the station's highest level. No one attempted to stop him on the way, though he met a couple of workers who flipped tentacles in casual recognition. The door of the observatory was not locked, as a trial push showed, and he entered, still without opposition. He was braced for a prompt request to depart, and was a little surprised when nothing at all was said. A moment later, when his eyes had become accustomed to the dimness of the big room, he realized to his chagrin that no one was there.

'No business secrets loose so far,' he muttered.

He was about to return the way he had come, when it occurred to him that he might as well make sure of that fact. There were not many places where paper work of any sort could be kept, at least at first glance; and these he rapidly covered. They were mostly cabinets built under instrument panels, and seemed to contain nothing but tables of the motions of the planets of this system. These seemed rather valueless; their most probable use would be in navigation, and Ken could not imagine anyone's wanting to navigate any-where in this system except to the world of Ice. They could also be used to direct the instruments, if anyone wanted to look at the planets in question; but that seemed even less helpful.

Under the beam setting controls was a small drawer which also contained two sets of numbers – again, spatial coordinates; but this time Ken froze to attention as he realized that one set at least did not refer to planets – they contained no cyclic term. The set was short, consisting of six groups of num-bers containing from six to ten digits each; but he *recognized* them. The first identified by spectrum a beacon star; the next three were direction cosines, giving the three-dimensional bearing to another sun; the fifth gave a dis-tance. Normally he might not have recognized or remembered the lengthy figures; but those were the coordinates of the blazing A-class sun which warmed Sarr, his home planet. The final number was another range; and beyond question it represented the distance from the present point of obser-vation to the listed star. Ken knew enough of the standard navigational notations to be sure of that.

The other set of numbers, then, must give the direction of the same sun relative to some local set of coordinates; and not only was he ignorant of the coordinates, but the numbers were too long to remember. To copy them would be suicide, if anything more than commercial secrecy were involved. For long minutes Sallman Ken stood frozen in thought; then, abruptly, he slipped the sheet back into the drawer, closed the latter, and as quickly as was compatible with caution left the observatory. Since the information was there, it would not do for anyone to get the idea he had been there for any great length of time. It would be better if no one knew he had been there at all, but he had been seen on the way up the ramp. He proceeded to get back to his own quarters and assume an attitude of repose, though his mind still raced furiously.

He knew his distance from home. Evidently the twenty-two days of the journey to this system had not been spent in straight-line flight; the distance was only two hundred twelve parsecs. Score one for Rade; that would be an expensive business precaution, but a normal criminal one.

The direction home *from* this system he did not know. It did not matter too much anyway; what the Narcotics Bureau would want would be the opposite direction, on Galactic coordinates, and there would be no mathematical connection between the two except a purely arbitrary formula which would be harder to memorize than the direction itself.

Of course, the beacon listed in the stellar coordinates was probably visible from here; but could he recognize it with any certainty without instruments? The instruments were available, of course, but it might not be wise to be caught using them. No, orientation was definitely the last job to be accomplished in his present location.

At any rate, one fact had been learned and one point of probability had been added to the Rade theory. Sallman Ken decided that made a good day's work, and allowed himself to relax on the strength of it.

6

Nearly three of Sarr's thirteen-hour days passed uneventfully before the relay station circling Earth picked up the approaching torpedoes. As Feth Allmer had predicted – and Laj Drai had confirmed, after checking with his tables – the signals from the planted homing unit were coming from the dark side of the planet. Drai phoned down from the observatory to the shop, where Ken and Allmer were engaged in decelerating their missile.

'You may as well drop straight down as soon as you swing around to the dark side,' he said. 'You will pick up the beacon if you spiral in, keeping between forty and fifty-five degrees above the plane of the planet's orbit, measured from the planet's center. The beam can be picked up by your torpedo more than forty diameters out, so you can't possibly miss it. You'd better ride the beam down automatically until you're into atmosphere, then go manual and move off a couple of miles if you plan to go all the way to the ground. If the natives are camping near the beam transmitter, it would be a pity to touch off your chemicals right in their midst.'

'True enough,' Ken replied. 'Feth is swinging around into the shadow now, still about five diameters out. I wish there were a vision transmitter in that machine. Some time I'm going down close enough to use a telescope, unless someone builds a TV that will stand winter weather.'

'You'll get worse than frostbite,' Drai responded sincerely. 'The time you were really looking at that world, you didn't seem quite so anxious to get close to it.'

'I hadn't gotten curious then,' responded Ken.

The conversation lapsed for a while, as Feth Allmer slowly spun the verniers controlling the direction of thrust from the torpedo's drivers. The machine was, as Ken had said, cutting around into the shadow of the big planet, still with a relative speed of several miles per second to overcome. Allmer was navigating with the aid of a response-timer and directional loop in the relay station, whose readings were being reproduced on his own board; the torpedo was still too far from Earth for its reflection altimeter to be effective. For some minutes Ken watched silently, interpreting as best he could the motions of the flickering needles and deft tentacles. A grunt of satisfaction from the operator finally told him more clearly than the instruments that the beam had been reached; a snaky arm promptly twisted one of the verniers as far as it would go.

'I don't see why they couldn't power these things for decent acceleration,' Feth's voice came in an undertone. 'How much do you want to bet that we don't run all the way through the beam before I can match the planet's rotation? With nine-tenths of their space free for drivers and accumulators, you'd think they could pile up speed even without overdrive. These cheap—' his voice trailed off again. Ken made no reply, not being sure whether one was expected. Anyway, Allmer was too bright for his utterances to be spontaneous, and any answer should be carefully considered purely from motives of caution.

Apparently the mechanic had been unduly pessimistic; for in a matter of minutes he had succeeded in fighting the torpedo into a vertical descent. Even Ken was able to read this from the indicators; and before long the reflection altimeter began to register. This device was effective at a distance equal to Sarr's diameter – a trifle over six thousand miles – and Ken settled himself beside the operator as soon as he noted its reaction. There was not far to go.

His own particular bank of instruments, installed on a make-shift panel of their own by Allmer, were still idle. The pressures indicated zero, and the temperatures were low – even the sodium had frozen, apparently. There had been little change for many hours – apparently the whole projectile was nearly in radiative equilibrium with the distant sun. Ken watched tensely as the altimeter reading dropped, wondering slightly whether atmosphere would first make itself apparent through temperature or pressure readings.

As a matter of fact, he did not find out. Feth reported pressure first, before any of Ken's indicators had responded; and the investigator remembered that the door was shut. It had leaked before, of course, but that had been under a considerably greater pressure differential; apparently the space around the door was fairly tight, even at the temperature now indicated.

'Open the cargo door, please,' Ken responded to the report. 'We might as well find out if anything is going to react spontaneously.'

'Just a minute; I'm still descending pretty fast. If the air is very dense, I could tear the doors off at this speed.'

'Can't you decelerate faster?'

'Yes, now. Just a moment. I didn't want to take all night on the drop, but there's only about twenty miles to go now. You're the boss from here in.' The needle of the altimeter obediently slowed in its march around the dial. Ken began warming up the titanium sample – it had the highest meeting point of all. In addition, he was reasonably sure that there would be free nitrogen in the atmosphere; and at least one of the tests ought to work.

At five miles above the ground, the little furnace was glowing white hot, judging from the amount of light striking the photocell inside the nose compartment. Atmospheric pressure was quite measurable, though far from sufficient from the Sarrian point of view, if the Bourdon gauge could be trusted; and Feth claimed to have worked out a correction table by calibrating several of them on the dark side of Planet One.

'Can you hold it at this height for a while?' Ken asked. 'I'm going to let this titanium act up here, if I possibly can. There's atmosphere, and we're high enough not to be visible, I should think.' Allmer gestured to the reading of the photocell.

'The door is open, and that furnace is shining pretty brightly. You'd do better to shut the door, only that would keep air pretty well out. A light like that so far from the ground must show for scores of miles.'

'I never thought of that.' Ken was a trifle startled. He thought for a moment, then, 'Well, let's close the door anyway. We have a pressure reading. If that drops, we'll know that some sort of action is taking place.'

'True enough.' Allmer snapped the toggle closing the door and waited silently while Ken manipulated his controls. Deprived of the opening through which a good deal of heat had been radiating, the compartment temperature began to climb. By rights, the pressure should have done the same; but to Ken's intense satisfaction, it did not – it fell, instead. At his request, the door was opened for an instant and promptly closed again; results were consistent. The pressure popped back to its former value, then fell off once more. Apparently the titanium was combining with some gaseous component of the surrounding atmosphere, though not violently enough for the reaction to be called combustion.

'If you're far enough to one side of the beam, let's go down to the surface,' the investigator finally said. 'I'd like to find out what percentage of the air will react this way, and for any sort of accuracy I'll need all the atmospheric pressure I can get to start with.'

Feth Allmer gave the equivalent of a nod.

'We're a couple of miles to one side,' he said. 'I can drop straight down whenever you want. Do you want the door open or closed?'

'Closed. I'll let the sample cool a little, so we can get normal pressure after landing without using it all up. Then I'll warm it up again, and see how much of the air in the compartment is used up.' Feth gestured agreement, and a faint whistling became audible as the torpedo began to fall without power – like the others, it had speaker and sound pickups, which Allmer had not bothered to remove. Four miles – three – two – one – with deceptive casualness, the mechanic checked the plunge with a reading of one hundred fifty feet on the altimeter, and eased it very cautiously downward. As he did so, he gestured with one tentacle at another dial; and Ken, after a moment, understood. The projectile was already below the level of the homing station.

'I suppose the transmitter is on a mountain, and we're letting down into a valley,' Feth elaborated, without taking his eyes from his work.

'Reasonable enough – this was always supposed to be a rough section of the planet,' agreed Ken. 'It's good – there's that much less chance of being visible from a distance. What's the matter – aren't you down, after all?'

The altimeter had reached zero, but nothing had checked the descent. Faint rustlings had become audible in the last few seconds, and now these were supplemented by louder snappings and cracklings. Descent ceased for a moment. Apparently an obstacle sufficient to reflect radar waves and take the machine's weight had been encountered; but when a little downward drive was applied, the crackling progress continued for some distance. Finally, however, it ceased – noise and motion alike – even when Allmer doubled and quadrupled the power for several seconds. He opened his drive switches and turned to Ken with a gesture equivalent to a shrug.

'We seem to be down, though I can't guarantee it's ground as we know it. It seems to be as low as we can get, though. There's the door switch, in case you didn't know. You're on your own, unless you don't mind my hanging around to watch. I suppose the boss will be here soon, too; he should have his machine in an orbit by this time.'

'Sure – stick around. I'll be glad to have you. Maybe we'll have to move the thing around, for all I can tell at the moment.' He had opened the door as he spoke, and watched with interest as the pressure gauge snapped up to a value about two thirds of Sarr normal. At the same instant, the temperature dial of the still hot titanium furnace began to rise spontaneously – apparently the greater atmospheric density was more than able to offset the slight amount of cooling that had taken place; the metal was actually burning. Ken hastily shut the door.

The temperature continued to rise a short distance, while the light intensity in the cargo compartment of the torpedo held at a value that would have been intense even to eyes accustomed to Sarr's fervent sun. The most interesting information, however, came from the pressure gauge; and it was on this that Ken kept his attention glued.

For perhaps twenty seconds the reaction continued unabated; then it began to die out, and in ten more the temperature began once more to drop. The reason was evident; pressure had dropped to less than two percent of its former value. There was literally nothing left to carry on the reaction.

Ken emitted the booming drone from his sound-diaphragm that was the Sarrian equivalent of a whistle of surprise.

'I knew molten titanium would react to completion in our atmosphere, but I didn't think it would possibly do it here. I guess I was wrong – I was rather expecting a mixture of compounds, whose heats of formation would prevent any such reaction. Still, I suppose at this planet's temperature, they wouldn't have to be very stable from our point of view ...' his voice trailed off.

'Means nothing to me, but it certainly burned,' Feth Allmer remarked.

'How about your other samples? Are you going to run them off right away, or wait for things to cool down again to planet-normal?' Another dial caught Ken's eye before he could answer.

'Hey – who lit the sodium?' he asked, heedless of Allmer's query. 'It's cooling now, but it must have been burning, too, for a while when there was air.'

'Let more in and see.' The toggle snapped over, and there was a distinct popping sound as air rushed into the rear-vacuum. The sodium continued to cool.

'Maybe a spark from the titanium pot lighted it up.' Without answering, Ken closed the door once more and began to warm up the sodium container. Apparently Feth's suggestion was not too far from the mark; very little additional heat was needed to ignite the metal. This time the reaction stopped after pressure had dropped about a sixth. Then the door was opened again, and another touch of artificial heat caused the reaction to resume. This time it continued, presumably, until the sodium was consumed.

'I want enough material to work on when we get it back,' Ken explained, 'I'm not the Galaxy's best analytical chemist.'

The crucible of carbon dust gave decidedly peculiar results. *Something* certainly happened, for the material not only maintained but even increased its temperature for some time after the heating current was cut off; but there was no evidence either of consumption or production of gas in the closed chamber. Both Ken and Feth were slightly startled. The former, in response to the mechanic's quizzical expression, admitted the fact was probably significant but could offer no explanation.

Samples of iron, tin, lead, and gold followed in due course. None of these seemed greatly affected by the peculiar atmosphere at any temperature, with the possible exception of the iron; there the pressure drop was too small to be certain, since in each of these cases the heating had caused an increase in pressure which had to be allowed for. Magnesium behaved remarkably like sodium, except that it burned even more brightly than the titanium.

Here again Ken decided to finish off the metal by relighting it with the door open; and here the testing program received a sudden interruption.

Both Sarrians were perfectly aware that with the door open a beam of light must be stabbing out into the darkness. Both had ceased to worry about the fact; it had been equally true, though perhaps the radiance was fainter, with the blazing sodium and almost as much so when the sheer heat of the samples of iron and gold had been exposed. They had completely ceased to worry about being seen; a full hour had already passed since they had landed the torpedo, owing to the cooling periods necessary between tests, and there had been no sign that any attention had been attracted. Ken should have remembered the difficulty that had been encountered in reaching the ground.

The possibility was brought back to their attention with the relighting of the magnesium sample. As the photocell reported the reestablishment of combustion, a shrill sound erupted from the speaker above the control board and echoed through the ship. Neither had to be told what it was; both had heard the recordings of the voice of the Third Planet native who had found the original torpedo.

For an instant both remained frozen on their racks, exploring mentally the possibilities of the situation. Feth made a tentative gesture toward the power switches, only to be checked by an imperious snap of Ken's tentacles.

'Wait! Is our speaker on?' The words were whispered.

'Yes.' Feth pulled a microphone down to chest level and retreated a step. He wanted no part in what Ken seemed about to do. Sallman himself, however, had once more become completely absorbed in the mystery of the World of Ice, to the exclusion of all other matters; he saw no reason for leaving the site where his activities had been discovered. It did not even occur to him not to answer the native who appeared to have made the discovery. With his speaking diaphragm close to the microphone, he emulated the 'boss' of so many years before, and tried to imitate the sounds coming from the speaker.

The result was utter silence.

At first neither listener worried; the native would naturally be surprised. Gradually, however, an expression of mild anxiety began to appear on Ken's features, while an 'I-told-you-so' air became manifest about Feth.

'You've scared him away,' the latter finally said. 'If his tribe stampedes with him, Drai won't be very happy about it.'

A faint crackling which had preceded the alien's call, and which his concentration of chemical problems had prevented reaching Ken's conscious mind, suddenly ballooned into recollection, and he snatched at the straw.

'But we heard him coming – the same sort of noise the torpedo made landing – and we haven't heard him leave. He must still be waiting.'

'Heard him coming? Oh – that? How do you know that's what it was? Neither of us was paying any attention.'

'What else could it have been?' This was a decidedly unfair question, to which Feth attempted no direct answer. He simply countered with another.

'What's he waiting for, then?' Fate was unkind to him; Ken was spared the necessity of answering. The human voice came again, less shrill this time; history seemed to be repeating itself. Ken listened intently; Feth seemed to have forgotten his intention of dissociating himself from the proceedings and was crowded as close as the detective to the speaker. The voice went on, in short bursts which required little imagination to interpret as questions. Not a word was understandable, though both thought they recognized the human 'no' on several occasions. Certainly the creature did not utter any of the names that the Sarrians had come to associate with trade items – Feth, who knew them all, was writing them on a scrap of paper. Ken finally grew impatient, took the list from the mechanic, and began to pronounce them as well as he could, pausing after each.

'Iridium – Flatinum – Gold – Osmium—'

'Gold!' the unseen speaker cut in.

'Gold!' responded Ken intelligently, into the microphone, and 'which one is that?' in a hasty aside to Feth. The mechanic told him, also in a whisper. 'There's a sample in the torpedo. We can't trade it off – I want to analyze it for traces of corrosion. Anyway it was melted a little while ago, and he'll never get it out of the crucible. What's the name for the stuff you get from them?'

'Tofacco.' Feth answered without thinking – but he started thinking immediately afterward. He remembered Drai's promise of the fate of anyone who gave Ken information about 'the stuff' obtained from Earth, and knew rather better than Sallman just how jocular Laj was likely to be. The memory made him itch, as though his hide were already coming loose. He wondered how he could keep news of his slip from reaching the higher levels, but had no time to get a really constructive idea. The speaker interrupted him again.

If the previous calls had been loud, this was explosive. The creature must have had his vocal apparatus within inches of the torpedo's microphone, and been using full voice power to boot. The roar echoed for seconds through the shop and almost drowned out the clanking which followed – a sound which suggested something hard striking the hull of the torpedo. The native, for some reason, seemed to have become wildly excited.

At almost the same instant, Ken also gave an exclamation. The thermometer dial for the gold sample had ceased to register.

'The blasted savage is stealing my sample!' he howled, and snapped over the switch closing the cargo door. The switch moved, but the door apparently didn't – at least, it failed to indicate 'locked.' There was no way of telling whether or not it had stopped at some partly-closed position.

The native was still jabbering – more than ever, if that were possible. Ken switched back to 'open' position, waited a moment, and tried to close again. This time it worked. The Sarrians wondered whether the relatively feeble motor which closed the portal had been able to cause any injury. There seemed little doubt about the cause of the first failure; if there had been any, the noise would have removed it.

'I don't think he was trying to steal,' Feth said mildly. 'After all, you repeated the name of the stuff more than once. He probably thought you were offering it to him.'

'I suppose you may be right.' Ken turned back to the microphone. 'I'll try to make clear that it's market day, not a wedding feast.' He gave a chirruping whistle, then 'Tofacco! tofacco! Gold – tofacco!' Feth shrivelled, internally. If he could only learn to keep his big diaphragm frozen—

44

'Tofacco! Gold – tofacco! I wonder whether that will mean anything to him?' Ken turned a little away from the microphone. 'This may not be one of the creatures you've been trading with – after all, we're not in the usual place.'

'That's not the principal question!' Feth's tentacles coiled tightly around his torso, as though he were expecting a thunderbolt to strike somewhere in the neighborhood. The voice which had made the last statement was that of Laj Drai.

7

Roger Wing, at thirteen years of age, was far from stupid. He had very little doubt where his father and brother had been, and he found the fact of considerable interest. A few minutes' talk with Edie gave him a fairly accurate idea of how long they had been gone; and within ten minutes of the time he and his mother returned from Clark Fork he had sharply modified his older ideas about the location of the 'secret mine.' Hitherto, his father had always been away several days on his visits to it.

'You know, Edie, that mine can't be more than eight or ten miles from here, at the outside.' The two were feeding the horses, and Roger had made sure the younger children were occupied elsewhere. 'I talked to Don for about two minutes, and I know darned well Dad was showing him the mine. I'm going to see it, too, before the summer's out. I'll take bets on it.'

'Do you think you ought to? After all, if Dad wanted us to know, he'd tell us.'

'I don't care. I have a right to know anything I can find out. Besides, we can do a better job of scouting if we know the place we're supposed to be protecting.'

'Well – maybe.'

'Besides, you know Dad sometimes sets things up just so we'll find things out for ourselves. After it's all over he just says that's what we have brains for. Remember he never actually *said* we weren't to go looking for the mine – he just said he'd tell us when the time came. How about that?'

'Well – maybe. What are you going to do about it? If you try to follow Dad you'll be picked up like a dime in a schoolroom.'

'That's what you think. Anyway, I'm not going to follow him. I'll lead him. I'll go out the first thing tomorrow morning and look for any traces they may have left. Then the next time they go, I'll be waiting for them at the farthest trace I could find, and go on from there. That'll work, for sure!'

'Who does the patrolling?'

'Oh, we both do, same as before. This won't take long. Anyway, like I said, since I'll be watching the trail they take, it'll be even better than the regular patrol. Don't you think?' Edie looked a little dubious as she latched the door of the feed bin.

'You'll probably get away with it, but I bet you'll have to talk fast,' was her verdict as they headed for the house.

46

Twenty-four hours later Roger was wondering whether any excuses would be needed at all. Things had not gone according to his sweepingly simple forecast.

In the first place, he had not had time to check any trail his father and Don might have left; for the two started out at daybreak the next morning. They did not follow the previous day's route, but the one Mr Wing had always taken in years past – the admittedly zigzag path specifically designed to permit his scouts to take short cuts to warn him, in the event that anyone followed. Roger and Edith were given stations which were to be watched for one hour after the two men had passed; each was then to intercept the trail and make a report, whether or not anyone had been seen. Roger looked suspiciously at his sister for an instant when those orders were received, but decided she would never have told his plans. His father was simply one jump ahead, as usual.

A good fraction of the morning had passed by the time he had made his report, and watched his father and brother disappear to the north. This was not the direction they had gone the day before, according to Edith; now the question was whether or not they had bothered to lay a false trail on that occasion, too. The only way to settle that appeared to be a straightforward search for traces. That was not too hopeless; as Roger had said while telling his father about the new patrol arrangements, there were places practically impossible to cross without leaving some sort of track, and the mere act of avoiding all those places would narrow down considerably the routes a person could take.

In spite of this, the boy had decided by dinner time that either he knew less about tracking than he had supposed or else the two he sought had spent the day in the attic. Certainly he had found nothing to which he could point with confidence as being evidence of their passage.

After the meal he had abandoned that line of research, and simply headed eastward. His sister had said they had taken this direction, and there was the remote chance that they might have abandoned precautions just that once. He travelled without pause for nearly half the afternoon, following what seemed to be natural trails, and finally stopped some eight miles from home.

He found himself in a valley, its center marked as usual by a noisy brook. The hills on either side were high, though by no means as high as some of their neighbors – six to seven thousand feet was a common height in this part of the range. He had not been here before, either alone or with his father, but still felt he had a good idea of his location. His principal worry was the fact that he had as yet seen no sign of his father or brother.

His intention was to work back toward the house from this point, zigzagging to cover as much territory as possible before dark. The first zig, he decided, should take him straight up the side of the hill to the south, thus crossing any possible trails cutting around this side of the mountain. After reaching the top, he could decide whether to go down the other side at once, or head west a short distance before sweeping back to the north. As it turned out, he never had to make that decision.

Roger Wing was not, of course, as competent a tracker as he liked to believe. As a matter of fact, he had crossed the trail he was so diligently seeking four times since leaving the house. His present location was at the foot of the hill bearing the open slope which the 'miners' had crossed the day before, and within a mile of the Sarrian homing station. The course he now took uphill would have led him within a few rods of the transmitter.

However, he didn't get that far. Donald had been perfectly correct in concluding that no one could cross that slope of loose rock without leaving traces. Roger failed to recognize the marks left by the two on the way out, but he did find where his brother had forced his way through an unusually thick patch of brush at the top of the scree on the way back. It was carelessness on the older boy's part, of course; his attention at the time had been mainly taken up with the search for tracks left by the possible followers, and he had paid no attention to those he himself was leaving. While the broken bushes gave Roger no clue to the traveller's identity, they indicated his direction very clearly; and the boy promptly turned westward. Had he stopped to think, it would have occurred to him that a trail in this direction hardly jibed with the assumption that his father and brother were going straight to the 'mine'; but he was not thinking at the moment. He was tracking, as he would have told anyone who might have asked.

Once out of the patch of brush, the trail was neither more nor less obvious than it had been all along; but Roger was able to follow it. Probably the assurance that there was a trail to follow had something to do with that. He still did not know whether the traces had been left by his father, his brother, or both. He also failed to recognize the point where the two had come together after covering both sides of the scree. He simply went on, picking out the occasional scuff in the carpet of fir needles or snapped twigs where the bushes were thicker. He descended the west side of the hill, after following it around from the point where the first traces had appeared. He crossed the narrow valley on this side, leaping the inevitable brook with little difficulty. Here he found the only assurance that he was actually following two people, in the indentations where they had landed on the bank after a similar leap. The marks were just dents, for the needles did not retain any definite shoe patterns, but there were four of them. They were in two pairs, one of each deeper than its fellow, as though the jumper had taken the shock of landing principally on one foot.

Up the side of the next hill the boy went. It was darker now under the trees, for the sun was already concealed by the peak ahead of him; and presently he began to wonder whether he were really on the right trail. He stopped, looking about, and saw first to one side and then the other marks of the sort he had been following. He could not, he found, convince himself that those ahead of him were the right ones.

He tried to go on, then hesitated again. Then he began to backtrack – and reached the brook many yards from the spot at which he had jumped it. He spent some minutes searching for the marks, and when he had found them realized that he had not even followed his own back trail with any accuracy.

He should, of course, have headed for home right then. Equally, of course, he did nothing of the sort. While the gloom on the mountain's eastward face grew ever deeper, he cast about for tracks. Every few minutes he found something, and spent long seconds over it before deciding to make sure – and then he always found something else. Gradually he worked his way up the mountain side, finally reaching open rock; and after deep thought, he moved around to the other side where it was lighter, and resumed his search. After all, the men had been heading westward.

He had crossed another valley – this time its central watercourse was dry, and there was no sign of anyone's jumping over – and was near the top of the unusually low hill on its farther side when he finally realized the time. He had been searching with a single-mindedness which had prevented even hunger from forcing itself on his attention. The sheer impossibility of seeing details on the shadowed ground was all that finally compelled him to consider other matters. He had no flashlight, as he had not contemplated remaining out this late. Worse, he had neither food, water, nor a blanket. The first two were serious omissions, or would be if his father heard of his venturing any distance into the woods without them.

It was quite suddenly borne in upon Roger Wing, as he saw the first stars glimmering in the deepening blue between the tree tops, that he was not another Daniel Boone or Kit Carson. He was a thirteen year old boy whose carelessness had gotten him into a situation that was certainly going to be uncomfortable and might even be serious.

Though rash, Roger was not stupid. His first action upon realizing the situation was not a wild break for home. Instead he sensibly stood where he was and proceeded to plan a course of action.

He was certainly going to be cold that night. There was no help for that, though a shelter of fir branches would make some difference. Also, there was no food, or at least none that he would be able to find in the dark. Water, however, should be findable; and, after all, it was the greatest necessity. Remembering that the valley he had just crossed lacked a stream, the boy started on again over the low top in front of him and began to pick his way down the other side. He was forced to rely almost entirely on touch before he reached the bottom, for the lingering twilight made little impression on the gloom beneath the firs. He found a brook, as he had hoped, partly by sound and partly by almost falling over the bank.

He did have a knife, and with this he cut enough fir branches to make a bed near the stream, and to lean against a fallen log beside it as a crude roof – he knew that anything at all to break air circulation immediately over his body would be a help. He then drank, loosened his belt, and crawled under the rude shelter. All things considered, he was not too long in going to sleep.

He was a healthy youngster, and the night was not particularly cold. He slept soundly enough so that the crackling and crashing of branches in the forest roof failed to awaken him, and even the louder crunching as Ken's torpedo settled through the underbrush forty yards away only caused him to mutter sleepily and turn over.

But he was awakened at last, by the stimulus which sends any forest resident into furious activity. The cargo door of the torpedo faced the boy's shelter. The light from burning sodium and glowing gold and iron did not disturb him – perhaps they only gave him bad dreams, or perhaps he was facing the other way at the time. The blazing radiance of the burning magnesium, however, blasted directly onto his closed eyelids, and enough of it got through to ring an alarm. He was on his feet yelling 'Fire,' before he was fully awake.

He had seen the aftermath of more than one forest fire – there had been a seventy-five hundred acre blaze the summer before north of Bonner's Ferry, and a smaller but much closer one near Troy. He knew what such a catastrophe meant for life in its path, and for several seconds was completely panic-stricken. He even made a leap away from the direction of the radiance, and was brought to his senses by the shock of falling over the tree trunk beside which he had been sleeping.

Coming to his feet more slowly, he realized that the light was not the flickering, ruddy glow of wood flames, that there was none of the crackling roar he had heard described more than once, and that there was no smell of smoke. He had never seen magnesium burn, but the mere fact that this was not an ordinary forest fire allowed his curiosity to come once more into the foreground.

The light was sufficient to permit him to clear the little stream without difficulty, and in a matter of seconds he had crashed through the underbrush to its source, calling as he went, 'Hello! Who's that? What's that light?'

The booming grumble of Sallman Ken's answer startled him out of his wits. The drumlike speaking diaphragm on the Sarrian torso can be made to imitate most human speech sounds, but there is a distortion that is readily apparent to any human ear; and the attempt to imitate his words in those weird tones sent prickling chills down the boy's spine. The fact that he *could* recognize his own words in the booming utterance made it, if anything, rather worse.

He stopped two yards from the torpedo, wondering. The blue-white glare from the rectangular opening had died away abruptly as he approached, and had been replaced by a fading yellow-white glow as the crucible which had contained the magnesium slowly cooled. He could just see into the door. The chamber beyond seemed to occupy most of the interior of that end of the structure, as nearly as he could tell from his inadequate view of the outside, and its door was covered with roughly cylindrical objects a trifle larger than his fist. One of these was the source of the white-hot glow, and at least two others still radiated a dull red. He had noticed only this much when Ken began to go through his precious-metals list.

Roger knew, of course, what platinum and iridium were, even when the former suffered from the peculiarities of the Sarrian vocal apparatus; but like many other human beings, it was the mention of gold that really excited him. He repeated the word instantly.

'Gold!'

'Gold.' The booming voice from the torpedo responded, and Roger found the courage to approach the still radiant doorway, and look in. As he had guessed, the little cylindrical crucibles were everywhere. The chamber was covered with white dust, the oxides of titanium and magnesium which had sprayed from the containers during the energetic reactions which had produced them. Tiny yellowish globules of sodium peroxide were spread almost as widely. A noticeable wave of heat could still be felt coming from the chamber along with a faint sulfurous smell, but when Roger laid a cautious hand in the dust of its floor the temperature proved to be bearable. He saw almost instantly what he supposed the hidden speaker had been talking about – the gold which had already solidified in its small container. The light was bright enough for him to recognize it, particularly since there was nothing else of even approximately the same color in the chamber.

The box acted instantly, but with more forethought than might have been expected. A dead branch which he picked up as he approached was put to use – the door of the compartment reminded him too much of a trap, and he propped it open. Then he made a grab for the pot of gold.

He did not see the wires which connected its heater to the power source of the torpedo. After touching the crucible, he did not even look for them, though they were the only reason he did not succeed in getting the container out. He had time for one good tug before the fact that the metal had only recently been melted made itself felt.

Roger, his face almost inside the compartment, yelled even more whole-heartedly then he had before, released the crucible, delivered a furious kick on the hull of the torpedo, and danced about, holding his scorched hand and hurling abuse at the unseen beings who had been responsible for the injury. He did not notice the stick which he had used as a prop suddenly snap as the door started to close, or the thud as the portal jammed against the fragments of wood. The sudden cutting off of nearly all the light, however, did catch his attention, and he saw what had happened when the door opened again. Without quite knowing why he did so, he swept the pieces out of the way with his uninjured hand, and a moment later he was left in darkness as the door closed completely. He had an uneasy idea that he was being watched.

Again the voice boomed out. He recognized the word 'gold' again, but the syllables which alternated with it were too much distorted for him to understand. He had, after all, no tobacco on his person, and there certainly was none in the torpedo, so that there was nothing to bring the substance to mind. He made no attempt to imitate the alien-sounding word, and after a moment the utterance ceased.

It was replaced by fainter sounds, which somehow did not seem to be directed at him, although they had the complexity of speech. Roger would not, of course, have analyzed them in just that way, but he got the distinct impression that they represented a conversation he could not understand.

This lasted for what seemed to the boy a long time; then the earlier refrain broke out again. 'Gold – tofacco – gold – tofacco!' Eventually it got on even Roger's nerves, and he yelled at the dark hulk.

'I don't know what you're saying, darn you! I'm darned if I'll touch your gold again, and I don't know what the other words are. Shut up!' He kicked the hull again, to emphasize his feelings, and was rather startled when the voice fell silent. He backed away a little farther, wondering what this presaged. It was well he did.

An instant later, without preliminary sound, the dark shape of the torpedo lunged upward, crashed through the overhanging branches, and vanished into the black sky with a whistle of protesting air. For minutes the boy stood where he was, gazing up through the gap smashed in the limbs; but nothing rewarded his efforts except the stars.

Roger Wing got very little sleep that night, and the fact that he got his feet wet finding his shelter was only partly responsible.

8

'No, that's not the principal question.' Laj Drai repeated the statement rather thoughtfully, as he glided into the shop and absently closed the door behind him.

'Sir, I—' Feth got no farther with his expostulation.

'Oh, don't let me interrupt. Go right ahead, Ken – you have a problem on your hands, I see. Get it out of the way, and we'll tackle the other afterwards. There'll be no interruptions then.'

Rather puzzled, for he had completely forgotten Drai's threat, Ken turned back to his microphone and resumed the apparently endless chant. While he did not understand the words with which Roger finally interrupted, the thing had gone on long enough so that he shared the boy's impatience to some extent. Also, the clank as Roger kicked the torpedo was at least suggestive.

It was Drai who drove the projectile into the air, an instant later. He had never heard those words, either; but they were different enough from the usual human conversation to start him shivering. The thought of strained or severed relations with Planet Three was one he could not face – and this being was definitely excited and more than probably angry. That blow on the hull of the torpedo—

Drai's tentacle whipped past Sallman Ken at the thought, and the main power and drive director switches closed as one. The investigator swivelled around on the control rack, and eyed his employer curiously.

'You seem almost as excited as the native. What's the matter?' Laj drew a deep breath, and finally got his voice under control. He was just beginning to realize that his dramatic entry had not been the wisest of moves. It was perfectly possible that his hired expert had learned the name of Earth's product quite innocently; and if that were the case he would be ill-advised to attach too much weight to the incident – publicly, at least. He shifted ground, therefore, as smoothly as he could.

'Your chemical analysis seems to have encountered complications.'

'It would seem so. Apparently your natives are not quite so completely diurnal as you gave me to understand.' Ken was not intentionally defending his actions, but he could have found no better answer. Laj Drai paused momentarily.

'Yes, that is a point that surprises me a little. For twenty years they have never signalled except during their daytime. I wonder if the flatlanders had anything to do with it? I can't imagine what or how, though. Did you finish your tests?'

'Enough, I guess. We'll have to bring the torpedo back here, so I can find out just what that atmosphere did to my samples. Some of them burned, we already know, but I'd like to know what was produced.'

'Of course it couldn't be sulfides. That's what one thinks of as the natural product of combustion.'

'Not unless frozen sulfur dust is suspended in the atmosphere in tremendous quantities. I hadn't thought of that, though – I'll check for it when the samples come back. Actually, I'm a little bothered by the results so far. I couldn't think of anything gaseous at that temperature which would support combustion, and something definitely does.'

'How about fluorine?' Laj was digging in the dim memories of an elementary science course.

'Maybe – but how come it exists free in the atmosphere? I should think it would be *too* active, even at that temperature. Of course, I suppose the same would be true of anything which would support combustion, so we'll simply have to wait until the samples are back. You know, I'm almost at the point where I'd be willing to risk a landing there, to *see* what the place is like.' Drai shrugged expressively.

'If you and Feth can figure out a way of doing it, I won't stop you. We might even see our way to offering a bonus. Well, it'll be nearly three days before your stuff is back here, and there won't be much to do in the meantime. Feth will cut it in on the beam when it's far enough from Three.'

Ken took this as a hint to leave, and drifted aimlessly out into the corridors. He had some thinking of his own to do. As Drai had said, nothing could be done about Planet Three until the return of the torpedo, and he had no excuse for not considering Rade's problem for a while.

The product was called 'tofacco.' That, at least, was information. Rade had had no name for the narcotic he sought, so the information was of questionable value so far.

This planetary system was relatively close to Sarr. Another fact. The precautions taken by Drai and his people to conceal that fact might or might not be considered reasonable for a near-legal commercial enterprise, but were certainly natural for anything as blatantly criminal as drug-running.

Planet Three was cold – to put it feebly – and the drug in question could not stand normal temperatures. That was a link of rather uncertain strength, reinforced slightly by Drai's tacit admission that 'tofacco' was a vegetable product.

Think as he would, he could recall no other information which could be of the slightest use to Rade. Ken was mildly annoyed at the narcotics chief anyway for involving him in such a matter, and was certainly more willing than

a professional policeman would have been to go back to the purely astronomical and ecological problem that was facing him.

How about his pesky Planet Three? Certainly it was inhabited – a fantastic
enough fact in itself. Certainly it was not well known; no vision transmitter
and no manned ship had ever gotten through its atmosphere. That seemed a
little queer, now that Ken considered the matter again. Granted the fearful
cold, and the fact that an atmosphere would conduct heat away as space
could not, he still found it hard to believe that a competent engineer could
not design apparatus capable of the descent. Feth was supposed to be a mechanic rather than an engineer, of course; but still it seemed very much as
though the organization were singularly lacking in scientific resource. The
very fact that Ken himself had been hired made that fact even more
evident.

Perhaps he was not so far from Rade's problem after all. Certainly any
regular interstellar trading organization could and always did have its own
ecological staff – no such concern could last without one, considering the
rather weird situations apt to arise when, for example, metal-rich Sarr traded
with the amphibious chemistry wizards of Rehagh. Yet he, Sallman Ken, a
general science dabbler, was all that Laj Drai could get! It was not strange; it
was unbelievable. He wondered how Drai had made the fact seem reasonable
even for a moment.

Well, if he found out nothing they would probably not bother him. He could
and would investigate Planet Three as completely as he could, go home,
and turn his information over to Rade – let the narcotics man do what he
wanted with it. Planet Three was more interesting.

How to land on the blasted planet? He could see keeping large ships out of
its atmosphere, after the trouble with the natives of the flat, bluish areas. Still,
torpedoes had been running the gauntlet without loss for twenty years, and
the only detectable flatlander activity had been radar beams in the last two or
three. Those were easily fooled by quarter wave coatings, as Drai had said.
No, the only real objections were the frightful natural conditions of the
world.

Well, a standard suit of engineer's armor would let a Sarrian work in a lake
of molten aluminum for quite a while. There, of course, the temperature difference was less than it would be on the Planet of Ice; but the conductivity of
the metal must be greater than that of the planet's atmosphere, and might
make up the difference. Even if it did not, the armor could be given extra
heating coils or insulation or both. Why had this never been tried? He would
have to ask Feth or Laj Drai.

Then, granting for the moment that a landing could not be made even this
way, why was television impossible? Ken refused to believe that the thin glass
of a television tube could not be cooled down sufficiently to match the world's

conditions without shattering, even if the electrical parts had to be kept hot. Surely the difference could be no greater than in the ancient incandescent bulbs!

He would have to put both these points up to Feth. He was heading purposefully back toward the shop with this plan in mind, when he encountered Drai, who greeted him as though there had been no suspicious thoughts in his own brain that day.

'Feth has cut you in to the main beam, and no piloting will be needed for nearly three days,' he said. 'You looked as though you were going back to your controls.'

'I wanted to talk to Feth again. I've been thinking over the matter of armor and apparatus withstanding Planet Three's conditions, and it seems to me something could be done.' He went on to give a censored version of his recent thoughts to his employer.

'I don't know,' the latter said when he had finished. 'You'll have to talk to Feth, as you planned. We've tried it, since he joined us, and the failures occurred just as he said in the matter of television. He was not with us on the original expedition, which did no investigating except as I originally told you – it was strictly a pleasure cruise, and the only reason there were so many torpedoes available was that the owner of the ship preferred to do his sightseeing in comfort – he'd send out a dozen at once, when we entered a planetary system, and keep the *Karella* in space until he found something he wanted to see or do personally.'

'I've never met him, have I?'

'No – he died long ago. He was pretty old when we hit this place. I inherited the ship and got into this trading business.'

'When did Feth join you?'

'A year or two after I got started – he's the oldest in the crew in point of service. He can tell you all about the engineering troubles, you see, and I certainly can't. You'd better see him, if he feels like talking.' Without explaining this last remark, Drai disappeared down the corridor. Ken did not wonder at the words – he had already come to regard Feth as a taciturn personality.

The mechanic did not appear to be busy. He was still draped in the rack in front of the torpedo controls, and seemed to be thinking. He rose as Ken entered the room, but said nothing, merely giving the equivalent of a nod of greeting. Not noticing anything unusual in his manner, Ken began immediately to spill forth his ideas. He was allowed to finish without interruption.

'Your points all sound good,' the mechanic admitted when he had heard them, 'and I certainly can't bring any theory against them. I can merely point out that the tubes do break. If you want to send down a suit of armor full of thermometers and pressure gauges, that's all right with me, but I trust you'll pardon a pessimistic attitude. I used up a lot of good TV equipment in that atmosphere.'

'Well, I admit your superior practical knowledge,' replied Ken, 'but I do think it's worth trying.'

'If the instruments read all right, who goes down in the armor the next time? The thought makes my knee-joints stiff. I'm scared of the idea, and don't mind admitting it.'

'So am I.' Ken remembered the uncontrollable emotion that had swept his being the first time he had seen Planet Three. 'It's a ghastly place, beyond doubt; but I still like to find things out, and I'm willing to take a chance on my health to do it.'

'Health – huh! You'd be a ready-made memorial statue five seconds after the first pinhole appeared in your suit,' retorted the mechanic. 'I almost feel it's a dirty trick to send good instruments down into that, even when I know they can take it. Well, I'll break out a suit of armor, if you really want to try it. There are plenty of torpedoes.'

'How can you carry it by torpedo? You can't possibly get it inside, surely.'

'No; there are rings on the outer hull, and we can clamp the suit to those. We'll just have to be careful and go through the atmosphere more slowly, this time.' He glided down the length of the shop to a set of lockers at the far end, and from one of these wrestled a suit of the much-discussed armor into view.

Even under Mercurian gravity it was difficult to handle. Owing to the peculiarities of the Sarrian physique, a greatly superior leverage could be obtained from inside the garment; but even knowing this, Ken began to wonder just what he was going to do if he succeeded in reaching the surface of the massive Planet Three in that metal monstrosity, under nearly four times his present gravity. That thought led to a question.

'Feth, what sort of body chemistry do you suppose these natives have? They move around – presumably – under a whopping gravity in a tempera-ture that should freeze any organic material. Ever thought about it?' The mechanic was silent for some time, as though considering his reply.

'Yes,' he said at last, 'I'll admit I've thought about it. I'm not sure I want to talk about it, though.'

'Why not? The place can't be that repulsive.'

'It's not that. You remember what Drai said he'd do if anyone gave you information about the stuff we got from the planet?'

'Yes, vaguely; but what does that have to do with it?'

'Maybe nothing, maybe not. He was pretty sore about my telling you the name of the stuff. I wouldn't have done it if I'd stopped to think. The situation just seemed to call for a quick answer, so I gave it.'

'But your ideas on the native chemistry could hardly tell – or I suppose perhaps they could. Still, Drai knows perfectly well I've never worked for another trading company and I'm not a trader myself – why should I be treated like a commercial spy? I don't care particularly what your stuff is – I'm interested in the planet.'

'I don't doubt it. Just the same, if I ever make any more slips like that, please keep whatever you learn to yourself. I thought there'd be a nuclear explosion when Drai walked in with you yelling "Tofacco!" into the mike.'

'He couldn't really do much, though.' This was a ranging question; Ken had started to think again.

'Well –' Feth was cautious about his answer – 'he's the boss, and this isn't such a bad job. Just do the favor, if you don't mind.' He turned back to the armor, with an expression on his face which indicated he was through talking for the time being. Ken found himself unable to get anything definite from the mechanic's answer.

He didn't think about it very hard anyway, for the other problem proved too interesting. Feth was certainly a good mechanic; as good as some rated engineers Ken had known. He had opened the armor completely and removed all the service plates, and started the job by giving it a full overhaul inspection. That completed, he refilled the zinc circulating system and replaced and safetied the plates he had removed, but left the armor itself open. One eye rolled questioningly at the watcher, and he spoke for the first time in two hours.

'Have you any ideas about instrument arrangement? You know best what you want to find out.'

'Well, all we really need to know is whether the suit can maintain temperature and pressure. I suppose a single pressure gauge anywhere inside, and thermometers at the extremities, would tell enough. Can you use telemetering instruments, or will we have to wait until this torpedo gets back, too?'

'I'm afraid we'll have to wait. The instruments themselves would be easy enough to install, but the voice transmitter in the armor couldn't handle their messages. I can put a multiple recorder in the body, connect the instruments to that, and arrange so you can turn it on and off by remote control – I'll simply tie it in to one of the suit controls. I suppose you'll want to be able to manipulate the suit heaters, as well?'

'Yes. If it takes anywhere near full power to maintain livable temperature, we ought to know it. I suppose extra heaters could be installed, if necessary?'

'I expect so.' For the first time, Feth wore an expression approximating a grin. 'I could probably mount blast furnaces on the feet. I'm not so sure you could walk around with them.'

'Even if I can't I can at least see.'

'If you don't have the same trouble with your visor that I did with TV tubes. Even quartz has its limitations.'

'I still think it can take it. Anyway, it won't cost *us* anything to find out. Let's go ahead and mount those instruments – I'm rather curious to see which of us is right. Is this recorder all right?' He took from a cabinet a minute machine whose most prominent feature was the double reel of sensitized tape, and held it up as he spoke. Feth glanced at it.

'Only one record. Get an L-7. You can recognize it by the reel – its tape is about five times as wide. I'm using the single barometer you suggested, and thermometers in head, trunk, one foot, and one sleeve as far out as I can mount it. That leaves a free band on the tape that you can use for anything you want.' The mechanic was working as he spoke, clamping tiny instruments from a well-stocked supply cabinet into the places he had mentioned. For a moment Ken wondered whether the existence of this more than adequate instrument stock did not invalidate his argument about the lack of scientific facilities; then he recognized that all the devices were perfectly standard engineering instruments, and represented nothing but a respectable financial outlay. Anyone could buy and almost anyone could use them.

In spite of Feth's evident skill, the job was a long one. They did not sleep, being Sarrians, but even they had to rest occasionally. It was during one of these rests that Ken happened to notice the time.

'Say,' he remarked to his companion, 'it must be daylight on that part of the planet by now. I wonder if Drai has made his landing yet?'

'Very probably,' Feth replied, one eye following Ken's gaze toward the clock. 'He is more than likely to be back in space again – he doesn't waste much time as a rule.'

'In that case, would I be likely to be skinned for dropping in to the observatory?' Feth gazed at him narrowly for long enough to let Ken regret the question.

'I probably would be if Drai found out I'd encouraged you,' was the answer. 'I think it would be better if you stayed here. There's plenty for us to do.' He rose and returned to his labors, although the rest period had scarcely started. Ken, realizing he did not intend to say any more, joined him.

The work turned out to be timed rather nicely. By the time the armor had survived a one-hour leakage and radiation-loss test in the vacuum of the shadowed airlock, had been clamped to the load rings of another torpedo, and launched into the void on automatic control, the other projectile was on the point of landing. The automatic control, in fact, was necessary – the second missile could not be handled by radio until the first had been docked, since the other controlling station was still being used by Drai to bring his own load back to Mercury.

A single rest period fitted nicely between the launching of the suit and the landing of the mobile laboratory; and Ken was awaiting the latter with eagerness when it finally drifted through the air lock under Feth's expert control.

He would have pounced on it at once, but was restrained by a warning cry from the mechanic.

'Hold on! It's not as cold as it was out on Planet Three, but you'll still freeze to it. Look!' A tentacle waved toward the gleaming hull, on which drops of liquid sulfur were condensing, running together and trickling to the floor, where they promptly boiled away again. 'Let that stop, first.'

Ken stopped obediently, feeling the icy draft pour about his feet, and backed slowly away. The air that reached him was bearable, but the hull of the torpedo must be cold enough to freeze zinc, if it had reached radiative equilibrium for this distance from the sun.

Long minutes passed before the metal was warmed through and the drip of liquid sulfur ceased. Only then did Feth open the cargo door, whereupon the process was repeated. This time the straw-colored liquid made a pool on the floor of the cargo compartment, flooding around the crucibles and making Ken wonder seriously about the purity of his samples. He turned on all the heaters at low strength to get rid of the stuff as fast as possible. Since there was a serious chance of further reaction with the air if a high temperature were attained, he opened the switches again the moment the hissing and bubbling of boiling air ceased; and at last he was free to examine his results. As Roger Wing could have told him, they were quite a sight!

9

Some of the little pots were full; most of these appeared to be unchanged. Others, however, were not. The contents of most of these were easy to find, but Ken could see that they were going to be hard to identify.

A white powder was literally over everything, as Roger had already seen. The yellow flecks of sodium peroxide were turning grayish as they decomposed in the heat. The gold crucible had been pulled from its base, but was otherwise unchanged; the iron had turned black; sodium, magnesium and titanium had disappeared, though the residue in each crucible gave promise that some of the scattered dust could be identified. There was still carbon in the container devoted to that substance, but much less of it than there had been.

All these things, however, interesting and important as they might be, only held the attention of Feth and Ken for a moment; for just inside the cargo door, imprinted clearly in the layer of dust, was a mark utterly unlike anything either had ever seen.

'Feth, dig up a camera somewhere. I'm going to get Drai.' Ken was gone almost before the words had left his diaphragm, and for once Feth had nothing to say. His eyes were still fixed on the mark.

There was nothing exactly weird or terrifying about it; but he was utterly unable to keep his mind from the fascinating problem of what had made it. To a creature which had never seen anything even remotely like a human being, a hand print is apt to present difficulties in interpretation. For all he could tell, the creature might have been standing, sitting, or leaning on the spot, or sprawled out in the manner the Sarrians substituted for the second of those choices. There was simply no telling; the native might be the size of a Sarrian foot, making the mark with his body – or he might have been too big to get more than a single appendage into the compartment. Feth shook his head to clear it – even he began to realize that his thoughts were beginning to go in circles. He went to look for a camera.

Sallman Ken burst into the observatory without warning, but gave Drai no chance to explode. He was bursting himself with the news of the discovery – a little too much, in fact, since he kept up the talk all the way back to the shop. By the time they got there, the actual sight of the print was something of an anticlimax to Drai. He expressed polite interest, but little more. To him, of course, the physical appearance of Earth's natives meant nothing whatever. His attention went to another aspect of the compartment.

'What's all that white stuff?'

'I don't know yet,' Ken admitted. 'The torpedo just got back. It's whatever Planet Three's atmosphere does to the samples I sent down.'

'Then you'll know what the atmosphere is before long? That will be a help. There are some caverns near the dark hemisphere that we've known about for years, which we could easily seal off and fill with whatever you say. Let us know when you find out anything.' He drifted casually out of the shop, leaving Ken rather disappointed. It had been such a fascinating discovery.

He shrugged the feeling off, collected what he could of his samples without disturbing the print, and bore them across the room to the bench on which a make-shift chemical laboratory had been set up. As he himself had admitted, he was not an expert analyst; but compounds formed by combustion were seldom extremely complex, and he felt that he could get a pretty good idea of the nature of these. After all, he knew the metals involved – there could be no metallic gases except hydrogen in Planet Three's atmosphere. Even mercury would be a liquid, and no other metal had a really high vapor pressure even at Sarrian temperature. With this idea firmly in mind like a guiding star, Ken set blithely to work.

To a chemist, the work or a description of it would be interesting. To anyone else, it would be a boringly repetitious routine of heating and cooling, checking for boiling points and melting points, fractionating and filtering. Ken would have been quicker had he started with no preconceived notions; but finally even he was convinced. Once convinced, he wondered why he had not seen it before.

Feth Allmer had returned long since, and photographed the hand print from half a dozen angles. Now, seeing that Ken had stopped working, he roused himself from the rack on which he had found repose and approached the work bench.

'Have you got it, or are you stumped?' he queried.

'I have it, I guess. I should have guessed long ago. It's oxygen.'

'What's so obvious about that? Or, for that matter, why shouldn't it be?'

'To the latter question, no reason. I simply rejected it as a possibility at first because it's so active. I never stopped to think that it's little if any more active at that temperature than sulfur is at ours. It's perfectly possible to have it free in an atmosphere – provided there's a process constantly replacing what goes into combination. You need the same for sulfur. Blast it, the two elements are so much alike! I should have thought of that right away!'

'What do you mean – a replacement process?'

'You know we breathe sulfur and form sulfides with our metabolic processes. Mineral-eating life such as most plants, on the other hand, breaks down the sulfides and releases free sulfur, using solar energy for the purpose. Probably there is a similar division of life forms on this planet – one forming oxides and the other breaking them down. Now that I think of it, I believe there are some microorganisms on Sarr that use oxygen instead of sulfur.'

'Is it pure oxygen?'

'No – only about a fifth or less. You remember how quickly the sodium and magnesium went out, and what the pressure drop was with them.'

'No, I don't, and I can't say that it means much to me anyway, but I'll take your word for it. What else is there in the atmosphere? The titanium took about all of it, I do remember.'

'Right. It's either nitrogen or some of its oxides – I can't tell which without better controlled samples for quantity measurement. The only titanium compounds I could find in that mess were oxides and nitrides, though. The carbon oxidized, I guess – the reason there was no pressure change except that due to heat was that the principal oxide of carbon has two atoms of oxygen, and there is therefore no volume change. I should have thought of that, too.'

'I'll have to take your word for that, too, I guess. All we have to do, then, is cook up a four-to-one mixture of nitrogen and oxygen and fill the caves the boss mentioned to about two-thirds normal pressure with it?'

'That may be a little oversimplified, but it should be close enough to the real thing to let this tofacco stuff grow – if you can get specimens here alive, to start things off. It would be a good idea to get some soil, too – I don't suppose that powdering the local rock would help much. I may add in passing that I refuse even to attempt analyzing that soil. You'll have to get enough to use.' Feth stared.

'But that's ridiculous! We need tons, for a decent-sized plantation!' Sallman Ken shrugged.

'I know it. I tell you clearly that it will be easier to get those tons than to get an accurate soil analysis out of me. I simply don't know enough about it, and I doubt if Sarr's best chemist could hazard a prediction about the chemicals likely to be present in the solid state on that planet. At that temperature, I'll bet organic compounds could exist without either fluorine or silicon.'

'I think we'd better get Drai back here to listen to that. I'm sure he was planning to have you synthesize both atmosphere and soil, so that we could set up the plantation entirely on our own.'

'Perhaps you'd better. I told him my limitations at the beginning; if he still expects that, he had no idea whatever of the nature of the problem.' Feth left, looking worried, though Ken was unable to understand what particular difference it made to the mechanic. Later he was to find out.

The worried expression was still more evident when Feth returned.

'He's busy now. He says he'll talk it over with you after that suit comes back, so that any alternatives can be considered, too. He wants me to take you out to the caves so you can see for yourself what he has in mind for making them usable.'

'How do we get there? They must be some distance from here.'

'Ordon Lee will take us around in the ship. It's about two thousand miles. Let's get into our suits.'

Ken heroically swallowed the impulse to ask why the whole subject should have come up so suddenly in the midst of what seemed a totally different matter, and went to the locker where the space suits were stowed. He more than suspected the reason, anyway, and looked confidently forward to having the trip prolonged until after the return of the trading torpedo.

His attention was shifted from these matters as he stepped onto the surface of Mercury, for the first time since his arrival at the station. The blistered, baked, utterly dry expanse of the valley was not particularly strange to him, since Sarr was almost equally dry and even hotter; but the blackness of the sky about the sun and the bareness of the ground contributed to a *dead* effect that he found unpleasant. On Sarr, plant life is everywhere in spite of the dryness; the plants with which Ken was familiar were more crystalline than organic and needed only the most minute amounts of liquid for their existence.

Also, Sarr has weather, and Mercury does not. As the ship lifted from the valley, Ken was able to appreciate the difference. Mercury's terrain is rugged, towering and harsh. The peaks, faults and meteor scars are unsoftened by the blurring hand of erosion. Shadows are dark where they exist at all, relieved only by light reflected from nearby solid objects. Lakes and streams would have to be of metals like lead and tin, or simple compounds like the 'water' of Sarr – copper chloride, lead bromide, and sulfides of phosphorus and potassium. The first sort are too heavy, and have filtered down through the rocks of Mercury, if they ever existed at all; the second are absent for lack of the living organisms that might have produced them. Sallman Ken, watching the surface over which they sped, began to think a little more highly even of Earth.

A vessel capable of exceeding the speed of light by a factor of several thousand makes short work of a trip of two thousand miles, even when the speed is kept down to a value that will permit manual control. The surface was a little darker where they landed, with the sun near the horizon instead of directly overhead and the shadows correspondingly longer. It looked and was colder. However, the vacuum and the poor conducting qualities of the rock made it possible even here to venture out in ordinary space suits, and within a few moments Ken, Feth and the pilot were afoot gliding swiftly toward a cliff some forty feet in height.

The rock surface was seamed and cracked, like nearly all Mercurian topography. Into one of the wider cracks Lee unhesitatingly led the way. It did not lead directly away from the sun, and the party found itself almost at once in utter darkness. With one accord they switched on their portable lamps and proceeded. The passage was rather narrow at first, and rough enough on both floor and walls to be dangerous to space suits. This continued for perhaps a quarter of a mile, and quite suddenly opened into a vast, nearly spherical chamber. Apparently Mercury had not always been without gases – the cave had every appearance of a bubble blown in the igneous rock. The crack through which the explorers had entered extended upward nearly to its top, and downward nearly as far. It had been partly filled with rubble from above, which was the principal reason the going had been so difficult. The lower part of the bubble also contained a certain amount of loose rock. This looked as though it might make a climb down to the center possible, but Ken did not find himself particularly entranced by the idea.

'Is there just this one big bubble?' he asked. Ordon Lee answered.

'No; we have found several, very similar in structure, along this cliff, and there are probably others with no openings into them. I suppose they could be located by echo-sounders if we really wanted to find them.'

'It might be a good idea to try that,' Ken pointed out. 'A cave whose only entrance was one we had drilled would be a lot easier to keep airtight than this thing.' Feth and Lee grunted assent to that. The latter added a thought of his own. 'It might be good if we could find one well down; we could be a lot freer in drilling – there'd be no risk of a crack running to the surface.'

'Just one trouble,' put in Feth. 'Do we have an echo-sounder? Like Ken on his soil analysis, I have my doubts about being able to make one.' Nobody answered that for some moments.

'I guess I'd better show you some of the other caves we've found already,' Lee said at last. No one objected to this, and they retraced their steps to daylight. In the next four hours they looked at seven more caves, ranging from a mere hemispherical hollow in the very face of the cliff to a gloomy, frighteningly deep bubble reached by a passageway just barely negotiable for a space-suited Sarrian. This last, in spite of the terrors of its approach and relative smallness, was evidently the best for their purpose out of those examined; and Lee made a remark to that effect as they doffed space suits back in the *Karella*.

'I suppose you're right,' Ken admitted, 'but I'd still like to poke deeper. Blast it, Feth, are you sure you couldn't put a sounder together? You never had any trouble with the gadgets we used in the torpedoes.'

'Now you're the one who doesn't realize the problem,' the mechanic replied. 'We were using heating coils, thermometers, pressure gauges, and photocells for the other stuff. Those come ready made. All I did was hook them up to a regular achronic transmitter – we couldn't use ordinary radio because the waves would have taken ten or twelve minutes for the round trip. I didn't make anything – just strung wires.'

'I suppose you're right,' Ken admitted. 'In that case, we may as well go back to the station and lay plans for sealing off that last cavern.' He kept a sharp look on his two companions as he said this, and succeeded in catching the glance Feth sent at the clock before his reply. It almost pleased him.

'Hadn't we better get some photographs and measurements of the cave first?' Ordon Lee cut in. 'We'll need them for estimates on how much gas and soil will be needed, regardless of how it's to be obtained.' Ken made no objection to this; there was no point in raising active suspicion, and he had substantiated his own idea. He was being kept away from the station intentionally. He helped with the photography, and subsequently with the direct measurement of the cave. He had some trouble refraining from laughter; affairs were so managed that the party had returned to the ship and doffed space suits each time before the next activity was proposed. It was very efficient, from one point of view. Just to keep his end up, he proposed a rest before returning to the base, and was enthusiastically seconded by the others. Then he decided to compute the volume of the cave from their measurements, and contrived to spend a good deal of time at that – legitimately, as the cave was far from being a perfect sphere. Then he suggested getting some samples of local rock to permit an estimate of digging difficulties, and bit back a grin when Feth suggested rather impatiently that that could wait. Apparently he had outdone the precious pair at their own game – though why Feth should care whether or not they stayed longer than necessary was hard to see.

'It's going to take quite a lot of gas,' he said as the *Karella* lunged into the black sky. 'There's about two million cubic feet of volume there, and even the lower pressure we need won't help much. I'd like to find out if we can get oxygen from those rocks; we should have picked up a few samples, as I suggested. We're going to have to look over the upper area for small cracks, too – we have no idea how airtight the darn thing is. I wish we could – say, Feth, aren't there a lot of radar units of one sort or another around here?'

'Yes, of course. What do you want them for? Their beams won't penetrate rock.'

'I know. But can't the pulse-interval on at least some of them be altered?'

'Of course. You'd have to use a different set every time your range scale changed, otherwise. So what?'

'Why couldn't we – or you, anyway – set one up with the impulse actuating a sounder of some sort which could be put in contact with the rock, and time *that* return-echo picked up by a contact-mike? I know the impulse rate would be slower, but we could calibrate it easily enough.'

'One trouble might be that radar units are usually not very portable. Certainly none of the warning devices in this ship are.'

'Well, dismantle a torpedo, then. They have radar altimeters, and there are certainly enough of them so one can be spared. We could have called base and had them send one out to us – I bet it would have taken you only a few hours. Let's do that anyway – we're still a lot closer to the caves than to the base.'

'It's easier to work in the shop; and anyway, if we go as far underground as this idea should let us – supposing it works – we might as well scout areas closer to the base, for everyone's convenience.' Ordon Lee contributed the thought without looking from his controls.

'Do you think you can do it?' Ken asked the mechanic.

'It doesn't seem too hard,' the latter answered. 'Still, I don't want to make any promises just yet.'

'There's a while yet before that suit comes back. We can probably find out before then, and really have some material for Drai to digest. Let's call him now – maybe he'll have some ideas about soil.'

The eyes of the other two met for a brief moment; then Lee gestured to the radio controls.

'Go ahead; only we'll be there before you can say much.'

'He told me you were going to manufacture soil,' reminded Feth.

'I know. That's why I want to talk to him – we left in too much of a hurry before.' Ken switched on the radio while the others tried to decide whether or not he was suspicious about that hasty departure. Neither dared speak, with Ken in the same room, but once again their eyes met, and the glances were heavy with meaning.

Drai eventually came to the microphone at the other end and Ken began talking with little preliminary.

'We've made measurements of the smallest cave we can find, so far at least, and figured out roughly how much air you're going to need to fill it. I can tell you how much soil you'll need to cover the bottom, too, if you plan to use all of it. The trouble is, even if I can analyze the soil – even as roughly as I did the air – you're facing a supply problem that runs into tons. I can't make that much in the laboratory in any reasonable time. You're going to have to get it ready-made.'

'How? We can't land a person on Planet Three, let alone a freighter.'

'That we'll see presently. But that's not the suggestion I wanted to make – I see we're nearly there, so we can finish this chat in person. Think this over while we're going in: whatever sort of atmosphere a planet may have, I don't see how the soils can be *too* different – at least in their principal constituents. Why don't you get a shipload of Sarrian soil?' Drai gaped for a moment.

'But – bacteria—'

'Don't be silly; nothing Sarrian could live at that temperature. I admit it would be safer to use soil from Planet Three, and we may be able to. But if we can't, then you have my advice, if you're interested in speed – even if I knew the composition, it would take me a lot longer than a week to make a hundred tons of dirt!' He broke the connection as the *Karella* settled to the ground.

10

Ken wasted no time donning his space suit and leaving the ship with the others. Once inside the station and out of the heavy garment, he hastened to the shop to see how far out the returning test suit was; then, satisfied with its progress as recorded there, he headed for the observatory to continue his conversation with Laj Drai. He met no one on the way. Lee had stayed on the ship, Feth had disappeared on some errand of his own the moment the lock had closed behind them, and the rest of the personnel kept pretty much to themselves anyway. Ken did not care this time whether or not he were seen, since he planned a perfectly above-board conversation.

He was interrupted, however, in planning just how to present his arguments, by the fact that the observatory door was locked.

It was the first time he had encountered a locked door in the station since his arrival, and it gave him to think furiously. He was morally certain that the trading torpedo had returned during the absence of the *Karella*, and that there was a load of tofacco somewhere around the building. If this were the only locked door – and it was, after all, the room Drai used as an office—

Ken pressed his body close to the door, trying to tell by sound whether anyone were in the room. He was not sure; and even if there were not, what could he do? A professional detective could probably have opened the door in a matter of seconds. Ken, however, was no professional; the door was definitely locked, as far as he was concerned. Apparently the only thing to do was seek Drai elsewhere.

He was ten yards down the ramp, out of sight of the observatory door, when he heard it open. Instantly he whirled on his toes and was walking back up the incline as though just arriving. Just as he reached the bend that hid the door from him he heard it close again; and an instant later he came face to face with Feth. The mechanic, for the first time since Ken had known him, looked restless and uneasy. He avoided Ken's direct gaze, and wound the tip of one tentacle more tightly about a small object he was carrying, concealing it from view. He brushed past with a muttered greeting and vanished with remarkable speed around the turn of the ramp, making no answer to Ken's query as to whether Drai were in the observatory.

Ken stared after him for seconds after he had disappeared. Feth had always been taciturn, but he had seemed friendly enough. Now it almost seemed as though he were angry at Ken's presence.

With a sigh, the pro tem detective turned back up the ramp. It wouldn't hurt to knock at the door, anyway. The only reason he hadn't the first time was probably a subconscious hope that he would find Drai somewhere else, and feel free to investigate. Since his common sense told him he couldn't investigate anyway, he knocked.

It was just as well he hadn't made any amateur efforts at lock-picking, he decided as the door opened. Drai was there, apparently waiting for him. His face bore no recognizable expression; either whatever bothered Feth had not affected him, or he was a much better actor than the mechanic. Ken, feeling he knew Feth, inclined to the former view.

'I'm afraid I'm not convinced of the usability of any Sarrian soil,' Drai opened the conversation. 'I agree that most of the substances present in it, as far as I know, could also be present at Planet Three's temperature; but I'm not so sure the reverse is true. Mightn't there be substances that would be solid or liquid at that temperature and gaseous at ours, so that they would be missing from any we brought from home?'

'I hadn't thought of that,' Ken admitted. 'The fact that I can't think of any such substances doesn't mean they don't exist, either. I can skim through the handbook and see if there are any inorganic compounds that would behave that way, but even that might miss some – and if their life is at all analogous to ours, there are probably a couple of million organic compounds – for which we *don't* have any catalogue. No, blast it, I guess you're right; we'll have to take the stuff from the planet itself.' He lapsed into silent thought, from which Drai finally aroused him.

'Do you really think you're going to be able to get to the surface of that world?'

'I still can't see why we shouldn't,' replied Ken. 'It seems to me that people have visited worse ones before, bad as that is. Feth is pessimistic about it, though, and I suppose he has more practical knowledge of the problem than I. We can make more definite plans in that direction when the suit comes back, which shouldn't be long now. According to the instruments it started back a couple of hours ago.'

'That means nearly three days before you're sure. There must be something else – say! You claim it's the presence of a conducting atmosphere that makes the heat loss on Planet Three so great, don't you?'

'Sure. You know as well as I that you can go out in an ordinary space suit light years from the nearest sun; radiation loss is easy to replace. Why?'

'I just thought – there are other planets in this system. If we could find an airless one roughly the same temperature as Three, we might get soil from that.'

'That's an idea.' Ken was promptly lost in enthusiasm again. 'As long as it's cold enough, which is easy in this system – and Three has a satellite – you showed it to me. We can go there in no time in the *Karella* – and we could pick up that suit in space while we're at it. Collect Feth, and let's go!'

'I fear Feth will not be available for a while,' replied Drai. 'Also,' he grimaced, 'I have been on that satellite, and its soil is mostly pumice dust; it might have come straight from the Polar Desert on Sarr. We'd better consider the other possibilities before we take off. The trouble is, all we've ever noted about the other planets of the system is their motions. We wanted to avoid them, not visit them. I do remember, I think, that Five and Six do have atmospheres, which I suppose writes them off the list. You might see where Four is just now, will you? I assume you can interpret an ephemeris.'

Ken decided later that courtesy was really a superfluous facet of character. Had it not been for the requirements of courtesy he would not have bothered to make an answer to this suggestion, and had not most of his attention been concentrated on the answer he would never have made the serious error of walking over to the cabinet where the table in question was located, and reaching for it. He realized just as he touched the paper what he was doing, but with a stupendous effort of will he finished his assurance that he could read an ephemeris and completed the motion of obtaining the document. He felt, however, as though a laboratory vacuum pump had gone to work on his stomach as he turned back to his employer.

That individual was standing exactly where he had been, the expression on his face still inscrutable.

'I fear I must have done our friend Feth an injustice,' he remarked casually. 'I was wondering how you had come to imply that a round trip to Sarr would take only a week. I realize of course that your discoveries were made quite accidentally, and that nothing was farther from your plans than vulgar spying; but the problem of what to do about your unfortunate knowledge remains. That will require a certain amount of thought. In the meantime, let us continue with the matter of Planet Four. Is it in a convenient position to visit, and could we as you suggested pick up the torpedo carrying your suit without going too far from course?'

Ken found himself completely at a loss. Drai's apparently unperturbed blandness was the last attitude he expected under the circumstances. He could not believe that the other was really that indifferent; something unpleasant must be brewing between those steady eyes, but the face gave him no clue. As best he could he tried to match his employer's attitude. With an effort he turned his attention to the ephemeris he was holding, found the proper terms, and indulged in some mental arithmetic.

'The planets are just about at right angles as seen from here,' he announced at length. 'We're just about between the sun and Three, as you know; Four is in the retrograde direction, roughly twice as far from us. Still, that shouldn't mean anything to the *Karella*.'

'True enough. Very well, we will take off in an hour. Get any equipment you think you will need on board before then – better use engineering armor for Planet Four, even if it doesn't have air. You'll have to point out where they are to whomever I get to help you.'

'How about Feth?' Ken had gotten the idea that the mechanic was in disgrace for betraying the secret of their location.

'He won't be available for some time – he's occupied. I'll give you a man – you can be picking out what you want in the shop; I'll send him there. One hour.' Laj Drai turned away, intimating that the interview was at an end.

The man he sent proved to be a fellow Ken had seen around, but had never spoken to. The present occasion did little to change that; he was almost as taciturn as Feth, and Ken never did learn his name. He did all he was asked in the way of moving material to the *Karella*, and then disappeared. The take-off was on schedule.

Ordon Lee, who evidently had his orders, sent the vessel around the planet so rapidly that the acceleration needed to hug the curving surfaces exceeded that produced by the planet's gravity; the world seemed to be above them, to the inhabitants of the ship. With the sun near the horizon behind and the glowing double spark of Earth rising ahead, however, he discontinued the radial acceleration and plunged straight away from the star. Under the terrific urge of the interstellar engines, the Earth-Luna system swelled into a pair of clearly marked discs in minutes. Lee applied his forces skilfully, bringing the vessel to a halt relative to the planet and half a million miles sunward of it. Drai gestured to Ken, indicating a control board similar to that in the shop.

'That's tuned in to your torpedo; the screen at the right is a radar unit you can use to help find it. There's a compass at the top of the panel, and this switch will cause the torpedo to emit a homing signal.' Ken silently placed himself at the controls, and got the feel of them in a few minutes. The compass gave rather indefinite readings at first because of the distance involved; but Lee was quickly able to reduce that, and in a quarter of an hour the still invisible projectile was only a dozen miles away. Ken had no difficulty in handling it from that point, and presently he and Drai left the control room and repaired to a cargo chamber in the *Karella*'s belly, where the torpedo was warming up.

This time it was the suit still clamped to the outside that took all their interest. The whole thing had been left at the bottom of the atmosphere for a full hour, and Ken felt that any serious faults should be apparent in that time. It was a little discouraging to note that air was condensing on the suit as well as the hull; if the heaters had been working properly, some sort of equilibrium should have been reached between the inner and outer layers of the armor during the few hours in space. More accurately, since an equilibrium had undoubtedly been reached, it should have been at a much higher temperature.

The trickling of liquid air did cease much sooner on the armor, however, and Ken still had some hope when he was finally able to unclamp the garment and take it in for closer examination.

The outer surface of the metal had changed color. That was the first and most obvious fact. Instead of the silvery sheen of polished steel, there was a definitely bluish tint on certain areas, mostly near the tips of the armlike handling extensions and the inner surfaces of the legs. Ken was willing to write off the color as a corrosion film caused by the oxygen, but could not account for its unequal distribution. With some trepidation he opened the body section of the massive suit, and reached inside.

It was cold. Too cold for comfort. The heating coils might have been able to overcome that, but they were not working. The recorder showed a few inches of tape – it had been started automatically by a circuit which ran from a pressure gauge in the torpedo through one of the suit radio jacks as soon as atmospheric pressure had been detectable – and that tape showed a clear story. Temperature and pressure had held steady for a few minutes; then, somewhere about the time the torpedo must have reached the planet's surface, or shortly thereafter, they had both started erratically downward – very erratically, indeed; there was even a brief rise above normal temperature. The recorder had been stopped when the temperature reached the freezing point of sulfur, probably by air solidifying around its moving parts. It had not resumed operation. The planet was apparently a heat trap; pure and simple.

There was no direct evidence that the suit had leaked gas either way, but Ken rather suspected it had. The bluish tint on portions of the metal might conceivably be the result of flame – flaming oxygen, ignited by jets of high-pressure sulfur coming from minute leaks in the armor. Both sulfur and oxygen support combustion, as Ken well knew, and they do combine with each other – he made a mental note to look up the heats of formation of any sulfides of oxygen that might exist.

He turned away from the debacle at last.

'We'll let Feth look this over when we get back,' he said. 'He may have better ideas about just how and why the insulation failed. We may as well go on to Planet Four and see if it has anything that might pass for soil.'

'We've been orbiting around it for some time, I imagine,' Dirai responded. 'Lee was supposed to head that way as soon as we got your suit on board, but he was not to land until I returned to the control room.' The two promptly glided forward, pulling their weightless bodies along by means of the grips set into the walls, and shot within seconds through the control room door – even Ken was getting used to non-standard gravity and even to none at all.

Drai's assumption proved to be correct; drive power was off, and Mars hung beyond the ports. To Sarrian eyes it was even more dimly lighted than Earth, and like it obviously possessed of an atmosphere. Here, however, the atmospheric envelope was apparently less dense. They were too close to make out the so-called canals, which become river valleys when observation facilities are adequate, but even rivers were something new to the Sarrians. They were also too close to see the polar caps from their current latitude, but as the *Karella* drifted southward a broad expanse of white came into view. The cap was nowhere near the size it had been two months before, but again it was a completely strange phenomenon to the gazing aliens.

Or, more accurately, almost completely strange. Ken tightened a tentacle about one of Drai's.

'There was a white patch like that on Planet Three! I remember it distinctly! There's *some* resemblance between them, anyway.'

'There are two, as a matter of fact,' replied Drai. 'Do you want to get your soil from there? We have no assurance that it is there that the tofacco grows on Planet Three.'

'I suppose not; but I'd like to know what the stuff is anyway. We can land at the edge of it, and get samples of everything we find. Lee?'

The pilot looked a little doubtful, but finally agreed to edge down carefully into atmosphere. He refused to commit himself to an actual landing until he had found how rapidly the air could pull heat from his hull. Neither Drai nor Ken objected to this stipulation, and presently the white, brown and greenish expanse below them began to assume the appearance of a landscape instead of a painted disc hanging in darkness.

The atmosphere turned out to be something of a delusion. With the ship hanging a hundred feet above the surface, the outside pressure gauges seemed very reluctant to move far from zero. Pressure was about one fiftieth of Sarr normal. Ken pointed this out to the pilot, but Ordon Lee refused to permit his hull to touch ground until he had watched his outside pyrometers for fully fifteen minutes. Finally satisfied that heat was not being lost any faster than it could be replaced, he settled down on a patch of dark-colored sand, and listened for long seconds to the creak of his hull as it adapted itself to the changed load and localized heat loss. At last, apparently satisfied, he left his controls and turned to Ken.

'If you're going out to look this place over, go ahead. I don't think your armor will suffer any worse than our hull. If you have trouble anywhere, it will be with your feet – loss through the air is nothing to speak of. If your feet get cold, though, don't waste time – get back inside!'

Ken cast a mischievous glance at Drai. 'Too bad we didn't bring two suits,' he said. 'I'm sure you'd have liked to come with me.'

'Not in a hundred lifetimes!' Drai said emphatically. Ken laughed outright. Curiously enough, his own original horror of the fearful chill of these Solar planets seemed to have evaporated; he actually felt eager to make the test. With the help of Drai and Lee he climbed into the armor they had brought from Mercury, sealed it, and tested its various working parts. Then he entered the air lock of the *Karella*, and observed his instruments carefully while it was pumped out. Still nothing appeared to be wrong, and he closed the switch actuating the motor of the outer door.

For some reason, as the Martian landscape was unveiled before him, his mind was dwelling on the curious discoloration of the suit that had been exposed to Planet Three's atmosphere, and wondering if anything of the sort was likely to happen here.

Curiously enough, one hundred sixty million miles away, a thirteen year old boy was trying to account for a fire which seemed to have burned over a small patch of brush, isolated by bare rock, on a hillside five miles west of his home.

11

Even to an Earth man, Mars is not a world to promote enthusiasm. It is rather cold at the best of times, much too dry, and woefully lacking in air – breathable or otherwise. The first and last of these points struck Ken most forcibly.

The landscape in front of him was very flat. It was also very patchy. In some spots bare rock showed, but those were few and far between. Much of the area seemed to be dark, naked soil, with bits of green, brown, red and yellow mingling in the general background. Nearly half of the landscape seemed to be composed of the patches of white, which had seemed to be a solid mass from space. Probably, Ken realized, they formed a solid covering closer to the center of the white region; they had landed on its edge, as planned.

He took a careful step away from the ship's side. The gravity was less than that of Sarr, but distinctly greater than on Mercury, and the armor was a severe burden. The two tentacles inside his right 'sleeve' forced the clumsy pipe of steel downward almost to the ground, and manipulated the handlers at the end. With some difficulty, he scraped loose a piece of dark brown soil and raised it to eye level. He locked the 'knees' of the armor and settled back on the tail-like prop that extended from the rear of the metal trunk, so that he could give all his attention to examining the specimen.

The glass of his face plate showed no signs of differential contraction so far, but he carefully avoided letting the soil touch it during the examination. He almost forgot this precaution, however, when he saw the tiny varicolored objects on the surface of the sample. Weird as they were in shape, they were unquestionably plants – tiny, oddly soft-looking compared to the crystalline growths of Sarr, but still plants. And they lived in this frightful cold! Already those nearest the metal of his handler were shrivelling and curling, cold as the outside of his armor already must be. Eagerly Ken reported this to the listeners inside.

'This life must have something in common with that of Three,' he added. 'Both must run on chemical energy of the same general sort, since there's no important difference in their temperatures. This soil must have all the elements necessary, even if the compounds aren't quite right for what we want – who ever heard of a life form that didn't have a good deal of latitude that way?' He looked back at the sample he was holding. 'It looks a little different around the edges, as though the heat of my armor were making some change in it. You may be right, Drai – there may be some volatile substance in this soil that's evaporating now. I wonder if I can trap it?' He lapsed into thought, dropping his specimen.

'You can try afterward. Why not investigate the white patches?' called Drai. 'And the rocks, too; they might be something familiar – and soils are made from rock, after all.' Ken admitted the justice of this, hitched himself off the rear prop, unlocked his leg joints, and resumed his walk away from the ship.

So far, he had felt no sign of cold, even in his feet. Evidently the soil was not a very good conductor of heat. That was not too surprising, but Ken made a mental note to be careful of any patches of solid rock he might encounter.

The nearest of the white areas was perhaps thirty yards from the air lock door. Reaching it quickly enough in spite of the weight of his armor, Ken looked it over carefully. He could not bend over to examine its texture, and was a little uneasy about picking it up; but remembering that the handlers of his armor extended some distance beyond the actual tips of his tentacles, as well as the fact that the first sample had been harmless, he reached down and attempted to scrape up a piece.

This seemed easy enough. The handler grated across the surface, leaving a brown streak behind – evidently the white material formed a very thin layer on the ground. Raising the sample to eye level, however, Ken discovered that he had nothing but dark-colored sand.

Excusably puzzled, he repeated the process, and this time was quick enough to see the last of the white material vanish from the sand grains. 'You were right, Laj,' he said into his transmitter. 'There's something here that's really volatile. I haven't got enough for a good look, yet – I'll try to find a deeper deposit.' He started forward again, toward the center of the white patch.

The expanse was perhaps fifty yards across, and Ken judged that the volatile coating might be thicker in the center. This proved to be the case, but it never became heavy enough to impede even his progress. His trail was clearly marked by bare soil, as the stuff faded eerily out of sight around each footprint. Ken, though he could have looked behind in his armor without turning his whole body, did not notice this, but the watchers from the ship did. Drai remarked on it over the radio, and Ken responded:

'Tell me if it stops – maybe that will be a place where it's thick enough to pick some of the stuff up. I'd like to get a close look at it before it evaporates. Right now, I can't imagine what it might be, and I need information badly in order to make even an educated guess.'

'The trail is getting narrower now – there are separate spots which outline the shape of the feet of your armor, instead of broad circular areas that blend into each other. A little farther ought to do it.'

A little farther did. Ken was not quite to the center of the white patch when Drai reported that he had ceased to leave a trail. He promptly stopped, propped himself as he had before, and scooped up a fresh handful of the evanescent substance. This time there was practically no sand included; the material was fully an inch deep. The mass on his handler began to shrink at once, but not so rapidly as to prevent his getting a fairly long look. It was crystalline, millions of minute facets catching and scattering the feeble sunlight; but the individual crystals were too tiny to permit him to determine their shape. It was gone before he was really satisfied, but there seemed little likelihood of his getting a better look. Somehow a sample would have to be obtained – and analyzed. He thought he saw how that might be done, but some careful preparation would be necessary. Announcing this fact over his suit radio, he prepared to return to the ship.

Perhaps, in the half-seated attitude he had been holding, his feet had been partly out of contact with the armor; perhaps in his single-minded interest in things outside he simply had not noticed what was happening. Whatever the cause, it was not until he stood up that the abrupt, stabbing blade of cold seared straight from his feet to his brain. For an instant he settled back on his prop, trying to draw his feet from the biting touch of what was supposed to be insulation; then, realizing that matters would only grow worse if he delayed, he forced himself into action. Barely able to bite back a scream of anguish, he strained every muscle forcing the unwieldy mass of metal toward the air lock; and even through his pain, the thought came driving – no wonder the trail had become narrower; the feet of his armor must be nearly at the temperature of their surroundings. From five hundred degrees above zero Centigrade to fifty below is quite a temperature gradient for a scant three inches of steel, vacuum space, fluid coils, and insulating fiber to maintain, even with a powerful heating coil backing up the high-temperature side of the barrier.

The pain grew less as he struggled toward the lock, but the fact did not make him any happier; it terrified him. If he should lose control of his feet, he would die within sight of the *Karella*'s crew, for there was not another suit of special armor aboard that could be worn to rescue him.

Now his face was cold, too – he must be losing radiation even through the special glass of the face plate. His tentacle tips were feeling the chill, but not so badly; the fact that the deadly whiteness had touched only the handlers, inches beyond the 'inhabited' parts of the sleeve, was helping there. He had reached the edge of the area of death, and only thirty yards of bare ground lay between him and the lock. That ground was cold, too. It must be as cold as the other area; but at least it did not seem to drink heat. The lock door was open as he had left it, a metal-lined cavern that seemed to draw away as he struggled forward. He was numb below the lower knees, now; for the first time he blessed the clumsy stiffness of the armor legs, which made them feel and act like stilts, for that was all that enabled him to control the feet. Once he stumbled, and had time to wonder if he would ever be able to get the clumsy bulk erect again; then he had caught himself in some way – he never learned how, and no one on the ship could tell him – and was reeling forward again. Ten yards to go – five – two – and he brought up against the hull of the *Karella* with a clang. One more step and he was inside the lock. Two, and he was out of the swing of the massive door. With frantic haste he swung the sleeve of his armor at the closing switch. He hit it – hit it hard enough to bend the toggle, but the circuit was closed and the door thudded shut behind him, the sound of its closing coming through the metal of floor and suit. Then came the air, automatically, pouring into the lock chamber, condensing on the body of his armor, freezing into a yellow crust on the extremities. With the pressure up, the inner door swung wide, revealing Drai and Ordon Lee in the corridor beyond. The former shrank from the fierce chill that poured from the chamber; the pilot, thinking faster, leaped to a locker nearby and seized a welding torch. Playing the flame of this ahead of him, he approached Ken carefully.

The crust of sulfur boiled away instantly in the flame, to be replaced almost as fast when the tongue of light swung elsewhere. Long seconds passed before the metal was warm enough to stay clear, and more before it could be touched, and the almost unconscious Ken extracted. Minutes more passed before the throbbing agony receded from his limbs, and he was able to talk coherently, but at last he was satisfied that no permanent damage had been done. He had not actually been frost-bitten, though judging by the color of his skin he had come dangerously near to it.

Drai and Lee, amazed and horrified at the results of the brief sortie, felt both emotions redoubled as they heard of his plans for another. Even Drai, interested as he was in obtaining useful information, made a halfhearted attempt to dissuade him from the project. Ken refused to be dissuaded, and his employer did not have too much difficulty in consoling himself – after all, it was Ken's health.

The instructions to bring 'whatever he thought he would need' had been obeyed, and Ken spent some time searching through the pile of apparatus from the Mercurian laboratory. What he found seemed to satisfy him, and he made a number of careful preparations which involved some very precise weighing. He then carried several items of equipment to the air lock, and finally donned the armor again, to Ordon Lee's undisguised admiration.

From the control room port, Drai and the pilot watched Ken's hasty trip back to the scene of his earlier trouble. He followed his earlier trail, which was still clearly visible, and carefully avoided touching the whiteness with any part of his armor. Arrived at the point where his cooling boots had been unable to boil their way down to solid ground, he stopped. The watchers were unable to make out his actions in detail, but apparently he set some object on the ground, and began rolling it about as the white substance evaporated from around it. Presently this ceased to happen, as its temperature fell to that of its surroundings; then Ken appeared to pick it up and separate it into two parts. Into one of these he scooped a quantity of the mysterious stuff, using an ordinary spoon. Then the two halves of the thing were fastened together again, and the scientist beat a hasty retreat toward the air lock.

Drai was promptly headed for the inner door of the chamber, expecting to see what was going on; but the portal remained closed. He heard the hissing of air as pressure was brought up, and then nothing. He waited for some minutes, wondering more and more, and finally went slowly back to the control room. He kept looking back as he went, but the valve remained sealed.

As he entered the control room, however, Lee had something to report.

'He's pumping the lock down again,' the pilot said, gesturing to a flaring violet light on the board. Both Sarrians turned to the port of the side toward the air lock, Lee keeping one eye on the indicator that would tell them when the outer door opened. It flashed in a matter of seconds, and the watchers crowded eagerly against the transparent panel, expecting Ken's armored figure to appear. Again, however, nothing seemed to happen.

'What in the Galaxy is the fellow up to?' Drai asked the world at large, after a minute or so. Lee treated the question as rhetorical, but did shift part of his attention back to the control board. Even here, however, fully five minutes passed without anything occurring; then the outer door closed again. Calling Drai's attention to this, he looked expectantly at the pressure indicator, which obediently flashed a report of rising pressure. They waited no longer, but headed down the corridor side by side.

This time Ken appeared to have finished his work; the inner door was open when they reached it. He had not permitted his suit to get so cold this time, it seemed; only a light dew dimmed its polish. Within a minute or so Lee was able to help him emerge. He was wearing a satisfied expression, which did not escape the watchers.

'You found out what it was!' Drai stated, rather than asked.

'I found out something which will let me figure out what it is, very shortly,' replied Ken.

'But what did you do? Why did you go out twice?'

'You must have seen me putting a sample into the pressure bomb. I sealed it in, and brought it inside so it would all evaporate and so that the pressure gauge on the bomb would be at a temperature where I could trust it. I read the pressure at several temperatures, and weighed the bomb with the sample. I had already weighed it empty – or rather, with the near-vacuum this planet uses for air inside it. The second time I opened the door was to let off the sample, and to make a check at the same temperature with a sample of the planet's air – after all, it must have contributed a little to the pressure the first time.'

'But what good would all that do?'

'Without going into a lot of detail, it enabled me to find out the molecular weight of the substance. I did not expect that to be very conclusive, but as it happened I think it will be; it's so small that there aren't many possible elements in it – certainly nothing above fluorine, and I think nothing above oxygen. I'll concede that I may be off a unit or so in mv determination, since the apparatus and observing conditions were not exactly ideal, but I don't think it can be much worse than that.'

'But what is it?'

'The molecular weight? Between eighteen and nineteen, I got.'

'What has that weight, though?'

'Nothing at all common. I'll have to look through the handbook, as I said. Only the very rarest elements are that light.'

'If they're so rare, maybe the stuff is not so important for life after all.' Ken looked at Drai to see if he were serious.

'In the first place,' he pointed out, seeing that the other had not been joking, 'mere rarity doesn't prove that life doesn't need it. We use quite respectable quantities of fluorine in our bodies, not to mention zinc, arsenic and copper. This other form of life may well do the same. In the second place, just because an element is rare on Sarr doesn't prove it would be so on Planet Three – it's a much bigger world, and could easily have held considerable quantities of the lighter elements during its original formation, even if they had been there as uncombined gases.' The group had been walking toward Ken's room, where he had stored most of his apparatus, as they talked. Reaching it at this point, they entered. Ken draped himself without apology on the only rack, and began to flip through the pages of the chemical handbook, in the section devoted to inorganic compounds. He realized that his mysterious substance could contain carbon, but it certainly could not contain more than one atom per molecule, so there was no danger of its being a really complex organic material.

There were, in fact, just eight elements likely to be present; and the laws of chemistry would put considerable restriction on the possible combinations of those eight. The lightest of these was hydrogen, of course; and to the hydrogen compounds Ken turned, since they came first in that section of the handbook.

Drai had moved to a position from which he could oversee the pages that Ken was reading; the less interested or less excitable Lee stayed near the door and waited silently. He was more prepared than his employer for a long wait while the scientist made his search; and he was correspondingly more surprised when Ken, almost as soon as he began reading, suddenly stiffened in a fashion which indicated he had found something of interest. Drai saw the action as well.

'What is it?' he asked at once. Both Ken and Lee realized that the 'it' referred to the substance, not the cause of Ken's interest; Drai assumed without thought that his scientist had found what he was seeking.

'Just a moment. There's something that doesn't quite agree – but the rest is too perfect – wait a minute—' Ken's voice trailed off for a moment; then, 'Of course. This is under normal pressure.' He looked up from the book.

'This appears to be the stuff – it's almost completely unknown on Sarr, because of its low molecular weight – most of it must have escaped from the atmosphere eons ago, if it ever was present. According to this handbook, it should be liquid through quite a temperature range, but that's under our atmospheric pressure. It's quite reasonable that it should sublime the way it did in this vacuum.'

'But what is it?'

'One of the oxides of hydrogen – H_2O, apparently. If it proves to be essential for the form of growth you're interested in, we're going to have a very interesting time handling it.'

'We have cargo shells that can be kept at outside conditions, and towed outside the ship,' Drai pointed out.

'I assumed you did,' replied Ken. 'However, normal "outside" conditions in the space near Planet One would almost certainly cause this stuff to volatilize just as it did from the comparatively faint heat radiating from my armor. Your shells will have to be sealed airtight, and you will, as I said, have an interesting time transferring their contents to any cave we may pick.'

Laj Drai looked startled for several seconds. Then he appeared to remember something, and his expression changed to one of satisfaction.

'Well,' he said, 'I'm sure you'll be able to figure that one out. That's what scientists are for, aren't they?' It was Ken's turn to look startled, though he had known Drai long enough by this time to have expected something of the sort.

'Don't you ever solve your own problems?' he asked, a trifle sourly. Drai nodded slowly.

'Yes, sometimes. I like to think them over for quite a while, though, and if they're scientific ones I don't have the knowledge to think with. That's why I hire people like you and Feth. Thanks for reminding me – I do have a problem at the moment, on which I have spent a good deal of thought. If you'll excuse me, I'll attend to the finishing touches. You can stay here and work on this one.'

'There's nothing more we can do on this planet for the present.'

'That I can believe. We'll head back for Planet One and the rest of your laboratory facilities. Come on, Lee – we'll leave the scientist to his science.'

Ken, unsuspicious by nature, did not even look up as the two left his room. He had just found ammonia on the list, and was wondering whether his measurement could have been far enough off to permit the true molecular weight to be only seventeen. Melting-point data finally reassured him. For safety's sake, however, he went through all the hydrogen, lithium, beryllium, boron, nitrogen, and oxygen compounds that were listed in the handbook. The faint disturbance incident to the vessel's takeoff did not bother him at all. The silent opening of his door made no impression on him, either.

In fact, the door had closed again with a crisp snap before anything outside the printed pages registered on his consciousness. Then a voice, coincident with the closing door, suddenly shattered the silence.

'Sallman Ken!' The mechanical speaker over the entrance boomed the words; the voice was that of Laj Drai. 'I said when we parted a moment ago that I occasionally solve my own problems. Unfortunately, you have come to represent a problem. There seems to be only one solution which will not destroy your usefulness. In a way I regret to employ it, but you have really only your own unwarranted curiosity to thank. When you wake up, we will talk again – you can tell me what you think of our commercial product!' The voice ceased, with a click which indicated that the microphone had been switched off.

Ken, fully aroused, had dropped the book and risen to his feet – or rather, left his rack and floated away from the floor, since they were in weightless flight. His eyes roved rapidly to all quarters of the room in search of something that might furnish meaning to Drai's rather ominous words. Several seconds passed before he saw it – a rectangular yellow brick, floating in the air near the door. For a moment he did not recognize it, and pushed against a wall to bring himself nearer to it; then, as he felt the chill emanating from the thing, he tried futilely to check his drift.

Already the brick was losing shape, its corners rounding with the heat and puffing off into vapor. It was frozen sulfur – harmless enough in itself if contact were avoided, but terrifying when considered with his background of knowledge and suspicion. With a frantic flailing of his tentacles, he managed to set up enough of an air current to cause the thing to drift out of his path; but an equally anxious look about the room for something which might serve as a gas mask disclosed nothing.

He found himself unable to take his eyes from the dwindling object, now a rather elongated ellipsoid. It continued to shrink remorselessly, and suddenly there was something else visible in the yellow – the end of a small white cylinder. As the last of the protective box vanished, this began to turn brown and then black over its entire surface, and a spherical cloud of smoke enveloped it. For an instant a wild hope flashed in Ken's mind; the thing had to burn, and a fire will not maintain itself in weightless flight. It requires a forced draft. Perhaps this one would smother itself out – but the cloud of smoke continued to swell. Apparently the thing had been impregnated with chips of frozen air in anticipation of this situation.

Now the edges of the smoke cloud were becoming fuzzy and ill-defined as diffusion carried its particles through the room. Ken caught the first traces of a sweetish odor, and tried to hold his breath; but he was too late. The determination to make the effort was his last coherent thought.

12

'So they decided to keep you.' There might or might not have been a faint trace of sympathy in Feth Allmer's tone. 'I'm not very surprised. When Drai raised a dust storm with me for telling you how far away Sarr was, I knew you must have been doing some probing on your own. What are you, Commerce or Narcotics?' Ken made no answer.

He was not feeling much like talking, as a matter of fact. He could remember just enough of his drug-induced slumber to realize things about himself which no conscientious being should be forced to consider. He had dreamed he was enjoying sights and pleasures whose recollection now gave him only disgust – and yet under the disgust was the hideous feeling that there had been pleasure, and there might be pleasure again. There is no real possibility of describing the sensations of a drug addict, either while he is under the influence of his narcotic or during the deadly craving just before the substance becomes a physical necessity; but at this moment, less than an hour after he had emerged from its influence, there may be some chance of his frame of mind being understandable. Feth certainly understood, but apparently chose not to dwell on that point.

'It doesn't matter now which you were, or whether the whole gang knows it,' he went on after waiting in vain for Ken's answer. 'It won't worry anyone. They know you're ours for good, regardless of what you may think at the moment. Wait until the craving comes on – you'll see.'

'How long will that be?' The point was of sufficient interest to Ken to overcome his lethargy.

'Five to six days; it varies a little with the subject. Let me warn you now – don't cross Laj Drai, ever. He really has the ship. If he keeps the tofacco from you for even half an hour after the craving comes on, you'll never forget it. I still haven't gotten over his believing that I told you where we were.' Again surprise caused Ken to speak.

'You? Are you—?'

'A sniffer? Yes. They got me years ago, just like you, when I began to get an idea of what this was all about. I didn't know where this system was, but my job required me to get engineering supplies occasionally, and they didn't want me talking.'

'That was why you didn't speak to me outside the observatory, just after we got back from the caves?'

'You saw me come out of the office? I never knew you were there. Yes, that was the reason, all right.' Feth's normally dour features grew even grimmer at the memory. Ken went back to his own gloomy thought, which gradually crystallized into a resolve. He hesitated for a time before deciding to mention it aloud, but was unable to see what harm could result.

'Maybe you can't get out from under this stuff – I don't know; but I'll certainly try.'

'Of course you will. So did I.'

'Well, even if I can't Drai needn't think I'm going to help him mass produce this hellish stuff. He can keep me under his power, but he can't compel me to think.'

'He could, if he knew you weren't. Remember what I told you – not a single open act of rebellion is worth the effort. I don't know that he actually enjoys holding out on a sniffer, but he certainly never hesitates if he thinks there's need – and you're guilty until proved innocent. If I were you, I'd go right on developing those caves.'

'Maybe you would. At least, I'll see to it that the caves never do him any good.'

Feth was silent for a moment. If he felt any anger at the implication in Ken's statement, his voice did not betray it, however.

'That, of course, is the way to do it. I am rather surprised that you have attached no importance to the fact that Drai has made no progress exploring Planet Three for the seventeen years I have been with him.'

For nearly a minute Ken stared at the mechanic, while his mental picture of the older being underwent a gradual but complete readjustment.

'No,' he said at last, 'I never thought of that at all. I should have, too – I did think that some of the obstacles to investigation of the planet seemed rather odd. You mean you engineered the television tube failures, and all such things?'

'The tubes, yes. That was easy enough – just make sure there were strains in the glass before the torpedo took off.'

'But you weren't here when the original torpedoes were lost, were you?'

'No, that was natural enough. The radar impulses we pick up are real, too; I don't know whether this idea of a hostile race living on the blue plains of Planet Three is true or not, but there seems to be some justification for the theory. I've been tempted once or twice to put the wrong thickness of anti-radar coating on a torpedo so that they'd know we were getting in – but then I remember that that might stop the supply of tofacco entirely. Wait a few days before you think too hardly of me for that.' Ken nodded slowly in understanding, then looked up suddenly as another idea struck him.

'Say, then the failure of that suit we sent to Three was not natural?'

'I'm afraid not.' Feth smiled a trifle. 'I overtightened the packing seals at knees, hips and handler joints while you were looking on. They contracted enough to let air out, I imagine – I haven't seen the suit, remember. I didn't want you walking around on that planet – you could do too much for this gang in an awfully short time, I imagine.'

'But surely that doesn't matter now? Can't we find an excuse for repeating the test?'

'Why? I thought you weren't going to help.'

'I'm not, but there's an awfully big step between getting a first hand look at the planet and taking living specimens of tofacco away from it. If you sent a person to make one landing on Sarr, what would be the chance of his landing within sight of a *Gree* bush? or, if he did, of your finding it out against his wish?'

'The first point isn't so good; this tofacco might be all over the place like *Mekko* – the difficulty would be to miss a patch of it. Your second consideration, however, now has weight.' He really smiled, for the first time since Ken had known him. 'I see you are a scientist after all. No narcotics agent would care in the least about the planet, under the circumstances. Well, I expect the experiment can be repeated more successfully, though I wouldn't make the dive myself for anything I can think of.'

'I'll bet you would – for one thing,' Ken replied. Feth's smile disappeared.

'Yes – just one,' he agreed soberly. 'But I see no chance of that. It would take a competent medical researcher years, even on Sarr with all his facilities. What hope would we have here?'

'I don't know, but neither of us is senile,' retorted Ken. 'It'll be a few years yet before I give up hope. Let's look at that suit you fixed, and the one I wore on Four. They may tell us something of what we'll have to guard against.' This was the first Feth had heard of the sortie on Mars, and he said so. Ken told of his experience in detail, while the mechanic listened carefully.

'In other words,' he said at the end of the tale, 'there was no trouble until you actually touched this stuff you have decided was hydrogen oxide. That means it's either a terrifically good conductor, has an enormous specific heat, a large heat of vaporization, or two or three of those in combination. Right?' Ken admitted, with some surprise, that that was right. He had not summed up the matter so concisely in his own mind. Feth went on: 'There is at the moment no way of telling whether there is much of that stuff on Three, but the chances are there is at least some. It follows that the principal danger on that planet seems to be encountering deposits of this chemical. I am quite certain that I can insulate a suit so that you will not suffer excessive heat loss by conduction or convection in atmospheric gases, whatever they are.'

Ken did not voice his growing suspicion that Feth had been more than a mechanic in his time. He kept to the vein of the conversation.

'That seems right. I've seen the stuff, and it's certainly easy to recognize, so there should be no difficulty in avoiding it.'

'You've seen the solid form, which sublimed in a near vacuum. Three has a respectable atmospheric pressure, and there may be a liquid phase of the compound. If you see any pools of any sort of liquid whatever, I would advise keeping clear of them.'

'Sound enough – only, if the planet is anything like Sarr, there isn't a chance in a thousand of landing near open liquid.'

'Our troubles seem to spring mostly from the fact that this planet *isn't* anything like Sarr,' Feth pointed out drily. Ken was forced to admit the justice of this statement, and stored away the rapidly growing stock of information about his companion. Enough of Feth's former reserve had disappeared to make him seem a completely changed person.

The suits were brought into the shop and gone over with extreme care. The one used on Planet Four appeared to have suffered no damage, and they spent most of the time on the other. The examination this time was much more minute than the one Ken had given it on board the *Karella*, and one or two new discoveries resulted. Besides the bluish deposit Ken had noted on the metal, which he was now able to show contained oxides, there was a looser encrustation in several more protected spots which gave a definite potassium spectrum – one of the few that Ken could readily recognize – and also a distinct odor of carbon bisulfide when heated. That, to the chemist, was completely inexplicable. He was familiar with gaseous compounds of both elements, but was utterly unable to imagine how there could have been precipitated from them anything capable of remaining solid at 'normal' temperature.

Naturally, he was unfamiliar with the makeup of earthly planets, and had not seen the fire whose remains had so puzzled Roger Wing. Even the best imaginations have their limits when data are lacking.

The joints had, as Feth expected, shrunk at the seals, and traces of oxides could be found in the insulation. Apparently some native atmosphere had gotten into the suit, either by diffusion or by outside pressure after the sulfur had frozen.

'Do you think that is likely to happen with the packing properly tightened?' Ken asked, when this point had been checked.

'Not unless the internal heaters fail from some other cause, and in that case you won't care anyway. The over-tightening cut down the fluid circulation in the temperature equalizing shell, so that at first severe local cooling could take place without causing a sufficiently rapid reaction in the main heaters. The local coils weren't up to the job, and once the fluid had frozen at the joints of course the rest was only a matter of seconds. I suppose we might use something with a lower freezing point than zinc as an equalizing fluid – potassium or sodium would be best from that point of view, but they're nasty liquids to handle from chemical considerations. Tin or bismuth are all right that way, but their specific heats are much lower than that of zinc. I suspect the best compromise would be selenium.'

'I see you've spent a good deal of time thinking this out. What would be wrong with a low specific heat liquid?'

'It would have to be circulated much faster, and I don't know whether the pumps would handle it – both those metals are a good deal denser than zinc, too. Selenium is still pretty bad in specific heat, but its lower density will help the pumps. The only trouble is getting it. Well, it was just a thought – the zinc should stay liquid if nothing special goes wrong. We can try it on the next test, anyway.'

'Have you thought about how you are going to justify this next trial, when Drai asks how come?'

'Not in detail. He won't ask. He likes to boast that he doesn't know any science – then he gloats about hiring brains when he needs them. We'll simply say that we have found a way around the cause of the first failure – which is certainly true enough.'

'Could we sneak a televisor down on the next test, so we could see what goes on?'

'I don't see how we could conceal it – any signal we can receive down here can be picked up as well or better in the observatory. I suppose we might say that you had an idea in that line too, and we were testing it out.'

'We could – only perhaps it would be better to separate ideas a little. It wouldn't help if Drai began to think you were a fool. People too often connect fools and knaves in figures of speech, and it would be a pity to have him thinking along those lines.'

'Thanks; – I was hoping you'd keep that point in mind. It doesn't matter much anyway – I don't see why we can't take the *Karella* out near Three and make the tests from there. That would take only a matter of minutes, and you could make the dive right away if things went well. I know it will be several days before the ship will be wanted – more likely several weeks. They get eight or ten loads of tofacco from the planet during the "season" and several days elapse between each load. Since all the trading is done by torpedo, Lee has a nice idle time of it.'

'That will be better. I still don't much like free fall, but a few hours of that will certainly be better than days of waiting. Go ahead and put it up to Drai. One other thing – let's bring more than one suit this time. I was a little worried for a while, there, out on Four.'

'A good point. I'll check three suits, and then call Drai.' Conversation lapsed, and for the next few hours a remarkable amount of constructive work was accomplished. The three units of armor received an honest preservice cheek this time, and Feth was no slacker. Pumps, valves, tanks, joints, heating coils – everything was tested, separately and in all combinations.

'A real outfit would spray them with liquid mercury as a final trick,' Feth said as he stepped back from the last suit, 'but we don't have it, and we don't have any place to try it, and it wouldn't check as cold as these are going to have to take anyway. I'll see what Drai has to say about using the ship – we certainly can't run three torpedoes at once, and I'd like to be sure all these suits are serviceable before any one of them is worn on Three.' He was putting away his tools as he spoke. That accomplished, he half turned toward the communicator, then appeared to think better of it.

'I'll talk to him in person. Drai's a funny chap,' he said, and left the shop.

He was back in a very few minutes, grinning.

'*We* can go,' he said. 'He was very particular about the plural. You haven't been through a period of tofacco-need yet, and he is afraid you'd get funny ideas alone. He is sure that I'll have you back here in time for my next dose. He didn't *say* all this, you understand, but it wasn't hard to tell what he had in mind.'

'Couldn't we smuggle enough tofacco aboard to get us back to Sarr?'

'Speaking for myself, I couldn't get there. I understand you don't know the direction yourself. Further more, if Drai himself can't smuggle the stuff onto Sarr, how do you expect me to get it past his eyes? I can't carry a refrigerator on my back, and you know what happens if the stuff warms up.'

'All right – we'll play the game as it's dealt for a while. Let's go.'

Half an hour later, the *Karella* headed out into the icy dark. At about the same time, Roger Wing began to feel cold himself, and decided to give up the watch for that night. He was beginning to feel a little discouraged, and as he crawled through his bedroom window a short time later – with elaborate precautions of silence – and stowed the rope under his bed, he was wondering seriously if he should continue the vigil. Perhaps the strange visitor would never return, and the longer he waited to get his father's opinion, the harder it would be to show any concrete evidence of what had happened.

He fell asleep over the problem – somewhere about the time the test torpedo entered atmosphere a few miles above him.

13

The *Karella* hung poised deep in Earth's shadow, well beyond measurable air pressure. The spherical compass tuned to the transmitter on the planet far below pointed in a direction that would have been straight down had there been any weight. Ordon Lee was reading, with an occasional glance at his beloved indicator board whenever a light blinked. This was fairly often, for Ken and Feth had put the testing of cold-armor on a mass-production basis. One of the suits had already returned and been checked; Feth was now in the open air lock, clad in an ordinary space suit, detaching the second from the cargo rings and putting the third in its place. He was in touch with Ken, at the torpedo controls, by radio. The scientist was holding the torpedo as well as he could partly inside the lock, which had not been designed for such maneuvers and was not large enough for the full length of the projectile. Feth was having his troubles from the same fact, and the lock-obstruction light on Lee's board was flashing hysterically.

With the torpedo once more plunging toward the dark surface below, things quieted down a little – but only a little. Feth brought the second suit inside, necessarily closing the outer door in the process and occasioning another pattern of colored light to disturb the pilot's reading. Then there was nothing but the fading proximity light as the torpedo receded, and the burden of divided attention was shifted to Ken. He had to stay at his controls, but he wanted desperately to see what Feth was doing. He already knew that the first of the suits was wearable – its interior temperature had dropped about forty degrees; which represented an actual heat loss his own metabolism could easily make up; and there was a governor on the heater unit which Feth had deliberately set down so that the heat loss should be measurable. With that limitation removed, he should be as comfortable on the Planet of Ice as anyone could expect to be while encased in nearly three hundred pounds of metal.

Knowing this, he was less worried about the second suit; but he found that he was still unable to concentrate completely on the job in hand. He was quite startled when a buzzer sounded on his own board, which proved to be announcing the fact that his torpedo had encountered outside pressure. As Ken had not reduced its speed to anything like a safe value, he was quite busy for a while; and when he had finally landed the messenger – safely, he hoped – Feth had finished his work. There were now two usable suits.

That removed the greatest load from the minds of both scientist and mechanic, and they were not too disappointed when the third unit failed its test. Ken had a suspicion of the reason – Feth found that leakage had occurred at leg and 'sleeve' joints, which would have been put under considerable stress by high acceleration. He did not volunteer this idea, and Feth asked no questions. Ken had an uneasy idea that the mechanic with the rather surprising chemical and physical background might have figured the matter out for himself, however.

This worry, if it could be dignified by such a name, was quickly submerged in the flurry of final preparations for the descent. Ordon Lee still refused flatly to lower his ship into the heat-trap of Earth's atmosphere, even after the success of two of the suits; it would therefore be necessary for Ken to ride down as the empty armor had done – clamped to the outside of a torpedo. The attachments would have to be modified so that he could manipulate them himself, and that took a little time. Ken ate a good meal, and took the unusual precaution of drinking – the Sarrians manufactured nearly all the liquid they needed in their own tissues.

If the scientist felt any slight doubts as he stepped into the metallic bulk which was to be his only shield for the next few hours from the ghastliest environment he could imagine, his pride prevented them from showing. He was silent as Feth carefully dogged the upper section in place – entry was effected through the top – and listened with a tiny stethoscope to each of the equalizer pumps as they were turned on. Satisfied, he nodded approval at the armored scientist, and Ken reached out, seized a stanchion with one of his handlers, and pulled his personal tank into motion toward the air lock. He had to wait in the corridor while Feth redonned his own suit, and then patiently inside the lock while the mechanic carefully attached the armor to the hull of the torpedo. Lee had finally become helpful, and was holding the projectile inside the lock against the pull of the meteor repellers, which he still refused to turn off for an instant.

Even when the outer door closed between Ken and the rest of the livable space within several million miles, he managed to keep his self control. He was now used to weightlessness, fortunately; the endless-fall sensation has serious mental effects on some people. Even the relative emptiness of the surrounding space he could stand, since he could see enough objects to keep himself oriented. There were about as many stars visible here as near his home planet, since two hundred parsecs mean little in the size of the galaxy.

In fact, he retained his calm until his eyes as well as his sense of balance agreed to tell him he was falling. The *Karella* had long since vanished behind – or above – him. The sun was in almost the same direction, since there had been no discussion needed to settle that the landing should be made on the day side of the planet. Rather more had been needed before the same old landing place had been selected – Ken, of course, wanted to see the natives, but even his scientific curiosity had been tempered with caution. Feth, regarding the trip chiefly as another test of the armor, had been rather against natives as an added complication; but curiosity had won out. Ken was falling toward the homing transmitter at which the trading was done, with the understanding that he would be carried a little to the west, as before – he was willing to meet 'his' native, but did not want to interfere more than necessary with trade. He realized, of course, that the creatures probably moved around, but he resolutely declined to think about the probable results if the one he had frightened had met the traders; he regarded it as profitless guesswork, which it certainly would have been.

The result of all the discussion, however, meant that he could see clearly the expanding world below – it felt like below, since Feth was now slowing the torpedo's descent. He could not see the torpedo at all easily, as his armor was facing away from it and the back view ports in the helmet were too close to the hull for real vision. He was beginning to feel, therefore, like a man hanging from the ledge of a high roof on a rope of questionable strength. If his vocal apparatus had been as closely connected with his breathing mechanism as is that of a human being, his state of mind would certainly have been betrayed by the radio to the listeners above. As it was they could not hear his tense breathing, and he endured his terror in silence and alone. It was probably just as well; Ordon Lee's reaction would hardly have been a sympathetic one, and whatever helpful feeling Feth might have had he would have been likely to express aloud.

There was air around him now – at least the gaseous mixture this world used for air. It was whistling upward, audible even through the armor. He could not be much more than five miles from the ground, and the descent was still rapid – too rapid, he was beginning to feel. As if in answer to the thought, his weight increased abruptly, and he knew that Feth far above had added power. With an effort greater than he had thought himself capable of making, Ken wrenched his attention from the rapid expansion of the landscape below and the creaking of the taut chains above, and concentrated on details. Once started, this proved easy, for there was more that was fantastic around him than mere temperature.

He could not see too far, of course. Eyes whose greatest sensitivity lies in the blue and near ultra-violet work are at a considerable disadvantage in Earth's hazy atmosphere. Still, the ground below was taking on detail.

It was rough, as they had deduced. Even though mountains do not show to best advantage from overhead, Ken was experienced enough to judge that these were quite respectable heights by Sarrian standards. The surface was buried in a riot of color, largely varying shades of green, brown, and gray. Here and there a patch of metallic sheen reminded him disquietingly of the vast, smooth areas where the mysteriously hostile intelligences of the planet dwelt. If these were outposts – but they had never interfered with the trading torpedoes which had been descending for years in this same area, Ken told himself.

As he dropped lower, he saw that some of the gray elevations were of remarkable shape and form – many of them were actually broader above than lower down. He was quite low before he could see that these objects were not part of the landscape, but were actually suspended in the air. The only clouds he had ever seen were the vast dust storms raised by Sarr's furious winds, but he judged that these must be of somewhat similar nature. Probably the particles were smaller, to permit them to remain in suspension – a planet this cold could hardly have very strong winds. He described the phenomena as minutely as he could to the listeners above. Feth reported that he was putting Ken's broadcasts on record, and added some more pertinent information.

'Your descent has been almost stopped, now. You are about one mile above the transmitter, and a few hundred feet higher above the place where the atmosphere tests were made. Do you want to go straight down now, or stay there and observe for a while?'

'Down with moderate speed, please. It is not possible to see too far, and I'd like to get down to where real details are visible. It seems to be mountainous country – I'll try to guide you in landing me near some peak, so that I can observe for a reasonable distance from a stable spot.'

'All right. You're going down.' Two or three minutes passed silently; then Ken spoke again.

'Are you moving me horizontally?'

'No. You are already away from over the transmitter – three or four miles.'

'Then this atmosphere has stronger currents than I expected. I am drifting visibly, though not rapidly. It's rather hard to specify the direction – the sun is not very far from straight up, and the torpedo hides it.'

'When you're nearly down, give me the direction with respect to the torpedo's orientation. I'll stop you before you touch.'

Gradually details grew clearer. The greenness seemed to be a tangled mass of material somewhat resembling chemical growths Ken had prepared in various solutions; he tentatively identified it as plant life, and began to suspect what had caused the crackling sound when the test torpedo had been landed.

Standing out from the green were areas quite obviously of bare rock. These seemed to be located for the most part at and near the tops of the mountains; and with infinite care Ken directed his distant pilot in an approach to one of these. Finally, hanging motionless twenty feet above a surface which even in this relatively dim light was recognizable as rock, he gave the order to lower away.

Six feet from the ground, he had the machine stopped again, and carefully released the leg chains. The lower part of his armor dropped, almost touching; a word into the microphone brought the metal feet into contact with the ground. Releasing one of the upper chains caused him to swing around, still leaning at a sharp angle with one side up toward the supporting hull. By a species of contortionism he contrived to make a workable tripod of his legs and the rear prop of the armor, and at last released the final chain. He was standing on the Planet of Ice, on his own two feet.

He felt heavy, but not unbearably so. His extreme caution not to land in a recumbent position was probably well founded – it was very unlikely that he could have raised himself and the armor to a standing posture with his own muscles in this gravity. Walking was going to be difficult, too – possibly even dangerous; the rock was far from level.

This, of course, was not the principal matter. For several minutes after he had severed connections with the torpedo, Ken made no attempt to move; he simply stood where he was, listening to the almost inaudible hum of his circulation motors and wondering when his feet would start to freeze. Nothing seemed to happen, however, and presently he began to take a few cautious steps. The joints of his armor were still movable; evidently the zinc had not yet frozen.

The torpedo had drifted away from overhead; apparently a slight wind was blowing. At Ken's advice, Feth brought the machine to the ground. Even with his fear lost in curiosity, Ken had no intention of becoming separated by any great distance from his transportation. Once assured that it was remaining in place, he set to work.

A few minutes' search located several loose rock fragments. These he picked up and placed in the torpedo, since anything might be of some interest; but he principally wanted soil – soil in which things were visibly growing. Several times he examined rock specimens as closely as he could, hoping to find something that might resemble the minute plants of Planet Four; but he failed utterly to recognize as life the gray and black crustose lichens which were actually growing on some of the fragments.

The landscape was not barren, however. Starting a few hundred yards from his point of landing, and appearing with ever-increasing frequency as one proceeded down the mountainside, there were bushes and patches of moss which gradually gave way to dwarfed trees and finally, where the rock disappeared for good beneath the soil, to full grown firs. Ken saw this, and promptly headed for the nearest clump of bushes. As an afterthought, he told Feth what he was doing, so that the torpedo could be sent along. There was no point, he told himself, in carrying all the specimens back up the hillside.

Progress was quite difficult, since a gap a foot wide between rocks presented a major obstacle to the armor. After a few minutes of shuffling punctuated with frequent pauses for rest, he remarked:

'The next time, we'd better have longer shoulder chains. Then I can hang right side up from the torpedo, and be spared all this waddling.'

'That's a thought,' replied Feth. 'It certainly will be easy enough. Do you want to come back up now and make the change, or collect a few things first?'

'Oh, I'll stay a while, now that I'm here. I haven't much farther to travel to get to these plants, if they are plants. The darned things are green, at least partly. I suppose, though, that objectively speaking there should be nothing surprising about that. Well, here we go again.'

He lifted his prop from the ground and shuffled forward once more. Another minute or two sufficed to bring him within reach of the strange growth. It was only about a foot high, and he was even less able to bend down to it than he had been on Planet Four; so he extended a handler to seize a branch. The results were a trifle startling.

The branch came away easily enough. There was no trouble about that. However, before he had time to raise it to his eyes a puff of smoke spurted from the point where the handler was touching it, and the tissue in the immediate neighborhood of the metal began to turn black. The memories aroused by this phenomenon caused Ken to drop the branch, and he would undoubtedly have taken a step backward had the armor been less cumbersome. As it was, he remembered almost instantly that no gas could penetrate his metal defenses, and once more picked up the bit of vegetation.

The smoke reappeared and grew thicker as he lifted it toward his face port, but he had several seconds to examine its structure before the smoldering wood burst into flame. Although this startled him almost as much as the earlier phenomenon had, he retained his hold on the fragment. He watched with interest as the main branch curled, blackened, glowed, and flamed away, the drier leaves following suit while the green ones merely browned slightly. He made an effort to capture some of the traces of ash that remained when the process was completed, but all he was able to save were some bits of charcoal from the less completely burned portions. This he also stowed in the torpedo, Feth guiding the little vessel over to him in response to spoken directions.

A bit of soil, scraped up from beneath the plant, smoked but did not burn. Ken obtained a number of airtight cans from the cargo compartment of the torpedo and spent some time scooping bits of soil up in these. He also compressed some of the air into a cylinder, using a small piston-type pump from which Feth had carefully removed all traces of lubricant. It leaked a trifle, but its moving parts moved, which was a pleasant surprise.

'There,' said Ken, when the task was completed. 'If there are any seeds in that earth, we should be able to build a little vivarium and find out at least something about this life and its needs.'

'Do you have a balance between makers and eaters?' asked Feth. 'Suppose these plants are all – what would you call them? oxidizers? – and you don't have the corresponding reducers. I should think you'd need a balance of some sort, with any sort of life – otherwise you'd have perpetual motion.'

'I can't tell that, of course, until we try. Still, I might go down this mountain a little farther and try to pick up a wider variety. There are still some empty cans.'

'Another point – I don't recall your making any arrangement to keep them at the proper temperature. I know they're almost as cold as outer space, but there's a difference between almost and all the way.'

'We'll leave the cans in the torpedo until we get back to One. With no air, they'll change temperature very slowly, and we can leave the torpedo somewhere on the twilight zone of One where it'll stay about the right temperature until we can build a chamber with thermostats and a refrigerator – it won't be very large; I have only a couple of cubic yards of air.'

'All right, I guess you win. If it doesn't work, it will be small loss anyway. Are your feet getting cold yet?'

'Not so far – and believe me, I'm looking for it!'

'I'm not sure I believe you. I have a pretty good idea of where most of your attention is. Have you seen any animal life? I've heard the old buzzing once or twice.'

'Have you? I hadn't noticed it. All I can hear comes from the mike in the torpedo, so I should get anything you do.'

'I told you where your attention was. Well, I'll call you if I hear it again.' He fell silent, and Ken resumed his laborious journey downhill. With frequent rests, he finally succeeded in filling and sealing all his containers and depositing them in the cargo space of the torpedo. He was interrupted once by Feth, who reported that the buzzing was again audible; but even though Ken himself could hear it when he listened, he was unable to find the source. Files are not very large creatures, and the light was very dim anyway by Sarrian standards. Since there was nothing very appetizing even for a fly in the cargo compartment above which the microphone was located, the buzzing presently ceased.

Ken took a final look at the landscape, describing everything as completely as he could so that the record being made far above would be useful. The peaks stood out far more prominently now, since some of them were higher than he was. By ignoring the vegetation with which their slopes were clothed and imagining that it was sunset just after a particularly good dust storm, he was even able to find something almost homelike in the scene – there were times when even Sarr's blue-white sun could look as dull as the luminary of this icy world. At such times, of course, there was always a wind which would put Earth's wildest hurricane to shame, and the silence around him was out of place on that score; but for just a moment his imagination was able to carry him across two hundred parsecs of emptiness to a world of warmth and life.

He came to himself with a little start. This place was nothing like home – it wasn't exactly dead, but it should be; dead as the vacuum of space it so greatly resembled. Its cold was beginning to creep into him, mentally in the form of a return of the horror he had felt the first time he had seen the planet and physically by a slight ache in his feet. Even the engineering miracle he was wearing could not keep out the fingers of the cold indefinitely. He started to call Feth, to have the torpedo lifted so that he could get at the chains and clamps; but the request was not uttered.

As suddenly as it had done a few days before, a human voice cut sharply through the stillness of the Planet of Ice.

14

It was not, in the end, his own discouragement which caused the cessation of Roger's nocturnal watchings. The night on which the Sarrians tested the armor was, indeed, the last of these journeys; but this was owing to reasons beyond the boy's control. When he descended in the morning, his father met him and accompanied him outside. There he pointed out certain footprints. Then they went up to Roger's room together, and the rope came to light. Mr Wing concluded the proceedings with a request for an explanation.

'Don't get the idea that anyone tattled,' he added. 'I don't know whether you have anyone in your confidence, even. Both your mother and I saw that you were getting most of your sleep done daytimes. Well, what's the story?'

Roger never even thought of lying. The family custom of proving questionable statements on challenge had taught him, as it had the other children, to recognize evidence and forego useless denial. The only question in his mind was whether to tell or not. He knew there would be no punishment if he refused; but also, there would be no help from his father on a problem that was decidedly beyond his own abilities, and there would most certainly be no more night journeys in search of landing torpedoes. He told what had happened, with all the detail the near-eidetic memory of childhood could evoke. His father was silent for a minute or two when he had finished.

'We'll say nothing about your following Don and me,' he said at last. 'You were never told in so many words not to, and curiosity is a healthy trait. Of course you let yourself get caught in the woods at night without food, water or light, and that is a more serious matter in view of the fact that you're supposed to know better. However, the story being as interesting as it is, I guess we'll suspend sentence on that offense.' Roger grinned.

'What would the sentence have been?'

'The logical one would be restriction to the half-mile circle for a week or two. You certainly behaved like a six-year-old. Let's consider that that's hanging over your head, and go on to more immediate matters. I suppose Edie knows all about this?'

'She knows about what happened that night. Not about the times I've gone out since.'

'All right. After breakfast, get her and come with me. We have a number of things to talk over.'

It turned out that Don was also at the meeting. This was held in a little

98

natural amphitheater a few yards uphill from the house, which had been fitted with split-log benches. Mr Wing wasted no time, but told the younger children the same story he had told Donald a few days before. Then Roger repeated his tale, mostly for his older brother's benefit. Don had, of course, seen a Sarrian torpedo by this time, as he had been present when the first load of tobacco had been delivered a few days before; and there seemed to be little doubt that the structure Roger had encountered was of the same origin.

'I don't understand why they're shifting their base of operations after all these years.' Mr Wing looked puzzled. 'They've been coming back to that same gadget which we think is a directional transmitter every summer since before Don was born.'

'You don't really know that they haven't landed anywhere else, though,' pointed out Donald. 'It just happened that Roger met one of their torpedoes. There might have been any number of others, anywhere on the earth.'

'That's true, of course. Rog, you didn't find any traces of other landings on these night walks of yours, did you?'

'I'm not sure, Dad. There's a little patch of bushes all by itself on a hilltop out that way, that's been burnt over. I couldn't find any sign of a campfire, and there haven't been any thunderstorms. I thought maybe one of the things had dropped something like the thing that burned my hand, and started the fire; but I couldn't find anything of the sort. I don't really know what started it.'

'I see. Then to sum up, we've been trading with creatures not native to this world for a long time; we may or may not be the only ones doing so; on at least one occasion they sent down a craft whose primary mission does not seem to have been trade.'

'Unless the light that Rog saw was intended to attract attention, as it did,' cut in Donald.

'In that case they would hardly have had their gold too hot to be touched. Furthermore, I've always refused gold – regular prospectors are competition enough without starting a rush of amateurs.'

'We don't know that other people, if there have been any, felt the same way. But I guess you're right about the temperature. They must have been conducting an experiment of their own, and the offer to trade was an afterthought when they heard Rog's voice.'

'It was a dirty trick,' commented Roger.

'It may have been unintentional. Their knowledge of our language is extremely limited, and apparently they can't see down here. Either they don't know about television or can't mount a transmitter in those torpedoes. Besides, if you came on them unexpectedly, they may have forgotten in the excitement of the moment that the gold would be hot. You said it was another container which was providing the light. However, that's a point there's not much use discussing.

'I had not planned to take this step until both Roger and Edie were older, and had had training enough to be of more help; but the matter seems to have been taken out of my control in that respect. What I want to do, and will need the help of all of you in doing, is to find out where these things are from, what sort of people are running them – and, if possible, how they work. I don't have to tell you how important that knowledge would be. I have never tried to get outside experts on the job, because, as I told Don, I was afraid they'd let curiosity overcome prudence. I don't want the torpedoes scared away by any hasty action. I'm too old to learn a new trade, for one thing.'

'Nuts!' It was Edie's first contribution to the discussion, though she had listened intently to all that had gone before.

'What are we going to do?' Roger asked, rather more practically.

'First of all, you two will come with us the next time we trade. I may take the younger kids along too, only it's quite a walk for them. You can listen in, watch, and generally see the whole thing for yourselves. After that, ideas will be in order. I was hoping, Rog, that you'd be an electronics expert by the time this happened. However, we'll use what we have.'

'Maybe my trouble the other night could be put to use,' Roger suggested. 'If they want tobacco badly enough to pay for it in platinum and iridium, they might be in a mood to apologize.'

'Supposing they realize they hurt you, and could think of a way to transmit the apology. I won't refuse an extra nugget or two if they choose to send them, but that won't be very informative.'

'I suppose that's so. Well, anyway, I'm going to go over the whole neighborhood of where I saw it and where you do your trading, by daylight. If they've made any other landings in the woods, I'll find 'em – that one broke a lot of branches, and left a dent in the ground the shape of the torpedo.'

'If you think it's worth doing,' remarked Don. 'Why should they have landed in this neighborhood? Earth's a pretty big place.'

'They did once, and I bet I know why!' retorted Roger. 'That transmitter is right here! If you were exploring a new world or a new country even, would you make one landing here and another five hundred miles away? You would not. You'd get to know one neighborhood first, and plant an outpost, and then spread out from there.'

There was silence for two or three minutes while the others absorbed this.

'You're assuming, then,' said Mr Wing at last, 'that after twenty years of mere trading, they suddenly are starting to explore? Why didn't they do it sooner?'

'Unfair question.'

'True enough. All right, it's certainly a usable working hypothesis. You may go ahead with your exploring – so may Edie if she wants. I'm not sold enough on your idea to spend the effort myself, but in a day or two I'll signal for another torpedo. That will give you time to do any looking you want, I suppose?'

'Well—' Roger's recent mapping activities had given him a much clearer idea than he had formerly held just what the examining of one square mile meant. 'We can look around a bit, anyway. I'm going right now, if no one has any real ideas. Coming, Edie?' The girl stood up silently, and followed him back to the house. Their father watched them go with some amusement.

'I wish I didn't have a nagging worry about Rog's theory,' he said suddenly to Donald. 'He might just be right – these creatures might be tired of paying for tobacco and they certainly know more of physical science than we do.'

'They'll have a fine time looking for the living weed in this neighborhood,' replied his son. 'They'll do better to stay on peaceful terms.'

'Just tell 'em that, will you?' murmured Mr Wing.

Roger and his sister wasted no time. This time there was no mistake in the matter of food; they hastily prepared some sandwiches – their mother had long since resigned herself to the fact that raids on the pantry were insepar- able from common-sense rules of forest life – and with a canteen of water apiece they set out eastward. Billy and Marge were playing somewhere out of sight, so there was no trouble about leaving them home. Their father's description had been clear enough so that they had no trouble in finding the Sarrian transmitter, and from there the two began their search. At Edie's sug- gestion they split up, she taking the southern slopes on the line back to their home and Roger taking the northern. They agreed to keep to high ground as much as possible, and thus remain in earshot of each other most of the time. There was little point, in the time available, to look for traces in the woods; but it might be possible to sight either burned spots such as Roger had already seen or traces of disturbance in the upper branches of trees while looking from above. At any rate, more territory could be examined. Neither youngster had spent any time debating the question of whether it was better to know about a small area or guess about a large one.

Neither Roger nor Edith was on the hill where Ken landed at the time of his descent. Nature had arranged that they should be in the neighborhood, but coincidence refused to carry matters farther. However, Nature still had a trick in reserve.

Roger, until that morning, had taken more or less for granted that any future visits of the torpedo would be at night, as the first had been. His father's story had changed that idea; and since he had heard it only three or four hours before, he had not given up taking rather frequent looks at the sky. It was not too surprising, therefore, that he saw the descending torpedo.

It was nearly a mile and a half away, and he could make out no details; but he was certain it was no bird. The irregularity caused by Ken's dangling form gave just a suggestion of oddness at that distance. Detailed or not, however,

Roger never thought of doubting what it was; and with a whoop that might or might not reach his sister's ears for all he cared at the moment, he headed downhill at a breakneck pace.

For a short time he made excellent speed, the irregularity of the rocks offering no obstacle that his alert eyes and active muscles could not overcome without trouble. Then he reached the forest, and was slowed considerably. For a short distance he kept up the furious effort with which he had started; then realizing that he had at least one hill to cross and another to climb, he eased off a little.

He had wet feet, thoroughly scratched legs, and a decided shortness of wind when he reached the hilltop toward which the torpedo had seemed to be descending, some three quarters of an hour later. He had seen no sign of Edith – he had, in fact, completely forgotten her. She might have come back to mind as he paused at the top of the small mountain to gain his breath and look around for the object of his search; but as it happened, the torpedo was in sight, only a short distance down the other side. So was Sallman Ken.

Roger had seen pictures of the tremendous pressure suits which have from time to time been constructed for deep-sea exploration. The sight of Ken, therefore, did not astonish him too much – certainly less than the sight of a Sarrian without armor would have done. The suit the scientist was wearing humanized his appearance considerably, since a human being would not have had to be too greatly distorted to get into it.

The legs, for engineering reasons, had only a single 'knee,' corresponding to the upper joint of the Sarrian limb; the body was about human size, and cylindrical in shape; there were only two upper limbs. These were more flexible than a human being would have needed in a similar suit, but they at least gave no indication that the creature wearing them was controlling them with two tentacles each. The handlers at their extremities were natural enough, though more complicated than the claw-like devices the boy had seen in the diving suit pictures.

At his distance, he could not see clearly through the transparent ports in the helmet; and so for some moments he failed to realize just how unhuman the wearer of the clumsy garment was.

For perhaps half a minute, Roger simply stared; then he unloosed the yell which interrupted Ken's 'embarkation.' The scientist's attention had been completely taken up with this task, and he had not seen Roger at all before the cry; after it, he saw nothing else. He himself was not facing the direction from which the sound had come, but one of the transparent ports in his helmet was; and he was much too interested to devote attention to anything like turning the armor, after his first look at the being charging downhill toward him. He simply stood, watching with the one eye he could bring to bear. It never occurred to him for an instant that the creature might be hostile.

Roger never thought of the possibility either. His mind resembled that of Ken much too closely, in spite of the overwhelming physical differences. They simply stood facing each other – Ken finally did swing his armor around, so he could use both eyes – and silently absorbed all the details their respective optics could pick out. Each had an advantage – Roger in the fact that the light was normal for him, Ken in that the boy was not concealed in a couple of hundred pounds of metal. Roger could see the Sarrian's face now, and his attention was taken up completely with the great, widespread, independently movable eyes, the blank where a nose should have been, and the broad, thin-lipped, surprisingly human mouth. The silence stretched out.

It was interrupted by Feth, whose anxiety had been increasing with each second that passed after Roger's call.

'What's happened? Is anything wrong? Are you all right, Ken?' The scientist found his voice.

'Perfectly all right. We have company, as I suppose you guessed.' He began to describe Roger as completely as possible, and was interrupted within a minute by the mechanic.

'It can't be done. We'll get a television set or a camera down there if I have to invent a whole new system. Never mind describing the thing – see if you can talk to it!'

Roger had heard none of this, since Feth had not energized the speaker in the torpedo. This oversight he now rectified, and Ken's next words reached the boy clearly.

'What in the Galaxy can I say? Suppose this one has heard about our mistake the other night – suppose it's even the same one? If I use the word "Gold" it'll either run or start fighting. I'm not afraid of it, but that certainly wouldn't help the process of getting acquainted.'

'Well, you've just used the word. How did he take it? I have the main speaker on.' Ken, who had had no means of knowing that fact, cast a startled glance at Roger.

The boy, of course, had understood just the one word 'Gold.' He probably would have missed that, except for the fact that Ken had accentuated it as one does a foreign word; but as it was, he thought that the previous conversation had been addressed to him. He had not distinguished the two voices, and all the sounds had come from the torpedo still poised just above Ken's head.

'I don't want any of your gold – not if it's like the last batch!' Again only one word was understood by the listener. Ken grew hopeful. Maybe this creature hadn't heard, or maybe they had completely misinterpreted the sounds he and Feth had heard during the atmosphere test.

'Gold?' he asked.

'NO!' Roger shook his head negatively and backed away as he gave the emphatic answer. The first gesture meant nothing to the watching Sarrian, but the second seemed clear enough.

'Did you get that last sound of his on record, Feth? Judging by his actions, that's the negative in their language. No gold!' he addressed the last two words after a brief pause. Roger relaxed visibly, but still spoke emphatically.

'No gold, no platinum, – I have no tobacco.' He spread empty hands and turned out his pockets, giving the Sarrian scientist a clue he had been waiting for on just how much of his covering was artificial.

'Point to things and name them!' Feth cut in from above. 'How else can you learn a language? This chatter sounds as silly as anything I've ever heard!'

'All right – only remember, I can see as well as hear. That makes a bit of difference. If you expect any results, keep quiet; how's this thing going to tell who's talking? It all comes from the same loudspeaker. I'll call you when I want to hear from you.' Feth gave no answer to this very sound point, and after waiting a minute Ken began to follow the mechanic's suggestion.

Since Roger had been thinking of exactly the same thing, he caught on at once, and thereby gave the Sarrian a higher opinion of human intelligence than his conversations with Laj Drai had caused him to hold previously. The English words for rock, tree, bush, mountain, cloud, and the numbers up to ten were learned in short order. A few verbs were managed easily enough. At this point operations seemed likely to be suspended, and Roger was rather relieved to have the subject changed by a distant hail.

'My gosh! I forgot all about Edie! She must think I fell off a cliff or something!' He turned in the direction from which the faint voice seemed to be coming, and put all the strength of his lungs into an answering hail. His sister heard it and responded; and ten or fifteen minutes of lung strain brought her to the scene. She seemed a little dubious about approaching Ken at all closely, to Roger's surprise.

'What's the matter with you? He just wants to talk, as far as I can see.'

'Haven't you got burned again?'

'No; why should I?'

'Can't you feel the heat?'

Oddly enough, Roger hadn't. He had never come closer than about fifteen feet to the scientist. The radiation from the armor was easily detectable at that distance without being uncomfortable, but he simply had not noticed it in the press of other interests. For Edith, whose strongest impression of the aliens had been derived from her brother's experience of a few nights before, it was the most prominent characteristic of the thing standing before them.

With the matter brought to his notice, Roger approached the alien more closely, and extended a cautious hand toward the metal. He stopped it more than a foot away.

'My gosh, he certainly *is* hot. Maybe that's what caused the trouble – they never thought the gold would burn me. Do you suppose that's it?'

'Maybe. I'd like to know how it can live when it's that hot, though. So would Dad. He ought to be here anyway. Had I better go tell him, while you keep the thing here?'

'I don't know how I'd keep it. Besides, it would be awful late by the time he got here. Let's try to make a date for tomorrow.' He turned back to Ken without waiting for Edie's rather sensible question, 'How?'

Actually the 'how' proved not too difficult. Time is an abstract quantity, but when it is measured by phenomena like the apparent movement of the sun it can be discussed in signs quite clearly enough for practical purposes. Ken understood without difficulty by the time Roger had finished waving his arms that the two natives would return to the present location shortly after sunrise the following day. The scientist was just as glad to break off the interview, since his feet were now quite numb with cold. He resumed the task of fastening himself to the hovering torpedo, and the children, turning back for a last look as they reached the trees, saw the odd-looking assemblage of suit and carrier drifting upward with ever-increasing velocity. They watched until it had dwindled to a speck and vanished; then with one accord they headed for home.

15

Mr Wing was not merely interested; he was enthralled by the youngster's report. He was sensible enough to realize that nothing any of his family had done could possibly be responsible for the aliens' starting to make personal exploration of the earth, but the fact that they were doing so seemed likely to be very helpful to his plans. The evening meal consisted very largely of conversation, for all attempts to keep the details from any of the family were abandoned. Mrs Wing, of course, had known everything from the beginning; Roger and Edie had been pretty well briefed that morning; but Billy and Marge lacked both specific information and basic knowledge to appreciate the situation. Their questions tended to break up the general train of thought, but only Roger showed any impatience. Since even he did not dare become openly contemptuous of their ignorance, the general tone of the conversation remained peaceful, and several important decisions were made.

'It seems to me,' Mr Wing said, 'that these things – maybe we can think of them as people, now that we have some idea what they look like – must at last have some scientists on the job. I can't even guess at the reason for the delay—'

'Look at an astronomical photo of the Milky Way some time, and you might guess,' cut in Don.

'Reason or no reason, the fact itself may be useful. There will be both explorers and apparatus coming down, beyond reasonable doubt; and they must expect to lose a certain amount of the latter. I don't mean to encourage dishonesty in my offspring, but if we could acquire some of that apparatus long enough to perform dissection I would be very pleased.'

'I take it you are no longer afraid of scaring them off?' Mrs Wing stated rather than asked.

'No. Whether they continue trading or not is out of my hands – it will probably depend on the results that their scientists get. I am not worried; they obviously want tobacco badly, and I doubt very much if it grows on any other planet. I could be surer of my ground, of course, if I knew what they wanted it for. I used to think they smoked it as we do, but this knowledge of their normal temperature makes that sound a trifle unlikely.

'But back to the original point. Anyone who talks to them from now on might well suggest that another transmitter be brought down, so they can home on this house. I see no point in walking five or six miles out and the same distance back just for a daily conversation. Incidentally, Rog, I'm wondering whether we mightn't have made a better impression if we'd tried learning their words for things instead of teaching them ours.'

'Maybe. I didn't think of that.'

'How about the trading, Dad?' asked Don. 'Are you going to keep it up as usual, or try to get these investigators to take our stuff?' His father considered for a moment.

'I think we'd better stick to the old routine,' he said finally. 'We have no assurance that the traders and scientists are in with each other, and it would be a pity to disappoint our customers. Perhaps, when we go to keep this date tomorrow, you'd better go on to the transmitter and give the signal. You'd better carry a pack of cigarettes with you; normally, of course, they're two or three days answering, but if they should be in with the science crowd they may be a lot closer at the moment. You'd better be prepared, in case they answer at once.'

'You mean I'd better stay by the transmitter all day, if necessary?'

'Well – no, not that. Hang around for a while, and then come back to where we'll be. We can keep an eye in the right direction in case another torpedo comes down – it can't be more than a couple of miles in a straight line, so we stand a fair chance of seeing it.'

'All right. I signal, and everybody talks, with emphasis on suggesting that another communicator be brought down – always supposing either party learns enough of the other's language to get any such idea across.' Don shifted the subject suddenly. 'Say, Dad, I just had an idea. You say it doesn't always take the same length of time between the signal and the arrival of the torpedo?'

'That's right. Never less than two days, never much more than three.'

'Could you give me any specific signalling dates, with the time of arrival? The more the better. I think I can do something with them.' Mr Wing thought for a moment.

'Some, anyway. I can remember those of the last couple of years pretty well, and probably some odd ones from earlier years if I try. What's your idea?'

'I'd rather not tell until I'm a little more certain of it. Let's have what you can recall.'

With the aid of the family, who were able to supply clues on his dates of absence – a diary kept by Edie was very helpful – about two dozen of the dates were fixed with sufficient accuracy to satisfy Don. He immediately went up to his room, carrying the notes he had taken.

From that point the conversation drifted by imperceptible degrees into pure fantasy, and by bed-time a number of wonderful pictures had been drawn about the home life of the fiery visitors. Little Margie's was the most interesting, if the least accurate.

Sallman Ken, however, was wasting no time on fantasy. He had not yet worked out a really detailed course of action, but certain ideas were gradually taking shape in his mind as he worked.

The moment he entered the *Karella* and had emerged from his bulky armor, he went into a close conference with Feth. Lee was present at first, even following them to Ken's quarters where the scientist began; but a glance of understanding passed between Ken and Feth, and the conversation took a remarkably abstruse turn. It had just enough meaning to give the impression that matters of highly advanced physics and chemistry were being covered, in connection with the problem of keeping the seeds – if any – in the soil samples alive and healthy. For a few minutes it looked as though Lee were going to stay and take it, but Feth suddenly had the inspiration to ask the pilot's opinion of occasional matters. After a little of this, Ordon Lee drifted back to his control room. 'He's not stupid,' Feth said, looking after his retreating form, 'but he certainly lacks confidence in his education! Now, what did you want to keep from Drai?'

'It has occurred to me,' Ken said, 'that our employer is going to want to hear everything that goes on on Planet Three, as soon as we are in halfway decent communication with the natives. I have some vague ideas about the uses to which those creatures can be put, and I'd rather not have Drai listening in to all our conversations. Since at the moment there's no way of preventing that, I'd like to know whether it might not be possible to connect me up with the speaker on the torpedo *without* having everything audible up here as well. It would be best, I suppose, if I could turn your contact on and off at will, so that he'll hear enough to keep him from getting suspicious.'

'I suppose it could be done, all right,' the mechanic said slowly. 'I'm afraid it would take more work than it's worth, though. Wouldn't it be a great deal simpler to take another set down with you in the torpedo? You already have means for tuning both transmitter and receiver in the armor, so you could switch from one set to the other whenever you pleased.'

'Wouldn't they miss the extra set?'

'Not unless Drai starts paying a great deal more attention to the technical supplies than he has in the past.'

'All right, let's do it that way. Now, let's see. I already suggested suspending the armor vertically instead of horizontally from the torpedo, so I can be carried around instead of having to lug that hardware against extra gravity, didn't I?'

'Yes. That will be easy enough.'

'It will have another good point, as well. The only discomfort I've felt so far on that planet has been in my feet, in spite of what we feared. This way we can keep them off the ground, so they don't lose so much by conduction.

'The only other thing I had in mind had to do with torpedo control. Could a unit be made small enough for me to carry, so I could move myself around down there instead of having to tell you where I want to go?'

Feth frowned at this suggestion. 'I thought of that, too, while I was trying to keep the torpedo near you this time,' he said. 'Frankly, I doubt it – not that the set could be made small enough, but that I could do it with the materials I have at hand. Still, I'll look into the possibility when we get back to One. I take it you have no objection to Drai's hearing about these last two suggestions?'

'Of course not. They ought to keep him happy. I suppose it would be too much to hope that he'd take a trip down there himself, once we showed it was safe enough?' Feth smiled broadly at the scientist's suggestion.

'It would take a better psychologist than either of us to endue him with that much trust in his fellows, I fear. Besides, what good would it do? We wouldn't gain anything by leaving him there, pleasant as the idea sounds, and there'd be no use trying to threaten him, since he'd never dream of keeping any inconvenient promises you might wring out of him.'

'I didn't really expect much from the idea. Well, with the other matter understood, I suppose we'd better take those samples back to One before they freeze, and get a vivarium knocked together. If we can grow anything at all, it ought to keep Drai quiet for a little while.'

The torpedo which had transported Ken and his specimens had been allowed to drift to the edge of the repeller field as soon as he had detached himself from it. Feth now returned to the control room and began to monitor the little vessel, holding it close against the hull of the large ship so that it would be dragged along in the *Karella*'s drive fields; and Lee, at Ken's request, headed sunward once more. A thousand miles from the surface of Mercury the torpedo was cast loose again, and Feth eased it down to a landing near the caves – a televisor had been set up there some time since, and he was able to guide the landing with the aid of this. He arranged matters so that about three feet of the torpedo's nose was in sunlight, while the rest was in the shadow of a large mass of rock. That, he judged, should maintain somewhere near the right temperature for a few hours at least.

As soon as the *Karella* was grounded, he and Ken adjourned at once to the shop. There, a metal case about a yard square and two feet high was quickly assembled. Feth very carefully welded all seams and tested them against full atmospheric pressure. A glass top was provided, sealed in place with a silicone vacuum wax that was standard equipment on any space ship; this also checked out against a pressure equivalent to an earthly barometric reading of twelve hundred fifty millimeters of mercury. A second, similar case large enough to enclose the first was under construction when Drai appeared. He had evidently noticed at last that the ship was back.

'Well, I understand from Lee that you actually talked to a native. Good work, good work. Did you find out anything about how they make their tofacco?'

'We haven't learned their language too well, yet,' Feth replied with as little sarcasm as he could manage. 'We were operating on a slightly different line of investigation.' He indicated the partly constructed vivarium. Drai frowned at it, as though trying to gather its purpose. 'It's a small chamber where we can reproduce Planet Three's conditions, we hope; more or less of an experiment. The larger one goes outside, and we'll maintain a vacuum between the two. Feth says one of the sulfur hexafluoride refrigerators he knocked together years ago will get the temperature low enough, and we got enough of the planet's air to fill it a couple of times at their pressure.' Drai looked puzzled still.

'But isn't it a little small for one of the natives? Lee said you'd described them as nearly five feet tall. Besides, I didn't hear about these plans at all.'

'Natives? I thought you wanted us to grow vegetation. What good would a native do us here?' The master's face cleared.

'Oh, I see. I didn't know you'd picked up vegetation already. Still, now that I think of it, it mightn't be a bad idea to have a native or two. If the race is at all civilized, they could be used for a really stupendous ransom in tofacco – and we could use them in the cave, once it was conditioned, to take care of the tofacco and harvest it. Thanks for the idea.'

'I don't know just how intelligent the natives are, as yet,' replied Ken, 'but I don't think they're stupid enough to walk into any sort of cage we might leave open for them. If you don't mind, I'll leave that as a last resort – we're going to have trouble enough getting our soil and seeds from their present containers into this thing without exposing them either to our atmosphere or to empty space. It would be a hundred times worse getting a native into one of those caves.'

'Well, you may be right. I still think it would get us more tofacco, though.'

'I'm sure it would, if they are at all civilized. I don't see why you're complaining about that, though – you're getting it cheap enough now, goodness knows.'

'I don't mind the price – it's the quantity. We only get a couple of hundred cylinders a year – one of Three's years, that is. That doesn't let us operate on a very large scale. Well, do what you think best – provided you can convince me it's best, too.' He left on that note, smiling; but the smile seemed to both Feth and Ken to have a rather unpleasant undertone. Feth looked after him a little uneasily, started to return to the job in hand, stopped once more, looked rather apologetically at Ken, and then went after Drai. The scientist remembered that Feth's last dose of the drug had come some time before his own.

That set him to wondering about when he himself could expect to feel the craving. Feth had said the interval was five or six Sarrian days – which were about thirteen Earthly hours in length. About half a day had been consumed after his first recovery in general talk, checking of the big suits, and travelling out to Three; rather more than a day in the actual tests and the meeting with which they had culminated; another half day since. Looking into the future, at least a full day must pass before the planned meeting with the natives of

Three. No one could tell how long that would last, but apparently he had a couple of days' leeway in any case. He stopped worrying and turned his attention back to the partly completed vivarium.

He was not an expert welder but the specimens waiting patiently two thousand miles away would only last so long, and he did not know how long Feth would be incapacitated. He took the torch and resumed work on the outer case. He had learned from watching Feth how the testing equipment was used, and was pleasantly surprised when his seams proved airtight. That, however, was as far as he could go; the mechanic had made no written plans, and Ken had no idea of his ideas on the attachment of the various refrigerating and pumping mechanisms. He stopped work, therefore, and devoted his mind to the problem he had mentioned to Drai – how to transfer the samples to the beautiful little tank after it was completed.

He spent some time trying to invent a remote-controlled can opener before the solution struck him. Then he kicked himself soundly for not having thought of it before – his double-kneed legs gave him a noticeable advantage in that operation. After that he relaxed until Feth returned, coming as close to sleep as his race ever did.

The mechanic was back in less than four hours, as a matter of fact. He seemed to be in fairly good shape; the tofacco apparently had few visible after-effects, even after years of use, which was a comforting thing to think about.

Ken showed him what had been done on the vivarium during his absence, and Feth expressed approval. He looked a little disappointed, however, at hearing the scientist's plan for stocking the device; as it turned out, he had had one of his own.

'I don't know why we were fools enough to get the specimens before we had a place to put them,' Ken said. 'We run the risk of ruining them in the cans, and have the transfer problem. We'd have been a lot smarter to make this thing first, and take it down to Three's surface for stocking on the spot. Why didn't we?'

'If you want an answer to that, we were probably too eager to make the trip,' was the plausible answer. 'Are you going to forget about the specimens we have, then?'

'We might check their temperatures. If those are still reasonable, we might as well take them back to Three and make the transfer there. It will be interesting to see how the seeds, if any, stood their trip – not that anything will be proved if they don't come up.'

'You could make a microscopic check for anything resembling seed,' Feth suggested, forgetting the situation for a moment.

'Do I cook the specimen or freeze the observer?' queried the scientist in an interested tone. Feth did not pursue the matter. Instead, he turned back to his work, and gradually the vivarium took shape under his skilled tentacles. Both the refrigerator and the pump were remarkably tiny devices, each solidly attached to a side of the box-like affair. Their controls were simple; an off-on toggle for the pump, and a thermostat dial for the refrigerator.

'I haven't calibrated that,' Feth said, referring to the latter. 'I'm mounting a thermometer inside where it can be seen through the lid, and you'll just have to fiddle with the knob until it's right.'

'That's all right – for supposedly haywire apparatus, you certainly turn out a factory job. There's nothing to apologize for that I can see.'

There were several hours yet to go before they were actually due at the meeting place on Planet Three. They loafed and talked for a while, Ken's plan coming gradually into more definite shape as they did so. They discussed the peculiarities of the Planet of Ice. Feth looked through his stock cabinets and reported that there was nothing he could turn into a portable control set so that Ken could handle his own torpedo. It was his turn to kick himself when the scientist suggested that he *wire* contacts to the controls – he (Ken) did not *insist* on sending the impulses by radio. Thirty minutes later a torpedo was sitting in the shop with a long cable extending from a tiny opening in its hull, and ending in a small box with half a dozen knobs studding its surface. Ken, manipulating the knobs, found no difficulty in making the projectile do whatever he wanted.

'I guess we're even in the matter of overlooking the obvious,' he said at last. 'Had we better be getting ready to go?'

'I suppose so. By the way, since you can't read the torpedo's instruments, maybe you'd better let me navigate you to the ground. Then you can do what you please.'

'That would be best. I certainly could not judge either distance or speed at three thousand miles from the surface.'

They donned space suits, and carried their apparatus out to the *Karella*. The vivarium they left in the air lock, since it was going to have to be fastened to the torpedo anyway; but Lee found it there a little later and delivered a vitriolic comment on people who obstructed the exits from a space ship. Ken humbly carted the box inside by himself, Feth having gone up to the control room to direct the newly modified torpedo to its cradle.

They were ready to go, except for one thing, and neither of them realized the omission. It was brought home to them only a minute before the planned take-off time, when another space-suited figure glided from the air lock of the station to that of the ship. Lee waited, apparently unsurprised; and a moment later Laj Drai entered the control room.

'We may as well go, if all your apparatus is on board,' he said.

Without comment, Ken nodded to the pilot.

16

Ken paused halfway into his armor to wave all four tentacles in expostulation.

'If you don't think I know what I'm talking about, why did you hire me?' he asked. 'I'll get and grow plants for you as fast as I can. Our tank is only so big – there are growths down there that wouldn't fit in this ship, whether you believe it or not. I don't know any better than you what tofacco looks like when it's growing – I'm not even as sure as you seem to be that it's a plant. Just get out of your head the idea that I'm going to pack plants into this case until thay have no room to breathe, and try to develop a little patience. It took two thousand years to explore Sarr, and the exploring was a darn sight easier than this!' He resumed the task of sliding into his metal shell.

'You'll do what you're told, Mr Ken. I don't care how you do it, as I said before; but if we're not growing tofacco in a reasonable time, someone's going to be awfully sorry.'

Ken's response was slightly muffled, as only his head was now protruding from the suit. 'That, of course, you can do; I can't stop you. However, if you'll let me do this my own way, I honestly think things will go faster. Use your head, after all – who does know this planet?' He paused too briefly for the question to have any but rhetorical significance, and went on: 'The natives, of course. They not only know the planet, they presumably know where the tofacco can be obtained, since they sell it to you. You'll have to work hard to convince me that there's any better way of learning what we want to know than getting the information from the natives.'

'But it takes so long to learn a language!'

'True. It also takes quite a while to explore two hundred million square miles of territory, even if you count out the three quarters of it that seems to be flatland – and you can't really do that; these natives may be on good enough terms with the flatlanders to get the tofacco from them by trade. How about that? I understand you had your fill of exploring the flatlands quite a while ago – what was it, nineteen out of nineteen torpedoes lost, or twenty out of twenty? The percentage was embarrassing in either case.'

'But suppose they don't want us to learn where it can be obtained? They might be afraid we'd get it ourselves, instead of paying them for it.'

'That would not be too stupid of them. Sure, they may suspect just that. I never denied that a certain amount of tact would be needed. If you don't think I can exercise it, I repeat – do it yourself. We have more suits. I want to go down anyway, to study the place, but come right along – the torpedo will carry you and me and the tank easily enough!'

'I may not be a genius, but I'm not completely insane. I'll be there by proxy. If I don't like your tact, you needn't bother to come back.'

'Don't you want the suit? I thought they were expensive,' Ken said sweetly, and pulled the massive helmet into place with a clang.

Feth, who had been listening in, dogged the piece in place. He was just a trifle worried; he himself had not talked to Drai like that for years, and still retained unpleasant memories of the last time he had done so. He knew, of course, the purpose behind Ken's attitude; the scientist wanted to annoy Drai sufficiently so that he would not suspect more than one thing at a time. That one thing was to be exactly what Ken wanted. Feth admitted to himself that that part of the conversation had been well handled. Nevertheless, he was not too sure he liked the expression of Laj Drai's face as that individual draped himself within easy earshot of the radio.

His attention was shifted from the matter as Ken called in from the air lock, reporting that he was attached.

'Let me get out of here with my own controls, and move around a bit while I'm close enough to judge results,' he finished. 'I'd better get the feel of this thing while I have just inertia for trouble, and before there's weight as well.'

'Sound enough,' Feth approved, and took his tentacles from his own controls. One eye remained on the indicators, while the other sought the nearest port. In a few seconds the cigar-shaped bit of metal came into view, darting this way and that, swinging the clumsy figure of the armored scientist from a point near its bow and the rectangular box of the vivarium a few feet farther aft – it, too, was too large to go into the cargo compartment. Ken seemed to be having no trouble in controlling the sloppy-looking assembly, and presently signified that he was ready for the dive.

'All right,' Feth replied, 'I have it. Be sure all your own controls are neutral – they're not cross-connected and impulses will add algebraically. By the way, *all* the stuff is in the cargo compartment.'

The other torpedo with the first batch of samples had been salvaged from its lonely perch on Mercury, and Laj Drai knew that; so Feth hoped he would not notice the slight accent on the 'all.' The mechanic had placed the extra radio in with the other objects, but had done so at the last moment and had had no time to tell Ken about it. He hoped the fellow knew how to operate the set.

Ken, as a matter of fact, had not realized what Feth was implying. He was much too occupied in bracing his nerves for the descent that had been so hard on them the previous time. He succeeded better on this occasion, largely because he was able to keep most of his mind on the problems that would be facing him after he was down. They were numerous enough.

He had little trouble finding the scene of the previous meeting, though Feth did not succeed in lowering him exactly over it. He was, he realized, early; the sun was barely up. All to the good. He reported his arrival to Feth to make sure, announced that he was resuming control, and went to work.

His first step was to guide the torpedo downhill to the edge of a fairly extensive patch of plant growth. Before doing anything else, he made sure that the patch was isolated; the reaction of the vegetable matter of this world to hot metal had impressed him strongly, and he had a good imagination. Then he lowered the carrier until the vivarium was touching the ground, and detached the clumsy box. The double lids opened without difficulty – Feth had allowed for the probable effect of low temperature on the mental hinges – and set to work.

The samples of earth came speedily from the cargo compartment, and were dumped into the box – all at one side. Using a strip of metal he had brought along for the purpose, Ken levelled out the dark pile into a layer some three inches deep and a foot wide along one side of the container; then he began to use the strip as a crude shovel. Tiny bushes, patches of moss, and other growths were pried out of the ground, the scientist carefully refraining from allowing his armor to contact them and laying the strip down to cool at frequent intervals. He investigated the widely varying root systems, and carefully dug an extra allowance of soil from the spot where each plant had been removed, so that there would be a sufficient depth in the box beneath it. One by one he transferred his specimens to the vivarium, placing them much too close together to have pleased a human gardener but setting them firmly into the soil so that they stood up as they had before. Once or twice he looked longingly at larger bushes, but gave up. They were too tall, and a brief investigation showed that their roots were too long.

He had covered perhaps two of the six square feet he had to fill when the Wings arrived. Roger and Edie were noticeably in advance of the rest; the two youngest would probably have been close behind them if the scene had not been so far from home. As it was, they had begun to get a little tired, and arrived at the same time as their parents.

Ken did not hear them coming; the microphone in the torpedo was not as sensitive as it might have been, and this time Roger did not call as soon as he saw the scientist. Instead, the children came as close as they dared, trying to see what he was up to. That proved obvious enough, but it was only after his curiosity was satisfied on that point that Roger gave an audible greeting.

'I see you're here early.'

'Why didn't you tell me they were coming?' snapped the voice of Laj Drai from the speaker.

'I didn't see them; I've been working,' replied Ken quietly. 'Now, if you expect us to get anywhere with communication, kindly keep quiet. They have no means of telling when I'm the one who's talking, and extra sounds will just confuse them.' He fell silent, and watched solemnly as the rest of the human beings arrived. The size of Mr and Mrs Wing surprised him a little; it took him some seconds to decide that the individuals he had seen first were probably children. The adults were more impressive, if one was impressed by mere size; Ken decided that either one would outweigh the average Sarrian by fully a quarter, assuming that they really filled their queer clothing and had flesh of comparable density. There was something a little more commanding about the manner of the older natives, also; a dignity and seriousness of purpose which he now realized had been decidedly lacking in the immature specimens. For the first time, Ken really thought of the natives of Earth as possibly civilized beings.

Certainly the actions of the largest one suggested a well disciplined mind. Mr Wing wasted little time. He seated himself in front of Ken, pulled out a notebook in which he had already noted the words Roger claimed to have taught the alien, and checked through them. He looked up at Ken as he pronounced each; the scientist responded by pointing to the appropriate object. Satisfied that these words were understood, the man promptly embarked on a language lesson with a singleness of purpose and efficiency of execution that had Ken regarding him as a fellow being long before they were in real communication. This was not accomplished at once, but it took far less time than many people would believe possible. As any proponent of Basic English will agree, most everyday matters can be discussed quite easily with a vocabulary of less than a thousand words. The present situation was not quite everyday in any sense of the term, but between Mrs Wing's sketching ability and the willingness of the children to illustrate practically any actions required, progress was quite satisfactory to both parties.

Since Ken had stood in the same place throughout the lesson, he had warmed up the rock around his feet; consequently it was fully three hours before he felt the first warning ache of cold. When he did, however, he suddenly realized that he had done nothing toward the filling of his specimen box since the natives had arrived; and waiting courteously until Mr Wing had finished an explanation, he indicated the dearth. The man nodded, and pointed to the ground beyond.

Ken had paid no attention to the actions of the smallest children since shortly after the lesson had started; he had judged that they were playing, as the children of his own race did. Now he was startled to see, spread out on the rock at a little distance from the case, several score plants of assorted shapes and sizes. Apparently the youngsters had seen what he was doing, and decided to help. With growing surprise, he discovered that there were no duplicates among the specimens. The race must really have brains; he had not seen either of the adults give instructions. With an oral expression of gratitude which he was sure must be lost on them, he began clumsily placing them in the box with the aid of his metal strip. As he picked up the first, he pointed to it with his free handler and said, 'Word!' All understood his meaning, and Roger replied, 'Fern.'

After watching his clumsy actions for a moment, Mr Wing waved him away from the box, and put the children to work. Ken watched them with tremendous interest, for the first time realizing what an efficient prehensile organ the human hand could be. The deft fingers of the girls in particular were setting the plants firmly in the earth at a rate and with an ease he himself could not have managed even without the handicap of armor and temperature difference. As each was picked up, a name was given it. It did turn out afterward that the same name had been used over several times in many cases for plants that bore either a merely superficial resemblance or none at all. It took him some time to solve that one, though he already knew that the native language had both particular and generic terms.

A very few minutes were required to cover the base of the box with neatly set plants; and not once had Ken heard the word that would have meant so much to the listening Drai. He himself was just as satisfied; the mention of 'tofacco' by a native in a place where Drai could have heard it would have put a serious crimp in Ken's now rapidly maturing plans.

In spite of his having taken the cans containing the earlier specimens from the cargo section of the torpedo, it was not until he was putting the empty containers back that Ken saw the other radio Feth had placed there. For a moment he was irritated both with himself and the mechanic, since by then he had forgotten the latter's words at the time of Ken's departure; then he decided that it might be for the best. If Drai had been listening ever since the start of the language lesson, he should by now be pretty well convinced that Ken was not up to any funny business. There had been no breaks to make him suspicious.

While these thoughts were passing through his mind, Mr Wing was also doing some thinking. It seemed fairly evident that the alien – they had not yet learned each other's names – was on the point of departure. This trip had been a pleasant enough outing for the family, it was true; but a daily repetition would be too much of a good thing, and there were more objects at their home which could be used in language instruction as well. It seemed, therefore, that it might be worth while to make the attempt he had suggested earlier to the family – persuading the aliens to land closer to the house. In consequence, when Ken turned from his task of replacing the empty cans and fastening the sealed vivarium back in place, he found the largest native facing him with a neatly drawn but quite unintelligible diagram in his hand and an evident desire to transmit intelligence of some sort.

It took four or five minutes to make clear exactly what the map represented, though Ken got the general idea after a few seconds. Scale was the principal difficulty. At last, however, the alien understood – he spent two or three minutes describing the map in detail to Feth, first, so that it could be studied and reproduced later – and then said, 'Yes,' to Mr Wing.

'Tomorrow – one day after now – *here*,' the man reiterated, and Ken nodded his head (he had not been too surprised to find that visual signs supplemented the spoken language of these creatures).

'Here.' He indicated the same spot as well as he could with a handler, and the paper turned brown before he hastily snatched it away. Then he remembered something else. 'Not tomorrow. Not one day after now. Two days.' Mr Wing frowned.

'Not tomorrow?'

'No. Two days. Go now; cold.' And Sallman Ken turned, took the extra radio from the cargo compartment, placed it on the ground, said, 'Carry!' and addressed himself to the task of attaching himself to the torpedo once more. He had detached himself, in spite of his original plan, when he found that he could not reach the cargo compartment while chained to the hull of the carrier.

The native mercifully said nothing as he completed this task. As a matter of fact, Mr Wing was too dumbfounded at this turn of events to say anything; and even the children wondered how he had done it. Ken rose into the air amid a dead silence, until the two youngest children remembered their training and shrilled, 'Goodbye!' after the vanishing form. He barely heard the words, but was able to guess at the meaning.

Back at the *Karella*, his first care was to get the vivarium inside. He had already evacuated the space between the walls by opening a small valve for a time during the journey through space; now he started the refrigerator, and refused to take his eyes from the inside thermometer until he had satisfied himself that all fluctuation had ceased. Then, and then only, did he start going over the tape record with Feth to make sure he remembered the hundred or so words he had been taught during his brief dive. Laj Drai, rather to Ken's surprise, forbore to interrupt, though Feth said he had listened carefully during the entire stay on the planet. During this session, Ken managed to tell the mechanic what he had done with the radio, and the latter agreed that it had been a wise move. There was now no need to fear a casual check on the contents of the torpedo by Drai or Lee.

It seemed that Ken had been more convincing than he had expected, in his speech to Drai just before leaving. He had been a little surprised when the boss had failed to interrupt him after his return; now he found that Drai had been itching to do just that, but had been afraid of putting himself in the wrong again. The moment the conference between Ken and Feth came to an end, he was at the scientist's side, asking for an eyewitness account to supplement what he had heard on the radio.

'I really need a camera to give a good idea of appearances,' Ken replied. 'I seem to have been wrong about their size; the ones I saw before appear to have been children. The adults are a trifle bulkier than we are.

'I don't think the language is going to be difficult, and it looks as though this group, at least, is very cooperative.' He told about the help he had received in making the plant collection.

'I was looking at that,' said Drai. 'I don't suppose any of those things is what we're after?'

'No, unless they use different names for the living plant and the product. They named each of these to me as they set them in, and you'd have heard as well as I if they'd said "tofacco" once.' Drai seemed thoughtful for a moment before he spoke again.

'Children, eh? Maybe if you can work with them and get rid of the adults you could find things out more easily. They should be easier to fool.'

'Something like that crossed my mind, too,' Ken said. 'Perhaps we ought to make a few more collection boxes to take down; I could give them to the kids to fill while I was having another language lesson, and then when they came back I'd have a good excuse to talk it over with each in turn. Something might very well crop up if the parents don't interfere.'

'Parents? How do you know?'

'I don't, of course; but it seems likely. But what do you think of the idea?'

'Very good, I should say. Can you get enough boxes for all the children ready by their next morning?'

'I'm not going down that soon. I was making allowances for what Feth told me was the effect of tofacco on the system, and thought I might not be able to make it.' Drai paused long enough to do some mental arithmetic.

'You're probably right. We'll have to go back to One to get your dose, too; I somehow can't bring myself to keep the stuff around where it might fall into the wrong hands.' He smiled, with the same ugly undertone that was making Ken hate the drug-runner a little more each time he saw it.

17

'Dad, will you kindly tell me just how on Earth you worked that?' Don stared at the Sarrian radio, which was all that was visible of the aliens by the time he got back from giving the trade signal. Roger chuckled.

'He didn't work it. He spends all afternoon teaching the thing to talk English, and just as it's going it turns around and puts this on the ground. "Carry" it booms, and takes off. What do you suppose it is, Dad?'

'I can't possibly be sure, Son, until he comes back. It may be a piece of apparatus he intends to use on his next visit; it may be a gift in return for your aid with the plant collection. I think we'd best take it home, as he seemed to want, and do nothing at all to it until he comes back.'

'But if he's not coming back until the day after tomorrow—'

'I know curiosity is a painful disease, Rog; I suffer from it myself. But I still think that the one who'll come out ahead in this new sort of trading is the one who steps most cautiously and keeps his real aims up his sleeve the longest. We're still not certain that this scientific investigation isn't aimed at just one end – to relieve them of the need for paying us for tobacco. After all, why did this fellow start with plants? There are lots of other things he might have shown interest in.'

'If he's as different from our sort of life as he seems to be, how would he know that tobacco is a plant?' countered Roger. 'It certainly doesn't stay unburned long enough at his temperature to let him look at the crumbs with a microscope or anything, and a cigarette doesn't much look like a plant.'

'That's true,' his father admitted. 'Well, I only said we don't *know* he hasn't that up his sleeve. I admit it doesn't seem likely.'

Curiously enough, Ken thought of one of those points himself before the next visit; and when he descended in the clearing by the Wing home with four collecting boxes attached to his torpedo, the first thing he did was to make clear he wanted minerals in one that was not equipped with refrigeration apparatus. Pointing to another similarly plain he said, 'Thing – good – hot – cold.' The Wings looked at each other for a moment; then Edith spoke.

'You mean anything that stays good whether its hot or cold? Stuff that you don't have to keep in a refrigerator?' There were too many new words in that sentence for Ken, but he took a chance. 'Yes. Hot, good.' He was still drifting a foot or two from the ground, having so arranged the load this time that he could detach it without first freeing himself. Now he settled lightly to the ground, and things began to happen.

The ground, like most of that in evergreen forests, was largely composed of shed needles. These had been cleared away to some extent around the house, but the soil itself was decidedly inflammable. Naturally, the moment Ken's armored feet touched it a cloud of smoke appeared, and only lightning-like action in lifting himself again prevented its bursting into flame. As it was, no one felt really safe until Roger had soaked the spot with a bucket of water.

That led to further complications. Ken had never seen water to his know-ledge, and certainly had never seen apparatus for dispensing apparently limitless amounts of any liquid. The outside faucet from which the bucket had been filled interested him greatly; and at his request, made in a mixture of signs and English words, Roger drew another bucketful, placed it on the flat top of one of the cement posts at the foot of the porch steps, and retreated. Ken, thus enabled to examine the object without coming in contact with any-thing else, did so at great length; and finished by dipping a handler cautiously into the peculiarly transparent fluid. The resulting cloud of steam startled him almost as much as the temporary but intense chill that bit through the metal, and he drew back hastily. He began to suspect what the liquid was, and mentally took off his hat to Feth. The mechanic, if that was all he really was, really could think.

Eventually Ken was installed on top of an outdoor oven near the house, the specimen boxes were on the ground, and the children had disappeared in various directions to fill them. The language lesson was resumed, and excel-lent progress made for an hour or so. At the end of that time, both parties were slightly surprised to find themselves exchanging intelligible sentences – crude and clumsy ones, full of circumlocutions, but understandable. A faint smile appeared on Mr Wing's face as he realized this; the time had come to administer a slight jolt to his guest, and perhaps startle a little useful infor-mation out of him. He remembered the conversation he had had with Don the night before, and felt quiet satisfaction in the boy – the sort of satisfaction that sometimes goes to make a father a major bore.

'You didn't have too many times, Dad,' his son had said, 'but there were enough. It ties in with other things, anyway. The intervals between signalling and the arrival of the trading torpedo have been varying in a period of just about a hundred and twenty days, taking several years into account. Of course, a lot of those "periods" didn't have any trading occur, but the period is there; first two days, then three. That hundred and twenty days is the syn-odic period of Mercury – the length of time it takes that planet to catch the Earth up on successive trips around the sun. I remembered Mercury's pos-ition when we studied it this spring, and did some figuring; your short times came when it was closest to us, the long ones when it was on the other side of the sun, about twice as far away. Those torpedoes seem to be coming from there at about one and a quarter G's of acceleration.' Mr Wing, though no physicist, understood this clearly enough. The concept had been publicized sufficiently in connection with airplanes.

He had looked over Don's figures, which were easy enough to follow, and agreed with his results; and the boy had, at his request, drawn a diagram of the orbits of inner planets of the Solar System showing the current positions of the planets themselves. This he now had in his pocket.

The word 'home' had just been under discussion, more or less as a result of chance. Mr Wing had made the concept reasonably clear, he believed; and it seemed to him that the time had come to put one of his cards on the table.

He began by waving an arm to encompass the whole horizon. 'Earth,' he said. The Sarrian repeated the word, but without any gesture of his own suggesting that he understood. The man repeated the word, stamping on the ground as he did so; then he took a new page in the notebook and made a sketch of the planet as he thought it would appear from space. As a final illustration, he molded a sphere from a lump of modeling clay which had been found in the playroom and had already been put to good use. Then he pointed to the sphere, drawing, and the ground, repeating the word after each in turn.

Ken understood. He proved it by scratching a picture of his own on the ground, reaching as far as he could over the side of the oven and using his strip of metal. It was a perfectly recognizable drawing of the sun and orbits of the first three planets. He knew he might be exceeding the local knowledge of astronomy, but the fact that the native seemed to know the shape of his world was encouraging.

Mr Wing promptly pulled out Don's diagram, which was substantially the same as Ken's except that Mars' orbit and position were shown. He spent some minutes naming each of the planets, and making the generic name clear as well. Then they spent some more time in a sort of game; Ken added Jupiter and Saturn to the diagram, in an effort to find out how much astronomy the human being knew. Mr Wing named those, and added Uranus, Neptune and Pluto; Don, who had made no contribution up to this point, made a correction in the orbit of Pluto so that it crossed that of Neptune at one point, and began adding satellites at a furious rate. They took the burst of Sarrian speech that erupted from the speaker as an indication of the alien's surprise, and were gratified accordingly.

Ken was surprised for more reasons than one.

'Drai, if you're listening, these folks are not any sort of savage. They must have a well-developed science. They seem to know of nine planets in this system, and we only knew about six; and there are an awful lot of moons one of them is busy telling me about right now – he's even put two with Planet Four, and we didn't notice any. They either have space travel or darned good telescopes.'

'We haven't seen a space ship here in twenty years,' Feth's voice reminded him. Ken made no answer; Mr Wing had started to talk again. He was pointing to Planet Three on his own diagram, and repeating the name he had given it.

'Earth – my home.' He indicated himself with one hand to emphasize the personal pronoun. Then he moved the finger to the innermost world. 'Mercury – your home.' And he pointed to Sallman Ken.

He was a little disappointed in the reaction, but would not have been had he known how to interpret Sarrian facial expressions. The scientist was dumbfounded for fully ten seconds; when he did regain control of his voice, he addressed the distant listeners rather than the Earthman.

'I'm sure that you will also be interested in knowing that he is aware we come from Planet One. I believe he thinks we live there, but the error is minor under the circumstances.' This time Drai's voice responded.

'You're crazy! You must have told him yourself, you fool! How could he possibly have learned that without help?'

'I did not tell him. You've been listening and ought to know. And I don't see why I should be expected to explain how he found out; I'm just telling you what's going on here at the moment.'

'Well, don't let him go on thinking that! Deny it! He knows too much!'

'What's wrong with that?' Ken asked, reasonably enough.

'Suppose they do have space travel! We don't want them dropping in on us! Why – I've been keeping this place a secret for twenty years.'

Ken forbore to point out the flaws in that line of reasoning. He simply said:

'Not knowing how certain they are of their facts, I think a denial would be foolish. If they are really sure, then they'd know I was lying; and the results might not be good.' Drai made no answer to that, and Ken turned back to the Earthman, who had been listening uncomprehendingly to the conversation.

'Mercury. Yes,' the Sarrian said.

'I see. Hot,' replied Mr Wing.

'No. Cold.' Ken paused, seeking words. 'Little hot. Hot to you. Hot to' – he waved a sleeve of his armor in a wide circle – 'plants, these things. Cold to me.'

Don muttered to his father, 'If he regards Mercury as too cold for comfort, he must come from the inside of a volcano somewhere. Most astronomers are satisfied that there's no planet closer to the sun, and he didn't show one on his diagram, you'll notice.'

'It would be nice if we knew just how hot he liked it,' agreed the older man. He was about to address Ken again in the hope of finding out something on this point when a burst of alien speech suddenly boomed from the torpedo's speaker. Even to Ken, it carried only partial meaning.

'Ken! This—' Just those two words, in Feth's voice; then the transmission ceased with the click that accompanies a broken circuit. Ken called Feth's name several times into his own microphone, but there was no response. He fell silent, and thought furiously.

He suspected from the fact that the natives were simply looking at him that they realized something had gone wrong; but he did not want to worry about their feelings just then. He felt like a diver who had heard a fight start among the crew of his air-pump, and had little attention for anything else. What in the Galaxy were they about, up there? Had Drai decided to abandon him? No, even if the drug-runner had suddenly decided Ken was useless, he would not abandon a lot of expensive equipment just to get rid of him. For one thing, Ken suspected that Drai would prefer to see him die of drug hunger, though this may have been an injustice. What then? Had Drai become subtle, and cut off the transmitter above in the hope that Ken would betray himself in some way? Unlikely. If nothing else, Feth would almost certainly have warned him in some fashion, or at least not sounded so anxious in the words he had managed to transmit.

Perhaps Drai's distrust – natural enough under the circumstances – had reached a point where he had decided to check personally on the actions of his tame scientist. However, Ken could not imagine him trusting himself in armor on the surface of the Planet of Ice no matter what he wanted to find out.

Still, there was another way of coming down personally. Lee would not like it, of course. He might even persuade his employer that it was far too dangerous. He would certainly try. Still, if Drai really had the idea in his mind, it was more than possible that he might simply refuse to listen to persuasion.

In that case, the *Karella*'s shadow might fall across them at any moment. That would fit in with Feth's attempt to warn him, and its abrupt interruption. If that were actually the case, he need not worry; his conscience was clear, and for all that was going on at the moment Drai was perfectly welcome to look on until his eyes froze to the ports. There had been no sign of tofacco anywhere, although the native children had been coming back at frequent intervals with new specimens for the boxes and had named them each time. He himself had not done a single thing in furtherance of his plan.

He had just relaxed with this realization firmly in mind when the native who had been doing most of the talking produced and lighted a cigarette.

Mr Wing had had no intention of doing anything of the sort. He had a pretty good idea of the value placed by these creatures on tobacco, and he did not want to distract the scientist from what might prove a valuable line of talk. As a matter of fact, he would have been perfectly satisfied to have the creature assume that it was someone else entirely who did the trading. Habit, however, defeated his good intentions; and he was only recalled from his speculations on the nature of this new interruption by the realization that he had taken the first puff.

The Sarrian had both eyes fixed on the little cylinder – an unusual event in itself; usually one was roving in a way calculated to get on the nerves even of someone like young Roger. The reason seemed obvious; Mr Wing could imagine the alien running mentally over the list of things he had brought with him, wondering what he could trade for the rest of the pack. He was closer to being right than he should have-been.

That line of thought, however, was profitless, and no one knew it better than Ken. The real problem of the moment was to get the infernal stuff out of sight before Drai arrived – if he were coming. For a moment Ken wondered if the other radio, which he had seen lying on the porch when be arrived, could be put to use in time. Common sense assured him that it could not; even if he could persuade one of the natives to bring it and tow the torpedo out of earshot, he certainly could not make his wish clear in time. He would have to hope – the cylinder was vanishing slowly, and there was a chance that it might be gone before the ship arrived. If only he could be sure that the receiver as well as the transmitter aboard the space ship had been cut off!

If Drai were still listening, the silence of the last few seconds would probably make him doubly suspicious. Well, there was nothing to be done about that.

As it happened, there was plenty of time for the cigarette to burn out, thanks to Ordon Lee. Feth had tried to give his warning the instant he realized what Drai was thinking; and the other's lashing tentacles had hurled him away from the board and across the control room before he could finish. When he had recovered and started to return, he had found himself staring into the muzzle of a pistol, its disc-shaped butt steadied against the drug-runner's torso.

'So the two of you *are* up to something,' Drai had said. 'I'm not surprised. Lee, find the carrier of that torpedo and home down on it!'

'But sir – into Three's atmosphere? We can't—'

'We can, you soft-headed field-twister. The tame brain of mine stood it for three hours and more in a suit of engineering armor, and you want me to believe the hull of this ship can't take it!'

'But the ports – and the outer drive plates – and—'

'I said *get us down there!* There are ports in a suit of armor, and the bottom plates stood everything that the soil of Planet Four could give them. And don't talk about risk from the flatlanders! I know as well as you do that the hull of this barrel is coated even against frequency-modulated radar, to say nothing of the stuff these things have been beaming out – I paid for it, and it's been getting us through the System patrol at Sarr for a long time. Now punch those keys!' Ordon Lee subsided, but he was quite evidently unhappy. He tuned in the compass with a slightly hopeful expression, which faded when he found that Ken's torpedo was still emitting its carrier wave. Gloomily he applied a driving force along the indicated line, and the gibbous patch of light that was Planet Three began to swell beyond the ports.

As the board flashed a warning of outside pressure, he brought the vessel to a halt and looked hopefully at his employer. Drai made a downward gesture with the gun muzzle. Lee shrugged in resigned fashion, switched on the heaters in the outer hull, and began feeling his way into the ocean of frigid gas, muttering in an undertone and putting on an I-told-you-so expression every time a *clink* told of contracting outer plates.

Feth, knowing he would get no further chance at the radio, glued his attention to one of the ports. One of Drai's eyes did likewise, but no change appeared in his expression as the evidence began to pile up that Ken had been telling the truth. Great mountains, hazy air, green vegetation, even the shiny patches so suggestive of the vast blue plains where the flatlanders had downed the exploring torpedoes; all were there, as the scientist had said, dimly illuminated by the feeble sun of this system but clearly visible for all that. Feth, heedless of the gun in Drai's hand, suddenly leaped for the door, shouting, 'Camera!' and disappeared down the corridor. Drai put the gun away.

'Why can't you be like those two?' he asked the pilot. 'Just get them interested in something, and they forget that there's anything in the universe to be afraid of.' The pilot made no immediate answer; apparently Drai expected none, for he strolled to the port without waiting. Then without looking up from his controls the pilot asked sourly:

'If you think Ken is interested in his job and nothing else why are you so anxious to check up on him all of a sudden?'

'Mostly because I'm not quite sure whose job he's doing. Tell me, Lee, just who would you say was to blame for the fact that this is the first time we're landing on this world which we've known about for twenty years?'

The pilot made no verbal answer, but one eye rolled back and met one of his employer's for a moment. The question had evidently made him think of something other than frostbite and cracked plates: Laj Drai may not have been a genius, as he had been known to admit, but his rule-of-thumb psychology was of a high order.

The *Karella* sank lower. Mountain tops were level with the port now; an apparently unbroken expanse of green lay below, but the compass pointed unhesitatingly into its midst. At five hundred feet separate trees were discernible, and the roof of the Wing home showed dimly through them. There was no sign of Ken or his torpedo, but neither being in the control room doubted for an instant that this was the house he had mentioned. Both had completely forgotten Feth.

'Take us a few yards to one side, Lee. I want to be able to see from the side ports. I think I see Ken's armor – yes. The ground slopes; land us uphill a little way. We can see for a fair distance between these plants.' The pilot obeyed silently. If he heard the shriek of Feth, echoing down the corridor from the room where the mechanic was still taking pictures, he gave no sign; the words were rendered indistinguishable by reverberation in any case. The meaning, however, became clear a moment later. The sound of the hull's crushing its way through the treetops was inaudible inside; but the other token of arrival was quite perceptible. An abrupt cloud of smoke blotted out the view from port, and as Laj Drai started back in astonishment a tongue of flame licked upward around the curve of the great hull.

18

Feth was not the only one who called to the pilot to hold off. Ken, realizing only too clearly that the hull of the vessel would be nearly as hot as his own suit in spite of its superior insulation, expressed himself on the radio as he would never have done before his pupils; but of course no one on board was listening. Mr Wing and Don, guessing the cause of his excitement, added their voices; Mrs Wing, hearing the racket, appeared at a window in time to see the glossy black cylinder settle into the trees fifty yards above the house. No one was surprised at the results – no one outside the ship, at least.

Don and his father raced at top speed for the stable, where the portable fire pumps were kept. Mrs Wing appeared on the porch, calling in a fairly well controlled voice, 'Don, where are the children?' This question was partially answered before either man could make a response, as Margie and Billy broke from the woods on opposite sides of the clearing, still carrying plants which they had forgotten to drop in their excitement.

'Daddy! See the fire!' the boy shrilled as soon as he saw his father.

'I know, Billy. Both of you go with your mother, start the pump, and help her spray everything near the house. I don't think the fire will come downhill with the wind the way it is, but we mustn't take chances.'

'Where are Roger and Edith?' Mrs Wing asked the younger children.

'They were going to get rocks for the fire-man,' Margie replied. 'I don't know where they were going to get them. They'll come back when they see the fire.'

'I suppose so.' Their mother was obviously unhappy about the matter, but she took the youngsters in tow and went after the hoses. Don and his father continued on their way, slung the always filled fire pumps across their shoulders, and headed back uphill toward the ever-thickening cloud of smoke and flame.

Ken had not waited for the human beings to go into action. Pausing only to make certain his armor was still firmly attached to the torpedo, he had seized the control spindle and shot straight upward. He was taking a chance, he realized; but with the relatively cold torpedo hull to smash the initial path through the thin overhanging branches he felt that he could avoid contact with any one of them except for periods too brief to set them ablaze. He succeeded, though a suspicion of smoke floated upward in his wake as he soared clear. The *Karella*, he noted, had done likewise; it now floated a quarter of a

mile above the blaze it had started. He wasted no further time on recrimina-
tions, even though the chances seemed good that those on board would be
listening again.

The fire was not spreading as rapidly as he had feared it might in most
directions. On the side toward the house it seemed to have made no progress
at all, while along the contours of the mountain its advance was very slow.
Upward, however, under the combined influence of its own convection currents and the breeze which had already been blowing in that direction, it was
leaping from growth to growth in fine style. Ken saw flaming bits of vegetable
tissue borne far aloft on the hot air pillar; some burned out in flight, others
settled into the trees farther up the mountain and gave rise to other centers
of combustion. A dark-colored growth, apparently dead, a few yards in
advance of the main blaze, smoked briefly in the fierce radiation and suddenly exploded with an audible roar, burning out in less than fifteen seconds
and crumbling into a rain of glowing coals. Ken, unmoved by the prospect of
being involved in the uprushing hot gases, maneuvered closer to the blaze.
At least part of the reason for the slow advance downhill became evident; the
two natives with whom he had been talking were visible through the trees,
spraying everything in sight with apparently tiny streams of a liquid at whose
nature Ken could only make an educated guess. He watched them for some
time, noting that they refilled their containers of liquid every few minutes at
a stream of the stuff flowing down near the house, which Ken had not noticed
earlier. He wondered where the liquid could have its source, and decided to
follow the stream uphill to find out.

As he rose, the extent of the forest country once more was impressed on
him, and he began to wonder at the magnitude of the catastrophe the *Karella*
had caused. If this combustion reaction were to spread over the whole countryside, the effect on the natives would undoubtedly be quite serious, he
decided. He noted that it had spread across the little stream a short distance
farther up; apparently the liquid had to be in actual contact with vegetation
in order to stop combustion. The flame and smoke made it impossible to follow the watercourse; Ken dropped lower, reasoning with some justice that
the temperature of his armor would do no damage to vegetation already
burning, and drifted along only a few feet above the stream bed, barely able
to see even then. For the first time he saw animal life other than the intelligent natives; tiny creatures, usually four-legged when they were moving
slowly enough for him to see the legs, all fleeing madly uphill. Ken wondered
that they could breath – the smoke suggested that the air should be full of
combustion products, and probably was too hot for them; he knew nothing
about the fairly common phenomenon of relatively pure air near the ground
ahead of a fire. Large scale conflagrations occurred on Sarr, but he was no
fireman.

He was ahead of the flames but still in smoke-filled air when he found the source of the stream. He had trouble realizing that it *was* the source; he was no geologist, and a real geologist of his race would have had difficulty in figuring out the mechanism of a spring. Ken rather suspected artificial backing for the phenomenon, but he did not dare touch the liquid to investigate very closely. He would have had grounds for serious worry had he known that a forest fire can sometimes cause a local rainstorm; but that, too, was too far outside his experience. The closest approach to such a thing on Sarr occurred near the poles, where on very rare occasions meteorological forces so combined as to raise the pressure and drop the temperature enough to cause a slight precipitation of liquid sulfur.

Realizing that nothing more could be learned here at the moment, Ken rose once more into clearer air. Downhill, the natives seemed to be winning; there was a narrow band of blackened vegetation at the edge of the region of flame which suggested that the fire had burned out in that direction. At the sides, progress was less obvious; but the fire in general had taken on the outline of a great fan, with its handle pointing toward the house and the ribs spreading to a breadth of three or four hundred yards at a roughly equal distance up the mountainside. Through the billowing smoke, Ken could see that the large trees were thinning out at this point, giving way to smaller growths which in turn seemed to follow the usual pattern of yielding to bare rock near the top of the hill. Ken, looking the situation over from his vantage point, decided that the blaze stood a very good chance of eating itself into starvation territory in a very few hours; the natives might very well dispose of the fringes without assistance.

The thought of possible assistance gave rise to another; the smoke was rising in a pillar that must be visible for many miles. Was this likely to bring other natives to help, or would it be mistaken for an ordinary cloud? Ken's eyes, with their color balance differing as it did from the human, could not be sure of the distinction in hue; but the shape of the smoke pillar seemed distinctive enough to attract attention. With this thought in mind, he decided to call the ship; but when he looked up, the vessel was nowhere in sight. He moved the torpedo back and forth rapidly enough to cause his armor to swing pendulum fashion and give him a glimpse of the sky directly overhead, but there was still no sign of the black cylinder. Apparently Laj Drai's brief taste of Planet Three had been enough. To make sure, Ken broadcast his thought on the matter of further natives arriving, and then returned to his examination of the fire. Within seconds, he had once more forgotten the vessel's existence.

He had found that little could be seen inside the fire itself. This time, therefore, he descended just ahead of the actual blaze, watching through the eddying smoke clouds as the leaves of bushes and small trees in its path shriveled, smoked, and burst into flame sometimes many feet from the nearest actual tongue of fire. Usually, he noticed, the thicker stems did not ignite until they were actually in contact with flame from some other source, but there were exceptions to this. He remembered the exploding tree. He regretted that he had no thermometer, with which he could get some idea of the kindling point of the growths. He wondered if the oxygen alone could be responsible for such a furious reaction, or whether the nitrogen which made up such a large part of the atmosphere might be playing a part. It had combined with his titanium specimen, after all. There seemed no way of collecting samples of the combustion gases, but perhaps some of the solid residue would tell. Ken landed in the midst of the fire, brought the torpedo down beside him, opened the cargo door, and threw in several pieces of charred wood. Then he went downhill a short distance, located some grayish ash, and added that to the collection. Satisfied for the moment, he rose clear of the ground again, wondering vaguely how much time, if any, his brief sojourn in the flames would add to the few hours he could remain down. He had heard the thermostats in his armor cutting off several of the heaters during those few minutes; the outer layers must have been warmed up considerably.

In an attempt to guess how long the fire would take to burn out, Ken moved fifty or sixty yards ahead of the flame front and began timing its rate of progress at several points. This proved deceptive, since the rate of travel varied greatly – as any forester could have told him. It depended principally on the sort of fuel available in a given spot and on the configuration of the ground, which influenced the air currents feeding the fire; and those points were both too difficult to observe for Ken to learn very much about them. He gave up that attempt, moved a little farther ahead, and tried to see what he could of the animals still scurrying away from the most frightful menace that ever threatened their small lives.

It was here that the torpedo microphone picked up a cracking that differed from that of the fire, and a heavy panting that reminded Ken of the sounds he had heard just after his first meeting with Roger. Remembering that he had not seen two of the natives just after the blaze had started, the scientist became a trifle anxious; and two or three minutes' search showed that his worry was only too well founded. Roger and Edith Wing, gasping and coughing from smoke and exhaustion, were struggling almost blindly through the bushes. The boy's original intention had been to travel across the path of the blaze, to get out of its way – the most sensible course under the circumstances. Several things, however, had combined to make this a trifle difficult. For one thing, after the smoke had become thick enough to prevent their seeing more than a few yards, they had blundered into a little hollow. Using the slope of the ground for guidance, they had made several complete circles of this spot before realizing what had happened. By that time the flames were actually in sight, and they had no choice but to run straight before them. They simply did not know by then how wide the flame front was; to parallel it at a distance of only a few yards would have been the height of insanity. They had been trying to work their way to one side while keeping ahead of the flames, but they were rapidly approaching a state of exhaustion where merely keeping ahead demanded all that their young bodies could give. They were nearly blind, with tears streaming down their soot-stained faces. In Edith's case the tears were not entirely due to smoke; she was crying openly from fatigue and terror, while the boy was having a good deal of trouble keeping his self-control.

None of these facts were very clear to the scientist, since even the undistorted human face was still quite strange to him; but his sympathy was aroused just the same. It is possible that, had the same situation occurred just after his first meeting with the natives, he might have remained an impassive observer in order to find out just what the creatures would and could do in an extremity. Now, however, his talk with Mr Wing and the evidence of culture and scientific knowledge the native had shown gave the Sarrian a feeling of actual intellectual kinship with the creatures below him; they were people, not animals. Also, they had fallen into their present plight while working for him; he remembered that these two had departed in search of specimens for him. He did not hesitate an instant after seeing them.

He dropped toward the stumbling children, using one of his few English verbs for all it was worth. 'Carry!' the torpedo speaker boomed, again and again. He stopped just ahead of the startled youngsters, poised just out of contact with the vegetation. Edith started to reach toward him, but Roger still retained some presence of mind.

'No, Edie! You'll be burned that way, too. We'll have to ride the thing that carries him, if we can get up to it.' Ken had already realized this, and was manipulating his control spindle in an effort to bring the torpedo's tail section within their reach, while he himself was still supported safely above the bushes. He had no intrinsic objection to igniting them, since they were doomed in a few minutes anyway, but it looked as though the young natives were going to have trouble enough without an extra fire right beside them. The problem was a little awkward, as his armored feet hung two yards below the hull of the torpedo, and the carrier itself contained automatic circuits designed to keep it horizontal while hovering in a gravitational field. It could be rotated on any axis, however; the main trouble was that Ken had had no occasion to do so as yet, and it took a little time to solve the necessary control combination. It seemed like an hour, even to him, before he succeeded in the maneuver, for he had thrown his full heart into the rescue and was almost as anxious as the children themselves; but at last the rear end of the yard-thick cylinder hung within its own diameter of the ground.

The children at once made frantic efforts to climb aboard. They had no luck; the composition was too slippery, the curve not sharp enough to afford a real grip, and they themselves too exhausted. Roger made a hand-stirrup for his sister, and actually succeeded in getting her partly across the smooth hull; but after a moment of frantic, futile clutching she slipped back and collapsed on the ground, sobbing. Roger paused, indecisive. A blast of hot, smoky air made him gasp for breath; there remained bare moments, it seemed to him, before the flames would be on them. For a second he stared enviously at the helpless being hanging from the other end of the torpedo, to whom the fire's breath was probably a cooling breeze; then he saw the clamps from which the specimen boxes had hung.

For a moment even these seemed useless. He doubted whether he could hang by hand grip alone from those small metal projections for any length of time, and was sure his sister in her present condition could not do so for a moment. Then he had an idea. The clamps were really hook-like, lockable devices rather like the clasp of a brooch; fastened, they made complete rings. Roger fastened the nearest, pulled his belt off with a savage jerk, threaded it through the ring, and buckled it again. Hastily urging Edie to her feet – she gained a little self-possession as she saw what he was doing – he did the same with her belt in another ring, not stopping to give thanks that she was wearing dungarees. All the children did in the woods. Then he helped support her while she held to one of the loops of leather and thrust both legs through the other. Some work would still be needed to hold on, but the leg-strap was carrying most of her weight. Satisfied, he waved the Sarrian off.

Ken understood, and his admiration for the human race went up another notch or two. He did not hesitate or argue, however; he knew perfectly well that the boy had found the only likely method of transporting either of them, and even if Ken could speak his language well enough argument would be a waste of time. He took off at once, the dazed girl hanging behind him.

He rose first out of the smoke, to give his passenger a chance to breath; then he took a good look at his surroundings, to be sure of finding the spot again. A momentary break in the smoke below showed Roger struggling uphill once more; and without waiting for further observation Ken sent the torpedo plunging downhill toward the house. Mrs Wing saw them coming, and he was on his way back for a second load in three quarters of a minute.

In spite of the brief interval and his careful observations, he realized as he arrived overhead that finding the other native was not to be an easy job. His original point of observation was reached easily enough; but he discovered when he arrived there that with the total lack of instruments at his disposal and the moderately strong and erratic air current obviously present there was no way for him to tell whether he had risen vertically to that point, or whether he would be descending vertically from it. He had, of course, seen

Roger after getting there, but the boy had already been in motion. He could also cut his lift entirely and fall vertically; but that line of action did not recommend itself. The torpedo was a heavy machine, and he had no desire to have it drop on his armor, especially in the gravity of this planet. He did the best he could, letting down to ground level as rapidly as seemed safe and starting a regular search pattern over the area.

Where he landed, the fire had not quite reached, though the bushes were beginning to smoke. There was no trail such as the boy might have left, or at least none that Ken could recognize. Playing safe, he moved downhill to the very edge of the fire and searched back and forth across it for fifty yards each way – a considerable distance, when the visibility was less than a tenth of that. Then he began moving his sweep gradually up the hill.

Roger had made more progress than might have seemed likely, considering the condition in which Ken had left him; it was fully ten minutes before the scientist found him, still struggling on but making practically no headway. He must have actually gained on the fire during at least part of that time, however, the Sarrian realized.

He sent his booming call downward, and once more lowered the tail of the torpedo. Roger, with a final effort, got his legs through one of the straps, and folded his arms through the other. His face was within an inch or two of the torpedo hull, which had been heated considerably by its recent passage along the flame front; but anything was better than staying where he was, and Roger was scarcely conscious of the blistering on his hands and face. Ken, once sure that the boy had a good grip, plunged up into clear air and bore his second burden down to the house. Roger was still holding on when they arrived, but it was hardly a conscious effort – his mother had to unlock his frantic grip by force.

Ken, knowing he could do no good around the house, went back uphill above the treetops to see how the others were making out in their fire fighting, leaving the presumably competent adult to care for the rescued children. The need for effort seemed to be decreasing; the lower portion was definitely burned out, it seemed to him, and the only activity was along the upper edge. The men were still at work soaking down the edges as they worked upward, but the really lively area had long since outrun them. It was, as Ken had rather expected, heading for bare rock and fuel starvation; but it would be many hours yet before it died completely. As the Wings were perfectly aware, it would be a source of danger for days if the wind should shift, and they did not let up for an instant in their effort until forced to do so by sheer exhaustion. Twice during that period Ken landed on bare patches near Mr Wing and sketched a rough map of the situation on the ground. Once he hugged ground between trees himself for many minutes while a stiff-winged, three-engined metal machine droned overhead; again he concealed himself as a group of men, bearing water pumps and other fire-fighting tools appeared on the trail from Clark Fork and passed on uphill to help. Ken remained in the vicinity of the house after that; he did not particularly want to be seen by these new natives, reasoning that much delay to his language progress would ensue. He may have been right.

It was shortly after the arrival of the new group that Mr Wing and Don appeared at the house, almost ready to drop. They were scratched, soot-stained, and scorched; even Ken could appreciate the difference from their former appearance, for they appeared in even worse shape than Roger and Edie had been. It was then, for the first time, that Mr Wing learned of the danger and rescue of the two, for Ken had made no attempt to apprise him of the matter – it was too difficult, with his limited grasp of English, to manu-facture adequate phrases.

Mr Wing had the same trouble, after he heard the story. Ken had already judged that the race must have strongly developed ties of affection; now he was sure of it. Mr Wing could not find the words to express himself, but he made the fact of his gratitude amply clear.

19

The *Karella* had indeed left the Earth's atmosphere, but had not returned to her previous height. Two-way communication had been reestablished – Ken wished he knew just when – and Feth was once more controlling the torpedo which carried the scientist. The process of getting aboard was no more complicated than usual. Ken left the two 'live' boxes in the air lock for the time being, having set their refrigerators to the same power as the first had seemed to require; the other two, partly filled with mineral specimens, he brought inside. Drai greeted him rather sourly as he emerged from his metal chrysalis.

'So you're finally back. What did you get, if anything?' Ken eyed him with the closest approach to a defiant expression he had yet worn.

'Very little. Thanks to the slight distraction you seem to have engineered, the natives had other things to do than talk to me.'

'How was I to know that the ship's hull would set off a chain reaction in the local vegetation? I should think if anything could to it, it would have happened long ago from some other cause.'

'I seem to recall telling you of the danger myself. And it may have happened before; the natives seemed to have fairly well organized means of dealing with it.'

'Then the fire is out?'

'Not quite. It will probably react for some hours yet. What I dislike is your habit of assuming that I am either a liar or a fool. I told you what happened to the piece of vegetation I picked up; I told you what I was doing with the native in the matter of learning his language. You were listening to me most if not all of the time. What possessed you to come down the way you did?'

'Because I doubted what you told me.' Drai made the statement without circumlocution; he apparently felt he was on secure ground. 'You said that there had been no talk between you and the native on the subject of tofacco; you even said that you doubted that this was the same native we've been trading with.'

'I said I wasn't sure he *was* the same. That's minor, though – go ahead.'

'The first day, while you were down talking to him, the signal came from the fixed transmitter, indicating that they were ready to trade.'

'I should think that would support my veracity. I was not near the transmitter. Ask Feth – he landed me.'

'That's what I thought, for a while. But today, which was the usual interval after a signal, I sent down another torpedo while you were having your "language lesson" – and nothing happened! There was no one there.'

'You mean no one gave you any tofacco.'

'No one took the metal, either. I'd be willing to believe they were trying to cheat me, if it had gone without anything in return; but that doesn't fit. I decided you had let something slip while I wasn't listening, and came down to see what you were up to.'

'Skipping for the moment the question of how I could possibly tell whether or not you were listening, I'm not sure whether to be glad you think me stupid rather than dishonest. I agree that my native may be your trader, in that case; he might have decided to go to the transmitter later in the day, after he had talked to me. He knew I couldn't stay long. In that case, you have only yourself to thank that he didn't go later – he was too busy. Also, a couple of the young ones were nearly killed by the chain reaction; he may not be too pleased with you now, if he's connected the ship and the trading business. After all, remember he knows we come from Planet One on these trips.'

'That I don't believe. He couldn't possibly know it. That's another reason I decided you were trying to cover up your own indiscretion. How do you know that two of the natives were endangered by the fire?'

'I saw them. As a matter of fact, I rescued them – rode them out of the way on the torpedo. I spent quite a while investigating the whole thing, since once you'd started it there there was nothing else for me to do. I can prove that – I got some specimens of vegetation residue that may give some more information about the planet.' Drai eyed him silently for some moments.

'I'm not convinced yet, and you'd better convince me before your next drug-hunger comes due. If they're going to stop trading, I'm going to stop distributing free samples.' Feth, in the background, emitted an uncontrolled sound that was the equivalent of a gasp of dismay; Ken permitted an anxious expression to reach his face for a moment. He had had one brief experience of tofacco-hunger now, and did not want a prolonged one. Drai nodded as he saw the expression. 'Yes. The stock is not very high, and if it's to be the last, I'm going to get value for it. I have been given an idea from what you just told me. If this tale of having rescued two natives from death by overheating is true, you can just go back down and play on their gratitude. You can make out that *you* want to trade for tofacco. Surely they will gratify the hero who pulled them from terrible death. Particularly if he makes it clear that he's in for a very uncomfortable time if they don't. You go right back down – your armor's warmed up by this time. We haven't pulled in the other torpedo yet; as soon as you go on local control down there, we'll send it over to you with the metal, and you can haggle to your heart's content.' He ceased, still wearing a definite sneer.

'That fact that my knowledge of the language is still fragmentary does not bother you?'

'No. I think you know more than you say.'

'How about the fact that there are, at the moment, many other natives at the scene of the fire? I kept among the trees when they arrived so as not to be seen, but I can't do that and trade at the same time. Do you want me to work out in the open? They'll all be fire-fighting for a while, but I suppose they'll want metal afterward.' He paused. 'I don't see how they can *all* be the one you've been trading with. But I suppose you don't mind opening new bargains with the others—' Laj Drai interrupted.

'You can wait.'

'Oh, it wouldn't take very many torpedo loads of metal to satisfy them all, I'm sure.'

'I said you could wait.' Drai must have seen the satisfied expression that flickered for an instant on the scientist's face, for he added, 'I have another idea. The *Karella* will go down with you, and both watch and listen. Possibly if the native becomes recalcitrant, we can suggest lighting another fire.'

'Now you want the natives to get a good look at a full-sized space ship. You don't care much about the law, do you?'

'You ought to know. Besides, they've seen it already. However, we'll wait – for a while. I rather think we'll land at a little distance from the scene of the fire, and drop in when it's out. That way,' both eyes fixed themselves on Ken, 'we'll be sure who talks, and for how long.' He turned, pushed off from a convenient wall, and glided out of sight along the corridor. Feth followed him with one troubled eye.

'Ken, you shouldn't use that tone of voice to him. I know you don't like him – no one could – but remember what he can do. I thought, after you'd had a taste of that, you'd calm down a bit. Now he's likely to hold out on you just for the fun of it.'

'I know – I'm sorry if I've gotten you in trouble too,' replied the scientist. 'I just think he's safer when angry. While he's gone, now, we'll have to talk fast. There's work to be done. First of all, was he telling the truth about the short supply of tofacco? Does he keep it all in that refrigerated safe that he hands out our doses from?'

'Yes. And he's probably telling the truth; most of the stuff goes back to the Sarrian system at the end of the season, and he doesn't keep much on hand.'

'How much constitutes a dose? I didn't get a really good look at what was inside the brick of frozen air, either time.'

'A little cylinder about so big.' Feth illustrated. 'It comes that way, only in longer sticks – he cuts them into ten sections, and freezes each one up for a separate dose.'

'All right – that's what I wanted to make sure of. Now, how good are the little refrigerators on those vivaria of mine? Will they freeze air?'

'Sure. Why?'

'You'll see. Right now, I imagine I have another acting job to do; I don't suppose anything would stop Drai from going down to the surface of Three, as he said.' Without explaining anything more, Ken headed toward the control room of the interstellar flyer.

He was quite right; the impatient drug-runner had already ordered the pilot down once more. Lee was making no objection this time, though his expression was not actually one of delight. The descent was uneventful, practically a repetition of the earlier one, except that they were homing on the fixed transmitter and consequently were some eight miles east of their former point of landing. They stopped at a height of two miles above the nearest peaks, and looked around for the smoke cloud. Rather to Drai's disappointment, they saw it; even their eyes could distinguish it from the regular clouds yithout much difficulty.

'It still seems to be burning,' Ken remarked innocently. 'Are we going to drift here in full sight until they put it out?'

'No. We'll go down and hide.'

'Among the plants? That doesn't seem to work so well, as a method of concealing this ship.' Drai eyed the scientist for some time, obviously near the limit of exasperation.

'I'm looking after the matter, thank you. The vegetation does not grow everywhere, as even you should be able to see. There, for example.' He pointed to the south. A triangular patch which gave a metallic reflection of the sky light lay in that direction. It was one of those Ken had noticed on his first descent. 'We'll look that over. It seems to be lower than the surrounding territory, and would make a very good hiding place. If it's really like the sort of ground the flatlanders live on, these other natives may very well avoid it. How about that, scientist?'

'You seem to have some logic on your side,' Ken replied equably. Drai made no answer to this; he simply gestured to Lee, and the pilot obediently slanted their line of descent toward the shiny patch.

With radio altimeter registering five hundred feet, Ken began a careful examination of the area. It was larger than he had guessed from a distance, and he found himself unable to decide on its nature. The planet had some queer minerals, of course; the brief look he had had of the specimens he had just brought in showed that. Directly below he could make out no details at all; but over near the edge of the area, the trees that rimmed it were reflected—

'Lee! *Hold up!*' The pilot obeyed without thought, stung by the urgency of his tone.

'What is it?' The eternal suspicion was lacking even from Drai's voice, this time.

'It's a liquid – see how the reflection at the edge trembles in the air currents!'

'So what?'

'The only liquid I've encountered on this planet behaved an awful lot like that queer oxide we found on Four – the one that nearly froze my feet. I saw some before here, and dipped a handler in it; the stuff vaporized instantly, and it was minutes before I could put a tentacle in the sleeve again. I think it's that heat-drinking stuff – hydrogen oxide.'

'Why didn't you mention this before?' The suspicion was back in Drai's tone.

'What chance have I had? Besides, I don't care if you leave yourself a frozen memorial on this planet – it's just that I'm with you at the moment. If you don't want to believe me, at least put a torpedo down on it first. You must have plenty of those.'

Even Drai could find no fault with this suggestion, and he gestured to Feth. The mechanic, with a censorious glance at Ken, went to his control board and without comment launched another of the projectiles. The one Ken had used was available, but it was the only one fitted with manual control, and he did not want to waste it. He was already convinced of the correctness of Ken's hypothesis.

The slim projectile appeared outside the control room port, and drifted gently down to the surface of the lake. It was still hot, having been stowed inside the ship; and contact with the liquid surface was heralded by a burst of steam. Feth hastily lifted it a short distance, and waited for it to cool somewhat.

'Hardly a fair test to cool it off that fast,' he said. 'Something's bound to give.'

Presently he lowered the machine again. This time only ripples marked the contact. Very cautiously Feth forced it still lover, while the others watched silently. Apparently the cold did not matter.

But something else did. Quite suddenly another cloud of steam arose, and a wave of considerable size spread from the place where the torpedo had been. *Had been* was the right expression; there was no response when the mechanic manipulated the controls to bring it up again. He glanced up, presently.

'It's a pity that only the cargo compartments of those things are airtight. Apparently the liquid bothers electrical machinery. Maybe it dissolves insulation.' Laj Drai was looking as though he had seen a ghost. He made no direct answer to the mechanic's remark.

'Ken!' he spoke suddenly, still looking preoccupied.

'When you first described this patch of stuff, you said its appearance reminded you of the flat country. Right?'

'Right.' Ken saw what the drug-runner had in mind.

'Would it – would it be possible for a planet to have so much liquid that three quarters of its surface would be covered?'

'I certainly can't say it's impossible. I admit it's hard to imagine. Any liquid at all – and particularly something as rare as that stuff is with us. Still, this is a larger planet than Sarr, and would have a greater velocity of escape, and is colder, so the average speed of the gas molecules would be slower – let's see—' His voice trailed off as he became involved in mental arithmetic. 'Yes, this planet would hold the stuff easily enough; and hydrogen and oxygen are common elements in the universe. I'm afraid it's very possible, Drai.' The other did not answer; everyone else knew what he was thinking. When he did speak, Ken felt smug – he had predicted the subject correctly.

'But the flatlanders – could they live in the stuff? – but maybe there aren't any; the liquid must have destroyed the torpedoes – but their radar beams! We've detected those!' He looked at Ken suddenly, as though he had made a telling point in an argument. Ken had been following his thoughts well enough to answer.

'You have no evidence whatever that those beams were not generated by the same race with which you have been trading. I have already pointed out that they are competent astronomers. I think you have been developing a very interesting mythology for the last twenty years, though I admit the idea could do with a little more proof.'

Keeping one eye on the enigmatic liquid beyond the port, Drai rolled the other toward the pilot.

'Lee, go up about ten miles, and start travelling. It doesn't matter which way, I guess.' He was obeyed in silence. Even though Lee did not take the shortest route to the ocean, the speed of the ship even within the atmosphere was such that only minutes passed before the fabulous 'flatland' lay beneath them – the closest any of them had dared to approach it in twenty Sarrian years. Dumbly the commander gestured downward, and presently they hung a few hundred feet above the waves. Drai looked for a long time, then spoke three words to Ken: 'Get a sample.'

The scientist thought for a moment; then he found the small bomb in which he had taken the frost sample on Mars, pumped out the air, and closed the valve. Redonning his armor, he clumped into the air lock after voicing dire warning to Lee about keeping the vessel level. He fastened a wire to the bomb itself and another to the valve handle; then, opening the outer door, he lowered away until the loss of weight told him the bomb was submerged. He pulled the other wire, waited a moment, pulled up the filled bomb, closed the valve again, and sealed the outer door of the air lock.

Naturally, the bomb exploded violently within a few seconds of the time that sulfur ceased condensing on its surface. Ken felt thankful that he had not yet removed the armor – parts of the bomb had actually scored the metal – and after some thought tried again. This time he let down a tiny glass wool sponge, hoping the liquid had a significant amount of natural capillary action. He placed the sponge in another bomb, and by the same method he had used with the Martian sample eventually determined the molecular weight of the substance. It came out higher than before, but eventually he found the deposit of salts on the sponge and allowed for their weight. The result this time left little doubt that the substance was indeed hydrogen oxide.

He looked down for a minute at the tossing blue expanse, wondering how deep it might be and whether it would have any real effect on the conditions of the Planet of Ice; then he turned, climbed out of the armor – he had stayed in it for the rest of his experiment, after the first blast – and went to report to Drai.

The drug-runner heard him in silence. He still seemed a little dazed by the overthrow of his former belief. It was many minutes before he spoke, and then he simply said, 'Take us back to One, Lee. I have to think.' Ken and Feth eyed each other, but kept all expression of glee from their faces.

20

'Well, you seem to have done it now.' Feth was still unhappy.

'In what way?' queried Ken. The two were ostensibly engaged in checking the mechanical adequacy of the refrigerated vivaria.

'I've been working for years to support this flatland myth – I realized it was never more than a theory, but Drai had to be shown the difference between that and fact – and I've been doing my level best to keep the production of tofacco down to a minimum.'

'Provided it was not cut off entirely,' Ken interjected rather unkindly.

'True. Now you blow up the story that kept him scared of really exploring the planet, and at the same time give him a tool for getting what he wants from the inhabitants by threats and force. If you had any ideas in mind at all, they seem to have flopped badly.'

'Oh, I wouldn't say that. You saw the way Drai was feeling when he left the ship.'

'Oh, yes, he was regretting the wasted years and the money that went with them, I suppose. That won't last much longer; he's been mooning for days now. Then he'll—' Ken had been thinking furiously as the me chanic delivered his gloomy discourse; now he interrupted abruptly.

'Then he'll be too late to do anything. Feth, I want you to take me on trust for a while. I promise you won't miss your sniff. I'm going to be very busy in the air lock for at least a couple of hours, I imagine. Lee is still aboard. I want you to find him, and keep him occupied in any way you see fit for at least that length of time. I don't want him to see what I'm doing. You have known him longer than I, and can figure out something to interest him. Just don't kill him; we're going to need him later.'

Feth looked at the scientist for several seconds, obviously doubtful. Ken wisely said nothing more, letting him fight his own battle with a perfectly natural fear. He was pleased but not too surprised when the mechanic finally said, 'All right,' and disappeared toward the control room. Ken waited a moment; then, reasonably sure of not being interrupted, he closed the inner door of the air lock, donned a regular space suit, and set briskly to work. He was rather regretful of the need for sacrificing some of his living specimens, but he consoled himself with the thought they could easily be replaced later. Then, too, the vivarium he had to use was the one containing only a few plants – the fire had interrupted before the human children had made much progress with it. That was foresight, not good fortune; he had had to decide which of them he was going to use, before he had left the planet.

In the control room, Feth did not find his task too difficult. He was not on the best of terms with the pilot, but had never held toward him the blazing hatred he had felt toward his chief. Lee was not particularly scrupulous, as he had shown in the past, but Feth knew of nothing in his record to call forth whole-souled detestation. In consequence, there was nothing strange in the mechanic's entering the control room and settling down for a talk. The pilot was reading, as usual when off duty; to his question concerning Ken's where-abouts, the mechanic responded that he was 'fooling with his vegetables in the air lock.'

'Why does he have to use the lock for a laboratory?' the pilot asked plain-tively. 'I've already told him it's bad practice. He's got a lab in the station – why doesn't he take them there?'

'I guess he figures if a refrigerator breaks down he can pump the air out of the lock and have a chance of the specimen's lasting until he can make repairs,' Feth replied. 'I imagine you'd have to ask him, to be really sure. I wouldn't worry – there are just the three of us aboard, and those cases aren't too big to get around if your engines start to get out of hand.' The pilot grunted, and returned to his reading; but one eye flickered occasionally to the board of telltale lights. He knew when Ken evacuated the lock and opened the outer door, but apparently did not consider it worth while to ask why. Feth, as a matter of fact, did not know either; he was wondering a good deal harder than Lee. Fortunately the pilot was used to his taciturnity and habitual glum-ness of expression, or his attitude might have aroused suspicion. It was, as a matter of fact, his awareness of this fact that had caused Ken to refrain from telling his whole plan to Feth. He was afraid the mechanic might look too happy to be natural.

The next interruption caused the pilot to put down his book and rise to his feet. 'What's that fool doing now?' he asked aloud. 'Drilling holes in the hull?' Feth could understand the source of his worry; the outer door of the air lock had been closed again, and pressure had returned to normal some time before – but now the pressure was dropping rapidly, as though through a ser-ious leak, and air was being pumped *into* the chamber. The outer door was still closed.

'Maybe he's filling some portable tanks,' suggested Feth hopefully.

'With what? There isn't a pump on board that could take air faster than the lock bleeders can deliver it, except the main circulators. He's not using those, where he is.'

'Why don't you call him and ask, then? I notice the inner door is sealed, too; he'll probably have a fit if you opened it in the middle of his work.'

'I'll have one myself if this goes on,' growled Lee. He watched the

144

indicators for another moment, noting that the pressure now seemed to be holding steady at about half normal. 'Well, if it's a leak, he had sense enough to plug it.' He turned to the microphone, switched to the local wavelength used in the suit receivers, and made the suggested call. Ken answered promptly, denying that he had bored any holes in the hull and stating that he would be through shortly. Lee was able to get nothing else from him.

'One would almost think you didn't trust him,' gibed Feth as the pilot turned away from the microphone. 'You have as much reason to believe him as you have to believe me, and I notice you don't worry much about me.'

'Maybe after he's had a few more sniffs I'll feel the same about him,' Lee replied. 'Right now, just listening to him makes me think he's not convinced yet about being under the influence. I never heard anyone talk like that to Drai before.'

'I did – once.'

'Yeah. But he's done it more than once. Drai feels the same way – he told me to camp in this control room as long as you two were on board. I don't think it matters, myself – I've got the key, and if anyone can short the whole control system out from under a Bern lock he's darned good. However, orders are orders.' He relaxed once more with his book. Feth resumed his gloomy train of thought.

'So they're trusting on just that one hold on us. As if I didn't know it. If Ken could figure out some means of getting at Drai's cold-safe – I certainly have never been able to – but then, we couldn't find Sarr anyway – if only we were looking for a sun like Rigel or Deneb, that a fellow could recognize at thousands of parsecs instead of having to get close enough to spot planets—' his thoughts rolled on, consisting largely of 'If only's' as they had now for years. The drug had won little if anything to Feth's mind, but the fact of his subjection to it had long since given him an apathetic attitude toward all suggestions for escape. He wondered why he had consented to do as Ken asked – how could the scientist possibly keep the assurance he had given?

Ken's own voice eventually interrupted this line of cogitation. 'Feth, could you come down here to help me for a moment? I'm nearly through; there's some stuff I want to take out of the lock.' Both Sarrians in the control room glanced at the indicators. The lock pressure was rising again.

'All right, I'm coming,' replied Feth. 'Get the inner door open as soon as pressure's up.' He started down the corridor, leaving the pilot behind. Ken's message had been well worded.

He was not gone long enough to make the pilot suspicious; within two or three minutes Lee heard both mechanic and scientist returning. They were not talking, and as they approached the pilot grew curious. He started to rise to meet them, but had time just to reach his feet before the two entered the door. The gloomy expression had left Feth's face, to be replaced by one much harder to decipher. Lee, however, spent no time trying to solve its meaning; his eyes were both drawn instantly to the object the two were carrying in a cloth sling between them.

It was roughly cubidal, perhaps a foot on a side. It was yellow in color. It trailed a visible stream of mist, and yellow droplets appeared and grew on its surface – droplets of a deeper, honey-colored hue; droplets that gathered together, ran down the sides of the block, soaked into the sling, and vanished in thin air. For an instant Lee, watching it, showed an expression of bewilderment; this changed almost at once to one of horror; then he regained control of himself.

'So that's where the air was going,' he remarked. 'What's the idea?'

Ken, who was clad in a space suit except for the helmet, did not answer the question directly. Instead, he asked one of his own.

'You know the coordinates of Sarr, and could get there from here, don't you?'

'Of course. I've made the trip often enough. So what – I hope you don't think I'm going to tell you in order to get out of a frostbite.'

'I don't care whether you want to tell us or not. I plan for you to do the piloting. And I don't plan to freeze you on this block – in fact, we'll put it down right here. You have until it evaporates to make up your mind. After that, we'll be in a position to make it up for you.' The pilot laughed.

'I was expecting that one. Am I supposed to believe you have some tofacco in the middle of that? You just made the block a couple of minutes ago.'

'Quite true. Since you bring up the matter, there *is* a cylinder of tofacco inside the block. I put it there myself – a few minutes ago, as you say.'

'I suppose you broke into Laj Drai's safe and borrowed it.' The pilot was obviously incredulous.

'No. However, Drai's suggestion of playing on the sympathies of the natives of Planet Three was a very good idea.'

'I suppose they gave you a hundred units for rescuing their kids.'

'As a matter of fact, it seems to be more like two thousand. I didn't exactly count them, but they're very neatly arranged; and if the unit you mean is one tenth of one of the cylinders they come in, that figure is about right.' The pilot might have been just a trifle uneasy.

'But there weren't any landings after Drai had the idea – you couldn't have asked for it.'

'Are you trying to insult me by saying I had to wait for Drai to have such an idea? I thought of it myself, but having been brought up with a conscience I decided against trying it. Besides, as I keep saying, I don't know their language well enough yet. As it happened, the native I'd been talking to gave me a container of the stuff without my mentioning it at all. He seems to be a nice fellow, and apparently knows the value we place on tofacco. I fear I forgot to report that to Drai.'

Lee looked positively haggard as the likelihood of the story began to impress him; Feth, on the other hand, had brightened up amazingly. Only a slight expression of doubt still clouded his features – could the scientist be running a bluff? It seemed impossible; it was hard to see how getting started for Sarr would do any good unless he had a supply of that drug, and he had made no mention of forcing Lee to help them get it from Drai's safe.

These points must have crossed the pilot's mind, too; he was looking at the dwindling lump of sulfur with a growing expression of terror. He made one last objection, knowing its weakness even before he spoke.

'You won't dare let it out – Feth has no suit, and you don't have a helmet.'

'What difference does it make to us?'

With that, Lee made a sudden, frantic break for the door. He dived head-long into Feth, and for a few seconds there was a nightmarish swirling of legs and tentacles. Ken stood by, but his assistance was not needed. The pilot suddenly rolled back almost to his control board, tentacles lashing madly; but when he regained his feet, he did not seem eager to renew the struggle.

'If I'd only had—'

'Yes – it would have been very nice if Drai had let anyone but himself carry a gun. The fact is, he doesn't; and you haven't too much time. How about it?' Feth emphasized his words by turning up the control room thermostat, which was within his reach.

The pilot gave in. If any shred of doubt about Ken's truthfulness remained in his mind, he did not dare gamble on it – he had seen drug addicts other than Feth, and remembered some harrowing details.

'All right – take it away!' he gasped. 'I'll do whatever you want!'

Without comment Ken picked up both ends of the sling and carried the now much lighter bundle back toward the air lock. He was back in two or three minutes.

'Made it!' he said. 'I was wondering if it might not boil through before I got there – you held out longer than I thought you would, Lee. However, the air is clear after all. I may mention that that particular block is the top one in my little refrigerator, and it will take remarkably little time to bring it into action.

'Well, let's make plans. I'd rather like to arrest our friend Drai, but I don't quite see how we're to go about it. Any ideas?'

'*Arrest* him?' A faint smile suddenly appeared on Feth's face.

'Yes. I'm afraid I'm some sort of deputy narcotics investigator – not that I asked for the job, and certainly I'm not a very efficient one. Maybe I ought to swear you in, too, Feth – I guess I can do it legally.'

'You needn't bother. It was done more than eighteen years ago. Apparently they didn't bother to tell you that the stunt of taking an innocent general science dabbler and trying to make a policeman out of him had been tried before, with no visible results?'

'No, they didn't. I'll have something to say to Rade when we get back. If he knew that—'

'Take it easy on him. Under the circumstances, I'm very glad he tried again. You haven't done such a bad job, you know.'

'Maybe not, but the job's not done. I see the reason now for a lot of things that puzzled me about you. As far as I'm concerned, this is your show as much as mine, from now on. How do we go about collecting Drai? I suppose the others aren't worth bothering with.'

'Why not leave him where he is? There's no other ship; he's stuck as long as we have this one, unless he wants to take a ride in a torpedo. Since there's nowhere else in this system where he could live for any length of time, I don't think he'll do that. My advice would be to take off right away, and let him worry about what's happened until we get back with official support.'

'The motion is carried – except for one thing. I have to run a little errand first. Feth, you keep an eye on our friend and pilot while I'm gone.' He disappeared toward the air lock before any questions could be asked.

As a matter of fact, his absence was quite long, and eventually the ship had to go after him. He was in a valley adjacent to that of the station, with a problem he could not handle alone. Sallman Ken liked to pay his debts.

None of the Wings, of course, felt that the strange 'fire-man' owed them anything. On the contrary. They did not blame him for the fire – he had been on the ground, talking to them, when the ship started it. The blaze was out by night, anyway, with the aid of the crew from Clark Fork. The only real concern the family felt was whether or not the alien would return.

It was not until evening that anyone remembered that a torpedo load of metal should have arrived that day. Don and Roger went out in the morning to the site of the transmitter, and found a torpedo, but its cargo door was closed and there was no answer to their shouts. This, of course, was the one Drai had sent down, and which he had completely forgotten in the rush of events. It had been operating on radio rather than achronic transmitter control, since the *Karella* had been so near at the time, and there was no way to switch it back from a distance even if the drug-runner's memory should improve. Ken himself, with his 'payment' safely on board the *Karella*, never thought of it; his attention had promptly switched to the obvious need for a survey of the Solar System before he left it. A full Earth day had been spent looking briefly over Sol's frozen family, before he could be persuaded to start for home – Feth did not try very hard to persuade him, as a matter of fact, since he had his own share of scientific curiosity. At last, however, they plunged back to make the final call at Planet Three. The transmitter was just emerging into sunlight; this time even Lee appeared willing to home down on it. A mile above the peaks, Ken guided him on a long downward slant to a point above the Wing home.

The natives had seen them coming; all seven of them were standing outside, watching the descent with emotions that Ken could easily guess. He waved Lee into a position that brought the air lock directly over the clearing in front of the house, and the lowest part of the ship's hull thirty feet above the treetops. Then he climbed into his armor, entered the air lock with his 'payment,' and opened the outer door without bothering to pump back the air. For a moment he was enveloped in a sheet of blue fire, which burst from the port and caused the natives to exclaim in alarm. Fortunately the flame of burning sulfur licked upward, and was gone in a moment. Then Ken, waving the natives away from directly below, rolled his payment over the sill of the lock. It made quite a hole in the ground. A carefully made diagram, drawn on the fluo-silicone material the Sarrians used for paper, followed; and when the Wings looked up after crowding around this, the *Karella* was a dwindling dot in the sky, and Ken was already preparing a report for the planetary ecologists and medical researchers who would return with them. Perhaps a cure for the drug could be found, and even if it weren't he was on good enough terms with the natives so that he needn't worry too much. Not, of course, that that was his only interest in the weird beings; they seemed rather likable, in their own way—

He even remembered to write a brief report for Rade.

On the ground, no one spoke for some time.

'I can't budge it, Dad,' were the first words finally uttered. They came from Roger, who had been vainly trying to move the grayish lump that had landed at their feet.

'It must weigh two hundred pounds or so,' supplemented Don. 'If it's all platinum—'

'Then we'll have a fine time breaking it up into pieces small enough to avoid comment,' finished his father. 'What interests me right now is this picture.' The others crowded around once more.

It was a tiny diagram of the Solar System, such as they had drawn before the fire two days ago. Beside it was the unmistakable picture of a space ship like the *Karella* – heading away from it. Then another diagram, apparently an enlarged view of the orbits of the inner planets, showed the arcs through which each would move in approximately a month; and finally a third picture reproduced the first – except that the space ship was pointing *toward* the system. The meaning was clear enough, and a smile broke out on Mr Wing's face as he interpreted it.

'I guess we continue to eat,' he remarked, 'and I guess our friend wants to learn more English. He'll be back, all right. I was afraid for a little while he'd take that carton of cigarettes in the wrong spirit. Well—' he turned to the family suddenly.

'Don – Roger – let's go. If he's going to be away a month, and that torpedo is still lying where you found it, we have a job of tinkering to do. Roger, by the time you're Don's age you may be able to pilot us on a return visit to your hot-blooded friend – we're going to find out how that gadget works!'

CYCLE OF FIRE

I

Logistics

Considering the general nature of a lava field the glider had no business looking as sound as it did. Its tail assembly was intact; its fuselage had suffered only the removal of fabric from the lower side; even the narrow wings appeared undamaged. Had there been a catapult within three thousand miles one would have been tempted to try launching the craft. Even Dar Lang Ahn might have been deceived, if his eyes had been his only source of information.

He had more than eyes, however. He had been the unfortunate who had ridden the machine in. He had seen the pitted black surface of the flow suddenly sweep toward him as an unexpected wind had dragged him toward the nameless volcano; he had felt the impact and the partial rebound as the springy wood frame of the aircraft had done its best to absorb the shock; and, most important, he had heard both main wing spars fail. The first question in his mind was not how to get aloft again but whether or not he should wreck the glider more obviously before he left it, and that was not really a question. The real problem was raised by the books.

There were not many of these, of course; Ree Pell Un had been far too foresighted to trust a very large fraction of the city's knowledge to one aircraft. Still, they could not be ignored; it was his duty to get them intact to the Ice Ramparts, and eight hundred years is quite long enough to develop a strong devotion to duty. Dar Lang Ahn had lived that long.

Fortunately they were not heavy. He set resolutely to work making as much as possible into a pack that could be carried without hampering either his walking or his use of weapons. When he finally straightened up and started purposefully away from the wreck he was laden with perhaps half his own weight in books, a tenth as much food, and the crossbow and bolts which had been his inseparable companions since early life. The greater part of his food remained behind, but no reading matter.

He had thought about the direction to take while loading up. A great circle course to his intended destination was a shade over two thousand miles, of which roughly half was ocean. The way he had planned to fly was much longer, because of the islands which made it possible to get across that ocean in stages never greater than fifty miles. He decided to stick to this route, because he had already traveled it several times and knew the way. To be sure, the landmarks would look different from the ground, but that should not prove a great difficulty to his photographic memory.

He did not, of course, start in the direction he intended to maintain. That would have led almost directly over the mountain on whose flanks he had crashed. Dar was a better mountain climber than any human being ever would be, owing to natural advantages of physique, but the top of this mountain was emitting a faint, steady plume of yellow smoke, and the lava under his feet was, it seemed to him, rather warmer than sunlight could account for. Therefore, while his immediate goal on the near shore of the ocean lay to the northeast and the nearest edge of the lava straight north, he turned until the crimson sun he called Theer was to his left and behind him and the smaller, blue Arren straight behind, and started into the northwest.

A lava field is not easy to cross on foot, even without a heavy load. Laden as Dar Lang Ahn was, it is torture. His feet were tough enough to resist the sharp bits of rock which he could not avoid, but there was no such thing as a level path. Again and again he had to revise his estimate of the time the journey would take, but he never admitted to himself that he might not complete it.

Twice he ate and drank, if the token sip and nibble that he took could be called by such names. Both times he kept walking. There were less than fifty miles between the place where the glider had crashed and the edge of the lava sheet, but if he were to fall asleep before crossing those miles he would almost certainly die of thirst. There was no water on the lava, so far as he knew, and with summer approaching he needed water as badly as a human being would in the same situation.

The first of his meals found him far enough from the mountain to turn northward, putting Theer directly behind him. Arren was catching up with the red sun, but shadows were still short. Accustomed though he was to two light sources, the presence of both suns made it a little more difficult to judge the terrain more than a few dozen yards ahead, and consequently he frequently missed short cuts.

Still, he made progress. The second 'meal' found him out of sight of the volcano and a few hours later he was sure he could see a line of green ahead. This might, of course, have been a mirage, with which Dar Lang Ahn was totally unfamiliar. It might also have been a denser covering of the spiky, pulpy, barrel-shaped plants which grew here and there on the lava itself. The traveler, however, felt sure that it was real forest – plants whose presence would mean a plentiful supply of the water he was beginning to want badly. He gave the equivalent of a grin of relief, resettled the pack of books across his shoulders, drank off the rest of his water, and started once more for the horizon. He discovered his mistake some time before he actually became thirsty again.

Traveling in anything like a straight line he could have walked the distance to the forest easily. Even with the sort of detours he had been forced to make on the lava field he could cover it before suffering too seriously from thirst. He simply had not counted on extraordinary detours, since he did not remember seeing from the air anything different from the general run of cracks and ridges on the lava flow. His memory did not betray him, as it turned out, but the terrain did.

Theer had nearly ceased his westward travel and was rising noticeably, preparing for his yearly swoop back toward Arren, when Dar Lang Ahn found the barrier. It was not a wall, which he would never have considered impassable in any case; it was a crack – a crack which must have formed after the lava mass as a whole had almost completely hardened, for it was far too deep and long to have been caused by the mere splitting of a bit of hardened crust under the pressure of fluid from below.

He had never noticed it from above simply because it was not straight; it snaked its way among the more ordinary irregularities of the region, so that he had traveled along it for more than an hour before he grasped the actual situation. That was when the crack began to curve back toward the now distant volcano.

When he did realize what was happening Dar Lang Ahn stopped instantly and sought the shade of an up-jutting slab of rock before he even began to think. He did not pause to berate his own foolishness, though he recognized it clearly enough; he concentrated on the problem that faced him.

The walls of the crevasse were unclimbable. Normally lava hardens in a surface rough enough to permit the claws of one of his people to get a grip on a nearly vertical surface, but this had been a split through the whole mass. True, the rock was full of gas bubbles and many of these had been opened by the crack and were large enough to furnish him support, but these occurred only near the surface. The opposite wall of the crevasse showed that only a few yards down the bubbles shrank to pinpoint size and, for practical purposes, vanished. Besides, the wall was not merely vertical. It 'waved' so that no matter where he started down – or from which side, had he had a choice – he would find an overhang before descending very far. No, climbing was out.

The gap was too wide to jump – in most places too wide even for one without a burden, and Dar Lang Ahn never thought of abandoning his load.

He had no rope and not enough harness on his body or pack to improvise a line that would reach even as far as he could jump. Nothing grew on the lava from which either a rope or a bridge could be fashioned. The plants proved to be of a pulpy texture inside, quite without woody tissue, and the skins were not even tough enough to resist his claws.

The thing that delayed him longest in finding a solution was, of course, his determination not to be separated from the books. It took him an unbelievably long time to get the idea that the separation need not be permanent; he could throw the books across the gap and then jump himself.

This disposed of nearly all the difficulties, since he recalled several places where he was pretty sure of being able to jump across the crack if he was unhampered. He simply had to find one where a reasonably flat area existed, within reach of his throwing arm, on the far side of the crevasse.

He found it eventually. For the moment he did not think of the hours that had passed; he simply slid his pack to the black surface, checked to make sure that it was securely fastened – he wanted no risk of books falling out as it flew – tested its weight calculatingly with one powerful arm, and then, swinging around completely after the manner of a hammer thrower, launched it across the crack. There never was any doubt that it would get there; actually it went a little farther than Dar Lang Ahn had hoped and for an instant he wondered whether it might not reach the rough ground just beyond his target area. It finally stopped rolling, however, in full view and apparently intact, and with that assurance he planned his leap and made it.

He would have given no more details than that, had he been preparing a report of the incident. Most men would have had difficulty in avoiding mention of their feelings as they rushed toward the edge, put every bit of effort they could raise into a leap as they reached it, looked for an instant into the sickening depth below, and then thudded painfully into rough, sharp, hard lava on the other side. One man did have a good deal to say about it, later. Dar Lang Ahn felt all the appropriate emotions as he went through this series of actions, but with the leap behind him he thought only of the books. He went on.

Theer was visibly higher when he encountered another crevasse between himself and the forest. This took less time to cross but still contributed its bit of delay; and finally, with the red sun well above the horizon and seemingly twice as large as it had appeared from the site of the glider crash, he was forced to admit to himself that he was going to be on the lava flow through the summer – and this was no time of year to spend a summer far from a large supply of water.

His death, then, would come somewhat earlier than he had expected, and something would have to be done about the books. Presumably there would be searchers when he failed to return home in a reasonable time, and he was close enough still to the usual air route between Kwarr and the Ice Ramparts for his location to be covered without the need for much imagination on any searcher's part. What was needed was something to make his position visible from the air. He considered trying to return to his glider but realized he could never make the journey – for one thing he would be too weak to get across the deep cracks by the time he reached them. Of course, if he had realized how small his chances of crossing the lava field actually were he would never have brought the books from the aircraft in the first place; it had simply never occurred to him to doubt his ability to make the trip. Now he had to rectify his error, or at least make it possible for someone else to do so.

He had left no visible trail on the rock, naturally, so that finding his glider would do no good to the searchers. They would know the general direction that he had taken, of course, but since they would not know the precise time of the crash there would be no way for them to tell how far he might have traveled. They would not guess, any more than he had, that he might not have reached the edge of the lava flow; no one had any first-hand knowledge of the conditions so near a volcano.

His own body would not show against the lava to an observer at any likely altitude, for neither his size nor his coloring rendered him conspicuous. Since all the rocks were of nearly the same color he could not make any sort of contrasting pattern which could be seen from the air. There was nothing in his pack which would make a decent-sized signal flag or serve to paint anything on the rocks. The only things about him which held any possibility of use in this problem, as far as Dar Lang Ahn could see, were the buckles of his harness.

These were flat and of polished iron; they might serve as mirrors, though they were pretty small. Still, where there was no other hope he would have to make them do. He reached this decision while still plodding northward.

The question that remained was whether he should stop where he was and devote his remaining time to perfecting an arrangement of buckles which would have a maximum chance of catching a passing flier's eye, or keep on until he was obviously near the end. The latter alternative had the advantage of giving him a chance to reach some particularly advantageous spot – perhaps some spire of rock or configuration of lava slabs which would help catch a searcher's eye. That it also included a possibility of his finding water in time to save his own life was a point he did not consider; so far as he thought about that matter he was dead already. The only advantage of stopping now was that he could spend the rest of his life in the shade, which might be more comfortable than traveling farther under the blaze of the two suns. As might have been expected, he elected to continue walking.

He walked, or scrambled, or climbed, as circumstances required, while the red sun continued to rise and grow. It was starting to swing back in an eastward direction, too, but Arren's steady motion toward the west made him, at least, still useful as a guide. Perhaps Dar's course corrections were a little vague; perhaps his path, toward the end, could hardly be called a course at all, for as time passed and temperature mounted his mind dwelt more and more on the torturing thirst messages which his body was sending it. A human being would have been dead long since – dead and baked dry. However, Dar Lang Ahn had no perspiration glands, since his nerve tissue could stand temperatures almost as high as the boiling point of water, and in consequence he did not lose the precious liquid nearly as rapidly as a man would. A little went, however, with each breath that passed out of his lungs, and the breaths were becoming ever more painful. He was no longer sure whether the wavering of the landscape in front of him was due to heat or his own eyesight; frequently he had to turn both eyes on the same object to be sure he was seeing it accurately. Short spurs of rock seemed, for brief instants, to take on a semblance of living creatures; once he caught himself starting to leave his chosen path in order to investigate a slab of lava. It took long seconds for him to convince himself that nothing could really have dodged behind it. Nothing lived here; nothing *could* move. The sounds which reached his ears were simply the crackings as new patches of lava were caught by the sunlight and warmed. He had heard them before.

Still, it had been a very convincing motion. Perhaps he should go back to see—

Go back. That was the one thing he must not do. That, of all possible actions, was the one provably useless one. If illusions were snatching at his mind in such a way as to tempt him into an act like that he must have come closer to the end than he thought. It was time to settle down and set up his reflector while he still had control of his muscles.

He wasted no time in regrets, but stopped where he was and looked around carefully. A few yards away a slab of hardened lava had been broken from the crust and tilted up almost perpendicularly by the pressure of liquid rock underneath. Its upper edge was a good ten feet above the surface in the immediate neighborhood. This was more than twice Dar Lang Ahn's height, but the sheet was rough enough to give a grip to his claws and he saw no reason to expect difficulty in setting up his buckles at the top.

He unslung the pack of books and lowered it to the hot rock. He made sure it was closed tightly and fastened it in position with one of the pack straps; it would probably rain even here when summer was over, and he could not afford to have the books spoiled or washed away.

Then he removed his harness and checked its individual straps with one eye, while he examined with the other the ridge where he planned to set the buckles. Two or three pieces of leather which seemed superfluous he laid beside the pack; the rest, with the buckles, he strapped once more about his body in order to leave both hands free for climbing.

The upper edge of the slab was as jagged as it had appeared from below and he had little difficulty in snagging the straps around the projections. He arranged one buckle so that its reflected beams pointed southward, rising at a small angle; the other he tried to set for the eyes of a searcher directly overhead. Neither, of course, was very likely to attract attention – they really depended only upon Arren's light, since the red sun would only be above the horizon for a short time before and after summer and the air lanes would be empty during the hot season itself. Still, it was the best that Dar Lang Ahn could do, and with the bits of metal arranged to his satisfaction he took one more look around before descending.

The landscape was shimmering more than ever. Once again he felt almost sure that he had seen something disappear behind a slab of rock, in the direction from which he had come. He dismissed the illusion from his mind and began to climb down, paying close attention to his hand and foot holds; he had no wish to spend his remaining few hours with the agony of a broken bone, even if there was no way to make the time really comfortable.

He reached the bottom safely and, after a few moments' thought, dragged his book pack into the shadow of the ridge. Then he settled himself calmly, using the pack as a pillow, folded his arms across his chest, closed his eyes, and relaxed. There was nothing more to do; perhaps his centuries-trained sense of duty was not exactly satisfied, but even it could not find a specific task to make him perform.

It would be nearly impossible to put his thoughts into words. No doubt he regretted dying earlier than his fellows. Quite possibly he considered the bleak landscape spread before him and wondered idly just how much farther he would have had to get in order to live. However, Dar Lang Ahn was not human, and the pictures which formed most of his thoughts, being shaped by an eyesight and cultural background drastically different from those of any human being, could never be properly translated to the mind of a person of Earth. Even Nils Kruger, as adaptable a young man as might be found anywhere and who certainly became as well acquainted with Dar Lang Ahn as anyone could, refuses to guess at what went on in his mind between the time he settled down to die and the time Kruger caught up with him.

The boy's approach went unheard by Dar, keen though his ears normally were. He was not entirely unconscious, however, for the scent of water affected him enough not only to snap his eyes open but to send him bounding to his feet. For just an instant his eyes roved wildly about in all directions, then they both fastened on the figure toiling over the rock a dozen yards away.

Dar Lang Ahn had never before had reason to distrust either his memory or his sanity, but this time he felt that something must be wrong with one or the other. This living thing was shaped correctly, more or less, but the size was unbelievable. It towered a good foot above his own four feet and a half, and that was simply *wrong*. The other oddities were minor – eyes in the front of its face, a beaklike projection above the mouth, pinkish coloration instead of purplish-black – but the height put it out of any class which Dar could drag from his memory. *People*, other than accident victims who had had to start over, were four and a half feet tall, just now; Teachers were a little under eight. There was nothing between those limits that walked on two legs.

Then even the size was driven from his thoughts by another fact. The smell of water that had roused him was coming from this creature; it must be literally drenched with the stuff. Dar Lang Ahn started to move toward the newcomer as this realization struck him, but he stopped after the first step. He was too weak. He groped backward, seeking support from the slab of rock in whose shadow he had been lying. With its aid he held up while the unbelievable thing approached; then, with the scent of water burning his nostrils, everything seemed to let go at once. A curtain dropped in front of his eyes and the rough stone at his back ceased to hurt. He felt his knees give, but not his impact with the lava.

II
Diplomacy

It was the taste of water that roused him, as its scent had a few minutes before. For long moments he let the liquid trickle into his mouth without opening his eyes or noticing anything peculiar in its taste. He could feel the strength flow back into his body along with the precious fluid and he simply enjoyed the sensation without even trying to think.

That, of course, could not last after his eyes were open, and finally he did open them. What he saw was sufficient to bring his mind to full alertness almost instantly.

It was not that the human face so close to his was weird in appearance; that appearance had already been engraved on his memory before he collapsed and it caused him no surprise now. It took only a few seconds of consciousness to allow him to realize that this creature was not a *person* as he understood the term, but that it evidently was not unfriendly and not entirely lacking in good sense. It was providing the water which was reviving him, after all. The tension Dar Lang Ahn felt at this point was due not to surprise at Kruger's presence or appearance, therefore, but to astonishment at the source of water. The strange thing was actually squeezing into his open mouth one of the pulpy plants. This act gave rise to the first of the misunderstandings which were to complicate the friendship of the two for a long time to come.

Dar Lang Ahn concluded instantly that Kruger must be a native of the volcano region, since he had such surprising knowledge of its plant life. This, naturally, caused him to regard the boy with more than a little uneasiness. Kruger, on his part, had been following the native from the time of the glider crash, had seen him ignore consistently the plants which so closely resembled Earth's cacti, and had only with the greatest difficulty been able to persuade himself that the little being's obvious distress was caused by thirst.

Had their positions been reversed Kruger would, of course, have felt properly grateful to anyone or anything which had supplied him with water, whether it was human or a walking pineapple, but he knew perfectly well that 'proper gratitude' was not a universal trait even with his own kind. Therefore the moment that Dar Lang Ahn's eyes opened the boy laid the partly squeezed cactus down within the native's reach and stepped backward. Personal caution was only part of his reason; he wanted to relieve any possible fear that the creature might feel.

Dar Lang Ahn handled immediate problems first. With one eye held on his strange helper – he did not know for a long time the uneasy sensation that very act could arouse in a human being – he used the other and one hand to find, pick up, and return to his mouth the plant whose juices had revived him. He kept it there for a long time, convinced that he would be able to use the last drop of fluid he could squeeze from it, but before it was quite empty another thought struck him. It made him pause.

Kruger saw the mangled plant leave his new acquaintance's mouth after what seemed a long time and found himself wondering a little tensely what would happen next. He was not really afraid, since the native was so much smaller than he, but he was experienced – or openminded – enough to realize that size and potentiality for damage might not go quite hand in hand. He hoped, naturally, that some move would be made which he could interpret beyond doubt as a friendly one, but he could not, offhand, imagine what action could be so free of uncertainty. Dar Lang Ahn managed to find one, however.

With an effort that was obvious even to the human being and which nearly dropped the little messenger back into unconsciousness, he rose to his feet. Carefully, still keeping one eye on Kruger, he made his way out into the sunlight to a point some twenty yards from his protecting rock. Here he stopped for a moment and gathered strength, then bent over, wrenched another cactus free, sucked briefly at the oozing base to make sure it was the same sort as the one he had just used up, returned to the rock – and gave the plant to Kruger. The boy mentally took off his hat to a mind apparently quicker than his own, accepted the gift, and drank from it. Five minutes later the two were seated side by side trying to make sense out of each other's sounds.

Each party, of course, had a few mental reservations about this developing friendship. Dar Lang Ahn could not forget the suspicion naturally engendered by his companion's familiarity with lava-field vegetation; Kruger was trying to make fit together the other's apparent ignorance of those same plants and what appeared to be an equally evident intelligence. It occurred to him that Dar was no more a native of this world than he himself, but he had seen the crash of the glider and spent some time examining the aircraft after the pilot had left it. It seemed beyond the pale of possibility that a visitor from another world would be traveling in such a conveyance; either he would be in his ship, or some auxiliary of it, or on foot like Kruger himself. There was a possibility on this line, though, at that. Perhaps this little manlike thing was a castaway like Kruger but had shown more ingenuity than the boy and managed to build the glider himself. That tied in with the speed of thought he – or she or it – had already shown, though it made Nils a trifle uncomfortable.

Human beings have a strong tendency to cling to whatever hypothesis they may evolve to explain some new situation. Hence, while the suggestion that Dar Lang Ahn was a member of a race foreign to this world and quicker-witted than his own hurt his pride, the notion stayed in Kruger's mind – and grew, during the days that followed, to something like a certainty.

Dar had an advantage over his new acquaintance in this respect. His strongest prejudices were not those in favor of his own ideas but those the Teachers and their books had instilled into him. Neither had ever mentioned anything like Nils Kruger, so he was free to form idea after idea concerning the strange creature's nature. He liked none of them. Therefore, he continued to think, while the strength flowed back into his muscles.

One thing was evident: this creature was intelligent and presumably had some natural means of communication. So far it had not shown evidence of possessing a voice, but that could easily be checked. Tentatively, Dar Lang Ahn spoke a few words to the larger being.

Kruger answered at once, producing a series of perfectly meaningless noises as far as Dar was concerned but at least showing that he did possess a language. This was one of the few experiences shared by the two which left them with the same impression; on this occasion they decided simultaneously that language lessons were in order and settled down to conduct them. It was too hot to travel, anyway, and Dar still needed to get some strength back.

The shadow of the rock ledge was growing narrower as the two suns separated – the near-eclipse had occurred during Dar's wait for death – but it was still broad enough to shield both of them. Kruger settled down with his back against the ledge; Dar resumed his former position, using the pack for a pillow.

There are several ways to learn a language. Unfortunately, there was only one possible with the resources at hand and even for that the material was a trifle scanty. A lava field with an occasional cactus, a respectable number of shadows, and two suns shining on it furnishes demonstration material for very few nouns and practically no verbs. Plenty of adjectives may apply to it, but it is decidedly difficult to make clear just which one is being used at the moment.

Kruger thought of drawing pictures, but he had neither pencil nor paper and the sketches he made on the lava surface with a broken bit of rock didn't look like much even to their author when he had finished. They certainly meant nothing to Dar.

Nevertheless a few sounds gradually acquired more or less the same meaning to both parties. To describe their exchange of ideas as a conversation would be rank deception, but ideas did get across. By the time the red sun had disappeared below the southeastern horizon it was mutually understood that they would proceed together to the edge of the lava field to find something more drinkable than cactus juice and more edible than the rather nauseating pulp of the plants.

Kruger was not too happy about this, as a matter of fact. In the months he had been on the planet he had walked some three thousand miles northward to get away from the periodically intolerable heat of the red sun, and in the last few hundred had realized that he was seeing progressively more of the blue one. The reason was obvious enough: the blue star was a 'circumpolar' in the northern part of the northern hemisphere – or, as the *Alphard*'s navigator would have to put it, its declination seen from this planet was at least several degrees north. The trouble was that Kruger had not the faintest idea of the motion of the planet relative to the blue star; he could not even guess whether it would produce a noticeable seasonal effect or not and if it did, how long the seasons would last.

He had been toying with the idea of heading southward again for several weeks before he had seen Dar's glider in flight. That was the first intimation he had had, other than the rather doubtful cases of lights seen from space by the *Alphard*'s observers, that there were people of any sort on the planet; he had set out in the direction the glider had been taking. It was sheer luck that he had been close enough to see Dar's crash – or rather that the crash had occurred so close to the spot where Kruger had happened to be. He had followed the little pilot for several days; he had leaped the same crevasses as Dar had, taking an even deadlier risk with his greater weight and not-so-much-greater strength, but not daring to lose track of the being; and he had been shocked profoundly to discover his guide down and apparently helpless in the midst of the lava desert. He had hoped even then, somewhat illogically, that he could learn from the creature of some place to the south, out of the permanent glare of the blue sun, where he could find shelter and civilized company; after all, while the glider had been going north, it must have been coming from somewhere.

Still, if the pilot wanted to continue to the north there seemed nothing to do but string along. Presumably he was trying to reach a place where he would be comfortable; Kruger realized that he himself had no means of telling just what that would mean in terms of temperature, food, and water, but at least his companion did not enjoy the lava plain any better than a human being would. With that much in common the risk of staying with him seemed well worth taking.

It was a good deal cooler when the red sun finally set, and Kruger knew from past experience that it would be seven or eight earthly days before it rose again in this latitude. They were both hungry, but far from starving, and Dar Lang Ahn had recovered much of his strength in the sixty or seventy hours since Kruger's arrival. The blue star had moved around to the southwest, but it would be quite a number of earthly days yet before it would hamper their travel by shining in their faces.

They traveled more slowly than Dar had when he thought he was alone. The principal reason lay in Kruger's physical make-up; no human being can be as agile as the small, loose-jointed natives of Abyormen. Enough of the travel was climbing for Dar's clawed hands and feet to make a good deal of difference, and weak though the native still was he had to hold back frequently for his bulkier companion.

Nevertheless they did make fair progress. No more major cracks were encountered, and after a few dozen hours of travel patches of soil began to appear here and there on the lava. Vegetation became thicker and from time to time pools of water stood in hollows in the lava. Evidently they were nearing the edge of the flow, since the lava itself was too porous to retain the liquid. The pools were scummed and crusted with rather smelly vegetation similar to the algae with which Kruger was familiar, and both travelers were willing to stick a little longer to cactus juice rather than drink from them; but their very presence improved morale. Dar hitched his pack of books a little higher and seemed to double his speed. The going became easier as more and more of the irregularities in the lava were filled with soil, though the soil itself was becoming more and more covered with vegetation. The plants at first were small in size, reminiscent to Kruger of lawn shrubs, but as the frequency of ponds increased and the amount of lava showing above the dirt grew smaller, the plants became larger, ranging finally to full-sized trees.

Most of these growths were as familiar to Kruger as to Dar, since the boy had seen them in profusion during his journey from the south; and he kept his eyes open for some whose stems or leaves he had learned were safe. He was in no mood to try any others; when Dar saw something he knew and offered it to his companion, Kruger shook his head.

'Nothing doing. Everything I've eaten on this world I had to try first, with no means of telling whether it would feed me or kill me. Out of five tries I got two bad bellyaches, and I'm lucky that was all. I'll wait until we see something I know, thanks.'

Dar understood absolutely nothing of this except the refusal, which he filed in his mind as something else requiring explanation. He took as a working hypothesis the idea that the boy knew and disliked the leaf in question; that supposition at least fitted in with the theory that Kruger was a native of the lava region.

By the time the blue sun had moved around to the west the trees were thick enough to shade them from it most of the time, and the undergrowth dense enough to impede them both quite seriously. Neither had any cutting tools except for a small sheath knife which had been part of Kruger's spacesuit kit, and this was virtually useless for cutting a path.

The result was that they traveled very slowly. The impatience Dar felt did not show in his outward expression, at least to one as unfamiliar with his facial expression as Kruger was.

Language lessons continued as they traveled, with somewhat more speed because of the better supply of referents. Kruger felt that they should by now be getting ideas across to each other quite well and couldn't understand why this didn't seem to be happening. A lot of nouns were clear to both and a fair number of verbs. Adjectives, now that a great many articles were at hand for comparison, were increasing in supply. Once there are trees of various sizes the meaning of 'big' and 'little' can get across; if the attempt is made with a big rock and a small cactus there is no way to tell whether size, color, shape, or something entirely different from any of these is under discussion.

Nevertheless something was wrong. Kruger was gradually coming to suspect that his companion's language contained only irregular verbs and that each noun belonged to a different declension. Dar, for his part, more than suspected that Kruger's language was richer in homonyms than any useful tongue should be; the sound 'tree,' for example, seemed to mean a vegetable growth with long, feathery, purplish leaves, and another with a much shorter trunk and nearly round leaves, and still another which actually varied in size from one specimen to the next.

They did not dare let the language problems occupy their full attention. The jungle contained animal life and not all of it was harmless. Dar's sense of smell warned them of some flesh-eaters but by no means all; several times he had to resort to his crossbow while Kruger stood by holding his knife and hoping for the best. On one or two occasions animals apparently were frightened off by the alien human odor. Kruger wondered whether any of them would refuse to eat his flesh for similar reasons but felt no impulse to solve this problem experimentally.

In their first hundred hours in the jungle Dar killed a medium-sized creature which he proceeded to dissect with his companion's knife and eat with great glee. Kruger accepted a piece of the raw flesh with some inner doubts but decided to take a chance. It was against all the rules, of course, but if he had obeyed the rules about testing all food before eating it he would have starved some months before. In the present case the stuff was edible if not delicious and after eight or ten hours of waiting he decided that he had added another item to his limited list of permissible foods.

When they first entered the jungle Dar had changed their course to the northeast. Kruger had endeavored to find out why and, as their stock of useful words increased, finally got the idea that his companion was trying to reach either a lake or sea – at any rate a great deal of water seemed to be involved. This seemed desirable, although there was no longer a drinking problem owing to the numerous brooks they crossed. Kruger had already found out that rain could be expected quite regularly this far north for a hundred hours or so before and perhaps half as long after the rising of the red sun. Where he had started his journey, much farther south, this star was in the sky all the time while the blue one followed a rising and setting pattern of its own; there the weather was much less predictable.

The rain he was expecting had not arrived, however, when he noticed that something seemed to have attracted Dar's attention. Kruger knew his companion could hear, though he was still unsure of the location of his ears, so he began to listen himself. At first nothing but the usual forest sounds were detectable – leaves and branches moving in the wind, the scurrying of thousands of tiny living things, the occasional drip of water from leaves, which never seemed to cease no matter how long a time had passed since it had rained – but Dar changed course a trifle; certainly he must hear something. They had gone another half-mile before it began to register on Kruger's ears.

When it finally did he stopped with an exclamation. Dar Lang Ahn swiveled one eye back toward him and stopped too. He knew as little of human facial expressions as Kruger knew of his, but even so he recognized the change of skin color that the sound produced in the boy's features.

'What?' Dar uttered the sound they had come to agree upon as a general interrogative.

'I think we'd better stay away from that.'

'What?' It was a repetition of the former question, not the more specific interrogative which would have suggested understanding of Kruger's words.

'It sounds like ...' The boy stopped; there were simply no available words. He fell back on signs. Unfortunately his first gesture was back in the direction from which they had come, and Dar took it to mean that Kruger had encountered this thing, whatever it was, before they had met. He was right but he did not grasp his companion's extreme reluctance to meet it again. After a few moments' silent regard of the boy's signals he gave it up and started on his way once more.

'Stop!' This was another word on which they had managed to agree, and Dar obeyed, wondering. They were far from the lava field; was it possible that this creature knew something about jungle that Dar himself didn't? The sound was strange to the native, of course; that was why he wanted to investigate it. Was the giant actually afraid of it? If so, some thought was indicated. If whatever was making this sound could harm Kruger it was more than likely to be able to do as much to Dar. On the other hand perhaps it was merely a matter of dislike. In that case Dar would be passing up a chance for knowledge which might prove worthwhile material for a book. The question seemed to lie, then, between a risk of losing what books he had and one of failing to improve them. The risk of life involved meant nothing, of course, but both the other points were serious.

Perhaps he could get a better measure of the risk by seeing how far Kruger was prepared to go to keep them from this phenomenon. With this thought in mind Dar Lang Ahn deliberately turned once more and again started walking toward the irregular, dull, 'Plop, plop, plop,' that was now coming clearly through the trees.

Kruger was in a quandary. He had never dreamed of having to impress his opinions on Dar by force; he was not sure what the result of trying it would be. In any case he did not want to do anything that might give rise to enmity or even any more distrust than could be helped. In the circumstances he did the only thing that was left. Dar, rolling an eye back toward the human being, saw him start to follow and proceeded on his way assured that there was no real danger. He increased his speed, so far as the undergrowth rendered that possible. In a few minutes the vegetation cleared enough so that real walking could take the place of the laborious pushing aside of branches and vines. To Dar, this was a help; to Kruger, a confirmation of a fact that the increasing sound had already proved.

'Dar! Stop!' The native obeyed, wondering what had happened to change the situation; then he watched in surprise while Kruger forged past him and took up the lead. With his own equivalent of a shrug, he followed. The human being was going more slowly than he would have liked but perhaps there was a reason for it.

There was. In another hundred yards the undergrowth vanished, and at almost the same point the trees stopped. In front of them lay a bare, smooth-surfaced clearing nearly fifty yards across.

To Dar, this was simply a spot in which travel was easy; he would almost certainly have plunged on into the open, eager to get across and resume his journey toward the source of the mysterious sound. However, he was stopped. For the first time in their relationship Kruger not only touched him but blocked his path firmly with an arm more than strong enough to do the job. Dar looked at his companion in surprise, then his eyes traveled on about the clearing. His efforts to force his way past his big companion ceased and both eyes focused on the center of the open space.

The source of the sound was there. The clearing, for the most part, seemed to be floored with some smooth, hard material, but the center was in a constant state of motion – a great cauldron of liquid, sticky mud, heaving upward every few seconds to give birth to a great bubble which burst with the 'plop' they had been hearing and released a cloud of vapor that drifted lazily away.

Kruger let his companion look for a minute or two; then, repeating his word to 'Stop!' he went back on their trail a few paces. Rocks are not ordinarily easy to find on a jungle floor, but they were still close enough to the big flow for occasional outcrops of lava to be present. He found one of these, with a good deal of effort knocked off a fair-sized corner, brought it back, and tossed it out onto the apparently hard surface. The crust of dried mud gave, and the lava boulder vanished with a splash.

'I don't like these places,' Kruger said firmly, indifferent to the fact that Dar could not understand him. 'I went through one myself a few months ago and when I got out by working back up the tree root that had stopped my sinking – and incidentally knocked me out for quite a while – I found my name carved on the tree with several remarks about what a nice young fellow I'd been. I don't blame them for leaving me; they have every reason to suppose I'm still sinking. Living through it once, though, doesn't mean I'm going to try it again; my space suit is a long, long walk from here!'

Dar said nothing but promised himself to heed the advice of his friend as long as they were anywhere near the big fellow's native volcanic region. This was certainly something for the book!

III
Pedagogy

The Mud Geyser, and several others, had been left miles behind, but an occasional lava outcrop still kept Dar following Kruger's lead. The direction of travel was still to the northeast – the boy had made no attempt to change that – but in some subtle fashion the relationship between the two had changed.

For one thing the inevitable mistrust that they had felt at the beginning was just as inevitably fading. Another change, less logical in origin, was due to the almost comical misunderstanding which had resulted in Dar's firm conviction that Kruger was a native of the little-known volcanic areas of Abyormen, while Kruger himself was just as sure that Dar Lang Ahn did not belong on the planet at all. As a result Dar was constantly looking to Kruger for advice. If he shot a new type of animal – new, that is, to him – he would wait for the boy's verdict before eating it. Naturally quite a lot of perfectly good meat was wasted, since Kruger was in no hurry to risk his health and life testing new types of food.

At last, however, Dar killed a creature of the same type as the one the human being had tried when they first entered the jungle. The pilot did not even ask questions about this one; he borrowed the knife and set to work. Kruger looked at his portion with some distaste when it finally came.

He did not like raw meat, though it had certainly not harmed him the other time. On that occasion he had not suggested stopping to make a fire, since Dar was the moral leader of the association and his idea of a meal was apparently to eat on the spot whatever could not be carried and nibble at the rest as he went along. Now, however, with matters waiting on Kruger's advice and opinions, he chose to cook his meal.

He had salvaged all the material from his space suit which seemed likely to be of use and which was not too awkward to carry. While a fire-lighter is in no sense normal space-suit equipment, he had improvised one from the tiny sun-battery and a coil and condenser from the radio. He used it now, to the utter fascination of Dar Lang Ahn. Satisfied that its spark was still good he went looking for dry fuel.

This is not too common in a rain forest, but Kruger had had plenty of practice locating it before he had reached the lava field. Dar, utterly ignorant of what he wanted, simply followed and watched, munching his own share of the meat as he did so. He was interested in a detached sort of way, feeling that possibly whatever was going on might be worth recording but that he wouldn't bet on it.

The detached attitude vanished as he felt the first wave of heat from Kruger's fire. He dropped his meat and sprang to the place where his crossbow was lying, snatching up the weapon as though his life depended on his speed. He made no sound, and Kruger, whose attention was focused on building up his fire, did not see what was going on. A struggle that quite literally involved his own life went on behind his back completely without his knowledge.

Dar had actually started to cock his bow when he stopped, one eye on his work and one on the preoccupied human being. For long moments he thought, wavering from one viewpoint to its opposite. Fire was the prime horror of Dar Lang Ahn's life; he had grown up with a terror of it. His people never used it, but lightning or accidental concentration of Arren's rays sometimes caused a blaze. The Teachers and the books had agreed in their endless admonitions to avoid it. It was the end of all life – was the end that would be taken by his own life, naturally, but that was not due for several years yet. Since reaching the edge of the lava field and thereby coming once more within reach of ample food and water, Dar had put his expectation of premature death out of his mind and it was quite a shock to have it brought back so suddenly.

Still, the giant did not seem to have Dar Lang Ahn in mind. Perhaps the fire was merely a part of Kruger's personal and private business, having nothing to do with Dar at all. After all, that would be a rather likely need for someone native to the neighborhood of a volcano. With this thought in his mind Dar relaxed enough to put the crossbow down, though he did not wander very far from the place where he laid it.

He continued to watch the human being, though his attitude bore no resemblance to the lackadaisical one he had shown while the firewood was being gathered. Mentally he was taking notes; the Teachers at the Ice Ramparts would be wanting to put this in a book, beyond all question.

The strange creature had first built his fire up until it was burning quite strongly, then he permitted it to die down until the flames had practically disappeared. A great deal of heat was still being radiated, however, and when it had reached what appeared to be a satisfactory state Kruger startled his companion still more by deliberately exposing his meat to it.

Dar knew that the boy was hungry; he had already formed a fairly exact idea of how much food a human being needed. Why the strange being should proceed to ruin his meal, then, was a mystery of the first order.

When Kruger completed his weird ritual by consuming the meat and then proceeded to extinguish the fire, Dar had long passed his capacity for further surprise. Seeing that the matter was finished he simply rose to his feet and resumed the journey, a sorely puzzled being.

As a matter of fact the notion that the ceremony was over was decidedly erroneous, though it was an error shared by both Dar and Kruger. The latter received the first intimations of the mistake within an hour after completing the meal, and shortly after the first twinges he was rolling helplessly on the ground. Dar, who had seen such symptoms among his own people but could imagine no cause for them this time, could think of nothing to do that might be helpful. Intermittently for more than an hour the cramps continued, giving Kruger just time between attacks to wonder whether he had made his final error in judgment. Eventually his outraged stomach returned the cause of the disturbance and, after a few more admonitory twinges, left him in peace. It was some time, however, before he was really able to give his mind to the problem of why meat which was perfectly wholesome raw should change in such a drastic manner when cooked. Could the smoke given off by the fire have anything to do with it? Perhaps something like the creosote that preserved smoked meat at home – but it would take a well-equipped organic chemistry lab to graduate any of his hypotheses to the theory class. The observed fact was enough for him now – slightly too much, in fact.

The rains had ceased at the usual time after the reappearance of Theer in the south and the temperature was rising again. Each time the red star made another of its odd loops through the sky Kruger wondered whether he would be able to stand the next one. Long months ago he had realized that he could not, at least in the midlatitudes where he had been at the time. On that part of the planet the loops were entirely above the horizon – Theer never set at all. It did, however, vary enormously in apparent size; it was merely Kruger's misfortune that its greatest apparent diameter, and with it the highest temperature of this sweat-box of a planet, occurred while it was at nearly the farthest north point of its loop. The misfortune lay in the fact that, from where he had been left, the loop itself was in the southern half of the sky and to get any part of it below the horizon was obviously best accomplished by going north. There had been, of course, the question of whether he could go far enough north; his knowledge of the geography of this world was confined to his memory of what he had seen during the landing orbit. That wasn't much. Still, there had seemed to be nothing to do but take the chance.

He was still not far enough north to be completely out of the red sun's reach, but there seemed a good chance that he might make it. It was now above the horizon for about eight days of its eighteen-day period, if Kruger's watch could still be trusted. He would have been quite happy if the question of Alcyone, which Dar Lang Ahn called Arren, were not forcing itself more and more prominently into his mind. It was all very well to turn a red dwarf sun from a permanent nuisance into an intermittent one, but the advantages tended to disappear when at the same time a blue giant changed from a periodic trouble into a constant fixture. With this matter steadily in the front of his mind Kruger was doing his utmost to get such concepts as temperature into their common language so that he could find out from his companion whether or not there was a spot on the planet which a human being would consider comfortable.

Dar's language was, very slowly, becoming less of a nightmare. As a result a picture was gradually building up in Kruger's mind of the goal that lay ahead of them.

Apparently Dar also wanted a cool place. That information was received by Kruger with unconcealed glee. A catch might lie in what constituted Dar's concept of 'cool,' but at least he seemed willing to apply the opposite adjectives to their present environment, which was an encouraging sign. Another was the pilot's persistent attempt to describe something which seemed, in the face of all probabilities, to be ice.

Kruger found this theory completely beyond belief at first and kept pestering his companion for a more careful description. However, Dar stuck to his terminology, and finally it occurred to his listener that perhaps the space ship which had brought Dar to Abyormen might be their goal. That should certainly have ice available, at least artificially.

There was the matter of the ocean in their path, whose existence he had gathered earlier. As the boy was not yet sure whether an actual ocean or simply a large lake was involved, he asked whether it would be possible to walk around it. The emphasis which Dar placed on his attempt to express the impossibility of such a move convinced him that 'ocean' must be the right word.

It was only at this point that Kruger thought of the possibility of maps. Granting that he had no artistic talent, he should still be able to make a sufficiently good plan of their route together from the lava field to their present position for Dar to grasp what he was trying to do; that would get the word 'map' across, and from there on the drawing problem would be Dar Lang Ahn's.

This meant interrupting their journey while the map was drawn, but the effort was an unqualified success. Not only did Dar understand the word and the request that followed its transmission, but he proved to be an excellent cartographer – a natural result of years in the air, since he tended to think of a map as an aerial picture anyway. He made sketch after sketch, clarifying the entire route they were to follow and displaying tremendous knowledge of the planet as a whole.

They were to proceed on their present northeast course until they reached the sea. That was not the closest way to the coast, but it brought them to a point at which a chain of islands stretched across to another continental mass. Getting across the ocean, they would head back along the coast to the left. Kruger assumed that this would be west, but actually it was east; he was already much closer than he realized to Abyormen's north pole, and would pass it before reaching the coast. Dar did not indicate this on his map. They would travel along the new coast for a considerable distance and then head inland. Their journey appeared to terminate shortly thereafter. Dar indicated a vast area with a satisfied air, said, 'Ice!' and sat back as though he had completed a great work. Kruger did not feel quite so happy. He indicated the area the other had just drawn.

'You mean – it's somewhere in this region? Here? or here?'

'Right here.' Dar indicated the point at which he had already terminated their course line.

'But what do you mean by the ice all over this place? You can't have ships covering half the planet.'

'I don't understand "ships." Ice is all over.'

'I still don't get it.'

Dar had had enough language trouble by this time not to feel particularly exasperated at Kruger's slowness; he proceeded to draw more maps. These were circular, and it quickly became evident that they were views of the whole planet from different directions. His ability to draw such charts was strictly in accord with Kruger's ideas about his origin, so the boy did not feel any surprise from this source. The details did bother him, however.

'You mean that there really is a very big area covered with ice.'

'Two of them.' Dar indicated his charts. Kruger frowned. Ice caps are noticeable features from space, and he had certainly seen none during the landing. Of course, he was not a trained observer, and had been paying more attention to the behavior of the pilot during the landing maneuver; and Abyormen's atmosphere has its share of clouds. He could quite possibly have missed them for any of those reasons. There was certainly no chance of their having been on the dark side of the planet; at the time of the landing the world's position with respect to the suns was such that there was no dark side.

At any rate the presence of a glacial area was extremely encouraging, particularly right now. The jungle did afford some protection from the approaching Theer which had been lacking on the lava desert, but the higher humidity pretty well offset this advantage. Kruger did not dare discard any more of his clothing because of the ultraviolet light coming from Arren.

As it turned out, he simply had to stop traveling for about fifty hours about the time of Theer's closest approach – the time for which Dar had a phrase in his language, which Kruger naturally translated as 'summer.' They camped by a stream which the boy hoped would not go dry while they remained, built a shelter whose thatched roof was meant to provide shade and was also kept wet to provide some evaporational cooling, and settled down to wait. Theer's crimson disk, partly visible through the trees, swelled slowly as it moved eastward and slightly higher; continued to swell as it arched across the top of its path and back toward the horizon which Kruger still considered the southeastern one, though his proximity to the pole had made it more like northeast; reached its maximum size, and began visibly to shrink once more before it finally disappeared. It had swung through fully a third of its apparent loop in the sky in only fifty hours, for which Kruger was duly thankful. With its disappearance the journey was resumed.

'Just how sure are you that we are heading toward the part of the coast nearest the island chain?' This question was finally understood.

'I can't be positive, but we're somewhere near right. I've flown over this route a lot.'

'You can't be using landmarks, though; we couldn't see anything much smaller than a mountain with all this jungle, and there haven't been any mountains. Couldn't we be working to one side or the other?'

'It is possible but doesn't matter greatly. There are low hills – volcanic cones – along the coast and you can climb one of those if we don't see any islands from the shore.' Kruger skipped for the moment the question of why he should be the one to do the climbing.

'But suppose even from a hilltop we can't see any of the island chain. Which way should we travel? Wouldn't it be better to strike for the coast now, so that there'll be no doubt of the direction after we get there?'

'But I don't know the route you suggest.'

'You don't know this one, either; you've never walked it before. If your maps are right there's no chance of getting lost, and much less chance than otherwise of wasting time once we reach the coast.'

Dar Lang Ahn pondered this bit of wisdom for a few moments and then agreed unreservedly. The course was changed accordingly. All went on as before. It did occur afterward to Dar that perhaps Kruger had been motivated by a desire to get back into a volcanic region sooner.

There were still several hundred miles to go, though Kruger was not sure of this – scale had been one feature left in considerable doubt on Dar's maps. A novelist of the nineteenth century could have made much of every mile of it; the way was made difficult by all the natural characteristics of a rain forest. Undergrowth and swamps delayed them; dangerous animals threatened them; time seemed to stretch onward endlessly and unchangingly. An occasional lava outcrop, usually heavily eroded, served to ease travel for a few miles, but the jungle always returned.

Very gradually, as they advanced, the portion of Theer's loop above the horizon diminished from the eight days near the mudpots to seven, and then to six. Simultaneously the tilt of Arren's diurnal circle changed. On the lava field it had been higher in the south than in the north; now the blue star held nearly even altitude all around the horizon. It was this observation which forced on Kruger's attention the fact that they must be very close to Abyor-men's north pole. That, in a way, was good, but in another it bothered him. If they were practically at the pole, where was this ice cap? Or, since Dar stuck to his claim that it was across an ocean in the direction they were traveling, why wasn't it at the pole? Kruger was sure that his problem could be solved in minutes by anyone with the training, but a sixteen-year-old cadet whose planned career involves piloting interstellar vessels simply doesn't get that kind of education.

In any case he was still not absolutely sure that he was interested in the ice cap itself; it seemed likely that Dar's people had simply landed their ship at its edge and Dar was using it as a reference point. The boy was not quite sure what he should do when he got to the ship, but there was no doubt in his mind about the advisability of going there.

All through the long journey the speed and clarity of their conversation improved. The language used was a hodge-podge of the two native tongues involved, but it contained a far larger proportion of Dar's words. This was deliberate on Kruger's part; when he did meet others of Dar's race he wanted to be able to speak to them without needing Dar as an interpreter. Before the pair reached the coast they were talking quite freely, though reiteration and sign language were still frequently necessary; but the basic misunderstand-ing was still present and seemed less likely than ever to be cleared up. The trouble now was that misunderstandings frequently went unrecognized; each party thought he had expressed himself clearly, or understood perfectly, as the case might be, when actually the thought received was very different from that transmitted. An example of this occurred one day when the ques-tion of possible rescue by some of Dar's people had arisen.

'You say that a good many of your people make the same trip in gliders that you were making when you crashed,' remarked Kruger. 'Mightn't it be a good idea, when we get to the point on the coast that's back under your regu-lar route, to light a smudge fire to attract their attention? We might be saved an awful lot of walking.'

'I'm afraid I don't see how attracting their attention would help us, even if you could make a big enough fire to be seen.'

'Wouldn't they come down and rescue us?'

'Well – yes, I suppose so. I'm afraid I don't want to reach the Ramparts quite that quickly, though.'

In this case, it is possible that the matter might have been cleared up if Kruger had pursued the conversation a little farther, but he had heard Dar speak of the Ramparts earlier and had gathered an impression that when he spoke of the ice region in that way it carried a religious significance which the little pilot was reluctant to discuss. Presumably these trips, then, were scheduled in a fashion which called for Dar's presence only at certain times.

Even mishaps such as those the pilot had suffered had their place in the program. This was a far-fetched idea, of course, but it fitted with many of the things Dar Lang Ahn had said and Kruger did not want to offend his little companion. Therefore the subject of the conversation was changed, and Dar assumed that he had explained what would happen, if by some mischance one of his friends were to examine the neighborhood of a fire closely and find Dar Lang Ahn beside it.

'What will you do after getting to the ice?' was Kruger's next question. If that was getting into a dangerous subject he assumed Dar could simply skip any matters he didn't want to discuss.

'There are a few years to go,' the other replied calmly. 'Twenty-two, if I remember the date correctly. If there is a glider available I suppose I will continue my regular work. If not, then whatever the Teachers say.'

Kruger had come to interpret the word 'year' as a cycle of the red sun; therefore the time Dar had mentioned was about thirteen months. Before he could ask another question the native put one of his own.

'What will *you* do? Will you actually come all the way to the ice and face the Teachers? I rather thought that you might be planning to stay at the coast when we get there.'

'I think it will be more comfortable for me to go on with you as long as you'll let me. They're your people, of course; if you don't want me to see them, that's up to you.'

'I very much want you but wasn't sure how you'd face the idea.'

'Why should it bother me? I am in worse need of help than you are, and perhaps your Teachers will be willing to give me the assistance I would like. I suppose your group is busy, if you expect to go right back to work, but I can wait. Perhaps after the time you mention is up they'll be free to give me a hand. I'll be willing to do what I can for you folks in the meantime.'

Dar did not answer this at once; by the time Kruger knew him well enough to have realized what a shock his words must have caused he had forgotten the details of the conversation. In all likelihood he never did realize Dar's feelings at that moment. The answer was as noncommittal a one as the little pilot could manage at the time.

'I'm sure something can be worked out.'

The basic misunderstanding was more firmly entrenched than ever, at least on one side.

Nevertheless a personal friendship was growing between the two. At any rate Kruger will swear to this; he knows how he felt about Dar, and has some pretty good evidence on how the alien felt about him. One piece of that evidence came during the journey, at the time they reached the coast – which they finally did, with several of the twenty-two 'years' Dar had mentioned used up on the way.

The jungle had thinned somewhat, and patches of lava and volcanic ash were exposed in greater numbers. Evidently the local volcanoes had been active fairly recently as geological phenomena go. There was a great deal more climbing than there had been for some hundreds of miles. None of the elevations was more than a few hundred feet high, but they were frequently fairly steep, the angle of repose for loose volcanic ash is of the order of thirty degrees. Remembering what Dar had said earlier, Kruger suspected that they would come in sight of the sea before very long, but it took him by surprise just the same.

They had reached the brow of one of the hills, apparently just like all the others, when they came to a clearing larger than most which gave them their first real view ahead for many miles. There was plenty to see.

Two fairly large volcanic cones, nearly a thousand feet in height, lay on either side of their course to the north. Between these sparkled a field of intense blue that could only be the body of water they had sought so long. Even this, however, did not claim much of the attention of either traveler. Instead, they both spent several minutes staring at the area between them and the sea – a region nestling in the cleft between the volcanoes and spreading part way up their slopes. Then they turned to each other almost simultaneously and asked, 'Your people?'

IV

Archaeology

Strictly speaking, there were no people to be seen, but they had rather evidently been there. Cities do not build themselves, and the area between the cones was a city whether seen by human or Abyormenite eyes. None of the buildings seemed very high. Three or four stories, judging by the window arrangement, was the maximum. The windows were apparently quite large – of course, at this distance, small ones would be pretty hard to see – but there was no reflection suggesting that any of them were glazed. This might, of course, be due to chance, but with both suns in the sky and thousands of windows, the chance that none of them would be reflecting light toward the travelers seemed pretty remote.

Kruger realized almost instantly that if his ideas about Dar were correct, such a place would hardly have been made by the pilot's fellows. However, he waited for an answer. This was several seconds in coming; Dar was expecting a reply to his own question. Kruger gave in first.

'No, that place was not built by my people. I have never seen it or anything much like it before.'

Dar took this statement with some reservations, but in turn denied any knowledge of the place.

'The shelters at the ice cap are below,' he said. 'These are built on the surface. My own place, Kwarr, is also on the surface, but the shapes and colors of the buildings are very different. I have never seen a place like this – either.' Dar hoped the last word was not too obviously an after-thought.

'The place looks deserted to me. Let's look it over, anyway.'

It was here that Dar gave evidence of the friendship he now felt for the human being. Left to himself, of course, he would have avoided the city by as wide a margin as possible. He was not as happy as he might have been about Kruger's remark concerning the city's deserted state; the Teachers had been rather mysterious about some phases of this fire matter. In spite of his doubts, which came very close to being fears, Dar Lang Ahn made no objection to Kruger's proposal, and the two started down the hill toward the city.

There were several more miles of jungle to pass before they reached it. Dar noted with interest that even the usual animal sounds from the vegetation around them seemed to be lacking. If Kruger noticed this he did not mention it. He might not have noticed it, Dar realized; he had long since learned that his own hearing was considerably more acute than that of his friend. A lack of wild animals might just possibly mean that the city was not as deserted as Kruger believed, and Dar kept his crossbow ready.

No reason to use the weapon developed, however. Eventually the two stood with the jungle behind them and only a few hundred yards of relatively open ground between them and the first buildings. They stopped where they were and examined them carefully.

Still nothing moved and no suspicious sound reached even Dar's ears. After several minutes of waiting Kruger started forward once more. He did not look back or ask whether Dar was following, but the pilot stayed with him – with thoughts quite indescribable to a human being seething in his head. If anything was going to happen – if his illogical trust of Nils Kruger was unjustified – now was the time it would happen. He still held his bow but, to his credit, it was not aimed anywhere near Kruger.

The ground underfoot changed suddenly to firm pavement, on which Dar's claws scraped faintly. Like the buildings, the pavement was made of lava blocks carefully squared and fitted. The buildings were not as high as Kruger had guessed from a distance – that is, not as high in absolute units; they did have the three or four stories that the window arrangement had suggested. Each story, however, averaged about five feet in height.

The buildings themselves hardly constituted houses, at least from Kruger's point of view. They were much too open for that. Not only was more than half the wall space taken up by unglazed windows, but the ground level seemed to consist mostly of doorways. They did have solid roofs and would presumably be some protection against rain, but there their usability as dwelling places seemed to stop.

The doors themselves were a little odd, if they could be called doors. Kruger, after examining the outside of half a dozen buildings, found himself unable to decide whether the lower stories could be said to have a bell-shaped door every few feet, or that the outer walls consisted of oddly shaped pillars. The latter seemed a slightly better way to put it, since calling an opening four feet wide at the bottom, three and a half feet high, and shaped like a probability curve a 'door' seemed stretching the usual meaning of the word.

Both travelers realized one thing rather quickly; each had been telling the truth in denying any connection with the city. The ceilings were too low for human beings, and while Dar could have moved about inside any one chamber without trouble, the doors had certainly not been built for his species either. This realization almost made Dar uncock his weapon – but not quite.

Kruger wanted to investigate the interiors of some of the buildings, but at Dar's suggestion decided to get a better idea of the entire city first. They moved on down the street on which they had found themselves when they first reached pavement.

This led toward the sea but did not appear to reach it. The plan of the city was sufficiently complicated so that no one street appeared to go entirely across it. Kruger kept on toward the sea, believing that the largest and most informative buildings should be at the waterfront.

He was partly right. The city did extend down to the sea, with more imposing structures appearing as they proceeded. However, the largest of these were not at the waterfront. They were well out in the harbor.

It took some little time for Kruger to digest this fact. Dar was even more startled; he had been willing to accept evidence that Kruger had no connection with the builders of this city, but he had been perfectly sure that the builders themselves were fire-lovers – the location as well as the structural materials used seemed to prove that. Such a hypothesis, however, did not square too well with buildings seemingly built under water with complete disregard of the change of environment. Dar knew little about fire, but even he was aware of this inconsistency. He drew a little closer to his large friend.

'I guess this place must be older than I thought,' Kruger remarked slowly. 'It must have taken a long time to drop the coast or raise the water level enough to submerge those buildings. It couldn't have been a sudden shock or the place wouldn't be standing.'

'What are we going to do, then?'

'Well, I'd still like to go through one of these buildings. There's no telling what we'll find that might prove useful, and anyway I'm curious.'

Dar found that he was curious too, in spite of the weight of eight centuries of tradition, and he followed Kruger without objection as the boy walked over to a nearby building, dropped to his hands and knees, and crawled through one of the openings in the wall. Inside, Dar was able to stand up with reasonable head clearance; he walked around freely while Kruger remained on his knees for some time looking about him.

The open structure of the outer wall had the advantage of letting in plenty of light, but it also meant that they had seen most of what there was to see from outside. In this case that was very little. A room, or hallway, about fifteen feet wide ran the full length of the building parallel to the street; it was completely devoid of furnishings of any sort. The inner wall of this passage possessed doors similar in size and shape to those leading from the street but not nearly so many of them. Kruger chose one at random and crawled through. Dar followed.

This room was also long and narrow, but its longer dimension was away from the street rather than parallel to it; the door through which they had entered was in one end. It was much smaller than the outer hall. At the far end was a dais raised about a foot from the floor. At four points, seemingly at random, on the floor itself were dome-shaped structures about two feet high and eighteen inches in diameter with fluted sides that made them look like inverted jelly-molds. They were made of some light-colored stone; Kruger was just barely able to slide one along the floor when he got between it and the wall and used his legs. Their purpose was certainly not obvious. Other furniture seemed easier to explain; there was a rectangular metal affair with sliding drawers and a mirror-smooth surface made of highly polished obsidian set into one of the side walls. The mirror, if that was its intended function, was about the same size and shape as the doors.

The drawers of the bureau, or filing cabinet, or whatever it was were fastened by simple latches. The top one was empty. The second was nearly full of metal objects, about half of which had no obvious function, while the others might very well have been drawing instruments. There was a pair of dividers, a straight edge marked off as a scale, a semicircular protractor divided into eighteen major parts by deep engraving in the metal, and several tools apparently for both cutting and engraving. One of these, a scalpel-like affair with a double-edged blade and a handle about three inches long, he pointed out to Dar with the suggestion that he take it along; he had been using Kruger's knife on his meat ever since he had discovered the advantages of a metal blade. The handle was not of a shape to fit his hand very closely, but neither was that of Kruger's knife, and this at least was nearer to the proper size.

Further examination of the room disclosed a small pipe emerging from one wall, with what appeared to be a burner nozzle at the tip. Kruger deduced a gas lighting fixture, with the corollary that the builders of the city possessed eyes.

The dais at the rear of the room contained two shallow, bowl-shaped depressions a little under four feet in diameter which might have been flower pots or bathtubs for all Kruger could guess. Approaching it, however, he seemed to feel an increase in temperature. Since he was always soaked with perspiration anyway, he wasn't sure at first, but when he touched the wall he jerked his hand away again with a startled exclamation; the surface was burning hot.

Dar preserved himself from hysterics only by a major exercise of will. He wanted nothing to do with sources of heat, artificial or not, and he withdrew to the door while Kruger finished his investigations alone. These took some time, for just as he had decided that there was nothing more to see, his eye caught a metal plate set flush with the floor. This was only about an inch square, and almost featureless, but careful examination disclosed a pair of tiny perforations near each of its sides.

Kruger went back to the drawer that held the drawing instruments, secured the dividers, and by inserting their points in two of the holes finally managed to pry up the plate. Its metal took no visible damage from what was presumably unorthodox treatment. This fact, however, did not hold Kruger's attention at the time.

What caught his eye was simple enough – merely a dull-colored surface with two small holes. After regarding these silently for several seconds Kruger went to work once more with his improvised pry-bar, and in a few minutes the dull plate came out beside its cover. Underneath it was exactly what the boy had expected to see – two silvery wires surrounded and separated by a black, flexible coating and leading to metal cups. With all due respect to the possibilities inherent in different culture backgrounds Kruger felt safe in concluding that he had been dissecting a plug receptacle designed to deliver current to whatever the inhabitant of the room chose. In short, an electric socket.

He looked at the wires, and up to the pipe and jet on the wall, and back to the wires, whistling tunelessly. Then he replaced the covers and relieved Dar's mind by leaving the room.

Kruger was not frightened but was sorely puzzled by what he had seen. A city, still in good repair although without any present inhabitants, presumably abandoned not long ago – yet running down into the ocean for a distance that implied centuries of land sinking, equipped with gas-lighting and electric wiring in the same building.

Dar was not able to throw light on the question. He recognized the weight of his friend's arguments in all matters except the gas-electricity question and was willing to accept a qualified opinion there. Kruger explained that situation as well as he could while they rested in the shade of the building's entrance hall. Theer was practically at his closest, and travel was impractical anyway. Dar understood without any trouble that a gas light was a form of fire and led the conversation hastily on to the question of electricity. Kruger did not expect to get much of this concept across and was pleasantly surprised to discover that Dar appeared to be following quite well. The explanation was long, of course, but by the time Theer had dropped once more behind the hills the boy was as sure as he ever became that he was understood.

The question then arose of just what they should do about it all. Kruger thought it would be best for them to examine at least one or two more buildings to make sure that the one they had seen was typical; then they would have some more or less organized information, which Dar could give to his people. Kruger's chance to report it to *his* people seemed a good deal more remote, but perhaps he could use the knowledge himself.

Dar had a more serious problem. His interest had been aroused, of course; he would like, in one way, to bring a group of his people and perhaps some Teachers back to this place so that they could learn more about the electricity that Kruger had described. At the same time there was the fact that he had violated firm and long-standing instructions – not merely orders of the Teachers but written material handed down in books from the time before his people were born – against having anything to do with fire. There could be no doubt that whoever had built this place had never heard of those laws. If Dar made a complete report at the Ice Ramparts would the result be an expedition, or censure? This was his problem, of course; he could not ask Kruger for advice. The human being obviously had never heard of the law either but could hardly be blamed for that; his background was different.

Still, what he was to do with the information made little difference in what he should do now about acquiring more. He followed Kruger's lead, therefore, and some hours were spent in going through a number of the structures.

These were no more identical than the buildings of a terrestrial city would have been, but none of the variations were particularly startling. The gas pipe-electric wiring anomaly seemed to exist everywhere; Dar pointed out that the pipes were only in inner rooms, whereas electrical outlets frequently appeared in entrance halls and even on outer walls. There seemed to be some prejudice on the part of the city dwellers against the use of electricity for lighting. Kruger refused to credit Dar's suggestion that they might not have invented electric lights. His opinion was that anyone who could construct a dependable current source, sufficient for a city, could at least strike an arc with it. He may have been right.

Although Theer had not been down very long, several thunder showers had passed over the city while they were investigating. When the two decided that they had seen enough and should probably continue their journey they found that another of the storms was just breaking. It would not have been impossible to travel in the rain – Kruger was usually soaking wet anyway – but visibility was not good and they decided to wait.

Like most of the others the shower did not last too long, and presently the sky began to lighten. Dar replaced his pack on his shoulders and they started out while rain was still hissing down. It struck the pavement loudly enough to make conversation difficult, and rivulets of water gurgled down the slope of the gutterless street toward the sea. Probably this was what kept Dar's ears from warning them. At any rate that was what he claimed later.

Whatever the reason, neither of them knew they were not alone until the company showed itself deliberately. The interruption to their journey involved both word and action; the word was 'Stop!' and the action took the form of a crossbow bolt which splintered against the street in front of them. Dar and Kruger, realizing that the projectile must have come from above, rapidly covered with their eyes the roof edges in their vicinity, but nothing moved.

The word had been in Dar's language, so the pilot took it on himself to answer. He very carefully refrained from raising his own crossbow. 'What do you want?'

'You must come with us.'

'Why?' Kruger had understood enough of the foregoing conversation to be able to ask this question.

'You are ———— ———— ———— the city.' The first and last parts of this sentence were all the boy could follow.

'What's their trouble?' asked Kruger.

'The trouble is ours. We are – we did – coming in the city was bad.'

'Why?'

'They do not say.' Dar did not mention that he thought he knew; this was no time for lengthy explanations.

'Do you have any ideas as to who these are?'

'Ideas, but I don't know.'

'What do you think we should do?'

'What they say.' Dar, standing in the middle of a bare street, was in no mood for a crossbow duel with an unknown number of antagonists, all under excellent cover. Nevertheless there was one question in his mind.

'What will be done to us for entering your city?'

'Whatever the Teachers say. It is not for us to decide.'

'What has happened in the past?'

'No one has disobeyed a Teacher for many years. At first, when people were young, some did; they suffered, and did not offend again.'

'But suppose we did not know we were offending?'

'You must have known; you are a person. The thing with you may be forgiven. The Teachers will decide.'

'But I never heard of this place; my Teachers never told me of it, and it is not in the books. How could I know?'

'You must have very stupid Teachers. Maybe you will not be blamed for that.' Dar was sufficiently indignant to make a retort which Kruger would have discouraged, had he been able to follow the conversation at all closely.

'Am I from your city?'

'No.'

'Did your Teachers tell you of my city?'

'No.'

'Then there must be two sets of stupid Teachers on Abyormen.' If Kruger had understood this remark he would have confidently expected to see it answered with a volley of crossbow bolts, but nothing of the sort happened. The unseen speaker simply returned to the original question.

'Will you come with us without fighting?'

'We will come.' Dar made the answer without any further consultation with Kruger. After all, the boy had already asked Dar what should be done, and presumably had no opinion of his own.

With Dar Lang Ahn's words the openings in the surrounding buildings gave forth some fifty beings. Kruger was able to take the revelation without particular surprise, but Dar was shocked beyond measure to find that the attackers were identical physically with himself. He was a well-traveled individual; he had met, on his official trips to the Ice Ramparts and elsewhere, members of his race from several score cities scattered over Abyormen's globe, and he had never heard of any except the uncaught savages living out of touch with the Teacher-ruled cities. Still, there was no questioning the facts; the beings surrounding him might have come straight from any city he had visited. Even the carrying harness they wore was virtually identical with his own, and the crossbows borne by most of them might have been made by Merr Kra Lar, home in Kwarr.

One who seemed to be in charge spoke as soon as he came up to them.

'You used a word that I never heard a little while ago. What is a book?' This question was not understood by Kruger; Dar had never told him what was in the pack he kept so carefully by him. Dar might not have been surprised at his human companion's ignorance of such matters, but that a member of his own species should never have heard of a book was quite unthinkable. Life could not go on without a record of the life that had gone before!

When he recovered from the astonishment that the question had caused him he tried to explain, but his listener seemed unable to digest the concept of writing. In an effort to clarify the point Dar removed one of the books from his pack and held it open before him while he tried to explain the significance of the marks, but this produced a result he had not foreseen.

'I do not quite understand why you need such a thing when you can ask Teachers for what you need to know, but perhaps our Teachers can tell why you do. We will show them your books; give them to me.'

V

Confiscation

There was nothing else to do; one crossbow can do nothing against two-score. For an instant Dar thought of making a wild break through the surrounding group to the shelter of the nearest building, but he abandoned the idea. Alive, he might recover the books.

'I would prefer to carry them and show them to your Teachers myself,' he suggested.

'There is no need to bring you to them at all unless they order it,' was the reply, 'but they will certainly want to see your books. I will go to them and show them the books and ask what is to be done to you.'

'But I want to see them, to explain why I did not know I was breaking their law.'

'I will tell them that. Since you have broken it what you want is not important.'

'But won't they want to see my companion? You have already said he was different from people.'

'Yes, I will take him.'

'Then you will need me. He knows very little proper speech, and I know some of his words.'

'If the Teachers wish to speak as well as look, and find that they need your aid, you will be sent for.' The speaker held out a hand and Dar reluctantly handed over his priceless pack.

Marching orders were given and the group headed back the way Dar and Kruger had come. However, instead of turning inland when they reached the avenue the pair had followed to the sea, they crossed it and headed toward the seaward side of one of the volcanoes – the one that had been on the left as the wanderers approached the city.

For the first time Dar regretted that he had not insisted on learning more of Kruger's language. The problem was to get the books back and get out of reach of these people, the sooner the better; failing that, to get out himself and get a report to the Ice Ramparts telling of their location. That *had* to be done in less than twenty years; no alternative was thinkable. With luck, Nils Kruger would help. Just now it would hardly be advisable to discuss the matter with him; too many of the words they would have to use would be understood by those surrounding them. Later, perhaps they would be left alone; if not, Dar would simply have to make use of the little English he had mastered. In that connection an idea struck him and he spoke to Kruger, using his English vocabulary to the utmost.

'Nils, talk while going. Your tongue. About anything.' He could not be more explicit; he wanted Kruger to discuss what they saw as they went along, in the hope that an occasional word would bear a sufficiently obvious meaning, when considered in connection with the words Dar already knew, for the native to grasp it. Kruger did not understand this, but he could see that Dar had something definite in mind, and endeavored to please. Since the most obvious subject for speech was just what Dar wanted, things did not go too badly.

It was a method which would not have been very practical, used by most human beings, but with the sort of memory Dar possessed it was not completely unreasonable. Even so, the little pilot's vocabulary increased very, very slowly indeed and frequently had to be corrected.

While this was going on the group passed the volcano, following the narrow beach of pulverized ash between it and the sea. On the other side the jungle came down practically to the shore in scattered tufts of vegetation, separated by piles of ejecta and occasional small sheets of lava. For a couple of hours they threaded their way through these patches of jungle, gradually working away from the sea. The ground did not rise again; they remained about at sea level and Kruger would not have been surprised to encounter another swamp. Instead they finally ran into a region of fog.

This was the first time in his months on Abyormen that Kruger had encountered this phenomenon and he was more than a little surprised. It did not seem to go with the air temperature. Nevertheless the drifting wisps of water vapor were there and as the group advanced they grew larger and more frequent. The boy had a sufficiently good background of physics to attribute the whole thing to one of two causes – either something cooling the nearly saturated air, or a body of water whose temperature was higher than that of the air above it. He was not too startled, therefore, when the second of these situations materialized. Pools of water appeared on both sides of their path, and presently the way led into a clearing two or three hundred yards across, dotted with more bodies of water which were giving off thick plumes of vapor. Some were bubbling violently, others lying quiet in the sunlight, but all seemed to be hot. Dar was visibly nervous – visibly to their captors, that is; Kruger still did not recognize the symptoms. The being who carried the pack was moved to inquire about it.

'Has your companion said something to trouble you?'

'No,' replied Dar, 'but it seems to me that if anyone is trespassing on forbidden ground, it is this group, right now.'

'Why? No one has forbidden this area; we were told to live here.'

'By your Teachers?'

'Of course.'

'With all this smoke?'

'It is water-smoke; it hurts no one. See, your friend is not bothered by it.'

Kruger had stepped aside to one of the hot pools, watched alertly but not prevented by his captors, and was examining both the water and the rock around it carefully. Up to now he had seen no limestone on the planet, but this pool was rimmed with travertine. The rim was a foot or so higher than the rock a short distance away.

Kruger looked over these factors and nodded to himself. Then he turned back to the rest – his captors had stopped, with remarkable complaisance, to let him finish his examination – and asked the individual with the pack, 'How often do these ———?' He had no word for the verb he wanted, but swung his hands up and outward in a fashion that was clear to everyone but Dar. The leader answered without apparent hesitation.

'No law. Sometimes once in two or three years, sometimes two or three dozen times a year.'

'How high?'

'Sometimes just overflows, sometimes tree-high. Lots of noise, lots of steam.'

There was nothing surprising, of course, about geysers in a volcanic area. However, Kruger had an impression that savage and semicivilized races usually avoided them, and he spent some time wondering whether the answer he had received told him anything about these beings. He decided ruefully that for practical purposes it didn't.

By the time he had reached this conclusion the journey was almost over. They had crossed the clearing where the geysers were located, and in the jungle on the far side was a collection of structures which proved to be the 'city' of their captors. It told a good deal more about the creatures than their words had.

The buildings were plain thatched huts, somewhat more complicated than the ones Kruger had built during the midsummer seasons along their route but much simpler than some that may be found in African kraals. The leader called out as they approached the village, and what turned out to be the rest of the population emerged from the huts to see them arrive.

Kruger had read his share of adventure novels and acquired most of what he thought he knew of primitive races from these. As a result he became distinctly uneasy about one aspect of the crowd which gathered about the captives. They were all the same size, as nearly as his eye could distinguish. The first impression this gave the boy was that this was a war party, with women and children strictly left at home. He relaxed slightly when he saw that only those who had been in the party that captured him and Dar were armed. However, the silence of the newcomers rather affected him after a while. Logically, they should all have been asking questions about the captives; instead they were merely staring at Kruger.

It was Dar who broke the silence, not because he particularly minded being ignored in the circumstances but because he was worried about his books.

'Well, when do we see these Teachers of yours?' he asked. The eyes of the being who had the pack swiveled toward him.

'When they say. We plan to eat first, but while food is being prepared I will report our return to them.'

One of the people who had not been with the party spoke up. 'It is reported; we heard you coming and could tell by the alien's voice that you had succeeded.'

Kruger understood enough of this sentence to see why the villagers were less surprised at their arrival than might have been expected. The party must have been sent out to capture the wanderers; Dar and he must have been seen crossing the clearing to the city. The times involved were reasonable.

'The Teacher who answered said that the party and the captives might eat and that both captives were then to be brought to him.' Neither Kruger nor Dar made any objection to this, though the boy had his usual doubts about the food.

Some of it, which was served first, was vegetation; it came in great baskets which were placed on the ground. Everyone sat around them and helped himself, so Kruger had no difficulty in selecting what he knew to be safe for him. While this was going on, however, a number of villagers had gone out to the geysers carrying other baskets containing cuts of meat. They returned with these and replaced the empty vegetable containers with those they had carried, and Kruger found to his dismay that the meat was hot – too hot to handle comfortably. Apparently it had been cooked in one of the springs.

Both he and Dar were still hungry, but neither dared try the meat after Kruger's earlier experience. They watched gloomily while the villagers gulped it down, until a point struck the boy.

'Dar, these people are the same as you. The cooking doesn't spoil the food for them; why don't you eat, at least? One of us should keep his strength up.' Dar was a little doubtful about his identity with the villagers, but the other point touched his sense of duty and after wrestling with his conscience for a few moments he agreed that his friend was right. His uneasiness as he ate was clear to the people around him and seemed to cause more surprise than Kruger's appearance had done.

Inevitably, he was asked what the trouble was and the surprised eyes turned back to Kruger as Dar related his unfortunate experience with cooked meat.

'I do not understand how that can be,' remarked one of the villagers. 'We have always cooked our meat; it is the rule. Perhaps your friend used a spring which had poison in the water.'

'He did not use a spring at all. There was only the river, which was cold, and we had nothing to hold water – at least, nothing big enough.'

'Then how could he possibly have cooked the meat?'

'He held it over a fire.'

The sudden buzz of conversation which greeted this word seemed to Dar to represent the first reasonable reaction he had obtained from these people, but he quickly found that he had been misunderstood.

'Was the fire near here?' was the next question. 'We are ordered to tell the Teachers whenever a volcano other than the ones near the Great City becomes active.'

'It was not a volcano. He made the fire himself.' The eyes swiveled back to Nils Kruger and a dead silence ensued. No one asked Dar to repeat his words; the average Abyormenite had too much confidence in his own hearing and memory to suppose that he might have misunderstood such a simple sentence. There was a distinct atmosphere of disbelief, however. Dar would almost have wagered his books on the question that would come next. He would have won.

'How is this done? He looks strange but not powerful.' The last word did not mean purely physical power; it was a general term covering all sorts of ability.

'He has a device which makes a very tiny fire when he touches it properly. With this he lights small bits of wood and when these burn he uses them to light larger ones.'

The creature had doubts. So did most of the others; there was a general grunt of agreement when he said, 'I will have to see this.' Dar carefully refrained from giving openly his equivalent of a smile.

'Will your Teachers be willing to wait until he has shown you, or should this thing be shown to them also?' This question caused some rapid discussion among the villagers, which culminated in a rapid journey by one of them to a small hut which stood near one side of the cluster of dwellings. Dar watched with interest as the fellow disappeared inside, and endeavored to decipher the faint mutters of speech that came out. He failed in this attempt and had to await the messenger's return.

'The Teacher says to bring wood, such as the strange one needs, and let him see the building of the fire.' The natives scattered at once to their huts, while Dar filled Kruger in on the numerous items he had missed in the conversation. By the time this was accomplished wood was arriving from all directions.

None of it had come straight from the jungle; it had evidently been cut some time before and been drying in the huts. There was no reason from the shape of the pieces to suppose that it had been originally obtained for firewood, and every reason from the background of the people to suppose that it had not, but there it was. Kruger selected a few pieces and shaved them into slivers with his knife, then made up a small armful of larger material and stood up, signifying that he was ready. Dar started to lead the way toward the hut where the messenger had gone.

Instantly he was interrupted.

'Not that way, stranger!'

'But is not that where your Teachers are?'

'In a little place like that? Certainly not. They *talk* there, it is true, but they wish to *see* you and your fire-maker. Come this way.' The speaker started to retrace the path by which they had come to the village and the prisoners followed him. The rest of the population trailed along.

A well-marked path wound among the hot springs. The captives followed it toward an unusually large pool near the side of the clearing away from the now distant sea. Apparently this one overflowed more frequently than the others or else had a greater supply of mineral in whatever subterranean source it sprang from, for its edge was nearly three feet high. The water within the rim steamed and bubbled furiously.

The area around the pool was clear except at one point, where an object that looked like a detached lump of travertine projected from the rim. It was dome-shaped except for the flattened top and was about as high as the rim and perhaps five feet in diameter. Its surface was mostly smooth, but there were a number of deep pits scattered around its sides.

Kruger would not have looked at it twice, except for the fact that they were stopped in front of it and the entire population of the village gathered around. This caused the boy to examine the outcrop more closely and he decided that someone had done a rather skillful bit of masonry. Presumably the Teachers were inside; the small holes must serve as spy-ports and ventilators. No entrance was visible. Perhaps it was inside the pool rim, where he could not see, or even some distance away and connected by a tunnel. He was not surprised to hear a voice come from the mound of stone.

'Who are you?' The question was not ambiguous; the grammatical arrangements of the language left no doubt that Kruger was the one addressed. For an instant the boy was not sure how to answer, then he decided simply to tell the truth.

'I am Nils Kruger, pilot-cadet of the cruiser *Alphard*.' He had to translate the nouns into similes in the Abyormenite language but was reasonably satisfied with the job. The next question made him wonder whether he was doing the right thing, however.

'When do you die?'

Kruger found himself at a slight loss for an answer to this question. It seemed to be nothing but a simple, straightforward one about how long he had to live, but he found himself unable to answer it.

'I do not know,' was the only response he could give. This led to a silence from the stone at least as long as the one his own hesitation had caused. With the next words the hidden speaker gave the impression of one who has shelved, for the time at least, a puzzling subject.

'You are supposed to be able to make fire. Do so.' Kruger, completely at a loss as to where he stood with the invisible questioner, obeyed. There was no difficulty to the job; the wood was dry and Arren furnished all the radiation the little battery needed. The snap of the high-tension sparks sent the nearer villagers back in momentary alarm, though to Kruger it sounded much like Dar's crossbow. The shavings caught instantly and sixty seconds later a very respectable little fire was blazing on the stone a few yards from the rock shelter of the Teachers. Throughout the operation questions had kept coming and Kruger had been answering them: why the wood had to be small at first, why he had chosen wood that was dry, and what was the source of the sparks. The answering was extremely difficult. Kruger faced roughly the same problem as would a high-school student asked to give a lecture on high-school-level physics or chemistry in French after perhaps a year's study of the language. As a result he was still trying to improvise signs and words when the fire burned out.

The creature within the rock shelter finally satisfied himself on fires – or, more probably, on what Kruger knew about them – and proceeded to a matter which seemed to interest him more.

'Are you from another world traveling about Theer, or from one circling Arren?'

Dar simply did not understand, but Kruger understood much too well. He was thunderstruck, after the usual fashion of human beings who find their pet theories suddenly untenable.

'Witch-doctor my eye!' he muttered under his breath, but was able to think of no coherent answer for the moment.

'What was that?' Kruger had forgotten for a moment that hyper-acute hearing seemed rather common on this world.

'An expression of surprise, in my own language,' he answered hastily. 'I do not think I understood your question.'

'I think you did.' Unhuman though the accents were Kruger had a sudden picture of a stern schoolmaster on the other side of the barrier, and decided that he might as well continue his policy of frankness.

'No, I do not come from Arren; I do not even know whether it has any planets, and Theer has no others.' The listener accepted the new word without comment; its meaning must have been obvious enough from context. 'My home world travels about a sun much fainter than Arren, but much brighter than Theer, whose distance from this system I cannot give in your language.'

'Then there are other suns?'

'Yes.'

'Why did you come here?'

'We were exploring – learning what other worlds and their suns were like.'

'Why are you alone?'

Kruger related in detail the accident that had dropped his space-suited form into a mud pot, the natural conclusion of his friends that he had perished, and his survival by means of a fortuitous tree root.

'When will your people return?'

'I do not expect them back at all. They had no reason to believe this world had inhabitants; the cities of Dar's people, which he has told me about, were not seen, and the village of these people of yours could not possibly have been detected. In any case the ship was on a survey trip which would last for quite a number of your years, and it might be fully as long after it returned home before the data on this system was even examined. Even then there will be no particular reason to come back; there is much to do a great deal closer to home.'

'Then to your people you are dead already.'

'Yes, I'm afraid so.'

'Do you know how your flying vessels work?' Kruger hesitated at this question, then remembered that he had described himself already as a pilot cadet.

'I know the forces and technology involved, yes.'

'Then why have you not tried to build one and return to your world?'

'Knowledge and ability are two different things. I know how this world came into being, but couldn't do the job myself.'

'Why are you with this one you call Dar?'

'I met him. Two people can get along better than one. Also, I was looking for a place on this world cool enough for a human being, and he said something about an ice cap to which he was going. That was enough for me.'

'What would you do about others of his kind if you met them at this ice cap?'

'Endeavor to get along with them, I suppose. In a way, they'd be the only people I'd have; I'd treat them as mine, if they'd allow it.' There was a pause after this answer, as though the hidden Teachers were conferring or considering. Then the questions resumed, but this time were directed at Dar Lang Ahn.

In reply, he stated that he was a pilot, normally assigned to the route between the city of Kwarr and the Ice Ramparts. The questioners asked for the location of the city, which Dar had to describe in great detail. He and Kruger both wondered whether the Teachers were really ignorant of it, or testing Dar's veracity.

No suggestion was made that Dar was not a native of the planet, and as the questioning went on Kruger grew more and more puzzled. It was some time before it occurred to him that since Dar was obviously of the same species as these people they must also be from another world. Why they were living as near-savages on this one was a mystery, but perhaps they had been marooned through damage to their ship. That would account for the questions about his own ability to build a space flier. In fact, for a moment it seemed to account for everything except why the 'Teachers' remained in concealment.

'What are these "books" you were carrying and about which you seem so anxious?' This question snapped Kruger's wandering attention back to the present. He had been wanting to ask the same thing for some time.

'They are the records of what our people have learned and done during their lives. The records which came down to us from those who went before were returned to safety at the Ramparts long ago, after we had learned what they contained, but it is the law that each people shall make its own books, as well, which must then be saved as those made before have been.'

'I see. An interesting idea; we shall have to consider it further. Now, another matter: you have given some of our people the impression that you consider it unlawful to have dealings with fire. Is that correct?'

'Yes.'

'Why?'

'Our Teachers have told us, and our books from times past have said the same.'

'Did they say it would kill you?'

'There was that, but it was something more. Being killed is one thing – we all die when the time comes, anyway – but this seemed to be something worse. I guess you're deader when you die from heat, or something. Neither the Teachers nor the books ever made it very clear.'

'Yet you accompany this being who makes fires whenever he wishes.'

'It worried me at first, but I decided that since he is not a real person he must have a different set of laws. I felt that bringing information about him back to my people at the Ice Ramparts would outweigh any violations I might commit in other directions. Besides, I kept as far as possible from the fires he made.'

There was another fairly lengthy silence before the Teacher spoke again. When he did, his tone and words were quite encouraging at first.

'You have been informative, cooperative, and helpful – both of you,' the hidden being said. 'We appreciate it; therefore we thank you.

'You will remain with our people for the time being. They will see that you are comfortable and fed; I fear we can do nothing now about the coolness the alien wants, but even that may be arranged in time.

'Place the books and the fire-lighting machine on the stone, and let everyone depart.'

VI

Investigation

A period of alternating rain and sunshine and the brief return and departure of Theer left the two travelers with the impression that the 'Teachers' of
the tribe which had captured them might be well disposed but were rather
opinionated beings. When they said anything it was so. Unfortunately they
had said that Nils Kruger and Dar Lang Ahn should remain available for talk,
and the village of creatures who obeyed them implicitly were quite able to
make it so.

Actually they were not completely prisoners. They could wander where
they pleased within the village and its immediate environs, except into the
hut where villagers went to talk to the Teachers. Also, when the unseen
beings learned about Kruger's watch, which was during the second interview,
they quite obligingly agreed that the two need not even remain nearby, provided that they appear at certain regular intervals which were determined by
mutual agreement on the spot. There was, Kruger realized, some pretty good
psychology at work; at the same time this freedom was granted, a half-prom-
ise was made to Dar that his books would be returned before too long – the
time was left vague. 'Just now they were being examined with great interest.'
Kruger noted that no request was made for Dar to give lessons in his written
language, but the important fact was that Dar was chained to the neighborhood by that promise as securely as though metallic shackles had been used.
He refused to consider for a moment any suggestion which involved desert-
ing his precious books.

More as an experiment than anything else, Kruger asked on one occasion
whether the law of the village forbidding entrance to the city applied to the
captives. He expected a curt refusal and was pleasantly surprised when they
were allowed to go there, on condition that nothing was removed or injured.
He said nothing about the knife that Dar had appropriated and cheerfully
made the required promise.

Dar was afraid that the villagers would resent this; it did seem a little odd,
permitting the captives to do something that was illegal for the captors. However, no sign of such a feeling appeared and they finally concluded that the
word of the Teachers must be the absolutely final authority for these people.

They took advantage of their permission several times, but found nothing
more surprising than the things that had turned up during their first

inspection. Kruger made a careful and well-planned search for the generating station that supplied power to the city wiring, but failed to find it. He was disappointed; he would have liked very much to know what the source of power of the city builders might have been.

The Teachers never asked how closely their condition was being followed, though one day the two had a bad scare during one of the conversations.

'Dar,' the speaker had asked, 'what is the substance of which those harness buckles of yours are made?' The pilot appeared not to be bothered by the question, but Kruger suddenly realized what might lie behind it and answered hastily, 'He had them before we came; they did not come from the city.'

'We realize that,' came the answer, 'but that is not what we wanted to know. Dar?'

'They are of iron,' the pilot replied, truthfully.

'So we thought. Would you mind explaining how a person who is forbidden to have anything to do with fire, and whose people all live under the same law, came by such articles?'

'I can tell, but not explain,' Dar answered precisely. 'I found them. A great deal of such material was found near and in the city when we first lived. We took what we wanted of it, since there was no law forbidding it. I did not know that iron had any connection with fire.' He looked uneasily down at the buckles.

This conversation ended there; as a matter of fact it was violently interrupted. One of the geysers a scant thirty yards from where the prisoners sat chose this moment to release some of its energy, and large quantities of boiling water began to appear. Dar and Kruger did not wait to say any farewells, they went, straight away from the disturbance and as rapidly as the clouds of vapor permitted.

Twice Kruger tripped over irregularities in the rock; both times he struggled back to his feet with scalding water almost on him. For what seemed to them both like hours, but which probably was rather less than a minute, no thought entered either of their minds except that of self-preservation; then they were safely beyond the reach of the disturbance.

Immediately, the instant they were sure of this, the two stopped; they both had the same thought, but it no longer dealt with their own safety. For a full hour, until long after the vapor had cleared away, they waited and watched, hoping to get a glimpse of the Teachers who would presumably have been driven out in the same way as their captives. Nothing moved in all that time, however, and when the clearing of the air was complete they could see the dome of rock sitting apparently unchanged with no sign that anyone or anything had moved in its vicinity. They went back and circled the pool beside which it lay, so as to see it from every side, for now if ever the entrance would be visible, but they found nothing.

Both were a trifle surprised when, on their return after the usual interval, discussion went on as though nothing had happened. Kruger wished he dared ask how the Teachers had escaped, but somehow failed to bring himself to the point of actually raising the question.

By this time he had told a good deal about his people. Dar had done the same. Kruger's facility with the language had grown far more rapidly than in any similar period of his companionship with Dar alone.

Dar, by this time, had realized his original error about Kruger, though his ideas of astronomy were distinctly sketchy. The boy, however, was by no means convinced that Dar and the villagers were natives of the planet; the Teachers had always shied away from direct answers on that subject and there was no direct evidence which tended to disprove the original notion that they were maroons like himself – none, at least, that Kruger recognized as such.

Their stay in the village was not entirely composed of exploration and conversation. Several times life became fairly exciting, in fact. On one occasion Kruger fell into a concealed pit which had rather obviously been made to trap animals; only the fact that it seemed to have been made for rather large game enabled him to miss the sharpened stake in the bottom. Again, while leaving a building at one edge of the city well up the side of one of the volcanoes, Kruger and Dar were nearly engulfed by a slide of volcanic ash which had apparently been loosened by recent rain. They had ducked back into the building barely in time, and afterward had to make their way painfully – for Kruger, that is – through the structure to find an exit on the other side, the uphill doors having been completely blocked.

Several times Dar renewed his request for the return of the books; his time was running out, in more senses than one. The Teachers still professed interest in the volumes, however, and failed to give any definite time when the interest might be expected to wane.

Several times when he and Dar were alone Kruger suggested, more or less forcefully, that they simply fail to return to the village some day, get to the Ice Ramparts, and return with enough assistance to compel the return of Dar's property; but the pilot refused to leave. It took a fairly complex combination of circumstances to change his mind.

They had covered the greater part of the city which lay toward the village but had done virtually nothing with the other side. Actually there was little reason to suppose that it would provide anything they had not seen already, and even Kruger was getting a little weary of rambling through deserted buildings, when Dar noticed that one street seemed to lead off from the farther side of the city around the second volcano, which they had never reached. This street was not noticeable from sea level; Dar saw it from the edge of the city well up the other hill – quite close, in fact, to the place where they had nearly been buried. The two decided to investigate immediately.

It took some time to descend one volcano, cross the level portion of the city, and climb the other to the point which Dar's memory indicated as being the start of the street in question; when they reached it, enough time had passed to suggest that they might possibly be late for their next conversation with the Teachers. They had always been careful not to overstay their leave, feeling quite logically that their freedom might suffer should they do so, but this time they decided to take the chance.

The street went up the hill rather steeply, angling at first toward the seaward side of the cone. From below they had not been able to tell whether it formed a switchback leading to the top of the volcano or a spiral going around it; they learned fairly soon that it was the latter.

They rather hoped to get to the top so that they could get a better idea of the local geography than their walks had given them. Dar could see no sense in building a street that led to a mountain top, but was willing to suspend judgment until the evidence was in.

'In any case,' the pilot pointed out, 'if you really want to get up there, there's no need to follow a road. We've both climbed hills before.'

'Yes, but I don't know about climbing this hill. Remember what happened over on the other side of town. It would be rather bad if another of those landslides started and we had no building to duck into.'

'I don't think we need worry. The ground on this cone looks a lot firmer than that on the other, and I haven't seen any marks suggesting recent landslides.'

'I didn't see any on the other side, either – and probably no one has been climbing this. Our disturbance might be all it was waiting for.'

They might have spared themselves the discussion; they never reached the top. The road ceased to climb at about the time the last of the city except the submerged portion was lost to view, and without even discussing the question the two continued to follow the paved way. The view was already extensive; when they looked back the bottom of the harbor revealed the extent to which it must once have been dry land, as the street pattern of the city showed through the clear water. Ahead, the nearly straight coastline vanished in distance many miles away.

Inland, the jungle extended as far as the eye could reach. Even from this height – which was not, after all, very great – they could not begin to see across the distance separating them from the lava field where they had met. There seemed no reason, so far, for building the road at all; it seemed to lead nowhere. With mounting curiosity they hastened along it.

A quarter of a mile beyond the point where even the harbor had vanished from view they came upon the crater. There was virtually no warning; one moment the hillside sloped up and down away from the road at the usual angle; the next, the region downhill had vanished and the road was running perilously along the edge of a three-hundred-foot cliff. A heavy metal guard rail was there and the two approached this and leaned over.

The crater, if that was what it had once been, was not in the top of the hill, but well to one side; the road had led them to the highest point of its rim and the cone went up several hundred more feet behind them as they stood looking into it. It was not a very orthodox crater; the inner walls were sheer cliffs, which at first made Kruger feel decidedly insecure. Then he saw that the inner wall of the pit was not made of the same material as the hillside in general, and very slowly it dawned on him that the whole thing was artificial.

The walls were of concrete, or some equivalent composition. They had been shaped by tools. The bottom was not the tapering cone of the usual small crater but neither was it completely level. There was a small lake, and vegetation floored most of the rest of the area. Around the edge the concrete wall material seemed to extend horizontally for a short distance, and on this there was no vegetation. Both watchers were able to see the mouths of caves or tunnels opening from the wall onto this ramp, and with one mind they started looking for a way down.

There was nothing remotely resembling a ladder anywhere on the inner wall, so the logical thing to do seemed to be to follow the road, which must have been built in connection with this pit This quickly gave promise of being the right course, as the path, instead of continuing around the mountain at the height which it had maintained for so long, began to curve downward in order to follow the rim of the pit. At the steepest part of the downhill slope the smooth surface of the pavement changed for about two hundred yards into something that might have been steps with very narrow treads and low risers or simply a corrugation to provide traction.

Shortly after this they reached a point where the trees grew right up to the edge of the road, overhanging both it and the pit. This had prevented their learning the course of the road from above; as it turned out, it had also prevented their seeing a number of buildings which were spaced at fairly regular intervals down the slope. These appeared to be built in the same style as the ones in the city except that they were all single-storied. Dar and Kruger wondered whether to examine them in detail now or find where the road led and come back later if there was time. The second alternative won.

However, it did not take long to find where the road led. Another two hundred yards down the slope it opened out into a paved space which Kruger labeled 'parking lot' in his mind without even thinking. Several minutes of thought and investigation revealed no better name for it, so the two explorers returned to the buildings. Once inside the first of these, all recollection of the fact that they were already late for their appointment with the Teachers vanished from Kruger's mind.

His first supposition was that this must be the city power plant. An electric generator is going to look pretty much the same whoever builds it and whatever causes it to turn, and the objects in the first building were quite plainly electric generators. They were large, though Kruger lacked the knowledge to tell whether they were large enough to supply the whole city. Their great armatures were mounted on vertical axles, and apparently the source of mechanical energy was below ground level. With this in mind the two made a rapid search and were rewarded by finding the head of a ramp that led downward as expected.

The only difficulty was that the ramp was both narrow and low. Kruger would have to go down on his hands and knees, and the slope was steep. Even if he worked his way down backward return would be difficult if not impossible, for the ramp was floored with smooth metal and traction was very poor. Dar was in even worse case; the size question bothered him less, but his claws for the first time in the history of their acquaintance were less suited to the situation than Kruger's feet. Kruger finally decided that discretion was the better part of valor, and postponed exploration of the lower level until the other buildings had been examined.

This took some time, for the place was fascinating. All sorts of technical equipment were to be found. All of it was much too big to move, to Kruger's disappointment, but it left no doubt that the city builders were a highly civilized race. The generators and motors, furnaces and machine tools told all that was really important to know about them – except what had forced them to leave, to abandon their city and their equipment. War would have ruined both; plague should have left some traces of bodies, unless they were soft-bodied beings such as mollusks. Kruger, as a young man who had grown up on Earth during the first decade of interstellar exploration, was quite prepared to believe this last possibility, but even he did not take it for granted.

Always there were the conflicting facts: a partly submerged city which must have been abandoned for centuries – and machines with only a thin film of dust, pavings still free of vegetation, walls straight and uncracked with sound mortar and firm masonry which must have been maintained with care until fairly recently. It looked as though most of the machines would run if they were simply cleaned and power supplied to them.

The group of buildings, given time, would have served as a school in which any competent archaeologist could have learned practically anything which could be asked about their makers; one of them, in fact, might almost have been designed as a school. It contained a beautiful relief model of the two volcanoes, the city between, the harbor – though it did not show any water level – and the great pit beside which the building itself stood. In addition, many of the machines present full-scale in the other buildings were here in model form; the two investigators would probably have spent hours here alone had it not been for one fact.

There was another ramp leading downward from the single floor of this structure, and this time it was large enough for Dar to walk upright without difficulty. Also, its slope was much less than that of the preceding one, and the floor formed of a rough composition in which the little native's claws could readily find a grip. Finally, it led in toward the pit; and without further ado, once this fact was digested, the two started down its gentle slope.

The light was not good, but enough came from the building they had left to enable them to see any branches in the tunnel. For some time there was none; then a number of open doorways appeared on each side. Judging by echoes, they led into empty rooms; it was now too dark to check this by sight. A moment later, however, a faint light appeared ahead of them.

They did not turn all their attention on this light at once, however. Another distracting circumstance arose. At almost the same moment that Dar caught the illumination a whistling roar sounded behind them and they felt a sudden wave of heat. As one they leaped forward; and as they did so, sound and heat subsided. A faint draft from the building they had left carried a cloud of water vapor around them and on toward the end of the tunnel.

'What in the Pleiades was that?' Kruger asked of no one in particular.

'Another geyser?' Dar's response was only half a question.

'Awfully brief.' Kruger started carefully back toward the source of the disturbance, ready to leap toward the pit once more if it seemed necessary.

It did. It happened again. And after some minutes of experiment it became evident that jets of live steam which played across the corridor were released by the weight of anyone standing or walking on the corridor floor approximately ten yards from the nozzles that supplied the steam.

'Which is interesting,' Kruger concluded. 'I suppose we should be thankful that they set the thing up to warn us. It would have been just as easy, I should think, to put the trigger right in front of their blasted pipes.'

'It would seem that they wanted to keep whatever was in here, inside,' was Dar's contribution, 'but didn't care if anyone or anything came in from outside. I find myself quite interested in what may be present at the other end of this tunnel. Do you have your knife, Nils?'

'I do. I'm right behind you, Robin Hood!'

With crossbow cocked and pointing forward the little Abyormenite strode down the slope toward the brightening light. Kruger followed. It occurred to both of them that the recent sounds would have destroyed any chance of taking whatever lay ahead by surprise, but neither mentioned this aloud.

VII
Engineering

They needn't have worried. It was decidedly an anticlimax, but after more than an hour of searching the crater floor they were forced to conclude that there was no animal in the enclosure larger than a squirrel. This was a relief in one way, but left the reason for the trap in the tunnel even more obscure than it had been. They discussed this as they rested beside the pond and ate meat which Dar's bow had provided.

'Finding nothing living here is reasonable, I suppose, with the city deserted, but you'd think that there'd at least be a skeleton,' Kruger remarked.

Dar scraped at the loamy soil with one claw.

'I don't know about that. Even bones from which flesh has been entirely eaten don't last very long, and if there's much meat left they go immediately. Still, you'd expect some traces of occupancy in those dens along the wall – the ones we saw from overhead.' These openings had all been explored in search of either the inhabitant of the pit or another way out of it, but were nothing but concrete caves.

Kruger's tendency was to sit and theorize about the possible function of the crater in the days when the city was inhabited; Dar had a rather more practical question.

'Whether it was to keep bad people or bad animals means little to us just now,' he said. 'The trouble is it seems adequate to keep *us*, too. Admittedly, we will not starve; there is food and water. However, I have too few years to live to want to spend them in this place, and I am far from my books. Would it not be better to be planning a way out?'

'I suppose it would,' Kruger admitted. 'Still, if we knew what was kept here we might have a better idea of how to do just that – if it was a lion cage and we knew it, we at least would know that the restraints were designed for lions. As it is—'

'As it is we know all about the restraints, as you call them. If we start up that tunnel it gets hot. I have no first-hand knowledge of what will happen if I walk into that steam, but I'm willing to assume that my Teachers had their reasons for keeping me away from such things. I notice that you, who are not afraid of fire, have shown no eagerness to get in front of those steam pipes either.'

'True enough. I'm not afraid of fire that I control, but that doesn't apply here. But wait a minute – you said something just then. If we go up the tunnel we hit that trigger section of the floor, but that's not right in front of the jets. It can't extend very close to them, either, or we'd have been blistered on the way in. It should be possible to go up the corridor, get past the part of the floor that controls the valves, and wait there until the steam cuts off again, and then just walk out.'

Dar was a little doubtful. 'It seems too simple,' he said. 'What could they have been trying to hold here that would simply be scared of the noise? That's all that was really keeping it in, if your idea is right.'

'Maybe that's just what it was,' retorted Kruger. 'Let's try it, anyway.'

Neither of them was surprised this time when the roar of steam answered their weight on the significant floor section. Kruger led the way as close as he dared to the blast of hot gas, which emerged from nozzles at one side of the corridor and vanished – for the most part – into larger openings in the other. Bits of the streaming vapor eddied out of the line and curled about the two in swirling wisps of hot fog, but there was enough air to breathe, and for minute after minute they waited at the very edge of the jet of death.

At long last Kruger was forced to admit that Dar had been right. They were much closer to the steam than they had been when it first started on their way in, but it seemed that it was not going to stop now. Apparently the machinery was more complicated than Kruger had believed.

There was, of course, another possible interpretation. Kruger did not want to consider it. Whether or not it had occurred to Dar he did not know and carefully refrained from asking when they were back at the side of the pool.

'Do you suppose that the trap was for these little things we've been eating?' asked Dar after a long silence.

'Coming around to my logic?' queried Kruger. 'I don't know, and don't see what good it will do us if it was.'

'Neither did I until you spoke as you did a little while ago. However, I started to wonder just how much weight it took to set off that valve. We know that our combined weights will; I think that yours alone would, but we don't know whether mine would and if it did, how little could be placed on that part of the floor without starting the works.'

'If yours touches it off what good would any further knowledge be?'

'It is not necessary to place all one's weight on one block, is it? It might be possible to place branches or logs on the floor so that we would—' Kruger was on his feet again; there was no need to finish the sentence. This time Dar led the way back up the tunnel, Kruger remaining several paces behind.

In due time the roar of steam showed that the trigger had been activated. Kruger stayed where he was, while Dar moved back toward him. The roar ceased; it was definitely Dar who had operated the valve. It was difficult to be sure of the precise position of the trigger block in the nearly dark passage.

Dar moved back and forth until he had located the edge of the sensitive area to the last inch; then he spoke to his companion.

'Nils, if you will go back to the open space and find some rocks of various weights we'll learn just how sensitive this thing is. I'll stay here and mark the place.'

'Right.' Kruger saw what the little fellow had in mind and obeyed without comment or question. He was back in five minutes with an armload of lava boulders whose total weight approximated Dar's fifty-five pounds, and the two proceeded to roll them one by one across the fatal line. Some minutes of alternate roaring and silence yielded evidence that the trigger was indeed operated by weight and that approximately fifteen pounds was required to open the valves. Further, the fifteen pounds could be applied at any point in the width of the corridor for a distance of at least ten feet. Merely spreading their weights would do no good, it seemed; as soon as the total reached the fifteen-pound limit the steam came on.

'We can still make a bridge right across the thing,' pointed out Dar when this conclusion was reached.

'It's going to be a job,' was Kruger's rather pessimistic reply. 'Two knives will mean quite a lot of whittling.'

'If you can think of something else I will be glad to try it. If not I suggest we start work.' As was so often the case Dar's words seemed too sensible to oppose and they returned to the sunlight to seek materials.

Unfortunately, Kruger had been right too. They had the two knives, neither one particularly heavy. The trees of Abyormen differ among themselves as widely as those of any other planet, but none of them is soft enough to be felled with a sheath-knife in half an hour – or half a day. The travelers hoped to find something thick enough to carry them without bending noticeably and thin enough to cut and transport. The patch of forest in the crater was not very extensive, and they might have to be satisfied with much less than they wanted; neither could remember noticing a really ideal trunk during their earlier search, though of course they had had other matters in mind at the time.

Kruger was still dubious as they wandered about the crater floor. He was no lazier than the average, but the thought of attacking even a six-inch trunk with his knife did not appeal to him. That situation has probably been responsible for most of the discoveries and inventions of the last half million years, so it is not too surprising that his mind was busy with other things as they hunted.

Nor is it surprising that some facts which had been available in the filing-case of his mind for some time should suddenly fall together; that seems to be the way ideas are usually born.

'Say, Dar,' he said suddenly, 'how come if this city is deserted, and the

205

power plants presumably shut down, there is still all this steam? I can understand a simple lever-and-valve arrangement's lasting this long, but what about the energy supply?'

'There is much steam around,' pointed out Dar. 'Might they not have gone far underground, to tap the same fire that fed these volcanoes or the hot water at the village?' Kruger's face fell a little, as he realized he should have thought of this himself.

'Just the same,' he said, 'it seems to me that there can be only so much steam there. Why shouldn't we leave some rocks on that trigger and just wait for the thing to run out?'

'It's been running, on and off, for quite a while now,' said Dar doubtfully, 'and hasn't shown any signs of running down. Still, I suppose there's a chance. Anyway, once the weight is in place it won't use any of our time; we can go back to this job. Let's do it.'

'It won't take both of us. I'll be right back.' Kruger returned to the tunnel, rolled one of the rocks they had left on the floor toward the trap until his ears told him it had gone far enough, and was back with Dar in less than two minutes.

By the perversity of fortune the only tree that seemed usable for their purpose was located about as far from the tunnel as it could be. Complaining about it would do no good, however, and the two set to work with their tiny blades. Its wood was softer than pine, but even so the seven-inch trunk took some time to cut through in the circumstances. They rested several times, and stopped to hunt and eat once, before the big plant came down.

This particular tree arranged its branches in more or less the fashion of a multi-layered umbrella, with four or five feet between layers. The plan was to save some of the branches from the layer nearest the base and from that nearest the top, so that they could serve as 'legs' to keep the weight of the main trunk and its burdens off the ground. Kruger would not have been too surprised had the job taken a year, but determination and increasing skill paid their dividends and only a few terrestrial days passed before the work was ready to be dragged to the tunnel. Throughout that time the howl of the steam never subsided; there was no need to visit the tunnel to check the jets' behavior. If there was any diminution in the sound it was too gradual for either of them to detect while they worked; the phenomenon that did attract their attention was its sudden stopping.

This happened just as they were starting to drag the log toward the tunnel. For a moment the echoes of the whistling roar played back and forth across the pit; then silence took their place. Dar and Kruger looked at each other for a moment, then, without pausing for discussion, started running toward the opening.

Dar reached it first in spite of his shorter legs; the undergrowth barring the way was sufficiently open to let him through fairly easily while Kruger had to force his way. The floor of the tunnel was wet with a trickle of near-boiling water, evidently from steam which had condensed on the walls and roof during the past few dozen hours. The air in the passage was only saved from being unbreathable by the draft entering it from the pit; only a few yards of the corridor could be seen in the swirling fog. Step by step they advanced as the current drove the mist curtain before it, and presently they reached the stones that had been left near the trigger block. Dar would have continued, but Kruger restrained him with a word of caution.

'Let's hold it a moment and see whether the rock I put on the trigger is still there. Maybe it got washed off by the stream; it wasn't very heavy.' Dar privately felt that a fifteen-pound boulder would need something more powerful than the trickle in the tunnel to shift it, but stopped anyway. Only a few moments were needed to see that the rock was still in place; presumably the trigger was still depressed, and therefore the steam had been shut off by some other cause. A little uneasily, Kruger shifted his own weight forward until he was beside the rock. Nothing happened, and for several seconds the two looked thoughtfully at each other. The same possibilities were passing through their minds.

Neither knew the details of the valve system that controlled the steam. There might be any number of safety devices for shutting it off before complete exhaustion of the supply – devices which could be overridden by other triggers if a determined effort was made to escape through the corridor. The trouble was that the makers were not human and, as far as could be told, not members of Dar's race either; there was simply no way of guessing what they might have considered logical design.

'I guess there's only one way to find out, Dar. You'd better let me go first; I could probably stand a brief dose if the thing started up, but from what your Teachers have said there's no telling what it would do to you.'

'That's true, but my weight is less. Perhaps it would be better if I were to start.'

'What good will that do? If it doesn't trip for you we still won't know that it won't for me. You just be set to come on the double if I make it.' Dar offered no further argument but helped his big companion make sure that the small amount of equipment he carried was securely fastened – neither one wanted to come back for anything that was dropped. With this accomplished Kruger wasted no more time; he set off up the tunnel as fast as his strength would allow.

Dar watched until he was sure that the boy was well past the steam jets; then he followed. He caught up with Kruger at the mouth of the tunnel, but the two did not stop until they were outside the building from which the passage led. No sound had come from behind them, and gradually Kruger's panting slowed as he waited and listened.

'I guess that did it,' he said at last. 'Now what do we do? We're something like half a year late for our talk with that Teacher back at the village; do you think we can persuade him that our lateness was accidental, and that he'll be in a mood to give back your books?'

Dar thought for some time. Even he had become a little tired of being put off each time he asked for his property, and Kruger's implied point was a good one. Dar was fair-minded enough to admit to himself that their lateness was not entirely accidental; they should have started back to the village well before the time they became trapped in the crater.

'I wonder why the villagers did not come after us?' he asked suddenly. 'They knew about where we were and they certainly were able to find us the other time.'

'That's a good question and I can't see any answer offhand. The steam shouldn't have scared them away; they were used to those geysers.'

'Do you suppose they could have known we were trapped and been satisfied to leave us where we were? A searching party could have heard the steam from a long distance and checked up on us by simply looking over the crater edge.'

'That's a distinct possibility – except that the trap was so easy to get out of that they would hardly suppose we could be permanently held by it. In that case there would still be guards around, and they'd probably have met us on the way out.'

'Perhaps there was only a single guard, who didn't think the noise would lead to anything – they might think of the jet as inexhaustible; I'm sure I would have. In that case he might only have just started for reinforcements. I'm armed, and he might not feel it his duty to attempt Our capture single-handed.'

'A possibility which we have no means of checking – except by waiting here to see whether the soldiers turn out. Should we do that?'

'I – guess not.' Dar was still a little reluctant in his answer. 'You were probably right all along. We have been wasting time and I have only sixteen years. We had better start for the Ice Ramparts once more and hope we can get there in time to return here with enough aid to get the books.'

'That suits me – it always has. This steam bath gets no more comfortable with time; in fact, I'd swear it got a little hotter each year. Let's go – and fast.' They suited action to the word and left mountain and city behind them without further discussion.

Travel was a little easier along the seacoast. The beach was usually of hard-packed sand, though it was almost always narrow – Abyormen had no moon massive enough to raise noticeable tides, and this close to the pole even those caused by Theer were not enough to measure. Kruger had been a little doubtful about their traveling on a surface that took their tracks so clearly, but Dar pointed out that they had told enough since their capture to give any would-be pursuers the proper direction. Speed, and speed alone, was all that would serve the fugitives at this point.

There were numerous animals in the forest, which came unbroken to the beach, and none of them seemed to have any particular fear of the travelers. Time and again Dar's crossbow knocked over their dinner, which was dissected on the spot and eaten either as they traveled or during the occasional stops which were needed for sleep.

Once or twice the tips of volcanic cones could be seen well inland, but only once did one of them hamper their travel in any way. Then they had to spend some hours working their way across a small field of lava which had flowed into the sea at some time in the past.

Usually they could see the coast for miles behind them, and oftener than not one of Dar's eyes was turned in that direction, but the only moving things he ever saw were wild animals, usually quite unconcerned with the travelers.

The trip became a monotony of walking in steaming heat or unpleasantly warm rain. Occasionally Kruger interrupted the traveling with a bath in the sea; warm though the water was, the refreshment resulting from the swim made him feel the risk was worth while. He did this only when Dar wanted to rest, since the Abyormenite had no use for swimming and seemed to think of little except the amount of time they were spending en route.

They had no precise means of measuring the distance they traveled, so that not even Dar could guess when the islands they were seeking would appear; but appear they eventually did. Dar gave a grunt of relief when the first of the little humps appeared far out on the horizon.

'Fifteen years to go. We'll make it yet.' His confidence may have been a trifle misplaced, but Kruger's ignorance of the scale of the maps he had seen kept him from realizing that the island chain by which Dar meant to proceed led across eight hundred miles of ocean, and that almost as much land lay between its end and the point on the ice cap which was their goal. He assumed the native's judgment to be sound and almost relaxed.

'How do we get across the sea?' he contented himself with asking.

'We float.' And Dar Lang Ahn meant it.

This worried Kruger, and his worry did not grow less as time went on. It became increasingly evident that Dar intended to make his trip on a raft, which was the only sort of craft their tools would allow them to build; and even his ignorance of the distance to be covered did not make the boy any happier at the prospect. There was no provision being made for sails; when Kruger mentioned this and finally managed to explain what sails were the pilot explained that the wind always blew against them anyway. They would have to paddle.

'Does the wind *never* change?' Kruger asked in dismay as he considered the task of moving by muscle power the unwieldy thing that was beginning to take shape on the beach.

'Not enough to matter.'

'But how do you know?'

'I have been flying this route all my life, and a glider cannot be flown by one who does not know what the currents are doing.'

'Didn't you say that this island chain marked the air route your gliders always take to the Ice Ramparts?' Kruger asked suddenly.

'Those coming from Kwarr, yes.'

'Then why haven't we seen any?'

'You have not been looking up. I have seen three since we reached this spot. If your eyes were only on the sides of your head and stuck out a little more—'

'Never mind my optical deficiencies! Why didn't you signal them?'

'How?'

'You were going to reflect sunlight from your belt buckles when I found you; or we could light a fire.'

'Your fire-lighter is in the keeping of our friends whom we have left behind, and even if we lighted one you should know by now that one of my people would not approach a fire. If the pilot saw the smoke he would avoid it and more than likely report it as a new center of volcanic activity.'

'But how about the reflection? Your buckles are still shiny!'

'How does one aim a beam of light from a mirror? I was using the method when you found me because it was the only possible one; I would have been as dead, had you not appeared, as I shall be less than fifteen years from now.'

'Can't you see the beam of light that the buckle reflects?'

'No. I once saw a mirror so perfectly flat that one could see the ray of sunlight coming from it if there were a little haze in the air, but my buckles are not in that class.'

'Then if they spread the beam it should be that much easier to hit something with it. Why do you not try, at least?'

'I think it would be a waste of time, but if you can suggest a way of pointing the beam reasonably closely you may try the next time a glider comes in sight.'

'Let me see the buckles, please.'

Dar complied with the air of one amusing a rather dull child. Kruger examined the plates of metal carefully. They were more nearly flat than Dar's words had led him to hope, rectangular in shape, about two inches wide and four long. Two holes about an inch square were present in each one, and between these a single small circular hole which in service held a peg for securing the leather straps threaded through the larger openings. Kruger smiled as he finished his examination, but handed them back to their owner without any comment except, 'I'll take you up on that offer. Let me know when another glider appears, if I don't see it myself.'

Dar went back to work with little interest in Kruger's idea, whatever it might be, but he obediently kept one eye roving about the horizon. He was a little annoyed that Kruger was now constantly lifting his head to do the same thing, but was fair-minded enough to admit that the poor creature couldn't help it. He was even more annoyed when Kruger proved the first to spot an approaching aircraft, but watched with interest as the boy prepared to use the buckles in signaling.

All he saw, however, was that a buckle was held before one of the small eyes, which apparently sighted through the center hole at the approaching glider. Dar could see no reason why this should give any assistance in aiming the reflected beam. He did see the spot of light shining through the same central opening on Kruger's face, but had no means of telling that the boy had so placed the mirror that the reflection of his own features in its back had taken a definite position – one which brought the spot of sunlight on the reflected face directly on the hole through which he was looking at the glider. Holding himself as motionless as possible, he spoke.

'Do you have any special signal that depends on flashes of light – something the pilot would definitely recognize?'

'No.'

'Then we'll just have to hope that he'll be curious about a constant blink.' Kruger began rocking the mirror back and forth as he spoke.

Dar Lang Ahn was astonished when the actions of the aircraft showed plainly that its occupant had seen the flashes and he made no secret of the fact. Kruger passed it off as an everyday occurrence. He was still young, after all.

VIII
Transportation

The glider did not land; its pilot was too cautious for that. Whatever might be making the flashes on the beach below was almost certainly not a launching catapult and if he touched the ground he would stay there. He had books of his own and had no intention of risking them. Nevertheless he skimmed low enough to make out the figures of Dar and Kruger and to be as puzzled by the latter as Dar had been.

One advantage of a glider is its silence. This characteristic, combined with the hyper-acute hearing of the Abyormenites, enabled a conversation to take place between Dar and the glider pilot. It was carried out in snatches as the aircraft swooped over and interrupted until it had passed on, turned into the updraft at the edge of the forest, picked up the altitude it had lost, and returned for another pass. Eventually, however, Dar got across the fact which he considered most important – the whereabouts of his books.

'I understand,' the pilot called down at length. 'I will go on, turn in my load, and give your report. You had better stay where you are. Is there anything else that should be known by the Teachers?'

'Yes. My companion. You can see he is not a person. He knows much that is not in the books; he should go to the Teachers himself.'

'Does he speak?'

'Yes, though not well. He has words of his own, which are different from ours, and has not learned all ours yet.'

'Do you know any of his?'

'Some, yes.'

'Then perhaps it would be best if we brought you along, too. It will save time and there is not too much more of that.'

'I am not sure, but I get the impression that he does not die at the proper time; he expects to live longer. There may be no need of haste.'

One of the frequent interruptions to regain altitude allowed this information to sink into the pilot's mind. When he swung past again:

'In any case remain with him. I will report all you have told me and someone will return to give you the decision of the Teachers. If you could improvise a catapult capable of launching a four-man glider it might expedite matters, since the portable ones are probably dismantled by now.' He passed on and began to circle in determined fashion for altitude, while Dar turned to

Kruger to answer his questions about the numerous parts of the conversation the boy had either not heard or not understood.

'I had suspected, but found it hard to believe,' Kruger said at the end.

'What?'

'That this "time" you have mentioned so often means the end of your life. How can it be that you know when you are going to die?'

'I have known it all my life; it is part of the knowledge in the books. Life starts, and continues for a measured time, and ends. That is why the books must go to the Ice Ramparts, so that the Teachers may use them to help instruct the people who come after.'

'You mean everyone dies at the same time?'

'Of course. Practically all lives started at the same time – except the few who have had accidents and had to start over.'

'How do you die?'

'We do not know, though the Teachers may. They have always told us the time but never the manner.'

'What sort of people are these Teachers?'

'Why, they are not people. They are – they are Teachers. That is, they look like people but are much bigger – bigger even than you.'

'Do they look more like your people than I do, or are there other differences like those between you and me?'

'They are exactly like me except for size – and the fact that they know so much, of course.'

'And they live on from one generation to the next – that is, through the time of one group of people and into that of the next – while all ordinary people die when the time comes?'

'So they, and the books, say.'

'How long is the time that you normally live?'

'Eight hundred and thirty years. We are now in the eight hundred and sixteenth.' Kruger thought this over and did a little mental arithmetic, and tried to imagine how he would feel knowing that he had just under nine months to live. He knew it would bother him; Dar Lang Ahn seemed to take it as a matter of course. Kruger could not help wondering whether his little friend had any secret washes concerned with a longer life span. He did not quite dare ask; it seemed to have the possibility of being a very touchy subject. He allowed the conversation to drift in the direction Dar was leading it. The little pilot seemed actually to pity him, Kruger finally realized, for *not* knowing when his own life was due to end; while he did not have the precise words to express his feelings, and they were a little too abstract to explain clearly, the boy got a definite impression that Dar considered the suspense of such a situation to be something he would not care to face.

'But enough of that.' Dar, too, seemed to feel that he was verging on what might prove an uncomfortable subject for his companion. 'The pilot suggested that we try to set up a catapult so that they can take you off. We should at least be able to get it started before they come back. All we really need is the stakes; they will certainly bring the cables when they come.'

'How does the catapult work?'

Dar gave an explanation. Apparently it was simply an overgrown slingshot. The complication in its construction lay first in the need for placing it so that it could hurl the glider into a reasonably dependable updraft, and second in making sure that the supporting structure to which the cable was hooked could stand the strain – a flimsily assembled mass of timber suddenly coming loose and snapping back toward the glider could be decidedly embarrassing. The first requirement was not difficult to satisfy on the seashore; the second was a matter of experience. The work was actually easier than the raft building had been, since the pieces of wood used were much thinner. Kruger cut most of them with his knife to Dar's specifications; the little native placed them and propped them with speed and skill.

Arren, circling lazily above the horizon, marked the passage of time, but neither workman noticed it particularly. They stopped to hunt and eat or for necessary rest, but Kruger never knew just how long it took the glider they had seen to complete its journey to the ice cap, and for the relief expedition to be organized and make the return. It was certainly less than a year – they never saw Theer at all between the two events – but when the first of the gliders skimmed in from over the sea the catapult was ready.

The machine settled reasonably close to the catapult. Two others followed it within the next half hour, and a single pilot climbed from each. Dar performed the introductions; all three were acquaintances of his. Neither then nor later was Kruger able to tell them apart, and he was embarrassed to find that he could not distinguish Dar from the others except by familiar stains, nicks, and scratches on his friend's leather harness and the iron buckles he had used for signaling. The others had bits of metal about them, but not serving the same functions; their harness buckles appeared to be of something like horn.

Their names were Dar En Vay, Ree San Soh, and Dar Too Ken. Kruger was bothered by the multiplicity of Dars, realizing that he could no longer indulge his habit of shortening his friend's name for convenience. He wondered if the names connoted any sort of family connection – though from what Dar Lang Ahn had been telling him that seemed unlikely.

One of the gliders was considerably larger than the other two; Kruger supposed it was the 'four-man' machine the other pilot had mentioned. Dar Lang Ahn called him over to it and the whole party went into consultation as to the best way of accommodating the relatively huge human body. The control seat, of course, had to be left in place for the pilot; if the three others were simply removed it left nothing to support Kruger except the frail envelope of the fuselage. No one of the seats was large enough to hold him, of course, though they were quite reasonably shaped from the human point of view. The final solution was an improvised support of slender branches, more like a mattress than a seat, which appeared to be strong enough to keep Kruger from going through to the fabric and light enough to meet the rather exacting balance requirements of the glider – requirements which were already being strained a trifle by the boy's physical characteristics.

Kruger gathered that some time elapsed between the dying off of one race and the appearance of the next, but when he put the question to the group no one was able to answer him. The three newcomers were startled at the question and from then on seemed to regard him as more of a freak than even his admittedly strange appearance warranted. The pilot of the large glider made no objection when it was suggested that Dar Lang Ahn fly it as long as Kruger was aboard.

With this arrangement completed Dar asked where the rest of the fleet might be, or whether a group this size was expected to raid the village where his books were held. Ree San Soh answered him.

'We are not going to that village yet. The Teachers wanted to get a more complete report on the situation, which could only be obtained from you, and they also want to see your companion Kruger. You said that he knew more than was in the books, so they feel that it is more important to get him to the Ice Ramparts, particularly if he suffers from heat.'

Dar Lang Ahn admitted the force of this reasoning, although a lifetime of habit prevented his being completely easy on the subject of his lost cargo. Kruger applauded the decision; every time he heard the word which he had decided must mean 'ice,' he felt homesick. A Turkish bath is all right now and then, but he had been in one for the best part of a terrestrial year.

There was no difficulty with the launching. Each glider in turn was anchored at the proper distance, the cable hooked to its nose, and a light, non-stretching line run up to the bracket, through a pulley, and back to a capstan. The latter was wound up until the stretching portion of the line reached the bracket, then the first line was detached and stowed and the glider was released. As it lunged forward over the bracket the hook disengaged from its nose and fell free, leaving the performance to be repeated with the next glider.

The only variation was with the last aircraft, which was the one used by Dar Lang Ahn and Kruger. In this case the detachable hook was fastened to the bracket instead of the craft, the capstan was installed on a support in the cockpit, and the glider was anchored by a slip knot that could be released by the pilot from his station. As a result the cable rode into the air along with them and was wound up by Kruger when they were safely airborne. Not until after this was finished did Dar comment on the consequences which would have ensued had the hook fouled in the launching bracket.

'But don't you have some means of releasing this end of the cable if that happens?' asked Kruger.

'It's been tried but usually the pilot doesn't react fast enough to get any good out of it. You don't know it's fouled until the cable jerks your nose down and breaks you out of your safety belt.' Kruger gulped and was silent.

The flight was interesting but relatively uneventful. It was slow, of course, by Kruger's standards; Dar could scarcely ever head straight toward an objective. He had to coast from one rising air current to the next and Kruger was by no means always sure just how he found his up-drafts. Dar, of course, could not always explain his knowledge; it had taken him a lifetime of about forty terrestrial years to pick it up and he could hardly impart it all in one flight.

One thing was certain: Dar Lang Ahn could have walked away with any sailplane prize ever offered on Earth without even realizing that he had been in a competition. The mere fact that the present flight covered over fifteen hundred miles was not the principal reason for this; rather it was the fact that he should take such a flight as a matter of course, with no more concern about the possibility of failure than a man considers when he starts to drive from Honolulu to New York. As the hours passed with no sign of the further shore Kruger began gradually to appreciate some of this.

When the coast finally did appear it was totally different in nature from the one they had left. That had been relatively flat, except for occasional volcanic cones; this was rugged. There were ranges of mountains produced quite obviously by both thrusting and block faulting – apparently young mountains, as geologists class such things. Steep cliffs, thousands of tiny streams rich in waterfalls and rapids, sharp, bare peaks – all told the same story. The air currents were incredibly complex and Dar used them with a skill bordering on the supernatural. The other gliders had long since disappeared; their lower wing loadings had enabled them to make 'jumps' from updraft to updraft which Dar had not been willing to risk.

With the coast in sight Dar had begun to work to the left, and crossed it on a long slant. Usually they were too high for any animals to be seen or even the details of the forests that clothed the lower slopes of the mountains, but sometimes the glider would drift along the leeward side of a valley to make use of the air currents being forced up the next ridge, and Kruger could see that the trees were different. One reason was fairly evident: the temperature was lower, as Kruger could easily feel. At the highest altitudes reached by the glider he had felt comfortable at the start of the flight, now the comfort point was much closer to the ground.

This grew worse as the hours passed. Kruger was not sure how far they traveled but realized that it must be hundreds of miles. He was tired, hungry, and thirsty. Dar seemed indifferent to all these ills, as well as to the cold which was beginning to make his human companion almost regret the jungle. They had spoken little for many hours but each time Kruger thought of asking how much longer the flight was to last he was stopped by his reluctance to appear complaining. Eventually it was Dar who spoke.

'We may not make it before dark,' he said suddenly. 'I'll have to land soon, and go on when the sun comes up again.' Kruger looked in surprise at the blue star, whose motions he had long since ceased to notice particularly. Dar was right, it seemed. Arren was almost on the horizon behind them and a little to the glider's right; it was very slowly going down. Kruger tried to use this fact to form an idea of his location on the planet – it must mean something, since he had seen the blue sun in the sky constantly for over six terrestrial months. One point seemed clear: Theer would not rise this year. They had crossed to the 'dark side' of Abyormen. An ice cap suddenly seemed a reasonable feature of the landscape.

Nevertheless, judging by the angle at which the star was setting it should not go very far below the horizon, Kruger decided. He put this point to Dar.

'It will not actually get too dark to see, will it?' he asked.

'No, but we do not habitually fly when neither sun is in the sky,' was the answer. 'Vertical air currents are much rarer and harder to identify from any distance. However, I will do my best to get to the Ramparts before the sun goes down; I have no great appetite for sitting on a hilltop for fifteen or twenty hours.' Kruger concurred heartily in this wish.

It was hard to tell just what the star was doing, since their altitude varied so widely and rapidly, but that it was setting there could be no doubt. His attention was so concentrated on the vanishing star that he failed to note the landscape below as he might otherwise have done, and the ice cap was in sight for some time before he noticed it. After that he noticed little else.

A great river flowing under their course toward the now distant sea was the first warning that caught his eye. Following it upstream he saw that it rose at the foot of a gigantic wall that gleamed pinkly in the nearly level rays of Alcyone. It took him several seconds to realized that the wall was the foot of a glacier. The river continued inland, but it was a river of ice. The mountains actually were higher toward the center of the continent, but to Kruger's view now they seemed to shrink, for their bases were buried in what looked like the accumulated snows of centuries. As far as the eye could reach from the highest point of the glider's flight the field of ice spread on. Most of it was held motionless by the great hills that strove to pierce it from beneath, but near the edge the glaciers oozed free and tried to make their way to the ocean. The ice was certainly a thousand feet or more thick here at the edge of the cap; Kruger wondered what it could be further inland.

But the sight of the ice cap meant that they could not be far from their goal; Dar would not have come so close to a fruitful source of downdrafts unless he had to. The pilot admitted this when Kruger asked him. 'We should make it, all right. About two more climbs, if I can find good enough updrafts, and we can coast the rest of the way.' The boy forbore to interrupt him any more and watched the landscape in fascination as forest gave way to patches of snow and ice, and soil to black and gray rock streaked with white.

Eventually the pilot pointed, and following his finger the boy saw what could only be their landing place. It was a level platform, apparently a natural terrace, far up the side of one of the mountains. The valley below was filled with ice, part of a glacier which remained solid for fully a dozen more miles after flowing beneath this point. The terrace was simply an entryway; the mouths of several huge tunnels which seemed to lead deep into the mountain were visible opening onto it. Several winged shapes lying near the tunnel mouths left no doubt of the nature of the place.

To Kruger it seemed as though they could glide to it from their present position, but Dar Lang Ahn knew only too well the fierce downdrafts present along the edge of the terrace when the sun was not shining on the mountain face, and took his last opportunity to climb. For two or three minutes as he circled, the glider was in the last rays of Alcyone and must have been visible to the watchers on the terrace below.

Then the star vanished behind a peak and the terrace swelled under the aircraft's nose. Dar brought the machine across the level space with five hundred feet to spare, made two tight slipping turns within its confines to get rid of the excess altitude, and settled like a feather in front of one of the tunnel openings. Kruger, half-frozen from the last climb, stumbled thankfully out of the machine and gratefully accepted the water jug which one of the waiting natives immediately presented him.

Apparently they were expected – naturally enough; the other gliders must have arrived long before.

'Do you need rest before talking to the Teachers?' asked one of those who had met them. Dar Lang Ahn looked at Kruger, who he knew had been awake much longer than he normally was, but to his surprise the boy answered, 'No; let's go. I can rest later; I'd like to see your Teachers and I know Dar Lang Ahn is in a hurry to get back to the village. Is it far to their office?'

'Not very distant.' Their questioner led the way back into the tunnel, which presently turned into a spiral ramp leading downward. They followed it for what seemed fully half an hour to the boy, who began to wonder just what their guide considered 'very distant,' but finally the slope eased off onto the level floor of a large cavern. The cave itself was nearly deserted, but several doors led into it, and their guide headed them toward one of these.

The room beyond proved to be an office and was occupied by two beings who were rather obviously, from Dar Lang Ahn's description, Teachers. As he had said, they were identical with him in appearance, with the single exception of their size. These creatures were fully eight feet tall.

They each took a step toward the newcomers and waited silently for introductions. Their motions were slow and a trifle clumsy, Kruger noted, and with that observation the suspicion he had entertained for some time grew abruptly in his mind to a virtual certainty.

IX
Tactics

Earth lies some five hundred light years from Alcyone and the star cluster in which it lies. This is not far as galactic distances go, so it must have been some time before Nils Kruger first met Dar Lang Ahn that the data gathered by the *Alphard* was delivered to the home planet. Since the survey vessel had obtained spectra, photometric and stereometric readings, and physical samples from some five hundred points in the space occupied by the Pleiades as well as biological and meteorological data from about a dozen planets within the cluster, there was a good deal of observational matter to be reduced.

In spite of this, the planet where Nils Kruger was presumed to have died came in for attention very quickly. There was not enough data on hand to make known its orbit about the red dwarf sun to which it was presumably attached or the latter's relationship to the nearby Alcyone, but a planet, a dwarf sun, and a giant sun all close together within a mass of nebular gas form together a situation which is rather peculiar by most of the cosmological theories. The astrophysicist who first came across the material looked at it again, then called a colleague; announcement cards went out, and a burning desire to know more began to be felt among the ranks of the astronomers. Nils Kruger was not quite as dead as he himself believed.

But Kruger himself was not an astronomer, and while he had by now a pretty good idea of the sort of orbit Abyormen pursued about its sun he knew no reason to suppose that the system should be of special interest to anyone but himself. He had put thoughts of Earth out of his mind – almost, for he had something else to consider. He expected to live out his life on Abyormen; he had found only one being there whom he considered a personal friend. Now he had been informed by the friend himself that their acquaintance could last only a few more of Kruger's months, that the other would die his natural death at the end of that time.

Kruger didn't believe it or, at least, didn't believe it was necessary. Dar Lang Ahn's description of the Teachers had aroused a suspicion in his mind. His sight of the great creatures had confirmed those suspicions, and he settled down to his first conversation with them possessed of a grim determination to do everything in his power to postpone the end that Dar Lang Ahn regarded as inevitable. It did not occur to him to question whether or not he would be doing a favor to Dar Lang Ahn in the process.

There is no way of telling whether the Teachers who questioned Nils Kruger sensed his underlying hostility to them; no one asked them during the short remainder of their lives, and they did not bother to record mere suspicions. They certainly showed none themselves; they were courteous, according to their standards, and answered nearly as many questions as they asked. They showed no surprise at the astronomical facts Kruger was forced to mention in describing his background; they asked many of the same questions that the Teacher of the villagers had put to him earlier. He pointed out that the previous Teacher had kept his fire-lighter, when the conversation went that way; he was prepared to defend Dar Lang Ahn's association with fire, but the Teachers did not seem bothered by the fact. Dar's relief at this was evident even to Kruger.

The Teachers showed him the Ice Ramparts in considerable detail – more than Dar Lang Ahn himself had ever seen. The caverns in the mountain were only an outpost; the main settlement was far underground and miles further inland. Several tunnels connected it with landing stages similar to the one on which they had arrived. It was here that the libraries were located; they saw load after load of the books which had come in from the cities scattered over Abyormen being filed for further distribution. Asked when this would take place the Teacher made no bones about the answer.

'It will be about four hundred years after the end of this life until the next starts. Within ten years after that the cities should be peopled again and the process of educating the populations begin.'

'Then you have already started to abandon your cities. Do all your people come here to die?'

'No. We do not abandon our cities; the people live in them to the end.'

'But the one Dar Lang Ahn and I found was abandoned!'

'That was not one of our cities. The people who lived near it were not our people and their Teachers were not of our kind.'

'Did you know about this city?'

'Not exactly, though those Teachers are not complete strangers to us. We are still undecided about what to do in that connection.' Dar interrupted here.

'We'll simply have to go back with enough people to take the books away – and I'm sure you want Nils's fire-lighter, too, even though we don't use fire. It is knowledge and should go into the libraries.'

The Teacher made the affirmative hand motion.

'You are quite right, up to a point. However, it is more than doubtful that we could force the return of the material. Did you not say that the books had been taken into a shelter among the hot-water pools?'

'Yes, but – they can't have been kept there!'

'I am less sure than you. In any case if we made an attack as you suggest they would have the time, and probably the inclination, to hide the things elsewhere.'

'But couldn't we make them tell where?' asked Kruger. 'Once we captured the place it could be a simple bargain – their lives for our property.'

The Teacher looked steadily at the boy for a moment, using both eyes.

'I don't think I could approve of taking their lives,' he said at last. Kruger felt a little uncomfortable under the steady stare.

'Well – they needn't know that we wouldn't actually do it,' he pointed out rather lamely.

'But suppose their Teachers still have the things? What good will threatening the people do?'

'Won't we have the Teachers too?'

'I doubt it.' The dryness of the answer escaped Kruger completely.

'Well even if we don't, don't they care enough about their people to give up the things in order to save them?'

'That might be.' The Teacher paused. 'That might – very – well – be. I am rendered a little uncomfortable by some of your ideas, but I must confess there are germs of value in that one. We need not threaten to kill, either; simply removing the people would be enough – or rather, threatening to do it. I must discuss this with the others. You may stay and examine the library if you wish, but I imagine you will want to be back at the outpost when a decision is reached.'

Kruger had seen all he wanted of the book-storing process and of the librarians, who were people of Dar's stature rather than Teachers, so he signified his intention of returning to the surface. Dar Lang Ahn came along and the long walk up the tunnel commenced. It was enough to keep Kruger warm, though the temperature was about forty-five Fahrenheit. He wondered as they traveled at the need for such a shelter – there was half a mile of rock and over three miles of ice overhead, according to the Teacher. Even more remarkable was the construction of such a place by people whose tools seemed to be of the simplest. But no doubt they had had tools when they first came; Kruger now believed that the accident which had marooned Dar's people on Abyormen must have occurred several generations before. For one thing there was obviously more than one shipload of them on the planet.

The discussion of Kruger's projects and its modification by the Teachers took quite some time, and the boy spent the interval seeing what he could do both inside the station and out.

The temperature outside was just about freezing, as might have been expected with so much ice in the vicinity. Kruger could not stay out for very long at a time, since his coveralls had been improvised with the thought in mind of keeping him cool. Fortunately the synthetic of which they were made was windproof, and by tightening the wrists, ankles, and neck he was able to gain some protection. Dar Lang Ahn, who accompanied him on most of his trips outside, seemed indifferent to the cold as he had been to the heat.

On one occasion Kruger did remain outside for a long time, but it was quite involuntary. He had gone out alone, and after plowing through drifts and over treacherous crust for half an hour or so had returned to find the door locked. He had not checked it on leaving to find what sort of latch it had, and apparently it was a spring lock. No amount of pounding attracted anyone's attention, since the door was a quarter of a mile from the main cavern on that level, and at last Kruger had to strike off around the mountain to the landing platform. He reached it more dead than alive, and thereafter was quite careful about doors.

Even inside he occasionally made mistakes, as well. Once he nearly suffocated in a food-storage bin he was examining, and on another occasion came within an ace of dropping through what later proved to be the trap of a rubbish-disposal chute. He learned later that the chute led to a narrow canyon full of melt-water which normally carried away the rubbish. Thereafter he went nowhere alone. He was decidedly relieved when the deliberations ended and the plan of attack was decided.

It was reasonably ingenious, he felt. He and Dar were to return to the city by glider, circling over the village to be sure they were seen. In the meantime a large force of bowmen were to land on the other side, far enough from the city to be assured of secrecy, and enter it. The two groups were to meet at a point which Dar selected, drawing a map with the aid of his photographic memory and marking the position on it.

The assumption was that the villagers would once more send a force to capture the intruders. This group would be led into a square by Dar and Kruger, which was surrounded by buildings in which the bowmen from the ice cap would be sheltered. There was the possibility that the two decoys would be held as hostages or even killed out of hand, but Dar did not appear worried and Kruger therefore preferred not to show his own feelings.

Kruger made sure that food and water were stowed in the big glider this time, though Dar appeared to consider them unnecessary for such a trip.

The return to the tropics, of course, pleased Kruger only briefly. After a very short time in the steamy air on the wrong side of the ocean he found himself thinking wistfully of the winds from the ice cap – quite humanly ignoring the fact that those winds had nearly been the death of him on one occasion. It is hard to imagine just how Dar Lang Ahn would have reacted had he known his companion's thoughts. Since Kruger kept them carefully to himself the pilot was able to concentrate on his business.

The volcanic cones were found without difficulty. Most of the other gliders were already down on the beach a few miles short of the mountains; as before, the lighter craft had made better time. Dar and Kruger could see the crews below them gathering for the trip to the city and decided to remain airborne for a while longer to make sure that the bowmen would have time to get into position.

They went on up the coast beyond the cones and cast about in an attempt to find the village of their captors from the air.

The huts themselves were too well concealed by the trees, it turned out, but the area of the geysers was easy enough to locate. The heat from this region provided a splendid updraft and Dar circled in it for several minutes while the two examined the area minutely, but there was no sign of life now. At length Dar took his glider back to the volcanoes and landed on the beach as close as he could get to the city.

They entered the place on foot, fully aware that they were leaving a plain trail in the sand of the beach but not worried about it. At least, Dar Lang Ahn was not worried; Kruger was beginning to wonder whether or not they might be getting just a little too blatant about the whole business. He suggested this to his companion, to whom the idea was wholly new.

'I don't think we need worry too much,' Dar said at length. 'They will see that we had to land on the beach; we certainly could not bring the glider down in the jungle, and there is no way of walking across sand without leaving a trail. We can be less obvious inside the city.'

'All right.' Kruger was coming to suspect that Dar Lang Ahn's people had had little practice in military matters. However, with luck, the villagers they sought to trap might prove equally naive; there was nothing much that could be done about it at this point.

The city lay silent, as it had before. There had been a recent rainstorm, and puddles of water were still present on the flatter portions of the pavement. Occasionally it was difficult to avoid wading through these, and wet footprints marked portions of their route to the square where the bowmen should be waiting for them. How long these would last in the nearly saturated air was a question that bothered Kruger slightly, though Dar did not appear to give it a thought.

They reached the designated point ahead of the others, in spite of the extra time spent in the air. When the force finally arrived no further time was wasted in placing the ambush. That completed, there seemed nothing for Dar and Kruger to do but start exploring buildings.

'I don't see what we're likely to find that will be of much interest,' the boy remarked. 'We've already been through most of the places around here. We should at least have picked a neighborhood we hadn't explored so thoroughly.'

'Then I could not have been sure that it would lend itself to our ambush,' pointed out Dar. 'I could go only by memory, you know.'

'I suppose that's so. Well, let's go in here and see what's to be seen.' Kruger led the way into a nearby structure and the routine they had developed earlier was repeated. As both had feared there was nothing new about the place above ground, and they both had a healthy dislike of the thought of going below.

And the hours passed. Every so often Dar Lang Ahn went back to the building in which the leader of the bowmen was concealed in order to discuss progress, but there was simply no progress to discuss. Kruger finally stated bluntly that the villagers or their Teachers must have outguessed them, and that the thing to do was take the whole group and proceed directly to the village. The thought, however, seemed to bother his companions seriously; it was not in accord with their instructions.

'We must wait for a time at least,' Ten Lee Bar, the leader of the group, insisted.

'But how much time do you have?' retorted Kruger. 'It doesn't matter so much to me, I suppose, though I'd like to be on the other side of the ocean before the last of your gliders is grounded for lack of pilots, but if you don't get those books soon you never will and the electrical apparatus that your Teachers want will be a long, long time getting to them.'

The native looked uncomfortable.

'In a way, no doubt you are right. Still, if we fail because we did not follow the plan …' His voice trailed off for a moment, then he brightened. 'I recall that you spoke of electrical equipment here in the city. Could you not use some of the time in obtaining samples of that? I will gladly help.' Kruger knew determination when he saw it, even in a nonhuman being. He shrugged.

'It's your funeral. Come along and I'll see what can be found.' He turned to the nearest building, Dar Lang Ahn and Ten Lee Bar following him, and led the way through the open entrance hall to one of the inner rooms. Like virtually every other room in the city it had the electric plugs, and with the natives watching, Kruger pried off the covering plates and exposed the connecting wires.

Dar Lang Ahn had heard his explanation before and did not pay as much attention through most of it, but toward the end even he was attracted. This was at the point where Kruger was explaining the need for two conductors and the results that would ensue if any easy path for the current was opened between them. This should have been strictly explanation, since no demonstration material was presumably around; unfortunately, when Ten Lee Bar brought wires together to see what the boy meant the strands of silver suddenly grew red hot, causing him to pull back his hand with a howl of surprised pain.

He was no more surprised than Nils Kruger. For several seconds the boy stared at the glowing wires; then he pried them apart with the insulating handle of his knife.

'Did you just feel heat, or something else?' Kruger asked sharply.

'I don't know. If that was heat I can see why the books have warned us against it.' The bowman had his hand at his mouth in an amazingly human fashion.

Realizing he could get no information from a being who did not even know what a burn felt like, Kruger experimented. After drawing a few sparks with his knife blade he concluded that the voltage must be very low. Making sure he was on the dry stone floor – as dry as stone was ever likely to be in this atmosphere, that is – he then bridged the gap with two fingers. He was unable to feel any shock, though a final check with the knife blade showed that the circuit had not picked that moment to go dead.

The question now stared him in the face: did the city normally run on very low voltage *and still have its generators going* or was this the last trickle from some emergency storage system? And also, did the Teachers in the nearby village know about this and was that why they had a general prohibition on the city? Kruger had come to feel a unity with Dar Lang Ahn's people, in spite of the hostility he felt toward their Teachers. If they would not move on their own initiative to obtain the information they needed Nils Kruger would make them! He turned abruptly to Ten Lee Bar.

'This changes matters. Dar Lang Ahn and I are going to that village; things need to be learned. You may come or not with your men, as you see fit.'

'But if you go what is the use of our waiting here?'

'I haven't the slightest idea. Use your own judgment. We're on our way.' Kruger started out of the building without even asking Dar if he was coming. Ten looked after them for a moment; then he, too, went outside and began to call his group from their hiding places. Looking back just once Kruger saw them starting after him; he smiled to himself but went on without comment.

The trail was easy to follow; they had been over it enough times before. Nothing occurred during the walk. No sign of animal or villager, either by sight or sound, could be detected. Even the clearing of the geysers was silent as they approached it. At the place where the trail forked, sending one branch to the point where they had always talked to the Teachers, Kruger turned toward the pool which had so nearly engulfed them in boiling water. A few moments later the whole party stood before the rock shelter which projected from one side of the rim.

Still the silence was broken only by the scrape of claws on the rock. After waiting for several minutes Kruger went boldly up to the shelter and began to examine it minutely for traces of an entrance. He started on the side toward the water, leaning over the rim to do so, since he had long since convinced himself that the door must be concealed there. However, he found no trace of any crack in the rock. Extending the search to the sides and front produced no better results.

The top was more fruitful. There were, here, a set of fine, almost invisible cracks outlining what might have been a square trapdoor, but the opening thus framed would barely have admitted Dar Lang Ahn himself. Never in the Universe could it have allowed the great body of one of the Teachers to pass. No doubt the books and fire-lighter had gone this way, but where the Teachers went was still a mystery.

Kruger extended the search for many yards around the pool, the rest of the group helping once they understood what he wanted and had overcome their nervousness at the sight of the steaming water. Numerous cracks were found, but all seemed to be random breaks produced by nature. An attempt to see through the small holes through which the Teachers had presumably looked out proved equally futile; none of them was more than a few inches deep. Kruger began to wonder whether the whole thing had not been a huge farce, a deliberate misdirection of attention. Perhaps the Teachers had been watching all the time from the edge of the forest, or some similar vantage point, while the conversations had been going on. In that case where were they now? Still no sign of villagers, still no sound of Teacher's voice – Kruger suddenly felt uneasy.

The others had given up their search and come back to him for further orders as he stood thinking, but he did not stop to feel pleased at having usurped command of the expedition. 'Let's go on to the village,' he said abruptly, and led the way.

There was no sign of life. They approached the edge of the clearing cautiously, stopping as they saw the first huts. At Kruger's order they spread out, to make poorer targets for possible hidden crossbows, and continued their advance until all were within the village.

Still there was neither sound nor motion. House after house was entered cautiously and searched, all with the same negative result. The place was indeed deserted.

'And I suppose my books went with them!' Dar Lang Ahn topped the conclusion bitterly.

'Seems likely. I'm afraid, unless you want to go back to the pool and pry open that trap door. Of course we still haven't been to the little hut where they reported to their Teachers. Though how a Teacher fitted into that I don't understand, now that I've seen one of them.'

'That's not the important point.' Dar was off toward the indicated hut like a bolt from his own crossbow. He vanished inside and an instant later called Kruger's name.

'What is it?' asked the boy as he broke into a run toward the hut. 'Did they leave your books as a gesture of good will?'

'Not the books. I can't describe the thing.' Kruger was inside the door with Dar's last words. For a moment he stopped while his eyes adjusted to the darkness; then he saw what the little pilot meant.

The hut was unfurnished except for a rude table in the center. On that table was lying a piece of apparatus. It was uncased, and contained coils and condensers and what must have been vacuum tubes, all exposed to view. Kruger realized what it must be almost instantly, but he was given no chance to voice his opinion. The device on the table spoke first.

'Come in, Nils Kruger. I have been waiting for you for quite a while. There is much we have to say to each other.'

X

Elucidation

The voice was that of the Teacher; there was no mistaking it. Equally, there was no mistaking the fact that Nils Kruger was going to have to revise a number of his ideas. Not even the race which had its headquarters at the ice cap and spread cities over most of the planet had radios, so far as he knew. Could this being have learned more electricity than seemed possible from the deserted city?

'Why were you waiting for me?' asked the boy. 'I didn't expect very much to come back, myself – or did you think I needed the fire-lighter too badly to leave it for long?'

'I was sure that Dar Lang Ahn would be back for his books; I know his people too well to doubt that. Later, I knew you would be with him.'

'How did you know?'

'I was told. I will explain that in due course. You may not believe it, but in spite of all that I have done which you may resent, I am not entirely your enemy. I am willing to allow you to live as long as your nature permits – provided that certain conditions are met.'

'And if they are not?' Kruger naturally resented the hidden being's words.

'Then accidents will continue to happen. You cannot escape all of them.'

Slowly the meaning of this dawned on the boy.

'You mean the landslide over by the city, and the pit, were done on purpose?'

'I mean just that. I also mean that a certain door did not lock itself accidentally, and a trap was left unguarded and unlocked with a purpose, and a certain geyser was allowed to feed its outlet instead of a heat exchanger. Be sensible, Kruger; you know too little of this planet, and I know too much.'

'But you couldn't—' Kruger stopped; the very fact that this thing knew about the events at the Ice Ramparts made his objection ridiculous. He changed his wording.

'How did you find out? Are you one of the Teachers from there?'

'I talk to them frequently.'

'Then did they cause those accidents at your request, or did they want to get rid of me on their own, or did you do it in spite of them?'

'They caused them at my order. They did not want you destroyed; from a purely personal viewpoint neither do I. Unfortunately you are too cooperative.'

'In what way? And why should that be a point against me?'

'I asked you many questions while you were a prisoner here, not only about yourself but about the technical knowledge you have. You answered them all, truthfully and, as far as I was able to tell, correctly. I am not an electrician myself, but I know enough to follow most of what you said.'

'What is your objection to that?'

'If you tell me, whom you had no reason to trust, you will presumably tell Dar Lang Ahn's people. I have no objection to the state of civilization which they now enjoy, but there are good and sufficient reasons why we do not want them to match the technology of your people.'

'How do you know what our technical level is?'

'You told me enough yourself merely by being here.'

'What is your objection to their learning our technology, if you learn it too?'

'Principally, we do not want them to leave this planet. We need them here.' Kruger began to develop a strong suspicion at this point and asked a question designed to check it.

'How about these people of yours who were here in the village? Would you object to their learning?'

'Very much. They are easier to control as they are.'

'How is it that you dare tell me all this with Dar Lang Ahn listening to the conversation?'

'His Teachers know it already. They did not want to help me get rid of you, but I was able to bring pressure to bear. When their attempts failed I had them send you back here, to be persuaded if possible, destroyed if not.'

Kruger, convinced that his idea was right, leaned forward and spoke with more anger than he had felt in his previous life. 'That does it. You are not the same race as Dar's people or as the people who lived in this village. You have the villagers to do as you want in the way of everyday labor, and the rest pretty much the same thing in more complicated matters. I don't know whether you or they are the original inhabitants of this world, but I can certainly see why you don't want them to leave it now. You might have to do some of your own work! Isn't that it?' Kruger was so furious by the time he reached the end of this speech that it was a wonder the hidden being could understand him, but it apparently did.

'You are partly right,' it answered calmly.

'Partly! I'm right from soup to nuts. I dare you to let me see you!'

'I'm afraid that's not possible just now.'

'Why not? Afraid I'll step on you?'

'Not quite that. However, our meeting under the same conditions would indeed result in the death of one of us. I could not survive in your environment and I am pretty sure you could not in mine – at least Dar Lang Ahn certainly could not.'

'Then he, and not you, is one of the natives of this world. You came and conquered it!'

'I do not know enough of the past to refute that belief, but I have reason to doubt it.'

'It's certainly plain enough.'

'You make an extremely positive statement on remarkably little data. Would you be willing to promise not to reveal any knowledge to Dar Lang Ahn's people, except what we approve—'

'No!'

'Let me finish – until you have learned enough about us to form a balanced opinion?'

'Who decides when my opinion is balanced?'

'I would agree to release you from your promise whenever you asked, with the understanding that I might then find it expedient or necessary to dispose of you.'

'How do you know I'll feel bound by a promise obtained under such terms?'

'I should not advise you to do or say anything which would give me reason to doubt the value of your word. I am sure you can see why.'

'How about Dar?'

'As I said, he may say what he wishes while he lives. He has no knowledge that I object to his people's sharing.'

'He heard me discuss electricity with you.'

'I remember.'

'All right, I will say nothing without giving you fair warning, but I assure you that you have some heavy convincing to do.' Something very like a sigh of relief came through the speaker.

'I much prefer it that way,' was the answer. 'Believe it or not, I would like to be on the same terms with you that Dar Lang Ahn seems to be.'

'After those engineered accidents that will take some doing – and some believing.'

'Your words make me begin to wonder whether your race can possibly be one that never makes mistakes. Mine is not. However, I had better get to my job of explanation.

'In the first place, your idea that we simply use Dar Lang Ahn's race for labor is quite wrong. It would be practically impossible for us to do that, since we cannot live under the same conditions they do. Their death, in a few years now, will mark the time when we can live normally on this world.'

'You mean you live during the time they die, and—'

'And most of us die during the time they live. That is correct.'

'Then that city between the volcanoes was built by your people!'

'It was. It is maintained, during our death time, by a few people of whom I am one.'

'So that's why the electricity was on in that building.'

'When? Just now?'

'Yes, when we were in the city just before coming here.' A succession of sounds quite beyond the power of human vocal cords to imitate spluttered from the speaker, and was followed by a brief silence. Then the invisible creature spoke again.

'Thank you. I had to turn on the power some time ago to handle a steam valve – I have you to thank for that, I suspect – and forgot to turn it off again. My own life is well past its prime, I fear.'

'You mean that thing in the crater across the city – you were handling that?'

'Not at first; it is automatic. The steam comes from the same underground heat source that maintains the geysers. The heat is virtually inexhaustible, but the water is not. I had to shut the valve manually because the loss of steam was threatening most of our other machinery. Am I correct in suspecting that you are the cause of the inconvenience?'

'I'm afraid so.' Kruger told the story, his good humor returning as he did so.

'I understand,' the other said at the end. 'I trust you will take the time to remove those stones before you go back to the ice cap. I could get my people here to do it, I suppose, but there are reasons why I do not want them there yet.'

'I'm willing as long as your manual valve stays off,' replied Kruger.

'We seem to be trusting each other,' was the answer. 'However, let us get back to the subject. As I said, we are different from your friends; we live under different conditions, use different tools, different buildings, different foods. In short, we do not compete with them – we might almost as well be living on a different planet.'

'Then what is your objection to *their* living on a different planet – or at least being able to do so?'

'That is as much in their interest as ours, as any of their Teachers will tell you. If they left this planet how likely would they be to find another just like it?'

'I don't know; there must be quite a number of them. There are vast numbers of planets in the galaxy.'

'But very few, if any, which would kill them at the proper time. I have gathered that you do not know when you are to die, and like it that way. Did you ever try to find out how your friend Dar would feel under such circumstances?' Kruger was silent; he had gathered already that Dar rather pitied the human state of eternal uncertainty. Then he remembered one of his numerous pet theories.

'I admit that Dar has been educated all his life to the idea that dying at a certain particular time is natural and inevitable, but it seems to be just a matter of education – some of his race seem to face quite happily the prospect of living longer.'

'They did not tell you that at the Ice Ramparts.' Kruger chose to interpret this answer as an admission that he was right.

'They didn't have to; I'm not blind. All Dar Lang Ahn's people, even your branch of them here, are the same size – and the same age. Their Teachers are also of a size, but much larger than Dar. It didn't take a genius to see the story: either these people grow throughout their lives, or else this dying time you talk about comes before they reach their full growth. Some live through that time, and keep on growing. They are the Teachers.'

'You are quite right in the main facts, but I think your remark about the attitude of the Teachers toward their prolonged lives must have been guesswork. Did you actually talk to any of the people at the Ice Ramparts who will be the Teachers for the next time of living?'

'What do you mean? I talked to a lot of their Teachers.'

'But surely you do not think that the present group of Teachers will live through this time of dying! The fact that they are all of a size, as you said, should show you that. The next group will come from among the people who started to live at the same time Dar Lang Ahn did.'

'But how were they chosen? Why cannot Dar here join them?'

'He could, but I am sure he does not wish to. The Ice Ramparts are the only place on Abyormen where his kind can live during the time my people hold the planet. They simply cannot accommodate the whole race; some selection must be made. Since long training is needed they are selected early in life.'

'You suggested that those chosen are not too happy about it. I find that hard to believe.'

'A chosen Teacher accepts from a sense of duty. Living beyond the natural time exacts a penalty; you saw that the Teachers at the Ice Ramparts moved slowly when they moved at all. You did not see them all; three out of four, by this time, are virtually cripples. Their size increases, but their strength does not keep up with it. Their joints become stiff, their digestion untrustworthy. Physical ills develop which make life far more of a burden than a pleasure. They accept this lot because if they did not each new group of their people would have to start from the beginning, and this world, during their time of living, would be inhabited by nothing but wild animals.'

'Is the same true for the Teachers of your race?'

'It is. However, I am not as near the end of my duty as are those at the ice cap; I must last through, or nearly through, my people's next time of living. Life is not too bad for me, so far.'

'But just what are the differences between your races? And what change in conditions kills off one and starts the other growing? Does it affect any other life forms on the planet?'

'The first question is difficult to answer unless we can work out some means of your seeing me, and I don't know how that would be possible. My environment would have to be separated from yours to permit us both to live, and I know of no barrier through which we could see.' Kruger started to suggest glass or quartz and discovered he did not know the word for either substance. Before he could invent a sentence to describe them the voice went on, 'The change in conditions is pretty thorough, but the most important factor is temperature. It gets much hotter (Kruger whistled gently) and the air changes.'

'Do you breathe air, or water, or both?' asked the boy. 'Your city extends into the ocean.'

'Only at the moment. During our living time the oceans disappear almost completely. We suppose that they travel as vapor to that portion of Abyormen on which neither sun shines and are there precipitated in either liquid or solid state. We have not been able to explore such regions, for fairly obvious reasons, but knowledge of the conditions at the Ice Ramparts lends support to this theory.'

'But the sun Arren shines on the Ramparts, most of the time.'

'Just now, yes; the region I mentioned is a quarter of the way around the planet from the point you speak of.'

'I begin to get the situation,' Kruger said. 'I had already realized that Abyormen was traveling in a pretty eccentric orbit around Theer; if what you say is correct Theer itself is doing much the same around Arren.'

'So we have deduced, though the precise size and shape of the path is not known for certain. We have been unable to devise measuring devices which would give us the needed values. We are sure, however, that both suns are much larger than Abyormen and very distant from it, so it seems reasonable to suppose that Abyormen rather than the suns is moving.'

'I can see the sort of thing that must happen to this place; I suppose my last question was wasted – if the temperature changes as you say, it must affect all the life on the planet. I've wondered why most of the trees and animals of a particular species seemed to be about the same size, now it's quite reasonable. Most of them must have started growing at about the same time.'

'I take it that this is not the case on your world.' The words were half a question. Kruger spent some time describing the seasonal changes of Earth and the way in which various forms of life adapted to them.

'It seems, then,' was the Teacher's comment to this information, 'that most of your creatures either continue through the full year at more or less normal activity, or else become dormant for the unsuitable season. On this world the first is not possible, at least not for us, and I find it hard to imagine a creature able to stand the full extremes of Abyormen's climate. The second seems to me to be extremely wasteful; if one type of life cannot stand the situation for part of the year why should not another take its place during that period?'

'It seems sensible,' admitted Kruger.

'Then what objection do you have to my race's sharing Abyormen with Dar Lang Ahn's?'

'None whatever. What bothers me is your treatment of them, forbidding me to tell them enough of the physical sciences to let them get out from under your control. You certainly don't seem to mind my giving *you* all the information I can.'

'To me personally, no. To my people, I would have the same objection that I do for Dar Lang Ahn's.'

'You mean you don't want your *own* people to be able to build space ships, supposing I were able to tell them how?'

'I mean just that.'

'But that doesn't make sense. What objection could you have to some of your people's *wanting* to go off and leave Dar's folk alone?'

'I said long ago that we need Dar's race, though you chose to interpret my words differently. What is more, his people need ours just as badly, even though Dar Lang Ahn doesn't know it – his Teachers do, at least.'

'Then why don't you treat them as friends instead of inferiors?'

'They are friends. I feel a particularly strong attachment for Dar Lang Ahn; that is one reason you were so well treated while you were in this place before, and why I sent my villagers away rather than risk violence when you came this time.'

'If you are so fond of Dar – whom you have never seen before in your life, as nearly as I can see – why did you keep his books? That has bothered him more than anything else that has happened since I have known him.'

'That was for experimental reasons, I am afraid. I wanted to learn more about you. I am sorry that Dar Lang Ahn suffered, but I am glad to have learned something of your capacity for sympathy and friendship. His books will be on the trap at the place where we used to talk as soon as I can get them there after ending this conversation.'

'How about my fire-lighter?'

'Do you really want it? I took it apart, I'm afraid, and am not sure that I could get it back together again. The condenser (he had to stop to explain this word) was, of course, quite familiar to us, but the part that turns the sun's heat into electricity was not. If you can spare it my scientists would be interested – when we have some.'

'I thought you didn't want your people to learn too much.'

'I don't, but I seriously doubt that this particular device will get any of them off the planet. I judge that it is less practical for our purposes than the generators we already use, which tap the volcanic heat of Abyormen.'

'Then you are living underground, near volcanoes where it is hot enough to suit you? I should think from what I saw of this continent that a good many of you must live through the cold time.'

'I am underground, as you say, but there are not many of us. Only four live in this area; similar numbers are in each of our other cities.'

'But you must have a lot more room to live in during your bad season than the others do. They're cramped under that ice cap—'

'Which is many hundreds of miles across at its smallest. It would be possible to dig caverns and, probably, store food enough for most if not all of the race.'

'And there are volcanoes for I don't know how many hundreds of miles down the length of that peninsula I followed from the place I was left. In short, there doesn't seem to be any reason why both races can't live at full strength all the time. What's wrong with the idea?'

'I have been giving you hints as to what is wrong with it all through this conversation. I told you each race was necessary to the other; you seem to believe that is due to our laziness. I mentioned that other planets would be unsuitable because they would not kill us at the right time; you appear to have put that down to superstition. I tell you that I have a strong personal interest in Dar Lang Ahn's welfare, and apparently you simply don't believe it. You remark on your own that there is no technical impossibility, or even great difficulty, in our remaining alive throughout the year if we choose. Instead of putting all those items together, you treat them as a group of separate impossibilities. I confess I have been trying ever since this conversation started to get some sort of idea of human intelligence, and you are certainly not giving me a high one. Can you honestly not think of an explanation that will embrace all those facts?'

Kruger frowned, and no one spoke for a minute or so; then Dar Lang Ahn made a remark.

'If you are testing intelligence, Teacher, you'd better compare his with mine. I've lived on Abyormen all my life and don't see what you're driving at.'

'Your training would prevent it.'

'Then I'd like to think that mine does the same thing,' snapped Kruger, somewhat annoyed. 'Why should I be able to win your guessing game if he can't?'

'Very well, I do not wish to cause you anger. The explanation will, I think, be easiest if you give me some words in your language. I understand that individuals of your race are directly concerned with the production of other individuals. What is the newly produced being called?'

'A child – son or daughter, according to—'

'The general term will be enough. Is there a word describing the relationship of two childs produced by the same individual?'

'Brother or sister, according—'

'All right, I will assume either word is usable. I have no child, since I am still alive, but Dar Lang Ahn is a child of my brother.'

The silence was much longer this time, while Nils Kruger fitted piece after piece of the jigsaw puzzle into place, and his attitude grew from one of sheer disbelief, through gradual recognition of the possibilities, to acceptance. 'You win – Uncle!' he said weakly, at last. 'But I still don't see—'

Kruger's sentence was interrupted – and not by the Teacher.

'I think I'll say "uncle" too.' The voice was a slow drawl that the boy had never to his knowledge heard before, but it was speaking English. 'I can stand,' it went on, 'an occasional word that sounds like good old English in any collection of random noises, and will gladly put it down to coincidence. However, when "child," "son," "daughter," "brother," "sister," and "uncle" all occur within the same thirty-second period, coincidence goes a long, long way out the window. Mr Nils Kruger, if you've been contributing heavily to the conversations we've been recording for the last couple of weeks, I hope you've developed a good accent. If not, a couple of philologists I know are going to be very, very angry indeed!'

XI

Astronomy; Diplomacy

Most human beings continue hoping long after any logical excuse for it has died. The man going into battle against impossible odds, the pilot who stays with a blazing airplane to guide it away from a city, the condemned criminal in the death cell – few of them give up while they breathe. Nils Kruger had not entirely relinquished hope of seeing Earth again. He did not, however, expect to be rescued. He had had faint ideas, which he would have admitted himself were illogical, that perhaps by combining Abyormenite technology with his own some sort of ship able to cross the five hundred light years to the solar system might be built. Even after he had gained a fairly accurate idea of the technical limitations of Dar Lang Ahn's race the thought had not entirely vanished; but unreasonable as he may have been in this respect, he never for an instant supposed that another terrestrial space ship would approach the Pleiades during his lifetime. There was too much else for them to do.

As a result the sound of an unmistakably human voice cutting in on his conversation with a creature who could hardly be less human gave Kruger quite literally the shock of his life. For some moments he was completely unable to speak. Several questions came from the radio, and when these were answered only by Dar Lang Ahn's rather unfortunate attempts at English the disturbance in the distant space ship was nearly as great as that in the hut.

'That can't be Kruger – he wouldn't talk like that, and anyway he's dead!'

'But where could they have learned English?'

'My year-old kid speaks better English than that!'

'Kruger, is that you or has the philology department gone off the rails?'

'I – I'm here all right, but you shouldn't do things like that. What ship is that? and how come you were listening in? and what are you doing in the Pleiades anyway?'

'It's your own ship, the *Alphard;* this is Donabed. That radio you have is pretty sad; I'm not sure of your voice either. We've been here a couple of weeks, and have been picking up and recording all the radio noise we could find in hopes of having some of the language in useful shape when we landed. I'm glad you were too sensible to expect us back; it seems that there's something about this system that had thrown the astronomers into fits, and they

238

had to come back to look for themselves. Is that radio a native product, or did you make it?'

'Strictly home grown.' Kruger was back in control of himself, though his knees still felt weak. 'Just a minute, we have an audience that doesn't speak English.' Kruger shifted back into the Abyormenite speech and explained to Dar and the Teacher what had happened. 'Now, while you're coming down, will you please explain to me just what is so peculiar about this place from the astronomer's point of view?'

'I'm not an astrophysicist, but here's the situation as I understand it,' returned Donabed. 'You know the elementary facts about the sources of stellar energy, and that main-sequence stars like the sun and this red dwarf should be able to keep radiating at their present rate for billions of years. However, there are a lot of stars in space which are a lot more luminous than Sol, sometimes by a factor of tens of thousands. Suns like that are using up their hydrogen so rapidly that they should not be able to last more than a few million, or a few tens of millions, of years at the most. Alcyone, like several other stars in the Pleiades, is such a sun.

'So far, that's all right. The Pleiades cluster is full of nebulous material, and presumably that is still combining to form other stars to add to the hundreds already in the group; but here we run into trouble. They've worked out to a fair degree of precision the sort of things that should happen to the condensing clouds. In some circumstances, with a certain amount of angular momentum, you can expect several stars to form, traveling in orbits about each other – a regular binary or multiple star system. In other cases, with less angular momentum, you get most of the mass in one star and the dregs left over forming a planetary system. It's a little surprising, though not impossible, to get a double or multiple star with planets as well; but to get a star like Alcyone with planets anywhere near it is queer as all get-out! A sun like that is putting out radiation tens of thousands of times as intense as Sol's; that radiation exerts pressure; and that pressure should easily be sufficient to push out of the neighborhood any solid particles that had any idea of coalescing into planets. That's one of the things that can be computed and checked experimentally, and it's hard to get around. For that reason the stargazers were not too bothered when they found from our data that Alcyone had a red dwarf companion, but when they learned that the companion had a planet they went wild. We had quite a time persuading some of them that we hadn't made some sort of silly mistake; we had to point out that we'd actually landed on the thing.'

'I'll say we did!' Kruger muttered.

'You should know. By the way, its name is officially Kruger, if you care.'

'I'm afraid its name is Abyormen, if we follow accepted usage,' replied the boy. 'But go on.'

'There's not much more to tell. They hated like poison to give up their pet theories, and I've heard them speculating all the way out here about the possibility of the red sun's having been captured by Alcyone after its planet or planets formed, and so on. There's lots of work to be done, and you can help a lot. I judge you've learned a good deal of the local language, and will save our time by acting as an interpreter.'

'Yes, up to a point; somehow whenever I talk to one of these people we get crossed up sooner or later. It may be happening without my even knowing it right now, since I haven't even seen this fellow I've been talking to on the radio.'

'How's that? Haven't seen him?'

'No, and haven't the faintest idea what he looks like. Look, Major, if you'll come down and get me out of this steam bath I'll be a lot better able to explain all this and, believe me, it will take quite a bit of explaining.'

'We're on the way. Will you be coming up alone?' Kruger explained the question briefly to Dar and asked if he would care to go along. The native was a trifle dubious for a moment, then realized that more book material would undoubtedly be involved and agreed to accompany his friend.

'Dar Lang Ahn will come with me,' Kruger reported to Donabed.

'Will he need any special accommodation?'

'I've seen him perfectly comfortable on an ice field, and he's made glider flights of fully two days without bothering to drink, so I don't think temperature and humidity will bother him. I don't know about pressure; as you say, it's higher here.'

'How high does he go on these glider flights?'

'I don't know. He hasn't any flight instruments, by our standards.'

'Did he ever get up near the top of the usual cumulus clouds?'

'Yes. I've been with him. He gets as high as he can whenever he can on long-distance flights.'

'All right. I don't think terrestrial pressure will hurt him. You'd better explain the risks to him if you can, though, and let him make his own decision.'

Kruger was never actually sure whether Dar completely understood him or not, but he was standing beside Kruger when the *Alphard*'s landing tender settled into the clearing of the geysers. The Teacher had been informed of what was going on, and the boy had promised to resume contact with him on the ship's radio equipment as soon as was practical. The hidden being had made no objection, though he must have realized that the move was taking Kruger out of his reach.

The flight back to the *Alphard*, which was circling safely beyond Abyormen's atmosphere, was uneventful to all except Dar Lang Ahn. He did not ask a single question while it lasted, but his eyes took in everything there was to see. One peculiarity of his behavior was noticed by most of the human crew. In most cases when a more or less primitive creature is taken for a ride off his planet he spends most of the time looking at the world as seen from outside. Nearly all Dar's attention, on the other hand, was devoted to the structure and handling of the tender. The only time he looked down for more than a moment at a time was when circular velocity was reached and the tender went weightless. Then he looked back at the surface for nearly a minute and, to the sincere astonishment of all watchers, took the phenomenon in his stride. Apparently he had convinced himself that the falling sensation did not represent an actual fall or, if it did, that the pilots would take care of the situation before it became dangerous. Major Donabed developed a healthy respect for Dar Lang Ahn in that moment; he had experienced too many educated human beings who had become hysterical in like circumstances.

Of course, reflected the boy, Dar is a flyer and gets plenty of brief low-weight jolts when he hits downdrafts or reaches the tops of updrafts, but they never last more than a second or two. The fellow was good; Kruger himself, after nearly an earthly year on the ground, was feeling a trifle queasy.

In due course the monstrous bulk of the *Alphard* was sighted, approached, and contacted, and the tender eased into the hull through its special lock. The group disembarked and a conference was called at once.

The meeting was held in the ship's largest lounge, since everyone wanted to hear Kruger's story. By common consent he made his report first, passing briefly over the way he had escaped death at the time he was abandoned and dwelling on his experiences as they applied to the plants, animals, minerals, and people of Abyormen. The lack of anything resembling fruit, the fact that the stems of many plants were edible but not very nourishing, the chances he had taken to find that they were at least not poisonous, and his determination to leave the hot, volcano-ridden area where he had been left and make his way to the pole, where it might be more comfortable, were woven into a reasonably concise account. Everyone who listened had some question or other when he was finished, however, and it was necessary for the *Alphard*'s commander to act as chairman.

'You must have had a bit of trouble setting up your direction, when you first started to travel.' This was one of the astronomers.

'It was a bit confusing.' Kruger smiled. 'If the red sun had merely kept changing in size it wouldn't have been bad, but it wobbled back and forth, at the place where I landed, from southeast to southwest and back again, in a way that took me quite a while to get used to. The blue one was easier – Alcyone rises in the east and sets in the west the way things ought to. At least, it does that far from the pole, and it was easy enough to see why it didn't when I got further north.'

'Right. The red dwarf's motions are natural enough, if you remember how eccentric the planet's orbit is. How much does the libration amount to, in your experience? I've only seen the planet through about one revolution.'

'I'd say about sixty degrees each side of the mean.'

The astronomer nodded, and yielded the floor. The captain gave the nod to a geologist.

'You say nearly all the country you saw was volcanic?'

'On the continent where you found me, yes. Actually I didn't cover too much of the planet, remember. The long peninsula I followed north—'

'About three thousand miles,' interjected a photographer.

'Thanks. Its full length was actively volcanic, and the continental region it projected from is largely covered with lava flows of various ages. Near the ice cap it's mountainous but not obviously volcanic.'

'Good. We've got to map some stratigraphic sequences as soon as possible, if we're to get any idea of the age of this world. I don't suppose you saw any fossils near the ice?'

'I was only on the ground near the settlement; I flew over the rest. Dar Lang Ahn, here, could probably help you, though.'

'Would he be willing to?'

'Probably. His curiosity bump is quite prominent. I gave you an idea of what he wants knowledge for – he puts it in books for the next generation, since his own won't last much longer.' Kruger did not smile as he said this; the prospect of losing Dar was weighing on him more and more heavily as time drew on.

'Would your friend tell us a little more about this alternation-of-generations business?' asked the biologist. 'We have animals on Earth that do much the same, though usually the two forms are not adapted to such drastically different environments, but the thing that bothers me right now is the question of these Teachers. When they finally do die, is the result a crop of the alternate-type descendant, or nothing, or what?'

'I don't know, and neither does Dar Lang Ahn. You'd better ask that "hot" form Teacher I was talking to when you heard me. I don't even know whether there is one offspring or a number of them in the normal state of affairs.'

'That's obvious enough – if there were only one, with no other method of reproduction the race would have died off long ago. There must be occasional accidental deaths.'

'Well, the person to ask is the Teacher, anyway. I'll do it for you when I talk to him.'

'Why do the Teachers keep most of their people in ignorance of this business, anyway?' Another questioner took over.

'You'll have to ask them. If I were in their place I'd do it to keep the peace, but this one claims that they don't mind having a definite death date.'

'I'd like to talk to your friend about it.'

'All right. I suspect someone will have to set up a schedule sheet, though.' The questions and answers went on and on, until Kruger gave up trying to stifle his yawns. The commander finally broke up the meeting; but even then the boy did not rest for some time. He proceeded to show Dar Lang Ahn over the *Alphard*, answering his little friend's questions as best he could.

He finally slept, enjoying weightlessness for the first time in many months. He did not notice whether or not Dar was able to sleep in the circumstances, but the native appeared adequately refreshed in the morning, so Kruger assumed that he had. Dar refused to try human foods, insisting he was not hungry, but Kruger consumed a breakfast so huge as to move some of his acquaintances to warn him. The relatively low nourishment value of Abyormenite plants had gradually accustomed him to eating far larger quantities at a meal while he was on the planet.

Hunger satisfied, he reported to the commander, who immediately called another conference, this time of scientists only. It was decided that top priority on Dar's time should be given the philologists, so that more interpreters would be available as soon as possible. The biologists were advised to take a landing boat and catch some animals of their own; they would have to get most of their knowledge the hard way. Kruger soothed them by promising to help them with the Teacher while Dar was giving language lessons.

The geologists, however, were going to need Dar's personal assistance. They could, of course, map the whole land surface of Abyormen and start checking likely spots for sedimentary outcrops in person, but the time which would be consumed that way could be put to much better uses. In consequence, Dar was shown colored pictures of the sorts of rock the specialists hoped to find and asked if he knew any places on the planet where they might be found.

Unfortunately he failed to recognize a single picture. The geologists might have given up after exhausting their photographs and gone back to the map plan, but Kruger noticed that one of the pictures was of a sample of travertine virtually identical with the material deposited around the geyser pool. He pointed this out to Dar.

'Your pictures are not very good,' was the response.

Twenty minutes later it had been established that Dar Lang Ahn could see light ranging in wave length from forty-eight hundred Angstroms to just under eighteen thousand – that is, not quite as far to violet as the average human being but more than an octave farther into the infra-red. The color pictures, balancing the three primary shades to make combinations which reproduced what the human eye saw of the original, simply did not duplicate more than half the color range that Dar saw. As he said, the color pictures were no good. The dyes in the film were the wrong colors, in that part of the spectrum.

'No wonder I never did get any of his words for colors,' muttered Kruger disgustedly. The problem was solved by making black and white prints and letting Dar concentrate on texture. Thereafter he was able to identify more than half the pictures and to tell where samples of most of them could be found. After a short geology lesson he even suggested areas of thrust and block-faulting and canyons which exposed strata to depths of hundreds or thousands of feet; the maps he drew were more than sufficient to enable the regions in question to be located. The rock specialists were delighted. So was Dar Lang Ahn, and so was Nils Kruger – the last for reasons of his own.

The boy had resumed radio contact with the Teacher while this was going on and told him everything that had happened. He explained what the visitors wanted in the way of information and offered to trade as much knowledge as the creature wanted. Unfortunately the Teacher still felt that too much scientific knowledge was not good for his people. He would not budge from his point that knowledge would, in time, lead to space travel, and space travel would inevitably lead to disruption of the Abyormenite life cycle, since it was ridiculous to suppose that another planet could match Abyormen's characteristics.

'But your people don't have to *stay* on other planets; why not just visit, to trade or learn or simply look?'

'I have showed you, Nils Kruger, that your ignorance of my people led you far astray before. Please believe me when I tell you that you are equally in error to think that leaving this world could help them in any way.' He remained stubborn on that point, and Kruger had to give up.

He reported his failure to Commander Burke and was somewhat surprised at that officer's answer.

'Aren't you just as fortunate that he didn't accept your offer?'

'Why, sir?'

'As I understand it you were virtually promising him any of our technical knowledge in which he might feel an interest. I admit that we are not as security conscious as we were a few generations ago when Earth still had wars, but it's generally considered inadvisable to be too free with a new race in the matter of potentially destructive techniques until we know them pretty well.'

'But I do know them!'

'I'll admit that you know Dar Lang Ahn. You have met a few others of his race, a number of his Teachers, and have spoken by radio to a Teacher of what I suppose we'll have to call the complementary race. I refuse to credit you with "knowing" the people in general, and still claim that you might have been in a rather equivocal position had that creature accepted your offer.'

'But you didn't object to everyone's telling Dar all he asked about.'

'For about the same reason that Teacher didn't object to your telling him.'

'You mean because he's going to die soon? Won't you let him go back to the Ice Ramparts before then? He expects to.'

'I suppose he does. I don't think it will do any harm; he will take no written material, and without that I am sure he could do no damage.'

Kruger checked himself; he had been on the verge of mentioning the native's memory. He wanted Dar Lang Ahn to learn things. He knew that what the little native was told or shown he would remember, and what he remembered he would tell his Teachers at the Ice Ramparts. The Teacher at the village might object, but there seemed little he could do; Kruger had kept their bargain.

But could that being do something? He had claimed to have influence over the Teachers at the ice cap – enough to make them attempt to murder Kruger against their own wills. Perhaps he could force them to ignore the information Dar brought, or even destroy Dar; that was definitely not part of Kruger's plan. What was the influence the being possessed, anyway? Could anything be done to reduce or eliminate it? He would have to talk to that Teacher again – and plan the talk very, very carefully indeed. The boy floated motionless for a long time, thinking, but at last his expression brightened a trifle. A few moments later he shoved himself into motion against the nearest wall and headed for the communication room.

The Teacher acknowledged the call at once.

'I suppose you have thought of some more arguments why I should favor the spread of your technology?'

'Not exactly,' replied Kruger. 'I wanted to ask a question or two. You said that there were four of you Teachers at that city. I'd like to know whether the others share your attitude in this matter.'

'They do.' The answer was prompt and disconcerted the boy a trifle.

'All right. How about the Teachers in the other cities? I assume you have been telling them about all that has been happening.' This time the answer was not so prompt.

'As a matter of fact, we have not. We do not maintain constant communication; simply check with each other every year. If I were to call now they would probably not be listening. It does not matter; there is no doubt how they would feel. After all, we have maintained for many long years the policy of limiting technology for ourselves and making sure that we were the source of knowledge for the others – the radios they have at the Ice Ramparts were made by us, for example; they do not know how to do it.'

'I see.' The cadet was a trifle discouraged but by no means ready to give up. 'Then you would not mind our visiting the other cities and contacting your fellow Teachers directly, to put the proposition to them.' He fervently hoped that it would not occur to the other to ask whether the human beings were all in accord on the matter.

'Certainly. You would, of course, explain the situation as you have to me; they would give the same answer.'

Kruger smiled wickedly.

'Yes, we might do that, or we might tell them a slightly different story – say, that your mind has become affected some way, and you had tricked some information out of us and were tired of the sacrifices involved in being a Teacher, and were going to build devices that would keep a larger part of the planet hot and stop your people's time of dying—'

'I never heard such nonsense in my whole year of life!'

'Of course you haven't. Neither have your friends in other cities. *But how will they know it's nonsense?* Will they dare take the chance?' He paused, but no answer came from the radio. 'I still think that there's no need for your people to fly off into space just because they learn a little physics. Aren't they as capable of seeing the dangers involved as you are?'

'Wait. I must think.' Silence reigned for many minutes, broken only by a faint crackle of static. Kruger waited tensely.

'You have taught me something, human being.' The Teacher's voice finally sounded again. 'I will not tell you what it is. But Dar Lang Ahn's Teachers may learn what they can.' He said no more.

Kruger relaxed, with a grin spreading over his face. The plan would work; it couldn't fail, now.

Dar Lang Ahn would soak up vast quantities of information, enough to fill many books – books which could not possibly be written before the time of dying. Dar Lang Ahn would return to the Ice Ramparts with his knowledge, and he would still be dictating it or writing it himself when the time came to seal the caverns against the rising temperature and changing atmosphere. He would still be inside when that happened, not out in the cities of the 'cold' people dying with his fellows. Dar Lang Ahn, by sheer necessity, would become a Teacher; and Nils Kruger would not lose his little friend.

XII

Geology; Archaeology

Abyormen is larger than the earth and has a smaller percentage of sea area even in the cold time, so the geologists had a great deal of territory to cover. They did not, of course, attempt to do it all; the basic plan was to attempt enough stratigraphic correlation to get a fair idea of its geological history and, if at all possible, find datable radio-actives in the series far enough down to get at least a minimum value for the age of the planet. The last was all the astronomers really wanted, but the biologists had considerably higher standards. They came along, prepared to analyze any fossils found by every technique known to their field.

Layer after layer of sedimentary rock was traced, sometimes for miles underground, sometimes only yards before it vanished – perhaps because quakes had shuffled it into a puzzle that took experience to solve, perhaps because the phenomena which had deposited it in the first place had covered only a limited area and the formation pinched out naturally. A limestone bed laid down over a million square miles at the bottom of a sea is one thing; a sandstone lens that was once the delta of a stream running into a small lake is something else – sometimes a rather inconvenient something else, when a problem of relative dates is in question.

Kruger thanked his luck that Commander Burke was not with this ground party and prayed constantly that he would not overhear any remarks made by the geologists, for Dar Lang Ahn was learning a good deal of English as time went on, and there are few places where a photographic memory can make itself more obvious or useful than in a stratigraphy problem. The geologists without exception regarded the native with awe and felt a friendship for him comparing strongly with Kruger's own. Sooner or later the commander would learn; the boy hoped that by then his little friend's popularity would have reached a point where the old officer would be moved to get rid of his suspicions.

Nowhere on the planet did there seem to be structures corresponding with the 'shields' which characterize certain parts of Earth. Apparently all the present land surface had been submerged in the not too distant past; there was more than a suggestion that Abyormen suffered much more seismic and orogenic activity than Earth. One of the specialists suggested that a reason for this might lie in the 'Long Year' seasonal changes, when the greater part of the sea water was deposited on the ice caps. A seismic check of the cap in the southern hemisphere (*not* over the south pole) indicated a thickness of nearly thirty-five thousand feet. It was snowing at the time the check was made, Theer never shone on this part of the planet, and Arren would not rise for several terrestrial years.

While several of Abyormen's short years passed before any absolute dating of strata was possible, the astronomers learned what they had feared rather quickly. From the beginning, of course, the geologists had kept their eyes open for pegmatites and other igneous intrusions which might contain radioactives suitable for dating, and fairly soon these were found at several places on the continent they were examining. It was not possible to correlate these rocks with the sedimentaries, at the time, but one of them had a uranium-lead ratio corresponding to an age of just under one and a half billion years. It was a large sample, and ten independent checks were run, none varying more than about twenty million years from the mean. Since the astronomers were not willing to believe that Alcyone had been in existence longer than something like one per cent of that time they accepted the information a trifle glumly.

But dated or not, the sedimentaries had their own fields of interest. If Dar Lang Ahn had ever seen a fossil in his life he had never given it a second thought. This omission was easily remedied, for the sediments had their share of organic remains. A lens of limestone some two hundred miles across, near the center of the continent, seemed to consist largely of a reef deposit, and several hundred different species were found at various points within it. Shellfish that might have come straight from Earth were present by the thousands – at least, so it appeared to Kruger; a biologist spent much time pointing out technical differences.

'I suppose,' he finished, 'that you could find a good many creatures virtually identical with these on the shores of your present oceans. There seems to be some ability in the mollusks and their relatives to ride out the changes of a planet. On Earth they've been around for half a billion years – changed, to be sure, but the basic plan seems to keep right on going.'

'I understand you in all but one point,' Dar Lang Ahn replied in his slow, careful English. 'I have been with you all along here, and have seen fossils like this in many different layers of rock, as you say is reasonable, but I have never seen a living creature which in any way resembles those fossils.'

'Have you ever spent any length of time at the seashore?'

'Much. Nils Kruger and I walked along one for about three hundred miles recently, if the occasions in my previous eight hundred years don't count.'

'That's right!' Kruger exclaimed excitedly. 'I knew there was something funny about that beach and never could put my finger on it. There weren't any seashells, or stranded jellyfish, or anything of that nature. No wonder it looked queer!'

'Hmph. I confess that is distinctly odd. How about other sea creatures?'

'I don't know. I think there are animals of various sorts living in the water, and I'm sure there are plants. I can't think of very many different kinds, though.' The biologist gave this bit of information to those of his colleagues engaged in field work; he himself was too busy with fossil correlation to follow it up.

Gradually he established order out of the chaos. For purposes of discussion, he divided Abyormen's past into periods whose boundaries in time seemed to have been established by the general flooding of this continent which had resulted in the limestone beds. The geologists could not find evidence for definite periods of mountain-building, which are usually better for such a purpose; on Abyormen, as they had already suspected, orogenic activity seemed to be fairly uniformly distributed through time.

There were, of course, many reasons why the world might be more active seismically than Earth. It was larger, for one thing – ninety-one hundred miles in diameter and forty per cent more massive, so that a one hundred seventy pound man weighed about one hundred eighty on its surface. The percentage difference was small, but the total tonnage of gravitational forces available for orogeny was much larger than on mankind's home world. At any rate there was the evidence – mountain-building periods were short, frequent, and local.

This should have made the biology department happy, even though it promised trouble for the astronomers. Unfortunately the vertebrate fossils had produced another headache.

It had not proved difficult to set up a general sequence almost certainly corresponding to the course of evolution on the planet, spanning what must have been several hundred million years, if Earth could serve as an example. This sequence started with things just barely possessed of hard-enough interior parts to preserve, ran through bony creatures comparable to the fishes, and led eventually to legged creatures which quite obviously breathed air and spent their lives, or most of them, on dry land. It would have been nice to have been able to put the simple end of this series at the bottom of a page and Dar Lang Ahn at the top, with logically intermediate forms in between, but this was rendered impossible by the fact that every fossil vertebrate found that was possessed of bony limbs at all had six of them. Dar was sufficiently human to have two arms and two legs, with no visible trace of any others.

At the biologists' urgent plea the native submitted to having a set of X-ray photographs made of himself. He was as interested as anyone in looking at the results, and was as able as any biologist to see that his skeleton bore no traces of a third pair of appendages.

Dar by now was as familiar with the general principles of evolution as the average educated human being and could see why the professionals were bothered. Even before anyone had asked he commented, 'It looks as though nothing you've found in the rocks could be a direct ancestor of my race. I suppose we might have come from some other world, as Nils once thought, but there is nothing in any book I have ever read, or that any Teacher has ever told me, to suggest such a thing.'

'That spikes that one,' remarked the biologist sadly.

'Not entirely; it is quite possible that it happened so long ago that either we kept no records or they have been lost in the meantime. However, I'm afraid it will be a little difficult to prove.'

'You're probably right. I think one thing that had better be done is to look for definitely recent formations.'

The geologists had listened to this conversation; it took place during one of the regular breaks for meals. One of them now spoke up.

'It's a little hard to look at a formation casually and say, "this is less than a million years old." We're keeping our eyes open, of course, but you know perfectly well that dating comes afterward – after excavation, and finding fossils and comparing them with other formations.'

'How about unconsolidated material on talus slopes or in caves?'

'Hardly our field, but we'll bore into any we find. I'm not sure I recall any really well-developed cave country, though some of these limestone layers might furnish the makings if the climate cooperated.'

'I have heard of caves on some of the other continents in which strange diagrams and drawings could be seen on the walls,' offered Dar Lang Ahn. The party turned toward him as one.

'Can you take us there?' Several voices asked the question almost simultaneously.

'Maybe. It would be safer if we went to one of the cities on that continent and had one of the local people act as guide.'

So it was arranged, after consulting with Commander Burke on the distant *Alphard*. Another flier was sent down to take the small party, so that the geologists would not be deprived of a means of travel, and several more specialists came down with the new vessel.

The continent in question lay far to the south and west of the place where the work had been going on but was still under the light of red Theer. Dar Lang Ahn found a city without difficulty and, after the usual explanations which sight of the human beings required, was able to obtain a guide. Actually, many of the citizens chose to come along to see the strangers at work; there was little of importance to be done, since all the books of this particular city had been taken to the Ice Ramparts and the people were simply awaiting death.

The caves were precisely as Dar had described; there was no doubt in the minds of any of the men that they had been inhabited by beings in the dawn of a civilization. Most of the visitors were attracted by the pictures on the walls, which Dar had mentioned, but those who knew what they were doing set to work with extreme care on the floors.

These were covered with hard-packed earth, which was carefully removed, layer by layer, and sifted for anything that might be present. The natives commented freely on everything that came to light; they had never thought of digging there themselves and apparently did not recognize any of the objects that were found. These might just as well have come from a similar cavern on Earth – tools of stone and bone and objects which might have been ornaments.

For days the digging went on. The scientists had hoped in the beginning that skeletons of the inhabitants might turn up, but they were disappointed. One of them mentioned this to Dar.

'It's not too surprising,' the native answered. 'I can see that these people lived in a way different from ours, but it can't have been that different. They either died at the proper time and left no trace, or died by violence, and that would hardly have happened in the caves here.'

'We don't really know that it was people like yours who lived here,' answered one of the scientists drily. 'Somewhere in the history of this planet of yours there seems to be a big break. I might have suspected that your people came from another planet and the "hot" ones were native to Abyor-men, if we didn't know about the father-son relationship you have with them.'

'Perhaps we both did,' suggested Dar. The biologist brightened.

'That's a possibility. I wish the people who lived in these caves had drawn a picture or two of themselves.'

'How do you know they didn't?' The scientist looked up at the weird creatures whose images sprawled across the limestone walls and ceilings.

'I don't,' he said sadly. 'You would bring that up. At least none of them are six-limbed, which at least *suggests* the animal life at the time this cave was inhabited was more closely related to you than what we found in the rocks can have been.'

The scientist went back to his work, and Dar Lang Ahn, for the first time since Kruger had known him, went off by himself. He saw the boy looking after him and called back with his equivalent of a smile, 'Don't worry, I just want to be alone for a while. I have a lot of thinking to do. Don't be afraid to call me if anything exciting happens.'

Kruger felt relieved but was not quite sure what would be listed as exciting by his little friend. At first, after the arrival of the *Alphard*, virtually everything had seemed to qualify; the native had difficulty in keeping his attention on one thing at a time, since everything in his vicinity demanded examination. As time went on that tendency had disappeared. Kruger wondered whether Dar could possibly be losing the interest in the sciences which the boy had been trying to develop. He decided that the risk was slight; this work *was* getting a trifle boring, even for Kruger. It had long since passed the point where every new fossil, flint knife, or piece of limestone added noticeably to their fund of knowledge.

He wondered whether it would be worth while to return to the *Alphard* with Dar to see what the astronomers were doing. It would be a change and if Dar's interest really was flagging, unlikely as that seemed, it might take a new turn for the better. He would make the suggestion when Dar emerged from his contemplation.

It turned out that the little native was not tired of geology, however. His natural courtesy made him suggest that they go back to the other party for 'just a little while' before returning to the ship; he would not have considered a return at all had he not realized that Kruger was getting bored.

The geology group, when they did get back to it, had made progress – more than they or anyone had a right to expect; so much that Kruger's boredom disappeared within seconds after landing at the current site of operations. Briefly, they had found the 'break' in the geological sequence.

It had dawned on one of the scientists, after much fruitless labor, that the drastic climatic change each long year should produce an effect similar to, but more pronounced than, the seasonal changes in such formations as varved clays on Earth. Lakes, for example, should dry up completely and alternate wind-blown with water-laid sediments in a much more distinct fashion than had ever been seen on the home planet. With this thought in mind they had selected a large, shallow lake. A series of cores from the edge compared with a similar series from the deepest part of the body of water had led to results which were fairly certain to make the astronomers very happy.

The seasonal changes as described by the Teacher in the distant village of the geysers had been going on, apparently, for just a trifle under six million years according to one worker's theory, or a trifle over ten million according to another's. The two schools of thought were about evenly divided, the first basing its figures on the assumption that the long year had always had its present length of about sixty-five terrestrial years, the second insisting that the seasonal period must have been more or less steadily decreasing in length. This group had no suggestions for explaining such a phenomenon but stuck to their interpretation of the data. Dar Lang Ahn was fascinated; it was the first time that he had realized that positive knowledge did not always result at once from scientific investigation.

It remained for the leader of the party to sum up the geological situation over the first meal after Dar and Kruger had returned.

'This seems to be the story of this planet, according to present evidence,' he said. 'It originated about as long ago as Earth, give or take a billion years, and as far as we can tell in the same manner. It passed through the usual stage of cooling, and eventually water was able to condense. Its primary atmosphere was probably retained a trifle better than Earth's, since the velocity of escape here is over twenty per cent higher. Life started, probably spontaneously in the usual manner but possibly from adventitious spores, and developed on a path comparable to that of the other planets with which we are familiar – that is, it drastically modified the primary atmosphere until it became more or less like that of Earth.

'During this period, which lasted for most of the planet's existence, the tremendous climatic changes now associated with its sun's periodic passage close to Alcyone do not seem to have been occurring; at least, no evidence whatever has been found to suggest they were, and a number of very significant facts indicate the contrary. For example, in some of the fossil beds great numbers of shellfish and other creatures of apparently identical species but widely differing size are found, without any layering which would suggest that the smaller ones died earlier. It would seem from such facts that the life of Abyormen, at that time, was normal from our point of view in its reproductive habits – creatures were born, grew old, and died pretty much at random.

'Life evolved to the stage of air-breathing vertebrates under these conditions, the characteristic types produced all being six-limbed. There is no evidence that intelligent beings evolved.

'Then somewhere between five and ten million years ago, the tremendous temperature changes produced by Alcyone began to occur and virtually all the life of the planet was wiped out. Either a few simple forms survived and gave rise to the present species, which get around the climate situation in the way we now know, or more spores arrived, or a totally new generation of life took place.

'We still know very little about these last few million years; it seems the consensus that we should actually drain this lake and conduct major excavations in its bed to find remains of the life of this period. However, we do know that at the moment the general life of the planet exists under a form of alternating generations which enable it to survive in two widely different environments. Are there any additions or corrections to this summary?'

'Just a comment; astronomical help is urgently needed,' came a voice.

'I agree. I have been recording this little speech and will send the tape up to the *Alphard* as soon as possible.'

The meal ended with no further contributions to science.

'What do you think of it, Dar?' Kruger asked later. 'Does this go very badly against what your Teachers have told you?'

'It doesn't conflict at all; they never told us anything about such possibilities. Knowing what the Teachers are, now, I can suppose that is because they never thought of them themselves.'

'Isn't there some chance of your Teachers' objecting to your telling all this? Or, if they don't object, at least some of the "hot" Teachers will.'

'I've been thinking about that. I think our own Teachers will be as interested as I am, and I have come to the conclusion that all the other Teachers know about our doings is what our own report to them by radio. The others couldn't live anywhere near the Ice Ramparts.'

'Not even underground?'

'A long way down, maybe, but they still couldn't watch very closely. For one thing, didn't that one at the geyser village mention that there was no way for you to see him or him to see you, since no barrier that would keep you both safe could be seen through?'

'I hadn't thought of that. But if he depends on reports from your Teachers, why couldn't they have just *said* they had killed me, instead of actually trying to carry out his orders?'

'Well, if that ever occurred to them they probably thought that the reason he wanted you killed was of such a nature that he was bound to detect the results if you weren't. If my people did learn a lot of your science right afterward, for example, it would be quite hard to hide.'

'I suppose so. Still, I'd certainly take a chance rather than kill a friend.'

'Perhaps they weren't sure how much of a friend you were. Remember, they hadn't been with you as long as I, and – well, you do have some rather odd characteristics, you know. I can understand that "hot" Teacher's feeling that way.'

'I suppose so. We know each other pretty well now, but we still find each other queer at times. It doesn't bother me any more, though.'

'Nor me.' The two looked at each other with a more nearly complete understanding, in that moment, than they had ever achieved before or were to attain later.

XIII

Astronomy; Xenology

The flier that took the geological report to the astronomers also carried Dar Lang Ahn and Nils Kruger back to the *Alphard*. Dar had followed the summary as far as it went, but he did not see just how astronomy was needed to check on the theories of the rock specialists. His curiosity about all matters allied to the physical sciences had reached a level that few human beings experience after leaving childhood.

He listened carefully as the record of the geologist's summary was played over by the astronomers, but heard nothing he did not remember from its original utterance. He listened carefully to the conversation of these new scientists and never considered that they might regard his insistent questions as a discourtesy – which, as a matter of fact, most of them did not.

'I am afraid I do not know exactly what you mean when you say that Arren may have "captured" Theer and Abyormen,' Dar would ask at one point.

'I think young Kruger explained something of Newton's laws to you,' was the beginning of the answer.

'Normally, any two bodies attract each other according to definite law, and that attraction, plus the ordinary fact of inertia – the thing that keeps a stone traveling after it leaves the hand that throws it – results in definite, predictable motions of those bodies, such as the *Alphard* around your planet at this moment. By "capture" we simply imply that originally Theer did *not* travel around Arren, but had its own path through space, and this path carried it close to Arren. The star's attractive forces changed the paths so that now they travel around each other.'

'That seems clear enough. But I gathered that some of you found fault with this idea?'

'Plenty of fault. Capture doesn't ordinarily occur; it calls, as a rule, for very special circumstances.'

'Why? If this force varies with distance as you say, I should think that all that would be needed would be for the two objects to get close enough together. In fact, I don't see why Theer and Arren haven't fallen into each other long ago, if what you say is right.'

'Good point. The trouble is, as two objects fall toward each other their speed increases – you can see that. Unless they are aimed exactly right to start with they won't collide, and unless they collide they'll start going apart again, slowing down just as fast as they picked up speed before. The out-bound path will be shaped just like the inbound one, so you won't see them spiraling together. Here, I'll show you.'

Since the *Alphard* was in free fall, demonstration of the point was easy enough. Two electrically charged pith balls in the evacuated air lock behaved in a manner that made the whole affair quite clear to the curious Abyormenite.

'Then how could a capture ever take place?' he asked when his instructor had re-entered the main part of the ship and doffed his space suit. 'I suppose it's possible some way or you wouldn't even have mentioned it.'

'It's possible – just. If a third object is present, moving exactly the right way with respect to the others, things may turn out just right, though the prob-ability of such an event is not awfully high; and if I'd let air into the lock a moment ago its friction would have caused the pith balls to spiral together.'

'I suppose the idea is that some of the other stars in this group served as the third body.'

'I hate to depend on such an idea, because they're pretty far apart, but that may account for the situation.'

'At any rate it is possible that this sort of thing may account for the begin-ning of the hot times on Abyormen.'

'Possible. I'd not like to say more.' The Abyormenite had to be content with that – for the time being.

Naturally it did not take very many answers involving the terms 'perhaps' and 'probably' to start Dar pondering on the 'how-do-you-know' type of question. Up to a point the astronomers bore with him even then, but even-tually they suggested as tactfully as possible that he have Kruger teach him a little elementary algebra.

It never occurred to Dar to be hurt. He was mildly annoyed at himself for not thinking of this before, since so many of his previous questions had involved bits of mathematics in their answers. He went gaily off to find Kruger, who no longer accompanied him everywhere since his great improve-ment in English.

Dar failed to notice the slight dismay that his request caused his human friend; he settled down and wanted to learn algebra at once. Kruger did his best, but was not the world's best teacher. He might have done better had he not been obsessed with a fear that this sort of thing was likely to destroy Dar's interest in science.

He need not have worried. Most people who suffer in mathematics do so because they treat it as something to be memorized, and memorization held no terrors for Dar Lang Ahn. Perhaps for that reason he was extremely slow in grasping the basic idea of algebra as a problem-solving tool; he could learn all the rules but, faced with a problem, had precisely the same trouble as so many high-school freshmen. However, it was Kruger rather than Dar who eventually sought relief from this task.

Finding a new subject to interest Dar was not difficult, but for private reasons Kruger felt that it should be a non-mathematical one this time. He shared the common belief about biology's being such a subject, and decided that it was about time to find out what the life scientists had learned about Abyormen.

It turned out that this team had been trying for some time to solve the problem of examining the only 'hot' life form available – one of the Teachers in the volcano-warmed refuges. The individual at the geyser village was still not exactly cooperative, but they felt that they knew him better than any of the others; it was this being who had been selected to play host to a televison-equipped robot which the *Alphard*'s engineers had improvised. Dar, seeing this device, was immediately off on a new track, and Kruger was faced with explaining television and remote control. He was still trying when everyone went aboard the landing boat with the robot.

Actually Dar felt he had a fairly clear picture of what the apparatus did, and he was beginning to get a very good idea of his chances of learning *how* it was done. He listened while Kruger talked to the Teacher on the boat's radio during the landing, but made no comments of his own.

'We would appreciate it if you would allow our robot to enter your retreat. We are sure it can stand the conditions.'

'Why should I do this? What good will it do either of us?'

'You have seen us, and must have formed some of your opinions as a result. Don't you think we might modify some of our beliefs after seeing you? After all, you have claimed many times that we do not understand you, since we do not agree with your views about the spreading of knowledge. It seems to me that you would be willing to do anything which will increase our understanding.'

'How do you know I have ever seen you? I told you that I knew of no substance which would keep our environments apart and which could also be seen through.'

'Then you didn't tell the whole truth – you have a television device of some sort. You saw clearly enough to ask about those iron belt buckles that Dar wears.'

'Very well. But how sure can I be that your seeing me will bring you strange people to your right minds?'

'I cannot tell; how can I promise what we'll conclude from evidence we don't yet possess? In any case you can learn more of us.'

'I have no particular interest in learning more about you.'

'You did when you were asking me all those questions a few years back.'

'I learned what I needed to know then.'

'Many of the people are learning about our science, not just Dar Lang Ahn.

There were scores of them watching while we investigated a cave far to the south.'

'There seems little I can do to stop it.'

'But if *you* will also learn from us, you could at least have some idea of what the others are finding out; and you would be able to exercise some control over what your own people learn when their time of living arrives.'

Dar was a trifle confused by this argument; he did not entirely understand what the boy was trying to do and understood even less the mental operations of the distant Teacher. He did not know whether or not to be surprised when this argument seemed to convince the creature, but he could tell that Kruger was satisfied with the result.

The robot, small though it was, was too big to go through the trap at the place where Dar and Kruger had talked to the Teacher. At the latter's direction, the flier was landed near the crater in which the two travelers had been trapped for so long and the machine carried to the building in which they had found the generators. The men returned to the flier, where they all gathered around the television screen tuned to the robot's transmitter.

'What next?' one of the men asked the Teacher.

'Send your machine down the ramp.' The operator complied; the little box rolled on its caterpillar treads down the slippery surface. The light grew dimmer as the bottom of the ramp was approached, and a bulb on the top of the robot was lighted to permit them to see.

'Along the corridor. Make no turns; there are other passages.' The machine advanced. The corridor was long and apparently led deep into the mountain; it was some time before the way was blocked by a fairly solid door.

'Wait.' They obeyed, and after a short time the door opened.

'Come quickly.' The robot rolled on through and the door swung shut behind it. 'Keep on; there are no more branches. I will come to meet your machine, but will travel slowly, as I have to bring my radio with me. I am still near the village.'

'You need not go to the trouble of traveling unless you would rather the robot did not see that part of your station,' replied one of the biologists. 'The machine can make the trip without anyone's being bothered.'

'Very well. I will wait here, and my companions can talk to you as well.'

There must have been a single long tunnel connecting the passages under the generator building with the area under the village by the geysers. It took a long time to traverse, but eventually the robot reached a point where the corridor suddenly expanded into a large chamber about eight feet high, from which a number of other openings branched. The spokesman, who had learned enough of the Abyormenite language to be independent of Kruger or Dar most of the time, informed the Teacher of the robot's location and requested further directions.

'You are very close; it will be easier to show you the way. Wait there, and I will be with you in a moment.' The men around the television screen watched intently.

In a few seconds a flicker of motion appeared in one of the openings and every eye fixed instantly on its screened image. Their attention did not waver as the newcomer walked toward the robot.

No one was particularly surprised. All except Dar had had more or less experience on Earth's exploring vessels, and had seen a wide variety of creatures turn out to be both intelligent and cultured.

This one was like nothing the Abyormenite had ever seen in his life. A melon-shaped body was supported on six limbs, so thick at the bases that they merged into each other but tapering nearly to points where they reached the floor. The human observers thought of an unusually fat-bodied starfish walking on the ends of its arms rather than spread out flat. In the light from the robot the upper third of the body appeared deep red to human eyes, with a stripe of the same color extending down to the end of each appendage; the rest was black. There were no visible eyes, ears, or similar items of equipment on the body, except for a spot at the very top which might have been anything from a closed mouth to a color peculiarity. Dar had no way of judging the size of the creature from its televised image; the operator of the robot, judging its distance with the usual focusing lights, found that it was about Dar's height and estimated that it must weigh eighty or ninety pounds.

'I take it you see me.' Dar got a distinct impression that the creature's tone was reflecting irony. There was no room for any doubt concerning this thing's identity, for the voice now coming from the robot's pick-up was the same that they had been hearing all along. 'If you will have your machine follow me we will be able to relax while you find out what you wish to know.' Without turning, the creature retraced its steps, and the robot followed. A short corridor led into a room about five feet high, very similar to one of those which Dar and Kruger had examined in the city. Dar watched eagerly, expecting to learn the uses of the various puzzling installations.

Some of them became obvious immediately. Three of the dome-shaped objects were occupied by creatures similar to their guide, their bodies centered on top and the six limbs draped down the side grooves. The guide himself went on to the end of the room and settled himself in one of the 'wash-bowls,' his limbs spread radially in all directions. It was not possible to tell from appearances that the creatures were examining the robot but there seemed little doubt that they were.

The guide, from his 'couch,' resumed the conversation.

'Here we are. Could you perhaps give us a more concrete idea of what you expect to learn by seeing us, and why that knowledge will make you more sympathetic with our ideas?'

'We hope to learn how you live, what you eat, what your abilities and limitations both physical and mental may be, and as much as possible about your connection with the "cold" people who are your children and ancestors. With that knowledge, we may understand better why you object to the spread of technical knowledge on this world. At the moment I must confess that your attitude reminds us of certain historical groups on our own world, and every time in the past that such a group has managed to curtail or control the spread of knowledge the result has been extremely unfortunate. If the people of Abyormen are so different from us that this result should not be expected we'd like to know it.'

'How have the people who have seen you at your work reacted to all this new information?'

'They are almost without exception interested. One at least has learned a good deal, and convinced us that your people are at least as intelligent as ours.'

'I suppose you mean Dar Lang Ahn. No doubt he is planning to expand the refuges of his Teachers or construct a flying machine like yours?'

'He has made no mention of it, but you may ask him. He is here with us.'

Dar was startled at this turn of the conversation, but spoke without hesitation.

'Of course I had not thought of such a thing. I have not learned enough for either task in any case.'

'There is something else I trust you have not learned from these creatures, which your friend Kruger has taught me. However, what you have learned yourself will soon be of little importance.'

'Of course.' Dar became silent and the conversation's subject changed.

'I suppose you control this machine by some modification of radio,' one of the beings on the dome-shaped 'chairs' remarked. The biologist admitted that this was so. 'What sort of waves do you use, that are effective through so much rock? The set with which we have been talking to you has a broadcasting antenna on the surface.'

'I cannot give that information in detail myself,' replied the biologist, 'as it is not my field of knowledge. The robot has an antenna, but it is not very noticeable; if you examine its body closely you will find a coil of wire wound many times about the upper part, just below the turret that carries the eye.' The questioner arose from his seat and walked toward the machine on all six limbs; Dar noticed that it betrayed none of the clumsiness or difficulty with motion so often showed, especially in the last few years, by his own Teachers. Arrived at the robot, the being stood on four of the legs and used the other two to grope over its surface. A bundle of small tendrils, which evidently served the purpose of fingers, became visible at the tip of each limb during this process.

'I can feel the coil,' it said after a moment, 'though it is too small – at least: in its individual wires – to see.'

'I'm afraid the light is not very well located for that purpose,' replied the biologist. 'We did not consider its use except for our own convenience.'

'What? You mean there is a light on this machine, too? When you started to speak I thought you referred to ours. If you will bring the robot over to it perhaps I can see a little better, but I doubt it; as I said, the wires are very fine.'

The biologists all saw what the trouble was, in general; the speaker said in a resigned tone, 'Yes, there is a light on the robot, at the very top, a small cylinder which you can probably feel even if you can't see it. Where is the one to which you were referring?'

'There.' Another limb left the floor and gestured. Dar Lang Ahn, following the indication, saw only the pipe-and-nozzle arrangement which Kruger had described as a gas light.

'You mean that pipe?' asked the biologist. Kruger hastily explained his idea, speaking a split-second before Dar would have.

'But if it's a gas jet why isn't it lighted?' was the objection.

'Maybe it is. Maybe it's a hydrogen flame that doesn't show up in the light from our robot.' Instantly the operator cut the light in question, but nothing was visible on the screen and he immediately restored it. During the brief exchange the Teacher had affirmed that the pipe in question was indeed what he meant.

'Apparently we see by different kinds of light,' the biologist said. 'Were you aware of that? Your "cold" people are a little different from us in that respect, but we are nearly enough alike to use the same lighting devices, so you must differ from them, too.'

'We knew that they could see smaller objects than we, but did not know the reason. We did not know that there were different kinds of light.'

'You are not aware that the waves your radio uses are the same, except for length, as those used for seeing?'

'Ridiculous! Radio waves travel too rapidly for the speed to be measured, if they take any time at all for transit. The waves of sight, if they are waves, travel little faster than those of sound.'

'Oh-ho-o-o.' The human speaker was buried in thought for a moment. Then he asked, 'Could you explain how that light of yours works?'

'It is simply a steam jet, expanding through a nozzle of a particular shape. It would be very difficult to describe the shape, at least in words that we both know.'

'Never mind; you have told me enough. What I fail to understand now is how you could possibly know anything about the suns; you certainly can't "see" them.'

'Of course not; they can only be felt.'

Dar Lang Ahn had been left behind some sentences before, and in hasty whispers the boy tried to explain what was going on.

'The "hot" people don't see the way we do at all; it's even worse than the difference between you and me. We at least see by the same general kind of light – electromagnetic waves. From what this one says, they use some form of sound – very high frequency, I guess, since he said something about its traveling a little faster than "ordinary" sound.'

'But how could anyone see with sound?'

'I suppose you could see, after a fashion, with anything that traveled in a straight line, and sound will do that if nothing interferes with it. The very short sound waves-ultrasonics – are better than the ones we talk with in that respect. Of course, they wouldn't show anything that was very small; he said the wires were too fine to see, you remember.'

The two brought their attention back to the radio conversation – at least, Kruger did. Dar, as usual, had something new to think about.

'You must have done some rather careful thinking yourselves to have deduced as much about this planetary system as you have,' the biologist was saying, 'since you can only detect objects outside Abyormen's atmosphere if they are radiating enough heat to feel.'

'The picture I gave to your Nils Kruger was only one of several theories,' the being replied calmly.

'It happens to be about right, as far as it goes. But if you can do that sort: of thing with scientific reasoning why are you so prejudiced against it?'

'I wish you would stop reiterating that question. To answer it, however, what good does it do us? Are we any better off for knowing that Abyormen goes around Theer and Theer around Arren? I admit that sort of knowledge is harmless, since it cannot lead to dangerous activity, but it is a waste of time.'

'In other words you divide scientific knowledge into two classes – useless items and dangerous ones.'

'Practically. There is an occasional exception; the person who invented these lights did some good, of course. However, it is necessary to examine each new item of knowledge to make sure that it will not be dangerous.'

'I begin to see your viewpoint. I take it, then, that you do not mind *our* wasting our time by finding things out about you.'

'I don't care what you do with your time. Ask your question.'

The scientists complied, and gradually Dar Lang Ahn began to understand the sort of beings his ancestors had been – and his children would be.

Their cities were scattered all over Abyormen, but they were invariably in volcanic areas where a few of their inhabitants could retreat underground and survive through the time of cold, so none of Dar's generation ever went near them – the fire taboo took care of that. It seemed likely, though the

Teacher never admitted it in so many words, that the taboo was another example of influence of the 'hot' Teachers over the 'cold' ones. No such prohibition existed for the 'hot' race, who lived and died where they chose; hence, metal articles such as Dar's belt buckles might be, and often were, found in or near low-temperature cities at the start of the 'cold' life cycle. Like Dar's generation the others took great pains to insure the transmission of knowledge from one cycle to the next, though they depended less on books than on the memory of their Teachers. When Dar interrupted the questioning to ask why it would not be better for the knowledge to go from 'hot' to 'cold' and back to 'hot' again, thus permitting both races to help in its development, the Teacher pointed out patiently that it would be virtually impossible to control the spread of information if this were done.

They were fairly competent electricians and excellent civil engineers. Their chemistry seemed good, surprisingly enough to a race whose chemists depended heavily on sight. Astronomy, naturally, was almost nonexistent and the deeper branches of physics quite beyond them so far. They had radioactive elements, of course, but had not the faintest idea of the cause of their behavior.

Many of the human questions puzzled Dar, of course, and in some cases this was not due to his ignorance of human science. As nearly as he could tell, the men were trying to find out how these Teachers felt about Dar's own people – that is, whether they liked them, respected them, hated them as necessary inferiors, or simply regarded them as a minor but important nuisance. Dar remembered that one of the beings present had claimed friendship with him on the basis of blood relationship, though he could not for the life of him see how such relationship had been determined.

This question also occurred to the biologist, who had been one of those listening in during the interception of Kruger's first radio conversation with the Teacher and had later asked for a translation of it. Rather to Dar's surprise the Teacher had an answer.

'We arrange for the circumstances, or at least the location, of many of our ancestors' deaths. In a short time the people of this village will be ordered to the crater where Dar and Kruger were trapped for a time; there we can observe the death and the beginning of the new lives, and can keep track of who is who's offspring. We also arrange to die ourselves at preselected places when the cold season is about to start, and try to learn from the "cold" Teachers the various places at which their new groups at the beginning of their time of living to catch the people are captured – they go out into the wilds in hunting new people, who are nothing more than wild animals at the time.'

'I should think they would miss some.'

'They do, as nearly as we can tell. Every now and then a member of our race turns up, or sometimes even a small group of them, whose parent must have survived the whole cold season as a wild animal; at least, we have no record of him.'

'Don't you know how many children a given person will have?'

'It is quite impossible to tell, depending on things such as his individual weight.'

'But that doesn't seem to vary much.'

'During normal life, no, but at the time of dying one may have gone for very long periods without food, or on the other hand have eaten very heavily and very recently – all according to the opportunities. Also it is impossible to tell whether any of the young children have been eaten by wild animals before they are caught, in the case of Dar Lang Ahn's people, since they do not take proper care of them as we do.'

'I see.' So did Dar. Good though his memory was it contained little of his brief existence before being 'caught,' but what little there was fitted in with what the Teacher said. He wondered why his own Teachers did not take precautions like those – and then realized that they had no chance; either the 'hot' people would have to cooperate, which they seemed unwilling to do, or his own race would have to keep a group of the others under control during the hot period, as this creature did with his villagers during the cold. This seemed difficult, to put it mildly; the other race had got far enough ahead technically to have pretty complete control of the situation. Dar began to suspect strongly that this Teacher had not been frank; there were reasons other than his personal disapproval of science behind his objections to the introduction of human knowledge.

That thought grew in his mind as the conversation went on, and gave birth to others. It was Dar Lang Ahn, after the robot had started back to the flier, who made the suggestion that some of the other Teachers in their volcanically warmed retreats be contacted and questioned; and even Kruger, who knew him better than any other human being ever would, did not realize just what he was trying to find out.

XIV
Biology; Sociology

Again and again Abyormen swung around its almost cometary orbit, and closer and closer Theer drew to its blazing primary. Abyormen, very slowly, grew hotter. To its natives this was a matter of little moment; the temperature had not yet reached the value which would activate the bacteria whose life processes would load the atmosphere with oxides of nitrogen. Until that happened Dar's people cared little whether the oceans of their planet were freezing or boiling.

The temperature did not bother the human scientists, either. Most of them had from the beginning been wearing complex protective garments which virtually air-conditioned them. Nevertheless they knew that more protection would be needed soon. Experiments with the native life, using not only bacteria but animals and plants large enough to be observed directly, had told them what to expect.

Kruger was more than satisfied with the situation. His friend had evidently become completely absorbed in the business of acquiring knowledge from the human visitors. Kruger could not always keep up with him, but the boy no longer cared much about that. If anything was certain, it was that Dar Lang Ahn had already collected far too much information to relay it all to his Teachers before the end of his normal life span. There would be no alternative to his remaining in the shelter under the ice cap when it was sealed, which meant that he would automatically become a Teacher himself.

Once or twice the boy's conscience bothered him a trifle; he wondered whether it would not have been fairer to point out to Dar what all this time spent with the human visitors must necessarily entail. Each time he thought of this, however, he managed to convince himself that the native was old enough to know what he was doing.

It might have helped had he brought the matter up, just the same.

While the human scientists could, of course, work even in the hot season of Abyormen, action would be much more awkward. Therefore they were trying to get their basic information before the change occurred. Dar watched everything that went on, as far as possible; Kruger was much less enthusiastic after seeing one of the biological tests.

This occurred after the chain-reaction effect of heat on the local bacteria had been discovered. A soil sample from the planet had been used to cover the floor of an airtight cage, and several small animals of the sort Dar and Kruger had encountered in the crater had been introduced. Several native plants were growing there as well; the biologists had tried to reproduce the planet's environment in miniature. This done, they proceeded to raise the temperature – gradually, to minimize the chance of thermal shock's complicating the situation.

The cage was well enough insulated to prevent steam from condensing on the walls, so it was still possible to see what went on within. Some water, of course, was still liquid, since the boiling of the rest had raised the pressure considerably; and quite suddenly a meter began to climb from the zero position.

It was simply a galvanometer, but it was mounted in series with a resistor consisting of a tiny, open vial of water inside the cage. The resistance of the liquid was dropping, and no one present doubted the cause. In a few seconds this became evident even to the naked eye, as the atmosphere within the cage took on a faint but unmistakable reddish-brown tint. The bacteria were at work; oxides of nitrogen were forming, acidifying any water that might still be present in liquid form – and doing something much more drastic to the life in the cage.

The animals had stopped moving, except for an uneasy turning of their heads. Each had drawn a little way from his neighbor, and stopped nibbling on the plants. For several seconds subjects and experimenters alike remained motionless while the suspense mounted.

Then the largest of the little creatures abruptly collapsed, and within the next thirty seconds the others had followed suit. Kruger stole a sidelong glance at Dar, but his little friend did not notice. He had both eyes fixed on the cage. The boy looked back at the animals, and suddenly felt sick. The tiny creatures were losing shape, melting into featureless puddles of protoplasm. The pools remained separate, even where two of the creatures had collapsed quite close together. A faint stirring motion became visible in the mounds of still-living jelly, and as he saw this Kruger's stomach failed him. He raced for the outdoors.

Dar did not seem affected; he remained for the next half hour, which was about the time it took the last of the pools to organize itself into about fifty tiny wormlike things which bore no resemblance whatever to the animal from whose body material they had been formed. These were crawling about the cage, apparently perfectly able to take care of themselves.

The plants had changed also, though not by the same process. The leaves of the larger ones dropped away and the trunks shriveled slightly. At first the watchers had supposed that the growths were simply being killed by the heat, but this hypothesis was eliminated by the appearance of hundreds of tiny knoblike excrescences on the withered trunks. These swelled slowly, apparently at the expense of the parent plant, and finally fell free in a rain of spheres which lasted several minutes.

Smaller, grasslike plants had simply withered, but other things were rapidly sprouting in their places. Less than an hour was required to transform the cage from a respectable representation of the landscape outside the flier to something utterly alien to all of the watchers – Dar Lang Ahn included.

'So that's the story!' one of the biologists breathed at last. Neither he nor any of his colleagues had been affected by the sight as Kruger had been. Of course, none of them had the same personal feeling about Dar. 'I suppose we should have expected quite a lot of offspring from each individual, if this is their only means of reproduction. The population of this planet must be something terrific right: after the season change.'

One of the other biologists shook his head negatively.

'That part is all right,' he said, 'but something else isn't. Right now we're just *before* one of the changes, and there are still plenty of animals around – carnivores as well as plant eaters – and the vegetation doesn't look particularly moth-eaten. I'm afraid I can't quite believe that there's no other method of reproduction here.'

'Wouldn't the need for that depend on the length of time between seasons? If this ratio is the usual one it simply means that about one individual out of fifty lives through the season.'

'Right, and the season now ending lasts about forty Earth years. I refuse to believe that such a large proportion of survivors could be expected in any wild animal over such a period. We know that they eat about as much, compared to their weights, as similar animals on Earth. How about it, Dar? Don't new animals get started at various times during your life span?'

'Certainly,' replied the native. 'Any part of an animal will grow a whole new one, provided it is big enough. The animals we use for food certainly do that, anyway; we always leave some of the creature, for that purpose. Isn't it that way with your animals?'

'Hmph. There are some creatures on Earth capable of that sort of thing, but they're fairly primitive forms. I don't see how anything on this planet could get killed.'

'Well, some animals don't leave enough of their prey to grow again, of course. Then there are always things like starvation or drowning, though starvation takes a long time to shrink anything down to the point where it can't live.'

One of the scientists looked thoughtfully at his own right hand, on which two fingers were represented by stumps – the relic of a childhood accident. 'I suppose, Dar, that it would be foolish to ask whether your own race shares this ability of regeneration.'

'I do not see why it is foolish. Yes, we have it; though in a civilized community there is, of course, very seldom any need for it. Occasionally a victim of a glider crash or something of that sort will have to replace an arm or leg.'

'Or head?'

'That is a special case. If the injury is one that interrupts the regular life processes the tissues go back to the "beginning" and reorganize to a completely new individual – or to several. As far as the original individual is concerned death has occurred. As I said, this sort of thing happens rarely.'

It rather surprised the biologists, that an explanation to the phenomenon was found. However, several weeks' work with all the facilities the *Alphard* had to offer did give a reasonable answer. Richter, head of the biological crew, was glad of the chance to explain it to Commander Burke. That officer had come to question him specifically on such matters; he was worried.

'I'm bothered a trifle about these people, Richter,' Burke opened the conversation. 'As you know, every ship commander that goes out from Earth gets a long briefing about the risk of introducing new species in any environment. They tell us about rabbits in Australia and Japanese beetles in North America, until we get sick of the whole business of ecology. It seems to me that we've run into something that might possibly be a serious competitor for humanity, if what I've been told about Dar Lang Ahn's people is correct.'

'I suppose you've read our summary about regeneration. I admit that these people are rather remarkable in some respects, but I shouldn't say they constituted any sort of danger.'

'Why not? Don't they fit right into the picture – a creature entering a new environment, where its natural enemies are absent, and multiplying unchecked? These beings would swamp men out in a few years.'

'I can't see it. Dar's people have the same natural enemies as men – any sort of meat-eating animal, as well as their usual diseases. They do have sickness, according to Dar. Anything like that would come with them.'

'But the primary killing agent that affects the race is heat. What's going to happen if they get established on Earth, or Thanno, or Hekla, or any of a score of other worlds you and I could name? They'd be virtually immortal.'

'Granting that they need heat to die "normally," I think you're forgetting something. They also need it to reproduce.'

'Either that, or dismemberment. What happened in the Chesapeake in the days when the oystermen thought they could get rid of starfish by chopping them up and throwing them back in the water?'

'You miss the point, Commander – and I'm afraid young Kruger has missed it, too. The really important fact is that *Dar Lang Ahn's people have to die in order to reproduce.* Have you thought of it that way?' There was a long silence before the commander answered.

'No, I can't say that I have. That does put another color to the whole situation.' He paused again in thought. 'Have you any idea of why this occurs – or rather, since it's an obvious evolutionary development for a planet like this, *how* it occurs?'

'We have. It was hard to figure, mostly because there is a good deal of evidence that this drastic climate change only started to occur in the last ten million years or so, but a certain organism of our own planet gave us the lead.'

'What? What creature of Earth is exposed to anything like the conditions met with here?'

'None, so far as I know; that wasn't the sort of lead. One of the men – Ellerbee, as I recall – was working with a group of "hot" animals that we'd obtained in the usual way, in one of our biggest conditioned cages. He was trying to determine whether the carnivores usually left enough of their victims to reproduce, and incidentally to see the regeneration process which Dar had told us about – we didn't really know whether it applied to the "hot" forms or not. Naturally Ellerbee was doing his best to keep track of the types and numbers of animals present, and he was a bit surprised, after a while, to find some creatures he hadn't seen before. Fortunately he didn't simply write the matter off as a slip in his earlier observations; he checked it carefully, and found that when the atmosphere and temperature change occurred it was possible to get animals from soil samples in which no "parents" had been present.'

'Which means?'

'That some of the "hot" forms reproduce by some form of microscopic spore which survives in the soil during the unfavorable season. Whether any of the "cold" ones can do the same is still uncertain; we haven't found any.'

'And what does this imply?'

'It got Ellerbee suspicious of the general theory that Dar Lang Ahn and those fire-blooded starfish are actually alternate generations of the same species. We talked over the matter at one of our regular discussion sessions and found that there was already some more evidence in. Dan Leclos had found in one type of animal a number of small, bony spheroids which experiment had showed to be the source of the "hot" generation for that particular species. If they were removed before exposing the creature to heat and nitrogen dioxide no descendants appeared, although the flesh behaved in the usual manner, while if the spheres themselves were exposed to the changed conditions they produced embryonic specimens of "hot" life.'

'I don't see what all that means.'

'It seems to mean that the "hot" and "cold" forms are completely alien types of life, which originally evolved independently. Each produced spores, or some equivalent, that were capable of surviving the unsuitable conditions.

'In the natural course of evolution some of them developed the trick of attaching or implanting their spores in the bodies of active animals of the other type – perhaps by arranging for them to be eaten, as some parasites on Earth still do.'

'But in that case you should be able to find the seeds, or whatever they are, in any of the creatures you examine. You said they were present in only one. How about that?'

'That's where the lead from Earth came in. You may know that there are some types of virus whose natural prey are bacteria. The virus makes contact with the germ, penetrates its cell wall, and after a while a hundred or so new viruses emerge from the deflated remains of the bacterium.'

'I didn't know that, but there seems nothing strange about it.'

'There isn't, so far. However, it sometimes happens that after the virus enters the body of its victim the latter goes on living as though nothing had happened.'

'Still reasonable. There's always a scattering of immunes in any population.'

'Let me finish. The bacterium lives out its time and divides in the usual fashion; its descendants do the same for ten or twenty or perhaps a hundred generations. Then, under the stimulus of radiation or chemicals or for no apparent reason at all most or all of the descendants of the original bacterium collapse – and clouds of virus particles emerge from the remains!'

'Eh?'

'Precisely. The original virus infected its first victim, all right, *in such a way that the reproductive material of the virus was divided when that of the bacterium did the same* and carried on to all the descendants of that first one. Eventually some change in conditions made them revert to their usual method of reproduction.'

'I see,' Burke said slowly. 'You think that a similar ability has developed here – that every cell of a being like Dar Lang Ahn has in its nucleus the factors which will produce one of those starfish under the proper conditions.'

'Exactly, and yet the relationship is no more a parent-and-child one than that between Jack Cardigan and his pet canary. There's a suspicion that the chloroplasts in earthly plants bear the same relation to them.'

'I don't see what difference it makes, really.'

'In a way, it might justify the attitude of the "hot" creatures toward Dar's people.'

'Perhaps. However, nothing you've said eases my first worry, except your point that both forms have to die to reproduce. You've added one thing that bothers me more.'

'What's that?'

'This business about the time in which adaptation to this climate has taken place. If you're right, one at least of these races has evolved from a standing start to intelligence comparable with our own in something under ten million years. It took Earth a hundred times as long to do the job – maybe twice that. These things must be among the most adaptable life forms in the universe – and that's the point where man has held the edge, so far.'

'You're afraid, I take it, that if they get access to human technology they'll spread out into the galaxy and start supplanting man?'

'Frankly, yes.'

'Just where would you expect them to settle?'

'For Heaven's sake, man – anywhere! Earth – Mars – Mercury – any of fifty worlds where we can live, and as many more where we can't! If they can't stand them now they soon will – it's that adaptability that has me worried. If we get into an argument with them how do we fight – how do you kill a creature that grows new arms and legs to replace the old, that produces a whole crop of descendants if you blow it to pieces with a bomb?'

'I don't know and I don't think it matters.'

'Why not?' Burke's voice sounded almost strangled by his emotion.

'Because, while Dar Lang Ahn could live on Earth and a lot of other worlds, and his fire-blooded opposite numbers could do the same in a higher temperature range, as you justly point out, none of the planets you mentioned provides *both* temperature ranges. If a group of Dar's people decides to migrate to Earth how will the "hot" folks *whose relatives are riding along with them* like it? Dar undoubtedly wants descendants as much as one of us; how will he feel at the thought of the starfish which develop from his body moving to Vega Two, or Mercury? What happens to his kids, then? No, Commander, I realize that most of us have decided, pretty much without discussion, that the Teacher down there by the hot springs is an opinionated, narrow-minded, dictatorial old fuddy-duddy whose opinion isn't worth the energy used to express it, but if you'll think a bit longer you'll realize that he's more far-sighted than a lot of others I could name!'

Burke shook his head slowly, keeping his gaze fixed on the biologist.

'I had thought of that point long ago, Dr Richter, and I suppose you're right in thinking that that Teacher has done the same. I'm a little disappointed, however, that you have gone no farther.'

'How's that?'

'Your point is well taken – only if these races lack technical knowledge! Dar won't mind having the gene structures which are to produce his offspring spend a few years anywhere the starfish carrying them wants to – if he knows that eventually that creature will either travel to a planet where they can develop or park himself in a mechanical refrigerator to achieve the same end. Remember, those creatures will have the same desires as regards offspring, and they will have to cooperate with Dar's race to satisfy them. If the natives of this planet get off it, on the basis of knowledge they've either picked up from us or acquired themselves, there's going to be one of the most cooperative teams in history spreading through the star clouds – and man is going to take a back seat, if he survives at all.'

'It seems to me that that very cooperation would be a good example to the rest of us, if it happens. These races certainly aren't very close to such a relationship right now.'

'No, and it's to our interest to see that they never get there. I don't like to do it any better than you do, or than young Kruger will, but I'm afraid the only thing we can reasonably do is prevent Dar Lang Ahn from taking the knowledge he has acquired back to his people. Unless we do that we've given them the galaxy.'

'You're right – I don't like it. How can we justify such a thing, after we ourselves have encouraged him to learn all he could?'

'We can't justify it,' Burke said grimly, 'but we're going to do it. Sure, I'll hate myself for the rest of my life, but in my considered judgment it is best for the human race that Dar Lang Ahn should not see his own people again.'

'I'm afraid you're right, though it doesn't make me any happier.'

'Nor me. Well, in common fairness we'd better tell him now. I'll call a meeting of the entire group and let anyone with any other helpful data present it. That's about as fair as I can be.'

'Young Kruger may not have data, but he'll have objections.'

'I realize that. He doesn't know what a favor I'll be doing him.' The biologist looked sharply at the old officer, but Burke had nothing more to say.

XV

Astronomy; Logic

Dar Lang Ahn heard the biological report with only his usual interest, since such phrases as fluorinated hydrocarbons and silicones still meant very little to him. He did react, however, to Commander Burke's announcement, and the reaction was not a mild one.

Devastating though his emotion was it did not become vocal, for Nils Kruger started talking first. Dar listened to precisely the points about fair play, honesty, and decency that had been discussed by Burke and Richter, but did not fully understand the terms used. In any case he did not pay full attention; he was trying to decide on his own line of action.

Argument would presumably be useless. The men would have formed their opinions on what they had learned of him and his people. He could not quite see why Abyormen constituted a danger to the galaxy, but had come to hold the opinions of the human scientists in high respect. In spite of this he found that his natural sense of duty was urging him to go against Burke's decision – to argue, lie, or commit violence to get what he considered vital information back to his own people. A third impulse was furnished by his natural curiosity; had it not been for duty, he would have liked nothing better than traveling to Earth with his friends – if he could still call them that – and seeing some of the worlds Kruger and the astronomers had described to him. He might have started to speak, bringing his dilemma out in the open, but Kruger never gave him a chance. The boy was forgetting all the discipline that cadet training had drilled into him and coming perilously close to using personal abuse on the commander. The full significance of this escaped Dar, of course, since he had only the vaguest knowledge of Kruger's background, but he did understand clearly that the boy wanted to let him go back to his people.

It seemed unlikely that Kruger would win his argument with the commander; Dar did have some idea of the relative ranks involved. Could he slip out while the argument was going on and steal one of the landing boats? He had watched carefully more than once while they were being flown; could he handle one himself? With his memory there was no question of his pushing the wrong button after he had once seen the right one pushed. However, his lifetime of flying preserved him from what would almost certainly have been a fatal error. He realized that there was much more to handling any sort of

273

space ship than he could possibly have learned by observation alone in a couple of dozen rides.

Could he stow away? Unlikely. These men, whatever else they might be, could not be called stupid. Once the commander had ordered that Dar Lang Ahn was not to return to Abyormen, steps would most certainly be taken to enforce the decision.

Could Kruger steal a boat and fly him down? Undoubtedly he could, since he could certainly fly the machines, but Dar was hampered in deciding the answer to this question by his ignorance of the weight of authority among human beings. There was no way to tell whether the boy *would*. He recognized this lack, and filed the idea for future checking when he could see Kruger alone.

Could he—

His reverie was interrupted at this point by the raised voice of Commander Burke.

'Mr Kruger! I called this meeting for intelligent discussion, not tear-jerking or personal abuse. Unless you have a meaningful argument to present, you will be silent. I understand your feelings, I share them, and I have weighed the moral issues involved at least as carefully as you have. Do me the favor to remember that I have a number of responsibilities which you do not as yet share and which you quite evidently have not considered. I did not ask for a vote or an expression of opinion from anyone. I stated a conclusion I have reached, to wit, that Dar Lang Ahn's race – or races, I suppose I should say – will constitute a danger to mankind if they leave their native planet. I firmly believe that the government will share that opinion. However, if you or anyone else has *information* which might require the modification of it, by all means speak up.'

Kruger was silent, realizing suddenly just how far he had gone and feeling gratitude to the officer for the relative mildness of the rebuke. Unfortunately he had nothing to say which could possibly be construed as information.

The silence was interrupted by another of Dar's friends, an astronomer named Murchison.

'I'm afraid that there is another point to be considered,' he said slowly, 'and I'm fairly sure it will not only cause the government to reach a different conclusion from yours, Commander, but will have them doing their level best to get both Abyormenite races educated as soon as possible.'

'Let's have it!' the commander replied instantly.

'The main fact is that if we leave these people on this planet, it will amount to an act of genocide. This planet is a poor home for us and at the moment a necessary home for its inhabitants, but before too long it's not going to be any sort of home for anyone.'

'How long? And why not?'

'Because this is not a stable system. Abyormen seems to have been formed in a more or less normal manner as a planet of the red dwarf sun the local natives call Theer, but at that time Alcyone was nowhere in the neighborhood. For one thing the light pressure of Alcyone is such that a planet could not have formed in its neighborhood.'

'I've heard that before, but didn't see how you were going to keep that theory going, since the planet is here.'

'I didn't for a while myself. However, there is geological evidence that what I say is true; the tremendous seasonal changes of this planet, due to the elliptical path of Theer about Alcyone, did not occur throughout the early portion of the world's history, but only in the last few million years. One of two things happened; either Theer was captured by Alcyone fairly recently, or the giant star actually formed in the neighborhood of the dwarf. I incline to the latter view; we are inside a star cluster where the space is loaded – relatively speaking – with gas and dust. It is more than likely that Theer's entrance into the cluster, if it was not originally a member of it, created enough turbulence to start a condensation in its neighborhood.'

'I can see how that fits in with the geological time scale, but doesn't it emphasize my point about the adaptability of these races?'

'In a way, yes, but I don't believe that any organic structure could adapt to the fate in store for this system. Remember what I said – the space in this vicinity is full of gas and dust. Therefore, it is not a frictionless medium. That is why the alternate theory – that Alcyone captured the Theer system – is possible. The friction is continually shortening Theer's orbit. More and more of each year is being spent in the hot zone, and less and less at a distance from the giant star which permits Dar's people to live. Unless Alcyone drifts out of the Pleiades cluster, which it doesn't seem about to do, another half million or million years will see the red sun, together with Abyormen, dropping into it.'

'That's a long time.'

'It's an indefinite time, and long before it expires Abyormen will be uninhabitable for even the "hot" form of life. It's our business to get these races off the planet or at least help them get themselves off; otherwise we're guilty of criminal negligence.'

'But if Alcyone's light pressure kept the matter which should have formed planets away from it, how can there be enough in the vicinity to create the friction you say?'

'The effect of light pressure on a particle, compared to that of gravity, is a function of the size and density of the particle. I assure you that we have made plenty of measurements throughout this volume of space and I'm not just guessing at what will happen. The only thing I'm seriously doubtful about is whether Theer itself will pick up enough matter so that its own increasing luminosity will sterilize this planet before the final fall occurs. I can't say which will happen first, but one of them will most certainly happen.'

'But where could we take these people? I doubt that there's a planet in the galaxy duplicating this seasonal situation.'

'I'd be willing to bet that there are thousands. I admit we haven't found them yet, but there's a lot of galaxy still unexplored. Even if there aren't any they could learn to live in ships – might even get along better that way, with numerous members of both races alive at once. I can see a ship with one portion hot and one cold, with people living in both parts and moving from one to the other when their lives reach the appropriate stage. That situation will certainly be better for the Abyormenites than settling on any Earth-type planet would be – and I'm sure the government will see it the same way. We'll be back here setting up technical schools before you're an admiral, Commander – setting them up for the both races. I don't care what the present crop of "hot" Teachers may think; a bit of astronomy will change their minds.'

'If you can teach any astronomy to a race that sees by means of sound waves,' Burke pointed out drily. 'However, that's a quibble. I agree with you.' Kruger's face showed his relief; no face could have shown what Dar felt. 'Dar Lang Ahn may continue learning from our scientists as long as he sees fit, and return to his own people with his information as soon as he wishes. In a way I am taking a slight chance in permitting this, but I have no serious doubt as to the official decision. Young fellow,' he turned abruptly to Kruger, 'this is an excellent example of the risk of reaching a decision on the basis of insufficient evidence. Just don't let it impress you too much. You never will get *all* the data bearing on any question, and you'll have to come up with an answer sometime – particularly if you are commanding any sort of space flier. You'll have to learn to accept the risk of making a premature judgment. If it kills you some time, don't let me hear you complain.'

'No, sir,' replied Kruger.

'Very well. Dar, I will not apologize for my previously announced policy. However, I will give you any assistance you may need while you are still with us, provided it lies within my power.'

'Thank you, Commander. My Teachers will appreciate your action.'

'Isn't it pretty nearly time for your refuge to be sealed?'

'One more year. I should return as soon as you will allow, however, since there is much for me to report.'

'We will take you down as soon as possible. Mr Kruger, I assume you will want to go with him. I will handle the flier; anyone else whose duties permit may come along, up to the capacity of the boat. We will stay down until the shelter is sealed, so anyone who wants to observe that operation can plan on a three-week stay away from the *Alphard*. The boat will depart in twenty hours, which should give anyone who wants to take apparatus plenty of time to get it aboard.

'Dar Lang Ahn, do you suppose your Teachers could find a use for a radio which does not operate on the same sort of wave as those of your fiery friends – one on which you could talk to us without their knowledge, if you wished?' Kruger restrained a grin with difficulty; the old coot was human, in spite of his devotion to duty.

'Such a device would quite possibly be of use, Commander. We would appreciate it very much.'

'All right, we'll see that a few of them are aboard the boat. Meeting adjourned.'

The approach to the landing platform at the Ice Ramparts was rather different this time. The space flier, supported and guided by fields similar to those which hurled the *Alphard* through interstellar space with total indifference to the law of the speed of light, did not have the maneuvering limitations of the gliders. This was just as well, for the platform was crowded with the aircraft in a way that might have made a landing difficult even for Dar Lang Ahn. For the first time Kruger saw Teachers on the surface, sometimes directing activities and sometimes simply watching.

The approach of the boat was noted, and a group of natives gestured toward one side of the platform, where gliders were being pulled aside to make a cleared space.

The instant the air lock of the little ship opened Dar and Kruger were outside, both burdened with the radio equipment Burke had donated. The native led the way into the tunnels and they started the long, long walk to the main body of the refuge located so far under the ice cap. Kruger no longer wondered at the reason for the location; he was still somewhat surprised that these people had been able to build it.

The whole place seemed far more active than it had been before, with scores and even hundred of the little natives scurrying about on their mysterious errands.

'There must be a lot of library work to be done,' Kruger remarked as he gestured at one of these groups.

'The books should all have come in long ago,' Dar replied. 'The problem now is food. Normally, there is enough on hand many years before the time comes, but no chances are taken. We keep bringing it in until the last possible moment.'

'What are you going to do?'

'Get together any Teachers who can devote their time to me and start reporting. There should be a number available, as they know that I am coming with knowledge.'

'I expect that reporting will keep you pretty busy from now on.'

'Yes, Nils. I suppose you would like to see this place once more as it is pre-pared for the time of dying, but I will not be free to act as your guide. No doubt some one will be found who can help you, though.'

Kruger stopped and laid a hand on the little native's shoulder.

'You'll not let the doors close without seeing me again, will you?' he asked. 'I don't want to interfere with the work that has to be done, but I don't want to see the last of you – at least, for a good many of my years – this soon.'

Both eyes swerved up and took in Kruger's anxious face for a moment.

'I will see you again before the Ramparts are sealed. I promise it,' said Dar Lang Ahn. They resumed the journey, the boy satisfied.

Dar's prediction that a committee would be awaiting him proved correct. It was composed, the boy noticed, of beings of his own stature – the new Teachers. One of the giants he had met before, however, offered to act as his guide, and under the tall being's leadership Kruger saw the now completely organized libraries, the food-storage bins in the upper levels only a few feet from the overlying ice, and great beds in the warmer lower levels where plants similar to terrestrial fungi grew.

At length, he was led upward to the landing platform, where activity con-tinued undiminished. Gliders lunged into the sky, bound for the distant cities and, if there was time after they arrived, another load of food. Others landed, in the relatively small space left for that purpose; busy ground crews were constantly dragging gliders either to one side of the platform or into the cavern to make room for the newcomers.

'Aren't I taking up a lot of your time?' Kruger asked when they reached the surface. 'This seems to be the busiest time of life for your people.'

'There is nothing more for me to do,' was the answer. 'My successor has taken over.'

'But don't you stay in the Ramparts this time?'

'No. My life is done. A few of us will stay to make sure that the seals are properly in place, but that is not one of my tasks. As soon as I can be of no more use to you I will leave.'

'But I thought they had dismantled all the gliders capable of carrying you.'

'They have. I will leave on foot. We do not return to the cities.'

'You mean—' Kruger stopped; he knew that Dar had told his people very little over the radio, and was not sure how much this being knew. The Teacher either knew or guessed what was in his mind, however.

'No, we do not return to the cities. It is not the custom; has not been for so long that I can no longer give you the precise details of the reason. However, it is better that we meet our ends where the heat is not very great – at least, not before our bodies are destroyed in other ways. When you no longer need me, I will – take a walk on the ice cap.'

Kruger found himself with nothing to say, except that he still felt the need of the Teacher's company. At his invitation the being entered the flier and was met with great interest by the biologists who had come down. One of these spoke enough of the native language to render the boy's presence unnecessary and he returned to the landing platform to watch for Dar. However, his little friend did not appear and the endless activity kept Nils's attention until he found it necessary to sleep.

So the time passed. Gradually the number of gliders diminished, as the arrivals ceased and those already present headed for the other hemisphere. The sight of the casual way in which these beings started their last flights was depressing, not only to Kruger but to the other human beings watching.

'I guess it's just the way you're brought up,' one of the men remarked, 'but if I knew I had a week to live I'd look a good deal soberer.'

'I think it's more like three weeks,' said Kruger. 'They seal this place a year in advance of the expected atmosphere change, just to play safe.'

'Don't quibble.'

'I didn't mean to. I got the impression from Dar, though, that he felt sorry for us – living from day to day without knowing when the end was to come. I suppose it's just as hard for him to realize that we're used to it, as it is for us to picture his attitude.'

'That's true.' It was a new voice that made this answer, and Kruger turned to see Commander Burke standing in the air lock. 'I should have liked to know your friend better, Mr Kruger, but I don't suppose we'd ever really *know* him – not even you.'

'Maybe not, sir, but I can't help feeling that I do.'

'Good luck to you. Isn't it nearly time for this sealing ceremony to take place?' Several more men were emerging from the little ship.

'I haven't kept close track, sir, but I guess it must be, at that. Nearly all the gliders are gone, and – and I've seen a number of the big Teachers leaving the platform and starting around the mountain.' His voice shook a little as he mentioned this and the commander nodded gravely.

'Yes. The one who acted as your guide went the last time you were asleep.'

'What? I didn't know that, sir.'

'I know you didn't. It was by my advice that he went then. I thought it was better that way.' Something in the tone of the officer's voice forbade further questioning.

Several more of the giant Teachers appeared on the platform at this point and the men stopped their conversation to watch them. One approached the group by the air lock and spoke.

'We are about to check the sealing of the outer gates. These are located some distance down the tunnel, as we have found it desirable to let ice come into the upper caverns later in the hot season. Would you care to come with us, to watch the operation?'

'Wait a minute! Dar Lang Ahn promised he'd see me before the doors were closed! Where is he?'

'He is coming. If you come with us you should meet him in the tunnel. I see his glider is waiting.' The being turned without further remark and the men followed, Burke watching the dazed Kruger with something like pity showing on his face.

The doors were about three hundred yards down the tunnel and, true to the Teacher's prediction, Dar Lang Ahn was waiting beside them.

'Hi, Nils!' he called as the boy came in sight. 'Sorry I was so long. There was a lot to do, believe me!'

'Dar! You can't have finished – but this Teacher said—'

'Sure I did. Had to. Come on up to the surface – I want to check my glider. Or would you rather watch them seal the door?'

'But they can't seal it yet! You can't possibly have told them all you learned from us! You've got to stay and be a Teacher for the next generation!' The little native was silent for a moment, then spoke in a softer voice.

'Come with me, Nils. Maybe I did something I shouldn't have, but it's done. I'll try to explain to you.' He gestured along the tunnel and the boy obeyed silently, staring at his little friend. Dar started talking as they went; the commander looked after them, shaking his head.

'Nils, I couldn't do it. I thought about the point you've just mentioned and when I first started to learn things from you I rather planned to do what you've just suggested. I didn't like it, of course, but it seemed to be my duty. Then I stayed with you and your people and – kept learning. Astronomy, geology, biology, archaelogy, mathematics, and all the other specialties that the men of your group represent. There was just too much of it.'

'Too much for *you* to remember?' Kruger stopped, his surprise momentarily covering his grief.

'Not too much to remember, no, but too much to grasp properly. I could have stayed down below and dictated scores of books about everything I had seen you do or heard you say, but even though I understood a good deal of it my people wouldn't. There was something else they needed more, and gradually I came to understand what it was.

'It's *method*, Nils. It's the very way you people go about solving problems – imagination and experiment together. That was the thing my people had to learn and the thing I had to show them. Their problems are different from yours, after all; they'll have to solve them for themselves. Of course, the facts are important, too, but I didn't give too many of those. Just scattered pieces of information here and there, so that they could check their answers once in a while.'

'Then – then it was my own fault you're doing this! I deliberately exposed you to as many different fields of knowledge as I could, so there'd be no chance of your getting it all recorded before the time of dying!'

'No! It's not your fault, if you can call it a fault at all. You showed, indirectly I admit, just what we need to know. I was looking for an excuse to avoid staying in the Ramparts; if you want to say you furnished it, all right – and thanks.' He paused; they had reached the platform and Dar began without preamble to make sure his glider was ready for launching.

'But – can't you come with us, instead? You don't have to go back to Kwarr and – and—' Kruger could not finish the sentence. Dar straightened from his task and looked at him narrowly. For a moment or two he seemed to struggle with some decision; then he shook his head in the negative gesture he had learned from Kruger.

'I'm afraid not. I think I see a little of how you feel, friend Nils, and in a way I am sorry to leave you behind, but – would *you* come with *me?*' He almost gave his equivalent of a smile as he asked this. Kruger was silent.

'Of course you wouldn't – you couldn't. You expect to live a long time yet, even though you don't know how long.' He gripped one of Kruger's hands with his small claw. 'Nils, many of your years from now there will be quite a lot of my people who are part of me. I will be gone, but you may still be around. Maybe with what you and I have done for them some of those people will be scientists, and will have learned to get respect instead of contempt from the "hot" ones, and to start something which may in time be a civilization like yours. I would like to think that you will be helping them.'

He vaulted into the seat of the glider and, without giving the boy time to say a word, tripped the catapult.

Kruger watched the little aircraft out of sight. It did not take long to vanish, for his eyes were not as clear as they should have been, but he was still facing the direction in which it had gone when he finally muttered, 'I will be!' He turned away as the thud of a great door sounded from the tunnel.

CLOSE TO CRITICAL

PROLOGUE
Investigation; Annexation

Sol, seen at a distance of sixteen light-years, is a little fainter than the star at the tip of Orion's sword, and it could not have been contributing much to the sparkle in the diamond lenses of the strange machine. More than one of the watching men, however, got a distinct impression that the thing was taking a last look at the planetary system where it had been made. It would be a natural thing for any sentient and sentimental being to do, for it was already falling toward the great dark object only a few thousand miles away.

Any ordinary planet would have been glaringly bright at that range, for Altair is an excellent illuminator and was at its best right then: Altair is not a variable star, but it rotates fast enough to flatten itself considerably, and the planet was in a part of its orbit where it got the maximum benefit from the hotter, brighter polar regions. In spite of this, the world's great bulk was visible chiefly as a fuzzy blot not very much brighter than the Milky Way, which formed a background to it. It seemed as though the white glare of Altair were being sucked in and quenched, rather than illuminating anything.

But the eyes of the machine had been designed with Tenebra's atmosphere in mind. Almost visibly the robot's attention shifted, and the whitish lump of synthetic material turned slowly. The metal skeleton framing it kept pace with the motion, and a set of stubby cylinders lined themselves up with the direction of fall. Nothing visible emerged from them, for there was still too little atmosphere to glow at the impact of the ions, but the tons of metal and plastic altered their acceleration. The boosters were fighting the already fierce tug of a world nearly three times the diameter of distant Earth, and they fought well enough so that the patchwork fabrication which held them suffered no harm when atmosphere was finally reached.

The glitter faded out of the diamond eyes as the world's great gas mantle gradually enfolded the machine. It was dropping slowly and steadily, now; the word *cautiously* might almost have been used. Altair still glowed overhead, but the stars were vanishing even to the hypersensitive pickups behind those lenses as the drop continued.

Then there was a change. Up to now, the thing might have been a rocket of unusually weird design, braking straight down to a landing on outboard jets. The fact that the jet streams were glowing ever brighter meant nothing; naturally, the air was growing denser. However, the boosters themselves should *not* have been glowing.

These were. Their exhausts brightened still further, as though they were trying harder to slow a fall that was speeding up in spite of them, and the casings themselves began to shine, a dull red. That was enough for the distant controllers; a group of brilliant flashes shone out for an instant, not from the boosters themselves but from points on the metal girders that held them. The struts gave way instantly, and the machine fell unsupported.

For only a moment. There was still equipment fastened to its outer surface, and a scant half-second after the blowoff of the boosters a gigantic parachute flowered above the falling lump of plastic. In that gravity it might have been expected to tear away instantly, but its designers had known their business. It held. The incredibly thick atmosphere – even at that height several times as dense as Earth's – held stubbornly in front of the parachute's broad expanse and grimly insisted on the lion's share of every erg of potential energy given up by the descending mass. In consequence, even a gravity three times that of Earth's surface failed to damage the device when it finally struck solid ground.

For some moments after the landing, nothing seemed to happen. Then the flat-bottomed ovoid moved, separating itself from the light girders which had held the parachute, crawled on nearly invisible treads away from the tangle of metal ribbons, and stopped once more as though to look around.

It was not looking, however; for the moment, it could not see. There were adjustments to be made. Even a solid block of polymer, with no moving parts except its outer traveling and handling equipment, could not remain completely unchanged under an external pressure of some eight hundred atmospheres. The dimensions of the block, and of the circuitry imbedded in it, had changed slightly. The initial pause after landing had been required for the distant controllers to find and match the slightly different frequencies now needed to operate it. The eyes, which had seen so clearly in empty space, had to adjust so that the different index of refraction between the diamond and the new external medium did not blur their pictures hopelessly. This did not take too long, as it was automatic, effected by the atmosphere itself as it filtered through minute pores into the spaces between certain of the lens elements.

Once optically adjusted, the nearly complete darkness meant nothing to those eyes, for the multipliers behind them made use of every quantum of radiation the diamond could refract. Far away, human eyes glued themselves to vision screens which carried the relayed images of what the machine saw.

It was a rolling landscape, not too unearthly at first glance. There were large hills in the distance, their outlines softened by what might have been forests. The nearby ground was completely covered with vegetation which looked more or less like grass, though the visible trail the robot had already left suggested that the stuff was far more brittle. Clumps of taller growths erupted at irregular intervals, usually on higher ground. Nothing seemed to move, not even the thinnest fronds of the plants, though an irregular crashing and booming registered almost constantly on the sound pickups built into the plastic block. Except for the sound it was a still-life landscape, without wind or animal activity.

The machine gazed thoughtfully for many minutes. Probably its distant operators were hoping that life frightened into hiding by its fall might reappear; but if this were the case they were disappointed for the moment. After a time it crawled back to the remains of its parachute harness and played a set of lights carefully over the collection of metal girders, cables, and ribbons, examining them all in great detail. Then it moved away again, this time with a purposeful air.

For the next ten hours it quartered meticulously the general area of the landing, sometimes stopping to play its light on some object like a plant, sometimes looking around for minutes on end without obvious purpose, sometimes emitting sounds of varying pitch and loudness. This last always happened when it was in a valley, or at least not on the very top of a hill; it seemed to be studying echoes for some reason.

Periodically it went back to the abandoned harness and repeated the careful examination, as though it were expecting something to happen. Naturally, in an environment having a three hundred-seventy-degree temperature, about eight hundred atmospheres pressure, and a climate consisting of water heavily laced with oxygen and oxides of sulphur, things started to happen soon enough; and great interest was shown in the progress of the corrosion as it steadily devoured the metal. Some parts lasted longer than others; no doubt the designers had included different alloys, perhaps to check this very point. The robot remained in the general area until the last of the metal had vanished in slime.

At irregular intervals during this time, the surface of the ground shook violently. Sometimes the shaking was accompanied by the crashes which had first greeted the robot's 'ears'; at other times it was relatively silent. The operators must have been bothered by this at first; then it became evident that all the hills in the neighborhood were well rounded with no steep cliffs, and that the ground itself was free of both cracks and loose stones, so there was little reason to worry about the effect of quakes on the fabulously expensive mechanism.

A far more interesting event was the appearance of animal life. Most of the creatures were small, but were none the less fascinating for that, if the robot's actions meant anything. It examined everything that appeared, as closely as it possibly could. Most of the creatures seemed to be scale-armored and eight-limbed; some appeared to live on the local vegetation, others, on each other.

With the harness finally gone, the attention of the robot's operators was exclusively occupied by the animals for a long time. The investigation was interrupted a number of times, but this was due to loss of control rather than distraction. The lack of visible surface features on Tenebra had prevented the men from getting a very precise measure of its rotation period, and on several occasions the distant ship 'set' as far as the important part of the planet was concerned. Trial and error gradually narrowed down the uncertainties in the length of Tenebra's day, however, and the interruptions in control finally vanished.

The project of studying a planet three times the diameter of Earth looked rather ridiculous when attempted with a single exploring machine. Had that been the actual plan, of course it *would* have been ridiculous; but the men had something else in mind. One machine is not much; a machine with a crew of assistants, particularly if the crew is part of a more or less world-wide culture, is something very different. The operators very definitely hoped to find local help – in spite of the rather extreme environment into which their machine had fallen. They were experienced men, and knew something of the ways of life in the universe.

However, weeks went by, and then months, with no sign of a creature possessing more than the rudiments of a nervous system. Had the men understood the operation of the lensless, many-spined 'eyes' of the local animals they might have been more hopeful; but as it was most of them grew resigned to facing a job of several lifetimes. It was sheer chance that when a thinking creature finally did turn up it was discovered by the robot. Had it been the other way around – if the native had discovered the machine – history could easily have been very different on several planets.

The creature, when they did see it, was big. It towered fully nine feet in height, and on that planet must have weighed well over a ton. It conformed to the local custom as regarded scales and number of limbs, but it walked erect on two of the appendages, seemed not to be using the next two, and used the upper four for prehension. That was the fact that betrayed its intelligence; two long and two shorter spears, each with a carefully chipped stone head, were being carried in obvious readiness for instant use.

Perhaps the stone disappointed the human watchers, or perhaps they remembered what happened to metals on this planet and refrained from jumping to conclusions about the culture level suggested by the material. In any case, they watched the native carefully.

This was easier than it might have been; the present neighborhood, many miles from the original landing point, was a good deal rougher in its contours. The vegetation was both higher and somewhat less brittle, though it was still virtually impossible to avoid leaving a trail where the robot crawled. The men guessed at first that the higher plants had prevented the native from seeing the relatively small machine; then it became apparent that the creature's attention was fully occupied by something else.

It was traveling slowly and apparently trying to leave as little trail as possible. It was also making allowance for the fact that to leave *no* trail was not practicable; periodically it stopped and built a peculiar arrangement consisting of branches from some of the rarer, springy plants and the sharp stone blades which it took in seemingly endless supply from a large leather sack slung about its scaly body.

The nature of these arrangements was clear, after the native had gotten far enough ahead to permit a close inspection. They were booby traps, designed to drive a stone point into the body of anything attempting to follow in the creature's footsteps. They must have been intended against animals rather than other natives, since they could easily be avoided merely by paralleling the trail instead of following it.

The fact that the precaution was being taken at all, however, made the whole situation extremely interesting, and the robot was made to follow with all possible caution. The native traveled five or six miles in this fashion, and during this time set about forty of the traps. The robot avoided these without trouble, but several times tripped others which had apparently been set earlier. The blades did no harm to the machine; some of them actually broke against the plastic. It began to look as though the whole neighborhood had been 'mined,' however.

Eventually the trail led to a rounded hill. The native climbed this quickly, and paused at a narrow gully opening near the top. It seemed to be looking around for followers, though no organs of vision had yet been identified by the human watchers. Apparently satisfied, it drew an ellipsoidal object from its sack, examined it carefully with delicate fingers, and then disappeared into the gully.

In two or three minutes it was back, this time without its grapefruit-size burden. Heading down the hill once more, it avoided with care both its own traps and the others, and set off in a direction different from that of its approach.

The robot's operators had to think fast. Should they follow the native or find out what it had been doing up the hill? The former might seem more logical, since the native was leaving, and the hill presumably was not, but the second alternative was the one they chose. After all, it was impossible for the thing to travel without leaving some sort of trail; besides, night was approaching, so it wouldn't get far. It seemed safe to assume that it shared the characteristic of Tenebra's other animal life, of collapsing into helplessness a few hours after nightfall.

Besides, looking at the hilltop shouldn't take too long. The robot waited until the native was well out of sight, and then moved up the hill toward the gully. This, it turned out, led into a shallow crater, though the hill bore no resemblance to a volcano; on the crater floor lay perhaps a hundred ellipsoids similar to that which the native had just left there. They were arranged with great care in a single line, and except for that fact were the closest things to loose stones that the men had yet seen on Tenebra. Their actual nature seemed so obvious that no effort was made to dissect one.

At this point there must have been a lengthy and lively discussion. The robot did nothing for quite a long time. Then it left the crater and went down the hill, picked its way carefully out through the 'mine field' on the trail of the native, and settled down to travel.

This was not quite as easy as it would have been in the day time, since it was starting to rain and visibility was frequently obstructed by the drops. The men had not yet really decided whether it was better, in traveling at night, to follow valleys and remain submerged or stick to ridges and hilltops so as to see occasionally; but in this case the problem was irrelevant. The native had apparently ignored the question, and settled for something as close to a straight line as it could manage. The trail ran for some ten miles, and ended at a clearing before a cave-studded cliff.

Details could not be seen well. Not only was the rain still falling, but the darkness was virtually absolute even to the pickups of the robot. More discussion must have resulted from this; it was two or three minutes after the machine's arrival at the clearing that its lights went on and played briefly over the rock.

Natives could be seen standing inside the cave mouths, but they made no response to the light. They were either asleep, in more or less human fashion, or had succumbed to the usual night-torpor of Tenebra's animal life.

No sign of anything above a stone-age culture level could be seen anywhere about, and after a few minutes of examination the robot cut off most of its lights and headed back toward the hill and the crater.

It moved steadily and purposefully. Once at the hilltop, several openings appeared in its sides, and from some of these armlike structures were extended. Ten of the ellipsoids were picked carefully from one end of the line – leaving no betraying gaps – and stowed in the robot's hull. Then the machine went back down the hill and began a deliberate search for booby traps. From these it removed the stone blades, and such of these as seemed in good condition – many were badly corroded, and some even crumbled when handled – disappeared into other openings in the lump of plastic. Each of these holes was then covered by a lid of the same incredibly stable polymer which formed the body of the machine, so that no one could have told from outside that the storage places were there.

With this task completed, the robot headed away, at the highest speed it could maintain. By the time Altair rose and began turning the lower atmosphere back into gas, the machine, the stolen weapons, and the 'kidnapped' eggs were far from the crater and still farther from the cave village.

I

Exploration; Expectation; Altercation

Nick pushed through the tall plants into the open, stopped, and used several words of the sort Fagin had always refused to translate. He was neither surprised nor bothered to find water ahead of him – it was still early in the morning – it was annoying, however, to find it on each side as well. Sheer bad luck, apparently, had led him straight out along a peninsula, and this was no time for anyone to retrace his steps.

To be really precise, he didn't *know* that he was being followed, of course; but it simply hadn't occurred to him to doubt that he was. He had spent two days, since his escape, in making as confused and misleading a trail as possible, swinging far to the west before turning back toward home, and he was no more willing than a human being would have been to admit that it might have been wasted effort. True, he had seen not the slightest sign of pursuers. He had been delayed by the usual encounters with impassable ground and wild animals, and none of his captors had caught up; the floating animals and plants which it was never safe to ignore completely had shown no sign of interest in anything behind him; his captors during the time he was with them had shown themselves to be hunters and trackers of superlative skill. Taking all these facts into account, he might have been excused for supposing that the fact of his continued freedom meant they weren't following. He was tempted, but couldn't bring himself to believe it. They had wanted so badly to make him lead them to Fagin!

He came to himself with a start, and brought his mind back to the present. Theorizing was useless just now; he must decide whether to retrace his steps along the peninsula, and risk running into his ex-captors, or wait until the lake dried up and chance their catching him. It was hard to decide which was the smaller risk, but there was one check he could make.

He walked to the water's edge, looked at the liquid carefully, then slapped it vigorously. The slow ripples which spread up the edge of the lake and out over its more or less level surface did not interest him; the drops which detached themselves did. He watched as they drifted toward him, settling slowly, and noted with satisfaction that even the largest of them faded out without getting back to the surface. Evidently the lake did not have long to go; he settled down to wait.

The breeze was picking up slowly as the plants awoke to the new day. He could smell it. He watched eagerly for its effect on the lake – not waves, but the turbulent hollows in the surface which would mark slightly warmer bodies of air passing over it. That would be the sign; from then on, the surface would probably drop faster down the lake bed than he could travel. The breeze should keep the air breathable, as long as he didn't follow the water too closely – yes, it couldn't be long now; the very point where he was standing was below the surface level of some parts of the lake. It was drying up.

The difference increased as he waited, the edge of the water slipping back in ghostly fashion. He followed it with caution until a wall of water towered on either side. It began to look as though the peninsula were really a ridge across the lake; if so, so much the better.

Actually, it didn't quite reach. He had to wait for a quarter of an hour at the ridge's end while the rest of the lake turned back to air. He was impatient enough to risk breathing the stuff almost too quickly after the change, but managed to get away with it. A few minutes more brought him up the slope to the tall vegetation on the east side of the erstwhile lake. Before plunging among the plants, where he would be able to see nothing but the floaters overhead, he paused a moment to look back across the dry bottom to the point where he had first seen the water – still no pursuers. Another floater or two were drifting his way; he felt for his knives, and slightly regretted the spears he had lost. Still, there was little likelihood of danger from a floater behind him as long as he traveled at a decent speed – and that's what he'd better be doing. He plunged into the brush.

Travel was not too difficult; the stuff was flexible enough to be pushed out of the way most of the time. Occasionally he had to cut his way, which was annoying less because of the effort involved than because it meant exposing a knife to the air. Knives were getting somewhat scarce, and Fagin was rather tight with those remaining.

The morning wore on, still without sight of pursuers. He made unusually good speed much of the time because of a remarkable lack of wild animals – par for a forty-mile walk being four or five fights, while he had only one. However, he more than lost the time gained when he ran into an area rougher than any he had ever seen. The hills were sharp and jagged instead of rounded; there were occasional loose rocks, and from time to time these were sent rolling and tumbling by unusually sharp quakes. In places he had to climb steep cliffs, either up or down; in others, he threaded his way through frighteningly narrow cracks – with no assurance that there was an opening at the other end. Several times there wasn't, and he had to go back.

Even here he left a trail, the local plant life being what it was; but with that area behind him he found it even harder to justify the feeling that he was being pursued. If his ex-captors really followed through that, they deserved to catch him! But still, however often he let his attention cover his rear, no sign of them appeared.

The hours passed, Nick traveling at the highest speed he could maintain. The one fight he had scarcely delayed him at all; it was a floater that saw him from ahead and dropped nearly to ground level in time to intercept him. It was a small one, so small that his arms outreached its tentacles; and a quick slash of one of his knives opened enough of its gas-bladders to leave it floundering helplessly behind him. He sheathed the weapon and raced on with scarcely diminished speed, rubbing an arm which had been touched lightly by the thing's poison.

The limb had ceased to sting, and Altair was high in the sky, when he finally found himself in familiar surroundings. He had hunted before this far from the home valley; rapid as changes were, the area was still recognizable. He shifted course a trifle and put on a final burst of speed. For the first time, he felt sure of being able to deliver a report of his capture, and also for the first time he realized that he had not tried to organize one. Just telling what had happened to him, item by item, might take too long; it was important that Fagin and the rest get away quickly. On the other hand, it would take a pretty complete explanation of the state of affairs to convince the teacher of that fact. Nick unconsciously slowed down as he pondered this problem. He was dragged from this reverie only by the sound of his own name.

'Nick! Is that really you? Where have you been? We thought you'd slept out once too often!'

At the first sound, Nick had reached for his knives; but he checked the movement as he recognized the voice.

'Johnny! It's good to hear proper talk again. What are you doing this far out? Have the sheep eaten everything closer to home?'

'No, I'm hunting, not herding.' John Doolittle pushed through the undergrowth into clear view. 'But where have you been? It's been weeks since you went out, and since we stopped looking for you.'

'You looked for me? That's bad. Still, I guess it didn't make any difference, or I'd have known it sooner.'

'What do you mean? I don't understand what you're talking about. And what did you mean about it's being good to hear "proper talk"? What other kind of talk is there? Let's hear the story.'

'It's a long one, and I'll have to tell everyone as quickly as possible anyway. Come along home; there's no point telling it twice.' He headed toward the valley they both called 'home' without waiting to hear any answer. John 'trailed' his spears and followed. Even without Nick's implication of trouble ahead, he would not willingly have missed the report. Fresh as he was, though, he had difficulty keeping up with the returned explorer; Nick seemed to be in a hurry.

They met two more of the group on the way, Alice and Tom, who were herding. At Nick's urgent but hasty words they followed toward the village as fast as their charge would permit.

Five more of the group were actually in the village, and Fagin was at his usual station in the center of the ring of houses. Nick called the teacher by name as he came in sight.

'Fagin! We're in trouble! What do we have for weapons that you haven't shown us yet?'

As usual, there was a pause of a couple of seconds before an answer came back.

'Why, it's Nick. We had about given you up. What's all of this about weapons? Do you expect to have to fight someone?'

'I'm afraid so.'

'Who?'

'Well, they seem to be people just like us; but they don't keep animals, and they don't use fire, and they use different words for things than we do.'

'Where did you run into these people, and why should we have to fight them?'

'It's a long story, I'm afraid. It will be better if I start at the beginning, I suppose; but we shouldn't waste any more time than we can help.'

'I agree; a complete report will make the most sense to all of us. Go ahead.' Nick settled his weight back on his standing legs and obeyed.

'I started south as we decided and went slowly, mapping as I went. Nothing much had changed seriously out to the edge of the region we usually cover in farming and grazing; after that, of course, it was hard to tell whether anything had changed at all recently, or in what way.

'The best landmark I saw by the end of the first day was a mountain, of quite regular conical shape and much higher than any I had ever seen before. I was tempted to climb it, but decided that detail mapping could be accomplished better later on; after all, my trip was to find new areas, not evaluate them.

'I passed to the east of the mountain shortly after sunrise the second day. The wind was remarkably strong in that region and seemed always to blow toward the mountain; I called it Storm Hill on the map. Judging by the wind, there ought to be a lot of night-growing plants there; any exploration should be planned to get off the hill before dark.

'As far as travel goes, everything was about as usual. I killed enough in self-defense to keep me in food, but none of the animals were at all unusual that day.

'The third morning, though, with the mountain out of sight, I got involved with something that lived in a hole in the ground and reached out an arm to catch things going by. It caught me around the legs, and it didn't seem to mind my spears very much. I don't think I'd have gotten away if I hadn't had help.'

'Help?' The startled question came without the pause characteristic of the teacher's remarks; it was Jim who asked it. 'How could you have gotten help? None of us was down that way.'

'So it wasn't one of us – at least, not exactly. He *looked* just like us, and used spears like ours; but when we finally managed to kill the thing in the hole and tried to talk to each other, his words were all different; in fact, it was quite a while before I realized that he was talking. He used the same sort of noises we do for words, but mixed them with a lot of others that we never learned from you.

'After a while I realized that the noises must be talk, and then I wondered why I hadn't thought of such a thing before – after all, if this person wasn't brought up by you, he'd have had to think up his own words for things, and it would be silly to expect them to be the same as ours. I decided to go with him and learn more; after all, this seemed a lot more important than just mapping. If I could learn his talk, he might know a lot more than we could find in months of exploring.

'He didn't seem to mind my trailing along, and as we went I began to catch on to some of his words. It wasn't easy, because he put them together in very strange ways; it wasn't just a matter of learning the noise he used for each object. We hunted together, though, and all the time we were learning to talk together. We didn't travel in a straight line, but I kept pretty good track of our path and can put his village on the map when I get the chance.'

'Village?' It was Jim once more who interrupted; Fagin had said nothing.

'That's the only word I know for it. It wasn't at all like ours; it was a place at the foot of a steep cliff, and there were holes all over the face of the stone. Some of them were very small, like the solution holes you can see in any rock; others were very much larger, and there were people living in them. The one I was with was one of them.

'They were very surprised to see me, and tried to ask me a lot of questions; but I couldn't understand them well enough to give any answers. The one I had traveled with talked to them, and I suppose told how he had met me; but they stayed interested, and a lot of them were always watching me, whatever I did.

'It was getting fairly late in the afternoon when we got to the cliff, and I was starting to wonder about camping for the night. I didn't realize just at first that these people lived in the holes in the rock, and when I finally caught on I wasn't very happy about it. There are even more quakes down that way than around here, I noticed, and that cliff seemed an awfully unhealthy neighborhood. When the sun was almost down, I decided to leave them and camp a little way out on a hilltop I'd found, and then I discovered that they didn't want me to go. They were actually prepared to get rough in order to keep me around. I had learned a few more of their words by that time, though, and I finally convinced them that I wasn't trying to get away completely, and just wanted to spend the night by myself. There was a surprising amount of firewood around, and I was able to collect enough for the night without much trouble – in fact, some of the little ones helped me, when they saw what I wanted.'

'Little ones? Weren't they all the same size?' Dorothy asked.

'No. That was one of the funny things I haven't had time to mention. Some of them weren't more than a foot and a half high, and some of them were nearly twice as tall as we are – nine feet or more. They all had the same shape as ours, though. I never found out the reason for that. One of the biggest ones seemed to be telling the others what to do most of the time, and I found that the little ones were usually the easiest to get along with.

'But that's getting off the story. When I built my fires a lot of them watched, but couldn't seem to make anything of it; when I lighted them, there was the biggest crowd of astonished people you ever saw. They didn't know anything about fire; that's why there was so much firewood near the cliff, I guess.

'Of course, it had started to rain by the time I lighted up, and it was funny to watch them; they seemed terribly afraid of being outside their holes in the rain, and still didn't want to miss watching the fires. They kept dithering back and forth, but gradually disappeared into their holes. After a while they were all gone, even though some of them stayed long enough to see what the fires did to the rain.

'I didn't see any more of them for the rest of the night. The water didn't get too deep along the face of the cliff, and they were out in the morning as soon as it had dried up.

'I could make a long story out of the rest of the time, but that will have to wait. I learned to talk to them pretty well – the way they put their words together makes a lot of sense once you catch on to it – and got to know them pretty well. The main thing is that they were interested in whatever things *I* knew that *they* didn't, like fire and keeping herds of animals and raising plants for food; and they wanted to know how I'd learned all these things. I told them about you, Fagin; and maybe that was a mistake. A few days ago their teacher, or leader, or whatever you can call him, came to me and said that he wanted me to come back here and bring you down to the cliff so you could teach all the things you know to his people.

'Now, that seemed all right to me. I judged that the more people you knew who could help in the things you want us to do, the better everything will be.' He paused, to give Fagin a chance to answer.

'That's true enough,' the voice from the robot agreed after the usual interval. 'What went wrong?'

'My answer wasn't worded just right, it seems. I interpreted the proposition as a request, and answered that I would gladly come back home and ask you whether you would come to help the cave people. The leader – his name means Swift, in their words; all their names mean something – became angry indeed. Apparently he expects people to do as he says without any question or hesitation. I had noticed that but had been a little slow in applying my knowledge, I fear. Anyway, I didn't see how he could expect *you* to obey his orders.

'Unfortunately, he does; and he decided from my answer that you and the other people of our village would probably refuse. When that happens, his first thought is the use of force; and from the moment I made my answer he began to plan an attack on our village, to carry you away with him whether you wanted to go or not.

'He ordered me to tell him how to find our village, and when I refused he became angry again. The body of a dead goat that someone had brought in for food was lying nearby, and he picked it up and began to do terrible things to it with his knives. After a while he spoke to me again.

'"You see what my knives are doing," he said. "If the goat were alive, it would not be killed by them; but it would not be happy. The same shall be done to you with the start of the new day, unless you guide my fighters to your village and its Teacher. It is too close to darkness now for you to escape; you have the night to think over what I have said. We start toward your village in the morning – or you will wish we had." He made two of his biggest fighters stay with me until the rain started. Even after all the time I'd been there no one ever stayed out of the caves after rainfall, so they left me alone when I lighted my fires.

'It took me a long time to decide what to do. If they killed me, they'd still find you sooner or later and you wouldn't be warned in time; if I went with them it might have been all right, but I didn't like some of the things Swift had been saying. He seemed to feel things would be better if there were none of your own people left around after he captured you. That seemed to mean that no matter what I did I was going to be killed, but if I kept quiet I might be the only one. That was when I thought of traveling at night; I was just as likely to be killed, but at least I'd die in my sleep – and there *was* a little chance of getting away with it. After all, a lot of animals that don't have caves or fire and don't wake up as early as some of the meat-eaters still manage to live.

'Then I got another idea; I thought of carrying fire with me. After all, we often carry a stick with one end burning for short distances when we're lighting the night fires; why couldn't I carry a supply of long sticks, and keep one burning all the time? Maybe the fire wouldn't be big enough to be a real protection, but it was worth trying. Anyway, what could I lose?

'I picked out as many of the longest sticks around as I could carry, piled them up, and waited until two of my three fires were drowned by raindrops. Then I picked up my sticks, lighted the end of one of them at the remaining fire, and started off as fast as I could.

'I was never sure whether those people stayed awake in their caves or not – as I said, water doesn't get up to them – but now I guess they don't. Anyway, no one seemed to notice me as I left.

'You know, traveling at night isn't nearly as bad as we always thought it would be. It's not too hard to dodge raindrops if you have enough light to see them coming, and you can carry enough wood to keep you in light for a long time. I must have made a good twenty miles, and I'd have gone farther if I hadn't made a very silly mistake. I didn't think to replenish my wood supply until I was burning my last stick, and then there wasn't anything long enough for my needs in the neighborhood. I didn't know the country at all; I'd started west instead of north to fool any of the cave people who saw me go. As a result I got smothered in a raindrop within a minute after my last light went out; and it was late enough by then for the stuff to be unbreathable. I'd kept to high ground all the time, though, so I woke up in the morning before any-thing had made breakfast of me.'

Nick paused, and like the other listeners – except Fagin – shifted himself to a more comfortable position on his resting legs as the ground shook underfoot. 'I made a good, wide sweep around to the west, then circled north and east again to get back here. I was expecting to be caught every minute; those people are marvelous hunters and trackers. I traveled for several hours after dark each night, but stopped in time to find wood and build permanent fires before my sticks went out, after the first time. I didn't get caught by rain again, and they never caught up with me. They'll still find the village here sooner or later, though, and I think we ought to move out as quickly as possible.'

For a moment there was silence after Nick finished his report; then the villagers began chattering, each putting forth his own ideas without paying much attention to those of his neighbor. They had picked up quite a few human characteristics. This noise continued for some minutes, with Nick alone waiting silently for Fagin to make some comment.

At last the robot spoke.

'You are certainly right about the cave-dwellers finding the village here; they probably know where it is already. They would have been fools to catch up with you as long as they had reason to suppose you were going home. I see nothing to be gained, however, by leaving; they could follow us anywhere we might go. Now that they know of our existence, we're going to meet them in very short order.

'I don't want you people fighting them. I'm rather fond of you all, and have spent quite a long time bringing you up, and would rather not see you butchered. You've never done any fighting – it's one thing I'm not qualified to teach you – and you wouldn't stand a chance against that tribe.

'Therefore, Nick, I want you and one other to go to meet them. They'll be coming along your trail, so you'll have no trouble finding them. When you meet Swift, tell him that we'll gladly move to his village or let him move to ours, and that I'll teach him and his people all he wants. If you make clear that I don't know his language and that he'll need you to talk to me, he'll probably be smart enough not to hurt any of us.'

'When shall we start? Right away?'

'That would be best, but you've just had a long trip and deserve some rest. Anyway, a lot of the day is gone, and there probably won't be much lost by letting you get a night's sleep before you start. Go tomorrow morning.'

'All right, Teacher.' Nick gave no evidence of the uneasiness he felt at the prospect of meeting Swift again. He had known that savage for several weeks; Fagin had never met him. Still, the Teacher knew a lot; he had taught Nick virtually all he knew, and for a whole lifetime – at least, Nick's whole lifetime – had been the final authority in the village. Probably everything would come out as Fagin predicted.

It might have, too, had not the men behind the robot grossly underestimated the tracking ability of the cave-dwellers. Nick had not even had time to get to sleep beside his watch-fire after lighting up at rainfall when a surprised yell, in Nancy's voice, sounded from a point four fires to his left; and a split second later he saw Swift himself, flanked by a line of his biggest fighters which disappeared around the hill on either side, sweeping silently up the slope toward him.

II

Explanation; Concatenation; Recrimination

'What do you do now?'

Raeker ignored the question; important as he knew the speaker to be, he had no time for casual conversation. He had to act. Fagin's television screens lined the wall around him, and every one showed the swarming forms of the fir-cone-shaped beings who were attacking the village. There was a microphone before his face, with its switch spring-loaded in the open position so that casual talk in the control room would not reach, the robot's associates; his finger was hovering over the switch, but he did not touch it. He didn't quite know what to say.

Everything he had told Nick through the robot was perfectly true; there was nothing to be gained by trying to fight. Unfortunately, the fight had already started. Even had Raeker been qualified to give advice on the defense of the village, it was too late; it was no longer even possible for a human being to distinguish the attackers from the defenders. Spears were sailing through the air with blinding speed – nothing merely tossed gets very far in a three-gravity field – and axes and knives flashed in the firelight.

'It's a good show, anyway.' The same shrill voice that had asked the question a minute earlier made itself heard once more. 'That firelight seems to be brighter than daylight, down there.' The casual tone infuriated Raeker, who was not taking the predicament of his friends at all casually; but it was not consideration of the identity or importance of the speaker that kept him from losing his temper and saying something unfortunate. Quite unintentionally, the onlooker had given him an idea. His finger stabbed at the microphone button.

'Nick! Can you hear me?'

'Yes, Teacher.' Nick's voice showed no sign of the terrific physical effort he was exerting; his voice machinery was not as closely tied in with his breathing apparatus as is that of a human being.

'All right. Fight your way into the nearest hut as quickly as possible, all of you. *Get out of sight of me.* If you can't reach a hut, get behind a woodpile or something like that – below the curve of the hill, if nothing better is possible. Let me know as soon as you've all managed this.'

'We'll try.' Nick had no time to say more; those in the control room could only watch, though Raeker's fingers were hovering over another set of switches on the complex panel before him.

'One of them's making it.' It was the high voice again, and this time Raeker had to answer.

'I've known these people for sixteen years, but I can't tell them from the attackers now. How can you identify them?' He let his glance shift briefly from the screens to the two nonhumans towering behind him.

'The attackers have no axes, only knives and spears,' pointed out the speaker calmly. The man hastily turned back to the screens. He could not be sure that the other was right; only three or four axes could be seen, and their wielders were not very clearly visible in the swirling press. He had not noticed any lack of axes in the hands of the attackers as they came up the hill, in the brief moments after they became visible to the robot and before battle was joined; but there was no reason to doubt that someone else might have. He wished he knew Dromm and its people better. He made no answer to the slender giant's comment, but from then on watched the axes which flashed in the firelight. These really did seem to be working their way toward the huts which rimmed the top of the hill. Some failed to make it; more than one of the tools which had so suddenly become weapons ceased to swing as the robot's eyes watched.

But some did get there. For half a minute a four-armed, scaly figure stood at one of the hut doors, facing outward and smashing the crests of all attack- ers who approached too close. Three others, all apparently injured, crawled toward him and under the sweep of the powerful arms to take shelter in the building; one of these remained in the doorway, crouching with two spears and guarding the axeman from low thrusts.

Then another defender battered his way to the side of the first, and the two retreated together inside the hut. None of the cave-dwellers seemed eager to follow.

'Are you all inside, Nick?' Raeker asked.

'Five of us are here. I don't know about the others. I'm pretty sure Alice and Tom are dead, though; they were near me at the beginning, and I haven't seen them for some time.'

'Give a call to those who aren't with you. I'll have to do something very soon, and I don't want any of you hurt by it.'

'They must either be safe or dead. The fighting has stopped; it's a lot easier to hear you than it was. You'd better do whatever it is without worrying about us; I think Swift's people are all heading toward you. Only a couple are out- side the door here; the others are forming a big ring around where I saw you last. You haven't moved, have you?'

'No,' admitted Raeker, 'and you're right about the ring. One of the biggest of them is walking right up to me. Make sure you are all under cover – preferably somewhere where light won't reach you. I'll give ten seconds.'

'All right,' Nick answered. 'We're getting under tables.'

Raeker counted a slow ten, watching the approaching creatures in the screens as he did so. At the last number his fingers tripped a gang bar which closed twenty switches simultaneously; and as Nick described it later, 'the world took fire.'

It was only the robot's spotlights, unused now for years but still serviceable. It seemed quite impossible to the human watchers that any optical organs sensitive enough to work on the few quanta of light which reach the bottom of Tenebra's atmosphere could possible stand any such radiance; the lights themselves had been designed with the possibility in mind that they might have to pierce dust or smoke – they were far more powerful than were really needed by the receptors of the robot itself.

The attackers should have been blinded instantly, according to Raeker's figuring. The sad fact slowly emerged that they were not.

They were certainly surprised. They stopped their advance for a moment, and chattered noisily among themselves; then the giant who was in front of the others strode right up to the robot, bent over, and appeared to examine one of the lights in detail. The men had long ago learned that the Tenebran vision organs were involved in some way with the spiny crests on their heads, and it was this part that the being who Raeker suspected must be Swift brought close to one of the tiny ports from which the flood of light was escaping.

The man sighed and shut off the lights.

'Nick,' he called, 'I'm afraid my idea didn't work. Can you get in touch with this Swift fellow, and try to get the language problem across to him? He may be trying to talk to me now, for all I can tell.'

'I'll try.' Nick's voice came faintly through the robot's instruments; then there was nothing but an incomprehensible chattering that ran fantastically up and down the scale. There was no way to tell who was talking, much less what was being said, and Raeker settled back uneasily in his seat.

'Couldn't the handling equipment of that robot be used for fighting?' The shrill voice of the Drommian interrupted his worries.

'Conceivably, under other circumstances,' Raeker replied. 'As it happens, we're too far away. You must have noticed the delays between questions and answers when I was talking to Nick. We're orbiting Tenebra far enough out to keep us over the same longitude; its day is about four Earth ones, and that puts us over a hundred and sixty thousand miles away. Nearly two seconds delay in reflex would make the robot a pretty poor fighter.'

'Of course. I should have realized. I must apologize for wasting your time and interrupting on what must be a very bothersome occasion.'

Raeker, with an effort, tore his mind from the scene so far below, and turned to the Drommians.

'I'm afraid the apology must be mine,' he said. 'I knew you were coming,

302

and why; I should at least have appointed someone to do the honors of the place, if I couldn't manage it myself. My only excuse is the emergency you see. Please let me make up for it by helping you now. I suppose you would like to see the *Vindemiatrix*.'

'By no means. I would not dream of taking you from this room just now. Anyway, the ship itself is of no interest compared to your fascinating project on the planet, and you can explain that to us as well here, while you are waiting for your agent's answer, as anywhere else. I understand that your robot has been on the planet a long time; perhaps you could tell me more about how you recruited your agents on the planet. Probably my son would like to be shown the ship, if someone else could be spared from other duties.'

'Certainly. I did not realize he was your son; the message telling us of your visit did not mention him, and I assumed he was an assistant.'

'That is perfectly all right. Son, this is Dr Helven Raeker; Dr Raeker, this is Aminadorneldo.'

'I am delighted to meet you, sir,' piped the younger Drommian.

'The pleasure is mine. If you wait a moment, a man is coming to show you over the *Vindemiatrix* – unless you would rather stay here and join conversation with your father and me.'

'Thank you, I would rather see the ship.'

Raeker nodded, and waited in silence for a moment or two. He had already pressed the call button which would bring a crewman to the observing room. He wondered a little why the younger being was with his father; presumably he was serving some purpose. It would be easier to talk without him, though, since the two were virtually indistinguishable to Raeker and it would be rather embarrassing to get them mixed up. Both were giants from the human point of view; standing on their hind legs – a highly unnatural attitude for them – they would have towered nearly ten feet tall. Their general build was that of a weasel – or better, an otter, since the slender digits which terminated their five pairs of limbs were webbed. The limbs themselves were short and powerful, and the webs on the first two pairs reduced to fringes of membrane along the fingers – a perfectly normal evolutionary development for intelligent amphibious beings living on a planet with a surface gravity nearly four times that of the earth. Both were wearing harnesses supporting sets of small gas tanks, with tubing running inconspicuously to the corners of their mouths; they were used to an oxygen partial pressure about a third greater than human normal. They were hairless, but something about their skins reflected a sheen similar to that of wet sealskin.

They were stretched in an indescribably relaxed attitude on the floor, with their heads high enough to see the screens clearly. When the door slid open and the crewmen entered, one of them came to his feet with a flowing motion and, introductions completed, followed the man out of the compartment.

Raeker noticed that he walked on all ten limbs, even those whose webs were modified to permit prehension, though the *Vindemiatrix*'s centrifugal 'gravity' could hardly have made it necessary. Well, most men use both legs on the moon, for that matter, though hopping on one is perfectly possible. Raeker dismissed the matter from his mind, and turned to the remaining Drommian – though he always reserved some of his attention for the screens.

'You wanted to know about our local agents,' he began. 'There's not very much to tell, in one way. The big difficulty was getting contact with the surface at all. The robot down there now represents a tremendous achievement of engineering; the environment is close to the critical temperature of water, with an atmospheric pressure near eight hundred times that of Earth. Since even quartz dissolves fairly readily under those conditions, it took quite a while to design machines which could hold up. We finally did it; that one has been down a little over sixteen of our years. I'm a biologist and can't help you much with the technical details; if you happen to care, there are people here who can.

'We sent the machine down, spent nearly a year exploring, and finally found some apparently intelligent natives. They turned out to be egg-layers, and we managed to get hold of some of the eggs. Our agents down there are the ones who hatched; we've been educating them ever since. Now, just as we start doing some real exploring with them, this has to happen.' He gestured toward the screen, where the huge Swift had paused in his examination of the robot and seemed to be listening; perhaps Nick was having some luck in his selling job.

'If you could make a machine last so long in that environment, I should think you could build something which would let you go down in person,' said the Drommian.

Raeker smiled wryly. 'You're quite right, and that's what makes the present situation even more annoying. We have such a machine just about ready to go down; in a few days we expected to be able to cooperate directly with our people below.'

'Really? I should think that would have taken a long time to design and build.'

'It has. The big problem was not getting down; we managed that all right with parachutes for the robot. The trouble is getting away again.'

'Why should that be particularly difficult? The surface gravity, as I understand it, is less than that of my own world, and even the potential gradient ought to be somewhat smaller. Any booster unit ought to clear you nicely.'

'It would if it worked. Unfortunately, the booster that will unload its exhaust against eight hundred atmospheres hasn't been built yet. They melt down – they don't blow up because the pressure's too high.'

The Drommian looked a trifle startled for a moment, then nodded in a remarkably human manner.

'Of course. I should have thought. I remember how much more effective rockets are on your own planet than ours. But how have you solved this? Some radically new type of reactor?'

'Nothing new; everything in the device is centuries old. Basically, it's a ship used long ago for deep-ocean exploration on my own world – a bathyscaphe, we called it. For practical purposes, it's a dirigible balloon. I could describe it, but you'd do better to—'

'Teacher!' A voice which even Aminadabarlee of Dromm could recognize as Nick's erupted from the speaker. Raeker whirled back to his panel and closed the microphone switch.

'Yes, Nick? What does Swift say?'

'In effect, *no*. He wants nothing to do with anything in this village but you.'

'Didn't you explain the language problem to him?'

'Yes, but he says that if I was able to learn his words you, who are my teacher, should be able to learn them more quickly. Then he will not have to depend on people he doesn't trust to tell him what you're saying. I hope he's right. He's willing to leave the rest of us here, but you have to go with him.'

'I see. You'd better agree, for now; it will at least keep those of you who are alive out of further trouble. It may be that we'll be able to arrange a little surprise for Swift in the near future. You tell him that I'll do what he says; I'll go along with him to the caves – I suppose he'll be starting back there tomorrow, though if he wants to stay longer don't discourage him. When they go, you stay where you are; find everyone who's still alive and get them back in shape – I suppose most of you are injured – and then wait until I get in touch with you. It may be some days, but leave it to me.'

Nick was a fairly fast thinker, and remembered at once that Fagin could travel at night without the aid of fire – rain did not suffocate him. He thought he saw what the teacher planned to do; it was not his fault that he was wrong. The word 'bathyscaphe' had never been used in his hearing.

'Teacher!' he called, after a moment's thought. 'Wouldn't it be better if we moved as soon as we could, and arranged some other place to meet you after you escape? He'll come right back here sure as rainfall.'

'Don't worry about that. Just stay here, and get things back to normal as soon as possible. I'll be seeing you.'

'All right, Teacher.' Raeker leaned back in his seat once more, nodding his head slowly.

The Drommian must have spent a good deal of time on Earth; he was able to interpret the man's attitude. 'You seem a great deal happier than you were a few minutes ago,' he remarked. 'I take it you have seen your way out of the situation.'

'I think so,' replied Raeker. 'I had forgotten the bathyscaphe until I mentioned it to you; when I did recall it, I realized that once it got down there our troubles would be over. The trouble with that robot is that it has to crawl, and can be tracked and followed; the bathyscaphe, from the point of view of the natives down there, can fly. It has outside handling equipment, and when the crew goes down they can simply pick up the robot some night and fly it away from the cliff. I defy Swift to do any constructive tracking.'

'Then isn't Nick right? Won't Swift head straight for the village? I should think you'd have done better to follow Nick's suggestion.'

'There'll be time to move after we get the robot. If they leave the village before, we'll have a lot of trouble finding them, no matter how carefully we arrange a meeting beforehand. The area is not very well mapped, and what there is doesn't stay mapped very well.'

'Why not? That sounds rather strange.'

'Tenebra is a rather strange planet. Diastrophism is like Earth's weather; the question is not whether it will rain tomorrow but whether your pasture will start to grow into a hill. There's a team of geophysicists champing at the proverbial bit, waiting for the bathyscaphe to go down so they can set up a really close working connection with Nick's group. The general cause we know – the atmosphere is mostly water near its critical temperature, and silicate rocks dissolve fairly rapidly under those circumstances. The place cools off just enough each night to let a little of the atmosphere turn liquid, so for the best part of two Earth days you have the crust washing down to the oceans like the Big Rock Candy Mountain. With three Earth gravities trying to make themselves felt, it's hardly surprising that the crust is readjusting all the time.

'Anyway, I think we're set up now. It won't be morning down there for a couple of days, and I don't see how much can happen until then. My relief will be here soon; when he arrives, perhaps you would like to see the bathyscaphe with me.'

'I should be most interested.' Raeker was getting the impression that either the Drommians were a very polite race or Aminadabarlee had been selected for his diplomatic post for that quality. He didn't keep it long.

Unfortunately, there was a delay in visiting the bathyscaphe. When Raeker and the Drommian reached the bay where the small shuttle of the *Vindemiatrix* was normally kept, they found it empty. A check with the watch officer – ship's watch, not the one kept on the robot; the organizations were not connected – revealed that it had been taken out by the crewmen whom Raeker had asked to show Aminadorneldo around.

'The Drommian wanted to see the bathyscaphe, Doctor, and so did young Easy Rich.'

'Who?'

'That daughter Councillor Rich has tagging along. Begging the pardon of the gentleman with you, political inspection teams are all right as long as they inspect; but when they make the trip an outing for their offspring—'

'I have my son along,' Aminadabarlee remarked.

'I know. There's a difference between someone old enough to take care of himself and an infant whose fingers have to be kept off hot contacts ...' The officer let his voice trail off, and shook his head. He was an engineer; Raeker suspected that the party had descended on the power room in the near past, but didn't ask.

'Have you any idea when the shuttle will be back?' he asked.

The engineer shrugged. 'None. Flanagan was letting the kid lead *him* around. He'll be back when she's tired, I suppose. You could call him, of course.'

'Good idea.' Raeker led the way to the signal room of the *Vindemiatrix*, seated himself at a plate, and punched the combination of the tender's set. The screen lighted up within a few seconds, and showed the face of Crystal Mechanic Second Class Flanagan, who nodded when he saw the biologist.

'Hello, Doctor. Can I help you?'

'We were wondering when you'd be back. Councillor Aminadabarlee would like to see the bathyscaphe, too.' The nearly two-second pause while light made the round trip from *Vindemiatrix* to tender and back was scarcely noticed by Raeker, who was used to it; the Drommian was rather less patient.

'I can come back and pick you up whenever you want; my customers are fully occupied in the 'scaphe.' Raeker was a trifle surprised.

'Who's with them?'

'I was, but I don't really know much about the thing, and they promised not to touch anything.'

'That doesn't sound very safe to me. How old is the Rich girl? About twelve, isn't she?'

'I'd say so. I wouldn't have left her there alone, but the Drommian was with her, and said he'd take care of things.'

'I still think—' Raeker got no further. Four sets of long, webbed, wire-hard fingers tightened on his shoulders and upper arm, and the sleek head of Aminadabarlee moved into the pickup area beside his own. A pair of yellow-green eyes stared at the image in the plate, and a deeper voice than Raeker had yet heard from Drommian vocal cords cut across the silence.

'It is possible that I am less well acquainted with your language than I had believed,' were his words. 'Do I understand that you have left two children unsupervised in a ship in space?'

'Not exactly children, sir,' protested Flanagan. 'The human girl is old enough to have a good deal of sense, and your own son is hardly a child; he's as big as you.'

'We attain our full physical growth within a year of birth,' snapped the Drommian. 'My son is four years old, about the social equivalent of a human being of seven. I was under the impression that human beings were a fairly admirable race, but to give responsibility to an individual as stupid as you appear to be suggests a set of social standards so low as to be indistinguish-able from savagery. If anything happens to my boy—' He stopped; Flanagan's face had disappeared from the screen, and he must have missed the last couple of sentences of Aminadabarlee's castigation; but the Drommian was not through. He turned to Raeker, whose face had gone even paler than usual, and resumed. 'It makes me sick to think that at times I have left my son in the charge of human caretakers during my years on Earth. I had assumed your race to be civilized. If this piece of stupidity achieves its most likely result, Earth will pay the full price; not a human-driven ship will land again on any planet of the galaxy that values Drommian feelings. The story of your idiocy will cross the light-years, and no human ship will live to enter Drom-mian skies. Mankind will have the richly earned contempt of every civilized race in—'

He was cut off, but not by words. A rending crash sounded from the speaker, and a number of loose objects visible on the screen jerked abruptly toward a near wall. They struck it loudly and rebounded, but without obey-ing the laws of reflection. They all bounced the same way – in the direction which Raeker recognized with a sinking feeling as that of the tender's air lock. A book flew past the pickup area in the same direction, and struck a metal instrument traveling more slowly.

But this collision went unheard. No more sound came from the speaker; the tender was silent, with the silence of airlessness.

III

Cerebration; Transportation; Emigration

Nick Chopper stood in the doorway of his hut and thought furiously. Behind him the seven other survivors of the raid lay in various stages of disrepair. Nick himself was not entirely unscathed, but he was still able to walk – and, if necessary, fight, he told himself grimly. All of the others except Jim and Nancy would be out of useful action for several days at least.

He supposed that Fagin had been right in yielding to Swift as he had; at least, the savage had kept his word about letting Nick collect and care for his wounded friends. Every time Nick thought of the attack, however, or even of Swift, he felt like resuming the war. It would have given him intense pleasure to remove Swift's scales one by one and use them to shingle a hut in full view of their owner.

He was not merely brooding, however; he was really thinking. For the first time in a good many years, he was questioning seriously a decision of Fagin's. It seemed ridiculous that the Teacher could get away from the cave village without help; he hadn't been able to fight Swift's people during the attack, and if he had any powers Nick didn't know about that was certainly the time to use them. Getting away at night didn't count; he'd be tracked and caught first thing in the morning.

But wait a minute. What could the cave-dwellers actually *do* to Fagin? The hard white stuff the Teacher was covered with – or made out of, for all Nick knew – might be proof against knives and spears; the point had never occurred to Nick or any of his friends. Maybe that was why Fagin was being so meek now, when his people could be hurt; maybe he planned to act more constructively when he was alone.

It would be nice to be able to talk it over with the Teacher without Swift's interference. Of course, the chief couldn't eavesdrop very effectively, since he couldn't understand English, but he would know that a conference was going on, and would be in a pretty good position to block any activity planned therein. If it were practical to get Swift out of hearing – but if that were possible, the whole thing would be solved anyway. The meat of the problem was the fact that Swift *couldn't* be handled.

Of course, it was night, and therefore raining. The invaders were being protected by the village fires, at the moment; however, Nick reflected, no one was protecting the fires themselves. He glanced upward at the thirty-to

309

fifty-foot raindrops drifting endlessly out of the black sky, following one of them down to a point perhaps three hundred yards above his head. There it vanished, fading out in ghostly fashion as it encountered the updraft from the village fires. It was not the drops straight overhead which were troublesome – not to Fagin's village.

Another, larger drop beyond the glowing protective double ring accomplished more. It settled to the ground fifty yards beyond one of the outer fires. The ground had been cooled enough by its predecessors to let it remain liquid, so for a short time it was visible as it drifted toward the blaze under the impulse of the fires' own convection currents. Then radiated heat made it fade out; but Nick knew it was still there. It had been crystal clear, free of suspended oxygen bubbles; it was now pure steam, equally free of combustion's prime necessity. Nick would have nodded in satisfaction, had his head been capable of free movement, when the fire in the path of the invisible cloud suddenly began to cool and within a few seconds faded from visibility.

If any of the attackers noticed the incident, they certainly did nothing. None of them moved, and the fire remained out. Five seconds later Nick had his plan worked out.

He emerged fully from the hut and walked over to the main fuel magazine. Here he loaded himself with as much as he could carry, and took it back to the building where the wounded were lying. None of the raiders stopped or questioned him; none had spoken to him since the truce had been concluded. Inside the hut, he quickly built and lighted a fire. When it had come to an even glow he lighted a torch from it and walked back to the woodpile. Casually he stuck the cold end of the torch into the pile, as though to illuminate his work; then he made several more trips carrying fuel to the hut, leaving the torch where he had placed it. Eventually the building could hold no more wood, so he ceased his labor.

But he left the torch.

Tenebran wood glows like punk; it does not flame. It took some time for the stick to burn down to its base, and still longer before the increase in brilliancy of the region around the village showed that the main stack had properly caught. Even then, there was no reaction from the invaders. These had gathered into a tight group surrounding the robot, which had remained in its usual position at the center of the village.

By this time, more than half of the peripheral fires were out, most of them in the outer ring. One or two of the inner ring had also been smothered, and Nick began to get an impression of uneasiness from the clustered cave-dwellers. When the last of the outer fires died, a mutter began to grow from their ranks, and Nick chuckled to himself. Swift just *might* have a little trouble handling his men as their protection from the rain vanished, and no caves were available. If the muttering continued, the chief would certainly have to take some action;

and all he could do, as far as Nick could see, would be to ask Nick himself for help. That should put quite a dent in his authority.

But Nick had underestimated the big fellow. From the vicinity of the robot his voice suddenly rapped out a series of orders; and obediently a dozen of his men ran from the outskirts of the group toward one of the fires which was still burning. There, to Nick's disgust, they seized sticks from the small wood-pile at its side, lighted their ends, carried the torches to the dead fires, and rekindled these without the slightest difficulty. Evidently the cave-dwellers didn't sleep *all* night in their holes; someone had watched his fire-technique long enough to get at least some of the idea. If they also knew about replen-ishing … They did. More wood was being put on all the fires. Nick noted with satisfaction, however, that it was far too much wood; he wouldn't have to wait too long before the small woodpiles beside each fire were extin-guished. The cave-dwellers seemed to have taken the now fiercely glowing main pile as another bonfire; Swift was going to have to do some fast think-ing when the reserves disappeared.

This he proved able to do. It was fortunate that Nick had been able to keep awake, for Swift's men did not announce their coming. They simply came.

They were unarmed, rather to Nick's surprise, but they approached the hut door without hesitation, almost as though they expected him to stand aside for them. When he didn't, they stopped, the foremost half a spear's length away. He may have intended to say something, but Nick spoke first.

'What do you want? My friends are all wounded and can't help you. There is no room in the hut. Go to the others, if you want shelter.'

'Swift sent us for wood.' It was a calm statement, with no 'or else' concealed in it, as far as Nick could tell by the tone.

'I have only enough to keep my own fire going for the night. You will have to use the other piles.'

'They are used up.'

'That isn't my fault. You know that wood burns up in a fire; you shouldn't have put so much on.'

'You didn't tell us that. Swift says that you should therefore give us your own wood, which we saw you taking, and tell us how much to use.'

It was evident that the chief had seen through at least part of Nick's scheme, but there was nothing to do now but carry it through.

'As I said, I have only enough for this fire,' he said. 'I shall not give it up; I need it for myself and my friends.'

Very much to his surprise, the fellow retreated without further words. Apparently he had gone as far as his orders extended, and was going back for more. Initiative did not flourish under Swift's rule.

Nick watched the group as it rejoined the main crowd and began to push its way through to the chief. Then he turned and nudged Jim.

'Better get up, you and Nancy,' he whispered. 'Swift can't let this go. I'll fight as well as I can; you keep me in ammunition.'

'What do you mean?' Nancy's thoughts were less swift than usual.

'I can't fight them with axes; they'd be through in two minutes. I'm tired and slow. I'm going to use torches – remember what it feels like to be burned? They don't; I warned them about it when I was at their village, and they were always very careful, so none of them has any real experience. They're going to get it now!'

The other two were on their feet by this time. 'All right,' agreed Jim. 'We'll light torches and pass them to you whenever you call. Are you going to poke with the things, or throw them? I never thought of fighting that way.'

'Neither did I, until now. I'll try poking first, so give me long ones. If I decide to throw, I'll call for really short ones – we don't want them throwing the things back at us, and they will if there's enough to hold on to. They're not too stupid for that – not by a long day's journey!'

Jim and Nancy gestured agreement and understanding, and turned to the piles of firewood that almost covered the floor. The fire was burning quite close to the doorway; Nick took his stand once more in the opening, and the other two on either side of the blaze, where they could hand torches to him as rapidly as he might need. Everything was ready when the party returned to the hut.

It was a little larger this time; Swift himself had joined it. They approached to within half a dozen yards, and spoke briefly and to the point.

'If you don't let us in to get the wood, my knives will take care of you. You have seen what I mean.'

'I have seen,' acknowledged Nick. 'That's why I want nothing to do with you. If you come any closer, it is at your own risk.'

He had never before seen Swift hesitant or uncertain, but for just a moment now the chief seemed to be running over the implications of Nick's words. Then he was himself again.

'Very well,' he said, and swept forward with four spears couched along his forearms.

Nick's battle plan had to be scrapped at the beginning; the spears were longer than his torches. He did succeed in striking their points aside before they touched him, but he could not reach Swift even with the spears out of the way. His hatred of the chief paralyzed his judgment for an instant, and he hurled both his left-hand torches at the giant's chest.

Swift ducked, barely in time. Those behind him were in a close-packed wedge whose central members were unable to dodge quickly enough, and howls of pain arose in several voices as the torches struck and scattered burning coals in all directions. The chief ducked backward to just beyond spear's length, resuming his attack stance.

'Half circle!' he snapped. The warriors obeyed with speed and precision, forming a thin line centered on Nick. 'Now, all at once – get him!' The semi-circle contracted, and the spear points came toward the door.

Nick was not too alarmed. None of the attackers was in a position to deliver the upward thrust which would get under scales; stone points were more likely to push him back than to penetrate. If he were pushed back against anything solid, of course, it would be a different story; the real danger at the moment, though, was that several of the fighters would get within knife range at once, and so occupy him that a spearsman could get close enough for long enough to strike from below. For just an instant he hesitated, wondering whether he should throw or strike; then he made up his mind.

'Short ones!' he ordered to the helpers behind him.

Nancy already had several foot-long sticks with their ends in the fire; she had them in his hands instantly, and was lighting others. For perhaps ten seconds Nick did his best to emulate a machine gun. More than half his projectiles missed, but a good many didn't; and after the first three or four seconds another factor complicated the fight. Still burning torches and fragments of glowing wood were being more and more thickly scattered before the doorway, and the attackers were getting involved with these. Feet were even more sensitive to the fire than were scales, and the effect was distracting, to put it mildly. Swift, to do him justice, stayed with his men and fought as hard as any; but at length even he had had enough and withdrew a few yards, limping slightly. Nick laughed aloud as he went.

'Better get your own firewood, Swift, my friend! Of course you won't find any within an hour's walk of the village; we've used it up long ago. Even if you know where the best places to get it are, you won't be able to get there and back through the rain. You needn't worry, though; we'll take care of you when you go to sleep. I wouldn't want anything to eat you, friend Swift!'

It was almost funny to watch Swift's fury. His hands tightened on the spear shafts, and he rose to full height on his walking legs, shaking all over with rage. For several seconds it seemed an even bet whether he would hurl the spears or charge the door across the scattered coals. Nick was perfectly ready for either, but was hoping for the latter; the mental picture of Swift with burned feet was a very attractive one.

But the chief did neither. In the midst of his fury he suddenly relaxed, and the spear points dropped as though he had forgotten them for a moment. Then he shifted the weapons backward until he was holding them near their centers of gravity, in 'carry' position, and turned away from the hut. Then, seemingly as an afterthought, he turned back and spoke to Nick.

'Thanks, Chopper. I didn't expect that much help. I'd better say good-bye, now; and so had you – to your Teacher.'

'But – you can't travel at night.'

'Why not? You did.'

'But how about Fagin? How do you know he can?'

'You told me he could do anything you could. You also said he'd agree to do what we said. If he forgets that, or changes his mind, we can thank you for showing us what to do. Do you suppose he'll like the touch of fire any better than we do?' Swift chuckled and strode swiftly back to the main group, bawling orders as he went. Nick began shouting at least as loudly.

'Fagin! Did you hear that? Fagin! Teacher!' In his anxiety he forgot the time it always took the Teacher to answer, and drowned the robot out for a moment. Then its answer became audible.

'What's the matter, Nick?' It was not possible to tell from the voice that Raeker was not at the other end; Nick's people had been given a general idea of the 'Teacher' situation, but not all the details, and they thought inevitably of the robot as an individual. This was virtually the first time it had made any difference; the man on watch knew the general picture, of course, having been briefed by Raeker when the latter had gone off duty, but he had not actually been present during Swift's initial attack or the subsequent truce. Consequently, Nick's words did not mean all they might have to him.

'Swift is going to start back for the caves right away; he says he'll use fire on you if you don't go with him. Can you stand that?'

There was a little more than the usual hesitation. No one had ever measured the temperature of a Tenebran fire, and the man on watch was not enough of a physicist to hazard a guess from its radiation output. The main consideration in his mind was the cost of the robot.

'No,' he answered. 'I'll go along with him.'

'What shall we do?'

Raeker's order for the villagers to stay put was one thing he had not mentioned to his relief; he had expected to be back on duty long before the start of the journey. The relief did the best he could under the circumstances.

'Use your own judgment. They won't hurt me; I'll get in touch with you again later.'

'All right.' Nick carefully refrained from reminding the Teacher of his earlier command; he liked the new one much better. He watched in silence as the invaders, under Swift's orders, collected what torches they could from the nearly spent fires. Then they clustered around the Teacher, leaving an opening in the crowd on the side they wished him to go. It was all done without words, but the meaning was plain enough. The robot swung around on its treads and headed south, the cave dwellers swarming after it.

Nick spent only a few moments wondering whether they'd find more torch wood before using up what they had. He had turned his mind to other matters even before the cavalcade was out of sight.

He had been given a free hand. Very well, he still felt that leaving the

314

village was best; they would do so as soon as possible. Of course, it wouldn't be possible for a few days, until everyone was able to travel again, but the time could be spent in planning. There was certainly the question of where to go, and the corollary one of how to get there – Nick began to realize with a shock just what leaving the village, with its lifetime accumulation of property and equipment, would mean – and how to get back in touch with Fagin when the move was accomplished. It was easy to tell oneself that the Teacher could always find them wherever they went; but Nick was mature enough to doubt the omniscience of anyone, including the robot. That meant, then, three problems to solve. Since Nick had no desire to resemble Swift in any way, he postponed solving them until the others would be awake and able to help in the discussion.

The fire lasted until morning, but only just, and only by virtue of Nick's running around the hut rapidly on a number of occasions to stir oxygen into an oncoming mass of dead steam. He got very little sleep after the last of the outer fires went, and that was pretty early in the night.

Morning brought no relief. The first task normally accomplished was to put a guard on the village herd, which was penned in a hollow near the village. The depression remained full of water a little later than the surrounding country, so the 'cattle' were normally safe from predators until the guards could arrive; but at the moment there simply weren't enough people in condition to guard both herd and village. They suffered several losses that morning as a result, until Nick could round up the reviving creatures by himself and herd them into the village. Then there was the problem of firewood for the next night; he had told the absolute truth to Swift in that respect. Someone had to get it. There was no choice but for the still battered Jim and Nancy to do the job together, dragging as best they could the cart on which they piled their fuel. They had never succeeded in training their cattle to pull the conveyance; the creatures stubbornly refused to budge under any sort of load.

By the second day, most of the others were on their feet if not at full efficiency, and matters were considerably easier. A consultation was held that morning, in which Nick proposed and defended vigorously the notion that they move to the viciously rough country he had crossed during his flight from the cave village. His chief point was the presence of so many spots which could only be approached from a single, narrow point, like a canyon or ridge, and could therefore be defended effectively by a small force. It was Nancy who answered the suggestion.

'I'm not sure that's a very good plan,' she said. 'In the first place, we don't know that any of the places you describe will still be that way when we get there.' A quake lent emphasis and support to her words.

'What if they aren't?' retorted Nick. 'There will always be others. I wasn't suggesting any of the specific spots I described, only the general area.'

'But how is Fagin to find us? Supposing one of us does get to the cave village and get a message to him, how are we to describe the way to him? We'd have to guide him directly, which would probably interfere with his own plans – you judged, and I think rightly, that he is planning to take advantage of his ability to travel at night without fire.'

Nick felt a very human surge of annoyance at this opposition, but remembered Swift in time to keep from yielding to it. He didn't want to be compared with that savage in anyone's mind, he told himself; besides, there was something to what Nancy was saying, now that he really gave his mind to it.

'What sort of place would you suggest?' he asked. 'You're right about getting back in touch with Fagin, but I certainly can't think of any place which we will ever defend as easily as those canyons in the west.'

'It seems to me that Fagin was right when he said it was foolish to fight Swift's people at all,' returned Nancy quietly. 'I was not thinking of defense; if we have to defend ourselves, we're already out of luck, I fear. What I had in mind was the sea.'

'What?'

'You know. You helped map it. Off to the east there's a body of water that isn't water – at least, it doesn't dry up entirely during the daytime. I don't remember just what Fagin called it when we reported it to him—'

'He said he supposed it was mostly sulphuric acid, whatever that is, but he didn't know how to make sure,' interjected the still crippled Dorothy.

'– Whatever it is, it stays there, and if we're on the edge of it Fagin can't help finding us if he simply travels along its border. Probably he can travel *in* it for a distance, too, so the cave people can't track him.' A hum of approving surprise greeted this notion, and after a few moments of thought Nick gestured agreement.

'All right,' he said. 'If no one has other ideas, we'll move to the edge of the sea; we can settle on the exact spot after we get there and have looked around. It's a year or two since we mapped the place, and I don't suppose we could trust information that old.

'The next problem is getting there. We'll have to decide how much we can take from the village here, and how we can carry it. I suppose we can start with the wood cart, but I'll bet there are places we won't be able to move it across. No matter how we figure it, there's a lot we'll have to leave behind.

'Then, finally, there's the matter of getting a message to Fagin. That we can leave until we're settled; there's no point telling him where we are before we know.

'I hope we can travel by tomorrow; in the meantime, the second question is the one to work on. Anyone who has more ideas, let's hear them at any time.' They dispersed, each to the tasks of which he was capable.

Jim and Nancy were practically whole again, and were now looking after the cattle. There had been no further losses since they had been able to take over the job. Dorothy was at the wagon, with all the articles they hoped to take stacked around her, arranging and rearranging them in the vehicle. No matter how she packed them, there was more outside than in, and nearly constant discussion and even argument was going on between her and the other members of the group. Each wanted his own belongings to go and it took a good deal of talk to convince some of them that since everything couldn't be taken the losses should be shared.

The argument was still going on, to a certain extent, when the journey started. Nick was beginning to feel a certain sympathy for Swift by that time; he had discovered that at times it was necessary for a group to have a leader, and that it was not always possible for the leader to reason his followers into the desired action. Nick had had to give his first arbitrary orders, and was troubled by the thought that half his friends must by now be comparing him with Swift. The fact that he had been obeyed should have clarified him on this point, but it didn't.

The cart was perilously overloaded, and everyone except those actually herding had to pull with all his strength. When fighting was necessary, hauling had to be stopped while weapons were snatched up and used. Actually, of course, there wasn't too much fighting; the average Tenebran carnivore wasn't very brainy, but most of them steered clear of such a large group. The chief exception was formed by the floaters, which were more vegetable than animal anyway. These creatures could be downed fairly safely by anyone having a spear longer than their tentacles; but even after their gas bladders were punctured they were dangerous to anyone coming within reach of the poisonous appendages. Several animals of the herd were lost when one of the monsters fell almost into it, and two of the party were painfully poisoned on the same occasion. It was some hours before they could walk unaided.

Contrary to Nick's pessimistic forecast, it proved possible to get the wagon all the way to the sea. Late in the second day of travel they reached it, after some hours of threading their way among ever larger pools of quiet, oily liquid.

They had seen such pools before, of course; they formed in hollows in their own valley toward the end of the day – hollows which were lakes of water at sunrise, but only tiny pools of oleum when the day reached its height. These were larger, filling a much bigger fraction of their beds.

The ground was different, too; vegetation was as thick as ever, but underfoot among the stems the ground was studded with quartz crystals. The cattle didn't seem to mind, but the feet of their owners were not quite so tough, and progress became decidedly difficult. Such masses of crystals did occur elsewhere, but usually in isolated patches which could be avoided.

The search for a stopping place was therefore briefer, and perhaps less careful, than it might otherwise have been. They agreed very quickly on a peninsula whose main body was a hill thirty or forty feet above the sea, joined to the mainland by a crystal-studded tombolo a dozen yards in width. Nick was not the only one of the party who was still considering the problem of physical defense; and in addition to its advantages in this respect, the peninsula was roomy enough for the herd. They guided and trundled their belongings down the sea and up the hill, and immediately settled down to the standard business of hunting for firewood. This was plentiful enough, and by dark a very satisfactory supply had been laid in. The watch fires were built, one of the herd animals slaughtered and eaten, and the group settled down for the night. It was not until the drops had appeared and the fires had been lighted that anyone thought to wonder what happened to the sea level during the nightly rain.

IV

Communication; Penetration; Isolation

Aminadabarlee fell silent, his eyes fixed on the vision screen; and, nasty as the creature had been, Raeker felt sympathetic. He himself would have been at least as unsociable under similar circumstances. There was no time for pity, however, while there was still hope; too much had to be done.

'Wellenbach! What's the combination of the bathyscaphe?' he snapped.

The communication watch officer reached over his shoulder. 'I'll get her for you, Doctor.'

Raeker pushed his hand aside. 'Wait a minute. Is it a regular set at the other end? An ordinary phone, I mean, or something jury-rigged into the panels?'

'Perfectly ordinary. Why?'

'Because if it weren't and you punched its combination, those kids might open their air lock or something like that in trying to answer. If it's standard in design and appearance, the girl will be able to answer safely.'

'I see. She won't have any trouble; I've seen her use the punch-combination sets here.'

'All right. Call them.' Raeker tried not to show the uncertainty he felt as the officer punched the buttons. It was not possible to tell yet just what had happened above Tenebra's atmosphere; *something* had evidently breached the air lock of the tender, but that might or might not have affected the bathyscaphe. If it had, the children were probably dead – though their guide might have had them in space suits, of course. One could hope.

Behind him, Aminadabarlee might have been a giant statue of an otter, cast in oiled gray steel. Raeker spent no time wondering at his own fate if bad news came back through the set and that statue returned to life; all his attention was concentrated on the fate of the youngsters. A dozen different speculations chased themselves through his mind in the few seconds before the screen lighted up. Then it did, and the worst of them vanished.

A human face was looking at them out of it; thin, very pale, topped by a mop of hair which looked black on the screen but which Raeker knew was red; a face covered by an expression which suggested terror just barely held under control, but – a living face. That was the important fact.

At almost the same instant a figure came hurtling through the door of the communications room and skidded to a halt beside the motionless figure of the Drommian.

'Easy! Are you all right?' Raeker didn't need the words to identify Councillor Rich. Neither did Aminadabarlee, and neither did the child in the screen. After the two-second pause for return contact, the terror vanished from the thin face, and she relaxed visibly.

'Yes, Dad. I was pretty scared for a minute, but it's all right now. Are you coming?'

For a moment there was some confusion at the set as Rich, Raeker, and the Drommian all tried to speak at once; then Aminadabarlee's physical superiority made itself felt, and he thrust his sleek head at the screen.

'Where is the other one – my son?' he shrilled.

She replied promptly, 'He's here; he's all right.'

'Let me talk to him.' The girl left the pickup area for a moment, and they heard her voice but not her words as she addressed someone else. Then she reappeared, with her dark hair badly disheveled and a bleeding scratch on one cheek.

'He's in a corner, and doesn't want to come out. I'll turn up the volume so you can talk to him there.' She made no reference to her injury, and, to Raeker's surprise, neither did her father. Aminadabarlee seemed not to notice it. He shifted into his own shrill language, which seemed to make sense to no one else in the room but Rich, and held forth for several minutes, pausing now and then for answers.

At first he received none; then, as he grew more persuasive, a feeble piping came back through the set. Hearing this restored the Drommian's composure, and he talked more slowly; and after a minute or so of this Aminadorneldo's head appeared beside Easy's. Raeker wondered whether he looked ashamed of himself; Drommian facial expressions were a closed book to him. Apparently one of the family had a conscience, anyway, for after a few moments' more talk from the elder one the child turned to Easy and shifted to English.

'I'm sorry I hurt you, Miss Rich. I was afraid, and thought you'd made the noise, and were trying to make me come out of the corner. My father says you are older than I, and that I am to do whatever you say until I am with him again.'

The girl seemed to understand the situation. 'It's all right, 'Mina,' she said gently. 'You didn't really hurt me. I'll take care of you, and we'll get back to your father – after a while.' She glanced at the pickup as she added the last words, and Raeker grew tense again. A glance at Councillor Rich confirmed his suspicion; the girl was trying to get something across, presumably without alarming her companion. Gently but firmly Raeker took the Drommian's place in the pickup field. Easy nodded in recognition; she had met him briefly on her own tour through the *Vindemiatrix* some time earlier.

'Miss Rich,' he began, 'we're still a little in the dark about just what happened down there. Can you tell us? Or is your guide there, to give a report?'

She shook her head negatively at the latter question. 'I don't know where Mr Flanagan is. He stayed in the tender to have a smoke, I suppose; he told us to be sure not to touch any controls – he must think we're pretty stupid. We stayed away from the board, of course – in fact, after the first look, we stayed out of the control compartment altogether, and looked through the other rooms. They're all observation or bunkrooms, except for the galley, and we were just going to suit up to go back to the tender when a call came from Mr Flanagan on the set he'd left tuned to suit radio frequency. He said he was at the outer lock, and would open it as soon as he closed the one on the tender – the two ships were so close together we could touch them both at once when we came across – and that we were to stay absolutely still and not do a thing until he came. 'Mina had just opened his mouth to answer when the jolt came; we were flung against the wall, and I was held there by what felt like three or four G's of acceleration. 'Mina could move around all right, and tried to call Mr Flanagan on the set, but there was no answer, and I wouldn't let him touch anything else. The acceleration lasted half a minute or so, I guess; you can tell better than we can. It stopped just before you called us.'

By this time the communication room was packed with men. Several of them began to work slide rules, and Raeker, turning from the set, watched one of these until he had finished; then he asked, 'Any ideas, Saki?'

'I think so,' the engineer replied. 'The kid's report isn't exact, of course, but judging from her estimate of acceleration and time, and the mass of the bathyscaphe, one full ring of the solid-fuel boosters was touched off somehow. That should give just over four G's for forty seconds – about a mile a second total velocity change. There's no way to tell where the ship is, though, until we get there and home on it; we can't compute, since we don't know the direction of acceleration. I wish the 'scaphe weren't so close to the planet, though.'

Raeker knew better than to ask the reason for this, but Aminadabarlee didn't.

'Why?'

The engineer glanced at him, then at the image of the other Drommian in the screen, and then apparently decided not to pull punches.

'Because a one-mile-a-second change in any of a good many directions could put it in an orbit which would enter atmosphere,' he said bluntly.

'How long to entry?' cut in Rich.

'Not my pigeon. We'll get it computed while we're under way. My guess would be hours at the outside, though.'

'Then why are we standing here talking?' shrilled Aminadabarlee. 'Why aren't preparations for rescue being made?'

'They are,' returned the engineer calmly. 'Only one shuttle was in regular use, but there are others here. One of them is being made ready, and will leave in less than ten minutes. Dr Raeker, do you want to come?'

'I'd just add mass without being useful,' Raeker replied.

'I suppose the same could be said for me,' said Rich, 'but I'd like to come if there's room. I certainly don't want to hamper the work, though.'

'It will be better if you don't,' admitted Sakiiro. 'We'll keep in touch with this ship and the 'scaphe, though, so you'll know what's happening.' He ran from the room.

Aminadabarlee had quite obviously meant to insist upon going; after Rich's words, however, he could hardly do that. He relieved his feelings by remarking, 'No one but a fool human being would have had takeoff boosters attached to an uncompleted ship.'

'The bathyscaphe is complete, except for final circuit checks and connections,' another engineer replied calmly, 'and the boosters were for landing as well as takeoff. As a matter of fact, they were not supposed to be connected until the last moment, and it will not be possible to tell what actually fired them until we salvage the ship. Until then, assigning blame is very much a waste of time.' He stared coldly at the Drommian, and Rich stepped into the breach. Raeker had to admit the fellow was good at his job; it had seemed a virtual certainty that the big weasel was going to clean the human beings out of the room, but Rich had him calmed down below boiling point in four or five minutes.

Raeker would have liked to hear the details, but he was occupied with the radio. The children on the bathyscaphe had heard, without understanding completely, most of the engineers' statements; and Raeker found himself doing his best to keep up their morale. They were, perfectly reasonably, frightened half to death. It wasn't as hard as he'd thought it might be, though; he hadn't talked long before he realized that the girl was doing exactly the same thing. He couldn't decide whether it was for the benefit of her father or her nonhuman companion, but his respect for the youngster went even higher.

The rescue ship was well on the way by this time, and as the minutes clicked by the hopes of everyone on all three vessels began to mount. If the 'scaphe were in an orbit that did not touch Tenebra's atmosphere, of course, there was no danger; food and air equipment were aboard and had been operating for some time. On a straight chance basis, it seemed to Raeker that the probabilities were at least three to one that this was the case, though he was no ballistician. The computer on the rescue boat was kept busy grinding out possible orbits; the worst seemed to call for atmospheric contact within three-quarters of an hour of the accident; and if this didn't occur within a little over two hours, it wouldn't.

There were view ports in the 'scaphe, and Easy was able to recognize some stars; but while this told them roughly which side of the planet she was on, the lack of precision measurements at her command made the information useless. At that time, there was only one side she *could* be on.

It was sixty-seven minutes after the accident that Easy reported acceleration. By that time, even Aminadabarlee knew all the implications of the fact. The rescue boat was 'there,' in the sense that it was within half a diameter of Tenebra and nearly motionless with respect to the planet – perfectly useless, as far as the trapped children were concerned. The engineers could get a fix on the 'scaphe's transmitter and locate it within a few miles; but they couldn't compute an interception orbit inside Tenebra's atmosphere. No one knew enough about the atmosphere. The certain thing was that no interception whatever could be accomplished before the 'scaphe was so low that rockets could not be used – atmospheric pressure would be too high for them. Saki-iro reported this to the *Vindemiatrix* within a minute of Easy's information; then, before Aminadabarlee could start to speak, he turned to the set which he had on the depth-boat's frequency.

'Miss Rich. Please listen carefully. Your acceleration is going to get much worse over the next few minutes; I want you to strap yourself in the seat before the control panel, and do what you can about your companion.'

'None of the seats fit him,' the girl answered.

'His normal weight is four G's,' Rich cut in from the *Vindemiatrix*,

'He'll be taking more than that; but he'll probably be able to stand it, in that case. Just tell him to lie down. Now, Miss Rich—'

'Call me Easy; it'll save time.'

'Tell me what you recognize on the board in front of you.'

'Not much. Light switches are labeled over on the left. The communicators are top center; air-lock controls under a guard near the light switches; about two square feet of off-on relay buttons, labeled with letters, that don't mean anything to me—' She let her voice trail off, and Saki nodded.

'All right. Now, near the top of the board, to the right of the communicators, you'll see an area about six inches square marked "Hunt." Have you found it?'

'Yes; I see it.'

'Make sure the master toggle at its lower left corner says "Off." Then put the three in the group labeled "Aero" in the "On" position. Then make sure that the big one marked "D.I." is off. Do you have that?'

'Yes, sir.'

'Now be sure you're strapped in. What you've been doing is to tie in a homing radio which is tuned to the transmission of the robot on the ground to the aerodynamic controls of the 'scaphe. I don't dare have you use any power, but with luck the autopilot will glide you down somewhere in the general vicinity of that robot. You don't have to worry about burning up in the atmosphere; the ship is designed for a power-off entry. It's a big planet, and if we can narrow down your landing area to even a five-hundred-mile radius it will be a big help in picking you up. Do you understand?'

'Yes. I'm strapped in the seat, and 'Mina is lying down.'

'All right. Now reach up to the "Hunt" region you've just been setting, and snap on the master switch. I hope you're not prone to motion sickness; it will be rough at first, I expect.'

Sakiiro from the rescue boat and the group in the message room of the *Vindemiatrix* watched tensely as the girl's hand went up and out of the pickup field. They could not see her actually close the switch, and to the surprise of the engineers they could not detect very easily the results of the act. They had expected the girl to be jammed into her seat by an abrupt acceleration change; but things proved not nearly so bad.

'I can feel it,' Easy reported. 'The ship is rolling – now the planet is on our left side – and I'm a little heavier in my seat – now we're leveling out again, and "Down" is forward, if this panel is at the front of the room.'

'It is,' replied the engineer. 'You should now be headed toward the robot, and will be slowing down until you're doing about five hundred miles an hour with respect to the air around you. The braking will be jerky; the ship had throw-away speed brakes to take it down through the heat barrier. Stay strapped in.'

'All right. How long will it take?'

'A couple of hours. You can stand it all right.'

Rich cut in at this point.

'Suppose the machine passes over your robot's location before getting rid of its speed, Mr Sakiiro? What will the autopilot do? Try to dive in at that point?'

'Certainly not. This is a vehicle, not a missile. It will circle the point at a distance which doesn't demand more than an extra half-G to hold it in the turn. If necessary, it will try to land the ship; but we should be able to avoid that.'

'How? You don't expect Easy to fly it, do you?'

'Not in the usual sense. However, when she's down to what we can call "flying" speed, the main buoyancy tanks of the 'scaphe should be full of the local atmosphere. Then I'll tell her how to start the electrolyzers; that will fill them with hydrogen, and the ship should float, when they're full, at an altitude where boosters can be used. Then she and her young friend can trim the ship so that she's hanging nose up, and fire the rest of the boosters. We can be waiting overhead.'

'I thought you said the boosters weren't connected to the control panel yet!'

Sakiiro was silent for a moment.

'You're right; I'd forgotten that. That complicates the problem.'

'You mean my kid is marooned down there?'

'Not necessarily. It's going to call for some tight maneuvering; but I should think we could rig boosters on this boat so as to be able to reach the 'scaphe when it's floating at its highest. The whole design object, remember, was for the thing to float high enough for hydroferron boosters to work; and if they'll work on one frame, they'll certainly work on another.'

'Then you can rescue her.' The statement was more than half a question. Sakiiro was an honest man, but he had difficulty in making an answer. He did, however, after a moment's hesitation, staring into the face of the middle-aged man whose agonized expression showed so clearly on his screen.

'We should be able to save them both. I will not conceal from you that it will be difficult and dangerous; transferring an engineer to the outside of the 'scaphe to finish up wiring, while the whole thing is floating like a balloon, from a rocket hanging on booster blasts, will present difficulties.'

'Why can't you transfer the kids to the rescue ship?'

'Because I'm pretty sure their space suits won't stand the pressure at the 'scaphe's floating height,' replied Sakiiro. 'I don't know about Drommian designs, but I do know our own.'

'Mr Sakiiro.' Easy's voice cut back into the conversation.

'Yes, Easy.'

'Is there anything more I can do? Just sitting here doesn't seem right, and – it scares me a little.'

Rich looked appealingly at the engineer. As a diplomat, he was an accomplished psychologist, and he knew his daughter. She was not hysterical by nature, but few twelve-year-olds had ever been put under this sort of stress. He himself was not qualified to suggest any reasonable occupation to hold her attention; but fortunately Sakiiro saw the need, too.

'There are pressure gauges to your left,' he said. 'If you can give us a running report on their readings, while your friend tells us when he can first detect signs of dimming in the stars, it will be of some help. Keep it up unless you get too heavy to be able to watch easily; that may not be too long.'

Rich looked his thanks; if Aminadabarlee was doing the same, no one was able to detect the fact. For long minutes the silence was broken only by the voices of the children, reading off numbers and describing the stars.

Then Easy reported that the ship was banking again.

'All right,' said Sakiiro. 'That means you're about over the robot. From now until your speed is killed, you're going to have to take better than three and a half gravities. Your seat folds back on its springs automatically to put you in the best position to stand it, but you're not going to be comfortable. Your friend can undoubtedly take it all right, but warn him against moving around. The ship's traveling fast in an atmosphere, and going from one air current to another at a few thousand miles can give quite a jolt.'

'All right.'

'The stars are getting hazy.' It was Aminadorneldo.

'Thanks. Can you give me another pressure reading?'

The girl obliged, with detectable strain in her voice. Until the last turn had started, the 'scaphe was in relatively free fall; but with its rudimentary wings biting what little there was of the atmosphere in an effort to keep it in a turn the situation was distinctly different. Why the vehicle didn't go into a frame-shattering series of stalls, none of the engineers could see; the turn had started at a much higher speed than had been anticipated by the designers of the machine. As it happened, the whole process was almost incredibly smooth – for a while.

Sakiiro, with no really objective data to go on, had about concluded that the vessel was down to gliding speed and was going to describe the location of the electrolysis controls to Easy when the motion changed. A series of shuddering jars shook the ship. The girl's body was held in the seat by the straps, but her head and limbs flapped like those of a scarecrow in a high wind; the young Drommian for the first time failed to stay put. The jolting continued, the thuds punctuated by the girl's sobs and an almost inaudibly high-pitched whine from Aminadorneldo. The elder Drommian rose once more to his feet and looked anxiously at the screen.

The engineers were baffled; the diplomats were too terrified for their children to have had constructive ideas even had they been qualified otherwise; but Raeker thought he knew the answer.

'They're hitting raindrops!' he yelled.

He must have been right, it was decided afterward; but the information did not really help. The bathyscaphe jerked and bucked. The autopilot did its best to hold a smooth flight path, but aerodynamic controls were miserably inadequate for the task. At least twice the vessel somersaulted completely, as nearly as Raeker could tell from the way the Drommian was catapulted around the room. Sheer luck kept him out of contact with the control switches. For a time the controls were useless because their efforts were overriden – a rudder trying to force a left turn will not get far if the right wing encounters a fifty-foot sphere of water, even though the water isn't much denser than the air. Then they were useless because they lacked enough grip on the atmosphere; the ship had given up enough kinetic energy to the raindrops to fall well below its stalling speed – low as that was, in an atmosphere seven or eight hundred times as dense as Earth's at sea level. By that time, of course, the ship was falling, in the oldest and simplest sense of the word. The motion was still irregular, for it was still hitting the drops; but the violence was gone, for it wasn't hitting them very hard.

The rate of fall was surprisingly small, for a three-G field. The reason was simple enough – even with the outside atmosphere filling most of its volume, the ship had a very low density. It was a two-hundred-foot-long, cigar-like shell, and the only really heavy part was the forty-foot sphere in the center which held the habitable portion. It is quite possible that it would have escaped serious mechanical damage even had it landed on solid ground; and as it happened, the fall ended on liquid.

Real liquid; not the borderline stuff that made up most of Tenebra's atmosphere.

It landed upside down, but the wings had been shed like the speed brakes and its center of gravity was low enough to bring it to a more comfortable attitude. The floor finally stopped rocking, or at least the Drommian did – with the vision set fastened to the ship, the floor had always seemed motionless to the distant watchers. They saw the otterlike giant get cautiously to his feet, then walk slowly over to the girl's chair and touch her lightly on the shoulder. She stirred and tried to sit up.

'Are you all right?' Both parents fairly shrieked the question. Aminador-neldo, his father's orders in mind, waited for Easy to answer.

'I guess so,' she said after a moment. 'I'm sorry I bawled, Dad; I was scared. I didn't mean to scare 'Mina, though.'

'It's all right, kid. I'm sure no one can blame you, and I don't suppose your reaction had much to do with your friend's. The main thing is that you're in one piece, and the hull's intact – I suppose you'd be dead by now if it weren't.'

'That's true enough,' seconded Sakiiro.

'You've had a rough ride, then, but it should be over now. Since you're there, you might take a look through the windows – you're the first non-natives ever to do that directly. When you've seen all you can or want to, tell Mr Sakiiro and he'll tell you how to get upstairs again. All right?'

'All right, Dad.' Easy brushed a forearm across her tear-stained face, unfastened the seat straps, and finally struggled to her feet.

'Golly, when are they going to cut the power? I don't like all these G's,' she remarked.

'You're stuck with them until we get you away from there,' her father replied.

'I know it. I was just kidding. Hmm. It seems to be night outside; I can't see a thing.'

'It is, if you're anywhere near the robot,' Raeker replied, 'but it wouldn't make any difference to your eyes if it were high noon. Even Altair can't push enough light for human eyes through that atmosphere. You'll have to use the lights.'

'All right.' The girl looked at the board where she had already located the light switches; then, to the surprised approval of the engineers, she made sure from Sakiiro that these *were* the ones she wanted. Saki admitted later that his hopes of rescuing the pair soared several hundred per cent at that moment.

With the lights on, both children went over to the windows.

'There isn't much to see,' called Easy. 'We seem to have splashed into a lake or ocean. It's as smooth as glass; not a ripple. I'd think it was solid if the ship weren't partly under it. There are big foggy globes drifting down, yards and yards across, but they sort of fade out just before they touch the surface. That's every bit I can see.'

'It's raining,' Raeker said simply. 'The lake is probably sulphuric acid, I suppose fairly dilute by this time of night, and is enough warmer than the air so the water evaporates before it strikes. There wouldn't be any waves; there's no wind. Three knots is a wild hurricane on Tenebra.'

'With all that heat energy running around?' Rich was startled.

'Yes. There's nothing for it to *work* on – I use the word in its physical sense. There isn't enough change in volume when the atmosphere changes temperature, or even changes state, to create the pressure differences you need for high winds. Tenebra is about the calmest place you'll find inside any atmosphere in the galaxy.'

'Does that jibe with your remarks about earthquakes a while ago?' It was a measure of Aminadabarlee's revived confidence that he could talk of something besides the stupidity of human beings.

'No, it doesn't,' admitted Raeker, 'and I'll have to admit, Easy, that there is a possibility that you *will* encounter some waves if you float there long enough. However, you won't be able to call them weather, and they won't carry you to any more interesting places. I'm afraid you've seen about all you can expect to, young lady; you may as well come up and be properly rescued.'

'All right. Only I'd like to know just what's going to make this thing float, and whether the trip up will be as rough as the one down was.'

'It won't. You'll go up vertically, and much more slowly. You're going to ride a balloon. The atmosphere there is mostly water, with enough ions loose to make it a decent conductor. The largest part of your hull is divided into cells, and each cell further divided in two by a flexible membrane. Right now, those membranes are squeezed flat against one wall of each cell by atmospheric pressure. When you start the electrolysis units, some of the water will be decomposed; the oxygen will be piped outside the hull, but the hydrogen will be released on the other side of the membranes and gradually drive the air out of the cells. The old bathyscaphe used the same idea, only it didn't need the membranes to keep the two fluids from diffusing into each other.'

'I see. How long will it take to make enough gas to lift us?'

'I can't tell; we don't know the conductivity of the atmosphere. Once you start things going, there's a bank of ammeters above the switches for each individual cell; if you'll give me their reading after things start, I'll try to calculate it for you.'

'All right. Where are the – Oh, here; you labeled them decently. Upper right, a bank of twelve toggles, with a gang bar and a master?'

'That's it. You can see the meters above them. Close the lot, hit the master, and give the readings.'

'All right.' The thin arm reached up and out of the field of vision, and everyone could hear the switches click. Easy pulled her hand back to her lap, settled back into the chair under her three hundred pounds of weight, eyed the dials one after another, and said, 'The readings are all zero. What do I do now?'

V

Peregrination; Consideration; Estivation

Nick had chosen a fire on the landward side of the hill, so he was the first to have to consider the sea-level problem. In the home valley, of course, the water at night had never gotten more than thirty or forty feet deep; slow as the runoff was, enough always escaped at the valley foot to keep the village itself dry. He knew, from Fagin's lectures, that the water which flowed away must eventually reach something like a sea or lake; but not even Fagin had stopped to think of what would happen then – naturally enough; the surface of Earth's oceans compared to the volume of an average day's rainfall doesn't correspond to much of a sea-level rise, to put it mildly.

On Tenebra, the situation is a trifle different. There is no single giant sea basin, only the very moderate-sized lake beds, which are even less permanent than those of Earth. What this difference could mean in terms of 'sea' level might possibly have been calculated in advance, but not by any of Nick's people.

At first, there was nothing to worry about. The great, cloudy drops drifted into sight from far above, settled downward, and faded out as the radiation from the fires warmed them a trifle. Then they came lower, and lower, until they were actually below the level of the hilltop on all sides.

Once a sharp quake struck and lasted for half a minute or more, but when Nick saw that the spit of land joining the hill to the shore was still there, he put this from his mind. Something much more unusual was starting to happen. At home, raindrops which touched the ground after the latter had been cooled down for the night flattened into great, foggy half-globes and drifted around until a fire obliterated them; here they behaved differently. Drops striking the surface of the sea vanished instantly and by Nick's standards, violently. The difference in pressure and temperature made the reaction between oleum and water much less noticeable than it would be in an Earthly laboratory, but it was still quite appreciable.

After each such encounter, it could be seen that further raindrops falling on the same area faded out a little higher than usual for a few minutes; Nick judged correctly that some heat was being released by the reaction.

He had been watching this phenomenon for some time, interrupted twice by the need to relight his fire when a particularly close drop smothered it, when he noticed that the hill was on an island. This startled him a trifle, and he turned all his attention to the matter. The quake hadn't done it; he particularly recalled seeing the tombolo intact after the shaking was done. It didn't take him too long to conclude that if the land wasn't sinking, the sea must be rising; and a few minutes' close watch of the shore line proved that something of that sort was happening. He called the others, to tell them of what he had seen, and after a few minutes they agreed that the same thing was happening on all sides of the hill.

'How far will it come, Nick?' Betsey's voice was understandably anxious.

'I don't see how it can get this high,' Nick answered. 'After all, it hasn't risen as much as the water in our own valley would have by this time of night, and this hill is nearly as high as the village. We're safe enough.'

It got a little harder to stick to this belief as the hours passed and the sea grew higher. They could see the pools on shore swell and overflow into the main body; as time went on, more than one great river formed, carrying runoff from no one knew what drainage area. Some of the rivers were frightening, their centers as high or higher than the hill itself before they spread out and merged with the sea. By this time the violence of water-meeting-acid had subsided; the sea, at least near the shore, was pretty dilute.

Of course, 'near the shore' might be too casual a statement. No one on the hilltop could tell for certain just where the shore was now. The route they had followed was deep under the acid sea, and the only evidence that dry land existed was the rivers which still came into view above sea level.

The island that had been a hill shrank steadily. The cattle seemed unperturbed, but were driven inside the ring of fires. Then this had to be drawn in – or rather, others had to be built closer to the hilltop; and at last people and animals huddled together behind a single ring of glowing heat, while the sea bulged upward at their feeble protection. The raindrops were clear now; they had fallen from high enough levels to lose their suspended oxygen, and inevitably the last fires succumbed. Their heat had for many minutes past been maintaining a hollow in the surface of the sea; and as they cooled, the ocean reclaimed its own. Seconds after the last spark died every living being on the hilltop was unconscious, and a minute later only a turbulent dimple in the surface of the sea showed where the slightly warmer hilltop was covered. Nick's last thought was to the effect that at least they were safe from animals; they would be uncovered long before anything could get at them.

Apparently he wasn't quite right. When they woke up the next morning and brushed the thin frost of quartz crystals from their scales, all the people were there, but the herd seemed to have diminished. A count confirmed this; ten cattle were gone, with only a few scales left behind. It was fortunate that the animals were of a species whose scale armor was quite frail, and which depended more on its breeding powers to survive; otherwise the meat-eaters who had come in the night might have made a different choice. The realization that things lived in the sea came as a distinct shock to the entire party. They knew just about enough physical science to wonder where any such creature got its oxygen.

But the new situation called for new plans.

'There seems to be a catch in the idea of telling Fagin just to hunt along the seashore until he finds us,' Nick commented after breakfast. 'The seashore doesn't stay put too well. Also, we can't afford to stay near it, if we're going to lose eight or ten per cent of our animals every night.'

'What we'll have to do is some more mapping,' commented Jim. 'It would be nice to find a place protected by sea but which *doesn't* get submerged every night.'

'You know,' remarked Nancy in a thoughtful tone, 'one could find a rather useful employment for this place right here, if the proper people could be persuaded to visit it.' Everyone pondered this thought for a time, and the tone of the meeting gradually brightened. This *did* sound promising. Idea after idea was proposed, discussed, rejected, or modified; and two hours later a definite – really definite – course of action had been planned.

None of it could be carried out, of course, until it was possible to get off the island, and this was not for a dozen hours after sunrise. Once the tombolo appeared, however, everyone went into furious activity.

The herd – what was left of it – was driven ashore and on inland by Betsey and Oliver. Nick, making sure he had his axe and fire-making equipment, started inland as well, but in a more southerly direction. The other five fanned out from the base of the peninsula and began mapping the country-side for all they were worth. They were to determine as closely as possible how much of the area was submerged by the sea at its highest and make their report no later than the second night following. The group was then to pick a more suitable campsite to the north of the previous night's unfortunate choice. They were to settle at this point, and send a pair of people each morning to the base of the peninsula until either Nick returned or ten days had passed; in the latter event, they were to think of something else.

Nick himself had the task of contacting Fagin. He alone of the group was just a trifle unclear on how he was to accomplish his job. Tentatively, he planned to approach the cave village at night, and play by ear thereafter. If Swift's people had gotten into the habit of moving around at night with torches, things would be difficult. If not, it might be easy – except that his own approach would then be very noticeable. Well, he'd have to see.

The journey was normal, with enough fights to keep him in food, and he approached the cliff on the evening of the second day. He had circled far around to the west in order to come on the place from the cliff top; but even so he halted at a safe distance until almost dark. There was no telling where hunting parties might be encountered, since there was a path up the cliffs in nearly constant use by them.

As darkness fell, however, Nick felt safe in assuming that all such groups would be back at their caves; and checking his fire-lighting equipment once more, he cautiously approached the cliff top. He listened at the edge for some time before venturing to push his crest over, but no informative sounds filtered up and he finally took the chance. The cliff was some three hundred fifty feet high at that point, as he well knew; and he realized that even a single spine would be quite visible from below by daylight. It might be somewhat safer now, since no fires appeared to have been lighted yet.

When he finally did look, there was nothing to see. There *were* no fires, and it was much too dark for him to see anything without them.

He drew back again to think. He was sure the village and its inhabitants lay below, and was morally certain that Fagin was with them. Why they had no fires going was hard to understand, but facts were facts. Perhaps it would be safe to try to sneak up to the village in the dark – but the rain would come soon, and that would be that.

Then he had another idea, found some small wood, and went to work with his fire-making tools, a drill and spindle made from tough wood. He rather expected some response from below when he got a small blaze going, since it lighted up the sky more effectively than daylight; but nothing happened until he executed the next portion of the idea, by tossing a burning stick over the edge of the cliff. Then everything happened at once.

The light showed Fagin, standing motionless fifty yards from the foot of the cliff. It showed an otherwise empty expanse of rock and vegetation; the people were in their caves, as usual. That, however, was only temporary.

With the arrival of the fire, a rattle of voices erupted from the caves. Evidently, if they ever slept, they weren't doing it yet. After a moment Swift's tones made themselves heard above the others.

'Get it! Get wood to it! Don't just stand there as if you were wet already!' A crowd of figures emerged from the rock and converged on the glowing twig; then they spread out again, as though they had all realized at once that no one had any wood and it would be necessary to find some. Plants were wrenched up from the ground by a hundred different hands and carried, or sometimes thrown, toward the spark. Nick was far more amused than surprised when it went out without anyone's succeeding in lighting anything from it, and was only academically curious as to whether it had burned out of its own or been smothered by its would-be rescuers. His attention was not allowed to dwell on the problem for long; Swift's voice rose again over the disappointed babble.

'There's a glow on top of the cliff, and that's where the fire came from! Someone up there still has some; come and get it!' As usual, obedience was prompt and unquestioning, and the crowd headed toward the trail up the cliff. Nick was a trifle surprised; it was close to rainfall time and the cave dwellers were carrying no fire. Something drastic must have happened, for them to overcome their lifelong habit of keeping to the caves at night. However, it was hardly the time to speculate on that subject; the cave men were seeking fire, and Nick happened to have all that there was around at the moment.

It took him about five seconds to dream up the rest of his idea. He lighted a stick at his small blaze and started toward the head of the trail from below, lighting all the plants he could reach as he went. When he reached the trail he tossed aside the nearly spent torch he had been using, made himself another which he hoped was small enough to shield with his body, and headed on along the cliff top. If the cave men were satisfied to take some fire, well enough; if they wanted him too, perhaps they'd look along the fire trail he had laid, which would lead them in the wrong direction. He wasn't really hopeful about this, knowing their skill at tracking, but anything seemed worth trying once.

He kept on along the cliff top, toward a point some two miles away where the cliff broke gradually away to the lower level. He was out of direct view from the head of the trail when Swift reached it, but did not let that fact slow him down. Once at the broken-rock region he picked his way carefully down, dodging boulders loosened by a sharp quake, and started back, hiding his little torch as well as he could from anyone overhead. Fifteen minutes after the disturbance had started he was beside Fagin, apparently unnoticed by any of Swift's people.

'Teacher! Do you hear me? It's Nick.'

'I hear you, all right. What are you doing here? Did you start this fuss? What's going on, anyway?'

'I threw the fire down the cliff, yes; I had to make sure you were here. The rest was a by-product. I'm here because we've found a way to get you out of Swift's hands without having to worry about his getting hold of you again afterward.'

'That's encouraging. I thought I had a way, too, but troubles have arisen in that direction. I need badly and quickly all the help I can get, and I can't see Swift being very helpful for some time. Let's hear your idea.'

Nick described the doings of his people since Fagin had been kidnapped, and dwelt particularly on the geography of the spot where they had spent their first night at the sea.

'We assume,' he said, 'that you can live under the sea the way you can in rain; so we thought if you fled to this hill, and Swift followed you, he'd be trapped there at night; and while he was asleep you could take away all the weapons of his people – which would be a help anyway, since we're getting so short – and if we couldn't figure out anything else to do with him, just shove him downhill to a point which stays submerged all day.'

'Would he last long in such a place?'

'Probably not, as there are animals in that sea that ate some of our cattle; but who cares? He didn't mind killing Tom and Alice, and would have done the same to the rest of us if he'd felt it necessary.'

'How about the rest of his people?'

'They helped him. I don't care what happens to them.'

'Well, I see your point, but I don't entirely share your view. There are reasons which might make you feel differently, but I can't go into them yet.

'Your plan, if it really rates the name yet, has some good points, but it also has some weak ones. If this place of yours is a day and a half's journey from here even for you, I'm not at all clear how I can keep ahead of Swift long enough to let me reach it; remember, you can travel faster than I. Also, now that you've brought them back the fire they'd lost, I'll be very surprised if it's as easy to get away at night as it would have been before.'

'What do you mean? They brought fire with them from our village.'

'They brought it, but didn't know how to make one fire except from another. They let what they had go out during the day after we arrived, and have been tireless ever since. They've been doing their best to teach me their language so I could show them how to make more, but I'm having a lot of trouble – for one thing, I can't make some of their shriller noises. Swift's been remarkably patient, though, I must say. Now he'll be even easier to get along with, I should imagine; but he certainly won't be easier to get away from.'

'Then maybe I shouldn't have come, Teacher. I'm sorry.'

'I'm not. My original plan for getting in touch with you again has already failed, so if you hadn't come we'd be in even worse shape. All I meant was that we have some heavy planning to do before we're out of this mess. You'd probably better get away for a few hours at least, while I think; there's no point in having you caught by Swift, too.'

'But how will I get back again? They have fire, now – for that matter, as soon as they come back they'll know I've been here, and probably start tracking me. I'd probably still be in sight, even if I started now; it's beginning to rain, and I can't travel without a torch, and that will be visible for miles. I was expecting you to come with me right away.'

'I see your trouble, but don't quite know what to do about it. It's hard to believe that Swift won't be back here in the next few minutes.' Fagin paused, as though in thought; Nick of course did not know that such pauses really meant a tense conference among several men a hundred and sixty thousand miles away. 'Look, Nick. There's a good deal of burnable material around, right?'

'Yes.'

'And there is only one path from the cliff top, and that a narrow cleft?'

'Yes, not counting the way around – a good four miles.'

'Hmph. I could wish it were longer. Do you think you can build a fire big enough to block the foot of that path for a while, so as to delay them while we get going? You'll have to work fast; they must be coming back by now, I should think, unless they're still looking for you on top.'

'I'll try.' Nick could see that this was no time for theorizing. 'Someone's probably looked over the edge and seen me by now, but there's nothing to lose. If I don't catch up to you, head east-northeast until you reach the sea, then follow along its daytime shoreline until you meet the others. I'll do what I can to interfere with Swift's trackers; you'd better get going now.'

Nick didn't wait for a reply; he was already racing toward the foot of the cliff trail, gathering fuel as he went. His torch was nearly gone, but he started a rough heap of wood a few yards inside the cleft, and managed to get it burning. Then he hunted around madly, tossing every bit of combustible matter he could find into the four-yard-wide crack.

A raindrop came squeezing its way down the gully and vanished as it neared the fire, but it was early enough in the evening for there still to be a good deal of oxygen in it. Nick was pleased; evidently no torch-bearing cave dwellers were yet on the path, or the drop would have been destroyed much sooner. That gave so much more time.

With the pile big enough to satisfy him, he set off along Fagin's trail. Even Nick could follow it, a five-foot-wide track of flattened and crumbled vegetation, except where it led through hollows already filling with liquid water. He could have gone through these with his torch, since the liquid was still fairly safe to breathe, but he chose to detour around. Even so, he caught up with Fagin within a mile.

'Keep going,' he said. 'I'm going to do a little trail erasing.' He applied his torch to a bush beside the trail, and to the crushed, brittle material on the track itself; then he started in a wide arc to the north, setting fire to every bush he passed. Eventually, a glowing belt of radiance extended from Fagin's trail almost east of the cave village around to the track down which the robot had been brought from the north. Nick thought he could hear excited voices from the caves, but wasn't sure. He raced northward at the top of his speed for another mile, and started another series of fires there. They should be visible from the cliff, too; and perhaps the cave dwellers would come out and search along the route to the old village rather than start tracking right away.

Then he raced back to intercept Fagin's trail, shielding his torch with his body in the hope that its glow would not be seen from the cliff. He found the trail with little trouble, though Fagin was sensibly keeping to the valleys as much as possible, and finally caught up with the Teacher. Fagin heard his report, and approved.

'It's probably the best you could have done,' he said. 'I'll be surprised if we get through the night without having company, though.'

'So will I,' admitted Nick.

In spite of this pessimism, the hours passed without any sign of pursuit. Nick's higher speed allowed him to keep up with the robot, even though he had to detour puddles which the machine took in its stride. The raindrops grew clear, and correspondingly dangerous; puddles and lakes larger, deeper, and harder to avoid as the bottom of Tenebra's atmosphere gradually underwent its nightly change in phase.

'Even with your staying on dry land and leaving such an open trail, they must be having trouble following by now,' remarked Fagin during one of the brief spells when they were together. 'A lot of the places where you went must be well under water by now, and they can't be boiling them off with torches at this hour; the water's too clear to let them get away with it. I'm starting to feel a little happier about the whole situation.'

'I'm not,' said Nick.

'Why not?'

'The pools are getting very big, and some of the valleys ahead are long and deep. I remember the night before last there were some pretty big rivers emptying into the sea. If we meet one of those, and I don't see how we can help it, we're stuck.'

'On the contrary, that seems to me the best thing that could happen. Swift can't follow through a river.'

'Neither can I.'

'Not under your own power. I can carry you, and it's pretty safe; we haven't met any creatures in sixteen years capable of living, or at least being active, in clear water – though I must admit I've always been expecting it.'

'There were some in the ocean.'

'That isn't water, for the most part, except late at night. Anyway, I think we needn't worry about ocean life. You've made me happier than I've been for some time; let's look for one of these rivers.'

'All right. I hope you're right.' Nick was accustomed enough to being knocked out by oxygen-free water, but somehow didn't like the idea of being carted around like a sack in that state. If Fagin thought it was all right, though ...

It looked for a while as though he needn't have worried. With the common perversity of the inanimate, once a river was wanted, none could be found. They kept on their original course, knowing the futility of zigzagging over unknown ground, and got closer and closer to the sea; but they actually reached it, not too many hours before day, without finding a river.

They had reached the 'shore' far south of the region where the others awaited them; Nick had selected their course so that there would be no question of which way to turn when they reached the coast. He had mapped enough to know what measuring uncertainties could mean.

Without hesitation, therefore, he directed Fagin to follow the 'shore' to the left. They were, of course, far inland from the hill which Nick had planned to use to trap Swift, but that was the least of their troubles at the moment. The chief annoyance was the lack of a river; a second one, which made itself apparent an hour or so after they reached the sea, was the appearance behind them of a distinct glow of light. There was no question what it was; the sun just didn't get that distinct, or even that bright.

'They're gaining on us. I wonder how long my fires delayed them?' muttered Nick when the glow caught his eye. Fagin had not seen it yet, apparently, and Nick saw nothing to be gained in calling his attention to it. He just looked that much more intensely for a river ahead.

The robot finally spotted the light as well, and understood its meaning as clearly as had Nick.

'If they get too close before we find a river, you'd better go on ahead at your best speed; you can probably outrun them.'

'What will you do?'

'Go into the ocean.'

'Why not take me with you? Won't that be as good as a river?'

'Not according to your own statement. I don't want you eaten right out of my arms, and I'm not very well suited to fighting things off if they attack.'

'That's true. I guess your idea is best, then.'

As it turned out, though, they didn't have to use it. By the time the glow of Swift's torches had resolved itself into separate points of light, and it could be seen that the cave dwellers were overhauling Fagin and his pupil at a rate that promised a scant hour of further freedom, a bulge had appeared on the landscape ahead; and in another minute or two this had taken on the shape of a low, rounded ridge snaking across the countryside. It had the dark hue of clear water; and well before they reached it there was no doubt that it was a river. Since it reached above Nick's crest, there was no way of telling its width; but it must certainly be wide enough to drown any torches Swift's people might be carrying.

Straight to its edge Fagin and Nick went. Ordinarily such a mass of clear water would be a frightening sight as it oozed slowly by toward the sea; but tonight neither of them felt afraid of it. Nick tossed his torch into it with a carefree gesture, noted with actual glee the way the glow died abruptly from its end, made sure his weapons and fire-drill were securely attached to his harness, and turned to the Teacher.

'All right, I'm ready.'

The white bulk of the robot slid toward him, and four appendages extended from openings in its smooth carapace. Gripping devices on the ends of these clamped firmly, but not painfully, onto two of Nick's arms and his walking legs, picked him up, and draped him over the machine's back.

'All right, Nick,' said Fagin. 'Relax. I'll get to high ground as quickly as I can on the other side and dodge raindrops, so you shouldn't be out long. Just relax.' Nick obeyed the injunction as well as he could as the machine slid into the river.

His body heat boiled a considerable volume of the liquid into gas as they entered; but the gas was oxygen-free and its physical state made no difference to Nick. He lost consciousness within half a minute.

Swift's warriors reached the spot where the trail entered the river fifteen minutes later. The chief was not philosophical enough to put the incident down to experience.

VI

Information; Navigation; Observation

'How much of a lead will that give you, Doctor?'

Raeker answered without taking his eyes from the robot's screens. 'Presumably the rest of the night, and a trifle more – however long it takes that river to dry up after sunrise. It's twenty hours or so to sunrise.'

'Maybe the plants will grow enough to hide the robot's trail in that time; will they?'

'I'm afraid I have no idea.'

'After observing the life of this planet for sixteen years? Really, Doctor, I should have supposed you'd know something in that time.'

'In all sixteen of those years I never had occasion to note just what kind of vegetation is on the north bank of this river,' Raeker retorted a trifle impatiently, 'and all I know from Nick about Swift is that he's a good tracker; I have no quantitative information as to just how good. Really, Councillor, I know you have been living in Hell the last three weeks; but if you can give only destructive criticism I can say that you won't be helping her much. You're getting to sound like Aminadabarlee.'

'I'm glad you mentioned that.' Rich did not sound at all offended. 'I know, Doctor, that it is difficult for you to bear up under Drommian mannerisms; they are a rather impulsive race, and while they are very courteous by their standards, those standards are not quite identical to ours. Aminadabarlee is an unusually restrained member of his race; that is why he holds the position he does; but I must suggest very strongly that you check your natural impulse to answer sharply when he gets insulting, as he occasionally does. There is no point in straining his capacity for tolerance. I assure you most solemnly that if he loses his self-control sufficiently to make an emotional report to Dromm, every word he has said about the results to Earth would be literally fulfilled. There wouldn't be a war, of course, but the result of a ninety per cent – or even a fifty per cent – cut in Earth's interstellar trade would be fully as disastrous as any war. You must remember that to most of the races we know, Earthmen and Drommians are equally alien; they are both "creatures from the stars," and what one race says about the other would have quite a ring of authority to most of them. This may sound a trifle exaggerated to you, but this little situation is potentially the most ticklish political and diplomatic affair that has occurred in my lifetime.'

That actually took Raeker's eyes from the screen for a moment.

'I didn't realize that,' he said. 'Also, I'm afraid I must admit that it will make no difference in my efforts to rescue Easy and 'Mina; I was doing my best already.'

'I believe that, and I'm grateful; but I had to tell you about the other matter. If Aminadabarlee weren't here it wouldn't have been necessary; but since you can't in decency avoid seeing him, it's very necessary that you understand him. Whatever he says, however intolerant or impatient or downright insulting he may be, you must keep your own control. I assure you he won't take your calmness as a sign of fear; his people don't think that way. He'll respect you the more for it – and so will I.'

'I'll do my best,' promised Raeker, 'but right now I'll be just as glad if he doesn't come in for a few hours. I'm busy juggling Nick across the river, and if you want to regard Nick as *my* child you won't be too far wrong. I don't mind talking as long as everything is going all right, but if I stop in the middle of a sentence don't be surprised. Have you been talking to the kids?'

'Yes. They're bearing up pretty well. It's lucky that Drommian is there; I'm afraid Easy would have let go all over the place if she didn't feel responsible for her 'Mina. He seems to feel that she's keeping everything in hand, so for the moment there's no morale problem. Did I tell you that Mr Sakiiro found that some of the inspection ports had been left open on the bathyscaphe, so that the electrolysis leads were undoubtedly corroded by outside atmosphere? He has some idea of getting your people down there to do a repair job.'

'I know. That's all I can think of at the moment, too; but to do that means I have to find *them*, and *they* have to find the 'scaphe. It's some comfort that the kids can stay alive almost indefinitely down there; the machine will keep them in food, water, and air.'

'That's true; but Easy won't last forever under three gravities.'

Raeker frowned. 'I hadn't thought of that. Have you any medical information on how long she's likely to hold out?'

'None at all. The problem has never come up for such a young person. Adults have stood it for a good many months, I know.'

'I see. Well, I should think you'd have a good excuse to be nastier than Aminadabarlee, at that rate. The gravity won't bother his youngster.'

'No, but something else will. The synthesizers in the bathyscaphe produce human food.'

'So what? Isn't Drommian metabolism like ours? They breathe oxygen, and I've seen them eat our food here on the *Vindemiatrix*.'

'In general, yes; in detail, no. Their vitamin requirements are different, though they do use fats, carbohydrates, and proteins as we do. 'Mina will almost certainly start suffering from vitamin deficiency diseases if he stays there long enough; and like me, his father has no exact medical information.'

Raeker whistled, and the frown stayed on his face. Rich thought for a moment that something had occurred on Tenebra to worry him, but the screens still showed nothing but river bed. The stream must have been fully a mile wide, judging by the time it was taking to cross it. The diplomat remained silent, and watched while the robot forged ahead and, finally, out on the far side of the great watercourse.

It was still raining, of course, and without Nick's torch it was necessary to use a spotlight to locate descending raindrops. After about ten minutes in normal air, Nick began to revive; and when he was once again himself, and had found and kindled a torch, the journey went on as before, except for the lack of anxiety over Swift's whereabouts.

Shortly after this, the relief operator appeared. Raeker didn't want to leave the controls, since the situation below was still rather ticklish, but he knew there was really no choice. The human being didn't live who could maintain decent alertness through a whole Tenebran night. He brought the other man up to date and, with several backward glances, left the observation room.

'I don't think I can sleep for a while,' he remarked to Rich. 'Let's go back to communications and see how Easy's making out.'

'She was asleep a couple of hours ago,' replied the girl's father. 'That's why I came to see what you were up to. No harm in checking, though.' He added after a moment's silence, 'I like to be there when she wakes up.' Raeker made no comment.

Nothing further had happened, according to the communication watch officer, but the two settled down in view of the bathyscaphe screen. No one had much to say.

Raeker was more than half asleep when Easy's voice came from the set.

'Dad! Are you there?' Rich might have been as drowsy as Raeker, but he answered instantly.

'Yes, dear. What is it?'

'We're moving. 'Mina's still asleep, and I didn't want to wake him, but I thought I'd better tell you.'

'Tell everything you can to Dr Raeker; he's here, and knows Tenebra better than anyone else.'

'All right. You remember the first night we landed I thought we were on solid ground and the lake was getting deeper, don't you?'

'Yes, Easy. We decided that the rain was diluting the acid in which you had fallen, so its density was going down and you weren't floating so high.'

'That's right. After a while the side windows were covered so we couldn't even see the rain, and each night before morning the top one is covered too; we're entirely under water.'

'That's using the word a bit loosely, but I see what you mean. In that case you can't see out at all, I should think; how do you know you're moving tonight?'

'We can see, with the lights on; we're at the bottom of the lake or ocean or whatever it is, and the lights show the rocks and some funny things I suppose are plants. We're going by them slowly, sort of bouncing, and the ship is rocking a little from time to time. I can hear the scrapes and bumps whenever we touch.'

'All right. I can't see that it's anything in particular to worry about, though I'd like to know why the change from the last five nights. When daylight comes the extra water will evaporate and you'll float again as usual, assuming you're still in the lake or sea. If, as seems rather likely, you're being carried down a river, you may find yourselves stranded on dry land somewhere when it dries up. At least you'll have a more interesting landscape to watch tomorrow, if that's the case.

'The only problem we have here is locating you. If you're going to start drifting around every night, directing our people to you is going to be hard, to say the least. You'll have to give us every bit of information you can on your surroundings, so we can pass it on to Nick and his friends. You were very smart to call us just now, the moment you discovered you were moving.'

'Thanks, Doctor. We'll keep our eyes open. I want to meet your friend Nick.'

'We're doing our best to see that you do. If, as we hope, you landed within a few dozen miles of the robot, the chances are you're being washed toward the same ocean that gave him trouble a couple of nights ago; we have reason to suspect that oceans don't get very large on Tenebra, at least by Earthly standards, so getting you together may not take too long.'

'Maybe I'd better stay awake for a while, so as to report to you if anything special happens, and then let 'Mina take a watch while I sleep.'

'That sounds perfect. We'll always have someone listening up here.' Raeker opened the mike switch and turned to Rich. The diplomat was eyeing him intently.

'How much of that was for Easy's morale, and how much for mine?' he asked.

'I made it sound as good as possible,' admitted Raeker, 'mostly for the kids. However, I didn't lie. I'm reasonably sure I can get my crew to the 'scaphe before too long; I admit I'm less sure what they can do after they find it. We really haven't the slightest idea of the conditions on the outside of that machine, remember; we'll have to wait for Nick's report before we decide what instructions to give him.'

Rich stared hard at the biologist for a moment, then relaxed slightly. 'That sounds reasonable,' he said. If he had planned to say any more, he wasn't given the chance.

'It doesn't sound reasonable to me!' The shrill voice needed no identification. 'Every human being in this place is dithering a lot of nonsense about teaching a bunch of savages to rewire a machine two thousand years ahead of their culture, and then risk not only a human but a Drommian life on their having done it properly. It's the sheerest nonsense I ever heard. It's hard to believe that anyone over three years old would fail to realize that nothing but another bathyscaphe has the slightest chance of making the rescue, but I haven't heard a single word about such an activity. I suppose men put the expense before the lives involved.'

'I haven't heard of any messages proposing such an activity going to Dromm, either,' snapped Raeker. 'I've heard that it has an industrial capacity at least equal to Earth's, and it's not a parsec farther from Altair. I suppose Drommians don't bother to repair situations that they feel are someone else's fault, whether lives are involved or not.'

None of the human beings present could tell just how Aminadabarlee reacted to this; Rich gave him no time to say anything.

'Dr Raeker, you're forgetting yourself,' he said sharply. 'If Councillor Aminadabarlee will come with me, I will discuss with him any points of value which may have been hidden in your words, as well as the very valuable suggestion he made himself. If you have any more courteous thoughts to add, get them to me. Please come, sir.' The diplomats stalked out, and the watch officer glanced uneasily at Raeker.

'You don't talk to Drommians like that,' he ventured at last.

'I know,' replied Raeker. 'Rich was telling me, a little while ago. I didn't like to do it, but it seemed to me that Rich needed something to take his attention off his kid.'

'You're taking a chance. That fellow could easily turn his whole race so anti-Earth that every human trader outside the solar system would be forced out of business.'

'So everyone seems to feel,' replied the biologist a trifle uneasily. 'I couldn't really believe that things were that critical. Maybe I was a little hasty. Anyway, Rich will be busy for a while, and so will the Drommian; let's concentrate on getting those kids out of trouble. I'll keep my nose out of interracial diplomacy after this.'

'Frankly, that relieves me. How about that suggestion – building a new 'scaphe?'

'I'm no engineer,' retorted Raeker, 'but even I have a pretty good idea how long that would take, even with the experience from the first one to help. I am a biologist, and my considered opinion is that both those youngsters would be dead before another bathyscaphe could be made ready. If Rich and the Drommian want to try it, I wouldn't discourage them; the new machine will be useful, and I might even be wrong about the time factors. However, I believe seriously that we will have to run this rescue along the lines already planned.'

'And the Drommian was right about those?'

'You mean, that we plan to get Nick's people to make the repairs? Yes. It's not as ridiculous as Aminadabarlee makes it sound. I've been bringing those people up for nearly sixteen years; they're as intelligent as human beings, judging by their learning rate, and they could certainly splice a few wires.'

The officer looked doubtful.

'As long as they splice the *right* wires,' he muttered. 'What will they use for insulation?'

'There's a glue they make – I showed them how, after some experiment – from animal scales. We'll have to make sure it's a nonconductor, but I'm not greatly worried about that.'

'Even though you think there's sulphuric acid in their body fluids?'

'I said, not *greatly* worried,' admitted Raeker. 'The main problem right now is bringing the parties together. You're sure you can't get me a closer fix on the robot and the 'scaphe?'

'Quite sure. They're putting out different wave lengths, and I have no means of finding the dispersion factor of the planet's atmosphere in that part of the spectrum, let alone getting the precise depth of the atmosphere itself or cutting down the inherent uncertainty of radio directional measurements. The chances, as I told you, are about fifty-fifty that the two are within forty miles of each other, and about nine out of ten that they're not over a hundred miles apart. Better than that I can't do, without radiations neither machine is equipped to transmit.'

'All right. I'll just have to get information from Easy, and try to match it in with Nick's maps. At least, they don't have to get too close under our guidance; Nick will be able to see the 'scaphe's lights for miles.' The officer nodded, and the two fell silent, watching the live screen. Nothing could be seen in it; if Easy was awake, as she had said she would be, she was not in the control room. Occasionally the men could hear a faint bumping or scraping sound; presumably the ship was still being carried with a current, but no landmark had attracted the girl's attention as being worth reporting.

Raeker finally went to sleep in his chair. The officer stayed awake, but the only message he received was to the effect that Easy was going to sleep and Aminadorneldo was taking over the watch. Nothing excited him, either, it seemed; the speaker remained silent after the human girl signed off.

For hour after hour the bathyscaphe bumped merrily on its way. Sometimes it stopped for a moment, sometimes for minutes on end; always the journey resumed, as vagaries in the current dislodged it from whatever barred its path. Easy woke up again, and attended to the problem of breakfast. Later she prepared a rather unappetizing dinner – so she said, anyway. Aminadorneldo was polite about it, blaming the deficiencies on the synthesizers. There's not too much one can do with amino acids, fats, and dextrose, even if vitamin powders are available for seasoning, Tenebra's long night wore on; Raeker served another watch in the robot's control room, bringing Nick and Fagin to a point which he believed was fairly close to the rest of the party from the village. A single night on a planet which takes nearly a hundred hours to rotate can become rather boring – though it doesn't have to be, Raeker thought wryly, as he recalled the one when Swift had made his raid.

Things looked up after sunrise – unfortunately, since he was getting sleepy again. Nick definitely recognized the ground over which they were passing, and stated flatly that they would meet his friends in another two hours; Raeker's relief arrived, and had to be given an extremely detailed briefing; and a message came from the communications room that the bathyscaphe seemed to have stopped.

'Will you please ask Lieutenant Wellenbach if he can have visual communication rigged up between his office and this room?' Raeker asked the messenger who brought this information. 'It begins to look as though I'll have to be talking to the bathyscaphe and my pupils at the same time in the near future.'

'Certainly, sir,' replied the messenger. 'There'll be no particular difficulty about that, I'm sure.'

'All right. I'm going up to the comm room now to hear Easy's report; I'll come back here when the set is rigged.'

'But shouldn't you get some sleep, Doctor?' asked his relief.

'I should, but I can't afford to for a while. You stay on duty after I come back, and stop me if I start to do anything really silly.'

'All right.' The graduate student shrugged his shoulders. Raeker knew he was not being very sensible, but he couldn't bring himself to leave the scenes of action at the moment. He headed for the communication chamber at top speed.

Rich and Aminadabarlee were there. The human diplomat had apparently calmed his Drommian colleague down, at least for the time being, since Raeker's entry produced no fireworks. Easy was speaking as the biologist came in, and he said nothing until she had finished.

'... minutes since we last moved. It's no lighter outside, but we're not being rocked so hard; I think the current is weaker. It's after sunrise, if I've been keeping track of time properly, so I guess the water's boiling away.' She paused, and Raeker made his presence known.

'I take it, Easy, that neither you nor 'Mina saw any living creatures in the water while you were drifting.'

'Nothing but plants, or what I guess were plants.'

'How about right now?'

'Still nothing.'

'Then my guess is you haven't yet reached the ocean. There were definitely animals there, according to Nick – of course, I suppose they might be frightened by your lights. Would you be willing to put them out for five minutes or so, then turn them on suddenly to catch anything which might have approached?'

'All right, as long as you don't mind the control room lights on. There aren't any windows here, so they shouldn't matter. I'd be afraid to turn them out; I might hit the wrong switch in the dark when it was time to turn them on again.'

'You're quite right. I never thought of that.'

'I've thought of a lot of things the last three weeks, down here.'

For an instant the light-hearted mask she had been holding for the benefit of her young companion slipped a trifle, and all the men saw a miserable, terrified twelve-year-old whose self-control was near its limit. Rich bit his lip and clenched his fists; the other human beings avoided his eyes. Aminadabarlee showed no emotion; Raeker wondered whether he felt any. Then the mask was back in place, and the merry-hearted youngster they had all known before the accident turned to the Drommian child.

''Mina, will you go to the window in the big lab? Call when you're there, and I'll turn off the outside lights.'

'All right, Easy.' The long body crossed the men's field of view and vanished again. Then his piping voice came from the other room, and the girl's fingers flicked the light switches.

'Is it dark outside now, 'Mina?'

'Yes, Easy. I can't see anything.'

'All right. Tell me if you do; we'll keep it dark for a while. Dr Raeker, is 'Mina's father there?'

'Yes, Miss Rich.' Aminadabarlee answered for himself.

'Perhaps you'd better tell me and Dr Raeker how long it takes your people's eyes to get used to the dark.' Not for the first time, Raeker wondered what combination of heredity and upbringing had given Rich such an amazing child. He had known students ten years her senior whose minds would have been lagging far behind – she was thinking of important points sooner than Raeker himself, and he didn't have her worries …

He brought his mind back to the present when she called his name.

'Dr Raeker, 'Mina couldn't see anything. Maybe five minutes wasn't enough for your sea animals to get over their scare, of course.'

'Maybe,' admitted Raeker. 'Maybe they're just not interested in the bathyscaphe, for that matter. However, I think we'll assume for the present that you haven't reached the sea yet. It will be interesting to see whether you're in a lake or stranded high and dry when the rain evaporates this morning. In either case, get us as complete a description of the country around as you possibly can.'

'I know. We'll do our best.'

'We're rigging up an arrangement that will let you talk more or less directly to Nick, when you're in a position to give him directions, so you won't have to trust my relaying of your reports. It should be ready soon.'

'That's good. I've wanted to talk to him myself ever since I saw you in the robot control room. It looked like fun. But can't I talk to him without going through you, if he finds me? Doesn't this ship have outside mikes and speakers?'

'Oh, yes. Mr Sakiiro will tell you how to turn them on. This is for the time before he finds you.'

'All right. We'll call you again as soon as the water's gone. 'Mina's hungry, and so am I.' Raeker sat back and dozed for a few minutes; then he realized that he, too, was hungry, and took care of the situation. By this time he really wanted to sleep; but a call on the intraship system informed him that the communication equipment he had requested was ready for use. Sleepy or not, he had to try it out, so he went back to the robot control room. It was a good many hours before he left it again.

Nick and Fagin had just rejoined their friends at the new camping spot, and Nick was bringing the others up to date on events. Naturally, Raeker had to listen carefully; there was always the chance that Nick had seen things in a different light from the human observer. It had been known to happen; a human education had not given the Tenebrites human minds.

This time Nick's report showed no signs of such difference, but Raeker had still to learn what the others had done. Since this, as Nick had planned, involved a great deal of mapping, some hours were spent hearing the various reports. It was customary for the maps to be shown to the robot for photographing in the *Vindemiatrix*; then each was explained in detail by the one who had drawn it, since not all the information could be crowded onto the paperlike leaves or summarized in conventional mapping symbols. These verbal accounts were recorded as spoken, and as a rule immediately pre-empted by the geological crew. Since the present area was very peculiar in that it lay close to the sea and was largely submerged each night, a great deal of time was spent in bringing the men's maps and charts up to date.

Too much time, in fact.

Raeker's relief had not received, perhaps, a really clear idea of the current danger from Swift; and Raeker himself had not given the matter a thought since his return to the observation room. Neither had thought to advise Nick to have anyone on the lookout for danger, and it was sheer chance that the danger was spotted in time.

Jane was telling her tale, and everyone else was listening and comparing her map with his own, when Betsey caught sight of something. It was just for an instant, and some distance away, showing among the shrubs on a hilltop.

She knew the Teacher could not have seen it; she was aware that her own vision equipment had superior resolving powers to his, though she didn't know the terminology. Her first impulse was to shout a warning, but fortunately before she yielded to it she got a better glimpse of the thing on the hill. That was enough for identification. It was a creature just like herself; and since all of Fagin's community was standing around the teacher, that meant it must be one of Swift's warriors. How he had gotten there so soon after things dried up she couldn't guess at the moment.

Speaking softly so as not to interrupt Jane, she called to Nick and John, who were closest.

'Don't make any move that would let him know you see him, but one of the cave men is watching us from the hill three quarters of a mile west-north-west. What should we do about it?'

Nick thought tensely for a moment.

'Just one is all I see. How about you?'

'Same here.'

'You've been around here, and I haven't. Is it possible to go down the south or east side of this hill we're on and make a long circuit so as to get on the other side of him without being seen?' Both John and Betsey thought for several seconds, reconstructing in their minds the regions they had mapped in the last day and a half. They spoke almost together, and in almost the same words.

'Yes, from either side.'

'All right, do it. Leave the group here casually – you'd both better go together; the herd is on the south side of the hill, and I would judge that some of the beasts are in his line of vision. You can go down and drive them around out of his sight, and we'll hope he thinks you're just doing an ordinary herding job. Once you and the cattle are out of his sight, get around behind him as best you can, and bring him here, preferably alive. I'd like to know how he got here so soon, and so would Fagin, I'm sure.'

'Are you going to tell him, or the others?'

'Not yet. They'll act more natural if they don't know. Besides, there are still a couple of reports to be given, and Fagin never likes that to be interrupted, you know.'

'I know he usually doesn't, but this seemed a sort of special case.'

'Special or not, let's surprise him with your prisoner. Take axes, by the way; they seemed to impress those folks a lot, and maybe he'll give up more easily.'

'All right.' John and Betsey pulled up their resting legs and started casually downhill toward the herd. None of the others appeared to notice them, and Nick did his best to imitate their attitude as the two scouts disappeared from sight.

VII
Acquisition; Inquisition; Instruction

Neither Raeker nor his assistant paid any attention to the departure of John and his companion. They were much too busy operating cameras and recorders, for one reason. Easy and her companion could now watch the group on the surface indirectly, but neither of them was familiar enough with the routine activities of Fagin's pupils to notice anything out of the ordinary. Besides, they were paying very close attention to the geographical reports, in the somewhat unreasonable hope of being able to recognize part of the land described.

For the bathyscaphe was now high and dry. The river down which it had been carried had vanished with the coming day, and the ship had rolled rather uncomfortably – though, fortunately, very slowly – to the foot of a hillock which Easy had promptly named Mount Ararat. The children were having a little trouble, since they had not only had their first visual contact with natives, via the observation room of the *Vindemiatrix*, but also their first look at the solid surface of Tenebra – if one excepts the bottom of a lake and a river. They were covering both scenes as well as they could, one at the windows while the other was at the plate, but each was trying to keep the other filled in verbally on the other part, with confusing results. Their shouted words were coming through to Raeker and the others in the observation room, and were adding their little bit to the confusion there. Raeker didn't dare cut them off, partly for reasons of their own morale and partly because it was always possible that the one at the windows would have something material to report. He hoped the recording of the native reports would be intelligible to the geologists.

Jane finished her account, was asked a question or two by Raeker on points he had not fully taken in, and then settled back to let Oliver show his map. Raeker's assistant photographed it, Raeker himself made sure that the recording tape was still feeding properly, and the two relaxed once more – or came as close to relaxation as the local confusion permitted. Raeker was almost ready to decide that he needn't stay, and to catch up on his overdue sleep.

He had not actually said anything about it, though, when the cave scout caught sight of John. Within three seconds after that, the biologist lost all intention of leaving.

The scout reacted practically instantaneously. He had been crouching as low in the vegetation as his anatomy permitted; now he leaped to his walking legs and started traveling. John was south and west of him, Fagin and the rest south and east; he headed north. Immediately Betsey rose into view in that direction, and he stopped in momentary confusion. Nick, who had never lost sight of the fellow's crest since Betsey had first pointed him out, interpreted the situation correctly even though he could not see John and Betsey. He sprang to his walking legs, interrupting Oliver unceremoniously, and began issuing orders. The others were surprised, but reacted with relatively little confusion; and within a few seconds the whole group was streaming down the hillside toward the point where the cave dweller had vanished, leaving the human observers to shout futile questions through the speakers of their robot. Seeing that words were useless, Raeker started the robot in the same direction as his pupils, and used language which made Easy raise her eyebrows as the machine was steadily left further and further behind. Nick and his friends disappeared over the hilltop where the scout had been hiding, and not even their shouts could be heard over Raeker's voice in the control room.

It was Easy who turned his words into more constructive channels, less because she was shocked than because she was curious.

'Dr Raeker! Did I hear one of them say that there was a cave dweller to catch? How did one get there so soon? I thought you said you'd left them behind at that river.' Her question was so exactly the one Raeker had been asking himself that he had nothing to say in reply for a moment; but at least he stopped talking, and had the grace to turn slightly red.

'That's what it sounded like to me, Easy. I don't know the way they found us any more than you do; I have always supposed this was a long way outside their home grounds, so I don't see how they could have known a short cut around the river – for that matter, I don't see how there could be such a thing; that river was over a mile wide. We'll have to wait until Nick and the others come back; maybe they'll have a prisoner we can question. I suppose that's his idea; I think he said "catch", not "kill".'

'That's right; he did. Well, we'll be able to see them in a minute or two, when the robot gets up this hill, unless they've gone over another one in the meantime.'

It turned out that they hadn't; the human watchers had a very good view of the chase, not that it was much to see. The valley into which the cave scout had fled was almost entirely ringed with the low, rounded hills so typical of much of Tenebra; John and Betsey had managed to get to the tops of two of these before being seen, so that they had a considerable advantage on the cave dweller when it came to running. He had made one or two attempts to race out through the wide gaps between Betsey and John and between them and the main group, but had seen after only a few moments on each dash that he was being headed off. When the robot came in sight he was standing near the center of the valley while Fagin's people closed in slowly around him. He was rather obviously getting ready for a final dash through any gap that might present itself, after his pursuers were close enough to have sacrificed their advantage of elevation. He might also be planning to fight; he was two feet taller than Nick and his friends, and had two efficient-looking short spears.

Nick seemed to have picked up a smattering of military tactics, not to mention diplomacy, however. He halted his people a good fifty yards from the big cave dweller, and spread them out into an evenly spaced circle. With this completed to his satisfaction, he shifted to Swift's language.

'Do you think you can get away from us?'

'I don't know, but some of you will be sorry you tried to stop me,' was the answer.

'What good will that do you, if you are killed?' The scout seemed unable to find an answer to this; in fact, the very question seemed to startle him. The matter had seemed so obvious that he had never faced the task of putting it into words. He was still trying when Nick went on, 'You know that Fagin said he was willing to teach Swift whatever he wanted to know. He doesn't want fighting. If you'll put your spears down and come to talk with him, you won't be hurt.'

'If your Teacher is so willing to help, why did he run away?' the other shot back. Nick had his answer ready.

'Because you had taken him away from us, and we want him to teach us too. When I came to your caves to get him, he came with me to help me get away. He carried me through the river, where I could not have gone alone. When you first attacked our village, he wanted us to talk to you instead of fighting; but you gave us no chance.' He fell silent, judging that his antagonist would need time to think. However, another question came at once.

'Will you do anything your Teacher tells you?'

'Yes.' Nick didn't mention the times he had hesitated about obeying Fagin's commands; quite honestly, he didn't think of them at that moment.

'Then let me hear him tell you not to harm me. He is coming now. I will wait here, but I will keep my weapons, until I am sure I won't need them.'

'But you don't know his language; you won't know what he's telling us.'

'He learned a few of our words while he was with us, though he couldn't say them very well. I think I can ask him if he is going to hurt me, and I'll know if he says yes or no.' The scout fell silent and stood watching the approach of the robot, still keeping a firm grip on his spears with two hands each. He was ready to stab, not throw.

Even Raeker could see that readiness as the robot glided into the circle, and felt a little uneasy; he would be a good two seconds slow in reacting to anything that happened. Not for the first time, he wished that the *Vindemi-atrix* were orbiting just outside Tenebra's atmosphere, with three or four relay stations to take care of horizon troubles.

'What's happened, Nick? Is he going to fight?'

'Not if you can convince him it isn't necessary,' replied Nick. He went on to give a précis of the scout's recent statements. 'I don't quite know what to do with him myself, now that we have him,' he finished.

'I wouldn't say you really had him, yet,' was Raeker's dry rejoinder, 'but I see the problem. If we let him go, Swift will be on us in a matter of hours, or in a day or so at the outside. If we don't, we'll have to keep a continuous watch on him, which would be a nuisance, and he might get away anyway. Killing him would of course be inexcusable.'

'Even after what happened to Alice and Tom?'

'Even then, Nick. I think we're going to have to put this fellow to a use, and face the fact that Swift will know where we are. Let me think.' The robot fell silent, though the men controlling it did not; plans were being proposed, discussed, and rejected at a great rate while the natives waited. Easy had not been cut off, but she offered no advice. Even the diplomats, able to hear from the communication room which they still haunted, kept quiet for once.

The cave dweller, of course had been unable to follow the conversation between Nick and the Teacher, and after the first minute or so of silence he asked for a translation. Somehow he managed to make the request in such a way that Nick felt he was repairing an omission rather than granting a favor when he provided the requested information.

'Fagin is deciding what is best to do. He says that we must not kill you.'

'Have him tell me that himself. I will understand him.'

'One does not interrupt the Teacher when he is thinking,' replied Nick. The cave dweller seemed impressed; at least, he said nothing more until the robot came back on the air.

'Nick.' Raeker's voice boomed into the dense atmosphere, 'I want you to translate very carefully what I have to say to this fellow. Make it word for word, as nearly as the language difference will allow; and think it over yourself, because there will be some information I haven't had time to give you yet.'

'All right, Teacher.' Everyone in the circle switched attention to the robot; but if the scout in the center realized this, he at least made no effort to take advantage of the fact. He, too, listened, as intently as though he were trying to make sense out of the human speech as well as Nick's translation. Raeker started slowly, with plenty of pauses for Nick to do his job.

'You know,' he began, 'that Swift wanted me at his place so that I could teach him and his people to make fires, and keep herds, and the other things I have already taught my own people. I was willing to do that, but Swift thought, from something Nick said, that my people would object, so he came fighting when it wasn't necessary.

'That's not really important, now, except for the fact that it delayed something important to Swift as well as to us. Up until now, all I've been able to give is knowledge. I was the only one of my people here, and I can never go back where I came from, so that I couldn't get more things to give.

'Now others of my people have come. They are riding in a great thing that they made; you haven't any words for it, since I never gave them to Nick's people and I don't think Swift's people have any such things. It was something we made, as you make a bucket or a spear, which is able to carry us from one place to another; for the place from which I came is so far away that no one could ever walk the distance, and is far above so that only a floater could even go in the right direction. The people who came were going to be able to come and go in this machine, so that they could bring things like better tools to all of you, taking perhaps things you were willing to give in exchange. However, the machine did not work quite properly; it was like a spear with a cracked head. It came down to where you live, but we found that it could not float back up again. My people cannot live outside it, so they aren't able to fix it. We need help from Nick's people and, if you will give it, from yours as well. If you can find this machine in which my friends are caught, and learn from me how to fix it, they will be able to go back up once more and bring things for you all; if you can't or won't, my people will die here, and there will not even be knowledge for you – for some day I will die, too, you know.

'I want you to take this message to Swift, and then, if he will let you, come back with his answer. I would like him and all his people to help hunt for the machine; and when it is found, Swift's people and Nick's can help in fixing it. There won't need to be any more fighting. Will you do that?'

Nick had given this talk exactly as it came, so far as his knowledge of Swift's language permitted. The scout was silent for half a minute or so at the end. He was still holding his spears firmly, but Raeker felt that his attitude with them was a trifle less aggressive. It may have been wishful thinking, of course; human beings are as prone to believe the things they wish were true as Drommians are to believe what occurs to them first.

Then the scout began asking questions, and Raeker's estimate of his intelligence went up several notches; he had been inclined to dismiss the fellow as a typical savage.

'Since you know what is wrong with your friends and their machine, you must be able to talk to them some way.'

'Yes, we – I can talk to them.'

'Then how is it you need to look for them? Why can't they tell you where they are?'

'They don't know. They came down to a place they had never seen before, and floated on a lake for five days. Last night they drifted down a river. They were at the bottom, and couldn't see where they were going; and anyway they didn't know the country – as I said, they never saw it before. The river is gone now, and they can see around, but that does no good.'

'If you can hear them talk, why can't you go to them anyway? I can find anything I can hear.'

'We talk with machines, just as we travel. The machines make a sort of noise which can only be heard by another machine, but which travels very much farther than a voice. Their machine can talk to one in the place where I came from, and then that one can talk to me; but it is so far away that it can't tell exactly where either of us is. All we can do is let them tell us what sort of country they can see; then I can tell you, and you can start hunting.'

'You don't even know how far away they are, then.'

'Not exactly. We're pretty sure it's not very far – not more than two or three days' walk, and probably less. When you start looking for them we can have them turn on their brightest lights, like these' – the robot's spots flamed briefly – 'and you'll be able to see them from a long distance. They'll have some lights on anyway, as a matter of fact.'

The cave dweller thought for another minute or so, then shifted the grip on his spears to 'trail.' 'I will give your words to Swift, and if he has words for you they will be brought. Will you stay here?'

The question made Raeker a trifle uneasy, but he saw no alternative to answering 'yes.' Then another point occurred to him.

'If we did not stay here, would it take you long to find us?' he asked. 'We noticed that you got to this side of the river and into sight of our group much more quickly than we had expected. Did you have some means of crossing the river before day?'

'No,' the other replied with rather surprising frankness. 'The river bends north not far inland from the place where you walked through it and goes in that direction for a good number of miles. A number of us were sent along it, with orders to stop at various points, cross as soon as it dried up, and walk toward the sea to find traces of you.'

'Then others presumably crossed our trail – all those who were stationed farther south – and located us.'

'No doubt. They may be watching now, or they may have seen you attack me and gone off to tell Swift.'

'You knew about the bend in the river. Your people are familiar with the country this far from your caves?'

'We have never hunted here. Naturally, anyone can tell which way a river is going to flow and where there are likely to be hills and valleys.'

'What my people call an eye for country. I see. Thank you; you had better go on and give the message to Swift before he arrives with another crowd of spears to avenge the attack on one of his men.'

'All right. Will you answer one question for me first? Sometimes you say I and sometimes "we" even when you obviously don't mean yourself and these people here. Why is that? Is there more than one of you inside that thing?'

Nick did not translate this question; he answered it himself.

'The Teacher has always talked that way,' he said. 'We've sometimes wondered about it, too; but when we asked him, he didn't explain – just said it wasn't important yet. Maybe Swift can figure it out.' Nick saw no harm in what he would have called psychology if he had known the word.

'Maybe.' The scout started south without another word, and the rest of the group, who had long since broken their circle and gathered around the teacher, watched him go.

'That sounded good, Dr Raeker. Should we keep the spot lights on just in case, from now on?' Easy Rich's voice broke the silence.

'I wouldn't, just yet,' Raeker said thoughtfully. 'I wish I could be sure I wanted Swift to find you, instead of merely wanting to keep him from attacking us.'

'What?' Aminadabarlee's voice was shriller, and much louder, even than usual. 'Are you admitting that you are using my son as bait to keep those savages away from your little pet project down there? That you regard those ridiculously shaped natives as more important than a civilized being, simply because you've been training them for a few years? I have heard that human beings were cold-blooded, and scientists even more so than the general run, but I would never have believed this even of human beings. This is the absolute limit. Councillor Rich, I must ask your indulgence for the loan of our speedster; I am going to Dromm and start our own rescue work. I have trusted you *men* too long. I am through with that – and so is the rest of the galaxy!'

'Excuse me, sir.' Raeker had come to have a slightly better grasp of the problem the Drommian represented. 'Perhaps, if you do not trust me, you will at least listen to Councillor Rich, whose daughter is in the same situation as your son. He may point out to you that the "ridiculous natives" whose safety I have in mind are the only beings in the universe in a position, or nearly in a position, to rescue those children; and he may have noticed that I did not tell the savage even the little I heard of Easy and 'Mina's description of the country around them. I am sure we will appreciate your planet's help, but do you think it will possibly come in time? Before the human girl is permanently injured by extra gravity, and your son has exceeded your race's time limit under vitamin and oxygen deficiency? I am not asking these questions to hurt you, but in an effort to get the best help you can give. If there is anything more you can do than keep your son's courage up by staying where he can see and hear you, please let us know.'

Rich's face was visible behind the Drommian's in the jury-rigged vision screen, and Raeker saw the human diplomat give a nod and an instantly suppressed smile of approval. He could think of nothing to add to his speech, and wisely remained silent. Before Aminadabarlee found utterance, however, Easy came in with a plea of her own.

'Don't be angry with Dr Raeker, please; 'Mina and I can see what he's doing, and we like Nick, too.' Raeker wondered how much of this was true; he wasn't as sure himself as he would like to have been of what he was doing, and the children had not yet talked directly to Nick, though they had been listening to him and his people for a couple of hours. Easy, of course, was a diplomat's daughter. Raeker had learned by now that her mother had died when she was a year old, and she had traveled with her father ever since. She seemed to be growing into a competent diplomat in her own right. 'It doesn't really matter if Swift does find us,' she went on. 'What can he do to hurt us, and why should he want to?'

'He threatened to use fire on the robot if it didn't come with him to the cave village,' retorted the Drommian, 'and if he does the same to the 'scaphe's hull when you fail to tell him something he wants to know, you'll be in some trouble.'

'But he knew that Fagin didn't speak his language, and was very patiently teaching it during the three weeks or so it was in his power; why should he be less patient with us? We're perfectly willing to teach him anything we know, and we can talk to him with less trouble than Dr Raeker could – at least, there won't be the delay.'

A burst of shrill sound from Aminadorneldo followed and, presumably, supported Easy's argument; Aminadabarlee cooled visibly. Raeker wondered how long it would last. At least, things were safe politically for the moment; he turned his attention back to Tenebra and to Nick.

That worthy had started his group back toward the original meeting place, with two running ahead – the herd had been unprotected quite long enough. Nick himself was standing beside the robot, apparently waiting for comment or instructions. Raeker had none to give, and covered with a question of his own.

'How about it, Nick? Will he come back? Or more accurately, will Swift go along with us?'

'You know as well as I.'

'No, I don't. You spent a long time with Swift and his people; you know him if any of us do. Was I right in playing on his desire for things we could bring him? I realize he wanted to know about things like fire, but don't you think it was for what he saw could be done with it?'

'It seems likely,' admitted Nick, 'but I don't see how it's possible to be sure of what anyone's thinking or what he's going to do.'

'I don't either, though some of my people keep trying.' The two started after the rest of the group, scarcely noticing the minor quake that snapped a few of the more brittle plants around them. Nick almost unthinkingly gathered firewood as he went, a habit of years which had developed in the old village after the more accessible fuel near the hilltop had been exhausted. He had quite a stack in his four arms by the time they rejoined the others. This was piled with the rest; the herd was checked and the strays brought back together; and then Fagin called a meeting.

'You all heard what I told Swift's man, about the machine which was stranded somewhere here with some of my people in it. If it is not found and fixed shortly, those people will die. You know as well as I that rescue of people in danger is of more importance than almost anything else; and for that reason, we are going to drop all other activities, except those needed actually to stay alive, while we look for that ship.

'I will give you a description, as completely as possible, of the place where they are. We'll check all our maps for similarity – I'll help you there; I can do it faster – and then you'll go out in pairs to check all likely spots. If we don't find them, mapping will proceed as rapidly as possible, to the exclusion of all other scientific activities.

'For the rest of today, Betsey and Nick will take care of camp and herd; search teams will be Oliver and Dorothy, John and Nancy, and Jim and Jane. I will assign an area to each of the teams as soon as the maps have been checked; in the meantime, you might all be gathering firewood for tonight.' The group scattered obediently.

The geologists in the *Vindemiatrix* had for some time been matching, or trying to match, Easy's not too complete description of the bathyscaphe's environs; they had come up with four or five possible locations, none of which made them really happy. However, when a sixth possibility was finally settled on, Raeker called the exploring teams back to the robot and assigned two of the hopeful areas to each team. These were all in the general direction of the old village, naturally, since the mapping had gone on radially from that point in the two or three years the cartography project had been going. They were all on the nearer side of that region, however, since the men who had done the matching had been influenced by the realization that the 'scaphe must have drifted seaward on the night that it moved. It seemed likely, therefore, that a day to go, a day to explore, and a day to return would suffice for this step of the plan. By that time, Swift might be back with his people, and the rate of search could be stepped up. That was why Nick had been kept behind at the camp site; he might be needed as an interpreter.

The instructions were heard, the villagers' own maps were checked, weapons were examined, and the parties set out. Nick and Betsey, standing beside the robot, watched them go; and far away, Raeker finally left the observing room to get some sleep. The diplomats stayed awake, chatting with their children as the latter described the animals which came into sight from time to time. In this relatively dull fashion the rest of the ship's day, a night, and part of another day were spent, while the search teams plodded sturdily toward their assigned areas.

This was the twenty-seventh ship's day since the accident to the bathyscaphe, the afternoon of the seventh day as far as Nick and his people were concerned. The children were understandably impatient; both fathers had to explain again and again how small were their chances of being found at the very beginning of the search. On this day, at least, human and Drommian were in remarkably close accord. In spite of this unity of effort, however, the children tended to spend more and more time at the windows as the day drew on, and from time to time even Easy brought up the subject of using the spotlights to guide the searchers who should be approaching. Her father kept reminding her that Raeker had advised against it; but eventually Raeker withdrew his objection.

'It'll make the kid feel more a part of the operation,' he said in an aside to Rich, 'and I can't see that there's much, if any, more chance of Swift's sighting them than of our own people's doing it at the moment. Let her play with the lights.'

Easy happily made full use of the permission and the bathyscaphe blazed far brighter than daylight – since daylight was utter darkness to human eyes – at Tenebra's surface. Rich was not too happy about the permission; it seemed to him encouraging the youngster in her unreasonable hope of an early rescue, and he feared the effects of disappointment.

'Listen to them,' he growled. 'Yelling to each other every time something moves within half a mile. If they could see any farther it would be still worse – thank goodness they're using their eyes instead of the photocells of the robot. That'll last until they get sleepy; then they'll start again when they wake up—'

'They should be under water by then,' pointed out Raeker mildly.

'And drifting again, I suppose. That's when everything will go to pieces at once, and we'll have a couple of screaming kids who'll probably start hitting switches right and left in the hope some miracle will bring them home.'

'I don't know about the Drommian, but I think you do your daughter a serious injustice,' replied Raeker. 'I've never known much about kids, but she strikes me as something pretty remarkable for her age. Even if *you* can't trust her, you'd better not let her know it.'

'I realize that, and no one trusts her more than I do,' was the weary answer. 'Still, she *is* only a kid, and a lot of adults would have cracked before now. I can name one who's on the edge of it. Listen to them, down there.'

Aminadorneldo's piercing tones were echoing from the speaker.

'There's something on this side, Easy! Come and see this one.'

'All right, 'Mina. Just a minute.' Easy's small form could be seen for an instant on the screen, passing through the control room from one side of the ship to the other, calling as she went, 'It's probably another of those plant-eating things that are about as big as Nick's people. Remember, the ones we want stand up on end.'

'This one does. Look!'

'Where?' Aminadorneldo must have been pointing; there was a moment of silence; then the girl's voice, 'I still don't see anything; just a lot of bushes.'

'It looked just like Nick. It stood beside that bush for a moment and looked at us, and then went away. I saw it.'

'Well, if you were right, it'll come back. We'll stand here and watch for it.'

Rich looked at Raeker and shook his head dismally.

'That'll—' he began, but got no further. His sentence was interrupted by a sudden shriek from the speaker, so shrill that for a moment neither of them could tell who had uttered it.

VIII
Radiation; Evaporation; Advection

John and Nancy made steady progress into the west. Their journey so far had not been particularly difficult, though most of it had been made over ground not yet surveyed. They had fought with floaters and other carnivores a reasonable number of times, eaten the fruits of their victories when they felt hungry enough, and talked more or less incessantly. The talk was mostly speculation; they had learned more about the nature of their Teacher in the last few days than in the preceding sixteen years, but what they had learned seemed only to give rise to more questions. They were young enough to be surprised at this; hence the steady conversation, which was interrupted only by their reaching a region which seemed to match part of their map.

'We must have kept our direction pretty well,' Nancy said after comparing the hills around them to those indicated on the sheet. 'We were trying to hit the mapped region about here,' she pointed, 'and seem to be only a dozen miles to the north. Oliver mapped this place; it hasn't changed enough to be really doubtful. We can head south, and be sure of ourselves in a few more miles.'

'All right,' agreed John. 'You know, even if we are still a good many miles from either of our search areas, it wouldn't actually hurt: to keep our eyes open for the machine.'

Nancy sent the ripple that passed for a shrug flickering down her scales. 'It's hardly worth making a special effort. We'll be able to see it miles away, if it's as bright as Fagin said. I think we'd better concentrate on the map, just now, until we're sure we're where we're supposed to be.'

'Fagin would have had something to say about that sentence,' muttered John, 'but I suppose you're right. Let's get on.'

Two miles, twenty-five minutes, one brief fight, and one longish quake later they were in a position to feel sure of themselves. Uniform as the solution-molded surface of Tenebra was, and rapid as its changes were, the present region matched the maps too closely to be coincidence. They spent a few minutes deciding whether it would be better to start gathering firewood for the night which was not too many hours away or move closer to their first search area so as to waste less time in the morning, settled on the second alternative, and went on.

Nightfall was even closer when they stopped simultaneously. Neither needed to speak, since it was quite evident to both that they had seen the same thing. Far to the south and somewhat to the west a light was shining.

For several seconds they stood looking at it. What they could see was not particularly brilliant – it was just enough to be noticeable; but light other than daylight on Tenebra can be explained only in a certain very few ways. So, at least, Fagin's students supposed.

After a moment's staring, they got out the maps once more and tried to judge where the source of the light might be. This was difficult, however, because it was next to impossible to estimate the distance. The source itself was not directly visible, just the glow which fires, spotlights, and Altair itself produced in Tenebra's soupy envelope. The direction was plain enough, but it seemed likely that the actual source was either outside mapped territory altogether or in the poorly covered region Nick had done during the trip which had discovered the cave village. It seemed equally likely that they could not possibly reach the place before rainfall, but after the briefest of discussions they agreed to start out.

The going was normal at first, but it gradually got rougher. This agreed with what they remembered of Nick's report on his trip. They also recalled his mention of a life form which lived in holes and was dangerous to passers-by, but they encountered no sign of it just then. The light kept getting brighter, which was encouraging, but for several hours they failed to get any better idea of what was making it.

Then they began to get an impression that it was coming from a point above their level, and after another half hour they were both quite sure of this. The fact was hard to understand; Fagin had said that the bathyscaphe couldn't fly because it was broken, and there had been no mention of a hill – at least, not of anything unusual in that respect – in the description of the machine's environment. As a matter of fact, they recalled, it had been stated to lie at the *foot* of a hill.

Then John remembered Nick's tale of a remarkably high hill in the region, and the two got out their maps once more. It seemed possible though far from certain, after careful checking, that the light was on the hill; but if that were the case it seemed to dispose of any remaining chance that they had found the bathyscaphe. Since the only other possibility they could envision was that Swift's people were there with a fire, a slight problem developed.

It would be raining before long, and travel without torches would be impossible. If the area ahead were actually a camp of Swift's cave dwellers, approaching it with torches would simply be asking for capture. Of course, the chief might have accepted Fagin's offer, so that they would technically be allies; but from what John and Nancy knew of Swift they didn't want to take the chance. From one point of view, there was no reason to approach at all, since they were searching for the bathyscaphe rather than scouting the cave men; but this phase of the matter didn't occur to either of them. If it had, they would probably have insisted that they weren't *sure* the light wasn't from the crippled machine. Anyway, they kept trying to plan a method of approach to the light.

It was Nancy who finally worked it out. John didn't like the plan and didn't trust it. Nancy pointed out truthfully that she knew more physics than he did, and even if he didn't know what she was talking about he ought to take her word for it. He replied, equally truthfully, that he might be a mathematician rather than a chemist but even he knew enough about rain not to accept ideas like hers uncritically. Nancy finally won her point by the simple process of starting toward the light alone, giving John the choice of coming or staying behind. He came.

Raeker would have liked to hear that argument. He had named the little creatures who had emerged from the stolen eggs quite arbitrarily, and still had no idea of the actual gender of any of them. Nancy's display of a human-feminine characteristic would have been fascinating if not very conclusive.

John watched the sky uneasily as they strode onward. Inwardly he knew perfectly well that the rain was not due for a while yet; but the mere fact of Nancy's defiance of the phenomenon made him abnormally conscious of it. By the time the first drops actually appeared far above, they were close enough to the light to see that something lay between them and the actual source – it was shining from behind a barrier of some sort, presumably a hill.

'Should we go over, or around?' John asked, when this fact became evident. 'If we go up, we'll run into the rain sooner.'

'That's a good reason for doing it,' retorted Nancy. 'If it is the cave people they won't be expecting us from that direction, and you'll see all the sooner that I'm right. Besides, I've never been up a really high hill, and Nick said this one was two or three hundred feet tall – remember?'

'I remember, but I'm not as sure as you seem to be that this is the hill he was talking about.'

'Look at your map!'

'All right, I know we're close to it, but his notes were pretty rough; you know that as well as I do. There never was time to make a decent map of the country he covered, after he got back. We've been fighting or moving practically ever since.'

'All right, you needn't make a thesis out of it. Come on.' She led the way without waiting for an answer.

For some time there was no appreciable rise in the general ground level, though the number of ordinary hillocks remained about as usual. The first implication that Nancy might be right about the nature of the hill was a change in the nature of the ground underfoot. Instead of the usual feldspar-rich granitic rock, heavily pitted with solution cavities, a darker, much smoother material became predominant. Neither of them had ever seen fresh lava, since Nick had brought back no specimens, and it took time for their feet to get used to it.

The rain was getting very close to the surface now. There was no difficulty in dodging drops, since there was more light corning from ahead than Altair gave at high noon; the trouble was that Nancy was not bothering to dodge them. Theoretically she was right enough; they were still cloudy with oxygen bubbles, and her body heat turned them into perfectly breathable air, but it took a while for John to follow her example. Habits are as hard to break for Tenebrites as for human beings.

Gradually the slope of the dark rock began to increase. They *were* on a hill, and the light was close ahead, now. Rocks were silhouetted sharply against it, not more than a mile in front. Nancy stopped, not because of the rain but to take a final look around; and it was then that they both noticed something else.

In the first place, the raindrops were not falling straight; they were drifting horizontally as they descended, drifting in the same direction as the two were traveling. That was reasonable when one stopped to think; they had known about convection and advection currents almost as long as they could remember. It was the speed that was remarkable; the drops were heading toward the fire at a good two miles an hour. The air current that impelled them could actually be *felt* – and that was a major hurricane, for Tenebra. If the thing ahead was a fire, it was a bigger fire than Fagin's pupils had ever lighted or ever seen.

'If Swift lighted that, he must have touched off a whole map section,' remarked John.

Nancy turned to him abruptly. 'Johnny! Remember what happened last night, when Nick got the Teacher away from the caves? He *did* light fires over a good part of a section! Do you suppose they could still be burning, and have spread like this?'

'I don't know.' John stood still and thought for a moment or two. Then he referred to the map, easily legible in the brilliant light. 'I don't see how it could be,' he said at length. 'We're a lot closer to the caves than we were this morning, but not that close. Besides, the clear rain late at night should have put any fire out if there was no one to tend it.'

'But if it were big enough, maybe it would stir up the air so there was always enough oxygen for it – feel this wind on our backs. Have you ever known anything like it?'

'No. Maybe you're right. We can go on and see, though; I still think it's more likely to be Swift. Are you still going to try that idea of yours?'

'Of course. It's all the better, with the wind carrying the drops as fast as this.'

'I hope you're as right as you are reasonable.' The two went on, somewhat more slowly since it was necessary to follow a rather tortuous path to keep their goal in sight among the drops. These were now reaching the surface in great numbers and remaining liquid, except for those parts most closely exposed to the body heat of the two travelers. It took a little longer than might have been expected, therefore, to get within two hundred yards of the rocks ahead, which from the absence of anything but light beyond them appeared to mark the top of the hill. At this point, Nancy decided that stealth was in order; so she brought the scary part of her plan into operation.

Finding an exceptionally large and still cloudy rain drop drifting downward at no great distance, she deliberately placed herself so as to be enveloped by it as it landed. Naturally, the bottom portion of the fifty-foot spheroid was obliterated at once by her body heat; but further descent of the drop finally hid her from view. The great, foggy blot of liquid began to follow the general pattern of activity of the others, moving slowly toward the light; and Nancy did her best to follow. This was not as easy as it might have been, even though the gas around her was perfectly breathable, since with no view of her surroundings it was nearly impossible to judge the rate of drift of the raindrop. The wind was some help, but not enough, and several times John could see her outline as she came too close to the edge of the volume of fog. He stayed where he was, not considering it cowardly to see how the experiment turned out before he tried it himself.

In one sense, the trial was a perfect success; that is, Nancy remained conscious as long as the drop lasted. In another, however, there was something lacking. This lay in the failure of the drop to last long enough. Suffering the assault of heat radiation both from Nancy within and the fire ahead, the thing abruptly faded out in a final surge of turbulence, leaving her in full view.

This turned out to be less of a catastrophe than it might have been. For three or four seconds after the vanishing of her concealment Nancy stood perfectly still; then she called out, making no effort to direct her voice away from the light ahead, 'Johnny! Here, quick!'

Her companion leaped forward, taking a little but not much less care to dodge raindrops, and came to a halt at her side.

She had stopped perhaps five yards from the edge of a nearly vertical-sided pit, fully two miles across. Her first few seconds of silence had been spent in telling herself how lucky she was that her shelter had not lasted a few seconds longer; then the blast of radiant heat corning from the floor of the crater, a scant hundred feet below, forced her to admit the matter was hardly one of luck. It could be seen from this vantage point that no raindrops at all approached the area except those which drifted up the slope of the hill from outside. The floor glowed visibly all over, and numerous patches were of almost dazzling brilliance. These last looked suspiciously like liquid, though the liquid possessed a remarkably sharp and well-defined surface.

Raeker, or even Easy, would have recognized a volcano at once; but the phenomenon was completely outside the experience and education of Fagin's pupils. Raeker had noted, in passing, Nick's earlier reference to the conical shape of the high hill he had reported; the geologists had also paid some attention to it, and even placed it on the list of things to be investigated more fully; but that was as far as matters had gone. Nick had said nothing to suggest that the thing was active – or rather, nothing the men had recognized as such evidence; he *had* mentioned wind. As a matter of fact, it had not been nearly so violent when he had passed, some three terrestrial months before. Only its size and shape had been worthy of note.

'You know,' John remarked after some minutes of silence, 'this would be a wonderful place for a village. We wouldn't need to keep fires going.'

'How about food?' countered Nancy. 'The plants growing on this dark rock are different from the ones we're used to; maybe the cattle wouldn't eat them.'

'That would be easy enough to find out—'

'Anyway, that's not the assignment just now. This light obviously isn't what we're looking for, though I admit it's interesting. We'd better get on with the job.'

'It's raining,' John pointed out, 'and there was no suggestion that we should search through the night as well as by day. This would seem a perfect place to sleep, at least.'

'That's true enough—' Nancy's agreement was interrupted suddenly. Some three hundred yards to their left, a segment of the pit's edge about fifty yards long and ten or fifteen deep cracked loose with a deafening roar and plunged downward. In that gravity even Tenebra's atmosphere was an ineffective brake, and a good ten or fifteen thousand tons of well-cemented volcanic detritus made its way effortlessly through the red-hot crust of nearly solid lava at the foot of the ledge. The results left no doubt about the liquid state of the hotter material – or would have left none had the two explorers still been watching. They weren't; they were on their way downhill in the direction from which they had come before the mass of rock was completely detached. Even as he ran, John had time to feel lucky that the incident had waited to happen until Nancy had agreed with him about what a good camping spot the place was. Needless to say, he did not mention this aloud. Even John was not bothering to dodge raindrops at the moment, much less talk on irrelevant subjects.

They covered nearly a mile down the slope before stopping. The light was still quite ample to permit reading the maps, and it took only a few minutes to convince them both that this was indeed the tall, conical hill which Nick had reported. With this settled, however, neither could quite decide what to do about it. The natural urge was to return to the camp to report the phenomenon to Fagin; against this, however, lay the fact that they had another assignment: to complete, which involved life and death.

'This can wait a day,' John pointed out. 'We can perfectly well camp right here, search our areas tomorrow, and then go back as was planned. We can't drop everything for one new discovery.'

'I suppose not,' agreed Nancy with some slight reluctance, 'but we certainly can't camp here. There isn't enough fuel for a dozen hours on this black stone, to say nothing of the rest of the night; and the raindrops are starting to get clear.'

'That I had noticed,' replied John. 'We'd better get going, then. Just a minute; there's enough here to make a torch. Let's get one started; we may be a little pressed for time later.'

Nancy agreed with this observation, and ten minutes later they were on their way once more with John carrying a glowing torch and Nancy the material for two more, all that the vegetation within convenient reach afforded. They headed toward a region which their maps showed as having slightly higher hills than usual, so as to avoid finding themselves in a lake bed before morning. Both were becoming a trifle uneasy, in spite of Nick's earlier success at all-night travel; but they were distracted once more before getting really worried.

Again a light showed ahead of them. It was harder to perceive, since the brilliance from behind was still great, but there was no doubt that a fire of some sort was on one of the hilltops ahead of them.

'Are you going to sneak up on this one the way you did on the other?' queried John.

Nancy glanced at the now dangerously clear raindrops and did not condescend to answer. Her companion had expected none, and after a moment asked a more sensible question.

'What about this torch? If we can see that fire, anyone near it can see us. Do you want to put it out?'

Nancy glanced upward – or rather, shifted her attention in that direction by a subtle alteration in the positions of her visual spines, which acted rather like a radio interferometer system, except that they were sensitive to much shorter wavelengths. 'We'd better,' she said. 'There's plenty of light to dodge the drops.'

John shrugged mentally and tossed the glowing piece of wood under a settling raindrop. The two slipped up toward the distant light.

It was an ordinary fire this time, they could see as they approached. Unfortunately, there was no one visible near it, and the vegetation was not dense enough to hide anyone of ordinary size unless he were deliberately seeking to use it for the purpose. This suggested possible trouble, and the two explorers circled the hill on which the blaze stood with the most extreme caution, looking for traces of whoever had been there in the past few hours. Not having the tracking skill of the cave dwellers, they found no signs of people. After two full circuits and some low-voiced discussion, they were forced to conclude that either whoever made the fire was still on the hill but remarkably well hidden, or else the fire itself had been started by something a trifle unusual. The latter hypothesis would probably not have occurred to them had it not been for their recent experience with the volcano. There seemed no way, however, to decide between the possibilities by reason alone. Closer investigation was in order and, with a constant expectation of hearing the sharp voice of Swift echoing about them, they set to it. Very carefully, examining every bush, they went up the slope.

The climb bore some resemblance to a scientific experiment, in that its completion eliminated both of the hypotheses and left them completely without ideas for a moment. It was only for a moment however; as the two loomed up beside the small fire, which had quite obviously been laid by intelligent hands, a shout sounded from the next hilltop, three hundred yards away.

'John! Nancy! Where did you come from?' The startled investigators recognized simultaneously the voice of Oliver and the fact that they had been a little hasty in eliminating possibilities; obviously they had missed a trail, since neither Oliver nor Dorothy could fly. Neither said anything about it aloud; each decided in private that the different vegetation of the area was responsible.

When Oliver and his companion came back to the fire from the separate hilltops to which they had taken on sighting John's torch, it quickly transpired that they, too, had seen the light of the volcano and had come to investigate it. Their adventures had been very similar to those of John and Nancy, except that neither of them had tried hiding in raindrops. Oliver and Dorothy had been an hour or so ahead of the others, and had found a good supply of fuel, so they were well set for the night.

'I'll bet Jim and Jane will be with us before the night's over,' remarked Nancy when both parties had completed their exchange of information. 'Their search areas were even closer to this place than yours, Oliver, and unless they went 'way off course coming across country they must have seen the big light, too.'

'Maybe they thought it was better to stick to their assigned job,' remarked John.

'Isn't investigating bright lights part of the job?' retorted his partner. 'As for me, if they're not here in an hour or two I'm going to start worrying about them. This fire-hill couldn't possibly be missed or ignored, and you know it.'

No one had a suitable answer for this, but no one was really impressed by the reasoning, since they had all spent some time in discussion before coming to check the mountain. At any rate, the hours passed without the predicted appearance. If Nancy was worrying, she failed to show it; certainly none of the others were. It was a very quiet night, and there was nothing to worry about. The hours were passing, but that was normal; the light was getting brighter, but there was the peculiar hill to account for that; the rain was decreasing, but the hill might account for that, too. The fire was using up its fuel with unusual speed, but there was plenty of fuel. Doubtless the wind was responsible – none of them had ever experienced such a wind, and an air current one could actually *feel* would no doubt do many queer things. The four explorers stood by their fire and dozed, while the wind grew fiercer.

IX

Deduction; Education; Experimentation

'Daddy! Dr Raeker! 'Mina's right; it's Nick!' Easy's voice was close to hysteria. The men glanced at each other, worried frowns on their faces. Rich gestured that Raeker should do the answering, but his expression pleaded eloquently for care. Raeker nodded, and closed his own microphone switch.

'Are you sure it's actually Nick, Easy?' he asked in as matter-of-fact a voice as he could manage. 'He's supposed to have stayed at the camp, you know. There are six others actually searching, supposedly in pairs; do you see two of them, there?'

'No,' replied Easy in a much calmer voice. Her father sank back in his chair with a thankful expression on his face. 'There was only one, and I saw him just for a second. Wait – there he is again.' Raeker wished he could see the girl's face, but she was shouting her messages from one of the observing chambers and was well out of pickup range of the vision transmitter. 'I can still see only one of them, and he's mostly hidden in the bushes – just his head and shoulders, if you can call them that, sticking up. He's coming closer now. He must see the 'scaphe, though I can't tell where he's looking, or what he's looking with. I'm not sure whether he's the same size, but he certainly is the same shape. I don't see how you'd ever tell them apart.'

'It isn't easy,' replied Raeker. 'After a few years, you find there are differences in their scale and spine arrangements something like the differences in human faces. Maybe you can tell me what this one is wearing and carrying; that should be a lot easier to describe.'

'All right. He has a sort of haversack slung over what would be his right hip if he had any hips; it's held by a strap running up around the other side of his body, over the arms on the left. The front of the sack has a knife hanging from it, and I think there's another on a sort of complex strap arrangement on the other side, but he's been working toward us at an angle and we haven't had a good look at that side. He's carrying four spears that look just like the ones Nick and his people had, and the more I see of him the more he looks like them.'

'Does he have an axe, or anything looking like one?' asked Raeker.

'If he has, it's hanging from his straps at the left rear, where we can't see it.'

'Then I'm afraid you're going to have to make good on your claim that you can get on all right with Swift's people. Mine carry only two spears, and the search teams took their axes with them. If that were one of our searchers he'd have an axe in one of his left hands, almost certainly. That means we'll have to change our plans a bit; we were hoping our folks would find you first. That's just luck; I suppose this is some hunter of Swift's. They'd hardly have had time to get an organized search going, even if he decided to run one on his own.'

'Isn't it going to be a long time before any of your search teams get back to the camp?' asked Easy after some seconds of thought.

'I'm afraid so; over a week of our time. Swift's answer should be back to Nick before then, though.'

'I wish the time didn't stretch out so on this darned four-days-for-one world. Didn't I hear you say you'd learned a little of Swift's language during the time he had the robot at his caves?'

'We did. Not very much, though; it's extremely hard for a human being to pronounce. We recorded a lot of it; we can give you the sounds, and as much as we could get of the meaning, if you think it will be any help. It'll help time to pass, anyway.'

Easy's face appeared in the screen, wearing an impish expression.

'I'm sure it will be very helpful. Won't it, Daddy?'

Even Rich was grinning. 'It will, Daughter. She'll learn any language she can pronounce nearly as fast as you can give it to her, Doctor.'

'Really? I've never heard her talk anything but English to her young friend there.'

'What human being can pronounce Drommian? She understands it as well as I do, though.'

'Well, I wouldn't bet very much that she could pronounce Tenebran, either. It's got some sort of pitch-inflected grammar, and a lot of the pitch is above human vocal range. Of course, she's young and female, but I'll bet she confines herself to understanding.'

'You may be right. Hadn't we better get back to the matter in hand? What's that native doing now, Daughter?'

'He's walking around, thirty or forty yards from the 'scaphe, looking it over, I suppose. If he's seen us through the ports he hasn't shown any sign of it. He's still alone – I guess you're right, Dr Raeker; I remember you sent your people out in pairs, and if anything had happened to one of a pair the other would surely report back to camp before going on with the search.'

'I'm not sure you're right there, but I *am* certain it's one of Swift's people,' replied Raeker. 'Tell us when and if he does anything new.'

'He is now. He's going out of sight the way he came. He definitely doesn't carry an axe; we've seen all sides of him now. He's getting hard to see; there's less of him visible above the bushes, and he's getting out of range of our lights. Now he's gone.'

Raeker glanced at a clock, and did some rapid mental arithmetic. 'It's about four hours to rainfall. Easy, did you say whether he was carrying a lighted torch, or fire in any form?'

'He definitely wasn't. He could have had matches, or flint and steel, or some such fire-making apparatus in his pouch, of course.'

'Swift's people don't know about them. Nick's group makes fire by friction, with a bow-drill, but I'm sure the others haven't learned the trick yet. They certainly hadn't yesterday – that is, three or four ship's days ago. Anyway, the point I'm trying to get at is that if the one you saw had no fire, he was presumably within about four hours march, or not too much more, of Swift's main group; and they'd almost have to be either at their caves or near the line between those caves and the point where Nick and the robot took to the river last night. He may be even closer, of course; you'd better keep your eyes open, and let us know immediately if the main body shows up. That would give us a still closer estimate.'

'I understand. We'll look out for them,' replied Easy. 'While we're watching, how about getting out those language tapes you have? The sooner we start listening to them, the more good they'll probably do us.'

Raeker agreed to this, and the next few hours passed without any particular incident. Nightfall, and then rainfall, arrived without any further sign of natives; and when the drops grew clear the children stopped expecting them. They ate, and slept, and spent most of their waking hours trying to absorb what little Raeker had gleaned of Swift's language. Easy did very well at this, though she was not quite the marvel her father had claimed.

A complication which no one had foreseen, though they certainly should have, manifested itself later in the evening. The bathyscaphe began to move again, as the river formed around it and increased in depth. The children were quite unable even to guess at the rate of motion, though they could see plants and other bits of landscape moving by in the glare of their lights; the speed was far too irregular. Even if they could have reported anything more precise than 'sometimes a fast walk, sometimes a creep, and sometimes not at all,' they were not even sure when the motion had started. They had had their attention drawn to it by an unusually hard bump, and when they had looked outside the few features visible were already unfamiliar. They might have been drifting a minute or half an hour.

Raeker took some comfort from the event, though Easy had been slightly disposed to tears at first.

'This gives us one more chance of getting our own people to you ahead of Swift's,' he pointed out. 'The cave men will have the job of hunting for you all over again, while we are getting you more closely located all the time.'

'How is that?' asked Easy in a rather unsteady voice. 'You didn't know where we were before we started moving, we don't know which way we're moving, how fast, or when we started. I'd say we know less than we did last night, except you can't know less than nothing.'

'We don't *know*,' granted Raeker, 'but we can make a pretty intelligent guess. We judged that you were within a few hours' walk – say twenty-five or thirty miles – of the line between Swift's caves and our people's camp. We are about as sure as we can be without having actually mapped the entire area that this region is in the watershed of the ocean Nick's people found. Therefore, you are being carried toward that sea, and I'll be greatly surprised if you don't wind up floating on it, if not tonight at least in the next night or two. That means that Nick will only have to search along the coast on land if you don't reach the ocean tonight, or look offshore for lights if you do. I shouldn't think you'd go far out to sea; the river will lose its push very quickly after getting there, and there's no wind to speak of on Tenebra.'

Easy had brightened visibly as he spoke. Aminadorneldo, also visible on the screen, had not made any change of expression detectable to the human watchers, but the girl had cast a glance or two his way and seemed to be satisfied with the effect of Raeker's words on him. Then a thought seemed to strike her, and she asked a rather pointed question.

'If we do get carried out on the sea, what do Nick's people or anyone else do about it?' she asked. 'We'll be out of his reach, and out of Swift's reach, and you say there aren't any winds on this planet, though I don't see why.'

'The pressure's so high that the atmosphere doesn't even come close to obeying the classical gas laws,' replied Raeker – he was no physicist, but had had to answer the question quite a few times in the last decade and a half – 'and the small percentage changes in temperature that do occur result in even smaller changes in volume, and therefore in density, and therefore in pressure. Little pressure difference means little wind. Even changing phase, from gas to liquid, makes so little change in density that the big raindrops just drift down like bubbles, in spite of the gravity.'

'Thanks, I'll remember to make sense of that when I get back to school,' said Easy. 'You're probably right, but you haven't answered my question about how Nick was going to reach us if we went out to sea. Forgive me if I'm spoiling an attempt to change the subject.'

Raeker laughed aloud, for the first time in some weeks.

'Good kid. No, I wasn't trying to change the subject; you just asked a question that every visitor for sixteen years has put to me, and I answer it without even thinking. You pushed a button. As far as your question goes, leave it to me. I'm going to talk to Nick first thing in the morning – he couldn't do anything right now.'

'All right,' said Easy. 'If you're that sure, I won't worry. Now how will we be able to tell when we reach the sea?'

'You'll float, the way you did in the lake, at least when some of the water toils off in the morning. I shouldn't be surprised if you were carried off the bottom even at night when the river reaches the sea, but I'm not certain of it. I don't know how completely or how far down the water dilutes the acid. Keep an eye on the landscape, and if you start to drift up from it let us know.'

'All right. That'll be easy.'

But they were still on the bottom when the 'scaphe stopped moving. The human beings at both ends of the communication line had slept in the meantime, but there were still some hours before local daylight was due. Something had slowed the current so that it was no longer able to push the big shell along, and Raeker suspected that the children had reached the ocean, but he admitted there was no way to be certain until day. The intervening time was used up with language work again; there was nothing else to do.

Then the ship began to rise gently off the bottom. The motion was so gradual that it was a minute or two before either of the youngsters was positive it was taking place, and more than three hours passed before the bottom could no longer be seen. Even then they had not reached the surface, or the surface had not reached them, depending on one's viewpoint. It was definitely day by this time, however, and Raeker had lost practically all his doubt about the ship's location. The river had dried up much more quickly, the day before. He told Easy what he was going to do, suggested that she listen in, and then called Nick.

There was no immediate answer, and a glance around the screens showed that both Nick and Betsey were with the herd, half a mile away. He sent the robot rolling toward them, meanwhile repeating his call in more penetrating tones. Both herders waved spears in token of understanding, and Nick began to trot toward the approaching machine. Raeker kept it coming, since he saw part of what he wanted at the foot of the hill.

Nick met him just before he reached it, and asked what had happened.

'I'll tell you in a few moments, Nick,' he replied. 'Could you go to the wagon and get a bucket, and then meet me at the pool down here?'

'Sure.' Nick loped back up the hill. Raeker had not had the robot bring the bucket because of a long-established habit of not using the machine's moving parts, such as the handling equipment, more than could conveniently be helped.

The pool he had mentioned lay in the bottom of a circular hollow, as was usually the case. Also as usual, it filled only a small part of the hollow, representing all that was left when the nightly lake which did cover the spot boiled almost dry by day. He had assumed for years, on rather inadequate data but without any contradicting evidence so far, that the stuff was oleum – principally sulphuric acid with a heavy lacing of metal ions from the surrounding rocks which had been dissolved in the nightly rain, and an equilibrium amount of the atmospheric gases. He ran the robot through it to make sure of its depth – the slope of the rock sometimes changed rather abruptly at the 'acid line,' so judging by eye was insufficient – and then waited until Nick returned with the bucket.

'Is that thing tight, Nick? Will it hold liquid without leaking?' In reply, Nick pushed the leather container beneath the surface of the pool, drew it up brimming, and waited for the fluid on the outer surface to drain away. This happened quickly, since the 'leather' was not wet by the oleum, and in a few seconds only a dozen or so hazily defined drops were clinging to the outer surface. Nick held the container up at the end of one arm for another minute or so, but nothing more fell.

'I guess it's tight, all right,' he said at length. 'Why is it important? We'll never have to carry this stuff very far; there are pools of it everywhere.'

'I'm not interested in keeping it *in* the bucket, Nick. Empty it again.' The student obeyed. 'Now set the bucket right side up in the pool, and let go of it – no, don't fill it.' The transmission delay made this warning a trifle late; Nick emptied what had gotten into the container and started over. 'That's right – *on top* of the pool. Now let go of it.' Nick obeyed. The weight of the strap that served as a handle promptly tipped it over, and three or four gallons of oleum poured in. This weighted the bottom sufficiently to bring the edge to the pool's surface, and there the bucket remained. Nick was startled; he had taken for granted that the thing would plummet to the bottom.

'I'm afraid I've been a trifle negligent with your education,' remarked Raeker, 'though I suppose the rather ambiguous nature of most of this planet's liquid gives me some sort of excuse for leaving out Archimedes' Principle. Try it again, Nick, and this time put a couple of stones in the bucket first.'

As might have been expected anywhere on Tenebra except the actively orogenic regions, there were no loose stones in the neighborhood; but by packing the bottom third of the container with broken-off shrubbery, Nick contrived to achieve the spirit of the Teacher's order. This time the bucket floated almost upright, and with a good deal of freeboard.

'See how much more you can put in it before it sinks,' said Raeker. Nick obeyed, without asking for the meaning of the new verb; it was clear enough from context. To his unconcealed astonishment, it proved possible to fill the bucket with the brittle growths without actually forcing it under, though a ripple half an inch high would have accomplished this end – a fact Raeker at once proceeded to demonstrate. At his order, Nick splashed vigorously in the pool with his feet; waves curled over the edge of the bucket, and it sank almost at once.

'Do you think it would be possible to make something on that general line, capable of keeping several people from sinking?' asked Raeker.

Nick wasn't sure. 'Just on the face of things, I'd say yes,' he replied, 'but I don't really see why that works at all. If I knew, I could answer more sensibly. What use would it be if we had such a thing?'

Raeker took this opportunity to give a rapid explanation of Archimedes' Principle, plus an account of Easy's reports, mentioning the brief appearance of the cave scout and concluding with the probability that the bathyscaphe had reached the sea. Nick could see the rest of the situation for himself, and, characteristically, went a trifle overboard in his enthusiasm.

'I see!' he exclaimed. 'The ship is in the ocean where no one can get at it, so you've showed us how to travel on the ocean itself. We could get out to the ship with this big bucket you want us to make, and pull the ship along with us to the other side, where Swift wouldn't bother us. It's a good idea. We'll start making the bucket as soon as the others come back – in fact, we can start collecting leather for it right now—'

'Hold up a minute, Nick. Crossing oceans, even oceans as small as Tenebra probably has, isn't something you do quite that casually. Also, there's another point to be considered. What if you were out in this – this bucket at night?'

Nick thought briefly. 'Why couldn't we carry firewood and torches?'

'You could; but that's not the point. What happens to the ocean at night?'

'It comes up; but wouldn't the bucket go up with it?'

'I'm afraid not. In going up, the ocean decreases enormously in density, and I'm afraid that rather early in the evening you'd find it oozing over the side of your bucket – and you saw what happened just now when the same thing occurred here in front of us.'

'Yes,' admitted Nick thoughtfully. He was silent for a time. Then he became enthusiastic again. 'Wait a minute. The bucket sinks because liquid gets into it, and it is no longer lighter than the liquid it displaces – right?'

'That's right.'

'Suppose, then, that instead of a bucket we have a closed bag of air? If it's tied shut the sea can't get in, no matter how much it rises.'

'But if the sea becomes no more dense than the air?'

'At least when the water boils out of the sea in the morning the bag will float once more.'

'All that is true only if your bag doesn't leak at all. I'd rather you didn't risk your lives by staying at sea during the night, though your idea of bags rather than buckets is a good one. It would be smart to make a ship of many bags tied together, so that if some of them do leak you will still float.'

'That's plain enough. But why shouldn't we stay out at night? What if night falls before we get the ship across the ocean?'

'You won't cross the ocean. You'll work on it during the daytime, and come ashore again at night.'

'But how about Swift?'

'I'll take care of him. Don't you plan to keep the agreement we offered to make with him?'

Nick thought for a moment. 'I suppose so, if he really agrees. If that was one of his scouts who found the ship last night, maybe he just decided to find it for himself.'

'I still think that find was sheer chance. If it should turn out that you're right, we'll solve that one when we face it. Easy is willing to face Swift, she says. Right, young lady?'

'Certainly.'

'Do you *like* Swift?' Nick asked her in some surprise. 'I can't forget that he killed two of my friends.'

'I've never met him,' Easy pointed out. 'I admit it was bad for him to attack your village that way, but probably he couldn't think of any other way to get what he wanted. If you're smart, Nick, I'll bet you could have him doing just what *you* want – and make him think it's his own idea all the time.'

'I never heard of such a thing!' exclaimed Nick.

'Well, listen in if Swift finds us again,' replied the girl, with a confident tone that surprised even her father. 'You'll learn something.'

Rich signed to Raeker to cut off his transmitter for a moment, and made a comment. 'I hope that young squirt isn't getting too cocky. I admit she's giving Nick just what I've given her on and off all her life; I just hope she's up to it if the occasion arises. That Swift isn't human, or Drommian either!'

Raeker shrugged. 'I'm hoping she won't have to try. In the meantime, I'd much rather have her confident than scared senseless.'

'I suppose you're right.' Rich looked at the screen, where his daughter's confident expression glowed as she enlarged on her theme to the surprised and still doubtful Nick. Raeker listened with amusement for a while, but finally suggested tactfully that she tell him something about boat-building; Nick knew even less about that than he did about diplomacy, and was more likely to need the information. Easy was perfectly willing to change the subject as long as she could keep talking.

Presently 'Mina, who had kept faithfully to his watchman's duties at one of the windows, called to her with the information that he thought he could see the surface. Easy broke off and left the control room hastily, calling back after a moment that her young friend seemed to be right. It was not until the upper observation windows of the bathyscaphe had actually emerged into the 'air' that Raeker remembered something; he had missed an opportunity to check on the mysterious sea life originally reported by Nick. Aminadorneldo had made no mention of any such creatures during his last period of watch, but Raeker didn't know the young Drommian well enough to feel sure he'd have reported them without special instructions. This was obviously not the time to ask; Easy's eager tongue was busy with more up-to-date reports.

'We're farther out to sea than you thought we would be, Dr Raeker,' she called. 'I can just barely see the shore, at the very limit of our hottest lights. I can't make out any details, really; but I think maybe there are some points, or maybe islands, sticking out our way.'

'Can 'Mina see anything more?'

'He says not,' came Easy's answer after a brief pause. 'He doesn't seem to see quite as well as I do, anyway, I've noticed.'

'I see. I suppose you can't tell whether you're moving or not.'

'The ocean is perfectly smooth, and there aren't any waves around us. There's nothing to tell by. The only things to see are those big jellyfish things floating in the air. They're moving slowly in different directions, more of them toward shore than away from it, I think. Let me watch them for a minute.' It was considerably more than a minute before she could make up her mind that the first impression had been right. Even then she admitted willingly enough that this was not evidence of the bathyscaphe's motion.

'All right,' said Raeker when this had been settled. 'Just keep an occasional eye on the ocean to make sure nothing happens, and give advice to Nick as long as he'll listen to you. He'll do what he and Betsey can about it, but that won't be much before the others get back. They'll probably be gone until tomorrow night, Tenebra time – between five and six days on your clock.'

'All right, Doctor. We'll be fine. It's rather fun watching those flying jelly-fish.' Raeker opened his mike switch and settled back thoughtfully, and with some satisfaction. Everything seemed to be progressing properly; perhaps somewhat more slowly than he would have liked, but as rapidly as could reasonably be hoped. This feeling must have showed on his face, for his thoughts were read quite accurately.

'Pleased with yourself, I take it, Man!' The speaker did not need to introduce himself. Raeker endeavored to control both his features and his feelings, with questionable success.

'Not exactly, Councillor—'

'Why *not exactly?*' shrilled Aminadabarlee. 'Why should you feel any remote sense of satisfaction? Have you accomplished anything at all?'

'I think so,' Raeker answered in some surprise. 'We know very nearly where your boy is, and we should have a rescue team out there in a week or ten days—'

'A week or ten days! And then you'll have to give the team members degrees in electrical engineering, and then hope the wiring of that ridiculous craft hasn't corroded beyond repair in the interval. How long do you think the actual *rescue* will take?'

'I'm afraid I couldn't hazard a guess,' Raeker answered as mildly as he could. 'As you point out so clearly, we don't know how much damage may have been done to wiring exposed by the inspection ports. I realize that it is hard to wait, but they've been getting on all right for a month now—'

'How stupid can even a human being get?' asked the Drommian of the world at large. 'You were talking to the ground just now, and heard as clearly as I did the human child's remark that my son didn't see as well as she did.'

'I heard it, but I'm afraid the significance escaped me,' admitted the man.

'Drommian eyesight is as good and acute as that of human beings, if not better, and my son's has always been normal for his age. If he can't see as well as the human with him, something's wrong; and my guess is that the low oxygen concentration is affecting him. I gather your engineers made no particular provision for altering that factor of the vessel's environment.'

'They probably didn't, since the crew was to be human,' admitted Raeker. 'I did not recognize the emergency, I must admit, Councillor; I'll try to find means of speeding up the operation – for example, I can probably get pictures of the wiring exposed by the ports from the engineers, and have Nick briefed on what to look for while he's waiting for the others. My relief is due in half an hour; as a matter of fact, he'd probably be willing to come now if I called him. Have you been able to get medical advice from Dromm yet? I understand a human doctor arrived a few hours ago, and has been finding out what he can about the diet available on the bathyscaphe.'

'Eta Cassiopeia is half a parsec farther from here, and I did not get a message off quite so quickly,' admitted the Drommian. 'One should be here shortly, however.'

Raeker felt that he had made a smart move in forcing the nonhuman to make such an admission; unfortunately, admitting mistakes under pressure does not improve the temper of the average human being, and Aminadabarlee's race was quite human in this respect. He could not be insultingly superior for the moment; even his standards prevented that; but the required repression of choler was a good deal more dangerous to peace than his usual superciliousness. He retired to his own room – which the 'incompetent' human engineers had at least set up with a decent atmosphere – and brooded darkly. There were many more message torpedoes.

With the Drommian gone, Raeker decided not to bring his relief on too early; but as soon as the fellow did show up, he made his way to the engineering section and outlined the proposal he had made on the spur of the moment to Aminadabarlee. Sakiiro and his colleagues agreed that it was worth trying, and they all settled down with their blueprints to decide what would be the best things to tell Nick and the easiest way to get the information across.

They spent some hours at this. Then Raeker went to eat, and back to his own room to sleep for a few hours. When he reappeared in the observation room, his relief rose gladly.

'Easy has something to report,' he said, 'but she wants to tell you personally.' Raeker raised his eyebrows, dived into his station, and energized the microphone.

'I'm here, Easy,' he said. 'What's happened?'

'I thought I'd better tell you, since you're the one who said we'd stay put,' the girl responded at once. 'We've been drifting closer to shore for five or six hours now.'

Raeker smiled. 'Are you sure the shore isn't just getting closer to you?' he asked. 'Remember, the sea level had a long way to go down even after you got to the surface.'

'I'm quite sure. We've been able to keep our eyes on one piece of shore, and the sea has stayed right by it while we got closer. It has a feature which makes it easy to recognize, though we weren't able to make out very clearly just what the feature was until now.'

'What is it?' asked Raeker, seeing that he was expected to.

Easy looked at him with the expression children reserve for adults who have made a bad mistake. 'It's a crowd of about fifty natives,' she said.

X

Comprehension; Construction; Inundation

Nick, for the hundredth time, looked toward the ocean and fumed. He couldn't see it, of course; to be out of its reach by night the camp had had to be placed well out of its sight by day, but he knew it was there. He wanted to see it, though; not only to see it but to ride on it. To explore it. To map it. That last idea presented a problem which occupied his mind for some time before he dropped it. Fagin would know the answer; in the meantime there was a boat to be built. That was the real annoyance. Nothing, really, could be done about that until the search teams got back. While it didn't actually take all of his and Betsey's time to watch the herd and gather firewood, neither could do any very effective hunting with those jobs in the background; and the boat was very obviously going to take a lot of skins.

Nick wasn't sure just how many, and to his surprise Fagin had refused to offer even a guess. This was actually reasonable, since Raeker, who was not a physicist, was ignorant of the precise densities of Tenebra's oceans and atmosphere, the volume of the average leather sack which might be used in the proposed boat, and even the weight of his pupils. He had told Nick to find out for himself, a remark which he had made quite frequently during the process of educating his agents.

Even this, however, called for a little hunting, since it had seemed a poor idea to sacrifice one of the herd to the experiment. Betsey was now scouring the surrounding valleys in the hope of finding something big enough to serve – the floaters of the vicinity had already learned to leave herd and herders alone, and those killed or grounded in the process had long since been disposed of by scavengers. Besides, their skins were much too frail to make good leather.

There was no serious doubt that Betsey would find a skin, of course, but Nick wished she'd be quicker about it. Patience was not one of his strong points, as even Easy had already noticed.

He was a little mollified when she came; she had brought not only the kill, but the skin already removed and scaled – a job which Nick didn't mind doing himself, but it was at least that much less time spent before the actual experiment. Betsey had kept in mind the purpose to which the skin was to be put, and had removed it with a minimum of cutting; but some work was still needed to make a reasonably liquid-tight sack. It took a while to prepare the glue, though not so long for it to dry – strictly speaking, the stuff didn't dry at all, but formed at once a reasonably tenacious bond between layers of materials such as leaves or skin. Eventually the thing was completed to their satisfaction and carried down to the pool where the bucket had floated a few hours before.

Nick tossed it in and was not in the least surprised to see that it, too, floated; that was not the point of the experiment. For that, he waded in himself and tried to climb onto the half-submerged sack.

The results didn't strike either Nick or Betsey as exactly funny, but when Raeker heard the story later he regretted deeply not having watched the experiment. Nick had a naturally good sense of balance, having spent his life on a high-gravity world where the ground underfoot was frequently quite unstable; but in matching reflexes with the bobbing sack of air he was badly outclassed. The thing refused to stay under him, no matter what ingenious patterns he devised for his eight limbs to enable them to control it. Time and again he splashed helplessly into the pool, which fortunately came only up to his middle. A ten-year-old trying to sit on a floating beach ball would have gone through similar antics.

It was some time before anything constructive came of the experiment, since each time Nick fell into the pool he became that much more annoyed and determined to succeed in the balancing act. Only after many tries did he pause and devote some really constructive thought to the problem. Then, since he was not particularly stupid and did have some understanding of the forces involved – Raeker felt he had not been a complete failure as a teacher – he finally developed a solution. At his instruction, Betsey waded into the pool to the other side of the sack and reached across it to hold hands with him. Then, carefully acting simultaneously, they eased the weight from their feet. They managed to keep close enough together to get all the members concerned off the bottom of the pool for a moment, but this unfortunately demonstrated rather clearly that the sack was not able to support both of them.

Getting their crests back into the air, they waded ashore, Nick bringing the bag with him. 'I still don't know how many of these we're going to need, but it's obviously a lot,' he remarked. 'I suppose six of us will go, and two stay with the herd, the way the Teacher arranged it this time. I guess the best we can do until the others get back is hunt and make more of these things.'

'There's another problem,' Betsey pointed out. 'We're going to have quite a time doing whatever job it is Fagin wants done while trying to stand on one or more of these sacks. We'd better pay some attention to stability as well as support.'

'That's true enough,' Nick said. 'Maybe now that we've done some experimenting, the Teacher will be willing to give us a little more information. If he doesn't, there's that other person whose voice he sends us – the one he says is in this ship we're to look for – By the way, Bets, I've had an idea. You know, he's been explaining lately about the way voices can be sent from one place to another by machines. Maybe Fagin isn't really with us at all; maybe that's just a machine that brings his voice to us. What do you think of that?'

'Interesting, and I suppose possible; but what difference does it make?'

'It's information; and Fagin himself always says that the more you know the better off you are. I suppose we don't really know this, but it's something worth keeping in mind until evidence comes in.'

'Now that you've thought of it, maybe he'll tell us if we ask him,' Betsey pointed out. 'He usually answers questions, except when he thinks it's for the good of our education to work out the answers ourselves; and how could we check on this one experimentally – except by taking the Teacher apart?'

'That's a point. Right now, though, the really important thing is to get this boat designed and built. Let's stick to that question for a while; we can sneak the other one in when there's less chance of getting a lecture about letting our minds wander.'

'All right.' This conversation had brought them to the top of the hill where the robot was standing, among the belongings of the village. Here they reported in detail the results of their experiment. Fagin heard them through in silence.

'Good work,' he said at the end. 'You've learned something, if not every-thing. Your question about stability is a good one. I would suggest that you build a wooden frame – oh, about the size and structure of one wall of a hut, but lying on the ground. Then the sacks can be fastened to the corners; any time one corner gets lower than the others, the buoyant force on it will increase, so the whole thing ought to be fairly stable.'

'But wood sinks. How can you make a boat out of it?'

'Just count it as part of the weight the sacks – let's call those floats, by the way – have to carry. You'll need even more floats, but don't let it worry you. I'd suggest that the two of you start the frame now; you might be able to fin-ish it by yourselves, since there's plenty of wood. Then you can start fastening floats to it whenever you can get hold of any; you make a few kills defending the herd every day, so you should make some progress.

'While you're doing that, you might lend your minds to another problem. The bathyscaphe is not staying at sea, but is drifting toward the shore.'

'But that's no problem; it *solves* our problems. We'll just have to travel south along the shore until we find it You had already decided it must be south of us, you said.'

'Quite true. The problem is the fact that Swift, with most of his tribe, seems to be standing on the shore waiting for it. Strictly speaking, Easy hasn't rec-ognized Swift, partly because she can't tell one of you from another yet and partly because they aren't close enough, but it's hard to imagine who else it could be. This raises the question of whether Swift is accepting our offer, or proposes to keep the bathyscaphe and those in it for his own purposes. I suppose it's a little early to expect an answer from him; but if we don't get one some time today, I think we'll have to assume we're on our own and act accordingly.'

'How?'

'That is the problem I suggest you attack right now. I suspect that whatever solution you reach, you'll find the boat will figure in it; so go ahead with it, as far as you can.'

The Teacher fell silent, and his students fell to work. As Fagin had said, there was plenty of wood around, since the camp had not been there very long. Much of it, of course, was unsuitable for any sort of construction, having the brittleness of so many Tenebran plants; but a few varieties had branches or stems both long and reasonably springy, and the two were able to locate in an hour what they hoped would be enough of these. The actual cutting of them with their stone blades took rather longer, and binding them into a framework whose strength satisfied all concerned took longest of all. When completed, it was a rectangle of some fifteen by twenty feet, made of about three dozen rods of wood which an Earth-man would probably have described as saplings, lashed at right angles to each other to form a reasonably solid grillwork. Thinking of it as a floor, neither Nick nor Betsey was particularly happy; the spaces were quite large enough to let their feet through, and the said feet were even less prehensile than those of a human being. They decided, however, that this was an inconvenience rather than a serious weakness, and shifted their attention to the problem of getting floats.

All this was reported to the Teacher, who approved. The approval was more casual than the two realized, for at the moment Raeker's attention was otherwise occupied. The bathyscaphe had now drifted within fifty yards of the shore and had there run aground, according to Easy. She had offered neither observation nor opinion as to the cause of the drift, and none of the scientists who had taken so many reels of data about the planet had been able to do any better. Easy herself did not seem bothered; she was now engaged in language practice across the narrow span of liquid that kept the bathyscaphe out of Swift's reach. Raeker lacked even the minor comfort of being able to hear the conversation. The microphones of the outside speakers were, somewhat sensibly, located by the observation ports, so that the girl had taken up her station where she would have to shout to be heard in the *Vindemiatrix*. She did not bother to shout; most of the time she didn't even think of Raeker or, to be embarrassingly frank, of her father. She had not been interested in the biology, geology, or the virtually nonexistent climatology of Tenebra; her interest in the rescue operation, while profound and personal, had reached the point where she could only wait for information which was always the same; but here were people, and people she could talk to – at least, after a fashion. Therefore, she talked, and only occasionally could anyone above get her attention long enough to learn anything.

She did find out that Swift was one of those present on the nearby shore, and Raeker duly relayed this information to Nick; but when questions were asked such as whether Swift planned to follow the suggestion he must by now have received via Nick's ex-prisoner, or how he had been able to find the bathyscaphe so quickly, no satisfactory answer was forthcoming. Raeker couldn't decide whether the trouble was Easy's incomplete mastery of the language, her lack of interest in the questions themselves, or a deliberate vagueness on Swift's part. The whole situation was irritating to a man who had exercised fairly adequate control over affairs on Tenebra for some years past; at the moment a majority of his agents were out of contact, what might be called the forces of rebellion were operating freely, and the only human being on the planet was neglecting work for gossip. Of course, his viewpoint may have been slightly narrow.

Things looked up toward the middle of the Tenebran afternoon. Jim and Jane returned, long before they had been expected, to increase the strength of the shipbuilding crew. They reported unusually easy travel and high speed, so they had reached their first search area on the initial day's travel, examined it, and been able to cover the other and return in something like half the expected time. They had found nothing in their own areas. They had seen a light to the south, but judged that John and Nancy would cover it, and had decided to stick to their own itinerary and get the desired report in. It was quite impossible, of course, for them to read any expression from the robot, and Raeker managed to keep his feelings out of his voice, so they never suspected that their report was in any way unsatisfactory. For a short time, Raeker toyed with the thought of sending them out again to check the light; but then he reflected that in the first place John and Nancy would, as Jim said, have done so, and in the second place the 'scaphe had effectively been located, and he decided the pair were of more use getting leather. The lack of initiative they had displayed tended to support this conclusion. He spoke accordingly, and the two promptly took their spears up again and went hunting.

'One point may have struck you, Nick,' Raeker said after they had gone.

'What is that, Teacher?'

'They saw the light to the south of their search area. That suggests strongly that the shore of this sea bends westward as it is followed south; and since the caves of Swift lie in the same direction, it is fairly likely that they are closer to the shore than we realized. This may account for Swift's finding the ship so quickly.'

'It may,' admitted Nick.

'You sound dubious. Where is the hole in the reasoning?'

'It's just that I hunted with Swift's people for a good many days, and covered a lot of territory around his caves in the process, without either encountering the sea myself or hearing it mentioned by any of his people. It seems hard to believe that the lights of your missing ship could be seen a hundred miles, and something like that would be necessary to reconcile both sets of facts.'

'Hmph. That's a point I should have considered. That light may call for more investigation, after all. Well, we'll know more when John and Nancy come in.'

'We should,' agreed Nick. 'Whether we actually will remains to be seen. I'm going to get back to fastening this float we've just glued onto the frame. I'm a lot surer that something constructive will come from that.' He went off to do as he had said, and Raeker devoted himself to listening. Thinking seemed unprofitable at the moment.

With two more hunters, the raft progressed more rapidly than anyone had expected. The region of the new camp was not, of course, as badly hunted out as had been the neighborhood of the old village, and skins came in about as fast as they could be processed. Float after float was fastened in place, each corner being supplied in turn to keep the balance – Nick and Betsey were very careful about that. By the late afternoon so many had been attached that it was less a matter of keeping track of which corner came next than of finding a spot not already occupied – the frame was virtually paved with the things. No one attempted to calculate the result of its stability. If anyone thought of such a problem, he undoubtedly postponed it as something more easily determined empirically.

The work was not, of course, completely uninterrupted. People had to eat, there was the need to gather firewood for the night, and the herd to be guarded. This last, of course, frequently helped in the 'shipyard' by providing leather without the need of hunting, but sometimes the fighting involved was less profitable. Several times the creatures attacking the herd were floaters, to everyone's surprise.

These creatures were reasonably intelligent, or at least learned rapidly as a rule to avoid dangerous situations. They were also rather slow-flying things – resembling, as Easy had said, the medusae of her home world in their manner of motion – so that after a fairly short time in any one spot, when a reasonable number of them had been killed, the survivors learned to leave the herd alone. Nick and his friends had believed this end accomplished for the present camp; but in the late afternoon no less than four of the creatures had to be faced by the herders in not much over an hour. The situation was both unusual and quite painful: while a competent spearsman could count surely enough, on grounding such a creature, it was nearly impossible to do so without suffering from its tentacles, whose length and poisonous nature went far to offset their owner's slow flight.

The attention of all four members of the group was naturally drawn to this peculiar state of affairs, and even the work on the raft was suspended while the problem was discussed. It was natural enough that an occasional floater should drift into the area from elsewhere, but four in an hour was stretching coincidence. The group's crests scanned the heavens in an effort to find an explanation, but the gentle air current toward the southwest was still too feeble at this distance from the volcano even to be felt, much less seen. The sky of Tenebra during the daytime is much too featureless to permit easy detection of something like a slow, general movement of the floaters; and the individual movement of the creatures didn't help. Consequently, the existence of the wind was not discovered until rainfall.

By this time, the raft seemed to be done, in that it was hard to see where any more floats could be attached. No one knew, of course, how many people it would support; it was planned to carry it to the ocean when the others returned, and determine this by experiment.

When the evening fires were lighted, however, it was quickly seen that the rain was not coming straight down. It was the same phenomenon that John and Nancy had observed the night before, complicated by the lack of an obvious cause. After some discussion, Nick decided to light three extra fires on the northeast side of the usual defenses, compensating for the extra fuel consumption by letting an equal number on the opposite side of the outer ring burn out. A little later he let go even more on the southwest, since no drops at all came from that direction even after the convection currents of the camp were well established. He reported the matter to Fagin.

'I know,' replied the Teacher. 'The same thing is happening where the ship is down, according to Easy. The drops are slanting very noticeably inland. I wish she had some means of telling direction; we could find out whether the coast is actually sloping east where she is, or the rain actually moving in a slightly different direction. Either fact, if we know it, could be useful.'

'I suppose she can't feel any wind?' asked Nick.

'Not inside the ship. Can you?'

'A little, now that the motion of the drops proves there must be some. I felt more around those fires I lighted when we getting away from the caves, but that's the only time. I think it's getting stronger, too.'

'Let me know if you become more certain of that,' replied Raeker. 'We'll keep you informed of anything from the other end which may have a bearing on the phenomenon.' Raeker's use of 'we' was apt; the observation and communication rooms were filling with geologists, engineers, and other scientists. The news that Tenebra was putting on its first really mysterious act in a decade and a half had spread rapidly through the big ship, and hypotheses were flying thick and fast.

Easy was giving a fascinating, and fascinated, description of events around the bathyscaphe; for while she and her companion had by now seen plenty of the nightly rainfall, they were for the first time at a place where they could actually observe its effect on sea level. The shore was in sight, and the way the sea bulged up away from it as water joined the oleum was like nothing either child had ever seen. Looking downhill at the nearby shore was rather disconcerting; and it continued, for as the bathyscaphe rose with the rising sea level it was borne easily inland with the bulging surface. This continued until the density of the sea fell too low to float the ship; and even then an occasional bump intimated that its motion had not stopped entirely.

'I can't see anything more, Dad,' Easy called at last. 'We might as well stop reporting. I'm getting sleepy, anyway. You can wake us up if you need to.'

'All right, Easy.' Rich made the answer for Raeker and the other listeners. 'There's nothing much going on at Nick's camp right now except the wind, and that seems more surprising than critical.' The girl appeared briefly on the screen, smiled good night at them, and vanished; Aminadorneldo's narrow face followed, and that station had signed off for the night.

Attention naturally shifted to the observation room, where the surface of Tenebra could actually be seen. Nothing much was happening, however. The robot was standing as usual in the middle of the rather unbalanced fire circle, with the four natives spaced around it – not evenly, tonight; three of them were rather close together on the northeast side and the fourth paced a beat that covered the remaining three-quarters of the circle. It was easy to see the reason with a few minutes' observation; for every fire snuffed out on the single man's beat, a full dozen went on the northeast. Someone was continually having to lope forward with a torch to relight one or two of the outer guard flames on that side. Occasionally even an inner fire would be caught, as a second drop blew too soon through the space left unguarded by the effect of a first. There seemed no actual danger, however; none of the natives themselves had been overcome, and their manner betrayed no particular excitement.

While Raeker had been eating, his assistant had had one of the pupils pace off a course which he compared with the robot's length, and then by timing the passage of a raindrop along it clocked the wind at nearly two miles an hour, which as far as anyone knew was a record; the information was spread among the scientists, but none of them could either explain the phenomenon or venture a prediction of its likely effects. It was an off-duty crewman, relaxing for a few minutes at the door of the observation chamber, who asked a question on the latter subject.

'How far from the sea is that camp?' he queried.

'About two miles from the daytime coast line.'

'How about the night one?'

'The sea reaches the valley just below that hill.'

'Is that margin enough?'

'Certainly. The amount of rainfall doesn't vary from one year to the next. The ground moves, of course, but not without letting you know.'

'Granting all that, what will this wind do to the shore line? With the sea not much denser than the air, the way it is late at night, I should think even this measly two-mile hurricane might make quite a difference.' Raeker looked startled for a moment; then he glanced around at the others in the room. Their faces showed that this thought had not occurred to any of them, but that most – the ones, he noted, most entitled to opinions – felt there was something to it. So did Raeker himself, and the more he thought of it the more worried he became. His expression was perfectly plain to Rich, who had lost none of his acuteness in the last month of worry.

'Think you'd better move them back while there's time, Doctor?' he asked.

'I'm not sure. It isn't possible to move the whole camp with just the four of them, and I hate to leave any of their stuff to be washed away. After all, they're fifty feet higher on that hill than the sea came before.'

'Is fifty feet much, to that sea?'

'I don't know. I can't decide.' The expression on Rich's face was hard to interpret; after all, he had spent his life in a profession where decisions were made whenever they had to be, with the consequences accepted as might be necessary.

'You'll have to do something, I should think,' he said. 'You'll lose everything if the sea gets them while they're there.'

'Yes, but—'

'But nothing! Look there!' It was the same crewman who had raised the wind question who cut into the exchange. His eyes were fixed on the screen which looked seaward, and both Raeker and Rich knew what he had seen in the split second before they were looking for themselves. They were quite right.

Hours before they were normally due, the oily tongues of the sea were creeping into sight around the bases of the eastern hills. For perhaps a second no words were uttered; then Raeker proceeded to destroy the image the diplomat had been forming of him – that of a slow-thinking, rather impractical, indecisive 'typical scientist.' With the safety of project and pupils in obvious and immediate danger, he planned and spoke rapidly enough.

'Nick! All of you! Take one second to look east, then get to work. Make sure that all the written material, maps especially, is wrapped securely and fastened to the raft. Make them firm, but leave enough rope to fasten yourselves to it as well. You and the maps are top priority, and *don't forget it*. With those as safe as possible, do the best you can at securing your weapons to yourselves or the raft. Hop to it!'

A question floated back from Nick; the transmission lag made it uncertain whether or not he had availed himself of the proffered observation time.

'How about the cattle? Without them—'

Raeker cut in without waiting for the end. 'Never mind the cattle! There's a big difference between what's nice to do and what's possible to do! Don't even think about anything else until you've taken care of yourselves, the maps, and your weapons!'

Nick's three companions had started to work without argument; the urgency in the Teacher's voice drove Nick himself to follow suit in silence, and a tense period of waiting ensued in the observation room. The distant watchers sat breathless as the work and the ocean raced each other – a race more deadly than any of them had even seen run on an Earthly track.

Raeker noticed that the streams of oleum were much higher in the center than at the edges, rather like greatly magnified trickles of water on waxed paper, even though they still showed a fairly distinct surface; evidently the sea had already been heavily diluted by the rain. That meant there was no point in expecting the raft to float. Its air-filled sacks were nearly half as dense as the straight acid; with this diluted stuff their buoyancy would be negligible.

He was almost wrong, as it turned out. The sea oozed up around the hill, snuffing the fires almost at a single blow, and for an instant blurred the picture transmitted from the robot's eyes as it covered the camp. Then the screens cleared, and showed the limp figures of the four natives on a structure that just barely scraped what had now become the bottom of the ocean. It moved, but only a few inches at a time; and Raeker gloomily sent the robot following along.

XI

Organization; Revelation; Declaration

Nights – Tenebran nights, that is – were hard on the Drommian, Aminada-barlee. They were even harder on any men who had dealings with him while they lasted. Seeing people engaged in work that had no direct bearing on the rescue of his son, and watching them for two Earthly days at a stretch, was hard for him to bear, even though he knew perfectly well that nothing could be done while the agents on the ground were immobilized or actually uncon-scious. This made no difference to his emotions; somebody, or everybody, should be doing *something*, his glands told him. He was rapidly, and quite unavoidably, coming to regard human beings as the most cold-blooded and uncooperative race in the galaxy. This was in spite of the skilled efforts of Rich, who had plenty to keep him professionally busy.

So far the great nonhuman had not descended to physical violence, but more than one man was carefully keeping out of his way. These were the ones least familiar with Drommians – so far. Raeker had noted that the number was increasing.

Raeker himself wasn't worrying; he wasn't the sort. Besides, he was occu-pied enough to keep his mind off Dromm and its impulsive natives. The robot, fortunately, had had no fighting to do, since nothing in the form of animal life had approached the raft and its helpless passengers, or had even been sighted by the carefully watching robot. This was a relief in one way, though Raeker was professionally disappointed. He had wanted to learn something of the creatures who were responsible for the loss of his students' herd a few nights before, and who could apparently live in a remarkably small oxygen concentration. Still, the four tied to the raft were fairly safe, though no one dared let them drift far from the robot; a constant watch was necessary.

As the night wore on, the vagrant currents which had been shifting raft and occupants became fewer, and so much weaker that they were no longer able to move the assembly, whose effective weight must have been only a few pounds. The man in control of the robot found it possible to leave the machine motionless for longer and longer periods; in fact, at one point Raeker almost went to sleep in the control chair. He was aroused from a doze by the shrill voice of the Drommian, however – 'And Earth-men expect people to work with them!' in what even a man could recognize as a contemptuous tone – and did not repeat the slip. It didn't matter; the raft's passengers were drifting unharmed when day arrived. This period was the hardest, as far as standing guard was concerned; as the water began to boil back out of the sea, the latter's density increased, and the raft began to float. It was extremely fortunate that there were by then no currents at all; raft and passengers went straight up. Unfortunately, but somewhat naturally, it turned upside down as it went, so that for a couple of hours the robot operator had the annoyance of seeing the natives hanging from the underside of the floating platform while they very gradually led the surface of the ocean back toward the ground. They had drifted away from the hilltop during the night, and eventually wound up floating in a relatively small pool in one of the nearby hollows. When it finally became evident that the pool would shrink no farther, the robot had to take action.

Fortunately, the oleum was shallow – so shallow that the raft was supported more by the bodies under it than by its own buoyancy. Raeker guided the machine through the liquid, pushing the four unconscious natives ahead of it to the other side. The raft naturally came along, but eventually the rather untidy heap was dripping at the edge of the oleum pool, with the foundation members struggling gradually back to consciousness.

By this time the bathyscaphe was also out of the sea. Like the raft, it had wound up in a pool at the bottom of a valley; unlike it, there was no question of its floating. The pool was too shallow. As a result, Easy and her friend found themselves in their pressure-tight castle fully equipped with a moat, which effectively prevented Swift and his crew from reaching them.

For Swift was there. He turned up within an hour of the time the pool had finished shrinking, in spite of the considerable distance the bathyscaphe must have drifted during the night. It was out of sight of the sea, Easy reported; the wind that had been moving everything else inland had brought the ship along. It didn't bother her; she said that they were getting along splendidly with Swift, and didn't seem too worried when told about Nick's reverses of the night. Rich lost his temper for the first time when he learned that Raeker had carelessly told the child about the destruction of the camp, and didn't regain it until the girl's voice made it perfectly clear that the story hadn't affected her morale.

Raeker himself was thinking less about her than about his rescue operation, at the moment; that was why he had been so careless with his words. Nick and Betsey, Jim and Jane were all safe; the maps had remained attached to the raft, and so had most of the weapons. However, it was going to take a little while to find just where they were, short as the distance they had drifted probably was; and when they did find the camp site, it seemed rather unlikely that they would find much else. The herd would be gone, or nearly so; the wagon – who could tell? A similar period under an Earthly ocean would write it off completely, even in the off chance that it could be found. Here, there was no saying, but Raeker was not optimistic.

Finding the site of last night's fire proved easier than expected. The wind proved to be a clue, when it finally occurred to someone – Jim, rather to Raeker's surprise. He and Jane, of course, had bucked it all the way back from their search areas, though they had not attached any meaning to it at the time; now it served to restore the 'sense of direction' which for Tenebrans as for humans was a compound of memory and the understanding of elementary natural phenomena. Once they knew the direction of the sea, there was no more trouble; there was no question that they had drifted pretty straight inland. The wagon and the remains of the watch fires were found in an hour. Raeker was really startled to find it and its contents intact; the mere fact that the two-mile hurricane had changed from gas to scarcely denser liquid had made no difference to most of the solid objects in its path.

'I think we can save a little time,' he said at length, when the status of the group's belongings had been determined. 'We can go back to the sea now, carrying the boat with us. We'll leave the cart, with a written message for the others; they can either follow us or start moving camp, depending on what seems best at the time they get back. Well test out the boat, and search as far south along the coast as time permits today.'

'What do you mean by that?' asked Nick. 'Do we search until dark, or until there's only enough time to get back here before dark?'

'Until nearly dark,' Raeker replied promptly. 'We'll go south until we decide it's far enough, and then go straight inland from wherever we are so as to get away from the ocean in time.'

'Then the others had better move camp no matter what time they get back, and head south with the cart. We're going to have a food problem, and so are they, with the herd gone.'

'Gone? I thought I saw quite a few, with Jim and Jane rounding them up.'

'That's true, they're not all gone; but they're down to where we can't afford to eat any until a few more hatch. We couldn't even find scales of the others, this time.'

'You couldn't? And I didn't see any creatures traveling around while you were in the sea, either. It seems to me that your missing cattle are more likely to have strayed than been stolen.'

'That may be, but they're gone in any case, as far as we're concerned. If all four of us are heading for the sea right away to test this boat, we won't be able to look for them.'

Raeker thought rapidly. Loss of the herd would be a serious blow to his community; remote-control education cannot, by itself, transform a group of people from nomadic hunters into a settled and organized culture with leisure time for intellectual activity. Without the herd Raeker's pupils would have to spend virtually all their time finding food. Still, they would live; and unless Easy and her companion were collected pretty soon *they* probably wouldn't. The question really, then, was not whether any could be spared from the cattle-hunt but whether one or two or all would be more useful in testing the boat and, if the test were successful, subsequently searching for the bathyscaphe from it.

Certainly two people were less likely to sink the thing than four. On the other hand, four could presumably drive it faster – Raeker suddenly recalled that neither he nor Nick had given any thought to the method of propulsion the raft was to have. He supposed paddles or something of that nature would be about the only possible means; the thought of trying to teach Nick the art of sailing on a world where the winds were usually nonexistent and the nearest qualified teacher sixteen light years away seemed impractical. With muscle power as the drive agent, though, the more muscles the better.

'All of you will come to the sea. We'll consider the herd problem later. If the boat won't carry all of you, the extra ones can come back and hunt for cattle. This search is important.'

'All right.' Nick sounded more casual than he actually felt; all his life, as a result of Raeker's own teaching, he had felt that the safety of the herd was one of the most important considerations of all. If this search were still more so, it must really mean something to the Teacher; he wished he could feel that it meant as much to him. He didn't argue, but he wondered and worried.

The four of them were able to carry the boat easily enough, though bucking the wind made matters a little awkward – the wind was even stronger today, Nick decided. In a way, that was good; a last backward glance at the deserted remnants of the herd showed that a huge floater was being swept past them by the savage current and, in spite of all its efforts, could not beat its way back to the relatively helpless creatures. Nick pointed this out to his companions, and they all felt a little better.

The two miles to the sea were covered fairly rapidly, and no formalities were wasted in testing the boat. It was carried out into waist-deep oleum and set down, and the four promptly climbed aboard.

It supported them – just. The floats were completely submerged, and the framework virtually so. The difficulty was not one of keeping on the surface, but of keeping more or less level. The four were all of almost the same age, but they did differ slightly in weight. One side of the raft persisted in settling deeper whenever they stopped moving; each time this happened they all, naturally, made a scramble for the rising portion, and each time they inevitably over controlled so that the raft rocked and tipped precariously first one way and then the other. It took several minutes and much misdirected action and speech before they learned the trick; then they took longer still to learn the use of the paddles Fagin had told them how to make. The robot itself was not too much use; if it stayed ashore its operators couldn't see things on the raft very clearly, and if it crawled into the sea to any point near the vessel it couldn't make itself heard – the boundary between oleum and air was sharp enough to reflect sound waves pretty completely.

'Why do you have them looking at all?' Aminadabarlee asked acidly at this point. 'The robot can travel along the shore as fast as they can paddle that ridiculous craft, and the bathyscaphe isn't at sea anyway. If you think those pupils are going to be of any use, why not have them *walk* with the machine?'

'Because, while all you say is true, the kids *are* inaccessible to the natives unless a boat is present. It doesn't seem likely that we'd save time by having Nick and his friends search on foot, and then have to go all the way back for the boat when they found the 'scaphe.'

'I see,' said the Drommian. Raeker cast a quick glance at him. The fellow was being unusually agreeable, all things considered; but the man had no time to ponder possible reasons. Nick and his companions were still too much in need of watching. He spoke over his shoulder, however, remembering Rich's injunction about being as courteous as possible to the big weasel. 'There's one thing that might help a great deal, though. You've been talking to your son all along, just as Councillor Rich and I have been talking to Easy; do you suppose he'd be the better for something constructive to do down there?'

'What?'

'Well, if he's as good at picking up languages as Easy was supposed to be, maybe he'd do a better job than she at finding something out from the cave dwellers. Swift quite obviously knows where both our camp and the bathyscaphe are; it would be most helpful if someone could worm a set of directions out of him for getting from the one to the other.'

The Drommian's face was unreadable to Raeker, but his voice suggested what from him was high approval.

'That's the first sensible remark I've heard from a human being in the last five weeks,' he said. 'I'll explain to Aminadorneldo what to do. There's no point in expecting the human girl to do it herself, or to help him.' The diplomat must be credited with what for him was the ultimate in tact, courtesy, and self-control – he had restrained himself from remarking that no human being could be expected to be helpful in a situation calling for intelligence.

He decided to go to the communication room in person, instead of working from Raeker's station – the relay system was efficient, but located in a corner which was rather inconvenient to him for anatomical reasons. Unfortunately, when he reached the other compartment it was even worse; the place was crowded with human beings. Rearing the front half of his long body upward he was able to see over them without any trouble, and discovered that the screen of the set tied in with the bathyscaphe was imaging the face of the human child. His own son was also visible, very much in the background, but only the human voice was audible – as usual, he reflected. The men were listening intently to her, and Aminadabarlee quite unthinkingly stopped to do the same before ordering the interfering creatures out of the way.

'No matter how we ask the question, we always get the same answer,' she was saying. 'At first, he seemed surprised that we didn't know; he's gotten over that now, but still says that Nick and Fagin told him where we were.'

'No matter how often you say that, it sounds silly to me,' retorted one of the scientists. 'Are you sure it's not language trouble?'

'Perfectly sure.' Easy showed no indignation, if she felt any at the question. 'You wanted to know how he found us so easily, and that's what I asked him. He claims he was given the information he needed by Nick, who had it from the robot, and that's what I told you. I don't remember exactly what was said to that prisoner when Nick's people had him; but you'd better play back the transcript and see what you can get out of it. Either the prisoner himself was able to figure it out from what Nick said to him, or Swift was able to do it from the prisoner's repetition. The first seems to make more sense, to me.'

There were few flies on Easy Rich. Aminadabarlee wouldn't have agreed with that, of course; her admission that she couldn't remember exactly what had been said in a conversation she had overheard lowered her considerably in his estimation. However, even he couldn't understand, any better than the listening scientists, what the cave dwellers had been able to learn from a brief description of country they had admittedly never seen.

Then an idea occurred to him, and he dropped back to the horizontal position for a few moments to think. This might really do some good; he almost felt guilty at the thought that he'd left all the serious planning in this matter to the human beings. If they'd only keep quiet for a minute or two and let him get his idea straight – But they didn't. They kept on calling excited remarks and questions to the child so far away.

'Wait a minute!' It was a geophysicist who suddenly came up with a point. Aminadabarlee thought, but he didn't pay enough attention to be really sure. 'This may be a little far-fetched; but a lot of fairly primitive peoples on Earth and other places get pretty darned good climate predictors – our ancestors knew when spring was coming, you know, and built places like Stonehenge.'

'What's the connection?' Several voices asked this question, though not all in the same words.

'This planet has no weather, in our sense of the word; but its geomorphology goes on at a time-rate which almost puts it in the climate class. I just remembered that Nick's prisoner was told that the bathyscaphe stayed on one lake, motionless, for several days, and only then started to drift down a river to the sea. If we're right about Tenebran weather, *that must have been a brand-new river!* The information was enough for any native – at least for any one who hadn't been cut off from the history or folklore or whatever the Tenebran equivalent may be of his race. They may never have been right on the scene of that river, but it was close enough to their regular stamping grounds so they could tell where it must be.'

'I'm going to check the lab alcohol,' commented one listener. The remark put the proponent of the new idea on his mettle.

'Easy!' he called. 'You heard what I just suggested. Ask Swift if it's not true that he knows when things like new rivers and rising hills are going to happen. Ask him how he dares to live in caves in a cliff – which as far as any of us can see is apt to be knocked down by a quake any day!'

'All right,' the girl said calmly. Her face vanished from the screen. Aminadabarlee was too furious to notice that she had gone. How dare these little monsters take his very own ideas right out of his mind, and claim them for their own? He hadn't quite worked out the details of his notion, but it was going to be the same as the one the human scientist had broached; he was sure of that. Of course, maybe it was a bit far-fetched – of course it was, now that he thought of it a little more carefully. The whole idea was the sheerest speculation, and it was a pity that the girl had been sent to waste time on it. He'd go in and show its weaknesses to his son, and suggest a more fruitful modification, as soon as he worked out its details – only then did he notice that Aminadorneldo had also disappeared from the view screen; he must have gone with the human girl. Well, that was all right; there was a little more thinking to be done, anyway. He kept at it for fifteen or twenty minutes, scarcely noticing the human conversation around him, until the children reappeared. They reported without preamble and without apparent excitement.

'You seem to be right,' Easy said. 'They seem surprised that anyone wouldn't know when a place was going to become active in quakes, or when a lake was going to spill, and in what direction. They know it so well themselves that they have a good deal of trouble telling me what they use for signs.' The geophysicist and his colleagues looked at each other almost prayerfully.

'Don't let them stop trying!' the first one said earnestly. 'Get down everything they say and relay it to us, whether you understand it or not. And we were going to use Raeker's students to learn the crustal dynamics of this planet!'

This irrelevance was the last straw, as far as Aminadabarlee was concerned. Without regard to rules of courtesy, either human or Drommian, he plowed into the communications room, his streamlined form dividing the human occupants as a ship divides water. He brought up in front of the screen and, looking past Easy's imaged face as though the girl were not there, he burst into an ear-hurting babble of his own language, directed at his son. None of the men interrupted; the creature's size and the ten-clawed limbs would have given most of them ideas of caution even if they had known nothing of

Drommians. As it was, Councillor Rich had spread some very impressive bits of information through the complement of the *Vindemiatrix*, so ideas weren't necessary.

The shrill sounds were punctuated by others from the speaker; apparently the son was trying to get an occasional word into the conversation. He failed, however; the older being's speech only stopped when he appeared to have run out of words to say. Then it was not Aminadorneldo who answered.

It was Easy, and she answered in her own language, since even her vocal cords couldn't handle Drommian speech.

'We've already told him, sir. Dr Raeker asked me to let you know when you showed up; you had just left his room when we got the information to him, and I didn't see you until just now. He's told Nick, and the boat should be as close as they can bring it on the sea well before night. They'll start to bring it inland then; Swift says they should be able to see our lights from the sea, so the robot has started back to the camp to meet the others and start them on the way here.'

The Drommian seemed stunned, but remembered enough of his manners to shift languages.

'You had already asked Swift to tell the way from the camp to where you are?' he asked rather lamely.

'Oh, yes. 'Mina thought of it some time ago. I should have told Dr Raeker or one of you sooner.' The news that it had been his son's idea calmed Aminadabarlee considerably; privately, most of the men in the room wondered how much truth the girl was speaking. They knew the effective age of the young Drommian, and they were coming to know Easy.

'How long will it take to get to you – for Nick, that is?' asked Aminadabarlee.

'Swift thinks by mid-afternoon, on foot; he doesn't know how fast the boat goes, though.'

'Did you tell him about the boat?'

'Of course. He was wondering how he could get over closer to the ship here; this pool we're in the middle of is too deep for his people to wade, and they don't seem to swim. I suggested floating over on a raft made of wood, but the wood on this crazy planet sinks, we found out.'

'You seem to be getting in a lot of talk with those people. Are you really good at their language?'

'Pretty good, but we're still very slow. If there's anything you want to ask Swift, though, let's have it.'

'No – nothing right now,' said the Drommian hastily. 'You didn't suggest that your friend Swift make a raft of the sort Nick has?'

'I did, but he can't do it. His people can get all the skins they'd need, of course, but they can't make tight enough – I was going to say air-tight – bags out of them. They don't know how to make the glue Nick used, and neither do I. He's waiting until Nick gets here with the boat.'

'And then will take it away from him, of course.'

'Oh, no. He has nothing against Nick. I've told him who Nick is – how the robot stole the eggs from the place where Swift's people leave them to hatch. I think he may be a little mad at the robot, but that's all right. I've said I'd teach him anything he wanted to know, and that Nick had learned a lot and would help. We're getting along very well.' The Drommian was startled, and showed it.

'Did Dr Raeker suggest all this to you?'

'Oh, no; I thought of it myself – or rather, 'Mina and I did. It seemed smartest to be friends with these cave people; they *might* not be able to hurt the ship if they got mad at us, but we couldn't be sure.'

'I see.' Aminadabarlee was a trifle dazed. He ended the conversation casually and courteously – he had never used toward Easy the mannerisms which were so natural with him when he talked to other human beings – and started to make his way back to Raeker's observation room. The scientists were questioning the girl once more before he was out of the room.

He seemed to be fated to choose bad times to move, that day. He had been in the corridors when Easy had given the bathyscaphe's location to Raeker and Nick; he was in them when the four explorers who had discovered the volcano returned and made their report to their teacher. He had stopped to eat, as a matter of fact, and didn't get back to the observation room until the report was finished. By that time the four natives and the robot were heading south with the cart in tow, answering a ceaseless flood of questions from the scientists, some of whom had been content to use the relay system while others had come down to the observation room. The bewildered Drommian found the latter compartment almost as crowded as the communication room had been a while earlier, and it took him some time to get up to date from the questions and comments flying around.

'Maybe we could get the distance by triangulation – the wind at camp and 'scaphe must be blowing right toward it.'

'But we don't know absolute directions at either place. Besides, the wind might be deflected by Coriolis action.'

'Not much, on a world like Tenebra. You have it backward, though; the mountain is already on the maps. With a little more data we could use the wind direction to pin down the 'scaphe—' That was what the Drommian heard as he came in; it confused him badly. A little later, when he had deduced the existence of the volcano, it made a little more sense; he could see how such a source of heat could set up currents even in Tenebra's brutally compressed envelope. By then it was another question that was perturbing him.

'How strong do you suppose the wind will get? If it brings the sea farther inland each night, and the sea carries the bathyscaphe with it, how close will those kids be carried to the volcano?'

'I don't think we need worry for quite a while. Wind or no wind, the sea that far inland will be mostly water, and won't float them very far. I'll bet if that thing keeps on, too, there won't even be liquid water within miles of it, by night or day.'

'Liquid or gas, it might still move the ship. The difference in density isn't worth mentioning.'

'The difference in viscosity is.' Aminadabarlee heard no more of that one, either; it had given him something to worry about, and he was good at worrying. He started back to the communicating room at top speed, which for him was high; he didn't want anything else to happen while he was out of touch. He managed to reach his goal without hurting anyone, though there was a narrow escape or two as his long form flashed along the corridors.

The scientists had left Easy for the new attraction, and the bathyscaphe screen was blank for the moment. Aminadabarlee didn't pause to wonder whether the children were asleep or just talking to the cave-dwellers; also, he didn't stop to wonder whether the question he had in mind should be mentioned in their hearing or not. He would have berated Raeker soundly for such a thing; but this, of course, was different.

'Miss Rich! 'Mina!' he shrilled unceremoniously into the microphone. For a minute or so there was no answer, and he repeated the call with what another member of his race would have recognized as overtones of impatience. Few human beings would have caught any difference from his normal tones. This time Easy appeared on the screen rubbing sleep out of her eyes, a gesture which either meant nothing to him or which he chose to ignore.

'Where's my son?' he asked.

'Asleep.' Easy would not normally have been so short.

'Well, you'll probably do. Did you hear that they've found out what caused the wind?'

'Yes; I gather it's a volcano. I went to sleep just after that. Has anyone come up with more news?'

'Not exactly news. It's occurred to some of those human fortune tellers that your ship may be blown a little closer to the volcano each night, until you're in serious trouble. What does your friend Swift think about that? He's supposed to be able to predict what his planet is going to do, and he seems to have been able to find you each morning so far.'

'Well, we certainly can't get there for several days; we can't see the light from the volcano from here.'

'You mean *you* can't; it's what the natives can see, and what they think, that counts. Have you asked Swift?'

'No. I didn't know about this until just now. Anyway, I'm not worried; if they'd seen the light they'd have mentioned it – they'd have thought it was the robot. We can't possibly reach the volcano for several of Tenebra's days – certainly not by tomorrow.'

'Who cares about just tomorrow? How you human beings ever achieved even the civilization you have is a mystery to me. Intelligent people plan ahead.'

'Intelligent people don't usually jump to conclusions, either,' snapped the girl, in the first display of temper she had shown since the accident. 'I'm not worried beyond tomorrow, because by the end of that day we'll be away from here. Please tell Mr Sakiiro to have the shuttle ready to meet us.' She turned her back and walked – stalked, rather – out of the field of view; and Aminadabarlee was too startled even to resent the discourtesy.

XII

Capitulation; Operation; Elevation

Easy was awake again by the time Nick reached the bathyscaphe. He had had no trouble finding it; the glow from its lights was quite visible from the coast. The wind was blowing straight toward the light, but Nick and his friends knew nothing of the volcano at the time and didn't have to worry about whether they were heading for the right light. They came ashore, shouldered the raft, and headed for their beacon.

Fagin and the other four pupils had arrived before them; travel on foot was a good deal faster, even for the robot, than by the decidedly clumsy raft. Swift seemed to be in a very tolerant mood. He didn't actually greet the newcomers effusively, but he was talkative enough. He took for granted that they were *his* people – people who had gone a trifle astray, and didn't always know just how to behave, but who might be expected to grow up properly if given time. As long as they treated him as chief, it seemed likely that there would be no trouble.

Within a few minutes of the arrival of John, Nancy, Oliver, Dorothy, and the robot, he had demanded to be shown how to make a fire. Easy, with her two-second advantage in reaction time, told John to go ahead before Raeker even knew the order had been given. John, knowing that the person in the bathyscaphe was one of his teacher's race, obeyed without question. He took out his friction gear and had a blaze going in two or three minutes.

Swift then demanded to be shown how to work the device himself; and by the time Nick, Betsy, Jim and Jane arrived with the raft the chief had succeeded in lighting his own fire and was in the highest of spirits.

This was more than could be said for anyone on the *Vindemiatrix*. Aminadabarlee was more than ever convinced that human beings were an ugly-tempered, uncooperative lot; and just now he had more than the usual reason for his opinion. Every human being in the ship was furious with the Drommian, taking their lead from Easy Rich. A night's sleep had not restored her usual sunny temper; she was indignant at the alien's insults of the evening before, and not only refused to explain to Aminadabarlee her justification for saying she would escape within a Tenebran day, but would say nothing more about it to anyone for fear he would hear. It was a childish reaction, of course; but then, Easy was a child, for all her adult speech and mannerisms. Her father had been asked to persuade her to talk; he had stared at her imaged face in the screen for a moment, but no word was spoken. Something must have passed between them, though, for after a moment he turned away and said, 'Please have Mr Sakiiro get the shuttle ready to meet the bathyscaphe. I understand it takes some time to install and adjust outside boosters.' He promptly left the room, ignoring the questions hurled at him, and disappeared into his own quarters.

'What do we do?' The question was not in the least rhetorical; the geophysicist who put it was a close friend of the Rich family.

'What he says, I should think,' answered another scientist. 'Rich seems to be sure the kid knows what she's talking about.'

'I know he's sure; but does *she*? He's her father; she's all the family he's had for ten years, and he's done a marvelous job of bringing her up, but he sometimes overestimates her. She convinced him, just then, that everything is all right; but I don't – *we* don't know. What do we do?'

'We do just what he asked,' pointed out another. 'Even if the kid's wrong, there's no harm in having the shuttle ready. Why is everything so shaken up?'

'Because we know what will happen to Easy and her father if she's wrong,' replied the geophysicist. 'If she's been speaking from her own knowledge, fine; but if that ten-legged weasel made her lose her temper and shoot her mouth off so as to justify her actions—' He shook his head grimly. 'She believes her own words *now*, all right, and so does her father. If they're disappointed – well, the kids have stayed alive down there so far because of the self-control of the Rich family.' He ended the discussion by cutting in another phone circuit and transmitting Rich's request to the engineers.

Raeker had been eating and, occasionally, sleeping in the observation room; he'd forgotten by now how long he had been there. The robot was rather out of things, but he could still watch. His pupils seemed to have been reabsorbed into Swift's tribe, and were being told what to do alternately by the chief himself and by Easy in the bathyscaphe. Nobody was asking Fagin what to do or how to do it, but in spite of this things were happening almost too fast for Raeker to keep track of them. He knew that Easy had had an argument with Aminadabarlee, though he wasn't clear as to the details; he had been told about her promise to be off the ground the next day, but had no more idea than anyone else how she expected to do it. He had had his share of Aminadabarlee's temper, for the Drommian had not by any means been silenced by Easy's flare-up, and had spent some time pointing out to Raeker the foolishness of separating his pupils from their own culture, and how much more would have been learned about Tenebra if contact had been made with Swift's people in the first place. Raeker had not actually been rude, but his answers had been rendered vague by his preoccupation with events on the ground, and he had thereby managed to offend the lutroid more than ever. He knew it, but couldn't bring himself to worry seriously about the prospect of severed relations between Sol and Dromm.

He knew in a general way what people were doing on the ground, but he couldn't understand all of it, and no one bothered to tell him. It never occurred to Raeker that this might have been at Easy's request; that she might be going to extremes to make sure that nothing like useful information got back to the *Vindemiatrix* and the being who had angered her so. He could only watch, photograph, record what conversation he could hear, and try to interpret what went on.

The raft was launched, and Nick and Betsey took Swift out on the surface of the pool to a point just outside one of the bathyscaphe's observation ports. Raeker could see the meeting between Tenebrans and the ship's two occupants, but could not hear their conversation – Easy was, of course, using the outside speakers, and the robot was too far away to hear these directly. The talk was long, and quite animated, for the gestures of all parties concerned could be seen – the port was large enough to let Raeker see fairly well into the 'scaphe even from the robot's vantage point. He tried to interpret the motions, but had no luck. Conversation did not end until nearly night; then the raft returned to the shore, and everyone began to pack up. A dozen cave dwellers helped carry the raft, others helped pull the cart. For the first time, Swift paid attention to the robot; he ordered it to come along, using Nick as an interpreter. Raeker agreed briefly; the journey was obviously to escape the sea, which would presumably come at least as far inland tonight as it had before.

'Where will the big ship go tonight?' he asked, more to secure a demonstration of the cave people's abilities than because the answer made any difference to him. He rather expected Swift would not bother to answer, but the chief was in a very good humor – everything had been going just as he wanted it all day. Once the group was under way, he walked beside the robot and talked quite cheerfully. Nick relayed his words, and he described in great detail the country which they were approaching and the point to which he expected the bathyscaphe to be washed. He also explained his reasons for this opinion, and the geophysicists listened, took notes, and watched with motherly care the recorders which were storing the conversation. For the first hour or two of that night there was more general happiness than the region of Altair had experienced for decades. About the only people not sharing in it were Aminadabarlee and Raeker.

Swift stopped his cavalcade after a scant two hours of rather slow travel. Night had fallen, and the rain was starting to do likewise; he set everyone to work gathering firewood, and ordered Nick to place the guard fires for a camp. Nick and his fellows obeyed without argument; Raeker suspected that they were human enough to enjoy the chance to show off their knowledge. Cave dwellers were at each of the fire sites practicing with friction drills, and one by one the piles of fuel began to glow.

For sixteen years, the lighting of the evening fires had been a signal for a forty-eight-hour period of relaxation on the *Vindemiatrix*, since nothing but rain ever happened at night on Tenebra. Now that was changed; discussion, sometimes verging on argument, went on full tilt. The engineers were busy festooning the outside of the shuttle with hydroferron boosters and their control lines. The diplomats wouldn't have been speaking to each other if they had followed their personal inclinations, but professional pride kept them outwardly courteous. People who knew them, however, listened to their talk very uneasily, and thought of jammed reactor control rods.

A few enthusiasts kept watch through the robot's eyes, partly in the hope that something would happen and partly to keep Raeker company. The biologist refused to leave the observation room; he felt sure that matters were building to some sort of climax, but couldn't guess just what sort. Even during the night this feeling grew worse – particularly at such times as he happened to see or hear one of the diplomats. Actually, Raeker was suffering badly from a sudden lack of self-confidence; he was wondering how he could possibly teach his students to make the necessary repairs on the bathyscaphe, even if they chose to listen to him. If they wouldn't, or couldn't, he didn't want to see or hear of Rich or Aminadabarlee again; he had convinced himself, quite unjustly, that his own arguments had caused them to pin their faith in him and not undertake any other steps toward a rescue.

In spite of the anxiety which let him sleep only for moments at a time, he managed to get through the night. The departure of the shuttle distracted him for a few minutes – at one point he almost convinced himself that he should go along with it, but common sense prevailed. Several times incidents occurred at the camp, and were pictured on the robot's screen, which would have made him laugh under different circumstances. The cave dwellers were not at all used to fires yet, and had some odd ideas of their properties, uses, and limitations. Several times Nick or one of the other human-educated natives had to make a rescue as someone ran blithely into the dead-air zone of a boiled-away raindrop to relight a fire. When they finally realized that a newly destroyed raindrop was like a newly boiled lake in the early morning, some of them took to waiting a long time before venturing near the extinguished fires, so that the fuel cooled too far to let the blaze spring back to life at the mere touch of a torch. Several of them grew worried about the fuel supply, which the experienced group had pronounced sufficient, and kept trying to persuade Swift to organize wood-collecting parties. Raeker could not, of course, understand these requests, but he heard a couple of his own people commenting on them with something like contempt in their voices. This made him feel somewhat better; if his pupils felt that way about the cave dwellers, perhaps they still had some attachment for their teacher.

Morning finally came without any serious incident in camp or at the bathyscaphe; and once the hill on which the camp was located ceased to be an island – it had been surrounded by the usual rainfall, but not by ocean, as far as anyone could tell – the group headed for the spot where the bathyscaphe was expected to be. This meant a walk nearly as long as that of the previous night, since Swift and his people had expected little motion on the part of the stranded machine. Raeker didn't know whether Easy had reported any drifting; he hadn't heard her voice very often during the last forty-eight hours.

Raeker himself wasn't sure how far to believe the predictions of the natives, and wasn't sure how far he wanted to believe them. If they proved right, of course, it would mean a lot to the geophysicists; but it might also mean that Easy had some grounding for her optimism about the day's events. That was good only if it was *solid* grounding; and Raeker could not for the life of him imagine how the girl expected the machine to be either flown, blown, or carried up to a point where the shuttle could meet it. On the few occasions that he had dozed, his sleep had been troubled by wild nightmares involving volcanoes, floaters, and forms of sea life whose shapes never became quite clear.

There was no question of how the geophysicists felt when the predicted spot was reached and the bathyscaphe found to be absent. They buzzed like a swarm of bees, hurling hypotheses at each other with scarcely time to listen to their neighbors. Aminadabarlee fainted, and constituted an absorbing first aid problem for several minutes until he revived by himself, none of the men having the slightest idea of what to do for him. Fortunately, the ship turned up after a quarter of an hour's search exactly where it had been left the night before, which made things easier on the fathers but left many human beings and quite a few Tenebrites rather at a loss for an explanation. The sea had certainly been there; Easy had reported as much. Apparently its transporting power had been lower than expected. Some of the scientists pointed out that this was obvious; this much farther from its natural bed, the sea would be correspondingly more diluted with water. It satisfied him and some of his friends, but Raeker wondered how a slightly greater dilution of something which must already have been pretty pure H_2O, as pure water went on Tenebra, could make that much difference. He wondered what excuse Swift was using, but couldn't find out.

Nor could he find, except by guesswork, the nature of the plan that was being executed before the robot's eyes.

Hunting parties – judging from their armament – were sent out in great numbers, each one accompanied by one of Fagin's pupils with his axe. The raft made trips to the bathyscaphe, and Swift and several others examined its surface with great care; Easy seemed to be talking to them while this went on, but Raeker and his companions couldn't hear what she said. The natives were greatly interested in the hot area at the top of the vessel, where its refrigerators pumped back overboard the calories they had drawn from the living quarters; they started to climb up the hull, by means of the numerous handholds, to examine this more closely. This act, since the craft was circular in cross section and just barely not floating, started the whole vessel rolling toward the raft; the climbers dropped back hastily. One of them fell into the lake, lost consciousness before he could grasp the paddles thrust down to him, and had to be shoved clumsily into shallow oleum by his fellows lying on the raft above him. This brought the raft itself closer to the robot, and Raeker was able to hear Nick remark to Betsey, 'This will save a lot of time. If the teachers inside don't mind, we can *roll* that thing over here where we can work on it.'

'We may do it whether they mind or not, if Swift gets the idea,' was the reply. 'We'd better ask in English first.'

'Right. Let's get back out there.' The two slid the raft back into the pool and paddled back toward the stranded vessel. This time Raeker knew what the conversation was about even though he couldn't hear it, and he knew how it came out – he could see Easy nod her head in assent. It was several seconds before a frightening thought struck him, and made him call the engineering department.

'Will turning that bathyscaphe over do any harm?' he asked without preamble. 'The natives are planning to roll it out of that pool.'

The men at the other end exchanged glances, and then shrugged at each other.

'Not as far as I can think at the moment,' one of them said. 'The ship was designed to fly, and it was assumed that inverted flight might be necessary. The kids may be bumped around a bit, and anything they've left loose will tumble, but nothing vital should suffer.'

'Thank goodness for that,' Raeker said feelingly, and turned back to his screens. The raft was on its way back to shore, and Nick was calling something to Swift. Raeker could catch only a word or two, since the native language was being used, but he could tell easily enough what was being discussed. Swift got aboard as soon as the raft reached wading depth, loading it to capacity. Back at the bathyscaphe, he and Betsey seized the handholds on the hull and began carefully to climb, Nick staying on the raft to keep it out of the way. Raeker expected some more accidents, but the climbers showed surprising skill and coordination, keeping just above the liquid surface as the ship slowly rocked toward them. It was lucky that the handholds extended all over the hull; Raeker was sure they hadn't checked this point before starting their stunt.

A quarter turn brough the hot 'exhaust area' into contact with the pool, and set the oleum bubbling furiously – or as close to bubbling as anything could come under Tenebra's atmospheric pressure. There was enough disturbance to attract the attention of the natives on the ship, but not to be visible from shore.

Two full rolls brought her to wading depth, and robbed her of enough buoyancy to make another climber necessary. Three turns brought her right side up at the shore line. A slight complication arose when the climbers dropped off and she started to roll back, and for the first time Raeker was able to make himself heard and listened to; he gave some rapid advice about placing chocks, which Nick heeded. With the hull stable and the children staring out at the robot a few yards away, Raeker thought he might learn what was going on, and he used the machine's speaker.

'Hello, Easy. We're finally together.'

'Hello, Doctor. Yes, your people are here. I thought we'd be able to do without them, but they've been a big help. Are you staying to watch the rest?'

The question startled the biologist, to put it mildly.

'Staying? We're just starting to work. I'll call the engineers and have them listen in while I explain the electrolysis circuits to Nick and the others; they'd be here now, only I didn't expect the ship to be available quite so quickly. We'll find whatever wires are corroded or disconnected, and—' Easy must have started talking before he got that far, but the transmission lag delayed his hearing her interruption.

'I'm sorry, Doctor, but I'd rather not have Nick fooling with the ship's wiring. I don't understand it myself, and I don't see how he possibly can keep from making mistakes. We're going up shortly, anyway, so please don't let him get into any of those inspection ports, if they're really open.' The girl spoke as pleasantly as ever, but there was a note of firmness which no human being who heard her could mistake. Raeker was surprised, and then indignant.

'What do you mean, you'd "rather not" have Nick work? Who else can? If you think he's ignorant of electricity, what good will it do for you to take over – or Swift? This plan has been under way for weeks, and you can't—'

'I don't care how long it's been organized, and I *can*,' replied the girl, still politely. 'Swift will do what I ask, and Nick will do what Swift orders. We're going to try Swift's idea first; I'm sure it will work, but if it doesn't perhaps we'll think about yours again.'

Raeker looked around helplessly; the kid was right. There was no way in the universe for him to enforce his will. Maybe her father – no; Rich was listening in the communication room, and the relay screen showed something like an expression of satisfaction on his face. The biologist surrendered.

'All right, Easy. Will you tell me what this plan of Swift's is? And how, if you don't trust me and Nick, you can possibly consider an ignorant savage like one of these cave dwellers worth listening to?'

'Your scientific friends do,' Easy replied pointedly. 'If I tell you, 'Mina's father will hear, and he'll start thinking of things wrong with it, and that'll get Dad worried. You just watch; it won't be long now.'

'How does your young friend feel about not telling his father?'

'He doesn't mind, do you, 'Mina?'

'No,' piped the young Drommian. 'Dad told me to do what Easy said, and besides, he was rude to her. We'll show him!'

Raeker raised his eyebrows at this, and somehow felt a little happier about the whole matter. If someone was going to make a fool of Aminadabarlee ...

And then Swift's plan became perfectly obvious. A group of hunters reappeared, towing among them the helpless form of a floater. The dangerous tentacles of the creature had been removed – it was obvious now why an axeman had accompanied each group – and enough of its gas cells punctured so that it could be held down; but some were still intact, and their intended use could easily be seen.

The hydrogen cells of the bathyscaphe possessed, naturally, pressure-equalizing vents on the lower side of the hull. While these vents opened into the cells on the wrong side of the plastic membrane designed to prevent hydrogen and air from mixing, the other side also had a plastic tube extending down to the same vent, for relief if too much electrolytic hydrogen was run into the cell. This tube was normally held shut, or rather flat, by outside pressure; but it was perfectly possible to push another tube into it from outside, and run gas or liquid into the compartment. This the natives proceeded to do; Raeker wasn't sure of the nature of the tube, but there was nothing surprising in their being able to improvise one. There must have been a good deal of gas wasted in the transfer process, but this didn't seem to bother anyone. There were, after all, plenty of floaters.

'I see,' he said through the robot after a few minutes. 'But I think I see a catch.'

'What?' Easy snapped the question with a speed which suggested she had some doubts of her own.

'That ship was computed around the lift of hydrogen. How do you know that stuff you're using will lift you high enough for your boosters to work, even if an engineer gets aboard to—'

'What makes you think this gas isn't hydrogen?'

'What makes you think it is?'

'What else is lighter than water, in the gas state, that's likely to be found on this planet?'

'Why, lots of things, I guess – I – I don't know; I hadn't thought of that.' Realization struck him. 'You've been talking to the engineers!'

'Of course. I don't mean to be rude, but where else could I learn anything useful about this ship? I'll admit you know the planet, but that wasn't enough.'

'I see,' said Raeker slowly. 'I hadn't thought as much as I should about the machine; but I did ask the engineers about its wiring – and say! won't you need that anyway? What are you going to do when they get enough gas into your cells to lift the ship out of their reach, but not enough to get you any higher? Hadn't you better have them tie the ship down, at least? You'd better wait until we—'

He was interrupted by laughter. It didn't come from Easy, who had looked impressed for a moment, but from the scientists in the observation chamber. Raeker realized that they were laughing at him, and for a moment was furious; then he realized he had asked for it. He put the best face he could on the matter while one of them carefully explained a little elementary physics.

And that, really, was all. Nick put to use the knowledge he had picked up in balancing on the experimental float, and made sure there were always more forward cells full than after ones. When the ship lifted, it naturally rode the wind toward the volcano; and it rose so slowly at first that the children had a good look at the terrifying sight. They dipped frighteningly toward the glowing mountain as it entered warmer air, but recovered in ample time as the hydrogen in its cells also warmed up. Gradually the glow faded out below them, and Easy and her friend waited happily to meet the shuttle.

EPILOGUE
Cooperation

'I told you human beings were helpless and useless.' Happy as he was, Aminadabarlee gave up his ideas with difficulty. 'You spend weeks trying to rig a rescue, and then are outsmarted by a savage with less education than either of these children. You spend a decade or two training agents of your own on the planet, and learn more useful facts in a week from natives you never bothered to contact directly.'

'Natives who would have tried to eat the robot if any such attempt had been made,' Easy pointed out. 'Remember, 'Mina and I know Swift. He respected the robot because it could talk and tell him things. He'd have ignored it or destroyed it otherwise.'

Aminadabarlee's eyes sought his son, who made a gesture of agreement. 'Well, anyway, the natives with their own culture are a lot more use, and I'll prove it soon enough.'

'How?' asked Raeker.

'I'll have a Drommian project here in three months. We can talk to Swift as well as you, and we'll see who learns more about geophysics in general and Tenebra in particular after that.'

'Wouldn't it be more profitable to run the projects jointly, and exchange information?'

'You'd certainly have to say that,' sneered the non-human. 'I've had enough of cooperation with human beings, and so has the rest of Dromm, if my opinion's good for anything. You learned Swift's language, didn't you, son?'

'Yes, Dad, but—'

'Never mind the but. I know you like Easy, and I suppose she's a little less poisonous than most human beings after the time she spent with you, but I know what I'm talking about. Here – use the robot voice and call Swift over to it; you can say something to him for me.'

'But I can't, Dad.' Even the human beings could see that the youngster was uncomfortable.

'Can't? What do you mean? You just said you'd learned enough of their language—'

'Oh, I understand it well enough. I just can't speak it.'

'You mean you just listened, and let that human girl do all the talking? I'm ashamed of you. You know perfectly well that no chance to learn the use of a new language should ever be missed.'

'I didn't miss it, Dad.'

Aminadabarlee seemed to swell slightly. 'Then, in the name of both suns, tell me what you did do!' His voice came closer to a roar than anyone in the room had ever heard from him. Aminadorneldo looked a little helplessly at Easy.

'All right, 'Mina,' the girl said. 'We'll show him.'

The two took their places before the microphone, which Easy snapped on. Then, keeping their eyes fixed on each other, they began to speak in unison. The sounds they produced were weird; sometimes both were together, sometimes the Drommian carried a high note alone, sometimes Easy took the deeper registers. A similar sound, which Raeker recognized perfectly well and understood slightly, cane from the speaker; Easy started an answer, using her hands to guide her 'little' companion on what words were coming next. They had apparently worked out a fairly satisfactory deaf-mute code between them; and while they spoke much more slowly than Swift, they were obviously perfectly clear to the native.

'He's here, Councillor,' Easy remarked after a moment. 'What did you want to say to him? This particular translating team is ready to go to work. I do hope you'll forgive 'Mina for cooperating with a human being. There really wasn't any other way, you know.'

Nobody laughed.

If you've enjoyed these books and would
like to read more, you'll find literally thousands
of classic Science Fiction & Fantasy titles
through the **SF Gateway**

✶

*For the new home of
Science Fiction & Fantasy . . .*

✶

*For the most comprehensive collection
of classic SF on the internet . . .*

✶

Visit the SF Gateway

www.sfgateway.com

Hal Clement (1922–2003)

Hal Clement is the *nom de plume* under which Harry Clement Stubbs wrote science fiction. Born in Massachusetts in 1922, he graduated from Harvard with a BSc. in astronomy, and later added degrees in chemistry and education. A former B-24 pilot who saw active service during the Second World War, he worked for most of his life as a high-school science teacher. He made his reputation as an SF writer with the work that appeared in *Astounding*, where his best-known novel, *Mission of Gravity*, first appeared in serialised form in 1953.